The Editor

DAVID SCOTT KASTAN is the Old Dominion Foundation
Professor in the Humanities at Columbia University. He is
the author of *Shakespeare and the Shapes of Time* (1982);
Shakespeare after Theory (1999); *Shakespeare and the
Book* (2001); coeditor of *Staging the Renaissance: Essays
on Elizabethan and Jacobean Drama* (1991) and of *The
New History of Early English Drama* (1997); and editor of
Critical Essays on Shakespeare's "Hamlet" (1995) and *A
Companion to Shakespeare* (1999). He serves as a General
Editor of the Arden Shakespeare, and his edition of
1 Henry IV for that series was published in 2002. He is
presently working on a book titled *The Invention of En-
glish Literature*.

A NORTON CRITICAL EDITION

Christopher Marlowe
DOCTOR FAUSTUS

A TWO-TEXT EDITION
(A-TEXT, 1604; B-TEXT, 1616)
CONTEXTS AND SOURCES
CRITICISM

Edited by

DAVID SCOTT KASTAN

COLUMBIA UNIVERSITY

W. W. NORTON & COMPANY
New York • London

W. W. Norton & Company has been independent since its founding in 1923, when William Warder and Mary D. Herter Norton first published lectures delivered at the People's Institute, the adult education division of New York City's Cooper Union. The Nortons soon expanded their program beyond the Institute, publishing books by celebrated academics from America and abroad. By mid-century, the two major pillars of Norton's publishing program—trade books and college texts—were firmly established. In the 1950s, the Norton family transferred control of the company to its employees, and today—with a staff of four hundred and a comparable number of trade, college, and professional titles published each year—W. W. Norton & Company stands as the largest and oldest publishing house owned wholly by its employees.

Every effort has been made to contact the copyright holders of each of the selections in this volume. Rights holders of any selections not credited should contact W. W. Norton & Company, Inc., 500 Fifth Avenue, New York, NY 10110, for a correction to be made in the next printing of our work.

The text of this book is composed in Fairfield Medium
with the display set in Bernhard Modern.
Composition by PennSet, Inc.
Manufacturing by the Courier Companies—Westford Division.
Production manager: Benjamin Reynolds.

Library of Congress Cataloging-in-Publication Data
Marlowe, Christopher, 1564–1593.
    Doctor Faustus: a two-text edition (A-text, 1604; B-text, 1616)
contexts and sources criticism / Christopher Marlowe; edited by
David Scott Kastan.
        p. cm.
    Includes bibliographical references.

ISBN 0-393-97754-4 (pbk.)

    1. Faust, d. ca. 1540—Drama. 2. Magicians—Drama.
3. Germany—Drama. 4. Devil—Drama. I. Kastan, David Scott.
II. Title.
PR2664.A2K64 2004
22'.3—dc28

                                                            2004053196

W. W. Norton & Company, Inc., 500 Fifth Avenue, New York, NY 10110-0017
www.wwnorton.com

W. W. Norton & Company Ltd., Castle House,
75/76 Wells Street, London W1T 3QT

4   5   6   7   8   9   0

Contents

Criticism

CONTENTS   vii

Introduction

In 1675, Edward Phillips in his *Theatrum Poetarum Anglicanorum* called Christopher Marlowe "a kind of second Shakspeare." High praise indeed; but, at the time of Marlowe's death in 1593, Shakespeare might well have been in fairness thought a kind of second Marlowe. Both were born in 1564, but by 1593 Shakespeare's hand could be seen on stage in only *The Comedy of Errors, Titus Andronicus, Two Gentlemen of Verona,* the *Henry VI* plays, and possibly *The Taming of the Shrew*. Marlowe had written *Dido, Queen of Carthage, The Massacre at Paris, The Jew of Malta,* the two parts of *Tamburlaine, Edward II,* and, of course, *Doctor Faustus*. In 1593, pride of place belonged to Marlowe, and the vector of influence seems clearly to move from him to Shakespeare rather than the other way round. Marlowe's imagination is certainly the more remarkable and daring, and in many ways, *Doctor Faustus* seems the most remarkable and daring manifestation of it at work—a tragedy that explores the very limits of human ambition.

It is difficult, however, to characterize the play's achievement, not least because of its complex textual history.[1] *Doctor Faustus* exists in two distinct editions. Written probably about 1590, it was not printed until 1604. In that year Thomas Bushell published what is now known to scholars as the A-text, a 1,517-line version of the play apparently printed from Marlowe's own drafts. Twelve years later John Wright (who had acquired the rights to the play in 1610) published a second edition of *Doctor Faustus* (unsurprisingly known as the B-text), this some 600 lines longer than the first. Adding to the complication is a note in Philip Henslowe's *Diary* dated November 22, 1602, about the payment of £4 to two playwrights, William Bird and Samuel Rowley, for "additions" to the play. We do not know whether these were the *only* additions made to the play between Marlowe's death and its appearances in print, but clearly additions were made. Seemingly, the 1616 B-text reflects the Bird and Rowley additions and possibly other new mate-

---

1. For the clearest and most compelling rethinking of the complex textual history of the play, see Eric Rasmussen's *A Textual Companion to Doctor Faustus* (Manchester and New York: Manchester University Press, 1993). For the relevant contemporary documents, see pp. 141–42 herein.

rial, including some expurgation of the text in accordance with the 1606 Act of Abuses, which prohibited references to God on the stage. The B-text, then, represents the play more or less as it came to be performed later in its stage history.

Nonetheless, the differences in the two texts do not reflect only the distinction between a largely "authorial" text and a "theatrical" one—that is, between the play as its author may have imagined it and the work as it survived and inevitably mutated in the theater. Much of that difference is indeed evident in the two texts (and as such, arguably is justification enough for insisting on a two-text edition of the play). But, even more, the two versions of the play in fact trace significantly different tragic trajectories, the B-text externalizing and theatricalizing what the A-text makes a matter of private conscience and conviction.[2] In both, Faustus suffers a terrifying damnation for daring "to practice more than heavenly power permits" (A- and B-text; Epilogue, line 8). But in the A-text, the choices Faustus makes are his own, and his suffering is largely psychological. In the B-text, he exists in a world where he is (mis)led by malign supernatural forces and his suffering is physical. In A, the Old Man exits, "fearing the ruin of [Faustus's] hapless soul" (5.1.61); in B, the Old Man quite differently fears "the enemy of thy hapless soul" (5.1.63). The A-text ends with Faustus alone, and only at the very end is he led off by devils. In B, there is another scene in which the scholars enter to find Faustus's dismembered body, torn by "the devils whom Faustus served" (5.3.8).

The psychological and theological differences between the two versions are indeed significant enough to make talking about *Doctor Faustus* almost meaningless without specifying which version of the play one is talking about. This Norton Critical Edition of *Doctor Faustus* is, therefore, a two-text version. The A-text and the B-text are each here, available to be read independently. Full notes are offered for each (even at the cost of the inevitable duplication) to facilitate the reading. It is not a parallel-text edition, however, which would highlight the differences between the texts but also would make those discontinuous differences the focus of the edition rather than the different experience of reading each play.

Doctor Faustus has long been recognized as one of the towering achievements of the Renaissance imagination, even if critics have not always been able to agree about its meaning. If it is a tragedy that clearly shows the Reformation sense of human depravity overwhelming the Renaissance dream of human perfectibility, much about its Reformation context remains at once uncertain and un-

2. See Michael Warren (pp. 142–52 herein), Leah Marcus (pp. 153–70), and Rasmussen (pp. 171–78).

settling. Is it finally an orthodox play, powerfully testifying to the inevitable and appropriate destruction of one who dares to challenge
the enduring moral laws of the universe, or is it a far more disturbing drama, in which those laws are themselves revealed as oppres-
sive? Is grace indeed always available to Faustus, as the Good Angel
insists, or is Faustus damned from the first, predestined to reject
what is seemingly offered? As Alan Sinfield asks, are we not forced
at least to "entertain the thought that Faustus is not damned because he is wicked, but wicked because he is damned?"[3]

That unnerving thought engages the very premise of a moral universe and a benign God, a thought that is perhaps reinforced by the
fact that only one supernatural agent of good ever appears (and
even that Good Angel disappears as the clock strikes eleven) but
that many devils appear to Faustus (and to us). Is the play, then,
a challenge not only to Renaissance confidence in the human intellect but also to Reformation comfort with the divine will? Is
Marlowe's own contemporary reputation as an atheist justified and
relevant to our sense of the play?[4] Is its final line (if indeed the line
does belong to the play proper)—*Terminat hora diem; terminat Author opus* (The hour ends the day; the author ends the work)—
perhaps the playwright's acknowledgment of his link to his transgressive hero? None of these questions is easily answered, and indeed *Doctor Faustus*, in both its versions, is a play that everywhere
and energetically resists easy answers—resists, perhaps, any answers at all. As its riddling textual history uncannily replicates, it
is in fact a play more about ignorance than knowledge, more
about doubt than understanding; and it is in its dramatizations of
that provocative uncertainty that *Doctor Faustus* achieves its
greatness.

In the preparation of any edition, enormous and unrepayable debts
are incurred, not least to the efforts of the editors who have come
before. My major debts here are to W. W. Greg and his magisterial
parallel-text edition of 1950 and to David Bevington and Eric Rasmussen's remarkable rethinking of the textual problems in their
two-text Revels edition of 1993. Other debts are perhaps less obvious in the final result but no less significant. If these, like the first
two, also are hardly repaid with mere mention, they also at least
must be recorded. Julie Crawford, Margreta de Grazia, Jonathan
Hope, András Kiséry, Laurie Maguire, Claire McEachern, Gordon
McMullan, Stephen Orgel, Richard Proudfoot, Jim Shapiro, Peter Stallybrass, Tiffany Stern, Keith Walker, and David Yerkes are

3. Sinfield, *Literature in Protestant England, 1550–1650* (London: Croom Helm, 1983),
   p. 14.
4. See pp. 127–30 herein.

among the numerous friends, colleagues, and students (the categories are not mutually exclusive) that over the years have discussed aspects of *Doctor Faustus* with me and ensured that my interest in the play has only grown. And then there are JE, AL, and, of course, MK—to them and all the rest, thank you.

Editorial Procedures

This two-text edition of *Doctor Faustus* is based on the 1604 and 1616 quartos. All substantive changes from those texts are recorded in the textual notes below. The texts presented here modernize the spelling and punctuation of the originals. Old *forms* of words are retained; old *spellings* are modernized (thus "professe" in 1.1.2 becomes "profess," but "fitteth" in line 11 is retained)—though the distinction often blurs (e.g., is "holla" a variant form or a variant spelling of "holler"?). Proper names are given in their usual modern forms, even when this may affect the meter. The flexibility of pronunciation and stress in early modern English permits various ways of understanding the metrical principles of particular lines, and little seems to be gained by retaining an idiosyncratic form of an otherwise recognizable name to preserve an uncertain metrical scheme. Punctuation is brought into line with modern practice, which, instead of the largely rhythmical punctuation of the early seventeenth century, attempts to clarify the logical relations between grammatical units. The Latin that is spoken by characters has been corrected, except when it is clear the errors are intentional. The argument that errors are deliberate and designed to be comic depends on subtle differences being heard on stage, and in general this seems to me unlikely.

The aim of this edition is to permit the two early texts of *Doctor Faustus* to be read easily and independently, and so I have been conservative in emending either text. The only major changes involve the repositioning of two comic scenes from the A-text (1604), which there are collapsed and appear between the Chorus and the action in the court of Charles V that the Chorus introduces. It is hard to see any way in which this order was either intended by the playwright or intelligible on stage. Here, following Bevington and Rasmussen (1993), they are relocated to 2.2 and 3.2, respectively. In the B-text, Wagner's Chorus appears between 2.1 and 2.2, and then an expanded version reappears again (seemingly in its correct place) at the beginning of Act 3. This edition omits the earlier version. The B-text attempts to fix the misplaced comic scenes of A, but, while correctly locating the second, places the first after 2.3 instead of before, where it apparently belongs.

Textual Notes

A-Text (1604)

The lists that follow record all substantive departures in this edition of the A-text (1604) and the B-text (1616). They do not record modernizations of spelling and punctuation, regularization of names, expansions of abbreviations, corrections of obvious typographical errors, or adjustments of lineation. The adopted reading in this edition is given first in boldface followed by the original reading of the relevant text (e.g., **Roda**   Rhodes). When the reading adopted here in either the A- or the B-text comes from the other, that fact is indicated parenthetically. Editorial stage directions are not collated but are placed within brackets in the text. The act and scene divisions are editorial, not appearing in either the A- or the B-text. For a full amount of the editorial assumptions and practices of this edition, see "Editorial Procedures," p. xiii herein.

PROLOGUE

1 SH **CHORUS**   not in A-text
12 **Roda**   Rhodes

I.I

6 **analytics**   Anulatikes
7 *logices*   logicis
12 *On kai me on*   Oncaymaeon
28 *legatur*   legatus
31 *Exhaereditare*   Ex haereditari
36 **Too servile** (B-text)   The deuill
90 **silk**   skill
112 **concise syllogisms**   Consissylogismes
129 **in the**   in their
130 **From** (B-text)   For
130 **drag**   dregge
139 **seen in**   seen

1.3

9 **anagrammatized** (B-text)   Agramithist
17 *aquatici*   Aquatani
19 *appareat* (B-text)   apariat
19 *Quid tu moraris*   quod tumeraris
22 *dicatus*   dicaetis
34 *redis*   regis
46 *accidens*   accident

1.4

11 **By'r Lady**   burladie
72–3 *vestigiis nostris*   vestigias nostras

2.1

18 **illusions, fruits**   illusious fruites
147 **no** (B-text)   not in A-text

2.2

The A-text places this scene after the Chorus that in this edition, as in most other modern editions, introduces Act 4. In the A-text, this scene is followed immediately by a second comic scene, which in this edition, as in the B-text and most modern editions, is located at 3.2.

2.3

19 **thunder**   thunders
55 *intelligentia*   Intelligentij

3.1

34–5 **Over . . . Rome** (B-text)   not in A-text
36 **Ponte**   Ponto
70 **ha't**   hate

3.2

See note on 2.2

4. CHORUS

SH **CHORUS**   not in A-text

4.1

127 **goodbye**   god buy
150 **hey-pass**   hey, passe
174 **hostry**   Oastrie

EPILOGUE

SH **CHORUS**   not in A-text

B-Text (1616)

THE TRAGEDY OF DOCTOR FAUSTUS

The title page of the B-text (1616) calls the play "The Tragicall History of the Life and Death of Doctor Faustus," but the first page of the text identifies it as "The Tragedie of Doctor Faustus." To help differentiate the two texts, I have adopted that title for the B-text.

PROLOGUE

1 SH **CHORUS**   not in B-text
12 **Roda**   Rhodes

1.1

7 *logices*   Logicis
26 *legatur*   legatus
29 *Exhaereditare*   Exhereditari
80 **India** (A-text)   Indian
88 **silk**   skill
108 **Swarm** (A-text)   Sworne
119 **Lapland**   Lopland

1.3

16 *dei*   dii
17 *aquatici*   Aquatani
19–20 *Quid tu moraris*   quod tumeris
22 *dicatus*   dicatis
22 SD **Dragon**   "Mephistiphilis Dragon" at 19 in B-text
44 *accidens*   accident

1.4

47 *vestigiis nostris*   vestigias nostras

2.1

14 SH **BAD ANGEL**   Euill An

2.2

2.2.   This scene is printed after the material that is 2.3 in the B-text. Following 2.1, the B-text prints a speech by Wagner that is substantially the same as the A-text's Act 3 Chorus and is apparently revised and expanded (and correctly located) as 3. Chorus below.

2.3

17 SH **BAD ANGEL**   Euill An
42 **erring** (A-text)   euening

3. CHORUS

1 SH **CHORUS**   not in B-text
7 **tropics**   Tropick
20 **coasts**   costs

3.1

6 **coasting**   costing
38 **Ponte**   Ponto
42 **match** (A-text)   watch
76, 80 **cunning**   comming
149 **rights**   rites

3.2

99 **on** (A-text)   not in B-text

4.1

71 **like a**   like
135 **is**   not in B-text

4.2

27 **heart's**   heart
70 **Ay, all**   I call

4.5

3 **guests**   Guesse

4.6

118 **guests**   guesse

5.2

72 **'tis** (A-text)   'ts
98 **must**   most
119 **boil**   broyle

EPILOGUE

1 SH **CHORUS**   not in B-text

The Texts of
DOCTOR FAUSTUS

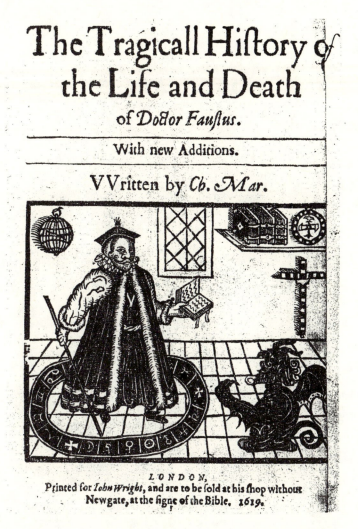

The Tragicall Hiſtory of the Life and Death

of *Doctor Fauſtus.*

With new Additions.

VVritten by *Ch. Mar.*

LONDON,
Printed for *Iohn Wright,* and are to be ſold at his ſhop without
Newgate, at the ſigne of the Bible. **1619.**

Title page of the second edition of the B-text (1619). This was the first printing to indicate that the text was presented "With new Additions." Used with
permission of the Princeton University Library.

The Tragical History of Doctor Faustus (A-Text, 1604)

List of Roles

CHORUS
Dr. John FAUSTUS
WAGNER   Faustus's servant
VALDES ⎫
CORNELIUS ⎬ Conjurors and Faustus's friends
ROBIN the ostler, a clown
RAFE
three SCHOLARS
The POPE
The CARDINAL of Lorraine
Charles V, EMPEROR of Germany
DUKE of Vanholt
DUCHESS of Vanholt
LUCIFER
BEELZEBUB
MEPHISTOPHELES
GOOD ANGEL
EVIL ANGEL
PRIDE ⎫
COVETOUSNESS ⎪
WRATH ⎪
ENVY ⎬ SEVEN DEADLY SINS
GLUTTONY ⎪
SLOTH ⎪
LECHERY ⎭
Spirits in the shapes of ALEXANDER THE GREAT, his Paramour, and HELEN of Troy
VINTNER

HORSE-COURSER
KNIGHT
OLD MAN
Devils, Friars, and Attendants

[Prologue]

Enter CHORUS.

CHORUS
Not marching now in fields of Trasimene,
Where Mars did mate the Carthaginians,
Nor sporting in the dalliance of love
In courts of kings where state is overturned,
Nor in the pomp of proud audacious deeds,   5
Intends our muse to daunt his heavenly verse.
Only this, gentlemen: we must perform
The form of Faustus' fortunes, good or bad.
To patient judgments we appeal our plaud
And speak for Faustus in his infancy.   10
Now is he born, his parents base of stock,
In Germany within a town called Roda.
Of riper years, to Württemberg he went,
Whereas his kinsmen chiefly brought him up.
So soon he profits in divinity,   15
The fruitful plot of scholarism graced,
That shortly he was graced with doctor's name,
Excelling all whose sweet delight disputes
In heavenly matters of theology;
Till swoll'n with cunning, of a self-conceit,   20
His waxen wings did mount above his reach,

Prologue
1. **Trasimene:** battlefield in Italy (near Lake Trasimeno in modern Umbria), where Carthaginian troops under Hannibal defeated the Romans in 217 B.C.E.
2. **Mars:** Roman god of war; **mate:** side with.
4. **state:** orderly government.
6. **daunt:** direct.
7. **gentlemen:** The audience of the theaters in which *Dr. Faustus* was performed was neither socially nor sexually homogeneous, as this would indicate.
9. **appeal our plaud:** make our case for applause.
12. **Roda:** the modern Stadtroda, near Weimar in Germany.
13. **Württemberg:** The A-text's rendering ("Wertenberg") of the town where Faustus was raised (unlike the B-text's "Wittenberg"). Württemberg was well known as a center of radical Protestantism.
15. **divinity:** theology.
16. **graced:** adorned.
17. **graced:** rewarded; although a *grace* was an official university term recognizing a student's eligibility for a degree.
18. **whose . . . disputes:** whose greatest pleasure comes from argumentation.
21. **waxen wings:** like those worn by Icarus (Ovid, *Metamorphoses* 8)—a familiar emblem of pride—who died when he flew too near the sun.

And melting heavens conspired his overthrow.
For, falling to a devilish exercise,
And glutted more with learning's golden gifts,
He surfeits upon cursèd necromancy.   25
Nothing so sweet as magic is to him,
Which he prefers before his chiefest bliss.
And this the man that in his study sits.   *Exit.*

[1.1]

Enter FAUSTUS *in his study.*

FAUSTUS
   Settle thy studies, Faustus, and begin
   To sound the depth of that thou wilt profess.
   Having commenced, be a divine in show,
   Yet level at the end of every art,
   And live and die in Aristotle's works. [*Picks up book.*]   5
   Sweet analytics, 'tis thou hast ravished me!
   [*Reads.*] "*Bene disserere est finis logices.*"
   Is to dispute well logic's chiefest end?
   Affords this art no greater miracle?
   Then read no more; thou hast attained the end.   10
   A greater subject fitteth Faustus' wit.
   Bid *On kai me on* farewell.
            [*Puts down book and picks up another.*]
                     Galen come.
   Seeing [*Reads.*] "*Ubi desinit philosophus, ibi incipit medicus,*"
   Be a physician, Faustus; heap up gold,
   And be eternized for some wondrous cure.   15

25. **necromancy:** forbidden magic.
27. **chiefest bliss:** i.e., hope of salvation.
[1.1]
1. **settle:** decide on.
2. **sound:** measure, explore; **profess:** choose as your area of expertise.
3. **commenced:** earned a degree; **divine:** theologian; **in show:** in appearance only.
4. **level . . . art:** consider the purpose of every discipline.
6. **analytics:** title of two of Aristotle's treatises on logic; here, however, most likely the discipline itself.
7. *Bene . . . logices*: i.e., the purpose of logic is to argue well (Latin; but from the *Dialectica* of Petrus Ramus [1515–1572], not Aristotle).
11. **wit:** understanding.
12. *On kai me on*: being and not being (Greek); i.e., philosophy.
12. **Galen:** Greek authority on medicine (2nd century C.E.).
13. *Ubi . . . medicus*: i.e., where the philosopher ends, the physician begins (Latin; Aristotle, *De Sensu* 436a).
15. **eternized:** immortalized.

[*Reads.*] *"Summum bonum medicinae sanitas."*
The end of physic is our body's health.
Why, Faustus, hast thou not attained that end?
Is not thy common talk sound aphorisms?
Are not thy bills hung up as monuments,   20
Whereby whole cities have escaped the plague
And thousand desperate maladies been eased?
Yet art thou still but Faustus, and a man.
Wouldst thou make men to live eternally
Or, being dead, raise them to life again,   25
Then this profession were to be esteemed. [*Puts down book.*]
Physic, farewell! Where is Justinian? [*Picks up another book
    and reads.*]
"Si una eademque res legatur duobus,
Alter rem, alter valorem rei, etc."
A pretty case of paltry legacies!   30
[*Reads.*] *"Exhaereditare filium non potest pater nisi,* etc."
Such is the subject of the *Institute*
And universal body of the Church.
His study fits a mercenary drudge
Who aims at nothing but external trash: 35
Too servile and illiberal for me. [*Puts down book.*]
When all is done, divinity is best. [*Picks up another book.*]
Jerome's Bible, Faustus; view it well.
[*Reads.*] *"Stipendium peccati mors est."* Ha!
Stipendium, etc. The reward of sin is death. That's hard.   40
[*Reads.*] *"Si peccasse negamus, fallimur,*
Et nulla est in nobis veritas."
If we say that we have no sin
We deceive ourselves, and there's no truth in us.

16. *Summum . . . sanitas*: i.e., health is the greatest good of medicine (Latin; Aristotle, *Nichomachean Ethics* 1094a).
17. **physic**: medicine.
19. **sound aphorisms**: reliable principles.
20. **bills**: medical prescriptions.
27. **Justinian**: Roman emperor (482–565) who codified the Roman law.
28–29. *Si . . .* etc.: i.e., if the one and the same thing is bequeathed to two people, one should have the thing itself and the other the value of the thing, and so forth (Latin; Justinian, *Institutes* 2.20).
31. *Exhaereditare . . . nisi*: i.e., a father may not disinherit his son unless (Latin; Justinian, *Institutes* 2.13).
32. *Institute*: the codification of Roman law ordered by Justinian (see note 27, above).
34. **His study**: i.e., studying Justinian.
38. **Jerome's Bible**: the Latin translation (the Vulgate) made by St. Jerome in the 4th century, although the biblical citations that follow do not use the Vulgate's wording and seem to be Marlowe's own translations into Latin from the English Geneva version.
39. *Stipendium . . . est*: i.e., the wages of sin are death (Latin; Romans 6:23). The rest of the verse, however, reads: "but the gift of God is eternal life through Jesus Christ our Lord."
41–42. *Si . . . veritas*: 1 John 1:8, translated from the Latin in the following two lines but ignoring the verse that follows: "If we confess our sins, he is faithful and just to forgive us our sins, and to cleanse us from all unrighteousness."

Why, then, belike we must sin and so consequently die.
Ay, we must die an everlasting death.
Why doctrine call you this? *Che serà, serà?*
What will be, shall be? Divinity, adieu! [*Puts down Bible.*]
[*Picks up book of magic.*] These metaphysics of magicians
And necromantic books are heavenly;   50
Lines, circles, scenes, letters, and characters—
Ay, these are those that Faustus most desires.
O, what a world of profit and delight,
Of power, of honor, of omnipotence,
Is promised to the studious artisan!   55
All things that move between the quiet poles
Shall be at my command. Emperors and kings
Are but obeyed in their several provinces,
Nor can they raise the wind or rend the clouds;
But his dominion that exceeds in this   60
Stretcheth as far as doth the mind of man.
A sound magician is a mighty god.
Here, Faustus, try thy brains to gain a deity.
Wagner!

    Enter WAGNER.

       Commend me to my dearest friends,
The German Valdes and Cornelius.   65
Request them earnestly to visit me.
WAGNER   I will, sir.   *Exit.*
FAUSTUS
  Their conference will be a greater help to me.
Than all my labors, plod I ne'er so fast.

    Enter the GOOD ANGEL *and the* EVIL ANGEL.
GOOD ANGEL
  O, Faustus, lay that damnèd book aside   70
And gaze not on it, lest it tempt thy soul
And heap God's heavy wrath upon thy head.
Read, read the Scriptures. That is blasphemy.
EVIL ANGEL
  Go forward, Faustus, in that famous art
Wherein all Nature's treasury is contained.   75

---

47. Che serà, serà: i.e., what will be, shall be (Italian; translated in following line).
55. studious artisan: skilled practitioner of an art.
56. quiet: motionless.
58. several: respective.
60. this: i.e., magic.
63. try: apply.
73. That: i.e., the book of magic.

Be thou on earth as Jove is in the sky,
Lord and commander of these elements.   *Exeunt* [ANGELS].

FAUSTUS

How am I glutted with conceit of this!
Shall I make spirits fetch me what I please,
Resolve me of all ambiguities,   80
Perform what desperate enterprise I will?
I'll have them fly to India for gold,
Ransack the ocean for orient pearl,
And search all corners of the new-found world
For pleasant fruits and princely delicates.   85
I'll have them read me strange philosophy
And tell the secrets of all foreign kings.
I'll have them wall all Germany with brass
And make swift Rhine circle fair Württemberg.
I'll have them fill the public schools with silk,   90
Wherewith the students shall be bravely clad.
I'll levy soldiers with the coin they bring,
And chase the Prince of Parma from our land,
And reign sole king of all the provinces.
Yea, stranger engines for the brunt of war   95
Than was the fiery keel at Antwerp's bridge
I'll make my servile spirits to invent.
Come, German Valdes and Cornelius,
And make me blest with your sage conference.

        Enter VALDES *and* CORNELIUS.

Valdes, sweet Valdes, and Cornelius,   100
Know that your words have won me at the last
To practice magic and concealèd arts.
Yet not your words only but mine own fantasy
That will receive no object for my head
But ruminates on necromantic skill.   105
Philosophy is odious and obscure;

78. **conceit of this**: the idea of being a magician.
80. **Resolve . . . ambiguities**: answer all my questions.
83. **orient**: i.e., precious (literally, from the East).
85. **delicates**: delicacies.
86. **read**: teach.
89. **Rhine . . . Württemberg**: Württemberg indeed was on the Rhine, unlike Wittenberg (see B-text), which is on the Elbe.
90. **public schools**: universities.
91. **bravely**: splendidly.
93. **Prince of Parma**: Alessandro Farnese, duke of Parma and Spanish governor of the Netherlands (ruled 1578–92).
95. **engines**: machines.
96. **fiery keel**: reference to the burning ship sent by Dutch forces in April 1585 to break the duke of Parma's blockade of Antwerp.
102. **concealèd**: occult.

Both law and physic are for petty wits;
Divinity is basest of the three:
Unpleasant, harsh, contemptible, and vile.
'Tis magic, magic, that hath ravished me.   110
Then, gentle friends, aid me in this attempt;
And I, that have with concise syllogisms
Gravelled the pastors of the German Church
And made the flowering pride of Württemberg
Swarm to my problems, as the infernal spirits   115
On sweet Musaeus when he came to hell,
Will be as cunning as Agrippa was,
Whose shadows made all Europe honor him.

VALDES

Faustus, these books, thy wit, and our experience
Shall make all nations to canonize us.   120
As Indian moors obey their Spanish lords,
So shall the subjects of every element
Be always serviceable to us three.
Like lions shall they guard us when we please,
Like Almain rutters with their horsemen's staves,   125
Or Lapland giants, trotting by our sides;
Sometimes like women, or unwedded maids,
Shadowing more beauty in their airy brows
Than in the white breasts of the Queen of Love.
From Venice shall they drag huge argosies   130
And from America the golden fleece
That yearly stuffs old Philip's treasury,
If learnèd Faustus will be resolute.

FAUSTUS

Valdes, as resolute am I in this
As thou to live; therefore, object it not.   135

CORNELIUS

The miracles that magic will perform

112. **concise syllogisms:** elegant arguments.
113. **Gravelled:** amazed.
116. **Musaeus:** legendary Greek poet, whom Virgil describes surrounded by admirers in the underworld (*Aeneid* 6.666–67).
117. **Agrippa:** Henry Cornelius Agrippa of Nettlesheim (1486–1535), famous German magician.
118. **shadows:** spirits raised from the dead.
121. **Indian moors:** the natives of the New World.
122. **subjects:** spirits.
125. **Almain rutters:** German cavalrymen.
128. **Shadowing:** harboring.
129. **Queen of Love:** i.e., Venus.
130. **argosies:** merchant ships.
131. **golden fleece:** the fabulous object sought by Jason and his argonauts.
132. **Philip's:** referring to King Philip II of Spain (1527–1598).
135. **object it not:** don't raise any objections.

Will make thee vow to study nothing else.
He that is grounded in astrology,
Enriched with tongues, well seen in minerals,
Hath all the principles magic doth require.   140
Then doubt not, Faustus, but to be renowned
And more frequented for this mystery
Than heretofore the Delphian oracle.
The spirits tell me they can dry the sea
And fetch the treasure of all foreign wrecks,   145
Ay, all the wealth that our forefathers hid
Within the massy entrails of the earth.
Then tell me, Faustus, what shall we three want?

FAUSTUS
Nothing, Cornelius. O this cheers my soul!
Come, show me some demonstrations magical   150
That I may conjure in some lusty grove
And have these joys in full possession.

VALDES
Then haste thee to some solitary grove
And bear wise Bacon's and Abanus' works,
The Hebrew Psalter, and New Testament;   155
And whatsoever else is requisite
We will inform thee ere our conference cease.

CORNELIUS
Valdes, first let him know the words of art,
And then, all other ceremonies learned,
Faustus may try his cunning by himself.   160

VALDES
First I'll instruct thee in the rudiments,
And then wilt thou be perfecter than I.

FAUSTUS
Then come and dine with me, and, after meat,
We'll canvass every quiddity thereof;
For, ere I sleep, I'll try what I can do.   165
This night I'll conjure, though I die therefore.   *Exeunt.*

---

138. grounded: well-educated.
139. tongues: languages; well . . . minerals: skilled in alchemy.
142. frequented . . . mystery: resorted to for this art.
143. Delphian oracle: the famous oracle of Apollo at Delphi in Greece.
148. want: lack.
151. lusty: pleasant.
154. Bacon's . . . works: the writings of Roger Bacon and Pietro d'Abano, 13th-century scientists reputed to be sorcerers.
164. canvass every quiddity: investigate in every detail.

[1.2]

Enter two SCHOLARS.

FIRST SCHOLAR   I wonder what's become of Faustus, that was wont to make our schools ring with *"sic probo."*

SECOND SCHOLAR   That shall we know, for see, here comes his boy.

Enter WAGNER [*with a bottle of wine*].

FIRST SCHOLAR   How now, sirrah! Where's thy master?   5

WAGNER   God in heaven knows.

SECOND SCHOLAR   Why, dost not thou know?

WAGNER   Yes, I know, but that follows not.

FIRST SCHOLAR   Go to, sirrah! Leave your jesting and tell us where he is.   10

WAGNER   That follows not necessary by force of argument, that you, being licentiate, should stand upon't. Therefore acknowledge your error and be attentive.

SECOND SCHOLAR   Why, didst thou not say thou knew'st?

WAGNER   Have you any witness on't?   15

FIRST SCHOLAR   Yes, sirrah, I heard you.

WAGNER   Ask my fellow if I be a thief.

SECOND SCHOLAR   Well, you will not tell us?

WAGNER   Yes, sir, I will tell you; yet, if you were not dunces, you would never ask me such a question; for is not he *corpus*   20 *naturale*? And is not that *mobile*? Then, wherefore should you ask me such a question? But that I am by nature phlegmatic, slow to wrath, and prone to lechery (to love, I would say), it were not for you to come within forty foot of the place of execution, although I do not doubt to see you both   25 hanged the next sessions. Thus, having triumphed over you, I will set my countenance like a precisian and begin to speak thus: truly, my dear brethren, my master is within at dinner with Valdes and Cornelius, as this wine, if it could speak, it would inform your worships. And so, the Lord bless you,   30 preserve you, and keep you, my dear brethren, my dear brethren.   *Exit.*

[1.2]
2. *sic probo*: i.e., thus I prove (Latin).
5. **sirrah**: term of address to an inferior.
9. **Go to**: expression of impatience.
12. **licentiate**: university designation for one eligible to study for the M.A.; **stand**: insist.
20–21. *corpus naturale*: natural body (Latin); **mobile**: able to move (Latin).
25. **place of execution**: i.e., the dining room (with obvious joke).
26. **sessions**: courtroom hearings.
27. **precisian**: one who is rigorous in religious observance; a Puritan.

FIRST SCHOLAR   Nay, then, I fear he is fallen into that damned
art for which they two are infamous through the world.

SECOND SCHOLAR   Were he a stranger and not allied to me,   35
yet should I grieve for him. But, come, let us go and inform
the Rector and see if he by his grave counsel can reclaim
him.

FIRST SCHOLAR   O, but I fear me nothing can reclaim him!

SECOND SCHOLAR   Yet let us try what we can do.   *Exeunt.*   40

[1.3]

Enter FAUSTUS [*preparing*] *to conjure.*

FAUSTUS
Now that the gloomy shadow of the earth,
Longing to view Orion's drizzling look,
Leaps from th'Antarctic world unto the sky
And dims the welkin with her pitchy breath,
Faustus, begin thine incantations   5
And try if devils will obey thy hest,
Seeing thou hast prayed and sacrificed to them.
[*Draws a circle.*]
Within this circle is Jehovah's name
Forward and backward anagrammatized,
The 'breviated names of holy saints,   10
Figures of every adjunct to the heavens,
And characters of signs and erring stars,
By which the spirits are enforced to rise.
Then fear not, Faustus, but be resolute
And try the uttermost magic can perform.   15
*Sint mihi dei Acherontis propitii! Valeat numen triplex
Jehovae! Ignei, aerii, aquatici, spiritus, salvete! Orientis
princeps Beelzebub, inferni ardentis monarcha, et*

---

37. **Rector:** head of a university.
[1.3]
2. **Orion's drizzling look:** the constellation Orion, whose prominent position in the late autumn sky heralded the stormy season (cf. *Aeneid* 1.565, 4.52).
4. **welkin:** sky; **pitchy:** pitch black.
6. **hest:** behest, command.
9. **anagrammatized:** made into anagrams; i.e., with the letters rearranged.
11. **Figures . . . heavens:** charts of all the heavenly bodies.
12. **characters:** symbols; **signs:** i.e., signs of the zodiac.
16–22. *Sint . . . Mephistopheles:* i.e., May the gods of Acheron be generous to me! Away with the threefold power of Jehovah! Hail spirits of fire, air, and water! The prince of the East, Beelzebub, monarch of burning hell, and Demogorgon, we beseech you that Mephistopheles may rise and appear. Why do you delay? By Jehovah, Gehenna, and the holy water I now sprinkle, and by the sign of the cross I now make, and by our vows, may Mephistopheles himself arise at our command (Latin).

Demogorgon, propitiamus vos, ut appareat et surgat
Mephistopheles! Quid tu moraris? Per Jehovam, Gehennam,
et consecratam aquam quam nunc spargo, signumque crucis   20
quod nunc facio, et per vota nostra, ipse nunc surgat nobis
dicatus Mephistopheles!

    Enter [MEPHISTOPHELES, *dressed as*] *a Devil.*

I charge thee to return and change thy shape;
Thou art too ugly to attend on me.
Go, and return an old Franciscan friar;   25
That holy shape becomes a devil best.

                                  Exit [MEPHISTOPHELES].
I see there's virtue in my heavenly words.
Who would not be proficient in this art?
How pliant is this Mephistopheles,
Full of obedience and humility!   30
Such is the force of magic and my spells.
No, Faustus, thou art conjuror laureate
That canst command great Mephistopheles.
Quin redis, Mephistopheles, fratris imagine?

    Enter MEPHISTOPHELES [*dressed as a friar*].

MEPHISTOPHELES
  Now, Faustus, what wouldst thou have me do?   35
FAUSTUS
  I charge thee wait upon me whilst I live,
  To do whatever Faustus shall command,
  Be it to make the moon drop from her sphere
  Or the ocean to overwhelm the world.
MEPHISTOPHELES
  I am a servant to great Lucifer   40
  And may not follow thee without his leave.
  No more than he commands must we perform.
FAUSTUS
  Did not he charge thee to appear to me?
MEPHISTOPHELES
  No, I came not hither of mine own accord.
FAUSTUS
  Did not my conjuring speeches raise thee? Speak.   45

---

27. **virtue:** power.
32. **laureate:** crowned with the laurel; i.e., preeminent, of recognized distinction.
34. ***Quin . . . imagine:*** i.e., Why don't you come back, Mephistopheles, in the shape of a friar?

MEPHISTOPHELES
   That was the cause, but yet *per accidens;*
   For, when we hear one rack the name of God,
   Abjure the Scriptures and his Savior Christ,
   We fly in hope to get his glorious soul;
   Nor will we come unless he use such means   50
   Whereby he is in danger to be damned.
   Therefore the shortest cut for conjuring
   Is stoutly to abjure the Trinity
   And pray devoutly to the prince of hell.
FAUSTUS
   So Faustus hath already done and holds this principle: 55
   There is no chief but only Beelzebub
   To whom Faustus doth dedicate himself.
   This word "damnation" terrifies not him,
   For he confounds hell in Elysium.
   His ghost be with the old philosophers.   60
   But, leaving these vain trifles of men's souls,
   Tell me, what is that Lucifer, thy lord?
MEPHISTOPHELES
   Arch-regent and commander of all spirits.
FAUSTUS
   Was not that Lucifer an angel once?
MEPHISTOPHELES
   Yes, Faustus, and most dearly loved of God.   65
FAUSTUS
   How comes it, then, that he is prince of devils?
MEPHISTOPHELES
   O, by aspiring pride and insolence,
   For which God threw him from the face of heaven.
FAUSTUS
   And what are you that live with Lucifer?
MEPHISTOPHELES
   Unhappy spirits that fell with Lucifer,   70
   Conspired against our God with Lucifer,
   And are for ever damned with Lucifer.
FAUSTUS   Where are you damned?
MEPHISTOPHELES   In hell.

---

46. cause . . . *per accidens:* i.e., the occasion but not the efficient cause.
47. rack: abuse, malign.
53. stoutly: resolutely.
59. confounds . . . Elysium: i.e., makes no distinction between the Christian hell and the classical Elysium.
60. old philosophers: i.e., the classical philosophers, who knew nothing of the moral judgments of the Christian afterlife.

FAUSTUS
  How comes it, then, that thou art out of hell?   75
MEPHISTOPHELES
  Why, this is hell, nor am I out of it.
  Think'st thou that I, who saw the face of God,
  And tasted the eternal joys of heaven,
  Am not tormented with ten thousand hells
  In being deprived of everlasting bliss?   80
  O, Faustus, leave these frivolous demands,
  Which strike a terror to my fainting soul!
FAUSTUS
  What, is great Mephistopheles so passionate
  For being deprivèd of the joys of heaven?
  Learn thou of Faustus manly fortitude   85
  And scorn those joys thou never shalt possess.
  Go bear those tidings to great Lucifer:
  Seeing Faustus hath incurred eternal death
  By desperate thoughts against Jove's deity,
  Say, he surrenders up to him his soul,   90
  So he will spare him four-and-twenty years,
  Letting him live in all voluptuousness,
  Having thee ever to attend on me,
  To give me whatsoever I shall ask,
  To tell me whatsoever I demand,   95
  To slay mine enemies and aid my friends,
  And always be obedint to my will.
  Go and return to mighty Lucifer,
  And meet me in my study at midnight,
  And then resolve me of thy master's mind.   100
MEPHISTOPHELES   I will, Faustus.   *Exit.*
FAUSTUS
  Had I as many souls as there be stars,
  I'd give them all for Mephistopheles.
  By him I'll be great emperor of the world
  And make a bridge through the moving air   105
  To pass the ocean with a band of men;
  I'll join the hills that bind the Afric shore
  And make that land continent to Spain,
  And both contributory to my crown.
  The Emperor shall not live but by my leave,   110
  Nor any potentate of Germany.
  Now that I have obtained what I desire,

91. **So:** on the condition that.
107. **bind:** border on, gird.
108. **continent to:** continuous with.

I'll live in speculation of this art
Till Mephistopheles return again.   *Exit.*

[1.4]

Enter WAGNER *and* [ROBIN]

WAGNER   Sirrah boy, come hither.

ROBIN   How, "boy"? Zounds, "boy"! I hope you have seen
many boys with such pickedevants as I have. "Boy," quotha?

WAGNER   Tell me, sirrah, hast thou any comings in?

ROBIN   Ay, and goings out too, you may see else.   5

WAGNER   Alas, poor slave, see how poverty jesteth in his
nakedness! The villain is bare, and out of service, and so
hungry, that I know he would give his soul to the devil for a
shoulder of mutton, though it were blood-raw.

ROBIN   How! My soul to the devil for a shoulder of mutton,   10
though 'twere blood-raw? Not so, good friend. By'r Lady, I had
need have it well roasted and good sauce to it, if I pay so dear.

WAGNER   Well, wilt thou serve me, and I'll make thee go like
"Qui mihi discipulus."   15

ROBIN   How, in verse?

WAGNER   No, sirrah; in beaten silk and stavesacre.

ROBIN   How, how, knaves-acre! [*Aside.*] Ay, I thought that was
all the land his father left him. [*To* WAGNER.] Do ye hear? I
would be sorry to rob you of your living.   20

WAGNER   Sirrah, I say in stavesacre.

ROBIN   Oho, oho, "stavesacre"! Why, then, belike, if I were
your man, I should be full of vermin.

WAGNER   So thou shalt, whether thou beest with me or no.
But, sirrah, leave your jesting and bind yourself presently   25
unto me for even years, or I'll turn all the lice about thee
into familiars, and they shall tear thee in pieces.

---

113. **speculation:** contemplation.
[1.4]
2. **Zounds:** by God's wounds; a mild oath.
3. **pickedevants:** short, pointed beards; **quotha:** i.e., said he.
4. **comings in:** income.
5. **goings out:** expenses (but punning on his flesh peeking out of his tattered clothes); **else:** if you do not believe me.
7. **out of service:** unemployed.
11. **By'r Lady:** by our Lady (the Virgin Mary); a mild oath.
15. *Qui mihi discipulus:* you who are my pupil. The opening line of a well-known Latin poem, *"Carmen de moribus,"* by William Lyly.
17. **beaten:** embroidered (but also, thrashed); **stavesacre:** a preparation made from delphinium seed used to exterminate lice and fleas.
25. **bind:** apprentice ("seven years" was the usual term of an apprenticeship).
27. **familiars:** evil spirits.

ROBIN   Do you hear, sir? You may save that labor. They are too familiar with me already. Zounds, they are as bold with my flesh as if they had paid for my meat and drink.   30

WAGNER   Well, do you hear, sirrah? Hold, take these guilders. [*Hands Robin coins.*]

ROBIN   Gridirons? What be they?

WAGNER   Why, French crowns.

ROBIN   Mass, but for the name of French crowns, a man were as good have as many English counters. And what should I   35
do with these?

WAGNER   Why, now, sirrah, thou art at an hour's warning whensoever or wheresoever the devil shall fetch thee.

ROBIN   No, no; here, take your gridirons again. [*Tries to hand them back.*]

WAGNER   Truly, I'll none of them.   40

ROBIN   Truly, but you shall.

WAGNER   [*To audience.*] Bear witness I gave them him.

ROBIN   Bear witness I give them you again.

WAGNER   Well, I will cause two devils presently to fetch thee away.—Baliol and Belcher!   45

ROBIN   Let your Balio and your Belcher come here, and I'll knock them. They were never so knocked since they were devils. Say I should kill one of them, what would folks say? "Do ye see yonder tall fellow in the round slop? He has killed the devil." So I should be called "Kill-devil" all the parish   50
over.

> *Enter two Devils; and* [ROBIN] *the Clown runs up and down crying.*

WAGNER   Baliol and Belcher! Spirits, away!   *Exeunt* [DEVILS.]

ROBIN   What, are they gone? A vengeance on them! They have vile long nails. There was a he-devil and a she-devil. I'll tell you how you shall know them; all he-devils has horns, and   55
all she-devils has clefts and cloven feet.

WAGNER   Well, sirrah, follow me.

ROBIN   But, do you hear? If I should serve you, would you teach me to raise up Banios and Belcheos?

---

31. guilders: Dutch coins (payment to mark Robin's acceptance of the apprenticeship).
32. gridirons: Robin's mishearing or deliberate corruption of the *guilders*.
33. French crowns: French coins (*écus*).
34. Mass: by the mass; a mild oath.
35. counters: tokens without monetary value.
45. Baliol and Belcher: names of devils. Baliol is a version of Belial. Belcher is perhaps a comic corruption of Beelzebub.
49. tall: valiant; **round slop:** baggy trousers.
56. clefts: split hooves (but also, vaginas).

WAGNER   I will teach thee to turn thyself to anything: to a dog,   60
or a cat, or a mouse, or a rat, or anything.

ROBIN   How! A Christian fellow to a dog, or a cat, a mouse, or
a rat! No, no, sir; if you turn me into anything, let it be in
the likeness of a little pretty frisking flea, that I may be here
and there and everywhere. O, I'll tickle the pretty wenches'   65
plackets! I'll be amongst them, i'faith.

WAGNER   Well, sirrah, come.

ROBIN   But do you hear, Wagner?

WAGNER   How? [*Calls.*] Baliol and Belcher!

ROBIN   O Lord! I pray, sir, let Baliol and Belcher go sleep.   70

WAGNER   Villain, call me "Master Wagner," and let thy left eye
be diametarily fixed upon my right heel, with *quasi vestigiis
nostris insistere.*   *Exit.*

ROBIN   God forgive me, he speaks Dutch fustian. Well, I'll follow him; I'll serve him, that's flat.   *Exit.*   75

[2.1]

Enter FAUSTUS *in his study.*

FAUSTUS
Now, Faustus, must thou needs be damned
And canst thou not be saved.
What boots it then to think of God or heaven?
Away with such vain fancies and despair.
Despair in God and trust in Beelzebub.   5
Now go not backward; no, Faustus, be resolute.
Why waverest thou? O, something soundeth in mine ears:
"Abjure this magic; turn to God again!"
Ay, and Faustus will turn to God again.
To God? He loves thee not.   10
The god thou servest is thine own appetite,
Wherein is fixed the love of Beelzebub.
To him I'll build an altar and a church
And offer lukewarm blood of new-born babes.

Enter GOOD ANGEL *and* EVIL [ANGEL].

GOOD ANGEL
Sweet Faustus, leave that execrable art.   15

66. **plackets:** slits in a skirt (and, by analogy, vaginas).
72. **diametarily:** diametrically.
72–73. ***quasi . . . insistere:*** i.e., as if to follow in our footsteps (Latin).
74. **Dutch fustian:** a coarse, cheap cloth; here, gibberish.
75. **flat:** certain, for sure.
[2.1]
3. **boots:** avails, helps.

FAUSTUS

    Contrition, prayer, repentance—what of them?

GOOD ANGEL

    O, they are means to bring thee unto heaven!

EVIL ANGEL

    Rather illusions, fruits of lunacy,

    That make men foolish that do trust them most.

GOOD ANGEL

    Sweet Faustus, think of heaven and heavenly things.   20

EVIL ANGEL

    No, Faustus; think of honor and wealth.   *Exeunt* [ANGELS.]

FAUSTUS

    Of wealth!

    Why, the seigniory of Emden shall be mine.

    When Mephistopheles shall stand by me,

    What god can hurt thee, Faustus? Thou art safe.   25

    Cast no more doubts.—Come, Mephistopheles,

    And bring glad tidings from great Lucifer.

    Is't not midnight? Come, Mephistopheles.

    Veni, veni, Mephistophile!

        Enter MEPHISTOPHELES.

    Now tell me what says Lucifer, thy lord?   30

MEPHISTOPHELES

    That I shall wait on Faustus whilst I live,

    So he will buy my service with his soul.

FAUSTUS

    Already Faustus hath hazarded that for thee.

MEPHISTOPHELES

    But, Faustus, thou must bequeath it solemnly

    And write a deed of gift with thine own blood,   35

    For that security craves great Lucifer.

    If thou deny it, I will back to hell.

FAUSTUS

    Stay, Mephistopheles, and tell me what good

    Will my soul do thy lord?

MEPHISTOPHELES   Enlarge his kingdom.

FAUSTUS

    Is that the reason he tempts us thus?   40

23. seigniory of Emden: governorship of Emden, a prosperous German port on the North Sea.
29. *Veni, veni, Mephistophile*: come, come, Mephistopheles (Latin).
32. So: provided that.

MEPHISTOPHELES
Solamen miseris socios habuisse doloris.
FAUSTUS
Have you any pain that tortures others?
MEPHISTOPHELES
As great as have the human souls of men.
But tell me, Faustus, shall I have thy soul?   45
And I will be thy slave, and wait on thee,
And give thee more than thou hast wit to ask.
FAUSTUS
Ay, Mephistopheles, I give it thee.
MEPHISTOPHELES
Then stab thine arm courageously
And bind thy soul, that at some certain day   50
Great Lucifer may claim it as his own,
And then be thou as great as Lucifer.
FAUSTUS.
[*Cuts his arm.*] Lo, Mephistopheles, for love of thee
I cut mine arm, and with my proper blood
Assure my soul to be great Lucifer's,   55
Chief lord and regent of perpetual night.
View here the blood that trickles from mine arm,
And let it be propitious for my wish.
MEPHISTOPHELES   But, Faustus, thou must write it in manner
of a deed of gift.
FAUSTUS   60
Ay, so I will. [*Writes.*] But, Mephistopheles,
My blood congeals, and I can write no more.
MEPHISTOPHELES
I'll fetch thee fire to dissolve it straight.   *Exit.*
FAUSTUS
What might the staying of my blood portend?
Is it unwilling I should write this bill?   65
Why streams it not, that I may write afresh:
"Faustus gives to thee his soul"? Ah, there it stayed!
Why shouldst thou not? Is not thy soul thine own?
Then write again: "Faustus gives to thee his soul."

Enter MEPHISTOPHELES *with a chafer of coals.*

---

41. Solamen . . . doloris: i.e., to the unhappy it is a comfort to have had company in misfortune (Latin).
42. Have . . . others: i.e., do you devils who torture others feel any pain yourselves?
49. certain: unavoidable (but also set, specified).
53. proper: own.
57. be propitious: be found acceptable.
64. bill: contract.
68. SD chafer: portable grate or grill.

MEPHISTOPHELES

    Here's fire; come, Faustus, set it on.   70

FAUSTUS

    So, now the blood begins to clear again;

    Now will I make an end immediately. [*Writes.*]

MEPHISTOPHELES

    [*Aside.*] O, what will not I do to obtain his soul?

FAUSTUS

    Consummatum est; this bill is ended,

    And Faustus hath bequeathed his soul to Lucifer.

    But what is this inscription on mine arm?   75

    "Homo, fuge!" Wither should I fly?

    If unto God, he'll throw me down to hell.

    My senses are deceived; here's nothing writ.

    I see it plain; here in this place is writ

    "Homo, fuge!" Yet shall not Faustus fly.   80

MEPHISTOPHELES

    [*Aside.*] I'll fetch him somewhat to delight his mind.   *Exit.*

        Enter [MEPHISTOPHELES] *with Devils, giving crowns and rich apparel to* FAUSTUS, *and* [*they*] *dance and then depart.*

FAUSTUS

    Speak, Mephistopheles; what means this show?

MEPHISTOPHELES

    Nothing, Faustus, but to delight thy mind withal

    And to show thee what magic can perform.

FAUSTUS

    But may I rise up spirits when I please?   85

MEPHISTOPHELES

    Ay, Faustus, and do greater things than these.

FAUSTUS

    Then there's enough for a thousand souls.

    Here, Mephistopheles, receive this scroll,

    A deed of gift of body and of soul,

    But yet conditionally that thou perform   90

    All articles prescribed between us both.

MEPHISTOPHELES

    Faustus, I swear by hell and Lucifer

    To effect all promises between us made.

FAUSTUS   Then hear me read them: [*Reads.*] *on these conditions following: first, that Faustus may be a spirit in form and*   95

---

73. *Consummatum est*: It is finished (Christ's last words on the Cross, John 19:30).

76. *Homo, fuge*: Man, flee. Cf. 1 Timothy 6:11 and Psalms 139:7–8.

83. withal: with.

*substance; secondly, that Mephistopheles shall be his servant
and at his command; thirdly, that Mephistopheles shall do for
him and bring him whatsoever; fourthly, that he shall be in his
chamber or house invisible; lastly, that he shall appear to the*   100
*said John Faustus at all times in what form or shape soever he
please. I, John Faustus of Württemberg, Doctor, by these presents, do give both body and soul to Lucifer, Prince of the East,
and his minister, Mephistopheles, and furthermore grant unto
them, that twenty-four years being expired, the articles above*   105
*written inviolate, full power to fetch or carry the said John
Faustus' body and soul, flesh and blood, or goods, into their
habitation wheresoever. By me, John Faustus.*

MEPHISTOPHELES
Speak, Faustus, do you deliver this as your deed?
FAUSTUS
Ay, take it, and the devil give thee good on't!
                    [*Hands* MEPHISTOPHELES *the deed.*]   110
MEPHISTOPHELES   Now, Faustus, ask what thou wilt.
FAUSTUS
First will I question with thee about hell.
Tell me, where is the place that men call hell?
MEPHISTOPHELES
Under the heavens.
FAUSTUS   Ay, but whereabout?
MEPHISTOPHELES
Within the bowels of these elements,   115
Where we are tortured and remain for ever.
Hell hath no limits, nor is circumscribed
In one self place, for where we are is hell,
And where hell is, there must we ever be.
And, to conclude, when all the world dissolves   120
And every creature shall be purified
All places shall be hell that is not heaven.
FAUSTUS   Come, I think hell's a fable.
MEPHISTOPHELES
Ay, think so still, till experience change thy mind.
FAUSTUS
Why, think'st thou, then, that Faustus shall be damned?
MEPHISTOPHELES   125
Ay, of necessity, for here's the scroll
Wherein thou hast given thy soul to Lucifer.

---

102. **presents:** legal documents.
105. **inviolate:** i.e., having not been violated.
117. **self:** particular, single.

FAUSTUS
  Ay, and body too. But what of that?
  Think'st thou that Faustus is so fond to imagine
  That, after this life, there is any pain?   130
  Tush, these are trifles and mere old wives' tales.
MEPHISTOPHELES
  But, Faustus, I am an instance to prove the contrary,
  For I am damned and am now in hell.
FAUSTUS   How? Now in hell? Nay, an this be hell, I'll willingly
  be damned here. What? Walking, disputing, &c. But, leaving   135
  off this, let me have a wife, the fairest maid in Germany, for
  I am wanton and lascivious, and cannot live without a wife.
MEPHISTOPHELES   How, a wife? I prithee, Faustus, talk not of
  a wife.
FAUSTUS   Nay, sweet Mephistopheles, fetch me one, for I will   140
  have one.
MEPHISTOPHELES
  Well, thou wilt have one? Sit there till I come.
  I'll fetch thee a wife in the devil's name.   [*Exit.*]

  Enter [MEPHISTOPHELES] *with a Devil dressed like a
  woman, with fire-works.*

MEPHISTOPHELES   Tell me, Faustus, how dost thou like thy
  wife?   145
FAUSTUS   A plague on her for a hot whore!
MEPHISTOPHELES
  Tut, Faustus, marriage is but a ceremonial toy;
  If thou lovest me, think no more of it.
  I'll cull thee out the fairest courtesans
  And bring them every morning to thy bed.   150
  She whom thine eye shall like, thy heart shall have,
  But she as chaste as was Penelope,
  As wise as Saba, or as beautiful
  As was bright Lucifer before his fall.
  Hold, take this book, peruse it thoroughly.
      [*Gives* FAUSTUS *a book and they look at it.*]   155
  The iterating of these lines brings gold;
  The framing of this circle on the ground
  Brings whirlwinds, tempests, thunder, and lightning;

128. **fond:** foolish.
146. **ceremonial toy:** trifling ceremony.
151. **Penelope:** Odysseus's faithful wife in Homer's *Odyssey.*
152. **Saba:** the Queen of Sheba (2 Chronicles 9:1–3; Vulgate spelling).
155. **iterating:** repetition.

Pronounce this thrice devoutly to thyself,
And men in armor shall appear to thee
Ready to execute what thou desir'st.   160

FAUSTUS

Thanks, Mephistopheles. Yet fain would I have a book wherein
I might behold all spells and incantations,
That I might raise up spirits when I please.

MEPHISTOPHELES   Here they are in this book.

                    [*They*] *turn to* [*the spells in the book*].

FAUSTUS

Now would I have a book where I might see   165
All characters and planets of the heavens,
That I might know their motions and dispositions.

MEPHISTOPHELES   Here they are too.   *Turn to them.*

FAUSTUS   Nay, let me have one book more—and then I have
done—wherein I might see all plants, herbs, and trees that   170
grow upon the earth.

MEPHISTOPHELES   Here they be.   *Turn to them.*

FAUSTUS   O, thou art deceived.

MEPHISTOPHELES   Tut, I warrant thee.   [*Exeunt.*]

[2.2]

Enter ROBIN *the ostler, with a book in his hand.*

ROBIN   O, this is admirable! Here I ha' stolen one of Doctor
Faustus' conjuring books, and i'faith, I mean to search some
circles for my own use. Now will I make all the maidens in
our parish dance at my pleasure stark naked before me, and
so by that means I shall see more than e'er I felt or saw yet.   5

Enter RAFE, *calling* ROBIN.

RAFE   Robin, prithee, come away; there's a gentleman tarries
to have his horse, and he would have his things rubbed and
made clean. He keeps such a chafing with my mistress about

161. **fain:** gladly.
166. **characters:** astrological symbols.
167. **dispositions:** situation of a planet in a horoscope.
174. **I warrant thee:** I assure you [that the book does contain all that has been promised].
2.2. On the placement of this scene here, which is printed in the A-Text (1604) after Faustus's visit to Rome (3.1), see p. 00 herein.
[2.2]
2.2. **SD ostler:** horsegroom, stableman.
3. **circles:** magic circles for conjuring.
7. **things rubbed:** saddle, bridle, and reins oiled (with sexual joke).
8. **chafing:** scolding.

it, and she has sent me to look thee out. Prithee, come away.   10

ROBIN   Keep out, keep out, or else you are blown up, you are dismembered, Rafe. Keep out, for I am about a roaring piece of work.

RAFE   Come, what doest thou with that same book? Thou canst not read.   15

ROBIN   Yes, my master and mistress shall find that I can read: he for his forehead, she for her private study. She's born to bear with me, or else my art fails.

RAFE   Why, Robin, what book is that?

ROBIN   What book? Why, the most intolerable book for con-   20
juring that e'er was invented by any brimstone devil.

RAFE   Canst thou conjure with it?

ROBIN   I can do all these things easily with it: first, I can make thee drunk with 'ippocras at any tavern in Europe for noth-ing; that's one of my conjuring works.   25

RAFE   Our Master Parson says that's nothing.

ROBIN   True, Rafe. And more, Rafe: if thou hast any mind to Nan Spit, our kitchen-maid, then turn her and wind her to thy own use as often as thou wilt, and at midnight.

RAFE   O, brave Robin! Shall I have Nan Spit, and to mine own   30
use? On that condition I'll feed thy devil with horse-bread as long as he lives, of free cost.

ROBIN   No more, sweet Rafe. Let's go and make clean our boots, which lie foul upon our hands, and then to our con-juring in the devil's name.   *Exeunt.*

[2.3]

[*Enter* FAUSTUS *and* MEPHISTOPHELES.]

FAUSTUS
    When I behold the heavens, then I repent
    And curse thee, wicked Mephistopheles,
    Because thou hast deprived me of those joys.

MEPHISTOPHELES
    Why, Faustus, think'st thou heaven is such a glorious   5
        thing?

11. **roaring:** riotous, dangerous.
16. **forehead:** a reference to the horns that were supposed to grow on the forehead of a cuckolded husband.
17. **bear:** tolerate (but also, give birth to a child).
19. **intolerable:** probably Robin's error for "incomparable."
20. **brimstone:** sulfurous; i.e., from hell.
23. **'ippocras:** i.e., hippocras; a spiced wine.
30. **horse-bread:** fodder, bran.

I tell thee, 'tis not half so fair as thou,
Or any man that breathes on earth.
FAUSTUS
How provest thou that?
MEPHISTOPHELES   It was made for man,
Therefore is man more excellent.
FAUSTUS
If it were made for man, 'twas made for me.   10
I will renounce this magic and repent.

          Enter GOOD ANGEL *and* EVIL ANGEL.

GOOD ANGEL
Faustus, repent; yet God will pity thee.
EVIL ANGEL
Thou art a spirit; God cannot pity thee.
FAUSTUS
Who buzzeth in mine ears I am a spirit?
Be I a devil, yet God may pity me;   15
Ay, God will pity me, if I repent.
EVIL ANGEL
Ay, but Faustus never shall repent.   *Exeunt* [ANGELS].
FAUSTUS
My heart's so hardened I cannot repent.
Scarce can I name salvation, faith, or heaven,
But fearful echoes thunder in mine ears,   20
"Faustus, thou art damned." Then swords and knives,
Poison, guns, halters, and envenomed steel
Are laid before me to despatch myself;
And long ere this I should have slain myself
Had not sweet pleasure conquered deep despair.   25
Have not I made blind Homer sing to me
Of Alexander's love and Oenone's death?
And hath not he that built the walls of Thebes
With ravishing sound of his melodious harp
Made music with my Mephistopheles?   30
Why should I die then or basely despair?
I am resolved: Faustus shall ne'er repent.
Come, Mephistopheles, let us dispute again

[2.3]
11. yet: even now, still.
21. halters: nooses; envenomed steel: poisoned blades.
26. Alexander's . . . death: i.e., the death of Paris in the Trojan war. He died in Oenone's arms; she then killed herself.
27–28. he . . . harp: Amphion, whose wonderful harp playing caused stones to rise and form the walls of Thebes.

And argue of divine astrology.
Tell me, are there many heavens above the moon?   35
Are all celestial bodies but one globe
As is the substance of this centric earth?

MEPHISTOPHELES
As are the elements, such are the spheres
Mutually folded in each other's orb,
And, Faustus, all jointly move upon one axletree,   40
Whose terminè is termed the world's wide pole;
Nor are the names of Saturn, Mars, or Jupiter
Feigned, but are erring stars.

FAUSTUS   But, tell me, have they all one motion, both *situ et*
tempore?   45

MEPHISTOPHELES   All jointly move from east to west in twenty-
four hours upon the poles of the world, but differ in their
motion upon the poles of the zodiac.

FAUSTUS
Tush, these slender trifles Wagner can decide.
Hath Mephistopheles no greater skill?   50
Who knows not the double motion of the planets? The first
is finished in a natural day; the second thus: as Saturn in
thirty years; Jupiter in twelve; Mars in four; the sun, Venus,
and Mercury in a year; the moon in twenty-eight days. Tush,
these are freshmen's suppositions. But, tell me, hath every   55
sphere a dominion or *intelligentia*?

MEPHISTOPHELES   Ay.

FAUSTUS   How many heavens or spheres are there?

MEPHISTOPHELES   Nine: the seven planets, the firmament, and
the imperial heaven.   60

FAUSTUS   Well, resolve me in this question: why have we not
conjunctions, oppositions, aspects, eclipses, all at one time;
but in some years we have more, in some less?

MEPHISTOPHELES   *Per inaequalem motum respectu totius.*

33. astrology: astronomy. A sharp separation of astrology from astronomy was not made
until the end of the 17th century.
35–36. Are . . . earth: i.e., do the stars and planets form a single, spherical structure, like
the earth itself that is at its center?
39. axletree: axis.
40. terminè: boundary.
42. erring stars: moving planets.
43–4. *situ et tempore*: in space and time (Latin).
54. freshmen's supposition: elementary facts given to beginning students.
55. dominion or *intelligentia*: angelic influence or intelligence, which was thought to
move the planets.
59. imperial heaven: the farthest sphere of the heavens, where God was thought to dwell.
(The B-text's "empyreal"—i.e., fiery—could be correct, and probably on stage no distinction
between the two words could be heard.)
61. conjunctions . . . aspects: astrological terms for, respectively, the proximity of two
planets; their location in directly opposite parts of the sky; their relative positions in the sky.
63. *Per . . . totius*: because of unequal motion in respect to the whole (Latin).

FAUSTUS   Well I am answered. Tell me who made the world?
MEPHISTOPHELES   I will not.   65
FAUSTUS   Sweet Mephistopheles, tell me.
MEPHISTOPHELES   Move me not, for I will not tell thee.
FAUSTUS   Villain, have I not bound thee to tell me any thing?
MEPHISTOPHELES   Ay, that is not against our kingdom; but this
is. Think thou on hell, Faustus, for thou art damned.   70
FAUSTUS   Think, Faustus, upon God that made the world.
MEPHISTOPHELES
    Remember this.   *Exit.*
FAUSTUS   Ay, go, accursèd spirit, to ugly hell!
    'Tis thou hast damned distressèd Faustus' soul.
    —Is't not too late?

            Enter GOOD ANGEL *and* EVIL [ANGEL].

EVIL ANGEL
    Too late.   75
GOOD ANGEL
    Never too late, if Faustus can repent.
EVIL ANGEL
    If thou repent, devils shall tear thee in pieces.
GOOD ANGEL
    Repent, and they shall never raze thy skin.   *Exeunt* [ANGELS].
FAUSTUS
    Ah, Christ, my savior,
    Seek to save distressèd Faustus' soul!   80

            Enter LUCIFER, BEELZEBUB, *and* MEPHISTOPHELES.

LUCIFER
    Christ cannot save thy soul, for he is just.
    There's none but I have interest in the same.
FAUSTUS
    O, who art thou that look'st so terrible?
LUCIFER
    I am Lucifer,
    And this is my companion prince in hell.   85
FAUSTUS
    O, Faustus, they are come to fetch away thy soul!
LUCIFER
    We come to tell thee thou dost injure us.
    Thou talk'st of Christ, contrary to thy promise.

67. **Move:** vex, anger (also urge).
78. **raze:** tear.
82. **interest in:** legal claim on.

Thou shouldst not think of God. Think of the devil
And of his dam, too.   90
FAUSTUS
    Nor will I henceforth. Pardon me in this,
    And Faustus vows never to look to heaven,
    Never to name God, or to pray to him,
    To burn his Scriptures, slay his ministers,
    And make my spirits pull his churches down.   95
LUCIFER   Do so, and we will highly gratify thee. Faustus, we
    are come from hell to show thee some pastime. Sit down,
    and thou shalt see all the Seven Deadly Sins appear in their
    proper shapes.
FAUSTUS   That sight will be as pleasing unto me as Paradise   100
    was to Adam, the first day of his creation.
LUCIFER   Talk not of Paradise nor creation, but mark this
    show. Talk of the devil and nothing else. [*Calls offstage.*]
    Come away!

           Enter the SEVEN DEADLY SINS.

    Now, Faustus, examine them of their several names and dis-   105
    positions.
FAUSTUS   What art thou, the first?
PRIDE   I am Pride; I disdain to have any parents. I am like to
    Ovid's flea. I can creep into every corner of a wench: some-
    times, like a periwig, I sit upon her brow; or, like a fan of   110
    feathers, I kiss her lips; indeed, I do—what do I not? But,
    fie, what a scent is here! I'll not speak another word, except
    the ground were perfumed and covered with cloth of arras.
FAUSTUS   What art thou, the second?
COVETOUSNESS   I am Covetousness, begotten of an old churl   115
    in an old leather bag, and, might I have my wish, I would de-
    sire that this house and all the people in it were turned to
    gold, that I might lock you up in my good chest. O, my sweet
    gold!
FAUSTUS   What art thou, the third?   120
WRATH   I am Wrath. I had neither father nor mother. I leaped
    out of a lion's mouth when I was scarce half an hour old,

90. **dam:** mother.
105. **several:** separate, different.
109. **Ovid's flea:** a Latin poem, "Elegia de pulice," wrongly ascribed to Ovid, notes the
flea's ability to go anywhere.
110. **periwig:** wig.
112. **except:** unless.
113. **cloth of arras:** fine tapestry. Arras, in Flanders, was a city renowned for its tapestry.
116. **bag:** purse, wallet.

and ever since I have run up and down the world with this
case of rapiers, wounding myself when I had nobody to fight   125
withal. I was born in hell, and look to it, for some of you
shall be my father.

FAUSTUS   What art thou, the fourth?

ENVY   I am Envy, begotten of a chimney-sweeper and an oyster-
wife. I cannot read and therefore wish all books were burned.   130
I am lean with seeing others eat. O, that there would come a
famine through all the world that all might die and I live
alone! Then thou shouldst see how fat I would be. But must
thou sit and I stand? Come down, with a vengeance!

FAUSTUS   Away, envious rascal! What art thou, the fifth?   135

GLUTTONY   Who? I, sir? I am Gluttony. My parents are all
dead, and the devil a penny they have left me but a bare pension, and that is thirty meals a day and ten bevers—a small
trifle to suffice nature. O, I come of a royal parentage! My
grandfather was a gammon of bacon, my grandmother a   140
hogshead of claret wine; my godfathers were these: Peter
Pickle-herring and Martin Martlemas-beef. O, but my godmother, she was a jolly gentlewoman and well-beloved in
every good town and city; her name was Mistress Margery
March-beer. Now, Faustus, thou hast heard all my progeny,   145
wilt thou bid me to supper?

FAUSTUS   No, I'll see thee hanged. Thou wilt eat up all my victuals.

GLUTTONY   Then the devil choke thee!

FAUSTUS   Choke thyself, glutton! What art thou, the sixth?

SLOTH   I am Sloth. I was begotten on a sunny bank, where I   150
have lain ever since, and you have done me great injury to
bring me from thence. Let me be carried thither again by
Gluttony and Lechery. I'll not speak another word for a
king's ransom.

FAUSTUS   What are you, Mistress Minx, the seventh and last?   155

LECHERY   Who? I, sir? I am one that loves an inch of raw mutton better than an ell of fried stock-fish; and the first letter
of my name begins with lechery.

124. case: pair.
133. with a vengeance: i.e., or else.
136. the devil a penny: i.e., not a damned cent.
137. bevers: snacks.
139. gammon of bacon: smoked ham.
140. **hogshead:** a large cask for liquor; **claret wine:** light red wine.
141. Pickled-herring: pickled herring (also, a buffoon); **Martlemas-beef:** salted beef, usually preserved around St. Martin's day (Martinmas, November 11).
144. March-beer: a strong beer, brewed in March; **progeny:** parentage.
157. ell . . . 45 inches; **stock-fish:** dried cod (often associated with sexual impotence); it is
not unlikely that the adjective "fried," as both the A-text and the B-text have it, is an error
for "dried."
158. lechery: many editors emend to "L," but the joke is that Lechery says his whole name.

FAUSTUS   Away, to hell, to hell!

                  Exeunt the [SEVEN DEADLY] SINS.

LUCIFER   Now, Faustus, how dost thou like this?   160

FAUSTUS   O, this feeds my soul!

LUCIFER   Tut, Faustus, in hell is all manner of delight.

FAUSTUS   O, might I see hell and return again, how happy
were I then!

LUCIFER   Thou shalt; I will send for thee at midnight. In mean-   165
time take this book; peruse it thoroughly, and thou shalt turn
thyself into what shape thou wilt.

FAUSTUS   Great thanks, mighty Lucifer! This will I keep as
chary as my life.

LUCIFER   Farewell, Faustus, and think on the devil.   170

FAUSTUS   Farewell, great Lucifer. Come, Mephistopheles.

                       Exeunt omnes.

[3.Chorus]

Faustus scene is more comical than normal

     Enter WAGNER, *Solus.*

WAGNER

Learnèd Faustus to know the secrets of astronomy
Graven in the book of Jove's high firmament
Did mount himself to scale Olympus' top,
Being seated in a chariot burning bright,
Drawn by the strength of yoky dragons' necks.   5
He now is gone to prove cosmography,
And, as I guess, will first arrive at Rome
To see the Pope and manner of his court
And take some part of holy Peter's feast,
That to this day is highly solemnized.   *Exit.*   10

[3.1]

Structurally a turning point

     Enter FAUSTUS *and* MEPHISTOPHELES.

FAUSTUS

Having now, my good Mephistopheles,

169. chary: carefully.
[3. Chorus]
2. Graven: engraved.
3. mount himself: i.e., take the reins of the chariot; scale Olympus' top: ascend to the
home of the gods on Mount Olympus.
5. yoky: yoked together.
6. prove: put to the test.
9. holy Peter's feast: St. Peter's feast day, June 29.

Passed with delight the stately town of Trier,
Environed round with airy mountain tops,
With walls of flint and deep entrenchèd lakes,
Not to be won by any conquering prince;   5
From Paris next, coasting the realm of France,
We saw the river Maine fall into Rhine,
Whose banks are set with groves of fruitful vines;
Then up to Naples, rich Campania,
Whose buildings, fair and gorgeous to the eye,   10
The streets straight forth and paved with finest brick,
Quarters the town in four equivalents.
There saw we learnèd Maro's golden tomb,
The way he cut an English mile in length
Through a rock of stone in one night's space.   15
From thence to Venice, Padua, and the rest,
In midst of which a sumptuous temple stands
That threats the stars with her aspiring top.
Thus hitherto hath Faustus spent his time.
But tell me now what resting place is this?   20
Hast thou, as erst I did command,
Conducted me within the walls of Rome?

MEPHISTOPHELES   Faustus, I have; and, because we will not be
unprovided, I have taken up his Holiness's privy chamber for
our use.   25

FAUSTUS
I hope his Holiness will bid us welcome.

MEPHISTOPHELES
Tut, 'tis no matter, man; we'll be bold with his good cheer.
And now, my Faustus, that thou mayst perceive
What Rome containeth to delight thee with,
Know that this city stands upon seven hills   30
That underprop the groundwork of the same.
Just through the midst runs flowing Tiber's stream
With winding banks that cut it in two parts,
Over the which four stately bridges lean,
That make safe passage to each part of Rome.   35

]3.1]
2. **Trier:** Treves, a German city on the river Mosel.
4. **entrenchèd lakes:** moats.
6. **coasting:** exploring.
9. **Campania:** region of Italy in which Naples is the principle city.
11. **straight forth:** in straight lines.
13. **Maro's golden tomb:** the tomb of Virgil (Publius Virgilius Maro), who was buried in Naples in 19 B.C.E.
17. **sumptuous temple:** probably St. Mark's in Venice.
21. **erst:** earlier.
24. **privy chamber:** private apartment in a palace.

Upon the bridge called Ponte Angelo
Erected is a castle passing strong,
Within whose walls such store of ordnance are,
And double cannons framed of carvèd brass,
As match the days within one complete year,   40
Besides the gates and high pyramides
Which Julius Caesar brought from Africa.

FAUSTUS
Now by the kingdoms of infernal rule,
Of Styx, of Acheron, and the fiery lake
Of ever-burning Phlegethon, I swear   45
That I do long to see the monuments
And situation of bright, splendent Rome.
Come, therefore, let's away.

MEPHISTOPHELES
Nay, Faustus, stay. I know you'd fain see the Pope
And take some part of holy Peter's feast,   50
Where thou shalt see a troop of bald-pate friars,
Whose *summum bonum* is in belly cheer.

FAUSTUS
Well, I'm content to compass then some sport
And by their folly make us merriment.
Then charm me that I   55
May be invisible, to do what I please
Unseen of any whilst I stay in Rome.
                        [MEPHISTOPHELES *casts a spell.*]
MEPHISTOPHELES   So, Faustus; now do what thou wilt, thou
shalt not be discerned.

> *Sound a sennet. Enter the* POPE *and the* CARDINAL *of Lor-
> raine to the banquet, with* FRIARS *attending.*

POPE   My Lord of Lorraine, will't please you draw near?   60
FAUSTUS   Fall to, and the devil choke you an you spare!
POPE   How now! Who's that which spake? Friars, look about.
FRIAR   Here's nobody, if it like your Holiness.
POPE   My lord, here is a dainty dish was sent me from the
Bishop of Milan.   65

36. **Ponte Angelo:** bridge built by Hadrian in 135 C.E.
37. **passing:** surpassingly.
41. **pyramides:** obelisk (in fact brought to Rome by Caligula from Heliopolis and moved in 1586 to the Piazza San Pietro). The noun is singular and pronounced with four syllables.
44–45. **Styx . . . Phlegethon:** three of the four rivers in the classical Greek underworld.
52. *summum bonum:* greatest good (Latin).
53. **compass:** contrive, invent.
59. **SD sennet:** flourish on a trumpet to signal a ceremonial entrance or exit.
61. **Fall to:** get on with it; **an you spare:** if you eat only sparingly.

FAUSTUS   I thank you, sir.   *Snatch[es the dish]*.
POPE   How now! Who's that which snatched the meat from
  me? Will no man look? My lord, this dish was sent me from
  the Cardinal of Florence.   70
FAUSTUS   You say true; I'll ha't.   *[Snatches the dish.]*
POPE   What, again! My lord, I'll drink to your Grace.
FAUSTUS   I'll pledge your Grace.   *[Snatches the cup.]*
CARDINAL   My lord, it may be some ghost, newly crept out of
  Purgatory, come to beg a pardon of your Holiness.
POPE   It may be so. Friars, prepare a dirge to lay the fury of   75
  this ghost.—Once again, my lord, fall to.
                  The POPE *crosses himself.*
FAUSTUS   What, are you crossing of yourself? Well, use that
  trick no more, I would advise you.
                      [The POPE] *cross[es himself] again.*
  Well, there's the second time. Aware the third, I give you fair
  warning.   80
                  [The POPE] *cross[es himself] again, and Faustus*
                  hits him a box of the ear; and they all run away.
  Come on, Mephistopheles; what shall we do?
MEPHISTOPHELES   Nay, I know not. We shall be cursed with
  bell, book, and candle.
FAUSTUS
  How! Bell, book, and candle; candle, book, and bell.
  Forward and backward, to curse Faustus to hell.   85
  Anon you shall hear a hog grunt, a calf bleat, and an ass bray,
  Because it is Saint Peter's holy day.

        Enter all the FRIARS *to sing the Dirge.*

FRIAR   Come, brethren, let's about our business with good de-
  votion.
                      [The FRIARS] *sing this.*
  Cursèd be he that stole away his Holiness's meat from the
    table: 90
      Maledicat Dominus!
  Cursèd be he that struck his Holiness a blow on the face:
      Maledicat Dominus!
  Cursèd be he that took Friar Sandelo a blow on the pate.

75. dirge: requiem sung at a burial (from the Latin *dirige*, the first word of the antiphon at
Matins in the Office of the Dead).
79. Aware: beware.
92. *Maledicat Dominus*: i.e., may God curse him (Latin).

> *Maledicat Dominus!*   95
> Cursèd be he that disturbeth our holy dirge.
> *Maledicat Dominus!*
> Cursèd be he that took away his Holiness's wine:
> *Maledicat Dominus et omnes Sancti!*
> Amen!

[MEPHISTOPHELES *and* FAUSTUS] *beat the* FRIARS *and fling fire-works among them, and so exeunt.*

(handwritten: Praying to God for Faustus to be damned)

[3.2]

Enter ROBIN [*with a book*] *and* RAFE *with a silver goblet.*

ROBIN   Come, Rafe. Did not I tell thee, we were for ever made by this Doctor Faustus's book? *Ecce signum!* Here's a simple purchase for horse-keepers. Our horses shall eat no hay as long as this lasts.

RAFE   But, Robin, here comes the vintner.   5

ROBIN   Hush! I'll gull him supernaturally.

Enter the VINTNER.

Drawer, I hope all is paid; God be with you! Come, Rafe.

VINTNER   Soft, sir; a word with you. I must yet have a goblet paid from you ere you go.

ROBIN   I, a goblet? Rafe, I, a goblet? I scorn you; and you are   10
but a etc. I, a goblet? Search me.

VINTNER   I mean so, sir, with your favor.   [*Searches* ROBIN.]

ROBIN   How say you now?

VINTNER   I must say somewhat to your fellow.—You, sir!

RAFE   Me, sir? Me, sir? [*Passes goblet to* ROBIN] Search your   15
fill. Now, sir, you may be ashamed to burden honest men with a matter of truth.

VINTNER   Well, t'one of you hath this goblet about you.

ROBIN   You lie, drawer, [*Aside.*] 'tis afore me.—Sirrah you, I'll teach you to impeach honest men. Stand by; I'll scour you   20
for a goblet. Stand aside you had best; I charge you in the

99. *et omnes Sancti*: and all his saints (Latin).
[3.2]
2. *Ecce signum*: behold the proof (Latin); **simple purchase**: easy profit.
3. **eat no hay**: because they will now be rich and be able to afford finer foods.
7. **Drawer**: waiter (an insult to the Vintner, who is the innkeeper).
8. **Soft**: i.e., wait a second.
11. **etc.**: a direction for the actor to improvise the expected insults.
12. **favor**: permission.
20. **impeach**: accuse.

name of Beelzebub. [*Whispers and hands goblet to* RAFE.]
Look to the goblet, Rafe.

VINTNER   What mean you, sirrah?

ROBIN   I'll tell you what I mean. [*He reads.*] "*Sanctobulorum*   25
Periphrasticon." Nay, I'll tickle you, vintner. Look to the goblet, Rafe. [*Reads.*] "*Polypragmos Belseborams framanto pa-
costiphos tostu Mephistopheles, &c.*"

Enter MEPHISTOPHELES, *sets squibs at their backs*[, *and
then exits*]. *They run about* [*transformed*].

VINTNER   O, *nomine Domine!* What meanest thou, Robin? Thou
hast no goblet?   30

RAFE   *Peccatum peccatorum!* Here's thy goblet, good vintner.
[*Throws the goblet after the* VINTNER, *who exits.*]

ROBIN   *Misericordia pro nobis!* What shall I do? Good devil,
forgive me now, and I'll never rob thy library more.

Enter to them MEPHISTOPHELES.

MEPHISTOPHELES   Vanish, villains! Th' one like an ape, another
like a bear, the third an ass, for doing this enterprise.   35
Monarch of Hell, under whose black survey
Great potentates do kneel with awful fear,
Upon whose altars thousand souls do lie,
How am I vexèd with these villains' charms?
From Constantinople am I hither come   40
Only for pleasure of these damnèd slaves.

ROBIN   How, from Constantinople? You have had a great journey. Will you take sixpence in your purse to pay for your supper and be gone?

MEPHISTOPHELES   Well, villains, for your presumption, I trans-   45
form thee into an ape, and thee into a dog; and so be gone!
Exit.

ROBIN   How, into an ape! That's brave. I'll have fine sport with
the boys; I'll get nuts and apples enow.

RAFE   And I must be a dog.

ROBIN   I'faith, thy head will never be out of the pottage pot.   50
Exeunt.

25–28. *Sanctabulorum . . .* **Mephistopheles:** Robin's nonsense Latin (but nonetheless effective in conjuring Mephistopheles—evidence of how little Faustus achieves).
29. *nomine Domine*: Here and in the lines below, the Latin phrases are garbled scraps of
the liturgy, here a jingling version of "the name of God."
31. *Peccatum peccatorum*: i.e., sin of sins.
32. *Misericordia pro nobis*: i.e., pity for us.
36. **survey:** gaze.
37. **awful:** i.e. full of awe.
47. **brave:** excellent.
48. **enow:** enough
50. **pottage:** porridge.

[4.Chorus]

Enter CHORUS

CHORUS
  When Faustus had with pleasure ta'en the view
  Of rarest things and royal courts of kings,
  He stayed his course and so returnèd home,
  Where such as bear his absence but with grief,
  I mean his friends and nearest companions,   5
  Did gratulate his safety with kind words;
  And in their conference of what befell,
  Touching his journey through the world and air,
  They put forth questions of astrology,
  Which Faustus answered with such learnèd skill   10
  As they admired and wondered at his wit.
  Now is his fame spread forth in every land.
  Amongst the rest the Emperor is one,
  Carolus the Fifth, at whose palace now
  Faustus is feasted 'mongst his noblemen.   15
  What there he did in trial of his art
  I leave untold; your eyes shall see't performed.   *Exit.*

[4.1]

Enter EMPEROR, FAUSTUS, [MEPHISTOPHELES,] *and a*
KNIGHT, *with* ATTENDANTS.

EMPEROR Master Doctor Faustus, I have heard strange report of thy knowledge in the black art; how that none in my empire nor in the whole world can compare with thee for the rare effects of magic. They say thou hast a familiar spirit by whom thou canst accomplish what thou list. This, therefore,   5 is my request: that thou let me see some proof of thy skill, that mine eyes may be witnesses to confirm what mine ears have heard reported, and here I swear to thee, by the honor of mine imperial crown, that, whatever thou doest, thou shall be no ways prejudiced or endamaged.   10
KNIGHT (*Aside.*) I'faith, he looks much like a conjurer.
FAUSTUS My gracious sovereign, though I must confess my-

[4. Chorus]
3. stayed his course: ended his travels.
6. gratulate: express joy at.
14. Carolus the Fifth: Charles V (1519–1556), king of Spain and emperor of the Holy Roman Empire until his abdication in 1555.

self far inferior to the report men have published and nothing answerable to the honor of your imperial Majesty, yet, for
that love and duty binds me thereunto, I am content to do   15
whatsoever your Majesty shall command me.

EMPEROR
   Then, Doctor Faustus, mark what I shall say.
   As I was sometime solitary set
   Within my closet, sundry thoughts arose
   About the honor of mine ancestors—   20
   How they had won by prowess such exploits,
   Got such riches, subdued so many kingdoms,
   As we that do succeed, or they that shall
   Hereafter possess our throne, shall,
   I fear me, ne'er attain to that degree   25
   Of high renown and great authority.
   Amongst which kings is Alexander the Great,
   Chief spectacle of the world's pre-eminence,
   The bright shining of whose glorious acts
   Lightens the world with his reflecting beams,   30
   As when I hear but motion made of him,
   It grieves my soul I never saw the man.
   If, therefore, thou, by cunning of thine art,
   Canst raise this man from hollow vaults below,
   Where lies entombed this famous conqueror,   35
   And bring with him his beauteous paramour,
   Both in their right shapes, gesture, and attire
   They used to wear during their time of life,
   Thou shalt both satisfy my just desire
   And give me cause to praise thee whilst I live.   40

FAUSTUS   My gracious lord, I am ready to accomplish your request, so far forth as by art and power of my spirit I am able
to perform.

KNIGHT   (*Aside.*) I'faith, that's just nothing at all.

FAUSTUS   But, if it like your Grace, it is not in my ability to   45
present before your eyes the true substantial bodies of those
two deceased princes, which long since are consumed to
dust.

KNIGHT   (*Aside.*) Ay, marry, Master Doctor, now there's a sign
of grace in you, when you will confess the truth.   50

[4.1]
13–14. **nothing answerable:** not at all equal.
14–15. **for that:** since.
19. **closet:** private room.
27. **Alexander the Great:** Alexander of Macedon (356–323 B.C.E.).
31. **motion:** mention.
49. **marry:** i.e., by the Virgin Mary; a mild oath.

FAUSTUS   But such spirits as can lively resemble Alexander and
    his paramour shall appear before your Grace, in that manner
    that they best lived in, in their most flourishing estate, which
    I doubt not shall sufficiently content your Imperial Majesty.

EMPEROR   Go to, Master Doctor; let me see them presently.   55

KNIGHT   Do you hear, Master Doctor? You bring Alexander
    and his paramour before the Emperor!

FAUSTUS   How then, sir?

KNIGHT   I'faith, that's as true as Diana turned me to a stag.

FAUSTUS   No, sir; but, when Actaeon died, he left the horns   60
    for you. Mephistopheles, be gone.   *Exit* MEPHISTOPHELES.

KNIGHT   Nay, an you go to conjuring I'll be gone.   *Exit.*

FAUSTUS   I'll meet with you anon for interrupting me so.
    ——Here they are, my gracious lord.

> *Enter* MEPHISTOPHELES *with* [SPIRITS *in the shapes of*]
> ALEXANDER *and his* PARAMOUR.

EMPEROR   Master Doctor, I heard this lady while she lived had   65
    a wart or mole in her neck. How shall I know whether it be
    so or no?

FAUSTUS   Your Highness may boldly go and see. [EMPEROR
    looks.]

EMPEROR   Sure, these are no spirits, but the true substantial
    bodies of those two deceased princes.   *Exeunt* [SPIRITS.]   70

FAUSTUS   Wilt please your Highness now to send for the
    knight that was so pleasant with me here of late?

EMPEROR   One of you call him forth.   *Exit* ATTENDANT.

> *Enter the* KNIGHT *with a pair of horns on his head.*

How now, sir knight! Why, I had thought thou hadst been
a bachelor, but now I see thou hast a wife that not only   75
gives thee horns but makes thee wear them. Feel on thy
head.

KNIGHT   Thou damnèd wretch and execrable dog,
    Bred in the concave of some monstrous rock,
    How dar'st thou thus abuse a gentleman?
    Villain, I say, undo what thou hast done!   80

FAUSTUS   O, not so fast, sir! There's no haste but good. Are

---

51. lively: vividly;
52. paramour: probably refers to Thais, Alexander's Athenian mistress, who, according to
legend, urged him to set fire to Persepolis; but possibly refers to Roxana, a princess of Bac-
tria, whom Alexander captured and married in 327 B.C.E.
59–60. Diana . . . Actaeon: In Greek mythology, Acteaon witnessed the goddess Diana and
her nymphs naked in their bath; as punishment he was changed into a stag and torn apart
by his own hounds (cf. Ovid, *Metamorphoses* 3.155–252).
63. meet with: get even with.
75–6. bachelor . . . them: see note at 2.2.11.

you remembered how you crossed me in my conference with
the Emperor? I think I have met with you for it.

EMPEROR　Good Master Doctor, at my entreaty release him.
He hath done penance sufficient.　　　　　　　　　　　　　85

FAUSTUS　My gracious lord, not so much for the injury he
offered me here in your presence, as to delight you with
some mirth, hath Faustus worthily requited this injurious
knight; which being all I desire, I am content to release him
of his horns. And, sir knight, hereafter speak well of schol-　90
ars. Mephistopheles, transform him straight. [MEPHISTOPHE-
LES *removes the horns.*] Now, my good lord, having done my
duty, I humbly take my leave.

EMPEROR
Farewell, Master Doctor. Yet, ere you go,
Expect from me a bounteous reward.　　　　　　　　　　　95

　　　　　　　　　　Exeunt EMPEROR, [KNIGHT, *and* ATTENDANTS.]

FAUSTUS
Now, Mephistopheles, the restless course
That time doth run with calm and silent foot,
Shortening my days and thread of vital life,
Calls for the payment of my latest years.
Therefore, sweet Mephistopheles, let us　　　　　　　　　100
Make haste to Württemberg.

MEPHISTOPHELES　What, will you go on horseback or on foot?

FAUSTUS　Nay, till I'm past this fair and pleasant green, I'll
walk on foot.

　　　　　Enter a HORSE-COURSER.

HORSE-COURSER　I have been all this day seeking one Master　105
Fustian. Mass, see where he is! God save you, Master Doctor!

FAUSTUS　What, horse-courser! You are well met.

HORSE-COURSER　Do you hear, sir? I have brought you forty
dollars for your horse.

FAUSTUS　I cannot sell him so. If thou likest him for fifty, take　110
him.

HORSE-COURSER　Alas, sir, I have no more!—I pray you, speak
for me.

MEPHISTOPHELES　I pray you, let him have him. He is an honest fellow, and he has a great charge, neither wife nor child.　115

FAUSTUS　Well, come, give me your money. [FAUSTUS *takes
money.*] My boy will deliver him to you. But I must tell you

---

91. **straight:** immediately.
104. **SD HORSE-COURSER:** horse dealer.
106. **Fustian:** his error for Faustus (see note at 1.4.74); **Mass:** a mild oath.
107. **You . . . met:** I am glad to see you.

one thing before you have him: ride him not into the water,
at any hand.

HORSE-COURSER   Why, sir? Will he not drink of all waters?   120

FAUSTUS   O, yes, he will drink of all waters, but ride him not
into the water. Ride him over hedge, or ditch, or where thou
wilt, but not into the water.

HORSE-COURSER   Well, sir. [*Aside.*] Now am I made man for
ever. I'll not leave my horse for forty. If he had but the qual-   125
ity of hey-ding-ding, hey-ding-ding, I'd make a brave living
on him. He has a buttock as slick as an eel.—Well, goodbye,
sir. Your boy will deliver him me? But, hark ye, sir; if my
horse be sick or ill at ease, if I bring his water to you, you'll
tell me what it is?   130

FAUSTUS   Away, you villain! What, dost think I am a horse-
doctor?   *Exit* HORSE-COURSER.
What art thou, Faustus, but a man condemned to die?
Thy fatal time doth draw to final end;
Despair doth drive distrust unto my thoughts.
Confound these passions with a quiet sleep.   135
Tush, Christ did call the thief upon the cross;
Then rest thee, Faustus, quiet in conceit.

[FAUSTUS] *sleep*[s] *in his chair.*

Enter HORSE-COURSER, *all wet, crying.*

HORSE-COURSER   Alas, alas! Doctor Fustian, quotha. Mass,
Doctor Lopez was never such a doctor! H'as given me a purgation: h'as purged me of forty dollars. I shall never see them   140
more. But yet, like an ass as I was, I would not be ruled by
him, for he bade me I should ride him into no water. Now I,
thinking my horse had had some rare quality that he would
not have had me known of, I, like a venturous youth, rid him
into the deep pond at the town's end. I was no sooner in the   145
middle of the pond, but my horse vanished away, and I sat
upon a bottle of hay, never so near drowning in my life. But
I'll seek out my doctor and have my forty dollars again, or
I'll make it the dearest horse! O, yonder is his snipper-
snapper.—Do you hear, you hey-pass? Where's your master?   150

119. **at any hand:** on any account.
120. **drink . . . waters:** i.e., go anywhere (proverbial).
125–27. **If . . . him:** i.e., if he were fertile, I'd make a good living (from stud fees).
137. **conceit:** this thought.
139. **Doctor Lopez:** a well-known Portuguese physician who attended Queen Elizabeth; he
was hanged in 1594 for his purported role in a plot to poison her.
139–40. **purgation:** a cathartic, a medicine that induces vomiting.
147, 149. **bottle:** bundle.
149. **dearest:** most expensive.
149–50. **snipper-snapper:** a conceited young man (cf. whipper-snapper).

MEPHISTOPHELES   Why, sir, what would you? You cannot speak
with him.

HORSE-COURSER   But I will speak with him.

MEPHISTOPHELES   Why, he's fast asleep. Come some other time.

HORSE-COURSER   I'll speak with him now, or I'll break his glass   155
windows about his ears.

MEPHISTOPHELES   I tell thee, he has not slept this eight nights.

HORSE-COURSER   An he have not slept this eight weeks, I'll
speak with him.

MEPHISTOPHELES   See where he is fast asleep.   160

HORSE-COURSER   Ay, this is he. God save you, Master Doctor,
Master Doctor, Master Doctor Fustian! Forty dollars, forty
dollars for a bottle of hay!

MEPHISTOPHELES   Why, thou seest he hears thee not.

HORSE-COURSER   (*Holler*[s] *in* [FAUSTUS's] *ear.*) So ho ho! So ho   165
ho! No, will you not wake? I'll make you wake ere I go.
            Pulls [FAUSTUS] *by the leg, and* [*it*] *comes away.*
Alas, I am undone! What shall I do?

FAUSTUS   O, my leg, my leg! Help, Mephistopheles! Call the
officers. My leg, my leg!

MEPHISTOPHELES   Come, villain, to the constable.   170

HORSE-COURSER   O Lord, sir, let me go, and I'll give you forty
dollars more!

MEPHISTOPHELES   Where be they?

HORSE-COURSER   I have none about me. Come to my hostry,
and I'll give them you.   175

MEPHISTOPHELES   Be gone quickly.
                HORSE-COURSER *runs away.*

FAUSTUS   What, is he gone? Farewell he! Faustus has his leg
again, and the horse-courser, I take it, a bottle of hay for his
labor. Well, this trick shall cost him forty dollars more.

        Enter WAGNER.

How now, Wagner! What's the news with thee?   180

WAGNER   Sir, the Duke of Vanholt doth earnestly entreat your
company.

FAUSTUS   The Duke of Vanholt! An honorable gentleman, to
whom I must be no niggard of my cunning.—Come, Mephistopheles, let's away to him.   *Exeunt.*   185

155–56. **glass windows:** probably Faustus wears spectacles (but possibly the windows of
the inn at which Faustus is staying).
174. **hostry:** inn, hostelry.
181. **Vanholt:** i.e., Anholt, a region in central Germany.

[4.2]

Enter [FAUSTUS, *with* MEPHISTOPHELES, *and*] *to them the*
DUKE [*of Vanholt*], *and the* [*pregnant*] DUCHESS.

DUKE Believe me, Master Doctor, this merriment hath much
pleased me.

FAUSTUS My gracious Lord, I am glad it contents you so well.
But it may be, madam, you take no delight in this. I have
heard that great-bellied women do long for some dainties or   5
other. What is it, madam? Tell me, and you shall have it.

DUCHESS Thanks, good Master Doctor. And, for I see your
courteous intent to pleasure me, I will not hide from you the
thing my heart desires. And were it now summer, as it is January and the dead time of the winter, I would desire no bet-   10
ter meat than a dish of ripe grapes.

FAUSTUS Alas, madam, that's nothing! Mephistopheles, be
gone.   *Exit* MEPHISTOPHELES.
Were it a greater thing than this, so it would content you,
you should have it.   15

    Enter MEPHISTOPHELES *with the grapes.*

Here they be, madam. Wilt please you taste on them?

DUKE Believe me, Master Doctor, this makes me wonder
above the rest, that being in the dead time of winter and in
the month of January how you should come by these grapes.

FAUSTUS If it like your Grace, the year is divided into two cir-   20
cles over the whole world, that, when it is here winter with
us, in the contrary circle it is summer with them, as in India,
Saba, and farther countries in the east; and by means of a
swift spirit that I have, I had them brought hither, as you
see. How do you like them, madam? Be they good?   25

DUCHESS Believe me, Master Doctor, they be the best grapes
that e'er I tasted in my life before.

FAUSTUS I am glad they content you so, madam.

DUKE
Come, madam, let us in,
Where you must well reward this learnèd man   30
For the great kindness he hath showed to you.

[4.2]
5. great-bellied: i.e., pregnant.
11. meat: food.
22. contrary circle i.e., the other half of the world.
23. Saba: i.e., the ancient country of Sheba (see 2.1.151) in the area of the modern Yemen.

DUCHESS

And so I will, my lord; and, whilst I live,
Rest beholding for this courtesy.

FAUSTUS

I humbly thank your Grace.

DUKE

Come, Master Doctor, follow us and receive your reward.   35

Exeunt.

[5.1]

Enter WAGNER *solus.*

WAGNER

I think my master means to die shortly,
For he hath given to me all his goods.
And yet, methinks, if that death were near,
He would not banquet, and carouse, and swill
Amongst the students, as even now he doth,   5
Who are at supper with such belly cheer
As Wagner ne'er beheld in all his life.
See, where they come! Belike the feast is ended.   [*Exit.*]

Enter FAUSTUS *with two or three* SCHOLARS, [*and* MEPH-
ISTOPHELES].

FIRST SCHOLAR   Master Doctor Faustus, since our conference
about fair ladies—which was the beautifullest in all the   10
world—we have determined with ourselves that Helen of
Greece was the admirablest lady that ever lived. Therefore,
Master Doctor, if you will do us that favor as to let us see
that peerless dame of Greece, whom all the world admires
for majesty, we should think ourselves much beholding unto   15
you.

FAUSTUS

Gentlemen, for that I know your friendship is unfeigned,
(And Faustus' custom is not to deny
The just requests of those that wish him well)
You shall behold that peerless dame of Greece,   20
No otherways for pomp and majesty
Than when Sir Paris crossed the seas with her

33. **rest beholding:** remain indebted.
[5.1]
4. **swill:** guzzle.
8. **Belike:** most likely.
21. **otherways:** different.
22. **Paris:** a Trojan prince whose abduction of Helen, the queen of Sparta, led to the Trojan war.

And brought the spoils to rich Dardania.
Be silent then, for danger is in words.

> *Music sounds, and* HELEN *[led by* MEPHISTOPHELES*] pass-eth over the stage.*

SECOND SCHOLAR
Too simple is my wit to tell her praise,   25
Whom all the world admires for majesty.
THIRD SCHOLAR
No marvel though the angry Greeks pursued
With ten years' war the rape of such a queen,
Whose heavenly beauty passeth all compare.
FIRST SCHOLAR
Since we have seen the pride of Nature's works   30
And only paragon of excellence,

> *Enter an* OLD MAN.

Let us depart; and for this glorious deed
Happy and blest be Faustus evermore!
FAUSTUS   Gentlemen, farewell. The same I wish to you.
                                              Exeunt SCHOLARS.   35
OLD MAN
Ah, Doctor Faustus, that I might prevail
To guide thy steps unto the way of life,
By which sweet path thou mayst attain the goal
That shall conduct thee to celestial rest.
Break heart, drop blood, and mingle it with tears,
Tears falling from repentant heaviness   40
Of thy most vile and loathsome filthiness,
The stench whereof corrupts the inward soul
With such flagitious crimes of heinous sins
As no commiseration may expel
But mercy, Faustus, of thy Savior sweet,   45
Whose blood alone must wash away thy guilt.
FAUSTUS
Where art thou, Faustus? Wretch, what hast thou done?
Damned art thou, Faustus, damned; despair and die!
Hell calls for right and with a roaring voice
Says: "Faustus, come; thine hour is come."   50
And, Faustus, will come to do thee right.

23. **Dardania:** i.e., Troy.
28. **rape:** abduction.
43. **flagitious:** villainous.

MEPHISTOPHELES *gives him a dagger.*

OLD MAN
  Ah, stay, good Faustus, stay thy desperate steps!
  I see an angel hovers o'er thy head
  And with a vial full of precious grace
  Offers to pour the same into thy soul.   55
  Then call for mercy and avoid despair.

FAUSTUS
  Ah, my sweet friend, I feel
  Thy words to comfort my distressèd soul!
  Leave me a while to ponder on my sins.

OLD MAN
  I go, sweet Faustus, but with heavy cheer,   60
  Fearing the ruin of thy hopeless soul.   [*Exit.*]

FAUSTUS
  Accursèd Faustus, where is mercy now?
  I do repent; and yet I do despair.
  Hell strives with grace for conquest in my breast.
  What shall I do to shun the snares of death?   65

MEPHISTOPHELES
  Thou traitor, Faustus, I arrest thy soul
  For disobedience to my sovereign Lord.
  Revolt, or I'll in piecemeal tear thy flesh.

FAUSTUS
  Sweet Mephistopheles, entreat thy Lord   70
  To pardon my unjust presumption,
  And with my blood again I will confirm
  My former vow I made to Lucifer.

MEPHISTOPHELES
  Do it, then, quickly, with unfeignèd heart,
  Lest greater danger do attend thy drift.

FAUSTUS
  Torment, sweet friend, that base and crooked age   75
  That durst dissuade me from thy Lucifer
  With greatest torments that our hell affords.

MEPHISTOPHELES
  His faith is great. I cannot touch his soul,
  But what I may afflict his body with
  I will attempt, which is but little worth.   80

FAUSTUS
  One thing, good servant, let me crave of thee,
  To glut the longing of my heart's desire:

60. **cheer**: disposition, mood.
68. **Revolt**: return (to your allegiance).
75. **crooked age**: bent, old man.

That I might have unto my paramour
That heavenly Helen which I saw of late,
Whose sweet embracings may extinguish clean   85
Those thoughts that do dissuade me from my vow,
And keep mine oath I made to Lucifer.

MEPHISTOPHELES
Faustus, this, or what else thou shalt desire,
Shall be performed in twinkling of an eye.

        Enter HELEN.

FAUSTUS
Was this the face that launched a thousand ships   90
And burned the topless towers of Ilium?
Sweet Helen, make me immortal with a kiss.   [*They kiss.*]
Her lips sucks forth my soul. See, where it flies!
Come, Helen, come, give me my soul again.   [*They kiss.*]
Here will I dwell, for heaven be in these lips,   95
And all is dross that is not Helena.

        Enter OLD MAN

I will be Paris, and for love of thee,
Instead of Troy shall Württemberg be sacked;
And I will combat with weak Menelaus
And wear thy colors on my plumèd crest.   100
Yea, I will wound Achilles in the heel
And then return to Helen for a kiss.
O, thou art fairer than the evening air
Clad in the beauty of a thousand stars.
Brighter art thou than flaming Jupiter   105
When he appeared to hapless Semele;
More lovely than the monarch of the sky
In wanton Arethusa's azured arms;
And none but thou shalt be my paramour!
        Exeunt [FAUSTUS, HELEN, *and* MEPHISTOPHELES].

OLD MAN
Accursèd Faustus, miserable man,   110
That from thy soul exclud'st the grace of heaven
And fly'st the throne of his tribunal seat!

85. **clean:** completely.
91. **topless:** immeasurably tall; **Ilium:** i.e., Troy.
99. **Menelaus:** Helen's husband, king of Sparta.
101. **wound . . . heel:** In mythology, Achilles was dipped in the river Styx by his mother, which rendered him invulnerable, except for the heel by which she held him.
106. **Semele:** one of Jupiter's human mistresses, who insisting on seeing the god in his divine form was consumed in flame (cf. Ovid, *Metamorphoses* 259–315).
107–8. **monarch . . . arms:** the beauty of the sun reflecting off a stream, though the specific reference is unclear. Arethusa was a nymph desired by the river god Alpheus, who changed into a fountain to avoid his lust (cf. Ovid, *Metamophoses* 5.577–641).

Enter the DEVILS.

Satan begins to sift me with his pride.
As in this furnace God shall try my faith,
My faith, vile hell, shall triumph over thee.   115
Ambitious fiends, see how the heavens smiles
At your repulse and laughs your state to scorn!
Hence, hell, for hence I fly unto my God.   *Exeunt.*

[5.2]

Enter FAUSTUS, *with the* SCHOLARS.

FAUSTUS   Ah, gentlemen!
FIRST SCHOLAR   What ails Faustus?
FAUSTUS   Ah, my sweet chamber fellow, had I lived with thee,
    then had I lived still! But now I die eternally. Look, comes he
    not? Comes he not?   5
SECOND SCHOLAR   What means Faustus?
THIRD SCHOLAR   Belike he is grown into some sickness by be-
    ing over-solitary.
FIRST SCHOLAR   If it be so, we'll have physicians to cure him.—
    'Tis but a surfeit; never fear, man.   10
FAUSTUS   A surfeit of deadly sin that hath damned both body
    and soul.
SECOND SCHOLAR   Yet, Faustus, look up to heaven; remember
    God's mercies are infinite.
FAUSTUS   But Faustus' offence can ne'er be pardoned. The ser-   15
    pent that tempted Eve may be saved, but not Faustus. Ah,
    gentlemen, hear me with patience and tremble not at my
    speeches! Though my heart pants and quivers to remember
    that I have been a student here these thirty years, O, would
    I had never seen Württemberg, never read book! And what   20
    wonders I have done all Germany can witness, yea, all the
    world—for which Faustus hath lost both Germany and the
    world, yea, heaven itself, heaven, the seat of God, the throne
    of the blessed, the kingdom of joy—and must remain in hell
    for ever, hell, ah, hell, for ever! Sweet friends, what shall be-   25
    come of Faustus, being in hell for ever?
THIRD SCHOLAR   Yet, Faustus, call on God.
FAUSTUS   On God whom Faustus hath abjured? On God
    whom Faustus hath blasphemed? Ah, my God, I would
    weep, but the devil draws in my tears. Gush forth blood in-   30

113. sift: cf. Luke 22:31: "behold, Satan hath desired to have you, that he may sift you as
wheat."

stead of tears. Yea, life and soul! O, he stays my tongue! I
would lift up my hands, but see, they hold them, they hold
them!

ALL   Who, Faustus?

FAUSTUS   Lucifer and Mephistopheles. Ah, gentlemen, I gave   35
them my soul for my cunning!

ALL   God forbid!

FAUSTUS   God forbade it, indeed; but Faustus hath done it.
For vain pleasure of twenty four years hath Faustus lost eternal joy and felicity. I writ them a bill with mine own blood.   40
The date is expired: the time will come, and he will fetch
me.

FIRST SCHOLAR   Why did not Faustus tell us of this before,
that divines might have prayed for thee?

FAUSTUS   Oft have I thought to have done so, but the devil   45
threatened to tear me in pieces if I named God, to fetch
both body and soul if I once gave ear to divinity. And now 'tis
too late. Gentlemen, away, lest you perish with me.

SECOND SCHOLAR   O, what shall we do to Faustus?

FAUSTUS   Talk not of me, but save yourselves and depart.   50

THIRD SCHOLAR   God will strengthen me. I will stay with Faustus.

FIRST SCHOLAR   Tempt not God, sweet friend; but let us into
the next room and there pray for him.

FAUSTUS   Ay, pray for me, pray for me; and what noise soever   55
ye hear, come not unto me, for nothing can rescue me.

SECOND SCHOLAR   Pray thou, and we will pray that God may
have mercy upon thee.

FAUSTUS   Gentlemen, farewell. If I live till morning, I'll visit
you; if not, Faustus is gone to hell.   60

ALL   Faustus, farewell.   *Exeunt* SCHOLARS.
                         The clock strikes eleven.

FAUSTUS
    Ah, Faustus, now hast thou but one bare hour to live,
    And then thou must be damned perpetually.
    Stand still, you ever-moving spheres of heaven,
    That time may cease and midnight never come.   65
    Fair Nature's eye, rise, rise again, and make
    Perpetual day; or let this hour be but
    A year, a month, a week, a natural day,

[5.2]
39. vain: worthless (but also with the sense of prideful).
40. bill: contract.
49. to Faustus: i.e., to help Faustus.
66. Fair Nature's eye: i.e., the sun.

That Faustus may repent and save his soul.
O lente, lente currite, noctis equi!   70
The stars move still, time runs, the clock will strike,
The devil will come, and Faustus must be damned.
O, I'll leap up to my God! Who pulls me down?
See, see, where Christ's blood streams in the firmament!
One drop would save my soul, half a drop. Ah, my Christ!   75
Ah, rend not my heart for naming of my Christ!
Yet will I call on him. O, spare me, Lucifer!
Where is it now? 'Tis gone. And see, where God
Stretcheth out his arm and bends his ireful brows!
Mountains and hills, come, come and fall on me,   80
And hide me from the heavy wrath of God.
No, no! Then will I headlong run into the earth.
Earth, gape! O, no, it will not harbor me.
You stars that reigned at my nativity,
Whose influence hath allotted death and hell,   85
Now draw up Faustus, like a foggy mist
Into the entrails of yon laboring cloud,
That, when you vomit forth into the air,
My limbs may issue from your smoky mouths,
So that my soul may but ascend to heaven.   90
                                    The watch strikes.
Ah, half the hour is past. 'Twill all be past anon.
O God, if thou wilt not have mercy on my soul,
Yet for Christ's sake, whose blood hath ransomed me,
Impose some end to my incessant pain.
Let Faustus live in hell a thousand years,   95
A hundred thousand, and at last be saved.
O, no end is limited to damnèd souls!
Why wert thou not a creature wanting soul?
Or why is this immortal that thou hast?
Ah, Pythagoras' *metempsychosis*—were that true,   100
This soul should fly from me and I be changed
Unto some brutish beast.
All beasts are happy, for when they die
Their souls are soon dissolved in elements,
But mine must live still to be plagued in hell.   105
Cursed be the parents that engendered me!
No, Faustus, curse thyself, curse Lucifer,

70. *O . . . equi:* O, run slowly, slowly, you horses of night (Latin; Ovid, *Amores* 1.13.40a).
90. **SD watch:** clock.
98. **wanting:** lacking.
100. *metempsychosis:* theory attributed to Pythagoras about the passing (transmigration) of the soul at death from one body to another.
105. **still:** ever.

That hath deprived thee of the joys of heaven.
                          The clock striketh twelve.
O, it strikes, it strikes! Now, body, turn to air,
Or Lucifer will bear thee quick to hell!   110
                          Thunder and lightning.
O soul, be changed into little water drops
And fall into the ocean, ne'er be found!

   Enter DEVILS.

My God, my God, look not so fierce on me!
Adders and serpents, let me breathe a while!
Ugly hell, gape not! Come not, Lucifer!   115
I'll burn my books! Ah, Mephistopheles!
                          Exeunt [DEVILS] *with him.*

[Epilogue]

Enter CHORUS.

CHORUS
   Cut is the branch that might have grown full straight,
   And burnèd is Apollo's laurel bough,
   That sometime grew within this learnèd man.
   Faustus is gone. Regard his hellish fall,
   Whose fiendful fortune may exhort the wise   5
   Only to wonder at unlawful things,
   Whose deepness doth entice such forward wits
   To practice more than heavenly power permits.   [*Exit.*]

   Terminat hora diem; terminat Author opus.

110. **quick:** alive.
[Epilogue]
2. **Apollo's laurel bough:** the worldly recognition that came to Faustus, the "conjuror laureate" (1.3.32).
3. **sometime:** formerly.
6. **Only to wonder:** i.e., to be content with wondering at (rather than engaging in).
7. **forward:** ambitious, eager.
Terminat . . . opus: The hour ends the day; the author ends his work (Latin). This conventional motto was most likely provided by the publisher rather than Marlowe.

The Tragedy of Doctor Faustus (B-Text, 1616)

List of Roles

CHORUS
Dr. John FAUSTUS
WAGNER   Faustus's servant
VALDES ⎫
            ⎬ Conjurors and Faustus's friends
CORNELIUS ⎭
ROBIN, the Clown
DICK
Three SCHOLARS
Two SOLDIERS
Pope ADRIAN
Pope BRUNO, the rival Pope
Cardinal of FRANCE
Cardinal of PADUA
Archbishop of RHEIMS
Bishop of LORRAINE
Charles V, EMPEROR of Germany
RAYMOND, King of Hungary
Duke of SAXONY
Duke of VANHOLT
DUCHESS of Vanholt
GOOD ANGEL
BAD ANGEL
MEPHISTOPHELES
LUCIFER
BEELZEBUB
PRIDE   ⎫
COVETOUSNESS   ⎪
ENVY   ⎪
WRATH   ⎬ The Seven Deadly Sins
GLUTTONY   ⎪
SLOTH   ⎪
LECHERY   ⎭

WOMAN DEVIL
ARGIRON
ASHTAROTH } Devils
BELIMOTH
Spirits in the shapes of ALEXANDER the great, his
PARAMOUR, DARIUS, and HELEN of Troy
MARTINO
FREDERICK
BENVOLIO
VINTNER
CARTER
HORSE-COURSER
HOSTESS
SERVANT
Monks, Friars, Cardinals, Devils, Soldiers, Officers,
Gentlemen, and Attendants.

[Prologue]

Enter CHORUS

CHORUS
  Not marching in the fields of Trasimene,
  Where Mars did mate the warlike Carthagens,
  Nor sporting in the dalliance of love
  In courts of kings where state is overturned,
  Nor in the pomp of proud audacious deeds,   5
  Intends our muse to vaunt his heavenly verse.
  Only this, gentles: we must now perform
  The form of Faustus' fortunes, good or bad.
  And now to patient judgments we appeal
  And speak for Faustus in his infancy.   10
  Now is he born of parents base of stock,
  In Germany, within a town called Roda.
  At riper years to Wittenberg he went,
  Whereas his kinsmen chiefly brought him up.

[Prologue]
1. **Trasimene:** battlefield in Italy (near Lake Trasimeno in modern Umbria), where Carthaginian troops under Hannibal defeated the Romans in 217 B.C.E.
2. **Mars:** Roman god of war; **mate:** side with.
4. **state:** orderly government.
6. **vaunt:** display.
7. **gentles:** i.e., gentlemen and gentlewomen; however, the audience of the theaters in which *Dr. Faustus* was performed was neither socially nor sexually homogeneous, as this would indicate.
12. **Roda:** the modern Stadtroda, near Weimar in Germany.
13. **Wittenberg:** the B-text's rendering of the town where Faustus was raised (unlike the A-text's "Wertenberg," i.e., Württemberg).

So much he profits in divinity   15
That shortly he was graced with doctor's name,
Excelling all, and sweetly can dispute
In th'heavenly matters of theology;
Till swoll'n with cunning, of a self-conceit,
His waxen wings did mount above his reach,   20
And melting, heavens conspired his overthrow.
For, falling to a devilish exercise,
And glutted now with learning's golden gifts,
He surfeits upon cursèd necromancy.
Nothing so sweet as magic is to him,   25
Which he prefers before his chiefest bliss.
And this the man that in his study sits.   [*Exit*]

[1.1]

FAUSTUS *in his study.*

FAUSTUS
Settle thy studies, Faustus, and begin
To sound the depth of that thou wilt profess.
Having commenced, be a divine in show,
Yet level at the end of every art,
And live and die in Aristotle's works. [*Picks up a book.*]   5
Sweet analytics, 'tis thou hast ravished me!
[*Reads.*] "Bene disserere est finis logices."
Is to dispute well logic's chiefest end?
Affords this art no greater miracle?
Then read no more; thou hast attained that end.   10
A greater subject fitteth Faustus' wit.
Bid *Oeconomy* farewell
                    [*Puts down book and picks up another.*]

15. divinity: theology.
20. waxen wings: like those worn by Icarus (Ovid, *Metamorphoses* 8)—a familiar emblem of pride—who died when he flew too near the sun.
24. necromancy: forbidden magic.
26. chiefest bliss: i.e., hope of salvation.
[1.1]
1. settle: decide on.
2. sound: measure, explore; profess: choose as your area of expertise.
3. commenced: earned a degree; divine: theologian; in show: in appearance only.
4. level . . . art: consider the purpose of every discipline.
6. analytics: title of two of Aristotle's treatises on logic; here, however, most likely the discipline itself.
7. Bene . . . logices: i.e., the purpose of logic is to argue well (Latin; but from the *Dialectica* of Petrus Ramus [1515–1572], not Aristotle).
11. wit: understanding.
12. Oeconomy: possibly Aristotle's term for the management of the household (cf. *Politics* 1258.a.28), though the emendation *"On kai me on"* (see A-text 1.1.12) is very attractive.

and Galen come.
Be a physician, Faustus. Heap up gold
And be eternized for some wondrous cure.
[*Reads.*] "*Summum bonum medicinae sanitas.*"   15
The end of physic is our body's health.
Why, Faustus, hast thou not attained that end?
Are not thy bills hung up as monuments,
Whereby whole cities have escaped the plague
And thousand desperate maladies been cured?   20
Yet art thou still but Faustus and a man.
Couldst thou make men to live eternally
Or, being dead, raise them to life again,
Then this profession were to be esteemed.
Physic, farewell! [*Puts down book.*] Where is Justinian?   25
[*Picks up another book and reads.*] "*Si una eademque res
    legatur duobus.*
Alter rem, alter valorem rei, etc.*"
A petty case of paltry legacies!
[*Reads.*] "*Exhaereditare filium non potest pater, nisi—*":
Such is the subject of the *Institute*   30
And universal body of the law.
This study fits a mercenary drudge,
Who aims at nothing but external trash;
Too servile and illiberal for me. [*Puts down book.*]
When all is done, divinity is best. [*Picks up another book.*]   35
Jerome's Bible, Faustus; view it well.
[*Reads.*] "*Stipendium peccati mors est.*" Ha!
Stipendium, etc. The reward of sin is death. That's hard.
[*Reads.*] "*Si peccasse negamus, fallimur,
Et nulla est in nobis veritas.*"   40

12. Galen: Greek authority on medicine (2nd century C.E.).
14. eternized: immortalized.
15. *Summum . . . sanitas*: i.e., health is the greatest good of medicine (Latin; Aristotle, *Nichomachean Ethics* 1094a).
16. physic: medicine.
18. bills: medical prescriptions.
25. Justinian: Roman emperor (482–565) who codified the Roman law.
26–27. *Si . . . etc.*: i.e., if the one and the same thing is bequeathed to two people, one should have the thing itself and the other the value of the thing, and so forth (Latin; Justinian, *Institutes* 2.20).
29. *Exhaereditare . . . nisi—*: i.e., a father may not disinherit his son unless—(Latin; Justinian, *Institutes* 2.13).
30. *Institute*: the codification of Roman law ordered by Justinian (see note to 25, above).
36. Jerome's Bible: the Latin translation (the Vulgate) made by St. Jerome in the 4th century, although the biblical citations that follow do not use the Vulgate's wording and seem to be Marlowe's own translations into Latin from the English Geneva version.
37. *Stipendium . . . est*: i.e., the wages of sin are death (Latin; Romans 6:23); the rest of the verse, however, reads: "but the gift of God is eternal life through Jesus Christ our Lord."
39–40. *Si . . . veritas*: 1 John 1:8, translated from the Latin in the following two lines but ignoring the verse that follows: "If we confess our sins, he is faithful and just to forgive us our sins and to cleanse us from all unrighteousness."

If we say that we have no sin,
We deceive ourselves, and there is no truth in us.
Why, then, belike we must sin
And so consequently die.
Ay, we must die an everlasting death.   45
What doctrine call you this? *Che serà, serà?*
What will be, shall be? Divinity, adieu!
          [*Puts Bible down and picks up book of magic.*]
These metaphysics of magicians
And necromantic books are heavenly.
Lines, circles, letters, and characters—   50
Ay, these are those that Faustus most desires.
O, what a world of profit and delight,
Of power, of honor and omnipotence,
Is promised to the studious artisan!
All things that move between the quiet poles   55
Shall be at my command. Emperors and kings
Are but obeyed in their several provinces,
But his dominion that exceeds in this
Stretcheth as far as doth the mind of man.
A sound magician is a demigod.   60
Here tire my brains to gain a deity.
Wagner!

          Enter WAGNER.

          Commend me to my dearest friends,
The German Valdes and Cornelius.
Request them earnestly to visit me.
WAGNER
    I will, sir.   *Exit.*   65
FAUSTUS
    Their conference will be a greater help to me
Than all my labors, plod I ne'er so fast.

          Enter the [GOOD] ANGEL *and* [BAD ANGEL].

GOOD ANGEL
    O, Faustus, lay that damnèd book aside
And gaze not on it, lest it tempt thy soul
And heap God's heavy wrath upon thy head.   70

---

46. *Che serà, serà*: i.e., what will be, shall be (Italian; translated in following line).
54. **studious artisan**: skilled practitioner of an art.
55. **quiet**: motionless.
57. **several**: respective.
58. **this**: i.e., magic.

Read, read the Scriptures. That is blasphemy.

BAD ANGEL

    Go forward, Faustus, in that famous art
    Wherein all Nature's treasure is contained.
    Be thou on earth as Jove is in the sky,
    Lord and commander of these elements.   *Exeunt Angels.* 75

FAUSTUS

    How am I glutted with conceit of this!
    Shall I make spirits fetch me what I please,
    Resolve me of all ambiguities,
    Perform what desperate enterprise I will?
    I'll have them fly to India for gold,   80
    Ransack the ocean for orient pearl,
    And search all corners of the new-found world
    For pleasant fruits and princely delicates.
    I'll have them read me strange philosophy
    And tell the secrets of all foreign kings.   85
    I'll have them wall all Germany with brass
    And make swift Rhine circle fair Wittenberg.
    I'll have them fill the public schools with silk,
    Wherewith the students shall be bravely clad.
    I'll levy soldiers with the coin they bring,   90
    And chase the Prince of Parma from our land,
    And reign sole king of all the provinces.
    Yea, stranger engines for the brunt of war
    Than was the fiery keel at Antwerp bridge,
    I'll make my servile spirits to invent.   95
    Come, German Valdes and Cornelius,
    And make me blest with your sage conference.

    Enter VALDES *and* CORNELIUS.

    Valdes, sweet Valdes, and Cornelius,
    Know that your words have won me at the last

71. **That:** i.e., the book of magic.
76. **conceit of this:** the idea of being a magician.
78. **Resolve . . . ambiguities:** Answer all my questions.
81. **orient:** i.e., precious (literally, from the East).
83. **delicates:** delicacies.
84. **read:** teach.
87. **Rhine . . . Wittenberg:** Wittenberg sits on the river Elbe not the Rhine, unlike Württemberg (see A-text), which was on the Rhine.
88. **public schools:** universities.
89. **bravely:** splendidly.
91. **Prince of Parma:** Alessandro Farnese, duke of Parma and Spanish governor of the Netherlands (ruled 1578–92).
93. **engines:** machines.
94. **fiery keel:** reference to the burning ship sent by Dutch forces in April 1585 to break the duke of Parma's blockade of Antwerp.

To practice magic and concealèd arts.   100
Philosophy is odious and obscure;
Both law and physic are for petty wits.
'Tis magic, magic that hath ravished me.
Then, gentle friends, aid me in this attempt,
And I, that have with subtle syllogisms   105
Gravelled the pastors of the German Church
And made the flowering pride of Wittenberg
Swarm to my problems, as th'infernal spirits
On sweet Musaeus when he came to hell,
Will be as cunning as Agrippa was,   110
Whose shadow made all Europe honor him.

VALDES

Faustus, these books, thy wit, and our experience
Shall make all nations to canonize us.
As Indian moors obey their Spanish lords,
So shall the spirits of every element   115
Be always serviceable to us three.
Like lions shall they guard us when we please,
Like Almain rutters with their horsemen's staves,
Or Lapland giants trotting by our sides;
Sometimes like women, or unwedded maids,   120
Shadowing more beauty in their airy brows
Than has the white breasts of the Queen of Love.
From Venice shall they drag huge argosies,
And from America the golden fleece
That yearly stuffed old Philip's treasury,   125
If learnèd Faustus will be resolute.

FAUSTUS

Valdes, as resolute am I in this
As thou to live; therefore, object it not.

100. **concealèd**: occult.
105. **subtle syllogisms**: clever arguments.
106. **Gravelled**: amazed.
109. **Musaeus**: legendary Greek poet, whom Virgil describes surrounded by admirers in the underworld (*Aeneid* 6. 666–76).
110. **Agrippa**: famous Henry Cornelius Agrippa of Nettlesheim (1486–1535), famous German magician.
111. **shadow**: a spirit raised from the dead.
114. **Indian moors**: the natives of the New World.
118. **Almain rutters**: German cavalrymen.
121. **Shadowing**: harboring.
122. **Queen of Love**: i.e., Venus.
123. **argosies**: merchant ships.
124. **golden fleece**: the fabulous object sought by Jason and his argonauts.
125. **old Philip's**: referring to King Philip II of Spain. (1527–98). The change to "stuffed" earlier in the line, from the A-text's "stuffs," apparently reflects the fact of Philip's death in 1598.
128. **object it not**: don't raise any objections.

CORNELIUS

    The miracles that magic will perform
    Will make thee vow to study nothing else.   130
    He that is grounded in astrology,
    Enriched with tongues, well seen in minerals,
    Hath all the principles magic doth require.
    Then doubt not, Faustus, but to be renowned
    And more frequented for this mystery   135
    Than heretofore the Delphian oracle.
    The spirits tell me they can dry the sea
    And fetch the treasure of all foreign wrecks,
    Yea, all the wealth that our forefathers hid
    Within the massy entrails of the earth.   140
    Then tell me, Faustus, what shall we three want?

FAUSTUS

    Nothing, Cornelius. O, this cheers my soul.
    Come, show me some demonstrations magical
    That I may conjure in some bushy grove
    And have these joys in full possession.   145

VALDES

    Then haste thee to some solitary grove
    And bear wise Bacon's and Abanus' works,
    The Hebrew Psalter, and New Testament;
    And whatsoever else is requisite
    We will inform thee ere our conference cease.   150

CORNELIUS

    Valdes, first let him know the words of art,
    And then, all other ceremonies learned,
    Faustus may try his cunning by himself.

VALDES

    First I'll instruct thee in the rudiments,
    And then wilt thou be perfecter than I.   155

FAUSTUS

    Then come and dine with me, and, after meat,
    We'll canvass every quiddity thereof;
    For ere I sleep I'll try what I can do.
    This night I'll conjure, though I die therefore.

                                    Exeunt omnes.

---

131. **grounded:** well educated.
132. **tongues:** languages; **well . . . minerals:** skilled in alchemy.
135. **frequented . . . mystery:** resorted to for this art.
136. **Delphian oracle:** the famous oracle of Apollo at Delphi in Greece.
141. **want:** lack.
147. **Bacon's . . . works:** the writings of Roger Bacon and Pietro d'Abano, 13th-century scientists reputed to be sorcerers.
157. **canvass every quiddity:** investigate in every detail.

[1.2]

Enter two SCHOLARS.

FIRST SCHOLAR   I wonder what's become of Faustus, that was
wont to make our schools ring with "*sic probo.*"
SECOND SCHOLAR   That shall we presently know; here comes
his boy.

Enter WAGNER.

FIRST SCHOLAR   How now, sirrah! Where's thy master?   5
WAGNER   God in heaven knows.
SECOND SCHOLAR   Why, dost not thou know, then?
WAGNER   Yes, I know, but that follows not.
FIRST SCHOLAR   Go to, sirrah! Leave your jesting and tell us
where he is.   10
WAGNER   That follows not by force of argument, which you,
being licentiates, should stand upon. Therefore, acknowledge your error and be attentive.
SECOND SCHOLAR   Then you will not tell us?
WAGNER   You are deceived, for I will tell you; yet, if you were   15
not dunces, you would never ask me such a question. For is
he not *corpus naturale*? And is not that *mobile*? Then wherefore should you ask me such a question? But that I am by
nature phlegmatic, slow to wrath, and prone to lechery (to
love, I would say), it were not for you to come within forty   20
foot of the place of execution, although I do not doubt but
to see you both hanged the next sessions. Thus having
triumphed over you, I will set my countenance like a precisian and begin to speak thus: truly, my dear brethren, my
master is within at dinner with Valdes and Cornelius, as this   25
wine, if it could speak, would inform your worships. And so,
the Lord bless you, preserve you, and keep you, my dear
brethren!   *Exit.*
FIRST SCHOLAR

O Faustus! Then I fear that which I have long suspected,
That thou art fall'n into that damnèd art   30
For which they two are infamous through the world.

[1.2]
2. *sic probo*: i.e., thus I prove (Latin).
5. **sirrah**: term of address to an inferior.
9. **Go to**: expression of impatience.
12. **licentiates**: university designation for those eligible to study for the M.A.; **stand**: insist.
17. *corpus naturale*: natural body (Latin); *mobile*: able to move (Latin).
21. **place of execution**: i.e., the dining room (with obvious joke).
22. **sessions**: courtroom hearings.
23–24. **precisian**: one who is rigorous in religious observance; a Puritan.

SECOND SCHOLAR
  Were he a stranger, not allied to me,
  The danger of his soul would make me mourn.
  But, come, let us go and inform the Rector.
  It may be his grave counsel may reclaim him.   35
FIRST SCHOLAR
  I fear me nothing will reclaim him now.
SECOND SCHOLAR   Yet let us see what we can do.   *Exeunt.*

[1.3]

    Thunder. Enter LUCIFER *and four Devils [above, and]*
    FAUSTUS *to them with this speech.*

FAUSTUS
  Now that the gloomy shadow of the night,
  Longing to view Orion's drizzling look,
  Leaps from th'Antarctic world unto the sky
  And dims the welkin with her pitchy breath,
  Faustus, begin thine incantations   5
  And try if devils will obey thy hest,
  Seeing thou hast prayed and sacrificed to them.
                                      [Draws a circle.]
  Within this circle is Jehovah's name
  Forward and backward anagrammatized,
  Th'abbreviated names of holy saints,   10
  Figures of every adjunct to the heavens,
  And characters of signs and evening stars,
  By which the spirits are enforced to rise.
  Then fear not, Faustus, to be resolute
  And try the utmost magic can perform.   *Thunder.* 15
  Sint mihi dei Acherontis propitii! Valeat numen triplex Jeho-
  vae! Ignei, aerii, aquatici, spiritus, salvete! Orientis prin-
  ceps Beelzebub, inferni ardentis monarcha, et Demogorgon,
  propitiamus vos, ut appareat et surgat Mephistopheles! Quid

---

34. **Rector:** head of a university.
[1.3]
2. **Orion's drizzling look:** the constellation Orion, whose prominent position in the late autumn sky heralded the stormy season (cf. *Aeneid* 1.565, 4.52).
4. **welkin:** sky; **pitchy:** pitch black.
6. **hest:** behest, command.
9. **anagrammatized:** made into anagrams; i.e., with the letters rearranged.
11. **Figures . . . heavens:** charts of all the heavenly bodies.
12. **characters:** symbols; **signs:** i.e., signs of the zodiac.
16–22. **Sint . . . Mephistopheles:** i.e., May the gods of Acheron be generous to me! Away with the threefold power of Jehovah! Hail spirits of fire, air, and water! The prince of the East, Beelzebub, monarch of burning hell, and Demogorgon, we beseech you that

tu moraris? Per Jehovam, Gehennam, et consecratam aquam   20
quam nunc spargo, signumque crucis quod nunc facio, et per
vota nostra, ipse nunc surgat nobis dicatus Mephistopheles!

> *Enter* [MEPHISTOPHELES, *like a Dragon.*]

I charge thee to return and change thy shape.
Thou art too ugly to attend on me.
Go, and return an old Franciscan friar;   25
That holy shape becomes a devil best.

> *Exit* [MEPHISTOPHELES].

I see there's virtue in my heavenly words.
Who would not be proficient in this art?
How pliant is this Mephistopheles,
Full of obedience and humility!   30
Such is the force of magic and my spells.

> *Enter* MEPHISTOPHELES [*dressed as a friar*].

MEPHISTOPHELES   Now, Faustus, what wouldst thou have me
do?
FAUSTUS
I charge thee wait upon me whilst I live
To do whatever Faustus shall command,   35
Be it to make the moon drop from her sphere
Or the ocean to overwhelm the world.
MEPHISTOPHELES
I am a servant to great Lucifer
And may not follow thee without his leave.
No more than he commands must we perform.   40
FAUSTUS
Did not he charge thee to appear to me?
MEPHISTOPHELES
No, I came now hither of mine own accord.
FAUSTUS
Did not my conjuring speeches raise thee? Speak.
MEPHISTOPHELES
That was the cause, but yet *per accidens,*
For, when we hear one rack the name of God,   45
Abjure the Scriptures and his Savior Christ,

Mephistopheles may rise and appear. Why do you delay? By Jehovah, Gehenna, and the
holy water I now sprinkle, and by the sign of the cross I now make, and by our vows, may
Mephistopheles himself arise at our command! (Latin).
22. SD a Dragon: following Boas and Bevington/Rasmussen, "Dragon," which appears following "Quid tu moraris" in the B-text, is taken to be a misplaced and fragmentary stage direction.
27. virtue: power.
44. cause . . . per accidens: i.e., the occasion but not the efficient cause.
45. rack: abuse, malign.

We fly in hope to get his glorious soul;
Nor will we come unless he use such means
Whereby he is in danger to be damned.
Therefore, the shortest cut for conjuring   50
Is stoutly to abjure all godliness
And pray devoutly to the prince of hell.

FAUSTUS

So Faustus hath already done, and holds this principle:
There is no chief but only Beelzebub,
To whom Faustus doth dedicate himself.   55
This word "damnation" terrifies not me,
For I confound hell in Elysium.
My ghost be with the old philosophers.
But, leaving these vain trifles of men's souls,
Tell me what is that Lucifer, thy lord?   60

MEPHISTOPHELES

Arch-regent and commander of all spirits.

FAUSTUS

Was not that Lucifer an angel once?

MEPHISTOPHELES

Yes, Faustus, and most dearly loved of God.

FAUSTUS

How comes it, then, that he is prince of devils?

MEPHISTOPHELES

O, by aspiring pride and insolence,   65
For which God threw him from the face of heaven.

FAUSTUS

And what are you that live with Lucifer?

MEPHISTOPHELES

Unhappy spirits that live with Lucifer,
Conspired against our God with Lucifer,
And are for ever damned with Lucifer.   70

FAUSTUS   Where are you damned?

MEPHISTOPHELES   In hell.

FAUSTUS

How comes it, then, that thou art out of hell?

MEPHISTOPHELES

Why, this is hell, nor am I out of it.
Think'st thou that I, that saw the face of God   75
And tasted the eternal joys of heaven,

---

51. stoutly: resolutely.
57. confound . . . Elysium: i.e., make no distinction between the Christian hell and the classical Elysium.
58. old philosophers: i.e., the classical philosophers, who knew nothing of the moral judgments of the Christian afterlife.

Am not tormented with ten thousand hells
In being deprived of everlasting bliss?
O, Faustus, leave these frivolous demands,
Which strikes a terror to my fainting soul!   80
FAUSTUS
What, is great Mephistopheles, so passionate
For being deprivèd of the joys of heaven?
Learn thou of Faustus manly fortitude
And scorn those joys thou never shalt possess.
Go bear these tidings to great Lucifer: 85
Seeing Faustus hath incurred eternal death
By desperate thoughts against Jove's deity,
Say, he surrenders up to him his soul,
So he will spare him four-and-twenty years,
Letting him live in all voluptuousness,   90
Having thee ever to attend on me,
To give me whatsoever I shall ask,
To tell me whatsoever I demand,
To slay mine enemies and to aid my friends,
And always be obedient to my will.   95
Go and return to mighty Lucifer,
And meet me in my study at midnight,
And then resolve me of thy master's mind.
MEPHISTOPHELES
I will, Faustus.   *Exit.*
FAUSTUS
Had I as many souls as there be stars,   100
I'd give them all for Mephistopheles.
By him I'll be great emperor of the world
And make a bridge through the moving air
To pass the ocean with a band of men.
I'll join the hills that bind the Afric shore   105
And make that country continent to Spain,
And both contributary to my crown.
The Emperor shall not live but by my leave,
Nor any potentate of Germany.
Now that I have obtained what I desired,   110
I'll live in speculation of this art,
Till Mephistopheles return again.
                    Ex[eunt FAUSTUS *below and Devils above].*

89. **So:** on the condition that.
105. **bind:** border on, gird.
106. **continent to:** continuous with.
111. **speculation:** contemplation.

[1.4]

Enter WAGNER *and* [ROBIN] *the clown.*

WAGNER Come hither, sirrah boy.

ROBIN "Boy"? O, disgrace to my person! Zounds, "boy" in your face! You have seen many boys with beards, I am sure.

WAGNER Sirrah, hast thou no comings in?

ROBIN Yes, and goings out too, you may see, sir.   5

WAGNER Alas, poor slave! See how poverty jests in his nakedness! I know the villain's out of service and so hungry that I know he would give his soul to the devil for a shoulder of mutton, though it were blood-raw.

ROBIN Not so neither. I had need to have it well roasted, and   10
good sauce to it, if I pay so dear, I can tell you.

WAGNER Sirrah, wilt thou be my man and wait on me, and I will make thee go like *"Qui mihi discipulus."*

ROBIN What, in verse?

WAGNER No, slave, in beaten silk and stavesacre.   15

ROBIN Stavesacre? That's good to kill vermin. Then, belike, if I serve you, I shall be lousy.

WAGNER Why, so thou shalt be, whether thou dost it or no; for, sirrah, if thou dost not presently bind thyself to me for seven years, I'll turn all the lice about thee into familiars and   20
make them tear thee in pieces.

ROBIN Nay, sir, you may save yourself a labor, for they are as familiar with me as if they paid for their meat and drink, I can tell you.

WAGNER Well, sirrah, leave your jesting and take these   25
guilders.   [*Gives money.*]

ROBIN Yes, marry, sir, and I thank you too.

WAGNER So, now thou art to be at an hour's warning whensoever and wheresoever the devil shall fetch thee.

ROBIN Here, take your guilders; I'll none of 'em.   30
                                        [*Tries to return money.*]

[1.4]

2. Zounds: by God's wounds; a mild oath.
4. comings in: income.
5. goings out: expenses (but punning on his flesh peeking out of his tattered clothes).
7. out of service: unemployed.
13. Qui mihi discipulus: i.e., you who are my pupil; the opening line of a well-known Latin poem by William Lyly, "*Carmen de Moribus.*"
15. beaten: embroidered (but also, thrashed); **stavesacre:** a preparation made from delphinium seed used to exterminate lice and fleas.
17. lousy: full of vermin (but also, abhorrent).
19. bind: apprentice ("seven years" was the usual term of an apprenticeship).
20. familiars: evil spirits.
26. guilders: Dutch coins (payment to mark Robin's acceptance of the apprenticeship).

WAGNER   Not I. Thou art pressed. Prepare thyself, for I will
presently raise up two devils to carry thee away.—Banio!
Belcher!

ROBIN   Belcher? An Blecher come here, I'll belch him. I am
not afraid of a devil.   35

        Enter two Devils.

WAGNER   How now, sir! Will you serve me now?

ROBIN   Ay, good Wagner. Take away the devil, then.

WAGNER   Spirits, away! Now, sirrah, follow me.

                                                    Exeunt [*Devils.*]

ROBIN   I will, sir. But hark you, master; will you teach me this
conjuring occupation?   40

WAGNER   Ay, sirrah, I'll teach thee to turn thyself to a dog, or a
cat, or a mouse, or a rat, or anything.

ROBIN   A dog, or a cat, or a mouse, or a rat! O, brave Wagner!

WAGNER   Villain, call me "Master Wagner," and see that you
walk attentively, and let your right eye be always diametrally   45
fixed upon my left heel that thou mayst *quasi vestigiis nostris
insistere.*

ROBIN   Well, sir, I warrant you.   *Exeunt.*

                        [2.1]

        Enter FAUSTUS *in his study.*

FAUSTUS
        Now, Faustus, must thou needs be damned?
        Canst thou not be saved?
        What boots it, then, to think on God or heaven?
        Away with such vain fancies, and despair.
        Despair in God and trust in Beelzebub.   5
        Now, go not backward, Faustus; be resolute.
        Why waver'st thou? O, something soundeth in mine ear:
        "Abjure this magic; turn to God again!"
        Why, He loves thee not.
        The god thou serv'st is thine own appetite,   10
        Wherein is fixed the love of Beelzebub.
        To him I'll build an altar and a church
        And offer lukewarm blood of new-born babes.

---

31. **pressed:** impressed, forced into service.
32–33. **Banio! Belcher:** names of devils (Banio is perhaps is a version of Belial;
Belcher perhaps a comic corruption of Beelzebub).
45. **diametrally:** diametrically.
46–47. *quasi . . . insistere:* i.e., as if to follow in our footsteps (Latin).
[2.1]
3. **boots:** avails, helps.

Enter the two ANGELS.

BAD ANGEL
Go forward, Faustus, in that famous art.
GOOD ANGEL
Sweet Faustus, leave that execrable art.   15
FAUSTUS
Contrition, prayer, repentance—what of these?
GOOD ANGEL
O, they are means to bring thee unto heaven.
BAD ANGEL
Rather illusions, fruits of lunacy,
That make them foolish that do use them most.
GOOD ANGEL
Sweet Faustus, think of heaven and heavenly things.   20
BAD ANGEL
No, Faustus; think of honor and of wealth.   *Exeunt* ANGELS.
FAUSTUS
Wealth! Why, the seigniory of Emden shall be mine.
When Mephistopheles shall stand by me,
What power can hurt me? Faustus, thou art safe.
Cast no more doubts. Mephistopheles, come   25
And bring glad tidings from great Lucifer.
Is't not midnight? Come, Mephistopheles.
Veni, veni, Mephistophile!

Enter MEPHISTOPHELES.

Now tell me what saith Lucifer, thy lord?
MEPHISTOPHELES
That I shall wait on Faustus whilst he lives.   30
So he will buy my service with his soul.
FAUSTUS
Already Faustus hath hazarded that for thee.
MEPHISTOPHELES
But now thou must bequeath it solemnly
And write a deed of gift with thine own blood;
For that security craves Lucifer.   35
If thou deny it, I must back to hell.
FAUSTUS
Stay, Mephistopheles, and tell me
What good will my soul do thy lord?
MEPHISTOPHELES   Enlarge his kingdom.

22. **seigniory of Emden:** governorship of Emden, a prosperous German port on the North Sea.
28. *Veni, veni, Mephistophile:* Come, come, Mephistopheles (Latin).
31. **So:** provided that.

FAUSTUS

    Is that the reason why he tempts us thus?   40

MEPHISTOPHELES

    Solamen miseris socios habuisse doloris.

FAUSTUS

    Why, have you any pain that torture others?

MEPHISTOPHELES

    As great as have the human souls of men.

    But tell me, Faustus, shall I have thy soul?

    And I will be thy slave, and wait on thee,   45

    And give thee more than thou hast wit to ask.

FAUSTUS

    Ay, Mephistopheles, I'll give it him.

MEPHISTOPHELES

    Then, Faustus, stab thy arm courageously

    And bind thy soul, that at some certain day

    Great Lucifer may claim it as his own;   50

    And then be thou as great as Lucifer.

FAUSTUS

    [*Cuts his arm.*] Lo, Mephistopheles, for love of thee

    Faustus hath cut his arm, and with his proper blood

    Assures his soul to be great Lucifer's,

    Chief lord and regent of perpetual night.   55

    View here this blood that trickles from mine arm

    And let it be propitious for my wish.

MEPHISTOPHELES

    But, Faustus, write it in manner of a deed of gift.

FAUSTUS

    [*Writes.*] Ay, so I do. But, Mephistopheles,

    My blood congeals, and I can write no more.   60

MEPHISTOPHELES

    I'll fetch thee fire to dissolve it straight.   *Exit.*

FAUSTUS

    What might the staying of my blood portend?

    Is it unwilling I should write this bill?

    Why streams it not, that I may write afresh:

    "Faustus gives to thee his soul." O, there it stayed!   65

    Why shouldst thou not? Is not thy soul thine own?

    Then write again: "Faustus gives to thee his soul."

---

41. Solamen . . . doloris: i.e., to the unhappy it is a comfort to have had company in misfortune (Latin).

42. have . . . others: i.e., do you devils who torture others feel any pain yourselves?

49. certain: unavoidable (but also, set, specified).

53. proper: own.

57. be propitious: be found acceptable.

63. bill: contract.

Enter MEPHISTOPHELES *with the chafer of fire.*

MEPHISTOPHELES
  See, Faustus, here is fire; set it on.
FAUSTUS
  So, now the blood begins to clear again.
  Now will I make an end immediately. [*Writes.*]   70
MEPHISTOPHELES
  [*Aside.*] What will not I do to obtain his soul?
FAUSTUS
  Consummatum est; this bill is ended,
  And Faustus hath bequeathed his soul to Lucifer.
  But what is this inscription on mine arm?
  "Homo, fuge"? Whither should I fly?   75
  If unto heaven, he'll throw me down to hell.
  My senses are deceived; here's nothing writ.
  O, yes, I see it plain; even here is writ
  "Homo, fuge." Yet shall not Faustus fly.
MEPHISTOPHELES
  [*Aside.*] I'll fetch him somewhat to delight his mind.   *Exit.* 80

    Enter Devils, giving crowns and rich apparel to FAUSTUS.
    They dance, and then depart. Enter MEPHISTOPHELES.

FAUSTUS
  What means this show? Speak, Mephistopheles.
MEPHISTOPHELES
  Nothing, Faustus, but to delight thy mind
  And let thee see what magic can perform.
FAUSTUS
  But may I raise such spirits when I please?
MEPHISTOPHELES
  Ay, Faustus, and do greater things than these.   85
FAUSTUS
  Then, Mephistopheles, receive this scroll,
  A deed of gift of body and of soul,
  But yet conditionally that thou perform
  All covenants and articles between us both.
MEPHISTOPHELES
  Faustus, I swear by hell and Lucifer
  To effect all promises between us both!   90
FAUSTUS   Then hear me read it, Mephistopheles: [*Reads.*] *on
these conditions following: first, that Faustus may be a spirit in
form and substance; secondly, that Mephistopheles shall be his*

67. **SD chafer:** portable grate or grill.
72. *Consummatum est:* i.e., It is finished (Christ's last words on the cross, John 19:30).
75. *Homo, fuge:* Man, flee! (cf. 1 Timothy 6:11; Psalm 139:7–8).

servant and be by him commanded; thirdly, that Mephistophe- 95
les shall do for him and bring him whatsoever; fourthly, that
he shall be in his chamber or house invisible; lastly, that he
shall appear to the said John Faustus at all times in what shape
or form soever he please. I, John Faustus of Wittenberg, Doctor, by these presents, do give both body and soul to Lucifer, 100
Prince of the East, and his minister, Mephistopheles, and
furthermore grant unto them that, twenty-four years being
expired, and these articles above written being inviolate, full
power to fetch or carry the said John Faustus' body and soul,
flesh, blood, into their habitation wheresoever. By me, John 105
Faustus.

MEPHISTOPHELES
Speak, Faustus; do you deliver this as your deed?

FAUSTUS
[*Gives paper.*] Ay, take it, and the devil give thee good of it!

MEPHISTOPHELES
So now, Faustus, ask me what thou wilt.

FAUSTUS
First I will question with thee about hell.   110
Tell me, where is the place that men call hell?

MEPHISTOPHELES   Under the heavens.

FAUSTUS
Ay, so are all things else, but whereabouts?

MEPHISTOPHELES
Within the bowels of these elements,
Where we are tortured and remain for ever.   115
Hell hath no limits, nor is circumscribed
In one self place, but where we are is hell,
And where hell is, there must we ever be.
And, to be short, when all the world dissolves,
And every creature shall be purified,   120
All places shall be hell that is not heaven.

FAUSTUS   I think hell's a fable.

MEPHISTOPHELES
Ay, think so still, till experience change thy mind.

FAUSTUS
Why? Dost thou think that Faustus shall be damned?

MEPHISTOPHELES
Ay, of necessity, for here's the scroll   125
In which thou hast given thy soul to Lucifer.

---

100. **presents**: legal documents.
103. **inviolate**: i.e., having not been violated.
117. **self**: particular, single.

FAUSTUS
   Ay, and body too; but what of that?
   Think'st thou that Faustus is so fond to imagine
   That after this life there is any pain?
   No, these are trifles and mere old wives' tales.   130
MEPHISTOPHELES
   But I am an instance to prove the contrary,
   For I tell thee I am damned and now in hell.
FAUSTUS
   Nay, an this be hell, I'll willingly be damned.
   What? Sleeping, eating, walking, and disputing?
   But, leaving this, let me have a wife, the fairest maid in Ger-   135
   many, for I am wanton and lascivious and cannot live with-
   out a wife.
MEPHISTOPHELES
   Well, Faustus, thou shalt have a wife.

      He fetches in a Woman Devil.

FAUSTUS
                                    What sight is this?
MEPHISTOPHELES
   Now, Faustus, wilt thou have a wife?
FAUSTUS
   Here's a hot whore indeed. No, I'll no wife.   140
MEPHISTOPHELES
   Marriage is but a ceremonial toy,
   And, if thou lov'st me, think no more of it.
   I'll cull thee out the fairest courtesans
   And bring them every morning to thy bed.
   She whom thine eye shall like thy heart shall have,   145
   Were she as chaste as was Penelope,
   As wise as Saba, or as beautiful
   As was bright Lucifer before his fall.
   Here, take this book, peruse it well.
      [*Gives* FAUSTUS *a book and they look through it.*]
   The iterating of these lines brings gold;   150
   The framing of this circle on the ground
   Brings thunder, whirlwinds, storm, and lightning;
   Pronounce this thrice devoutly to thyself,

128. **fond:** foolish.
141. **ceremonial toy:** trifling ceremony.
146. **Penelope:** Odysseus's faithful wife in the *Odyssey*.
147. **Saba:** the queen of Sheba (2 Chronicles 9:1–3, Vulgate spelling).
150. **iterating:** repetition.

And men in harness shall appear to thee
Ready to execute what thou command'st.   155
FAUSTUS
Thanks, Mephistopheles, for this sweet book.
This will I keep as chary as my life.   *Exeunt.*

[2.2]

Enter [ROBIN,] *the clown* [*with a book*].

ROBIN   What, Dick! Look to the horses there till I come again.
I have gotten one of Doctor Faustus' conjuring books, and
now we'll have such knavery as't passes.

Enter DICK.

DICK   What, Robin! You must come away and walk the horses.
ROBIN   I walk the horses? I scorn't, faith. I have other matters   5
in hand. Let the horses walk themselves an they will.
[*Reads.*] "A" *per se* "a"; "t," "h," "e"—"the"; "o" *per se* "o";
"Deny orgon gorgon." Keep further from me, O thou illiter-
ate and unlearned ostler!
DICK   'Snails, what hast thou got there? A book? Why, thou   10
canst not tell ne'er a word on't.
ROBIN   That thou shalt see presently. [*Draws a circle.*] Keep
out of the circle, I say, lest I send you into the hostry with a
vengeance.
DICK   That's like, faith! You had best leave your foolery, for, an   15
my master come, he'll conjure you, faith.
ROBIN   My master conjure me? I'll tell thee what: an my master come here, I'll clap as fair a pair of horns on's head as
e'er thou sawest in thy life.
DICK   Thou need'st not do that, for my mistress hath done it.   20

154. **harness:** armor.
157. **chary:** careful.
2.2. On the placement of this scene here, which is printed in the B-text (1616) after the
material of 2.3, see p. xiii herein.
3. **as't passes:** as one can best imagine.
7. *per se*: by itself (Robin is trying to read, sounding out the words letter by letter).
8. **Deny orgon gorgon:** presumably Robin's effort to read and pronounce the word *demogorgon.*"
9. **ostler:** horse groom.
10. **'Snails:** By his nails, referring to the Crucifixion; an oath.
11. **tell:** understand, read.
13. **hostry:** inn, hostelry.
15. **That's like:** i.e., some chance (sarcastic).
15, 17. **an:** if.
18. **horns:** i.e., the horns that were supposed to grow on the forehead of a cuckolded husband.

ROBIN   Ay, there be of us here that have waded as deep into
matters as other men, if they were disposed to talk.

DICK   A plague take you! I thought you did not sneak up and
down after her for nothing. But, I prithee, tell me in good
sadness, Robin, is that a conjuring book?   25

ROBIN   Do but speak what thou'lt have me to do, and I'll do't.
If thou'lt dance naked, put off thy clothes, and I'll conjure
thee about presently; or, if thou'lt go but to the tavern with
me, I'll give thee white wine, red wine, claret wine, sack,
muscadine, malmsey, and whippincrust—hold, belly, hold—   30
and we'll not pay one penny for it.

DICK   O, brave! Prithee, let's to it presently, for I am as dry as
a dog.

ROBIN   Come, then, let's away.   *Exeunt.*

[2.3]

Enter FAUSTUS, *in his study, and* MEPHISTOPHELES.

FAUSTUS
When I behold the heavens, then I repent
And curse thee, wicked Mephistopheles,
Because thou hast deprived me of those joys.

MEPHISTOPHELES
'Twas thine own seeking, Faustus; thank thyself.
But think'st thou heaven is such a glorious thing?   5
I tell thee, Faustus, it is not half so fair
As thou, or any man that breathe on earth.

FAUSTUS   How prov'st thou that?

MEPHISTOPHELES
'Twas made for man; then he's more excellent.

FAUSTUS
If heaven was made for man, 'twas made for me.   10
I will renounce this magic and repent.

Enter the two ANGELS.

GOOD ANGEL
Faustus, repent; yet God will pity thee.

21. **of us:** some of us.
24–25. **in good sadness:** in earnest.
29. **sack:** a strong white wine imported from Spain and the Canary Islands.
30. **muscadine:** a white wine imported from Tuscany made from muscat grapes; **malmsey:**
a strong sweet wine, imported from Madeira; **whippencrust:** a spiced wine (hippocras, see
A-text, 2.2.23).
[2.3]
12. **yet:** still, even now.

BAD ANGEL

  Thou art a spirit; God cannot pity thee.

FAUSTUS

  Who buzzeth in mine ears I am a spirit?

  Be I a devil, yet God may pity me;   15

  Yea, God will pity me, if I repent.

BAD ANGEL

  Ay, but Faustus never shall repent.   *Ex[eunt]* ANGELS.

FAUSTUS

  My heart is hardened; I cannot repent.

  Scarce can I name salvation, faith, or heaven.

  Swords, poison, halters, and envenomed steel   20

  Are laid before me to dispatch myself;

  And long ere this I should have done the deed,

  Had not sweet pleasure conquered deep despair.

  Have not I made blind Homer sing to me

  Of Alexander's love and Oenone's death?   25

  And hath not he that built the walls of Thebes

  With ravishing sound of his melodious harp

  Made music with my Mephistopheles?

  Why should I die then or basely despair?

  I am resolved; Faustus shall not repent.   30

  Come, Mephistopheles, let us dispute again

  And reason of divine astrology.

  Speak; are there many spheres above the moon?

  Are all celestial bodies but one globe,

  As is the substance of this centric earth?   35

MEPHISTOPHELES

  As are the elements, such are the heavens,

  Even from the moon unto the empyreal orb,

  Mutually folded in each other's spheres,

  And jointly move upon one axletree,

  Whose terminè is termed the world's wide pole;   40

  Nor are the names of Saturn, Mars, or Jupiter

  Feigned, but are erring stars.

20. halters: nooses; **envenomed steel:** poisoned blades.
25. Alexander's . . . death: i.e., the death of Paris in the Trojan war. He died in Oenone's arms; she then killed herself.
26–27. he . . . harp: Amphion, whose wonderful harp-playing caused stones to rise and form the walls of Thebes.
32. astrology: astronomy. A sharp separation of astrology from astronomy was not made until the end of the 17th century.
34–35. Are . . . earth: i.e., do the stars and planets form a single spherical structure, like the earth itself that is at its center?
37. empyreal orb: the outermost sphere of heaven (supposedly where God dwells), though the aural suggestion of "imperial" (see A-text, 2.3.59) is impossible to avoid.
39. axletree: axis.
40. terminè: boundary.
42. erring stars: moving planets.

FAUSTUS   But have they all one motion, both *situ et tempore*?

MEPHISTOPHELES   All move from east to west in four-and-
   twenty hours upon the poles of the world, but differ in their   45
   motions upon the poles of the zodiac.

FAUSTUS
   These slender questions Wagner can decide.
   Hath Mephistopheles no greater skill?
   Who knows not the double motion of the planets?
   That the first is finished in a natural day;   50
   The second thus: Saturn in thirty years;
   Jupiter in twelve; Mars in four; the sun,
   Venus, and Mercury in a year; the moon in twenty-eight days.
   These are freshmen's questions. But tell me, hath every
   sphere a dominion or *intelligentia*?   55

MEPHISTOPHELES   Ay.

FAUSTUS   How many heavens or spheres are there?

MEPHISTOPHELES   Nine: the seven planets, the firmament, and
   the empyreal heaven.

FAUSTUS   But is there not *coelum igneum et crystallinum*?   60

MEPHISTOPHELES   No, Faustus, they be but fables.

FAUSTUS   Resolve me, then, in this one question: why are not
   conjunctions, oppositions, aspects, eclipses all at one time,
   but in some years we have more, in some less?

MEPHISTOPHELES   *Per inaequalem motum respectu totius.*   65

FAUSTUS   Well I am answered. Now tell me who made the
   world?

MEPHISTOPHELES   I will not.

FAUSTUS   Sweet Mephistopheles, tell me.

MEPHISTOPHELES   Move me not, Faustus.   70

FAUSTUS   Villain, have I not bound thee to tell me anything?

MEPHISTOPHELES
   Ay, that is not against our kingdom;
   This is. Thou are damned; think thou of hell.

FAUSTUS
   Think, Faustus, upon God that made the world.

MEPHISTOPHELES   Remember this.   *Exit.*   75

---

43. *situ et tempore*: in space and time (Latin).
54. freshmen's questions: i.e., easy questions.
55. dominion or *intelligentia*: angelic influence or intelligence, which was thought to
move the planets.
59. emphyreal heaven: see note at 2.3.59.
60. *coelum . . . crystallinum*: i.e., the fiery and crystalline spheres (Latin).
63. conjunctions . . . aspects: astrological terms for, respectively, the promixity of two
planets; their location in directly opposite parts of the sky; their relative positions in the sky.
65. *Per . . . totius*: because of unequal motion in respect to the whole (Latin).
70. Move: vex, anger (also, urge).

FAUSTUS
  Ay, go, accursèd spirit, to ugly hell!
  'Tis thou hast damned distressèd Faustus' soul.
  —Is't not too late?

  Enter the two ANGELS.

BAD ANGEL   Too late.
GOOD ANGEL
  Never too late, if Faustus will repent.   80
BAD ANGEL
  If thou repent, devils will tear thee in pieces.
GOOD ANGEL
  Repent, and they shall never raze thy skin.   *Exeunt* ANGELS.
FAUSTUS
  O Christ, my Savior, my Savior,
  Help to save distressèd Faustus' soul!

  Enter LUCIFER, BEELZEBUB, *and* MEPHISTOPHELES.

LUCIFER
  Christ cannot save thy soul, for he is just.   85
  There's none but I have interest in the same.
FAUSTUS
  O, what art thou that look'st so terribly?
LUCIFER
  I am Lucifer,
  And this is my companion prince in hell.
FAUSTUS
  O Faustus, they are come to fetch thy soul!   90
BEELZEBUB
  We are come to tell thee thou dost injure us.
LUCIFER
  Thou call'st on Christ, contrary to thy promise.
BEELZEBUB
  Thou shouldst not think on God.
LUCIFER   Think on the devil.
BEELZEBUB And his dam, too.
FAUSTUS
  Nor will Faustus henceforth. Pardon him for this,   95
  And Faustus vows never to look to heaven.
LUCIFER
  So shalt thou show thyself an obedient servant,
  And we will highly gratify thee for it.

82. **raze:** tear.
86. **interest in:** legal claim on.
94. **dam:** mother.

BEELZEBUB   Faustus, we are come from hell in person to show
    thee some pastime. Sit down, and thou shalt behold the   100
    Seven Deadly Sins appear to thee in their own proper shapes
    and likeness.
FAUSTUS   That sight will be as pleasant to me as Paradise was
    to Adam the first day of his creation.
LUCIFER   Talk not of Paradise or creation, but mark the show.   105
    Go, Mephistopheles; fetch them in.
                                    [*Exit* MEPHISTOPHELES.]

        Enter [MEPHISTOPHELES *with*] *the* SEVEN DEADLY SINS.

BEELZEBUB   Now, Faustus, question them of their names and
    dispositions.
FAUSTUS   That shall I soon. What art thou, the first?
PRIDE   I am Pride. I disdain to have any parents. I am like to   110
    Ovid's flea. I can creep into every corner of a wench: some-
    times, like a periwig, I sit upon her brow; next, like a neck-
    lace, I hang about her neck; then, like a fan of feathers, I
    kiss her; and then, turning myself to a wrought smock, do
    what I list. But, fie, what a smell is here! I'll not speak a   115
    word more for a king's ransom, unless the ground be per-
    fumed and covered with cloth of arras.
FAUSTUS   Thou art a proud knave, indeed. What art thou, the
    second?
COVETOUSNESS   I am Covetousness, begotten of an old churl   120
    in a leather bag; and, might I now obtain my wish, this
    house, you, and all should turn to gold, that I might lock you
    safe into my chest. O my sweet gold!
FAUSTUS   And what art thou, the third?
ENVY   I am Envy, begotten of a chimney-sweeper and an   125
    oyster-wife. I cannot read and therefore wish all books
    burned. I am lean with seeing others eat. O, that there
    would come a famine over all the world, that all might
    die and I live alone! Then thou shouldst see how fat I'd be.
    But must thou sit and I stand? Come down, with a
    vengeance!   130
FAUSTUS   Out, envious wretch! But what art thou, the
    fourth?

---

111. **Ovid's flea:** a Latin poem, "Elegia de pulice," wrongly ascribed to Ovid, notes the
flea's ability to go anywhere.
112. **periwig:** wig.
114. **wrought smock:** embroidered undergarment;
115. **list:** like.
117. **cloth of arras:** fine tapestry. Arras, in Flanders, was a city renowned for its tapestry.
121. **bag:** purse, wallet.
129–30. **with a vengeance:** i.e., or else.

WRATH   I am Wrath. I had neither father nor mother. I leaped
out of a lion's mouth when I was scarce an hour old and ever
since have run up and down the world with these case of
rapiers, wounding myself when I could get none to fight   135
withal. I was born in hell, and look to it, for some of you
shall be my father.

FAUSTUS   And what art thou, the fifth?

GLUTTONY   I am Gluttony. My parents are all dead, and the
devil a penny they have left me but a small pension, and that   140
buys me thirty meals a day and ten bevers—a small trifle to
suffice nature. I come of a royal pedigree: my father was a
gammon of bacon and my mother was a hogshead of claret
wine; my godfathers were these: Peter Pickled-herring and
Martin Martlemas-beef. But my godmother, O, she was an   145
ancient gentlewoman; her name was Margery March-beer.
Now, Faustus, thou hast heard all my progeny; wilt thou bid
me to supper?

FAUSTUS   Not I.

GLUTTONY   Then the devil choke thee!   150

FAUSTUS   Choke thyself, glutton! What art thou, the sixth?

SLOTH   Heigh-ho! I am Sloth. I was begotten on a sunny
bank. Heigh-ho! I'll not speak a word more for a king's ransom.

FAUSTUS   And what are you, Mistress Minx, the seventh and
last?   155

LECHERY   Who, I? I, sir? I am one that loves an inch of raw
mutton better than an ell of fried stock-fish, and the first letter of my name begins with lechery.

LUCIFER   Away to hell, away! On, piper!

Exeunt the SEVEN SINS.

FAUSTUS   O, how this sight doth delight my soul!   160

LUCIFER   But, Faustus, in hell is all manner of delight.

FAUSTUS   O, might I see hell and return again safe; how happy
were I then!

---

134. **case:** pair.
139–40. **the devil a penny:** i.e., not a damned cent.
141. **bevers:** snacks.
143. **gammon of bacon:** smoked ham; **hogshead:** a large cask for liquor.
143–44. **claret wine:** light red wine.
145. **Martlemas-beef:** salted beef, usually preserved around St. Martin's day (Martinmas, November 11).
146. **March-beer:** a strong beer, brewed in March.
147. **progeny:** parentage.
157. **ell:** 45 inches; **stock-fish:** dried cod (often associated with sexual impotence); it is not unlikely that the adjective "fried," as both the B-text and A-text have it, is an error for "dried."
158. **lechery:** many editors emend to "L," but the joke is that Lechery says his whole name.

LUCIFER

    Faustus, thou shalt; at midnight I will send for thee.

                             [*Hands him a book.*]

    Meanwhile peruse this book and view it thoroughly,

    And thou shalt turn thyself into what shape thou wilt.   165

FAUSTUS

    Thanks, mighty Lucifer!

    This will I keep as chary as my life.

LUCIFER   Now, Faustus, farewell.

FAUSTUS   Farewell, great Lucifer. Come, Mephistopheles.   170

                    Exeunt omnes, several ways.

[3.Chorus]

Enter CHORUS.

CHORUS

    Learnèd Faustus, to find the secrets of astronomy

    Graven in the book of Jove's high firmament,

    Did mount him up to scale Olympus' top,

    Where, sitting in a chariot burning bright,

    Drawn by the strength of yokèd dragons' necks,   5

    He views the clouds, the planets, and the stars,

    The tropics, zones, and quarters of the sky,

    From the bright circle of the hornèd moon

    Even to the height of *Primum Mobile;*

    And, whirling round with this circumference,   10

    Within the concave compass of the pole,

    From east to west his dragons swiftly glide

    And in eight days did bring him home again.

    Not long he stayed within his quiet house

    To rest his bones after his weary toil,   15

    But new exploits do hale him out again,

    And, mounted then upon a dragon's back,

    That with his wings did part the subtle air,

---

168. chary: carefully.

[3.Chorus]

2. Graven: engraved.

3. scale Olympus' top: ascend to the home of the gods on Mount Olympus.

7. tropics . . . quarters: various terms for the structure of the heavens: the "tropics," Cancer and Capricorn, were the two major divisions of the sky, which was also understood to be divided up into five "zones," as well as into "quarters," which corresponded to the four seasons on earth.

9. *Primum Mobile*: the outermost sphere (literally, the first mover).

10–11. whirling . . . pole: i.e., on a circular path around the axis on which all the universe turns.

18. subtle: rarefied.

He now is gone to prove cosmography,
That measures coasts and kingdoms of the earth,   20
And, as I guess, will first arrive at Rome,
To see the Pope and manner of his court
And take some part of holy Peter's feast,
The which this day is highly solemnized.   *Exit.*

[3.1]

Enter FAUSTUS *and* MEPHISTOPHELES.

FAUSTUS
    Having now, my good Mephistopheles,
    Passed with delight the stately town of Trier,
    Environed round with airy mountain tops,
    With walls of flint, and deep-entrenchèd lakes,
    Not to be won by any conquering prince;   5
    From Paris next, coasting the realm of France,
    We saw the river Maine fall into Rhine,
    Whose banks are set with groves of fruitful vines;
    Then up to Naples, rich Campania,
    Whose buildings, fair and gorgeous to the eye,   10
    The streets straight forth and paved with finest brick.
    There saw we learnèd Maro's golden tomb,
    The way he cut an English mile in length
    Through a rock of stone in one night's space.
    From thence to Venice, Padua, and the east,   15
    In one of which a sumptuous temple stands
    That threats the stars with her aspiring top,
    Whose frame is paved with sundry colored stones
    And roofed aloft with curious work in gold.
    Thus hitherto hath Faustus spent his time.   20
    But tell me now what resting place is this?
    Hast thou, as erst I did command,
    Conducted me within the walls of Rome?

19. **prove:** put to the test.
23. **holy Peter's feast:** St. Peter's feast day, June 29.
[3.1]
2. **Trier:** Treves, a German city on the river Mosel.
4. **deep-entrenchèd lakes:** moats.
6. **coasting:** exploring.
9. **Campania:** the region of Italy in which Naples is the principal city.
11. **straight forth:** in straight lines.
12. **Maro's golden tomb:** the tomb of Virgil (Publius Virgilius Maro), who was buried in Naples in 19 B.C.E.
16. **sumptuous temple:** probably St. Mark's in Venice.
22. **erst:** earlier.

MEPHISTOPHELES
   I have, my Faustus. And, for proof thereof,
   This is the goodly palace of the Pope,   25
   And, 'cause we are no common guests,
   I choose his privy chamber for our use.
FAUSTUS
   I hope his Holiness will bid us welcome.
MEPHISTOPHELES
   All's one, for we'll be bold with his venison.
   But now, my Faustus, that thou mayst perceive   30
   What Rome contains for to delight thine eyes,
   Know that this city stands upon seven hills
   That underprop the groundwork of the same.
   Just through the midst runs flowing Tiber's stream,
   With winding banks that cut it in two parts,   35
   Over the which two stately bridges lean
   That make safe passage to each part of Rome.
   Upon the bridge called Ponte Angelo
   Erected is a castle passing strong,
   Where thou shalt see such store of ordnance   40
   As that the double cannons, forged of brass,
   Do match the number of the days contained
   Within the compass of one complete year,
   Beside the gates and high pyramides
   That Julius Caesar brought from Africa.   45
FAUSTUS
   Now, by the kingdoms of infernal rule,
   Of Styx, of Acheron, and the fiery lake
   Of ever-burning Phlegethon, I swear
   That I do long to see the monuments
   And situation of bright splendent Rome.   50
   Come, therefore, let's away.
MEPHISTOPHELES
   Nay; stay, my Faustus. I know you'd see the Pope
   And take some part of holy Peter's feast,
   The which, this day with high solemnity
   This day is held through Rome and Italy   55
   In honor of the Pope's triumphant victory.

27. privy chamber: private apartment in a palace.
38. Ponte Angelo: bridge built by Hadrian in 135 C.E.
39. passing: surpassingly.
44. pyramides: obelisk (in fact brought to Rome in Caligula from Heliopolis and moved in 1586 to the Piazza San Pietro); the noun is singular and pronounced with four syllables.
47–48. Styx . . . Phlegethon: three of the four rivers in the classical Greek underworld.
53. holy Peter's feast: see 3.Chorus 23.
56. victory: i.e., the victory over the German emperor and the capture of Bruno, the rival pope.

FAUSTUS

    Sweet Mephistopheles, thou pleasest me.
    Whilst I am here on earth, let me be cloyed
    With all things that delight the heart of man.
    My four-and-twenty years of liberty   60
    I'll spend in pleasure and in dalliance,
    That Faustus' name, whilst this bright frame doth stand,
    May be admirèd through the furthest land.

METPHISTOPHELES

    'Tis well said, Faustus. Come, then, stand by me,
    And thou shalt see them come immediately.   65

FAUSTUS

    Nay; stay, my gentle Mephistopheles,
    And grant me my request, and then I go.
    Thou know'st, within the compass of eight days
    We viewed the face of heaven, of earth, and hell.
    So high our dragons soared into the air,   70
    That, looking down, the earth appeared to me
    No bigger than my hand in quantity.
    There did we view the kingdoms of the world,
    And what might please mine eye I there beheld.
    Then in this show let me an actor be,   75
    That this proud Pope may Faustus' cunning see.

MEPHISTOPHELES

    Let it be so, my Faustus. But, first, stay
    And view their triumphs as they pass this way,
    And then devise what best contents thy mind,
    By cunning in thine art, to cross the Pope   80
    Or dash the pride of this solemnity—
    To make his monks and abbots stand like apes
    And point like antics at his triple crown,
    To beat the beads about the friars' pates
    Or clap huge horns upon the cardinals' heads,   85
    Or any villany thou canst devise,
    And I'll perform it, Faustus. Hark! They come.
    This day shall make thee be admired in Rome.

                             [They move aside.]

60. **liberty:** (1) ability to act without restraint; (2) freedom from hell.
62. **bright frame:** splendid universe.
78. **triumphs:** processions, celebrations.
83. **antics:** clowns, grotesques; **triple crown:** the distinctive papal tiara (cf. "triple diadem," 3.1.181).
84. **beads:** prayer beads.

Enter the Cardinals [of FRANCE *and* PADUA] *and Bishops,
some bearing crosiers, some the pillars; Monks and Friars,
singing their procession; then the* POPE *[Adrian],* RAY-
MOND, *King of Hungary, the Archbishop of* RHEIMS, *with*
BRUNO *led in chains, and Attendants.*

POPE
    Cast down our footstool.
RAYMOND   Saxon Bruno, stoop,
    Whilst on thy back his Holiness ascends   90
    Saint Peter's chair and state pontifical.
BRUNO
    Proud Lucifer, that state belongs to me.
    But thus I fall to Peter, not to thee.   *[He kneels.]*
POPE
    To me and Peter shalt thou grovelling lie
    And crouch before the papal dignity.   95
    Sound trumpets, then, for thus Saint Peter's heir,
    From Bruno's back, ascends Saint Peter's chair.
                A Flourish while he ascends.
    Thus, as the goods creep on with feet of wool
    Long ere with iron hands they punish men,
    So shall our sleeping vengeance now arise   100
    And smite with death thy hated enterprise.
    Lord Cardinals of France and Padua,
    Go forthwith to our holy consistory
    And read amongst the statutes decretal
    What, by the holy council held at Trent,   105
    The sacred synod hath decreed for him
    That doth assume the papal government
    Without election and a true consent.
    Away, and bring us word with speed.
FRANCE   We go, my Lord.   *[Exeunt Cardinals.]* 110
POPE   Lord Raymond—
FAUSTUS
    Go, haste thee, gentle Mephistopheles.
    Follow the cardinals to the consistory,
    And, as they turn their superstitious books,
    Strike them with sloth and drowsy idleness,

88. SD crosiers: ceremonial staffs carried by Church officials; **SD pillars:** portable ceremonial columns; **SD procession:** i.e., liturgical songs chanted during the procession.
92. state: throne.
103. consistory: senate (as at 3.1.188).
104. statues decretal: papal decrees (as at 3.1.182).
105. holy . . . Trent: The Council at Trent, held intermittently between 1545 and 1563,
was charged with reforming the Church in response to the challenge of the Reformation.
106. sacred synod: Church council.

And make them sleep so sound that in their shapes   115
Thyself and I may parley with this Pope,
This proud confronter of the Emperor,
And, in despite of all his holiness,
Restore this Bruno to his liberty   120
And bear him to the states of Germany.

MEPHISTOPHELES   Faustus, I go.

FAUSTUS   Despatch it soon.
The Pope shall curse that Faustus came to Rome.

Ex[eunt] FAUSTUS *and* MEPHISTOPHELES.

BRUNO
Pope Adrian, let me have some right of law;   125
I was elected by the Emperor.

POPE
We will depose the Emperor for that deed
And curse the people that submit to him.
Both he and thou shall stand excommunicate
And interdict from Church's privilege   130
And all society of holy men.
He grows too proud in his authority,
Lifting his lofty head above the clouds
And, like a steeple, overpeers the Church.
But we'll pull down his haughty insolence,   135
And, as Pope Alexander, our progenitor,
Trod on the neck of German Frederick,
Adding this golden sentence to our praise,
"That Peter's heirs should tread on Emperors,
And walk upon the dreadful adder's back,   140
Treading the lion and the dragon down,
And fearless spurn the killing basilisk,"
So will we quell that haughty schismatic
And, by authority apostolical,
Depose him from his regal government.   145

BRUNO
Pope Julius swore to princely Sigismund,
For him and the succeeding Popes of Rome,
To hold the emperors their lawful lords.

---

125. **Adrian:** Pope Adrian IV, the only Englishman to serve as pope (1154–59).
128. **curse:** excommunicate.
130. **interdict:** barred.
136–37. **Pope . . . Frederick:** Pope Alexander III (actually Adrian's successor) excommunicated Frederick in 1165.
142. **basilisk:** a mythological lizardlike beast whose glance and breath were fatal.
146. **Pope . . . Sigismund:** This is not historical, but Sigismund was the Holy Roman Emperor from 1411 to 1437, and Julius II was Pope (1503–13) and Julius III from 1550 to 1555.

POPE

    Pope Julius did abuse the Church's rights,
    And therefore none of his decrees can stand.   150
    Is not all power on earth bestowed on us?
    And therefore, though we would, we cannot err.
    Behold this silver belt whereto is fixed
    Seven golden seals, fast sealed with seven seals,
    In token of our seven-fold power from heaven,   155
    To bind or loose, lock fast, condemn or judge,
    Resign or seal, or what so pleaseth us.
    Then he and thou and all the world shall stoop,
    Or be assurèd of our dreadful curse
    To light as heavy as the pains of hell.   160

    Enter FAUSTUS *and* MEPHISTOPHELES, *[dressed] like the Cardinals [of* FRANCE *and* PADUA].

MEPHISTOPHELES   Now tell me, Faustus, are we not fitted well?
FAUSTUS

    Yes, Mephistopheles, and two such cardinals
    Ne'er served a holy pope as we shall do.
    But, whilst they sleep within the consistory,
    Let us salute his reverend Fatherhood.   165
RAYMOND

    [*To the* POPE.] Behold, my lord, the cardinals are returned.
POPE

    Welcome, grave fathers. Answer presently:
    What hath our holy council there decreed
    Concerning Bruno and the Emperor
    In quittance of their late conspiracy   170
    Against our state and papal dignity?
FAUSTUS

    Most sacred patron of the church of Rome,
    By full consent of all the synod
    Of priests and prelates, it is thus decreed
    That Bruno and the German Emperor   175
    Be held as Lollards and bold schismatics
    And proud disturbers of the Church's peace.

149. **rights:** The B-text prints "rites," though the meaning seems to be "privileges" rather than "ceremonies."
152. **though we would:** even if we wanted to.
154. **Seven . . . seals:** a reference to the absolute power and mysterious authority of the Pope; cf. Revelation 4–8.
157. **Resign:** unseal.
160. **light:** alight, land on.
170. **quittance of:** retaliation for.
176. **Lollards:** i.e., heretics; literally, followers of the English reformer John Wyclif (1320–1384).

And if that Bruno, by his own assent,
Without enforcement of the German peers,
Did seek to wear the triple diadem   180
And by your death to climb Saint Peter's chair,
The statutes decretal have thus decreed
He shall be straight condemned of heresy
And on a pile of fagots burnt to death.

POPE
It is enough. Here, take him to your charge,   185
And bear him straight to Ponte Angelo,
And in the strongest tower enclose him fast.
Tomorrow, sitting in our consistory
With all our college of grave cardinals,
We will determine of his life or death.   190
Here, take his triple crown along with you
                                   [*Gives them the crown.*]
And leave it in the church's treasury.
Make haste again, my good Lord Cardinals,
And take our blessing apostolical.

MEPHISTOPHELES
So, so; was never devil thus blessed before.   195

FAUSTUS
Away, sweet Mephistopheles; be gone.
The cardinals will be plagued for this anon.
            Exeunt FAUSTUS *and* MEPHISTOPHELES [*with* BRUNO].

POPE
Go presently and bring a banquet forth,
That we may solemnize Saint Peter's feast
And with Lord Raymond, King of Hungary,   200
Drink to our late and happy victory.   *Exeunt.*

[3.2]

A *sennet while the banquet is brought in. And then enter*
FAUSTUS *and* MEPHISTOPHELES *in their own shapes.*

MEPHISTOPHELES
Now, Faustus, come prepare thyself for mirth.
The sleepy cardinals are hard at hand
To censure Bruno, that is posted hence
And, on a proud-paced steed, as swift as thought

180. **triple diadem:** see 3.1.83.
181. **Saint Peter's chair:** i.e., the papal throne.
184. **fagots:** sticks, branches.
189. **college:** council.
3.2. **SD sennet:** trumpet flourish.

Flies o'er the Alps to fruitful Germany,   5
There to salute the woeful Emperor.
FAUSTUS
The Pope will curse them for their sloth today,
That slept both Bruno and his crown away.
But now, that Faustus may delight his mind
And by their folly make some merriment,   10
Sweet Mephistopheles, so charm me here
That I may walk invisible to all
And do whate'er I please, unseen of any.
MEPHISTOPHELES
Faustus, thou shalt; then kneel down presently,
Whilst on thy head I lay my hand   15
                    [MEPHISTOPHELES *casts a spell*.]
And charm thee with this magic wand.
First, wear this girdle; then appear
Invisible to all are here.
The planets seven, the gloomy air,
Hell, and the Furies' forkèd hair,   20
Pluto's blue fire, and Hecate's tree,
With magic spells so compass thee
That no eye may thy body see.
So, Faustus, now, for all their holiness,
Do what thou wilt; thou shalt not be discerned.   25
FAUSTUS
Thanks, Mephistopheles. Now, friars, take heed,
Lest Faustus make your shaven crowns to bleed.
MEPHISTOPHELES   Faustus, no more. See, where the Cardinals
come.

        Enter POPE *and all the Lords. Enter the Cardinals with a*
        book.

POPE
Welcome, lord Cardinals; come sit down.   30
Lord Raymond, take your seat. Friars, attend
And see that all things be in readiness,
As best beseems this solemn festival.

6. **woeful:** grieving (because of Bruno's capture).
8. **slept:** i.e., lost through their inattention.
17. **girdle:** belt.
20. **Furies' forkèd hair:** i.e., the entwined snakes that were the hair of the avenging goddesses in Greek mythology.
21. **Pluto's blue fire:** i.e., the flames of the underworld; **Hecate's tree:** perhaps the gallows; Hecate was a goddess of magic.
22. **compass:** surround, encompass.

FRANCE

    First, may it please your sacred Holiness

    To view the sentence of the reverend synod   35

    Concerning Bruno and the Emperor?

POPE

    What needs this question? Did I not tell you

    Tomorrow we would sit i'th'consistory

    And there determine of his punishment?

    You brought us word even now it was decreed   40

    That Bruno and the cursèd Emperor

    Were by the holy council both condemned

    For loathèd Lollards and base schismatics.

    Then wherefore would you have me view that book?

FRANCE

    Your Grace mistakes; you gave us no such charge.   45

RAYMOND

    Deny it not; we all are witnesses

    That Bruno here was late delivered you,

    With his rich triple crown to be reserved

    And put into the Church's treasury.

PADUA and FRANCE   By holy Paul, we saw them not.   50

POPE

    By Peter, you shall die

    Unless you bring them forth immediately.——

    Hale them to prison; lade their limbs with gyves.——

    False prelates, for this hateful treachery

    Cursed be your souls to hellish misery.   55

                  [*Exeunt attendants with the Cardinals.*]

FAUSTUS

    So, they are safe. Now, Faustus, to the feast.

    The Pope had never such a frolic guest.

POPE

    Lord Archbishop of Rheims, sit down with us.

RHEIMS   I thank your Holiness.

FAUSTUS   Fall to; the devil choke you an you spare!   60

POPE

    Who is that spoke? Friars, look about.

    Lord Raymond, pray, fall to. I am beholding

    To the Bishop of Milan for this so rare a present.

FAUSTUS   I thank you, sir.   [*Snatches the dish.*]

POPE

    How now! Who snatched the meat from me?   65

35. **reverend synod:** holy council.
48. **reserved:** put aside for safekeeping.
53. **lade:** weigh down, burden; **gyves:** shackles.

Villains, why speak you not?
My good Lord Archbishop, here's a most dainty dish
Was sent me from a cardinal in France.

FAUSTUS   I'll have that too.   [*Snatches the dish.*]

POPE

What Lollards do attend our Holiness   70
That we receive such great indignity?
Fetch me some wine.

FAUSTUS   [*Aside.*] Ay, pray, do, for Faustus is a-dry.
                                    [*Attendant brings in wine.*]

POPE   Lord Raymond, I drink unto your Grace.

FAUSTUS   [*Snatches the cup.*] I pledge your Grace.   75

POPE

My wine gone too! Ye lubbers, look about
And find the man that doth this villany,
Or, by our sanctitude, you all shall die!
I pray, my lords, have patience at this troublesome banquet.

ARCHBISHOP   Please it your Holiness, I think it be some ghost   80
crept out of purgatory and now is come unto your Holiness
for his pardon.

POPE   It may be so.
Go then; command our priests to sing a dirge
To lay the fury of this same troublesome ghost.   85
                    [*Exit an Attendant. The* POPE *crosses himself.*]

FAUSTUS   How now! Must every bit be spiced with a cross?
Nay, then, take that.   [*Strikes the* POPE.]

POPE

O, I am slain! Help me, my lords!
O, come and help to bear my body hence.
Damned be his soul for ever for this deed.   90
                                    Exeunt the POPE *and his train.*

MEPHISTOPHELES   Now, Faustus, what will you do now? For I
can tell you you'll be cursed with bell, book, and candle.

FAUSTUS

Bell, book, and candle; candle, book, and bell,
Forward and backward, to curse Faustus to hell!

        Enter the FRIARS, *with bell, book, and candle, for the
        dirge.*

FIRST FRIAR   Come, brethren, let's about our business with   95
good devotion.   [*They chant.*]

---

76. **lubbers:** oafs.
84. **dirge:** requiem sung at a burial (from the Latin *dirige*, the first word of the antiphon at
Matins in the Office of the Dead).

Cursèd be he that stole his Holiness's meat from the table:
  Maledicat Dominus!
Cursèd be he that struck his Holiness a blow on the face:
  Maledicat Dominus!   100
Cursèd be he that struck Friar Sandelo a blow on the pate:
  Maledicat Dominus!
Cursèd be he that disturbeth our holy dirge:
  Maledicat Dominus!
Cursèd be he that took away his Holiness's wine: 105
  Maledicat Dominus!

  [MEPHISTOPHELES *and* FAUSTUS] *beat the* FRIARS, *fling*
            fireworks among them, and exeunt.

[3.3]

  Enter [ROBIN] *and* DICK *with a cup.*

DICK   Sirrah Robin, we were best look that your devil can answer the stealing of this same cup, for the vintner's boy follows us at the hard heels.
ROBIN   'Tis no matter; let him come. An he follow us, I'll so
  conjure him as he was never conjured in his life, I warrant   5
  him. Let me see the cup.
DICK   Here 'tis [*Gives the cup to* ROBIN.] Yonder he comes.
  Now, Robin, now or never show thy cunning.

  Enter VINTNER.

VINTNER   O, are you here? I am glad I have found you. You are
  a couple of fine companions. Pray, where's the cup you stole   10
  from the tavern?
ROBIN   How, how! We steal a cup? Take heed what you say.
  We look not like cup-stealers, I can tell you.
VINTNER   Never deny't, for I know you have it; and I'll search
  you.   15
ROBIN   Search me? Ay, and spare not. [*Whispers.*] Hold the
  cup, Dick. [*Gives him the cup.*]—Come, come, search me,
  search me. [VINTNER *searches him.*]
VINTNER   [*To* DICK.] Come on, sirrah, let me search you now.
DICK   Ay, ay, do, do. [*Whispers.*] Hold the cup, Robin. [*Gives* 20
  him the cup.]—I fear not your searching; we scorn to steal
  your cups, I can tell you. [VINTNER *searchs him.*]

98. *Maledicat Dominus*: May God curse him (Latin).
[3.3]
3. at . . . heels: close by, at our heels.

VINTNER   Never outface me for the matter, for sure the cup is
between you two.

ROBIN   Nay, there you lie; [*Holds the cup up.*] 'tis beyond us   25
both.

VINTNER   A plague take you! I thought 'twas your knavery to
take it away. Come, give it me again.

ROBIN   Ay, much! When, can you tell? Dick, make me a circle,
and stand close at my back, and stir not for thy life. Vintner,   30
you shall have your cup anon. Say nothing, Dick. [*Chants.*]
"O" *per se* "O"; Demogorgon, Belcher, and Mephistopheles!

    Enter MEPHISTOPHELES.

                                      [*Exit* VINTNER.]

MEPHISTOPHELES
You princely legions of infernal rule,
How am I vexèd by these villains' charms!
From Constantinople have they brought me now,   35
Only for pleasure of these damnèd slaves.

ROBIN   By Lady, sir, you have had a shrewd journey of it! will
it please you to take a shoulder of mutton to supper and a
tester in your purse, and go back again?

DICK   Ay, I pray you heartily, sir, for we called you but in jest,   40
I promise you.

MEPHISTOPHELES
To purge the rashness of this cursèd deed,
[*To Dick.*] First, be thou turnèd to this ugly shape,
For apish deeds transformèd to an ape.

ROBIN   O, brave! An ape! I pray, sir, let me have the carrying of   45
him about to show some tricks.

MEPHISTOPHELES   And so thou shalt. Be thou transformed to a
dog and carry him upon thy back. Away! Be gone!

ROBIN   A dog! That's excellent! Let the maids look well to
their porridge pots, for I'll into the kitchen presently. Come,   50
Dick, come.   *Exeunt the two clowns.*

MEPHISTOPHELES
Now with the flames of ever-burning fire
I'll wing myself and forthwith fly amain
Unto my Faustus, to the great Turk's court.   *Exit.*

23. outface: boldly maintain a falsehood.
32. *per se*: by itself.
37. By Lady: By our Lady, i.e., the Virgin Mary; a mild oath; shrewd: unpleasant.
39. tester: a sixpence coin.
53. amain: at full speed.
54. great Turk: In *The History of the Damnable Life* (see pp. 182ff), Faustus flies to Constantinople and visits with the Turkish Emperor. The episode does not appear in the play.

94

[4.1]

Enter MARTINO *and* FREDERICK [*with Attendants*] *at several doors.*

MARTINO
What, ho, officers, gentlemen!
Hie to the presence to attend the Emperor.
Good Frederick, see the rooms be voided straight;
His Majesty is coming to the hall.
Go back and see the state in readiness. [*Exeunt officers.*]   5

FREDERICK
But where is Bruno, our elected Pope,
That on a Fury's back came post from Rome?
Will not his Grace consort the Emperor?

MARTINO
O, yes, and with him comes the German conjurer,
The learnèd Faustus, fame of Wittenberg,   10
The wonder of the world for magic art.
And he intends to show great Carolus
The race of all his stout progenitors,
And bring in presence of his Majesty
The royal shapes and warlike semblances   15
Of Alexander and his beauteous paramour.

FREDERICK
Where is Benvolio?

MARTINO   Fast asleep, I warrant you;
He took his rouse with stoups of Rhenish wine
So kindly yesternight to Bruno's health
That all this day the sluggard keeps his bed.   20

FREDERICK   See, see, his window's ope. We'll call to him.

MARTINO   What, ho, Benvolio!

Enter BENVOLIO *above at a window, in his nightcap, buttoning.*

BENVOLIO   What a devil ail you two?

[4.1]
2. **presence:** presence chamber, reception hall.
3. **voided straight:** emptied immediately.
5. **state:** throne.
7. **post:** swiftly.
8. **consort:** accompany.
12. **Carolus:** Charles V (1519–1556), king of Spain and emperor of the Holy Roman Empire until his abdication in 1555.
13. **race . . . progenitors:** i.e., line of his noble dynasty.
18. **took his rouse:** went on a drinking binge; **stoups:** tankards, flasks.

MARTINO
    Speak softly, sir, lest the devil hear you,
    For Faustus at the court is late arrived,   25
    And at his heels a thousand Furies wait
    To accomplish whatsoever the doctor please.
BENVOLIO   What of this?
MARTINO
    Come, leave thy chamber first, and thou shalt see
    This conjurer perform such rare exploits   30
    Before the Pope and royal Emperor
    As never yet was seen in Germany.
BENVOLIO
    Has not the Pope enough of conjuring yet?
    He was upon the devil's back late enough.
    An if he be so far in love with him,   35
    I would he would post with him to Rome again!
FREDERICK
    Speak. Wilt thou come and see this sport?
BENVOLIO   Not I.
MARTINO
    Wilt thou stand in thy window and see it, then?
BENVOLIO
    Ay, an I fall not asleep i'th'mean time.
MARTINO
    The Emperor is at hand, who comes to see   40
    What wonders by black spells may compassed be.
BENVOLIO   Well, go you attend the Emperor. I am content, for
    this once, to thrust my head out at a window, for they say if
    a man be drunk over night the devil cannot hurt him in the
    morning. If that be true, I have a charm in my head shall   45
    control him as well as the conjurer, I warrant you.

        Ex[*eunt* FREDERICK *and* MARTINO; BENVOLIO *remains above*].

        A sennet. [*Enter*] *Charles the German* EMPEROR, BRUNO,
        [*the Duke of*] SAXONY, FAUSTUS, MEPHISTOPHELES, FRED-
        ERICK, MARTINO, *and Attendants.*

EMPEROR
    Wonder of men, renowned magician,
    Thrice-learnèd Faustus, welcome to our court.
    This deed of thine, in setting Bruno free
    From his and our professèd enemy,   50

---

25. late: lately.
41. compassed: accomplished.
45–46. I . . . conjurer: i.e., my hangover would overpower the devil as well as Faustus can.
50. professèd: declared.

Shall add more excellence unto thine art
Than if by powerful necromantic spells
Thou couldst command the world's obedience.
Forever be beloved of Carolus,
And if this Bruno thou hast late redeemed   55
In peace possess the triple diadem
And sit in Peter's chair, despite of chance,
Thou shalt be famous through all Italy
And honored of the German Emperor.

FAUSTUS
These gracious words, most royal Carolus,   60
Shall make poor Faustus to his utmost power
Both love and serve the German Emperor
And lay his life at holy Bruno's feet.
For proof whereof, if so your Grace be pleased,
The doctor stands prepared by power of art   65
To cast his magic charms, that shall pierce through
The ebon gates of ever-burning hell
And hale the stubborn Furies from their caves
To compass whatsoe'er your Grace commands.

BENVOLIO   [*Aside*.] Blood, he speaks terribly! But, for all that,   70
I do not greatly believe him. He looks as like a conjurer as
the Pope to a costermonger.

EMPEROR
Then, Faustus, as thou late didst promise us,
We would behold that famous conqueror,
Great Alexander, and his paramour   75
In their true shapes and state majestical,
That we may wonder at their excellence.

FAUSTUS
Your Majesty shall see them presently.
Mephistopheles, away,
And with a solemn noise of trumpets' sound   80
Present before this royal Emperor
Great Alexander and his beauteous paramour.

MEPHISTOPHELES   Faustus, I will.   [*Exit* MEPHISTOPHELES.]

BENVOLIO   Well, Master Doctor, an your devils come not away
quickly, you shall have me asleep presently. Zounds, I could   85
eat myself for anger to think I have been such an ass all this
while to stand gaping after the devil's governor and can see
nothing!

55. **late redeemed:** recently set free.
67. **ebon:** black, ebony.
70. **Blood:** By Christ's blood; an oath.
72. **costermonger:** fruit seller.

FAUSTUS

    I'll make you feel something anon, if my art fail me not.

    [*To* EMPEROR.] My lord, I must forewarn your Majesty,   90

    That when my spirits present the royal shapes

    Of Alexander and his paramour

    Your Grace demand no questions of the King,

    But in dumb silence let them come and go.

EMPEROR

    Be it as Faustus please; we are content.   95

BENVOLIO   Ay, ay, and I am content too. An thou bring Alexander and his paramour before the Emperor, I'll be Actaeon
and turn myself to a stag.

FAUSTUS   And I'll play Diana and send you the horns presently.

    [*Enter* MEPHISTOPHELES.]

    Sennet. Enter at one [door] the Emperor ALEXANDER, *at
the other,* DARIUS. *They meet;* DARIUS *is thrown down;*
ALEXANDER *kills him, takes off his crown, and, offering
to go out, his* PARAMOUR *meets him. He embraceth her
and sets* DARIUS' *crown upon her head; and, coming back,
both salute the [German]* EMPEROR, *who, leaving his
state, offers to embrace them, which* FAUSTUS *seeing,
suddenly stays him. Then trumpets cease, and music
sounds.*

    My gracious lord, you do forget yourself;   100

    These are but shadows, not substantial.

EMPEROR

    O, pardon me! My thoughts are so ravishèd

    With sight of this renownèd Emperor

    That in mine arms I would have compassed him.

    But, Faustus, since I may not speak to them   105

    To satisfy my longing thoughts at full,

    Let me this tell thee: I have heard it said

    That this fair lady whilst she lived on earth

    Had on her neck a little wart or mole.

    How may I prove that saying to be true?   110

FAUSTUS

    Your Majesty may boldly go and see.   [EMPEROR *looks.*]

EMPEROR

    Faustus, I see it plain,

    And in this sight thou better pleasest me

    Than if I gained another monarchy.

99. SD **offering**: about to.
104. **compassed**: embraced.

FAUSTUS   [*To the Spirits.*] Away! Be gone!   *Exit Show.* 115
   See, see, my gracious lord, what strange beast is yon that
   thrusts his head out at window.

EMPEROR
   O, wondrous sight! See, Duke of Saxony,
   Two spreading horns most strangely fastenèd
   Upon the head of young Benvolio!   120

SAXONY   What, is he asleep or dead?

FAUSTUS   He sleeps, my lord, but dreams not of his horns.

EMPEROR   This sport is excellent. We'll call and wake him.
   What ho, Benvolio!

BENVOLIO   A plague upon you! Let me sleep a while.   125

EMPEROR   I blame thee not to sleep much, having such a head
   of thine own.

SAXONY   Look up, Benvolio; 'tis the Emperor calls.

BENVOLIO   The Emperor! Where? O, zounds, my head!

EMPEROR   Nay, an thy horns hold, 'tis no matter for thy head, 130
   for that's armed sufficiently.

FAUSTUS   Why, how now, sir knight. What, hanged by the
   horns? This is most horrible. Fie, fie, pull in your head for
   shame. Let not all the world wonder at you.

BENVOLIO   Zounds, doctor, is this your villany?   135

FAUSTUS
   O, say not so, sir. The doctor has no skill,
   No art, no cunning to present these lords
   Or bring before this royal Emperor
   The mighty monarch, warlike Alexander.
   If Faustus do it, you are straight resolved   140
   In bold Actaeon's shape to turn a stag.
   And therefore, my lord, so please your Majesty,
   I'll raise a kennel of hounds shall hunt him so
   As all his footmanship shall scarce prevail
   To keep his carcass from their bloody fangs.   145
   Ho, Belimoth, Argiron, Ashtaroth!

BENVOLIO   Hold, hold! Zounds, he'll raise up a kennel of devils, I think, anon. Good my lord, entreat for me. [*He is attacked.*] 'Sblood, I am never able to endure these torments.

EMPEROR
   Then, good Master Doctor,   150
   Let me entreat you to remove his horns;
   He has done penance now sufficiently.

FAUSTUS   My gracious lord, not so much for injury done to me

129. **zounds:** By Christ's wounds; a mild oath.
130. **an:** if.
144. **footmanship:** ability to run.

as to delight your Majesty with some mirth hath Faustus
justly requited this injurious knight; which being all I desire,   155
I am content to remove his horns. Mephistopheles, transform him. [MEPHISTOPHELES *removes the horns*.] And hereafter, sir, look you speak well of scholars.

BENVOLIO   Speak well of ye! 'Sblood, an scholars be such
cuckold makers to clap horns of honest men's heads o' this   160
order, I'll ne'er trust smooth faces and small ruffs more. But
an I be not revenged for this, would I might be turned to a
gaping oyster and drink nothing but salt water.

EMPEROR
Come, Faustus. While the Emperor lives,
In recompense of this thy high desert   165
Thou shalt command the state of Germany
And live beloved of mighty Carolus.   *Exeunt omnes.*

[4.2]

Enter BENVOLIO, MARTINO, FREDERICK, *and Soldiers.*

MARTINO
Nay, sweet Benvolio, let us sway thy thoughts
From this attempt against the conjurer.
BENVOLIO
Away! You love me not to urge me thus.
Shall I let slip so great an injury
When every servile groom jests at my wrongs   5
And in their rustic gambols proudly say,
"Benvolio's head was graced with horns today"?
O, may these eylids never close again
Till with my sword I have that conjurer slain.
If you will aid me in this enterprise   10
Then draw your weapons and be resolute;
If not, depart. Here will Benvolio die
But Faustus' death shall quit my infamy.
FREDERICK
Nay, we will stay with thee, betide what may,
And kill that doctor if he come this way.   15

160. of: upon;
160–61. o' this order: in this manner.
161. smooth . . . ruffs: the unshaven faces and starched collars (i.e., the mark of
young and supposedly innocent students).
[4.2]
5. groom: serving man.
13. But: unless; quit: repay.
14. betide: come.

BENVOLIO

   Then, gentle Frederick, hie thee to the grove
   And place our servants and our followers
   Close in an ambush there behind the trees.
   By this, I know the conjurer is near.
   I saw him kneel and kiss the Emperor's hand   20
   And take his leave laden with rich rewards.
   Then, soldiers, boldly fight. If Faustus die,
   Take you the wealth; leave us the victory.

FREDERICK

   Come, soldiers, follow me unto the grove.
   Who kills him shall have gold and endless love.   25

                       Exit FREDERICK *with the Soldiers.*

BENVOLIO

   My head is lighter than it was by th'horns,
   But yet my heart's more ponderous than my head
   And pants until I see that conjurer dead.

MARTINO

   Where shall we place ourselves, Benvolio?

BENVOLIO

   Here will we stay to bide the first assault.   30
   O, were that damnèd hellhound but in place,
   Thou soon shouldst see me quit my foul disgrace.

     Enter FREDERICK.

FREDERICK

   Close, close! The conjurer is at hand
   And all alone comes walking in his gown.
   Be ready, then, and strike the peasant down.   35

BENVOLIO

   Mine be that honor, then. Now, sword, strike home!
   For horns he gave I'll have his head anon.

     Enter FAUSTUS *with the false head.*

MARTINO

   See, see, he comes!

BENVOLIO   No words. This blow ends all.
   Hell take his soul! His body thus must fall.

                    [*Strikes* FAUSTUS.]

FAUSTUS   O!   40

FREDERICK   Groan you, Master Doctor?

---

18. **Close:** hidden.
19. **By this:** by this time.
31. **in place:** on the spot, here.

BENVOLIO
  Break may his heart with groans! Dear Frederick, see,
  Thus will I end his griefs immediately.
MARTINO
  Strike with a willing hand.
                    [BENVOLIO *cuts off* FAUSTUS's *false head.*]
                    His head is off!
BENVOLIO
  The devil's dead; the Furies now may laugh.   45
FREDERICK
  Was this that stern aspect, that awful frown,
  Made the grim monarch of infernal spirits
  Tremble and quake at his commanding charms?
MARTINO
  Was this that damnèd head, whose heart conspired
  Benvolio's shame before the Emperor?   50
BENVOLIO
  Ay, that's the head, and here the body lies
  Justly rewarded for his villanies.
FREDERICK
  Come, let's devise how we may add more shame
  To the black scandal of his hated name.
BENVOLIO
  First, on his head, in quittance of my wrongs,   55
  I'll nail huge forkèd horns and let them hang
  Within the window where he yoked me first,
  That all the world may see my just revenge.
MARTINO   What use shall we put his beard to?
BENVOLIO   We'll sell it to a chimney-sweeper. It will wear out   60
  ten birchen brooms, I warrant you.
FREDERICK   What shall his eyes do?
BENVOLIO   We'll pull out eyes; and they shall serve for buttons
  to his lips, to keep his tongue from catching cold.
MARTINO   An excellent policy! and now, sirs, having divided   65
  him, what shall the body do?
                                        [FAUSTUS *rises.*]
BENVOLIO   Zounds, the devil's alive again!
FREDERICK   Give him his head, for God's sake!

---

46. awful: terrifying, awe-inspiring.
57. yoked: confined, held in place (as oxen in yoke).
60. wear out: outlast.
61. birchen: made of birch twigs.
65. policy: strategy.

FAUSTUS
    Nay, keep it. Faustus will have heads and hands,
    Ay, all your hearts, to recompense this deed.   70
    Knew you not, traitors, I was limited
    For four-and-twenty years to breathe on earth?
    And had you cut my body with your swords,
    Or hewed this flesh and bones as small as sand,
    Yet in a minute had my spirit returned,   75
    And I had breathed a man made free from harm.
    But wherefore do I dally my revenge?
    Ashtaroth, Belimoth, Mephistopheles!

        Enter MEPHISTOPHELES, *and other Devils.*

    Go horse these traitors on your fiery backs
    And mount aloft with them as high as heaven;   80
    Thence pitch them headlong to the lowest hell.
    Yet stay. The world shall see their misery,
    And hell shall after plague their treachery.
    Go, Belimoth, and take this caitiff hence,
    And hurl him in some lake of mud and dirt.   85
    [*To* ASHTAROTH.] Take thou this other; drag him through the
        woods
    Amongst the pricking thorns and sharpest briers,
    Whilst, with my gentle Mephistopheles,
    This traitor flies unto some steepy rock
    That, rolling down, may break the villain's bones   90
    As he intended to dismember me.
    Fly hence. Dispatch my charge immediately.
FREDERICK   Pity us, gentle Faustus! Save our lives!
FAUSTUS   Away!
FREDERICK   He must needs go that the devil drives.   95
        Exeunt [MEPHISTOPHELES *and Devils*] *with the Knights.*

        Enter the ambushed SOLDIERS.

FIRST SOLDIER
    Come, sirs. Prepare yourselves in readiness.
    Make haste to help these noble gentlemen.
    I heard them parley with the conjurer.
SECOND SOLDIER
    See where he comes. Dispatch, and kill the slave.
FAUSTUS
    What's here? An ambush to betray my life?   100
    Then, Faustus, try thy skill. Base peasants, stand!

77. **dally:** delay.
84. **caitiff:** scoundrel.
99. **Dispatch:** hurry.

[*A wall of trees appears in front of the* SOLDIERS.]

For, lo, these trees remove at my command
And stand as bulwarks 'twixt yourselves and me
To shield me from your hated treachery.
Yet to encounter this your weak attempt,   105
Behold, an army comes incontinent!

> FAUSTUS *strikes the door, and enter a Devil playing on a*
> *drum; after him another, bearing an ensign; and divers*
> *with weapons;* MEPHISTOPHELES *with fire-works. They set*
> *upon the* SOLDIERS, *and drive them out.*

> [*Exeunt.*]

[4.3]

> *Enter, at several doors,* BENVOLIO, FREDERICK, *and* MAR-
> TINO, *their heads and faces bloody and besmeared with*
> *mud and dirt, all having horns on their heads.*

MARTINO
  What, ho, Benvolio!
BENVOLIO   Here! What, Frederick, ho!
FREDERICK
  O, help me, gentle friend! Where is Martino?
MARTINO
  Dear Frederick, here,
  Half smothered in a lake of mud and dirt
  Through which the Furies dragged me by the heels.   5
FREDERICK
  Martino, see! Benvolio's horns again.
MARTINO
  O, misery. How now, Benvolio?
BENVOLIO
  Defend me, heaven! Shall I be haunted still?
MARTINO
  Nay, fear not, man; we have no power to kill.
BENVOLIO
  My friends transformèd thus! O, hellish spite!   10
  Your heads are still all set with horns.

102. **remove:** move, change places.
106. **incontinent:** immediately.

FREDERICK   You hit it right;
  It is your own you mean; feel on your head.
BENVOLIO
  [*Feels his head.*] Zounds, horns again!
MARTINO   Nay, chafe not, man; we all are sped.
BENVOLIO
  What devil attends this damned magician
  That, spite of spite, our wrongs are doubled?   15
FREDERICK
  What may we do that we may hide our shames?
BENVOLIO
  If we should follow him to work revenge,
  He'd join long asses' ears to these huge horns
  And make us laughing-stocks to all the world.
MARTINO
  What shall we then do, dear Benvolio?   20
BENVOLIO
  I have a castle joining near these woods,
  And thither we'll repair and live obscure
  Till time shall alter this our brutish shapes.
  Sith black disgrace hath thus eclipsed our fame,
  We'll rather die with grief than live with shame.   25

                                              Exeunt omnes.

[4.4]

Enter FAUSTUS, *and the* HORSE-COURSER, *and*
MEPHISTOPHELES.

HORSE-COURSER   I beseech your worship, accept of these forty
  dollars.
FAUSTUS   Friend, thou canst not buy so good a horse for so
  small a price. I have no great need to sell him, but, if thou
  likest him for ten dollars more, take him, because I see thou
  hast a good mind to him.   5
HORSE-COURSER   I beseech you, sir, accept of this. I am a very
  poor man and have lost very much of late by horse flesh, and
  this bargain will set me up again.

[4.3]
13. chafe: worry; **sped:** done for.
15. spite of spite: in spite of anything we can do.
24. Sith: since, seeing that.
[4.4]
4.4. SD HORSE-COURSER: horse dealer.

FAUSTUS   Well, I will not stand with thee. Give me the money.   10
    [*Takes money.*] Now, sirrah, I must tell you that you may ride
    him o'er hedge and ditch and spare him not, but (do you hear?)
    in any case, ride him not into the water.

HORSE-COURSER   How, sir? Not into the water? Why, will he
    not drink of all waters?   15

FAUSTUS   Yes, he will drink of all waters, but ride him not into
    the water—o'er hedge and ditch, or where thou wilt, but not
    into the water. Go bid the ostler deliver him unto you, and
    remember what I say.

HORSE-COURSER   I warrant you, sir! O, joyful day! Now am I a   20
    made man forever.   *Exit.*

FAUSTUS
    What art thou, Faustus, but a man condemned to die?
    Thy fatal time draws to a final end.
    Despair doth drive distrust into my thoughts.
    Confound these passions with a quiet sleep.   25
    Tush, Christ did call the thief upon the cross;
    Then rest thee, Faustus, quiet in conceit.
                                            He sits to sleep.

        Enter the HORSE-COURSER, *wet.*

HORSE-COURSER   O, what a cozening doctor was this! I, riding
    my horse into the water, thinking some hidden mystery had
    been in the horse, I had nothing under me but a little straw   30
    and had much ado to escape drowning. Well, I'll go rouse
    him and make him give me my forty dollars again. Ho, sirrah
    Doctor, you cozening scab! Master Doctor, awake and rise,
    and give me my money again, for your horse is turned to a
    bottle of hay. Master Doctor! (*He pulls off his leg.*) Alas, I am   35
    undone! What shall I do? I have pulled off his leg.

FAUSTUS   O, help, help! The villain hath murdered me.

HORSE-COURSER   Murder or not murder, now he has but one
    leg. I'll outrun him and cast this leg into some ditch or other.
                                            [*Exit.*]

FAUSTUS   Stop him, stop him, stop him! Ha, ha, ha! Faustus   40
    hath his leg again, and the horse-courser a bundle of hay for
    his forty dollars.

        Enter WAGNER.

---

10. **stand:** haggle, negotiate.
23. **fatal time:** i.e., the time allowed by fate.
25. **Confound:** defeat, get rid of.
27. **conceit:** thought.
33. **cozening scab:** cheating scoundrel.

How now, Wagner. What news with thee?

WAGNER   If it please you, the Duke of Vanholt doth earnestly
entreat your company and hath sent some of his men to at-   45
tend you with provision fit for your journey.

FAUSTUS   The Duke of Vanholt's an honorable gentleman and
one to whom I must be no niggard of my cunning. Come,
away.   *Exeunt.*

[4.5]

Enter CLOWN [ROBIN], DICK, *the* HORSE-COURSER, *and a*
CARTER.

CARTER   Come, my masters. I'll bring you to the best beer in
Europe. What, ho, Hostess! Where be these whores?

Enter HOSTESS.

HOSTESS   How now! What lack you? What, my old guests,
welcome!

ROBIN   [*To* DICK.] Sirrah Dick, dost thou know why I stand so   5
mute?

DICK   [*To* ROBIN.] No, Robin; why is't?

ROBIN   [*To* DICK.] I am eighteen pence on the score. But say
nothing; see if she have forgotten me.

HOSTESS   Who's this that stands so solemnly by himself?   10
What, my old guest?

ROBIN   O, Hostess, how do you? I hope my score stands still.

HOSTESS   Ay, there's no doubt of that, for methinks you make
no haste to wipe it out.

DICK   Why, Hostess, I say, fetch us some beer.   15

HOSTESS   You shall presently.—Look up into th'hall there, ho!
                                                        [*Exit.*]

DICK   Come, sirs, what shall we do now till mine Hostess
comes?

CARTER   Marry, sir, I'll tell you the bravest tale how a conjurer
served me. You know Doctor Fauster?   20

HORSE-COURSER   Ay, a plague take him! Here's some on's have
cause to know him. Did he conjure thee, too?

CARTER   I'll tell you how he served me. As I was going to Wittenberg t'other day with a load of hay, he met me and asked

48. no niggard of: not stingy with.
[**4.5**]
8. on the score: in debt (a mark or "score" was made to record a patron's debt in inns and
taverns).
19. bravest: best.
21. on's: of us.

me what he should give me for as much hay as he could eat.   25
Now, sir, I, thinking that a little would serve his turn, bade
him take as much as he would for three farthings. So he
presently gave me my money and fell to eating, and, as I am
a cursen man, he never left eating till he had eat up all my
load of hay.   30

ALL   O, monstrous! Eat a whole load of hay?

ROBIN   Yes, yes, that may be, for I have heard of one that has
eat a load of logs.

HORSE-COURSER   Now, sirs, you shall hear how villainously he
served me. I went to him yesterday to buy a horse of him,   35
and he would by no means sell him under forty dollars. So,
sir, because I knew him to be such a horse as would run over
hedge and ditch and never tire, I gave him his money. So,
when I had my horse, Doctor Fauster bade me ride him
night and day and spare him no time; "but," quoth he, "in   40
any case, ride him not into the water." Now, sir, I, thinking
the horse had had some quality that he would not have me
know of, what did I but rid him into a great river? And when
I came just in the midst my horse vanished away, and I sat
straddling upon a bottle of hay.   45

ALL   O, brave doctor!

HORSE-COURSER   But you shall hear how bravely I served him
for it. I went me home to his house, and there I found him
asleep. I kept a-hollering and whooping in his ears, but all
could not wake him. I, seeing that, took him by the leg and   50
never rested pulling till I had pulled me his leg quite off, and
now 'tis at home in mine hostry.

ROBIN   And has the doctor but one leg, then? That's excellent,
for one of his devils turned me into the likeness of an ape's
face.   55

CARTER   Some more drink, Hostess!

ROBIN   Hark you, we'll into another room and drink awhile,
and then we'll go seek out the doctor.   *Exeunt omnes.*

---

29. **cursen:** i.e., Christian, a dialect form (though the sense of "cursing" or "cursed" seems
unavoidable); **eat:** eaten (pronounced 'et').
52. **hostry:** inn, hostelry.

[4.6]

Enter the Duke of VANHOLT, *his* DUCHESS, FAUSTUS,
MEPHISTOPHELES, [*and Attendants*].

VANHOLT   Thanks, Master Doctor, for these pleasant sights;
nor know I how sufficiently to recompense your great de-
serts in erecting that enchanted castle in the air, the sight
whereof so delighted me as nothing in the world could
please me more.   5

FAUSTUS   I do think myself, my good lord, highly recom-
pensed in that it pleaseth your Grace to think but well of
that which Faustus hath performed. But, gracious lady, it
may be that you have taken no pleasure in those sights;
therefore, I pray you tell me, what is the thing you most de-   10
sire to have? Be it in the world, it shall be yours. I have
heard that great-bellied women do long for things are rare
and dainty.

DUCHESS   True, Master Doctor; and, since I find you so kind,
I will make known unto you what my heart desires to have.   15
An were it now summer, as it is January, a dead time of the
winter, I would request no better meat than a dish of ripe
grapes.

FAUSTUS   This is but a small matter.—Go, Mephistopheles;
away!   [*Exit* MEPHISTOPHELES.]   20
Madam, I will do more than this for your content.

Enter MEPHISTOPHELES *again, with the grapes.*

Here; now taste you these. They should be good, for they
come from a far country, I can tell you.

DUKE   This makes me wonder more than all the rest, that at
this time of the year, when every tree is barren of his fruit,   25
from whence you had these ripe grapes.

FAUSTUS   Please it your Grace, the year is divided into two circles over the whole world, so that, when it is winter with us,
in the contrary circle it is likewise summer with them, as in
India, Saba, and such countries that lie far east, where they   30
have fruit twice a-year. From whence, by means of a swift
spirit that I have, I had these grapes brought, as you see.

[4.6]
12. great-bellied: pregnant.
16. An: if.
17. meat: food.
27–28. two circles: two halves (imagined as an eastern and western hemisphere, rather
than northern and southern).
29. contrary: opposite.
30. Saba: i.e., the ancient country of Sheba, in the area of the modern Yemen.

DUCHESS   And, trust me, they are the sweetest grapes that e'er
I tasted.

*The Clown[s—*ROBIN, DICK, *the* CARTER *and the* HORSE-
COURSER—] *bounce at the gate, within.*

DUKE
What rude disturbers have we at the gate?   35
[*To* SERVANT.] Go, pacify their fury; set it ope
And then demand of them what they would have.

They knock again and call out to talk with FAUSTUS.

SERVANT   Why, how now, masters! What a coil is there! What
is the reason you disturb the Duke?
DICK   [*Within.*] We have no reason for it; therefore, a fig for   40
him!
SERVANT   Why, saucy varlets, dare you be so bold?
HORSE-COURSER   [*Within.*] I hope, sir, we have wit enough to
be more bold than welcome.
SERVANT   It appears so. Pray be bold elsewhere and trouble   45
not the Duke.
DUKE   What would they have?
SERVANT   They all cry out to speak with Doctor Faustus.
CARTER   [*Within.*] Ay, and we will speak with him.
DUKE   Will you, sir?—Commit the rascals.   50
DICK   [*Within.*] Commit with us? He were as good commit
with his father as commit with us.
FAUSTUS
I do beseech your Grace, let them come in.
They are good subject for a merriment.
DUKE
Do as thou wilt, Faustus; I give thee leave.   55
FAUSTUS
I thank your Grace.

Enter [ROBIN], DICK, CARTER, *and* HORSE-COURSER.

Why, how now, my good friends?
'Faith, you are too outrageous. But come near;
I have procured your pardons. Welcome all.
ROBIN   Nay, sir, we will be welcome for our money, and we
will pay for what we take. What, ho! Give's half a dozen of   60
beer here, and be hanged!

34. SD **bounce:** knock loudly.
38. **coil:** disturbance.
51. **Commit:** The Duke's "commit" in the previous line means "lock up," but Dick impu-
dently takes "commit" in a colloquial sense to mean "have sex with."

FAUSTUS   Nay, hark you, can you tell me where you are?

CARTER   Ay, marry, can I. We are under heaven.

SERVANT   Ay; but, Sir Saucebox, know you in what place?

HORSE-COURSER   Ay, ay, the house is good enough to drink in.   65
Zounds, fill us some beer, or we'll break all the barrels in the
house and dash out all your brains with your bottles!

FAUSTUS
Be not so furious. Come, you shall have beer.
My lord, beseech you give me leave a while.
I'll gage my credit 'twill content your Grace.   70

DUKE
With all my heart, kind Doctor; please thyself.
Our servants and our court's at thy command.

FAUSTUS
I humbly thank your Grace. [*To Servant.*] Then fetch some beer.

HORSE-COURSER   Ay, marry, there spake a doctor, indeed! And,
'faith, I'll drink a health to thy wooden leg for that word.   75

FAUSTUS
My wooden leg? What dost thou mean by that?

CARTER   Ha, ha, ha! Dost hear him, Dick? He has forgot his
leg.

HORSE-COURSER   Ay, ay. He does not stand much upon that.

FAUSTUS
No, faith, not much upon a wooden leg.   80

CARTER   Good lord, that flesh and blood should be so frail
with your worship! Do not you remember a horse-courser
you sold a horse to?

FAUSTUS   Yes, I remember I sold one a horse.

CARTER   And do you remember you bid he should not ride him   85
into the water?

FAUSTUS   Yes, I do very well remember that.

CARTER   And do you remember nothing of your leg?

FAUSTUS   No, in good sooth.

CARTER   Then, I pray you, remember your court'sy.   90

FAUSTUS   I thank you, sir.

CARTER   'Tis not so much worth. I pray you, tell me one thing.

FAUSTUS   What's that?

CARTER   Be both your legs bedfellows every night together?

FAUSTUS   Wouldst thou make a Colossus of me, that thou ask-   95
est me such questions?

---

70. gage: risk.
79. stand much upon: Attach much importance to (but the literal meaning is obviously
part of the joke).
90. court'sy: courtesy (but also "curtsy," another meaning of "leg" in line 88).
95. Colossus: the Colossus of Rhodes, one of the wonders of the ancient world, a giant
statue whose legs straddled the harbor.

CARTER   No, truly, sir; I would make nothing of you, but I
would fain know that.

    Enter HOSTESS *with drink.*

FAUSTUS   Then, I assure thee, certainly they are.
CARTER   I thank you; I am fully satisfied.   100
FAUSTUS   But wherefore dost thou ask?
CARTER   For nothing, sir. But methinks you should have a
wooden bedfellow of one of 'em.
HORSE-COURSER   Why, do you hear, sir? Did not I pull off one
of your legs when you were asleep?   105
FAUSTUS   But I have it again now I am awake. Look you here,
sir.
ALL   O, horrible! Had the doctor three legs?
CARTER   Do you remember, sir, how you cozened me and eat
up my load of—   110
                    FAUSTUS *charms him dumb.*
DICK   Do you remember how you made me wear an ape's—
                  [FAUSTUS *charms him dumb.*]
HORSE-COURSER   You whoreson conjuring scab, do you remember how you cozened me with a ho—
                  [FAUSTUS *charms him dumb.*]
ROBIN   Ha' you forgotten me? You think to carry it away with
your "hey-pass" and "re-pass." Do you remember the dog's
fa—   115
                  [FAUSTUS *charms him dumb.*]
                    Exeunt Clowns.
HOSTESS   Who pays for the ale—hear you, Master Doctor—
now you have sent away my guests? I pray, who shall pay me
for my a—
                [FAUSTUS *charms her dumb.*]
                    Exit HOSTESS.
DUCHESS
My lord, we are much beholding to this learnèd man.   120
DUKE
So are we, madam, which we will recompense
With all the love and kindness that we may.
His artful sport drives all sad thoughts away.
                    Exeunt.

97. **make nothing of:** a literal reply to Faustus's question, but also "make light of"; **fain:**
gladly.
114. **carry it away:** be successful, carry the day.
115. **"hey-pass" and "re-pass":** familiar conjuring terms.

[5.1]

Thunder and lightning. Enter Devils with covered dishes.
MEPHISTOPHELES *leads them into* FAUSTUS's *study. Then enter* WAGNER.

WAGNER
   I think my master means to die shortly.
   He has made his will and given me his wealth:
   His house, his goods, and store of golden plate,
   Besides two thousand ducats ready coined.
   I wonder what he means. If death were nigh,   5
   He would not frolic thus. He's now at supper
   With the scholars, where there's such belly-cheer
   As Wagner in his life ne'er saw the like.
   And see where they come. Belike the feast is done.

                                                    Exit.

    Enter FAUSTUS, MEPHISTOPHELES, *and* two *or* three
    SCHOLARS.

FIRST SCHOLAR   Master Doctor Faustus, since our conference   10
about fair ladies—which was the beautifullest in all the
world—we have determined with ourselves that Helen of
Greece was the admirablest lady that ever lived. Therefore,
Master Doctor, if you will do us so much favor as to let us
see that peerless dame of Greece, whom all the world ad-   15
mires for majesty, we should think ourselves much beholding
unto you.

FAUSTUS
   Gentlemen, for that I know your friendship is unfeigned,
   It is not Faustus' custom to deny
   The just request of those that wish him well.   20
   You shall behold that peerless dame of Greece,
   No otherwise for pomp or majesty
   Than when Sir Paris crossed the seas with her
   And brought the spoils to rich Dardania.
   Be silent then, for danger is in words.   25

    Music sound. MEPHISTOPHELES *brings in* HELEN. *She pass-
    eth over the stage.*

[5.1]
3. **golden plate:** gold bullion.
4. **ducats:** gold coins.
9. **Belike:** most likely.
23. **Paris:** a Trojan prince whose abduction of Helen, the queen of Sparta, led to the Trojan war.
24. **Dardania:** i.e., Troy.

SECOND SCHOLAR
  Was this fair Helen, whose admirèd worth
  Made Greece with ten years' wars afflict poor Troy?
THIRD SCHOLAR
  Too simple is my wit to tell her worth,
  Whom all the world admires for majesty.
FIRST SCHOLAR
  Now we have seen the pride of nature's work,   30
  We'll take our leaves, and, for this blessèd sight,
  Happy and blest be Faustus evermore.   *Exeunt* SCHOLARS.
FAUSTUS   Gentlemen, farewell. The same wish I to you.

        Enter an OLD MAN.

OLD MAN
  O gentle Faustus, leave this damnèd art,
  This magic, that will charm thy soul to hell   35
  And quite bereave thee of salvation.
  Though thou hast now offended like a man,
  Do not persever in it like a devil.
  Yet, yet thou hast an amiable soul,
  If sin by custom grow not into nature.   40
  Then, Faustus, will repentance come too late;
  Then thou art banished from the sight of heaven.
  No mortal can express the pains of hell.
  It may be this my exhortation
  Seems harsh and all unpleasant. Let it not,   45
  For, gentle son, I speak it not in wrath
  Or envy of thee, but in tender love
  And pity of thy future misery;
  And so have hope that this, my kind rebuke,
  Checking thy body, may amend thy soul.   50
FAUSTUS
  Where art thou, Faustus? Wretch, what hast thou done?
  Hell claims his right and with a roaring voice
  Says, "Faustus, come; thine hour is almost come."

        MEPHISTOPHELES *gives him a dagger.*

  And Faustus now will come to do thee right.
OLD MAN
  O, stay, good Faustus, stay thy desperate steps!   55

39. **amiable:** worthy to be loved.
40. **custom:** habitual behavior.
47. **envy of:** malice toward.
50. **Checking:** restraining.
55. **stay:** stop.

I see an angel hover o'er thy head,
And with a vial full of precious grace
Offers to pour the same into thy soul.
Then call for mercy and avoid despair.

FAUSTUS

O friend, I feel thy words to comfort my distressèd soul.   60
Leave me a while to ponder on my sins.

OLD MAN

Faustus, I leave thee, but with grief of heart,
Fearing the enemy of thy hapless soul.   *Exit.*

FAUSTUS

Accursèd Faustus, wretch, what hast thou done?
I do repent and yet I do despair.   65
Hell strives with grace for conquest in my breast.
What shall I do to shun the snares of death?

MEPHISTOPHELES

Thou traitor, Faustus, I arrest thy soul
For disobedience to my sovereign lord.
Revolt, or I'll in piecemeal tear thy flesh.   70

FAUSTUS

I do repent I e'er offended him.
Sweet Mephistopheles, entreat thy lord
To pardon my unjust presumption,
And with my blood again I will confirm
The former vow I made to Lucifer.   75

MEPHISTOPHELES

Do it, then, Faustus, with unfeignèd heart,
Lest greater dangers do attend thy drift.

FAUSTUS

Torment, sweet friend, that base and agèd man,
That durst dissuade me from thy Lucifer,
With greatest torments that our hell affords.   80

MEPHISTOPHELES

His faith is great; I cannot touch his soul.
But what I may afflict his body with
I will attempt, which is but little worth.

FAUSTUS

One thing, good servant, let me crave of thee
To glut the longing of my heart's desire: 85
That I may have unto my paramour
That heavenly Helen which I saw of late,
Whose sweet embraces may extinguish clear

70. **Revolt:** return (to your allegiance).
88. **clear:** completely.

Those thoughts that do dissuade me from my vow,
And keep my oath I made to Lucifer.   90
MEPHISTOPHELES
This, or what else my Faustus shall desire,
Shall be performed in twinkling of an eye.

  Enter HELEN *again, passing over* [*the stage*] *between two
  Cupids.*

FAUSTUS
Was this the face that launched a thousand ships
And burned the topless towers of Ilium?
Sweet Helen, make me immortal with a kiss. [*They kiss.*]   95
Her lips suck forth my soul; see, where it flies!
Come, Helen, come, give me my soul again. [*They kiss.*]
Here will I dwell, for heaven is in these lips,
And all is dross that is not Helena.
I will be Paris, and for love of thee   100
Instead of Troy shall Wittenberg be sacked;
And I will combat with weak Menelaus,
And wear thy colors on my plumèd crest;
Yea, I will wound Achilles in the heel
And then return to Helen for a kiss.   105
O, thou art fairer than the evening air
Clad in the beauty of a thousand stars;
Brighter art thou than flaming Jupiter
When he appeared to hapless Semele;
More lovely than the monarch of the sky   110
In wanton Arethusa's azure arms;
And none but thou shalt be my paramour.   *Exeunt.*

---

94. topless: immeasurably tall; **Ilium:** i.e., Troy.
102. Meneleus: Helen's husband, king of Sparta.
104. wound . . . heel: In mythology, Achilles was dipped in the river Styx by his mother,
which rendered him invulnerable, except for the heel by which she held him.
109. Semele: One of Jupiter's human mistresses, who insisting on seeing the god in his divine form was consumed in flame (cf. Ovid, *Metamorphoses* 259–315).
110–11. monarch . . . arms: the beauty of the sun reflecting off a stream, though the specific reference is unclear; Arethusa was a nymph desired by the river-god Alpheus, and
changed into a fountain to avoid his lust (cf. Ovid, *Metamophoses* 5.577–641).

116

[5.2]

Thunder. Enter [above] LUCIFER, BEELZEBUB *and*
MEPHISTOPHELES.

LUCIFER
  Thus from infernal Dis do we ascend
  To view the subjects of our monarchy,
  Those souls which sin seals the black sons of hell,
  'Mong which as chief, Faustus, we come to thee,
  Bringing with us lasting damnation   5
  To wait upon thy soul. The time is come
  Which makes it forfeit.
MEPHISTOPHELES   And this gloomy night
  Here in this room will wretched Faustus be.
BEELZEBUB
  And here we'll stay
  To mark him how he doth demean himself.   10
MEPHISTOPHELES
  How should he, but in desperate lunacy?
  Fond worldling, now his heart-blood dries with grief;
  His conscience kills it, and his laboring brain
  Begets a world of idle fantasies
  To overreach the devil. But all in vain.   15
  His store of pleasures must be sauced with pain.
  He and his servant Wagner are at hand.
  Both come from drawing Faustus' latest will.
  See, where they come!

Enter FAUSTUS *and* WAGNER.

FAUSTUS
  Say, Wagner, thou hast perused my will.   20
  How dost thou like it?
WAGNER   Sir, so wondrous well
  As in all humble duty I do yield
  My life and lasting service for your love.

Enter the SCHOLARS.

FAUSTUS   Gramercies, Wagner. Welcome, Gentlemen.
             [*Exit* WAGNER.]

[5.2]
1. Dis: Roman god of the underworld.
6. wait upon: (1) serve; (2) wait for.
10. demean: (1) conduct; (2) degrade.
12. Fond: foolish.
24. Gramercies: thank you.

FIRST SCHOLAR
   Now, worthy Faustus, methinks your looks are changed.   25
FAUSTUS O, gentlemen!
SECOND SCHOLAR   What ails Faustus?
FAUSTUS Ah, my sweet chamber fellow, had I lived with thee,
   then had I lived still, but now must die eternally. Look, sirs,
   comes he not? Comes he not?   30
FIRST SCHOLAR
   O my dear Faustus, what imports this fear?
SECOND SCHOLAR
   Is all our pleasure turned to melancholy?
THIRD SCHOLAR
   He is not well with being over-solitary.
SECOND SCHOLAR   If it be so, we'll have physicians, and Fau-
   stus shall be cured.   35
THIRD SCHOLAR   'Tis but a surfeit, sir; fear nothing.
FAUSTUS A surfeit of deadly sin that hath damned both body
   and soul.
SECOND SCHOLAR   Yet, Faustus, look up to heaven and remem-
   ber mercy is infinite.   40
FAUSTUS But Faustus' offence can ne'er be pardoned. The
   serpent that tempted Eve may be saved, but not Faustus. O
   gentlemen, hear with patience and tremble not at my
   speeches! Though my heart pant and quiver to remember
   that I have been a student here these thirty years, O, would   45
   I had never seen Wittenberg, never read book. And what
   wonders I have done, all Germany can witness, yea, all the
   world—for which Faustus hath lost both Germany and the
   world, yea, heaven itself, heaven, the seat of God, the throne
   of the blessed, the kingdom of joy, and must remain in hell   50
   for ever. Hell, O, hell, for ever! Sweet friends, what shall become of Faustus, being in hell for ever?
SECOND SCHOLAR   Yet, Faustus, call on God.
FAUSTUS On God, whom Faustus hath abjured? On God,
   whom Faustus hath blasphemed? O my God, I would weep,   55
   but the devil draws in my tears. Gush forth blood instead of
   tears! Yea, life and soul! O, he stays my tongue! I would lift
   up my hands, but see, they hold 'em, they hold 'em.
ALL   Who, Faustus?
FAUSTUS Why, Lucifer and Mephistopheles. O, gentlemen, I   60
   gave them my soul for my cunning!

---

31. imports: implies, signifies.
36. surfeit: a sickness caused by overeating or drinking.

ALL   O, God forbid!

FAUSTUS   God forbade it indeed; but Faustus hath done it. For the vain pleasure of four-and-twenty years hath Faustus lost eternal joy and felicity. I writ them a bill with mine own blood. The date is expired. This is the time, and he will fetch me. 65

FIRST SCHOLAR   Why did not Faustus tell us of this before, that divines might have prayed for thee?

FAUSTUS   Oft have I thought to have done so, but the devil threatened to tear me in pieces if I named God, to fetch me body and soul if I once gave ear to divinity. And now 'tis too late. Gentlemen, away, lest you perish with me. 70

SECOND SCHOLAR   O, what may we do to save Faustus?

FAUSTUS   Talk not of me, but save yourselves and depart. 75

THIRD SCHOLAR   God will strengthen me; I will stay with Faustus.

FIRST SCHOLAR   Tempt not God, sweet friend, but let us into the next room and pray for him.

FAUSTUS   Ay, pray for me, pray for me. And what noise soever you hear, come not unto me, for nothing can rescue me. 80

SECOND SCHOLAR   Pray thou, and we will pray that God may have mercy upon thee.

FAUSTUS   Gentlemen, farewell. If I live till morning, I'll visit you; if not, Faustus is gone to hell. 85

ALL   Faustus, farewell.   *Exeunt* SCHOLARS.

MEPHISTOPHELES

Ay, Faustus, now thou hast no hope of heaven;
Therefore despair. Think only upon hell,
For that must be thy mansion, there to dwell.

FAUSTUS

O thou bewitching fiend, 'twas thy temptation 90
Hath robbed me of eternal happiness.

MEPHISTOPHELES

I do confess it, Faustus, and rejoice.
'Twas I that, when thou wert i'the way to heaven,
Dammed up thy passage. When thou took'st the book
To view the Scriptures, then I turned the leaves 95
And led thine eye.
What, weep'st thou? 'Tis too late; despair. Farewell.
Fools that will laugh on earth must weep in hell.   *Exit.*

65. **bill:** contract.
69. **divines:** priests.
72. **divinity:** i.e., thoughts of God.

Enter the GOOD ANGEL *and the* BAD ANGEL *at several doors.*

GOOD ANGEL
    O Faustus, if thou hadst given ear to me
    Innumerable joys had followed thee.   100
    But thou didst love the world.
BAD ANGEL   Gave ear to me
    And now must taste hell's pains perpetually.
GOOD ANGEL
    O, what will all thy riches, pleasures, pomps,
    Avail thee now?
BAD ANGEL   Nothing but vex thee more,
    To want in hell that had on earth such store.   105
                      Music while the throne descends.

GOOD ANGEL
    O, thou hast lost celestial happiness,
    Pleasures unspeakable, bliss without end.
    Hadst thou affected sweet divinity,
    Hell or the devil had had no power on thee.
    Hadst thou kept on that way, Faustus, behold   110
    In what resplendent glory thou hadst set
    In yonder throne, like those bright-shining saints,
    And triumphed over hell. That hast thou lost,
    And now, poor soul, must thy good angel leave thee.
    The jaws of hell are open to receive thee.   *Exit.* 115
                      Hell is discovered.

BAD ANGEL
    Now, Faustus, let thine eyes with horror stare
    Into that vast perpetual torture house.
    There are the Furies tossing damnèd souls
    On burning forks. Their bodies boil in lead.
    There are live quarters broiling on the coals,   120
    That ne'er can die. This ever-burning chair
    Is for o'er-tortured souls to rest them in.
    These that are fed with sops of flaming fire
    Were gluttons, and loved only delicates,
    And laughed to see the poor starve at their gates.   125
    But yet all these are nothing. Thou shalt see
    Ten thousand tortures that more horrid be.

108. **affected:** been drawn to.
111. **set:** sat.
120. **quarters:** i.e., quartered pieces of bodies.
124. **delicates:** delicacies.

FAUSTUS
   O, I have seen enough to torture me!
BAD ANGEL
   Nay, thou must feel them, taste the smart of all.
   He that loves pleasure must for pleasure fall.   130
   And so I leave thee, Faustus, till anon;
   Then wilt thou tumble in confusion.   *Exit.*
                              The clock strikes eleven.
FAUSTUS
   O Faustus, now hast thou but one bare hour to live
   And then thou must be damned perpetually.
   Stand still, you ever-moving spheres of heaven,   135
   That time may cease and midnight never come.
   Fair Nature's eye, rise, rise again, and make
   Perpetual day, or let this hour be but
   A year, a month, a week, a natural day,
   That Faustus may repent and save his soul.   140
   O lente, lente currite, noctis equi.
   The stars move still. Time runs. The clock will strike,
   The devil will come, and Faustus must be damned.
   O, I'll leap up to heaven. Who pulls me down?
   One drop of blood will save me. O, my Christ!   145
   Rend not my heart for naming of my Christ.
   Yet will I call on him. O, spare me, Lucifer.
   Where is it now? 'Tis gone.
   And, see, a threatening arm, an angry brow.
   Mountains and hills, come, come and fall on me,   150
   And hide me from the heavy wrath of heaven.
   No? Then will I headlong run into the earth.
   Gape, earth! O, no, it will not harbor me.
   You stars that reigned at my nativity,
   Whose influence hath allotted death and hell,   155
   Now draw up Faustus like a foggy mist
   Into the entrails of yon laboring cloud,
   That when you vomit forth into the air
   My limbs may issue from your smoky mouths,
   But let my soul mount and ascend to heaven!   160
                              The watch strikes.
   O, half the hour is past! 'Twill all be past anon.
   O, if my soul must suffer for my sin

132. **confusion:** ruin, destruction.
137. **Fair Nature's eye:** i.e., the sun.
141. ***O . . . equi:*** O, run slowly, slowly, you horses of night (Latin; Ovid, *Amores* 1.13.40).
155. **influence:** the supposed effect of the stars on individual character and fate.
160. **SD watch:** clock.

Impose some end to my incessant pain.
Let Faustus live in hell a thousand years,
A hundred thousand, and at last be saved.   165
No end is limited to damnèd souls.
Why wert thou not a creature wanting soul?
Or why is this immortal that thou hast?
O, Pythagoras' *metempsychosis*—were that true,
This soul should fly from me, and I be changed   170
Into some brutish beast.
All beasts are happy, for when they die
Their souls are soon dissolved in elements,
But mine must live still to be plagued in hell.
Cursed be the parents that engendered me.   175
No, Faustus, curse thyself; curse Lucifer,
That hath deprived thee of the joys of heaven.

                                    The clock strikes twelve.

It strikes, it strikes! Now, body, turn to air,
Or Lucifer will bear thee quick to hell.
O soul, be changed into small water drops   180
And fall into the ocean, ne'er be found!

          Thunder, and enter the Devils.

O, mercy, heaven! Look not so fierce on me!
Adders and serpents! Let me breathe a while!
Ugly hell, gape not! Come not, Lucifer!
I'll burn my books! O, Mephistopheles!   *Exeunt.*   185

[5.3]

          Enter the SCHOLARS.

FIRST SCHOLAR
     Come, gentlemen, let us go visit Faustus,
     For such a dreadful night was never seen
     Since first the world's creation did begin.
     Such fearful shrieks and cries were never heard.
     Pray heaven the Doctor have escaped the danger.   5
SECOND SCHOLAR
     O, help us, heaven! See, here are Faustus' limbs
     All torn asunder by the hand of death.

---

167. **wanting:** lacking.
169. **metempsychosis:** a theory attributed to Pythagoras about the passing (transmigration) of the soul at death from one body to another.

THIRD SCHOLAR
   The devils whom Faustus served have torn him thus;
   For, twixt the hours of twelve and one, methought
   I heard him shriek and call aloud for help,   10
   At which self time the house seemed all on fire
   With dreadful horror of these damnèd fiends.
SECOND SCHOLAR
   Well, gentlemen, though Faustus' end be such
   As every Christian heart laments to think on,
   Yet, for he was a scholar once admired   15
   For wondrous knowledge in our German schools,
   We'll give his mangled limbs due burial,
   And all the students, clothed in mourning black,
   Shall wait upon his heavy funeral.   *Exeunt.*

[Epilogue]

Enter CHORUS.

CHORUS
   Cut is the branch that might have grown full straight,
   And burnèd is Apollo's laurel bough,
   That sometime grew within this learnèd man.
   Faustus is gone. Regard his hellish fall,
   Whose fiendful fortune may exhort the wise   5
   Only to wonder at unlawful things,
   Whose deepness doth entice such forward wits
   To practice more than heavenly power permits.   *Exit.*

Terminat hora diem; terminat Author opus.

[5.3]
11. **self:** same.
15. **for:** since.
[Epilogue]
2. **Apollo's laurel bough:** the worldly recognition that came to Faustus, the "conjuror lau-reate" (A-text, 1.3.32).
3. **sometime:** formerly.
6. **only to wonder:** i.e., to be content with wondering at (rather than engaging in).
7. **forward:** ambitious, eager.
Terminat . . . opus: The hour ends the day; the author ends his work (Latin). This conven-tional motto was most likely provided by the publisher rather than Marlowe.

SOURCES AND CONTEXTS

"Sources and Contexts" consists of original documents and modern scholarship chosen to illuminate the intellectual, theatrical, and literary worlds in which *Doctor Faustus* was written, performed, and read. The material in the following section, "Criticism," was picked with several interrelated goals in mind: primarily to give readers access to essays that will increase their understanding and appreciation of Marlowe's play but also to provide a representative sample of the best criticism of *Doctor Faustus* over time and to suggest something of the range of critical questions that might usefully be asked of Marlowe's play as well as of any literary text. If some of the "early" criticism now seems dated in its vocabulary, if not its concerns, it nonetheless testifies to the enduring power of Marlowe's play (and, if read carefully, may prove surprisingly prescient about aspects that may seem to us uniquely modern). Many other worthy critics have not been included here only for reasons of space, but all the essays that are here, plus the material listed in the Selected Bibliography, provide compelling evidence of how criticism itself is one of the means by which the literary past remains part of our cultural present.

Because of the textual complexity of *Doctor Faustus*, which different critics have differently understood, it is impossible to bring their citations to the play in line with the present edition. I have, therefore, retained their citations and other aspects of the original essays, except for renumbering the footnotes when necessitated by the excerpting.

Christopher Marlowe

RICHARD BAINES

Baines (b. 1566?) was a member of the Middle Temple and worked as some kind of government informer and spy. This letter, exposing Marlowe's heretical beliefs, was sent first to the Privy Council and then to the queen in the spring of 1593. It is unclear, however, whether the letter accurately reports Marlowe's blasphemous opinions or if it is a false accusation designed to curry favor with government officials by giving them the heretic they sought (or if Marlowe was himself working as a spy and indeed said what is recorded but only to entrap others into betraying their own heresies).

Letter†

A note containing the opinion of one Christopher Marly Concerning his damnable Iudgment of Religion, and scorn of Gods word.

That the Indians and many Authors of antiquity have assuredly written of above 16 thousand yeares agone wheras Adam is proved to haue liued within 6 thowsand yeares.

He affirmeth that Moyses was but a Jugler & that one Heriots being Sir W Raleighs man Can do more than he.

That Moyses made the Iews to travell xl yeares in the wildernes (which Journey might have bin done in lesse then one yeare) ere they Came to the promised land to thintent that those who were priuy to most of his subtilties might perish and so an everlasting superstition Remain in the hartes of the people.

That the first beginning of Religioun was only to keep men in awe.

That it was an easy matter for Moyses being brought up in all the artes of the Egiptians to abuse the Iewes being a rude and grosse people.

That Christ was a bastard and his mother dishonest.

That he was the sonne of a Carpenter and that if the Iewes

---

† BM Harl ms. 6848, fo. 185–6; rpt. in *The Life of Marlowe and The Tragerly of Dido, Queen of Carthage*, ed. C. F. Tucker Brooke (New York: Dial Press, 1930), pp. 98–100.

among whome he was borne did Crucify him theie best knew him and whence he Came.

That Christ deserued better to dy than Barrabas and that the Iewes made a good Choise, though Barrabas were both a thief and a murtherer.

That if there be any god or any good Religion, then it is in the papistes because the service of god is performed with more Cerimonies, as Eleuation of the mass, organs, singing men, Shauen Crownes & etc. That all protestantes are Hypocriticall asses.

That if he were put to write a new Religion, he would undertake both a more Exellent and Admirable methode and that all the new testament is filthily written.

That the women of Samaria & her sister were whores & that Christ knew them dishonestly.

That St John the Evangelist was bedfellow to Christ and leaned alwaies in his bosome, that he vsed him as the sinners of Sodoma.

That all they that love not tobacco & Boyes were fooles.

That all the apostles were fishermen and base fellowes neyther of wit nor worth, that Paull only had wit but he was a timerous fellow in bidding men to be subject to magistrates against his Conscience.

That he had as good Right to Coine as the Queen of England and that he was aquainted with one Poole a prisoner in Newgate who hath greate skill in mixture of mettals and hauing learned some thinges of him he ment through help of a Cunninge stamp maker to Coin ffrench Crownes pistoletes and English shillinges.

That if Christ would have instituted the sacrament with more Ceremoniall Reverence it would have bin had in more admiration, that it would haue bin much better being administered in a Tobacco pipe.

That the Angel Gabriell was baud to the holy ghost, because he brought the salutation to Mary.

That on Ric Cholmley hath Confessed that he was perswaded by Marloe's Reasons to become an Atheist.

These things, with many other shall by good and honest witnes be aproved to be his opinions and Comon Speeches and that this Marlow doth not only hould them himself, but almost into euery Company he Cometh he perswades men to Atheism, willing them not to be afeard of bugbeares and hobgoblins, and utterly scorning both god and his ministers as I Richard Baines will Iustify & approue both by mine oth and the testimony of many honest men, and almost al men with whome he hath Conversed any time will testify the same, and as I think all men in Christianity ought to indeuor that the mouth of so dangerous a member may be stopped, he saieth likewise that he hath quoted a number of Contrarieties oute of the Scripture which he hath giuen to some great men who in Convenient time shalbe named. When these things shalbe Called in question the witnes shalbe produced.

Richard Baines

THOMAS BEARD

Beard (d. 1632) was a well-known Puritan divine who served as master of the Huntingdon Hospital and grammar school (where Oliver Cromwell was a student); he was later a canon at Lincoln Cathedral from 1612 until his death. His *Theatre of God's Judgements*, published in 1597, was an enormously influential collection of examples of God's providential activity in human history. His account of the death of Marlowe is the first in print.

From The Theatre of God's Judgements†

Not inferiour to any of the former in Atheisme & impiety, and equal to all in maner of punishment was one of our own nation, of fresh and late memory, called *Marlin* [marginal note: *Marlow*.], by profession a scholler, brought vp from his youth in the Vniuersitie of Cambridge, but by practise a play-maker, and a Poet of scurrilitie, who by giuing too large a swinge to his owne wit, and suffering his lust to haue the full raines, fell (not without iust desert) to that outrage and extremitie, that hee denied God and his sonne Christ, and not only in word blasphemed the trinitie, but also (as it is credibly reported) wrote bookes against it, affirming our Sauiour to be but a deceiuer, and *Moses* to be but a coniurer and seducer of the people, and the holy Bible to be but vaine and idle stories, and all religion but a deuice of pollicie. But see what a hooke the Lord put in the nosthrils of this barking dogge: It so fell out, that in London streets as he purposed to stab one whome hee ought a grudge vnto with his dagger, the other party perceiuing so auoided the stroke, that withall catching hold of his wrest, he stabbed his owne dagger into his owne head, in such sort, that notwithstanding all the meanes of surgerie that could be wrought, hee shortly after died thereof. The manner of his death being so terrible (for hee even cursed and blasphemed to his last gaspe, and togither with his breath an oath flew out of his mouth) that it was not only a manifest signe of Gods iudgement, but also an horrible and fearefull terrour to all that beheld him. But herein did the iustice of God most notably appeare, in that hee compelled his owne hand which had written those blas-

† London, 1597, sig. K5$^{r\text{-}v}$.

phemies to be the instrument to punish him, and that in his braine, which had deuised the same. I would to God (and I pray it from my heart) that all Atheists in this realme, and in all the world beside, would by the remembrance and consideration of this example, either forsake their horrible impietie, or that they might in like manner come to destruction: and so that abominable sinne which so flourisheth amongst men of greatest name, might either be quite extinguished and rooted out, or at least smothered and kept vnder, that it durst not shew it head any more in the worlds eye.

WILLIAM VAUGHAN

Vaughan (1577–1641) was a minor poet and prose writer, and elder brother of the better-known poet Henry Vaughan. William was also involved in the English settlement of Newfoundland, owning land and visiting there in 1622. His *Golden-Grove, Moralized in Three Books* (1600) was, as the title page explained, "A Work very necessary for all such as would know how to governe themselves, their houses, or their countrey."

From The Golden-Grove, Moralized in Three Books†

Not inferiour to these was one Christopher Marlow by profession a play-maker, who, as is reported, about 7. yeeres a-goe wrote a booke against the Trinitie: but see the effects of Gods iustice; it so hapned, that at Detford, a little village about three miles distant from London, as he meant to stab with his ponyard one named Ingram, that had inuited him thither to a feast, and was then playing at tables, he quickely perceyving it, so auoyded the thrust, that withall drawing out his dagger for his defence, hee stabd this Marlow into the eye, in such sort, that his braines comming out at the daggers point, hee shortlie after dyed.

ANTHONY À WOOD

Anthony à Wood (1632–1695) was an English historian and antiquary. Educated at Oxford, where he did not distinguish himself, he lived mainly off his inheritance, living in two rooms in the family house opposite Merton College, Oxford. He obtained access to the university archives, which enabled him to study the university's history. His *Athenae Oxonienses* was published in two volumes (1691–92) and pro-

† London, 1600, sig. C4^v-5^r.

vides biographies of the distinguished graduates of Oxford from 1500 to 1690.

From Athenae Oxonienses†

Christop. Marlo, sometimes a Student in *Cambridge*; afterwards, first an actor on the stage, then, (as *Shakespeare*, whose contemporary he was,) a maker of Plays. . . . But in the end, so it was, that this *Marlo* giving too large a swing to his own wit, and suffering his lust to have the full reins, fell to that outrage and extremity, as *Jodelle* a French tragical poet did, (being an Epicure and an Atheist,) that he denied God and his Son Christ, and not only in word blasphemed the *Trinity*, but also (as it was credibly[1] reported) wrote divers discourses against it, affirming our *Saviour* to be a deceiver, and *Moses* to be [a] conjurer: The holy Bible also to contain only vain and idle stories, and all religion but a device of policy. But see the end of this person, which was noted by all, especially the Precisian. For so it fell out, that he being deeply in love with a certain Woman, had for his rival a bawdy serving man, one rather fit to be a Pimp, than an ingenious *Amoretto* as *Marlo* conceived himself to be. Whereupon *Marlo* taking it to be an high affront, rush'd in upon, to stab, him, with his dagger: But the serving man being very quick, so avoided the stroke, that withal catching hold of *Marlo*'s wrist, he stab'd his own dagger into his own head, in such sort, that notwithstanding all the means of surgery that could be wrought, he shortly after died of his wound, before the year 1593.

DAVID RIGGS

From Marlowe's Quarrel with God‡

*   *   *

III

Like everyone who prepared for a career in the ministry, schools, or universities, Marlowe was trained to function as a closet atheist within the Church. Alexander Nowell's *Catechism of First Instruction and Learning of Christian Religion* (1573) taught Elizabethan

† London, 1691, pp. 288–89.
1. See in Tho. Beard's *Theatre of God's Judgments*, lib. 1, chap. 23 [in original].
‡ From *Marlowe, History, and Sexuality: New Critical Essays on Christopher Marlowe*, ed. Paul Winfield White (New York: AMS Press, Inc., 1998), pp. 25–33. Copyright © 1998 by AMS Press, Inc. All rights reserved. Reproduced by permission.

schoolboys that most of them were predestined to sin and therefore could not experience the ecstatic "renning of the spirit" that assured the fortunate few of their place among the elect. But the *Catechism* further assured them that it was perfectly acceptable to pretend otherwise: "Many by hypocrisie and counterfaiting of godlinesse do joyne them selves to this fellowship, which are nothing lesse than true members of the Chirch." The *Catechism* did require reprobate scholars to retain a "generall" or "dead" faith in the God who had consigned them to everlasting torment; at the same time, however, the all-embracing criterion of conformity made it exceedingly easy to carry on as a hypocrite within the establishment. Bacon contended that "the great *Atheists*, indeed, are *Hypocrites*: which are ever Handling Holy Things, but without Feeling; so as they must needs be cauterized in the End."[1]

During his six years at Cambridge, Marlowe learned the intellectual foundations of speculative atheism. The disputations that comprised the core of the B.A. course exposed inconsistencies within the Bible and subjected individual texts to contradictory interpretations. "[T]he whole Scriptures," complained Henry Barrow, "must in these their schooles and disputations, be unsufferably corrupted, abused, wrested, perverted" by the disputers, who "must handle, divide, utter and discusse, according to their vaine affected arts of logick and rhetorick." The M. A. course offered extensive training in natural philosophy (astrology, cosmology, medicine) and introduced Marlowe to the ancient sources for modern atheism: Aristotle's *de Anima*, Pliny, Lucretius, and Lucian. This curriculum was supposed to produce a Protestant ministry fortified by a deep understanding of God's word and works; but since belief, "the gift of God," could not be learned, the system could just as easily produce a sophisticated unbeliever like Doctor Faustus. John Case, a Fellow of New College, Oxford from 1572 to 1600, encountered swarms of these "scorpions and locusts" during his time at the university.[2]

From a professional standpoint it did not matter whether or not these students believed in God: so long as there was no record of any impropriety, closet atheists were free to seek employment within the conformist establishment. But in Marlowe's case there was impropriety. Shortly before he was to receive his M.A., in the summer of 1587, the Cambridge authorities were informed that he

1. *Catechism*, 49 ("renning of the spirit"), 23 ("dead" faith), and 47 (hypocrisy); Francis Bacon, "Of Atheism," in *The Essayes or Counsels, Civill and Moral*, ed. Michael Kiernan (Cambridge, Mass.: Harvard University Press, 1985), 53.
2. Henry Barrow, *A Brief Discovery*, 345. For a similar critique see *The Writings of Robert Harrison and Robert Browne*, ed. Leland Carlson and Albert Peel (London, 1953), 173–93; John Case, *Ancilla Philosophiae* (Oxford, 1599), sig. A-AV, as cited in Don Cameron Allen, *Doubt's Boundless Sea* (Baltimore: Johns Hopkins University Press, 1964).

intended to join the English seminary at Rheims. When the university transmitted this report to the Privy Council, the Council replied that Marlowe "had no such intent, but that in all his actions he had behaved himself orderly and discreetly, whereby he had done her majesty good service and deserved to be rewarded for his faithful dealing." By commissioning Marlowe to spy on dissident Catholics, the government scripted him into two roles—loyal servant and subversive other—that were diametrically opposed to one another. The Privy Council's letter to Cambridge smoothes over this double insertion by equating the real Marlowe with the loyal subject ("he had no such intent"), indicating that the seditious Marlowe was merely playing a part. But such distinctions did not hold up in practice. Sir Francis Walsingham, the head of Elizabeth's spy system, routinely recruited informants by "turning" individuals who were already involved with the Catholic underground; here the spy's loyalty to the state was suspect from the start. Moreover, even the most zealous spy could be persuaded to do business with his victims—it was all in a day's work. The Privy Council valued Marlowe because of his contacts in the recusant community, and because of his willingness to betray it. These were equally reasons not to trust him. The original informant could have been right.[3]

Sequestered in a no man's land that was both Protestant and Catholic, double agents personified the godless creed of "politic religion." In describing his own evolution from seminarian to spy, Marlowe's accuser Richard Baines recalled that he "began to deride what was seen as important to our religion . . . a sure road to heresy, infidelity, and atheism." When Baines himself recruited English seminarians at Rheims in 1582, he did not appeal to their residual sense of patriotism. Instead, he tried to persuade them that religion consisted of fictions imposed on gullible believers; that "the mystical ceremonies of dreadful sacrifice . . . were no more than pretty gestures, performing which even a Turk would look holy"; that "there was no fire by which souls may be tortured but it was the worm of conscience"; that he "could teach a more useful method of prayer—reciting the twenty four letters of the alphabet."[4]

3. For the Privy Council's letter, see A. D. Wraight, *In Search of Christopher Marlowe* (London: Macdonald, 1965), 88; Jonathan Goldberg, "Sodomy and Society: The Case of Christopher Marlowe," *Southwest Review* 69 (1984): 373; Charles Nicholl, *The Reckoning: The Murder of Christopher Marlowe* (London, 1992), 94–168; John Michael Archer, *Sovereignty and Intelligence: Spying and Court Culture in the English Renaissance* (Stanford, 1993), 67–93 and passim.

4. *Concertatio Ecclesiae Catholicae in Anglia adversus Calvinopapistus et Puritanos*, ed. John Gibbons and John Fenn (Trier, 1588), 240. Translation supplied by Roy Kendall in "Richard Baines and Christopher Marlowe's Milieu," *English Literary Renaissance* 24 (1994): 507–52.

In the meantime, Marlowe began to write scripts for the London acting companies. In 1576 the actors had erected the first purpose-built theater since Roman times and begun offering commercial entertainment to metropolitan audiences on a daily basis. During the decade that followed, the militant wing of the Puritan faction initiated a strident debate about the cultural significance of these facts. Taking their case to the public in sermons and pamphlets, John Northbrooke, John Field, Philip Stubbes, Stephen Gosson, Anthony Munday and William Rankins characterized the playhouse as a site of anti-Christian rites and performances. Field accused the actors of raising "flagges of defiance against God." Reminding his readers that plays were "invented by the devil, practiced by the heathen gentiles and didicat to their false idols, Goddes and Goddesses," Stubbes argued that modern theaters "renue the remembrance of heathen idolatrie": "if you will learne to contemne God and all his lawes, to care neither for heaven nor hel . . . you need goe to no other school." The fact that the actors performed plays based on Scripture only made matters worse, according to Munday, since "the reverend word of God & histories of the Bible, set forth on the stage by these blasphemous players, are so cor-rupted with their gestures of scurrilitie, and so interlaced with un-cleane, and whorish speeches, that it is not possible to drawe anie profite out of the doctrine of their spiritual moralities." When Northbrooke's Youth reminds Age that "many times they play histo-ries out of the Scriptures," Age replies: "Assuredly that is very evill so to doe, to mingle scurrilitie with Divinitie, that is, to eate meate with unwashed hands."[5]

Like other Elizabethan allegations about the spread of godless-ness, these claims can neither be proved nor disproved. Very few of the many plays written for the public stage during this decade are extant; and in any case, the charges mainly refer to performance practice and spectatorial license. The closet remains closed. Never-theless, the antitheatrical critics put the compromise position of "closet" atheism under a new kind of strain: for the thrust of the Puritan case against the theater was precisely that it took place in public, on the sabbath, and so gave scandal to God. Since God is not mocked, these performances were bound to bring divine retri-bution, not only on players and playgoers, but on the city and na-tion as well. The collapse of the galleries at Paris Garden on Sunday, 13 January 1583, a misfortune that claimed the lives of at

5. John Field, *A Godly Exhortation by Occasion of the Late Judgement of God, Shewed at Paris Garden* (1583), sig. B5ᵛ; Philip Stubbes, *The Anatomy of Abuses* (1583), sig. L6ʳ; Anthony Munday qtd. in E. K. Chambers, *The Elizabethan Stage*, 4 vols. (Oxford, 1923), 4: 211; John Northbrooke, *A Treatise Wherein Dicing, Dancing, Vain Plays . . . are Re-proved* (1577), 65.

least seven spectators, confirmed this hypothesis in spectacular fashion. Field, Stubbes, and Rankins demanded that performances come to a halt before God struck again. "For as the majestie of God is impatient of any aspiring mind to be partaker of his deitie," Rankins warned, "so dooth hee with a sharpe whippe scourge those blasphemers, that attribute anie dignitie belonging to heaven his head, or the earth his footstoole to any other but himselfe."[6]

Tamburlaine the Great, which the Lord Admiral's Men performed in the year Rankins' pamphlet appeared, is the first extant play to challenge the antitheatrical critics on their own ground. Tamburlaine's famous paean to the "aspiring mind" at once defines his stance and recapitulates two of the seminal Renaissance texts on atheism. The first half of his oration echoes and reaffirms Ovid's account of creation in Book I of the *Metamorphoses*, where "Nature" fashions humanity out of the four elements. Just as the elements are "Warring in our breasts for regiment," Ovid's Nature teaches the strong to displace the weak, the son, Jove, "To thrust his doting father from the Chaire." What the orthodox moralist stigmatizes as evil, the play implies, embodies the violence and desire that constructed the social order in the first place. The second half of Tamburlaine's speech echoes and repudiates Calvin's account of the soul in *The Institutes of the Christian Religion*. Replying to natural philosophers who would "destroy the immortality of the soul and deprive God of his rights," Calvin emphasizes the soul's innate desire for celestial knowledge. He praises the "manifold nimbleness" with which it "surveyeyth heaven and earth," "measure[s] the skie," and "gather[s] the number of the starres . . . with what swiftness or sloweness they go their courses." The soul ascends the heavens because it wishes "to clime up even to God and to eternall felicity," for man's own "felicite . . . is that he be joined with God, and therefore it is the chief action of the soule to aspire thereunto." In Tamburlaine's revision of this much-traveled itinerary, "Our soules" proceed along the same course, comprehending "the wondrous architecture of the world / And measuring every wandring planet's course"; but Tamburlaine's journey ultimately leads not to God, but to "That perfect bliss and sole felicity, / The sweet fruition of an earthly crowne."[7]

In subordinating religion to force, Tamburlaine exposes the cen-

6. William Rankins, *A Mirror of Monsters* (1587), sig. G1^V. Compare Stubbes, *Anatomy*, sig. P4^{r-v}; Field, *A Godly Exhortation*, passim.

7. *Tamburlaine the Great*, ed. J. S. Cunningham (Manchester, 1981), *Part One*, II.vii.1329. All citations to *Tamburlaine* in my text are from this edition. Anthony Brian Taylor, "Notes on Marlowe and Golding," *Notes and Queries* 34 (1987), 192–93; Taylor, "Tamburlaine's Doctrine of Strife and John Calvin," *English Language Notes* 27 (1989), 30–31. See also Jonathan Crewe, "The Theater of the Idols: Marlowe, Rankins, and Theatrical Images," *Theater Journal* 34 (1984): 321–33.

tral contradiction in the Protestant theory of the state. Although Romans 13:1 prohibits rebellion ("Let every soul be subject unto the higher powers"), the relentlessness of Paul's logic compels him to enfranchise a successful usurper ("for the powers that be are ordained of God"). The stereotypical figure of the "scourge of God" is an attempt to resolve this contradiction by reducing the usurper to a doomed and unthinking instrument of God's justice. But Tamburlaine invokes the orthodox doctrine of obedience in a sophisticated defense of his own right to disobey. Since he is termed "The scourge of God and terror to the world," he concludes that "I must apply myself to fit those terms / . . . / And plague such peasants as resist in me / The power of heaven's eternal majesty."[8] Marlowe's hero is God's double agent, licensed by divine authority to wreak havoc in his name. From a theological standpoint, such agents can never act autonomously, for they are constrained by predestination, bondage of the will, and innate belief enforced by the fear of punishment. On the stage—as Tamburlaine and Kyd's Hieronimo both discover—the role liberates the scourge from the very God who enfranchises him.

Tamburlaine's attack on God reaches a crescendo shortly before the end of Part Two, when he burns the Koran and defies its author: "Now Mahomet, if thou have any power / Come down and work a miracle." Since Tamburlaine dies two scenes later, pious commentators have inferred that God does, finally, give him his comeuppance. But atheists were supposed to die horrific deaths—railing, convulsing, frantic at the prospect of divine correction; such performances offered irrefutable proof that the wicked did indeed possess an innate fear of God, however involuntary. But Tamburlaine dies at peace with himself, in serene assurance that his sons "Shall retain my spirit though I die / And live in all your seeds immortally" (V.iii.173–74).

Although *Tamburlaine* became the most widely imitated play in the Elizabethan repertory, its success left Marlowe in a vulnerable position. Shortly after *Tamburlaine*'s debut, Robert Greene publicly taxed "mad and scoffing poets, that have propheticall spirits as bold as Merlin's [Marlowe's] race," for "daring God out of heaven with that atheist Tamburlaine" and for wantonly uttering "such impious instances of intollerable poetry."[9] Although Greene makes these allegations in a spirit of affable raillery, they do indicate the nature of Marlowe's predicament. He had now come under adverse scrutiny twice in the same year—first for sedition, then for public impiety.

8. *Tamburlaine, Part Two*, IV.i.155–58. Lynette and Eveline Feasey, "Marlowe and the Homilies," *Notes and Queries*, 195 (1950), 7–10.
9. Qtd. in Millar MacLure, ed., *Marlowe: the Critical Heritage* (London, 1979), 29–30. Hereafter cited as MacLure.

IV

During the last eighteen months of his life, Marlowe was subjected to a devastating series of accusations. In January of 1592, Richard Baines, now his chamber-fellow at Flushing, accused him of counterfeiting and of intending "to goe to the Ennemy"— Spain—"or to Rome." Marlowe responded by leveling the same accusations at Baines. The terms under which the two men were released remain unclear, but the government continued to receive intelligence reports about Marlowe. When an anonymous rhymester subsequently nailed a seditious libel based on *Tamburlaine* to the door of the Dutch Church in London, the Privy Council launched a full-scale investigation. The most spectacular charges involved the crime of blasphemy. In the course of ransacking the belongings of Thomas Kyd, another ex-roommate, the authorities found a handwritten transcript of "vile heretical conceits denying the divinity of Jesus Christ" copied from *The Fall of the Late Arian*. Although sections of the manuscript are written in the italic hand that Kyd—a scrivener—would have used, he told Lord Keeper Puckering that it belonged to Marlowe, and had been "shuffled" with his papers by mistake. In the meantime, the London gangleader Richard Chomeley informed one of the Council's spies "that one Marlowe is able to showe more sounde reasons for Atheisme then any devine in Englande is able to prove divinitie & that Marloe told him he had read the Atheist lecture to Sir Walter Raleigh and others" (undated spy's report, 1592–93).[1]

Was Marlowe now a *bona fide* atheist? Was he being falsely accused? Or was he attempting to entrap others who were suspected of that crime—Raleigh, for example, whom Father Parsons had recently accused of heading a "school of atheism"? Within the fluid, opportunistic world of the double agent, it is hard to imagine what sort of evidence could categorically exclude any of these alternatives. As a spy, Marlowe served the state by voicing what the crown regarded as treason and heresy; the state retained the capacity to determine whether he counted as a loyal servant or subversive other. In this instance, the Council ordered a professional informer named Thomas Drury to procure testimony from Marlowe's former chamber fellow and enemy twin Richard Baines. Bear in mind that Baines had already concocted, used, and confessed to his own version of the atheist lecture, which was published on the continent in 1583 and again in 1588, that someone in the government had

---

1. R. B. Wernham, "Christopher Marlowe in Flushing in 1592," *English Historical Review* 91 (1976), 344–45; Arthur Freeman, "Marlowe, Kyd, and the Dutch Church Libel," *English Literary Renaissance* 3 (1973), 44–52; for Kyd's letters see Wraight, 238–39, 314–15; for the unnamed spy's report on Chomeley, see Wraight, 354–55; Baines' Note is in MacLure, 36–38.

questioned Baines about Marlowe when the two of them were sent back from Flushing, and that Drury was in regular communication both with Baines, who "did use to resort" unto him, and with the Council, whom he supplied with intelligence. In other words, the Council knew all along what Baines could tell them about Marlowe. The fact that Kyd's allegations about Marlowe's atheism are similar to those in Baines' Note lends credence to Baines' story; but Kyd's testimony was extracted under torture, and the men who obtained it were in communication with both him and Drury at approximately the same time. The authorities did not merely seek the Baines Note; they produced it.[2]

Baines' report on Marlowe's "damnable Judgment of Religion, and scorn of God's word" contains the first written exposition of atheism in early modern Europe. The informant cites some eighteen separate theses. Taken in sequence, these proceed from a literalistic critique of the Bible to the claim that religion consists of persuasive fictions to the conclusion that Marlowe can "write a new religion" based on "a more Excellent and Admirable method" than either Catholicism or Protestantism. Baines offers Marlowe's interpretations of John 13:23 and Romans 13:1 as illustrations of this excellent new method. Marlowe's gloss on the passage from John preserves the literal sense of the text ("Nowe there was one of his disciples [i.e. John], which leaned on his bosom, which Jesus loved") but glosses it according to a logic of carnal desire: "St. John the Evangelist was bedfellow to Christ and leaned always in his bosom . . . he used him as the sinners of Sodoma." This reading entails a new precept: "That all they that love not boys and tobacco are fools." The precept brings Marlowe's new religion into conflict with the law. Where the letter of Romans 13:1 requires obedience, the ungodly interpreter appeals to the internalized voice of the spirit, arguing that "Paul was a timerous fellow in bidding men to be subject to magistrates against his conscience." Although Marlowe's conclusions are outrageous, his premises are orthodox: he takes the Protestant stress on the prerogatives of the inspired lay interpreter to its natural destination. Luther had foreseen this outcome when he wrote that "The ungodly out of the gospel do seek only a carnal freedom, and become worse thereby, therefore not the Gospel but the Law belongeth unto them." Marlowe's new religion uses the gospel to overturn the law. Marlowe "doth not only hould [these opinions] himself," Baines concluded, "but almost into every Company he Cometh he perswades men to Atheism, willing them not to be afeard of bugbeares and hobgoblins, and utterly scorning

2. For Drury, Baines, and Puckering see E. S. Sprott, "Drury and Marlowe," *Times Literary Supplement* 2 August 1974; and Roy Kendall, "Richard Baines and Christopher Marlowe's Milieu," *English Literary Renaissance* 24 (1994): 507–52.

both god and his ministers." Kyd corroborated these allegations: "[I]t was his custome," he wrote, "in table talk or otherwise to jest at the devine scriptures gybe at praiers, & strive in argument to frustrate & confute what hath byn spoke or wrytt by prophets & such holie men."[3]

Baines' Note defines the moment when blasphemy unites with sodomy, steps out of the closet, and coalesces around an actual figure of opposition. Open atheism cannot be the thought of an anonymous other; it requires a real subject. By the Spring of 1593, Marlowe was ready to fill this role. He had been taken with a counterfeit shilling in Flushing; Robert Greene had publicly accused him of saying "(like the fool in his heart) There is no God"; the Dutch Church libeler had used *Tamburlaine* as the model for a genuine popular uprising; the government had assembled a dossier of spy's reports, culminating in the Note itself. Although the full extent of Marlowe's atheism only becomes legible within the state security apparatus, its appearance there signals a genuine crisis in sixteenth-century Protestantism. By making fear the ultimate guarantor of belief, Calvin's God had staked his prestige on the impossibility of an open atheism that went unpunished. The handful of ancient blasphemers who had dared God out of heaven (Caligula, Diagoras, Dionysius) were the exceptions that proved the rule: for, as Calvin put it, no one "ever trembled with greater distress at any instance of divine wrath" than they. Rankins explains why:

> [T]he mighty Jehova inkindled his wrath and sent wormes to devoure the guts of this Arius. . . . And Dionisius Aropagita, for blaspheming the name of God, suddainly sanck into the earth . . . unhappy wife of Job, that willed him to curse God and die, with her children, and all the rest of her substance, was suddainly wasted and consumed. . . .[4]

Tamburlaine, and now Marlowe, put this axiom into play.

Blasphemers trembled because death could come either at the hands of the law or of God Himself, intervening through agents raised up by Him for that purpose. This overdetermined punitive apparatus meant that Marlowe was subject to the combined forces of state power, casual violence, and divine wrath. All three factors came into play at the end of his life. The killing occurred under the aegis of state power, was subsequently represented as an act of

3. Goldberg, "Sodomy and Society"; *Selections from the Table Talk of Martin Luther*, trans. Captain Henry Bell (1892), qtd. in Christopher Hill, *The World Turned Upside Down* (New York, 1972), 125–26. For Kyd, see Wraight, 316; for Baines, see MacLure, 36–38.
4. David Wooten, "The Fear of God in Early Modern Political Theory," Canadian Historical Association, *Historical Papers* 18 (1983): 56–79; Bacon, "Of Atheism"; John Calvin, *Institutes of the Christian Religion*, trans. John Allen, 2 vols. (Philadelphia: Presbyterian Board of Christian Education, 1936), 1:55–56, 61; Rankins, *A Mirror of Monsters*, sig. G1^{r-v}.

causal violence in which Marlowe struck the first blow, and thus became an apt occasion for divine intervention. Indeed, during the months leading up to Marlowe's death, Robert Greene publicly predicted that God would soon strike down the "famous gracer of tragedians." Four years later the Puritan minister Thomas Beard rearticulated this version of Marlowe's demise in his popular book *The Theater of God's Judgements*. The story appealed to Beard because of its transparent exemplary force. Marlowe had "denied God and his sonne Christ . . . But see what hooke the Lord put in the nosthrils of this barking dogge." Three years later the conformist minister William Vaughan reiterated this providential narrative in *The Golden Grove:* "one Christopher Marlow by profession a playmaker . . . about 7. yeeres a-goe wrote a booke against the Trinitie: but see the effects of Gods iustice . . . ." The divines rejoiced in Marlowe's killing for the same reason that Field, Stubbes, and Rankins revelled in the collapse of the Bear House at Paris Garden. These occurrences demonstrated that their Lord and Master was, as Greene put it, "a God that can punish enemies."[5]

This last version does justice neither to Marlowe nor to God, who need not be held responsible for the lethal acts that continue to be done in His name. Baines' atheist lecturer still offers the most vivid image of Marlowe's predicament. The lecturer knows too much for his own good. Like Baines, he has taken in the atheist critique of mainstream religion; unlike Baines, who had been paid off with a church living at Waltham,[6] he does not enjoy the option of conformity and hypocrisy. He can incorporate his forbidden knowledge into a strategy of self-presentation, as Marlowe does in *Tamburlaine*, but this is a dangerous game. When Tamburlaine entered the real world of oppositional politics, he took Marlowe with him. The atheist lecturer continues to play despite the risk. He recognizes that his dissidence has been produced within a Protestant theocracy, but he does not accept the corollary that his rebellion is doomed or ineffectual. Like Marlowe—and here the two figures converge at last—he is silenced at the moment when he becomes visible as a figure of opposition. The leading question, then, is how to undo that silencing? This essay makes a start in that direction.

5. MacLure, 30, 41–42, 47.
6. Constance Kuriyama, "Marlowe, Shakespeare, and the Nature of Biographical Evidence," *University of Hartford Studies in Literature* 20 (1988), 9.

Composition and Publication

Following are contemporary records relating to *Doctor Faustus*. The first two are from the guild that organized the publishing industry. Publishers paid a small sum (here six and seven pence) to the clerk of the Stationers Company to establish their ownership of the text that they sought to publish. (Copyright at this time belonged to publishers, not to authors.) The third item is from the account book of Philip Henslowe, who was the manager of the acting company that first performed *Doctor Faustus*; here he records his payment (forty shillings, which equals two pounds) to two dramatists, William Bird and Samuel Rowley, for providing new material for *Doctor Faustus*. We are not sure what parts of the play may have been written by these two, although many scholars have argued that it is the additional comic material in the B-text (see pp. 160–61 and 171–79 herein).

Document 1: Stationers' Register, January 7, 1601†

Thomas Busshell: Entred for his copye vnder the handes. of Mr Doctor Barlowe, and the Wardens. A booke called *the plaie of Doctor Faustus* vj^d

Document 2: Stationers' Register, September 13, 1610‡

John Wrighte: Assigned ouer to him from **Thomas Bushell** and with Consent of master **Adames** warden vnder his hand, these 2 Copyes followinge xij^d

> *The gate of Syon or religious meditations of the Deathe of Christ Jesus.*
> *The tragicall history of the horrible life and Death of Doctor FFaustus*, written by C.M.

† Edward Arber, ed. *A Transcript of the Registers of the Company of Stationers of London, 1554–1640 AD* (London: Privately Printed, 1875), III, 178.
‡ Arber, III, 442.

Document 3: Henslowe's Diary, November 22, 1602†

Lent vnto the companye the 22 of novmb₃ 1602⎫

Lent vnto the companye the 22 of novmb3 1602⎫
++ to paye vnto w^m Bvrde & Samwell Rowle[4] ⎬ iiij^li
for ther adicyones in docter fostes the some of ⎭

MICHAEL J. WARREN

From Doctor Faustus: The Old Man and the Text‡

* * *

The A-text is 1517 lines long. Although its corrupt truncated state is generally assumed, it has been frequently acclaimed for its dramatic brevity and precision, for its heroic verse, for its vigorous language, for its subtle exploitation of image patterns, and for the robust comic scenes which present a harsh commentary upon the main action of the play. It has also been viewed as a reported text, a bad quarto, revealing the standard attributes of a bad quarto: disorder of scene and disjointedness of episode; irregularity in the verse; a proliferation of connective phrases, repetitions, recollections, and anticipations; substitutions of the commonplace for the distinctive phrase; and the introduction of low jokes and gags. Most scholars would agree that there is probably a scene missing where the sequence involving the signing of the bond leads directly into the passage prior to the presentation of the Seven Deadly Sins (A627–28); that the two comic scenes printed consecutively (A949–84, 985–1037) probably belong apart; that the jokes about "Doctor *Lopus*" (A1176–77) and "french crownes" (A394–95) postdate Marlowe's death; and that the middle scenes of the play seem brief and fragmentary.

The B-text by contrast is 2121 lines long. It has usually been described as well plotted, well structured, and well proportioned, and as generally harmonious in its presentation of the life and death of Faustus. It involves a wide range of theatrical devices, far more than the A-text. Although none claims that it is all Marlowe, Greg at least suggests that "structurally at any rate the B-text preserves the more original . . . version of the play" (p. 29), though Bowers now disagrees with Greg on this point. Kuriyama detects in it the

---

† *Henslowe's Diary*, ed. R. A. Foakes and R. T. Rickert (Cambridge: Cambridge University Press, 1961), p. 206.
‡ From *English Literary Renaissance* 11 (1981): 111–29. Reprinted by permission of the editors.

additions of 1602, discerning acutely the hand of Rowley, and possibly of Birde also. All admit, however, that it has been edited in places, and that its blasphemous elements have been either removed or at least muted. Nevertheless, its comparative regularity of form and line have commended it to many scholars. Other scholars, however, point to that regularity as indicative of the interference of other hands; the places where its readings are pedestrian by contrast to those of the A-text have been similarly interpreted. Some scholars judge the elaborate use of the devils and of diabolical machinery in the play to be non-Marlovian while others perceive them as part of the author's design; the misplacement of the Chorus Speech of A810–20 to fill a gap at B558–68 when a fuller version is actually printed at B778–801 is noted as confusing; the apparent muddle of the Duke of Vanholt scene with the eruption of the scene at the inn is seen as likely to moderate one's enthusiasm for B's reliability.

Apart from the numbers, all these statements reflect matters of judgment rather than of scientific observation. Indeed, most of the criticisms are made with a conscious norm, a hypothetical Marlovian perfection, in mind. Even without any illustrative examples the two plays appear to be very different and the possible reconciliation of the texts would appear to be a matter of reconciling objects that are extremely unlike in general aspects. Yet if the contrast of the two is avoided, and each text is approached on its own terms, each may be seen to contain some distinctive coherence that precludes its association with the coherence of the other, and questions of superiority and relation to the hypothetical Marlovian original can be allowed to recede for a brief while. Moreover, when assumptions of superiority and inferiority are temporarily disregarded it becomes possible to accept readings that have been dismissed, and consequently to doubt the local weakness and to question the extent of the general corruption. At one point Greg says that "once revision in the prompt-book is established it is possible to see other instances" (p. 81). But one should try not to listen to the siren-call of one's own hypotheses; after all, the contrary is equally true and equally valid: once one recognizes that a line may not be corrupt, many others cease to look corrupt, a process that I shall demonstrate in arguing that neither text is as corrupt locally as criticism has previously suggested.

It is valuable then to examine the A-text initially, and to turn to those "weaknesses" that Greg cites as evidence to confirm his hypothesis that it is a reported text of the collaborative original that he perceives behind the B-text.[1] Kuriyama has already made a

---

1. W. W. Greg, ed., *Marlowe's "Doctor Faustus," 1604–1616: Parallel Texts* (Oxford: Clarendon Press, 1950), p. 37 ff. In discussing Greg's study at length I do not intend to criticize Greg alone, but the whole tradition of thought about the play that he fostered.

strong case for the quality of some A readings. However, although she suggests that the examples Greg cites as evidence of reporting are "subject to counter-interpretation, so that the writer of B may be seen to be borrowing from A (or as Bowers suggests, from a text of which A is a report), expanding and condensing," she still concludes that A is "a heavily cut and otherwise debased text."[2] However, I would argue, building upon her conclusions, that it is also important to recognize the extent to which the criticism of details of A is often unfounded; moreover, that while it would be hard to deny that A appears fragmentary, we do not know whether it may not perhaps be unfinished rather than cut, and that consequently we should be cautious in presuming the extent of the corruption; estimates of that debasement may vary. In this regard it is useful to consider some of those passages from A that Greg cites as inferior to those in B, and to show not necessarily their superiority or originality but at least their theatrical and dramatic viability, and therefore their artistic and intellectual integrity; and to demonstrate in consequence the weakness of the negative arguments for which they have constituted evidence. For instance, in the pageant of the Seven Deadly Sins: immediately prior to their appearance Lucifer says in the A-text, presumably to Faustus, "talke of the diuel, and nothing else: come away" (A737), while in the B-text he says "go *Mephostoph.* fetch them in" (B677). Greg comments, "Simpson has commented upon the absurdity—'clumsiness' is his word—of the order 'come away' when nobody leaves the stage" (p. 38). But the phrase is neither clumsy nor absurd, and it need not indicate a departure from the stage; it can be reasonably interpreted as Lucifer calling Faustus to his part of the stage to make room for the pageant. For Greg, however, this passage bolsters his theory of textual origin: "I suggest that 'come away' is an insertion intended to replace B's 'fetch them in' and to close the scene at this point should the pageant prove beyond the capacity of the company or the time available be insufficient for its exhibition" (p. 38).[3] Yet another example appears in the same scene. Greg states that "at the end of the same show there is a little variant that is an epitome of the character of A. In B Lucifer dismisses the Sins with the words (730): 'Away to hell, away on piper.' Instead A has 'Away, to hell, to hell' [sic] but the words instead of being given to Lucifer, and although they retain their indentation, are tacked on to the speech of Lechery. The piper, who evidently led the procession, disappears in accordance with A's habit of pruning all theatrical display"

2. Constance Kuriyama, *Hammer or Anvil: Psychological Patterns in Christopher Marlowe's Plays* (New Brunswick, N.J.: Rutgers University Press, 1980), pp. 176–77.
3. Greg here conceives of possible performance without the pageant of the Sins, something which I find hard to imagine.

(pp. 49–50). I would suggest that theatrically there is no evident superiority to B's readings, and that Glynne Wickham's[4] and Kuriyama's research indicates that there is certainly no historical priority that must be accorded to them. But Greg, led by his sense of B's priority and convinced of A's reduced staging, sees the piper as "evidently" leading the procession, even though the above is the sole reference to it. A's "Away, to hel, to hel" is indeed indented, but one should not jump to a simple conclusion that it is Lucifer's line; it is awkwardly placed in A, beginning where the speech prefix should have begun, and as it stands it could belong as easily to Lechery or even to all the Sins in chorus as to Lucifer. Moreover, the lines which follow present problems that are primarily interpretive rather than being merely editorial:

> Away, to hel, to hel.   *exeunt the sinnes.*
> *Lu.* Now Faustus, how dost thou like this?
> *Fau.* O this feedes my soule.
>   (A795–97)

> *Luc.* Away to hell, away on piper. *Ex. the 7 sinnes.*
> *Faust.* O how this sight doth delight my soule.
>   (B730–31)

Greg does not refer to this succeeding exchange in his introduction but in his notes he states that the "omission" of the speaker's name before "Away, to hel, to hel" "may somehow be connected with its insertion of a question by Lucifer designed to make less abrupt the transition to Faustus' exclamation of delight. The latter differs widely in the two versions without there being any internal indication which is the more original" (p. 343). I will return to the last point later; it is sufficient here to observe that Greg's whole mode of thought predisposes him to regard A not merely as inferior to B but as poor; distracted by his preference for B, he attributes significance to an indentation, but his conclusion, the absence of the speech prefix appropriate to Lucifer, is not necessary. I would argue that both texts appear "good" here; and that they are simply very different, requiring different but equally satisfactory stagings.

In these two examples I have shown how Greg's belief in the priority of B's composition leads him to discern its superiority over A, only to display the limits of Greg as interpreter rather than any difference in quality of text. Limitation of response in an interpreter

---

4. In "*Exeunt to the Cave*: Notes on the Staging of Marlowe's Plays," *Tulane Drama Review*, VIII (1964), 184–94, Glynne Wickham dealt a largely unrecognized death-blow to Greg's thesis that the fuller staging of the B-text is the original while the A-text represents a reduced version for a touring company by pointing out that no London theater of 1593 had the equipment to stage the B-text.

always produces problems, but in editors who are determined to discriminate between readings it is a major handicap. Further examples appear in relation to the opening Chorus of the play:

> Excelling all, whose sweet delight disputes
> In heauenly matters of *Theologie*
> (A19–20)

> Excelling all, and sweetly can dispute
> In th'heauenly matters of Theologie
> (B18–19)

In his notes Greg reviews the history of emendation of this passage, but argues that A "is undoubtedly right, *disputes* being a substantive and 'is' (i.e., consists in) being understood after *delight*. And this, I conjecture, was also the reading of MS; but it is certainly awkward and apparently tempted the editor of B to substitute his own superficially specious version" (p. 297). Greg is here taking a chance, pursuing the "awkward" A-text reading over the "perfectly smooth—suspiciously so" (p. 43) B-text reading, but his own explanation or justification is needlessly complicated. The elliptical construction which he suggests is extraordinary and to my mind unlikely. Far simpler is a reading of the words as a standard subject-predicate clause in which "delight disputes," a not unreasonable metaphorical construction in connection with scholars who take pleasure in debate. I find the A reading less "awkward" than Greg, although I would be reluctant to call it "undoubtedly right." A similar example appears a few lines earlier:

> To patient Iudgements we appeale our plaude,
> And speake for *Faustus* in his infancie
> (A10–11)

> And now to patient iudgements we appeale,
> And speak for *Faustus* in his infancie.
> (B10–11)

Greg's argument about these lines is lengthy, complex, and fanciful: where in the last example the A reading was found acceptable in its awkwardness, here the lines from A are declared to be "just such semi-sense as an actor or reporter might produce" (p. 42); and with respect to B10 he hypothesizes that "now" is not a repetition from B8 (such as might occur in a reported text) but an authorial mis-writing of "And so" (p. 42). What is evident here is the presence in Greg's mind of a powerful image of what Marlowe's *Doctor Faustus* should look like, what Marlowe must have written; the editor here is dominated not by logic but by fantasy. Awkwardness is permissible in one place, not in another; "appeale our plaude" is undeniably a strange phrase, but it is not unintelligible, certainly not in the context of a play in which language is used inventively, or at least idiomatically.[5] I myself still puzzle over the Chorus' use of the word "for" in the phrase "speake for *Faustus* in his infancie," but neither I nor any editor I have come across would suggest an emendation.

If "errors" are said to abound in A, few that are commonly cited as evidence that it is a reported text seem more than matters of taste. Greg talks of "injury to the sense . . . particularly, and perhaps significantly, in the case of auxiliaries" (p. 45), and he subjects several uses of "will" in the A-text to intense scrutiny; however, none of them bears the weight he puts on it. For instance: "I writ them a bill with mine owne bloud, the date is expired, the time wil come, and he wil fetch mee" (A1427–28). For "the time wil come" B reads "this is the time"; neither is nonsense, neither is poor dramatic language. Greg, however, criticizes A: "Obviously, if the date was expired, the time had come" (p. 45). Equally obviously, one might reply, even if the "date" has "expired," Faustus still awaits Lucifer's arrival. Both texts betray Faustus' confused, hysterical anticipation of the awful event by the clash of present and future tenses. Again, where the A-text has Mephostophilis say "If thou deny it, I wil backe to hel" (A477), Greg prefers the B-text's "I must backe to hell" (B425), commenting that Mephostophilis "is not his own master, but is merely executing the commands of Lucifer" (p. 45). But the fact is not evident from the play, nor would it prevent Mephostophilis from presenting himself as having choice. In each text Faustus confronts a crisis; the A-text can be read as exploiting Faustus' personal attachment to Mephostophilis while the B-text stresses the simple absolutes of Lucifer's company.

Minor theological issues provide the basis for small discriminations between the texts also, and Greg argues the deficiencies of A from his certainty concerning the exact purport of characters' statements. At A708 the Good Angel says "Neuer too late, if Faustus can repent"; Greg prefers the B-text's "will repent" (B649) on the grounds that "it is not a matter of the possibility of repentance—that is assumed—but of the will to repent" (p. 45). But the word "can" is often used in the sense of "find the capacity to achieve," and "will" is often a matter of simple futurity, even in a stressed position. No great theological point is in dispute here, though B's reading may be more cautious, less colloquial. The same is true of two passages concerning the second scholar: when the second scholar learns of Faustus' predicament he says:

5. Hazelton Spencer had no difficulty in glossing "our plaude": "For our applause"; he then quotes the B-text line and comments "typical of that ed.'s efforts to smooth the original version" (*Elizabethan Plays*, [Boston, 1933], p. 41).

O what shal we do to Faustus?
(A1435)

O what may we do to saue *Faustus*?
(B1971)

Greg declares that A's line "makes no sense," and concludes that "the omission of 'saue' was doubtless accidental" (p. 45). Even if one should give assent to that not indubitable hypothesis, one still need not assent to Greg's next observation: "However, it is not a question which of several courses the students will choose, but what possible course is open to them" (p. 45). But it may fairly be answered that in A the second scholar is acting as if that were not the issue, and as an impulsive faithful disciple he is presuming that he has the power to effect Faustus' rescue. Greg, however, mistakes characterization for error. When the second scholar later reminds Faustus in the A text that "gods mercies are infinite" (A1400-01), Greg again argues for the correctness of B's reading "mercy is infinite" (B1936) on the grounds that A "misses the point: it is not a question of how abundant are the mercies that God bestows on mankind, but that His mercy extends even to the greatest sinner" (p. 46). But there is no need to posit nicety of expression in the second scholar; as in the previous example from A, he is driven by a desire to influence and help Faustus, not to be precise in his terminology; and I might add, the statement "gods mercies are infinite" would not be found improper or irrelevant in a society accustomed to think of God's generous forgiveness in phrases such as the following from the Geneva Bible, where David is conscious of his sin: "And David said vnto Gad, I am in a wonderful straite: let vs fall now into the hand of the Lord, (for his mercies *are* great) and let me not fall into the hād of man."[6] One last point of this kind. While Faustus says "Ah Christ my Sauiour, seeke to saue distressed Faustus soule" at A711-12, he says in B "O Christ my Sauiour, my Sauiour, / Helpe to saue distressed *Faustus* soule" (B652–53), and Greg comments: "To seek to do something implies a doubtful issue: but whereas it is heretical to question Christ's power to save, it is true belief that that power is only exercised in aid of the sinner's own endeavour" (p. 46). Greg is presumably arguing for the B reading here, thus making Faustus temporarily into an orthodox Christian; but if one attends to the A reading one finds that it contains that characteristic element of demanding challenge that Faustus reveals elsewhere; in A Faustus wants Christ to make a special effort to save him, rather than just to

---

6. *The Geneva Bible: A facsimile of the 1560 edition*, ed. Lloyd E. Berry (Madison, Wis., 1969): the text is 2 Samuel 24:14. Compare also Nehemiah 9:28; Psalms 77:9; and Psalms 69:16.

help him perform a proper act of repentant appeal as in B. Greg's desire for theological orthodoxy of expression prejudices him towards the doctrinal propriety of utterances in the B-text, leading him to ignore the contextual validity of A's readings.

None of these examples from Greg's study is found to have any substance under examination. The professed objectivity of investigation is quite spurious; each decision has been shown to be a consequence of a preconceived view of the play and its language. The section of Greg's introduction from which most of them have been drawn begins as follows: "But it often happens that what at first sight look like indifferent variants yet on further consideration offer some valid ground of choice" (p. 44). I would suggest that Greg's own example indicates that variants are rarely indifferent and that valid choice is not possible in any simple way. By choosing, the editor invests a reading with value, determines his choice of further readings, and starts the process by which he chooses into being, personally *creates* the play that he conceives mentally. And such a mental conception is limited by the quality of mind of the editor, his sense of language, of theatrical action, his taste. To say of the absence from A of the word "now" in the line "Well, I am answer'd: now tell me who made the world?" (B636) that "A's apparently trivial omission of 'now' is really a distinct loss" (p. 44) is to fail to imagine what an actor could do with an abrupt, unsignalled change of direction to the most important question of all for Faustus; such a criticism as Greg's is interesting in relation to its absence from the discussion of "now" at B10, which was discussed earlier. It may also be true that "B's 'reason' is slightly more dignified than A's 'argue' " (p. 44) in "let vs dispute againe, / And argue of diuine *Astrologie*" (A662–63), but dignity in relation to Faustus' character is not necessarily an apt ground for authority. One may take greater delight in the "suggestion of a dimly apprehended form" (p. 44) apparent in B's "O what art thou that look'st so terribly" (B657) than in A's use of "who" in the question "O who art thou that lookst so terrible?" (A716), but one can equally prefer A's "terrible" to B's "terribly." And lastly, to say that "at A810ff. 'Learned Faustus, / To know the secrets of *Astronomy* . . . / Did . . . scale *Olympus* top,' will pass; but B's 'to find the secrets seems more appropriate" (p. 44) is to persuade oneself that one is engaging in intellectual activity when one is not.

Such instances are advanced by Greg to justify his sense of the "weaknesses" of A; succeeding editors have endorsed these views. Spurred by his success he proceeds to "prove" A's memorial origin by discerning metrical flaws, examples of inversion, repetition, and exaggeration, all of them highly subjective opinions, susceptible of contrary interpretation. The evidence that Greg adduces is useful only in supporting a previously established conviction of the priority and superiority of the B-text, and is available only to one who fails to read the A-text on its own terms, for its own meaning. Once one disabuses one's mind of the idea of "reported text," one finds merely difference of meaning.[7]

By contrast with A, the deficiencies of B for Greg are the consequences of the problems that the play's compiler, "the editor," confronted: a copy of A3, a manuscript which "was not only in all probability incomplete, mutilated, and illegible, but also contained a text that was at some points unrevised" (p. 85), and the editor's own desire to "bowdlerize" and to censor profanity; all these problems preceded the work of the printer in introducing error. But Greg's criticisms concentrate mostly on single line or word readings; he is confident that the play as printed in 1616 represents the form of the play that Marlowe devised, even if some of it was actually written by a collaborator; and in this most editors have followed him. But to other critics, especially those desirous of incorporating A readings into their interpretations, B reveals weaknesses that put its value into question. Kuriyama documents these charges best, although J. B. Steane is more vociferous.[8] I will examine her arguments to show that some of B's "failings" are not necessarily as gross as they have been described. The comic scenes of the third and fourth acts are an immediate object of concern. Kuriyama is swift in her denunciation of their excessive detail and unimaginative quality,[9] yet in themselves they generally seem quite proportionate to and consistent with the play they appear in. She is right to observe the anomaly when Robin refers to his "Apes face" at B1631 since it is Dick who has been turned into an ape and Robin into a dog.[1] But like Greg in respect to the text that he does not favor, she perceives "numerous gross lapses in continuity which are conspicuous"[2] where to my mind some of those lapses are merely pieces of wrongly interpreted stagecraft. For instance, she comments that "B's Wagner appears to know what is in Faustus' will when he introduces the last phase of the action, but fewer than 150 lines later he seems to be discovering its contents for the first time (B1778; 1912–19)."[3] Repetition between the two scenes is evident, but it is not necessarily either a foolish error or an inconsistency. Wagner does indeed know what is in the will at B1778, but we do not see him conversing with Faustus about it at that point;

7. Kuriyama also rejects the "reported text" hypothesis (p. 177).
8. Kuriyama, *passim*, but esp. pp. 177–80; J. B. Steane, *Marlowe: A Critical Study* (London: Cambridge University Press, 1970), pp. 117–26.
9. Kuriyama, pp. 185–86.
1. Kuriyama, p. 178.
2. Kuriyama, p. 178.
3. Kuriyama, p. 178.

his musing—"I wonder what he means, if death were nie, he would not frolick thus" (B1781–82)—suggests that he has no clear sense of what is to come. When the second conversation occurs, Wagner is being informed by Faustus of the will's contents for the first time, and his response is not without irony with its protestations of Christian sacrifice and love: "in all humble dutie, I do yeeld / My life and lasting seruice for your loue" (B1918–19). It is solely Mephostophilis' introductory statement that produces uncertainty: "He and his seruant *Wagner* are at hand, / Both come from drawing *Faustus* latest will" (B1912–13). But even this may merely indicate the activity as Faustus finally signs the will, or shows the will to Wagner and seeks his approval and consequently comfort; alternatively, the word "latest" may even indicate that Faustus is compulsively writing a sequence of wills. Any way it seems to me no "flaw." Elsewhere, Kuriyama finds B tending "to confuse the theological issues even more than A, at one moment presenting Faustus as willful and culpable (' 'Twas thine owne seeking *Faustus*, thanke thy selfe') and at the next moment presenting him, rather superstitiously, as a helpless victim of diabolical machinations (' 'Twas I, that when thou wer't i'the way to heauen, / Damb'd vp thy passage')."[4] But the two passages are perfectly compatible. In the first (B573) Mephostophilis is reinforcing Faustus' despair of heaven by stressing that it is by an act of Faustus' own will that he has rejected God, and that he has thus damned himself. In the second (B1988–90) he is increasing Faustus' sense of the impotence of his will by gloating over him, asserting that he has tricked him at all times, and baiting him in his despair. So long as Mephostophilis is perceived throughout as a vivid character, a skilled tempter in the service of the "father of lies," ready to use any rhetorical strategy in order to maintain Faustus in desperate subjection, no inconsistency appears. Again, Kuriyama dismisses B's presentation of the conjuration as "manifest nonsense": "In B Lucifer and four devils enter first; then Faustus enters, and according to the stage direction ("*Faustus to them with this speech*") informs *the devils* that it is night, even though such business is patently absurd and contradicts Faustus' lines further on in the speech, where he is obviously anxious to see if he can make any devils appear (B226, 231–33)."[5] One may not particularly like the extensive introduction of devils as an aspect of the B-text but it is not "patently absurd." In the B-text the devils are shown onstage at this point and also in Act V, but in neither place can Faustus see them. The audience of the B-text sees what Faustus apprehends in the actual world and also what is

4. Kuriyama, p. 177.
5. Kuriyama, p. 178.

actually happening in the spiritual-diabolical world. What Mephostophilis tells him in response to his question "Did not my coniur-
ing raise thee? speake" (B271) is apt for the occasion: although we
know that Faustus has been watched expectantly throughout his
conjuration, Mephostophilis makes him perceive the proceedings
in a way that explains to Faustus the behavior of devils, emphasizes
to him the awesome and profane power of his spell, and does not
mention the vigilance of the diabolical world, its readiness to trap
the rashly daring:

> That was the cause, but yet *per accident*:
> For when we heare one racke the name of God,
> Abiure the Scriptures, and his Sauiour Christ:
> We flye in hope to get his glorious soule;
> Nor will we come vnlesse he vse such meanes,
> Whereby he is in danger to be damn'd
> (B272–77)

Mephostophilis is characteristically telling a partial and conve-
niently seductive truth here. This speech does not sound the same
way here as it does in the A-text where the context makes it appear
much more direct, but neither text is nonsensical.[6]

I have tried to suggest that the B-text may not be worthy of all
the scorn which Kuriyama lays upon it. However, her refutation of
Greg's dating of the B-text provides a further attack upon the
soundness of Greg's argument for its exclusive authoritative value
as a text. The same qualities that were identified as characteristic in
A of a reported text are discussed in relation to B by Greg without
a similar conclusion being drawn (p. 68). The whole thesis of
Greg's reconstruction involving MS with A3 is shaky in the extreme. Although it is very likely that such a combination may have
been used, MS is never incontrovertibly established as original.
Greg's theory is based on the observations that the MS was used
only intermittently, that it was "incomplete" (p. 79), that "the probability is that MS was generally in a rather dilapidated condition"
(p. 79), that "it will be charitable and reasonable to assume that in
most instances damage to or illegibility of MS rendered correction
impossible" (p. 79), that "the manuscript used in the preparation of
the B-text was not only in all probability incomplete, mutilated, and
illegible, but also contained a text that was at some points unrevised" (p. 85), and that "the only sort of dramatic manuscript likely
to exhibit these features would be a bundle of what were known as
'foul papers,' that is, the draft of the play in the hands of the authors, from which the prompt-copy was prepared" (p. 85). Such a

6. For an excellent discussion of Mephostophilis' behavior in the play, see Robert H. West,
   "The Impatient Magic of Dr. Faustus," *English Literary Renaissance*, IV (1974), 218–40.

complex theory boggles the mind with its carefully constructed narrow systems of thought about textual recension, its detailed identification of a fragmentary original, its staggering optimism about the survival of a bundle of "foul papers" twenty-three years after the author's death, and its insistence that *only* "foul papers" among dramatic manuscripts would be likely to exhibit such features when any decayed version of a manuscript text which had suffered heavy use in its lifetime could do so; even indeed a "reported text."[7] Greg's reconstruction of B's origin is itself an expose of the elaborate application of a system of categories so precisely limited and determined that they produce false confidence in the powers of reason amid a chaos of alternative probabilities; to contemplate it is to wonder how one ever took its certainties seriously.

In sum, both texts have their obscurities and their problems and their misprints, and both are probably faulty in relation to any authorial original, but of that authorial original we can know nothing. A may well not be a reported text, and the MS behind B may well not be authorial; the original may never have been complete. And that authorial original cannot be recovered with any confidence by any bibliographical tools currently available.

* * *

LEAH MARCUS

From Textual Instability and Ideological Difference: The Case of *Doctor Faustus*†

Here is a wish-fulfillment scenario for Marlovian editors and biographers: in the bricked-off attic of a suburban London cottage, workmen clearing the way for a car park discover a parcel of old manuscripts, among them several letters dating from the 1590s and directed to "Christopher Marley" or "Marlowe." They are partly in code but decipherable, and turn out to contain passages detailing his duties as an intelligencer in Her Majesty's service. In the bundle are also several papers, apparently in the hand of Marlowe himself, elucidating such mysteries as the nature of his religious belief and the reasons for his brush with the Privy Council in 1593. There are also drafts of letters sent by Marlowe; one of them, dated

---

7. By contrast with Greg, Roma Gill writes that "some kind of M.S., certainly, was used in preparing the B-text, but the detailed stage directions which this apparently provided suggest rather a theatrical book than the author's foul papers" (*Doctor Faustus*, 2nd ed., New Mermaid Series [New York: W. W. Norton, 1965], p. xv).

† Rev. from *Renaissance Drama* 20: 38–54. Copyright © 1990 by Northwestern University Press. Reprinted by permission of Northwestern University Press.

later than the rest, hints at his fears of assassination, thus lending support to time-honored speculation that his violent death was not just the result of private feuding. Also in the packet are fair copies in the same hand of several of Marlowe's known works, among them *Hero and Leander* in the unfinished version of the 1598 printed edition but including a note affirming the author's intent to leave it unfinished; among them also an autograph copy of *The Tragicall Historie of Doctor Faustus* inscribed at the end "as written by me, Christofer Marley, 1592. *Terminat hora diem, Terminat Author opus.*" The *Faustus* manuscript—perhaps the most sensational find of all—allows scholars to settle once and for all the vexing textual problems surrounding the play by establishing a definitive authorial version that is polished and close to flawless, far superior to either the quarto of 1604 or the quarto of 1616 over which modern editors of Marlowe have puzzled and wrangled for over a century.

This imaginary cache of manuscripts fills many blank spaces in Marlowe scholarship and undoes many ambiguities; with one fell stroke, it also sweeps away the scholarly industry devoted to the recovery or reconstruction of a lost Marlovian "original" for *Doctor Faustus*. The present chapter will analyze the shape of the editorial controversy surrounding the play in order to critique some of its guiding assumptions—particularly its futile pursuit of the "lost original." My wish-fulfillment fantasy set aside, the *Faustus* problem is this: we have two early printed versions of the play, each with features lacking in the other, each displaying gaps that the other seems to fill. The first existing quarto version of the play was published in 1604, after which there were several reprintings of that text; in 1616 a second version of the play was printed, with subsequent quartos following it rather than the 1604 version until 1663, when yet a third version of *Doctor Faustus* appeared in quarto.

In twentieth-century editorial practice, the 1604 and 1616 printed versions have become bitter rivals: to choose one text as closer to "Marlowe" has invariably meant devaluing and debasing the other. The A text (the quarto of 1604) is closer in time to Marlowe in terms of publication but (much like a "bad" quarto of Shakespeare) too short and seemingly truncated to appear a satisfactory play—whole episodes that exist in the later 1616 version do not exist in the A text; moreover, the A text includes topical references to the Lopez affair of 1594, which postdated Marlowe's death. The B text (the quarto of 1616) is fuller and longer than A, but filled out for the most part with "low" comic scenes that appear, to some readers at least, insufficiently Marlovian.[1]

---

1. For a full spectrum of views, see Sylvan Barnet, ed., *Doctor Faustus* (1969; reprinted New York: New American Library, 1980); Fredson Bowers, ed., *The Complete Works of Christopher Marlowe*, vol. 2 (Cambridge: Cambridge University Press, 1973); and Bow-

For anyone trained in traditional methods of critical analysis, the experience of reading the two versions of the play in W. W. Greg's parallel text edition (1950) induces a sense of textual paradise lost. The edition is valuable in that, like any good parallel text edition, it facilitates comparison of the A and B versions of the play. But this edition in particular, in progress at the time that Greg's important paper on "The Rationale of Copy-Text" was delivered before the English Institute in 1949 and published the same year as the paper was, seems designed to offer graphic evidence of the major point made in Greg's paper—that it is usually necessary to conflate early texts to achieve a satisfactory edition of a work of Elizabethan literature.

Greg's introduction whets the reader's appetite for the reconstruction of Marlowe's "original" version of the play—a version assumed to be unencumbered by infelicities and ambiguities that mar the surviving printed playbooks. The 1604 and 1616 quartos, if approached through a modern conception of authorship, offer extraordinary "evidence" of Marlowe's original control over his materials. Both quartos end with the enigmatic comment "*Terminat hora diem, Terminat Author opus*," which, for twentieth-century readers at least, has evoked a seductive image of the author working intensely and in solitude on his masterwork, which he finished and "signed" with a majestic gesture of authorial finality. But in the absence of the wish-fulfillment evidence offered at the beginning of this chapter, we have no certainty that the line was actually Marlowe's. Some editors have speculated that it could have been added by the printer or someone else close to the publication process. Even more disconcertingly for our modern ideas of authorship, the

---

ers, "Marlowe's *Doctor Faustus*: The 1602 Additions," *Studies in Bibliography* 26 (1973): 1–18; Walter Cohen, *Drama of a Nation: Public Theater in Renaissance England and Spain* (Ithaca: Cornell University Press, 1985), pp. 23–25; Roy T. Eriksen, *"The Forme of Faustus Fortunes": A Study of* The Tragedie of Doctor Faustus, *1616* (Atlantic Highlands, New Jersey: Humanities Press, 1987); Roma Gill, Review of *The Complete Works of Christopher Marlowe*, ed. Fredson Bowers, *Review of English Studies* n.s. 25 (1974): 459–64; and Gill, ed., *Doctor Faustus*, vol. 2 of *The Complete Works of Christopher Marlowe* (Oxford: Clarendon Press, 1990); W. W. Greg, *A Bibliography of the English Printed Drama to the Restoration*, vol. 1 (London: Oxford University Press, 1939); and Greg, ed., *Marlowe's* Doctor Faustus, *1604–1616: Parallel Texts* (Oxford: Clarendon Press, 1950); John D. Jump, ed., *Doctor Faustus* (London: Methuen, 1962); Michael Keefer, ed., *Doctor Faustus: A 1604-version edition* (Peterborough, Ontario, and Lewiston, New York: Broadview Press, 1991); Leo Kirschbaum, "The Good and Bad Quartos of *Doctor Faustus*," *Library*, 4th series 26 (1945–46): 272–94; Constance Brown Kuriyama, "Dr. Greg and *Doctor Faustus*: The Supposed Originality of the 1616 Text," *English Literary Renaissance* 5 (1975): 171–97; and E. D. Pendry, ed., *Christopher Marlowe, Complete Plays and Poems* (London: Dent, 1976). On formulaic elements in both versions of the play, see also Thomas Pettitt, "Formulaic Dramaturgy in *Doctor Faustus*," in Kenneth Friedenreich, Roma Gill, and Constance B. Kuriyama, eds, *"A Poet and a filthy Playmaker": New Essays on Christopher Marlowe* (New York: AMS, 1988), 167–91.

Citations from *Doctor Faustus* in my text will be to line numbers from Greg's parallel text edition, since modern facsimiles of A and B are less than readily available. There are a few small errors but it offers a reasonably accurate transcription of the quarto texts.

line appears at the end of both versions of the play, so that both, although different, have the same claim to authenticity.

Greg's parallel text edition of *Doctor Faustus* encourages readers to think in terms of recapturing the single authentic *opus* that we can so vividly imagine Marlowe writing. The edition gives passages that exist in one early text but not in the other "absent presence" in the text from which they are "missing" through blank spaces—even in the middle of lines—that interrupt the flow of reading and make each version appear fragmentary by itself. The editor offers his readers a strong temptation to escape from the anxiety created by the apparent lacunae through a process of selection and consolidation that chooses one reading as "superior" and rejects its rival version across the page, thus actively constructing a composite version that will be better than either flawed quarto. Indeed Greg published his own "Conjectural Reconstruction" of the play in the same year as his parallel text edition.[2] His two editions of *Doctor Faustus*, together with the nearly simultaneous article on "Copy-Text," offered a formidable and influential display of an editorial method that was to freeze into dogma during the next several decades.

For most readers, however, the two texts of *Doctor Faustus* have proven curiously resistant to assimilation, and do not mesh satisfactorily to form a single composite whole. In the case of Shakespeare plays with both good and bad quartos, twentieth-century editions have for the most part settled into comfortable consensus. Readers encounter only minor textual differences in moving from one edition of a given play to another, or at least they did before the publication of the controversial new Oxford Shakespeare. Indeed, it could be argued that the elaborate apparatus of dictionaries, concordances, and even the *OED* itself built up around the text of Shakespeare has required the texts to remain stable so that the apparatus could preserve its accuracy. Not so with Marlowe. Different editors of *Doctor Faustus* have offered us markedly different versions of Marlowe's intended *opus*. The usual editorial practice of creating a composite text from elements of A and B have brought us no closer to a Marlovian original because editors have seldom agreed as to what is Marlowe and what isn't. Greg's efforts notwithstanding, we are left with an array of different reconstructions of *Doctor Faustus* that tell us more about the personal tastes and unspoken value-systems of individual editors than they do about the elusive "original."

---

2. W. W. Greg, ed., *The Tragical History of the Life and Death of Doctor Faustus: A Conjectural Reconstruction* (Oxford: Clarendon Press, 1950). It is noteworthy that this edition, despite its reliance on B, is more balanced than the parallel text edition in its assessment of A.

Michael Warren has argued persuasively that we need to set aside the passion for textual syncretism and take a harder look at the early quarto texts of *Doctor Faustus* we actually have.[3] There is much to be gained by keeping the two separate and distinct. They are profoundly different—much more unlike than the quarto and folio versions of *King Lear*, for which Warren and others have proposed a similar separation. Merely to read each in its original quarto edition (or a facsimile or modern edited version thereof) is to get a much stronger sense of the textual integrity of each than if they are read in Greg's fragmenting parallel columns. If we read each text of *Doctor Faustus* on the assumption that it is sufficient in itself rather than a deficient simulacrum of the other, we will find that each has its own distinctive atmosphere and dramatic logic. We will not, however, find ourselves moving closer to the absent authorial presence we call Marlowe.

It is time to step back from the fantasy of recovering Marlowe as the mighty, controlling source of textual production and consider other elements of the process, particularly ideological elements that the editorial tradition has, by the very nature of its enterprise, suppressed. I would like to second Warren's call for a separation of the two texts of *Doctor Faustus*, but carry his argument further by contending that for *Faustus*, and for Renaissance drama more generally, a key element of textual instability is ideological difference. Except for minor shifts in wording, the disparities between the 1604 and 1616 versions of *Doctor Faustus* are not random; they form a rough but fairly coherent pattern of "relocation" that alters the site of dramatic conflict. The A text places the magician in "Wertenberg" and within a context of militant Protestantism; the B text situates him instead in "Wittenberg," within a less committedly Calvinist, more theologically conservative and ceremonial millieu. Each placement of Faustus carries different implications in terms of the play's engagement of political and religious controversy. More interesting for us, perhaps, are the implications for modern editorial practice: to a significant degree, twentieth-century editorial opinion has organized itself around a secularized version of the same ideological polarities.

Wittenberg and Wertenberg

The attempt to reconstruct a pristine Marlovian "original" has been, in part, an attempt to separate Marlowe from historical process and from the contingency of meaning that historical interpretation usually implies; it is an attempt to give the Marlovian text

3. Michael J. Warren, "*Doctor Faustus*: The Old Man and the Text," *English Literary Renaissance* 11 (1981): 111–47.

a fixity and permanence it certainly did not have in the Elizabethan theater. Interestingly enough, the key New Bibliographical work on the play appeared in the five years after World War II, at a time when traditional philological scholarship was on the wane among leaders of the discipline of English. Greg's editions and Leo Kirschbaum's seminal 1946 article (see n. 1 [p. 154, above]) defining the 1604 text as a "bad" quarto of the play can be seen in retrospect as part of the postwar effort to stabilize and preserve important cultural monuments. But the play we call *Doctor Faustus* was malleable and unfixed from the outset, acted in different "local" versions which can be correlated with different historical moments; it was, as I shall argue, dependent upon those moments to achieve its full power in the theater.

I will speculate here about the origins and significance of the A and B quartos of *Doctor Faustus* in order to demonstrate the inevitable historicity of our editorial practice, but also to make a plea for the recovery of "local" differences in Renaissance texts more generally. In the case of *Doctor Faustus*, the differences between early printed versions are more flamboyant than they are for early printed versions of most Shakespearean plays, and lead us farther away from the playwright as authority over the meaning of his work. Most of the discrepancies between quarto and folio versions of Shakespeare that recent textual revisionists have brought to our attention could at least conceivably have been created during the author's lifetime and could therefore have been the product of authorial revision; the different versions of Marlowe I will discuss almost certainly were not.

Doctor Faustus enjoyed a long and colorful theatrical history in the late sixteenth and early seventeenth centuries. Its illicit acts of conjuring were able to "ravish" and terrify audiences, as is witnessed by the numerous tales of demonic interference during performances of the play: at Exeter, an extra devil suddenly appeared among the actors on stage, causing a panic; in London the "old Theater crackt and frighted the audience" during one performance, at others, the "visible apparition" of the devil appeared on stage "to the great amazement both of the Actors and Spectators."[4] The play did not hold its ability to spellbind English audiences for nearly half a century by remaining always the same. For Renaissance audiences of *Doctor Faustus*, to the extent that they took notice of the playwright at all, watching "Marlowe" meant watching a theatrical

4. See John Russell Brown, "Marlowe and the Actors," *Tulane Drama Review* 8.4 (1964): 155–73; E. K. Chambers, *The Elizabethan Stage* (Oxford: Clarendon Press, 1923), 3: 423–24; and Michael Goldman, "Marlowe and the Histrionics of Ravishment," in *Two Renaissance Mythmakers: Christopher Marlowe and Ben Jonson*, ed. Alvin Kernan, Selected Papers from the English Institute, 1975–76 (Baltimore: Johns Hopkins University Press, 1977), pp. 22–40.

event balanced on the nervous razor edge between transcendent heroism and dangerous blasphemy—transgression not only against God but also against cherished national goals and institutions.

The "Marlowe effect," as we can perhaps term it, is particularly fully documented in terms of audience response to *Doctor Faustus*, but was probably part of the appeal of other Marlowe plays as well (*Tamburlaine* will be mentioned later on). I would like to contend that the differences between the A and B quartos of *Faustus* functioned to keep the "Marlowe effect" alive—to keep the play, amidst shifting conditions in church and state, on the same "ravishing" razor edge between exaltation and transgression. As I have argued elsewhere, the different early texts of a Shakespeare play often seem to disperse authorial identity, at least to the extent that authorial identity is associated with consistency of method and purpose, in that they alter the ideological message of the play in subtle but significant ways.[5] In the case of Marlowe, or at least of *Doctor Faustus*, just the opposite is true. The different versions of the play carry different ideological freight—the A text could be described as more nationalist and more Calvinist, Puritan, or ultra-Protestant, the B text as more internationalist, imperial, and Anglican, or Anglo-Catholic—but each version places the magician at the extreme edge of transgression in terms of its own implied system of values.

In order to consider the quartos of *Doctor Faustus* in terms of ideological difference, we need first of all to temporarily suspend the almost inevitable tendency to rank one version higher than the other—a judgment usually made in aesthetic terms but masking an array of other concerns. By attempting to winnow out "Marlowe" from the chaff of non-authorial intrusions, editors uphold an elite cultural ideal: the text judged more defective than the other is almost invariably associated with a lowering of social standards. Editors disagree, however, about which version of the play is too "low" to be genuine Marlowe. W. W. Greg opted for the 1616 version (the B text) as closer to Marlowe on grounds that it has a more coherent plot and more "orderly succession of scenes," as well as greater polish and more effective theatricality. The 1604 quarto (the A text), by contrast, is for Greg a jumble of "merely disjointed episodes," the "mutilated remains" of an "original form" which B more nearly reflects. The A text "lacks" many of the comic episodes of the B text, it also "lacks" the episode of Faust's intervention in the struggle between the Emperor and the Pope and many of the visual elements (the final appearance of the Good and Bad Angels, the vi-

---

5. Leah S. Marcus: *Puzzling Shakespeare: Local Reading and Its Discontents* (Berkeley and London: University of California Press, 1988), pp. 44–50, 156–59.

sion of the heavenly throne, the hell mouth) in the play's closing moments. The A text's "feebleness," "gibberish," and "inapposite rant" are, for Greg, the probable effects of popularization and professional decline. In the course of time, the text of the play was "progressively adapted to the needs of a declining company and the palate of an uncultivated audience" (G pp. 20–39).

This is precisely the style of argument we would expect from the innovative New Bibliographer who argued for memorial reconstruction as the source of Shakespeare's "bad" quartos. It was followed (albeit more temperately) by Fredson Bowers, who in his own edition of the play disagreed with Greg's conviction that the scenes unique to the B text were Marlovian, but nevertheless used B as the copytext on grounds that A was "corrupt" and B "purer," more "textually coherent," and "superior."[6] What makes the case of *Faustus* particularly interesting, however, is that other reader-critics have used similar criteria to reach the opposite judgment about what is "genuine" Marlowe. Constance Brown Kuriyama, for example, has complained that "acceptance of the B text as 'original' or authoritative leaves us with a work that is, to put it plainly, an aesthetic monstrosity and a critical nightmare." A has an "aesthetic integrity" far superior to B. B is full of "infelicitous bungling," it confuses the play's theology, and "because of its authors' fatal attraction to the coarser episodes of the *Faustbook*" it "tends to reduce Faustus' struggle to terms that I find hopelessly lurid and vulgar."[7] Roma Gill uses more cautious language but similarly prefers the A text on grounds that the B "additions" are "trivial" and the serious scenes in A are "clearly superior."[8]

The case of *Doctor Faustus* throws into stark relief the relativity of editorial judgment, the ease with which we construct an "original" that will satisfy our own tastes and assumptions. The critic's chosen version of the play is idealized or at least given the benefit of elaborate explanation of what might otherwise be perceived as its "defects"; the rejected version, like its dark, monstrous double, is perceived as formless, fragmentary, *basse classe* and uncouth, attributable to inferior authorship. And so, we find, Greg goes to considerable lengths to defend the comic scenes and Papal-Imperial episodes of his preferred B text as closer to the play as Marlowe originally wrote it; Kuriyama, like most editors before Greg and a growing number since him, identifies these scenes instead as the non-Marlovian "adicyones in doctor fostes" for which Philip

6. See Bowers, ed., *Doctor Faustus*, pp. 142–43.
7. Kuriyama, pp. 177–80.
8. Gill, ed., *Doctor Faustus*, pp. xxii, 141. Gill represents a particularly interesting case in that she has altered textual allegiance over time. Her 1965 edition of *Doctor Faustus* (reprinted New York: Hill & Wang, 1966) followed Greg in preferring B as copytext; her new Oxford edition prefers A.

Henslowe paid Samuel Rowley and William Birde or Borne £4 in
1602 (G p. 11, Kuriyama pp. 180–81; see n. 1 [p. 154, above]).

Part of the conflict I have sketched out here can be correlated
with postwar generational differences. Greg speaks for what we
used to call "establishment" opinion, preferring smoothness, polish,
a brand of theatricality which relies on spectacle and special effects
to communicate widely accepted cultural ideals. The B text, with
its imperial hijinx and busy damnation scene, a "huge phantas-
magoria of scenic properties, emblematic costumes, allegorical actions on all three levels of the Elizabethan stage," does that far
more successfully than the A text. Greg also finds more sympathetic
the ceremonial style of Anglicanism in B; to him the more iconoclastic A text registers as jarringly uncouth.[9] The work of somewhat
younger critics like Warren, Kuriyama, Michael Keefer, David Bevington, and Stephen Greenblatt (who also prefers A) postdates the
heyday of the theatrical avant-garde in the 1960s and early 1970s
and the broader critique of "the establishment" with which both
the avant-garde theater and an emerging generation of young scholars of the Vietnam era were associated. These scholars display more
tolerance, even active preference, for theatrical starkness, iconoclasm, dissonance. They are happier with the A text, which far
more often relies on a bare, unadorned stage and casts Faustus's
conflict in a more introspective, psychological mode. The A text has
recently appeared on its own in three published editions—additional evidence of the rise in its status.[1] Editorial preference for ei-

9. See Johannes H. Birringer, "Between Body and Language: 'Writing' the Damnation of
Faustus," *Theatre Journal* 36 (1984): 335–55; quotation is from p. 351. Like Greg, G. K.
Hunter also defends the artistry of the B text in his "Five-Act Structure in *Doctor Faustus*," *Tulane Drama Review* 8.4 (1964): 77–91. On Greg's at least implicit prejudice
against Calvinist doctrine, see Keefer, ed., pp. lxiv–lxv.
1. See Warren; Kuriyama; and Stephen J. Greenblatt, "Marlowe and Renaissance Self-
Fashioning," in Kernan, ed., p. 64 n. 2; and *Renaissance Self-Fashioning: From More to
Shakespeare* (Chicago and London: University of Chicago Press, 1980), p. 290 n. 2. Edward A. Snow and C. L. Barber have expressed the same preference: see Snow, "Marlowe's *Doctor Faustus* and the Ends of Desire" in Kernan, ed., pp. 70–110; and Barber,
"The Form of Faustus' Fortunes Good or Bad," *Tulane Drama Review* 8.4 (1964):
92–119, reprinted in somewhat different form in *Creating Elizabethan Tragedy: The
Theater of Marlowe and Kyd*, ed. Richard P. Wheeler (Chicago: University of Chicago
Press, 1988), pp. 87–130.
    For the new editions, see David Ormerod and Christopher Wortham, eds, *Dr Faustus:
The A-Text* (Nedlands: University of Western Australia Press, 1985); Keefer, ed.; and
David Bevington and Eric Rasmussen, eds, *Doctor Faustus: A- and B-texts (1604, 1616)*
(Manchester and New York: Manchester University Press, 1993). I am grateful to the
editors of the second and third of these for sending me welcome early copies of their
work. Perhaps even more indicative of the recent shift is the fact that the most recent
edition of *The Norton Anthology of World Masterpieces*, vol. 1, now uses the A text rather
than Boas's composite edition for its widely used teaching text of the play (New York and
London: W. W. Norton, 1992).
    In terms of both age and aesthetic preference, I too belong to the pro-A-text group.
However, I am less interested in choosing between texts than in demonstrating relationships between them. To the extent that my work here displays the iconoclasm characteristic of my generation of scholars, I am directing it not against the B text, but against the
idea that we can recover a genuine "Marlowe."

ther version of *Doctor Faustus* will continue to alter along with
other cultural forms and dominant ideologies.

There are interesting correlations between the generational differences I have identified here and a much earlier controversy surrounding the figure of Faustus which has left its mark on the A and
B quartos of the play. The two versions differ as to Faustus's base of
operations: as I have noted, he hails from Wittenberg in the B text,
from Wertenberg in the A text. All editors of the play (even those
who prefer A) have at least tacitly accepted "Wertenberg" as a corruption or, in Greg's phrase, a "nominal perversion" (G p. 39) of the
"correct" location, Wittenberg. We all know, or think we know, that
the historical Dr Faustus lived in Wittenberg, a prominent university town, a haven for lingering elements of late-medieval
scholasticism but also the intellectual center of Lutheranism. In
maintaining this knowledge, we are following an editorial line
which has so dominated thinking about the play that the A text's locale of "Wertenberg" is editorially speaking, nowhere. If we look up
"Wertenberg" in a standard topographical dictionary to the Elizabethan drama, we will find (in a circularity familiar to us from our
earlier discussion of the "blue-eyed hag") that "Wertenberg," is
listed only in reference to *Faustus* as the A text's error for "Wittenberg," with the English Faustbook cited as an authority.[2]

And yet in the Renaissance (as today) Wertenberg was not
nowhere; "Wertenberg" or "Wirtenberg," in its standard sixteenth-
century spellings, was the independent Rhineland Duchy of
Württemberg, well known to English Protestants through its
associations with the uprisings by radical Zwinglian Protestants
during the early sixteenth century which caused Martin Luther and
his followers to retreat from the most revolutionary implications of
Reformation doctrine. The Duchy of Württemberg took a consistently anti-Imperial stance during the late sixteenth century and
was one of the foreign powers with which England was on the most
intimate terms. The Duke of Württemberg (or "Wirtemberg," as he
himself signed it), was ostensibly a Lutheran, but of a theological
school that Wittenberg branded as heretical; he was widely suspected of crypto-Calvinism, and some modern historians call him a
Calvinist. He lent his support to the English side in the French
wars; he visited England himself and was a familiar enough figure
at least in court circles to be satirized (we think) in Shakespeare's

2. See Edward H. Sugden, *A Topographical Dictionary to the Works of Shakespeare and His
Fellow Dramatists* (Manchester: Manchester University Press, 1925), p. 570. The traditional objection that "Wertenberg" is no more than a printinghouse error has recently
been restated by Robert F. Fleissner in " 'Wittenberg,' not 'Wertenberg': A Nominal Discrepancy in the A-text of *Doctor Faustus*," *Papers of the Bibliographical Society of America* 89 (1995):189–92; however, Fleissner offers no new evidence supporting the
traditional view.

Merry Wives of Windsor. English actors also visited his court in Württemberg.[3]

Moreover, even in relation to the historical figure of Faustus, Wertenberg was not nowhere. In the late sixteenth century there was an alternate tradition associating Faustus with Württemberg (and its University of Tübingen) rather than with Wittenberg. According to Philipp Melanchton of Wittenberg, who was eager to dissociate such a marginal figure as the magician from the intellectual center of Lutheranism, Faustus perished in Wertenberg, not in Melanchton's own Wittenberg; later Lutheran propagandists followed Melanchton in attempting to undo the abuse and slander of the "school and church of Wittenberg" that placed the magician as a Doctor of Divinity there. A similar association is made in *The Merry Wives of Windsor*: the folio version of the play calls the three "cozen Germans," one of whom appears to be a satirical portrait of the Duke of Württemberg, "three German devils, three Doctor Faustuses."[4] Nor is the Faustbook itself as consistent as editors have claimed; in at least one instance, it gives the magician's place of residence as "Wirtenberg."[5] So the A text, in placing Faustus in "Wertenberg," may not be marred by "nominal perversion" after all. Rather, it draws on an alternate tradition associating Faustus

3. On the Duke and Württemberg, see William Brenchley Rye, *England as Seen by Foreigners in the Days of Elizabeth and James the First* (London: John Russell Smith, 1865), pp. lv–cvii, 7; H. J. Oliver, ed., *The Merry Wives of Windsor*, The Arden Shakespeare (London: Methuen, 1971), pp. xlvi–xlix; James Allen Vann, *The Making of a State: Württemberg 1593–1793* (Ithaca: Cornell University Press, 1984), p. 54; Gerald Strauss, *Law, Resistance, and the State: The Opposition to Roman Law in Reformation Germany* (Princeton: Princeton University Press, 1986), p. 265; A. W. Ward, *et al., The Cambridge Modern History*, vols 2–3 (Cambridge: Cambridge University Press, 1903–04); and the account of the history and culture of Württemberg in Johannes Janssen's multi-volume study of the Reformation, *History of the German People at the Close of the Middle Ages*, trans. M. A. Mitchell and A. M. Christie, 17 vols (London: Kegan Paul, 1900–25), especially vols 2–9. Janssen's account is strongly anti-Reformation in its bias but wonderfully detailed. Since Württemberg was officially Lutheran rather than Calvinist the parallel between Marlowe's "Wertenberg" and the historical Württemburg obviously cannot be pressed too far. My argument here is more about English perceptions of kinship than it is about precise historical congruence.

4. On Wittenberg and Melanchthon, see Keefer, ed., pp. xxxiii–xlv; and William Empson, *Faustus and the Censor: The English Faust-book and Marlowe's Doctor Faustus*, ed. John Henry Jones (Oxford: Blackwell, 1987), pp. 6–14; Melanchthon himself had spent time at the University of Tübingen and taken the M.A. degree there, but later broke with it over theological matters: through most of the sixteenth century, Tübingen adhered to "heretical" doctrines that denied the sacrificial nature of the Eucharist (Janssen, 7:74–77, 313).

For the topicality of *Merry Wives*, see Oliver, ed., p. 125 (*Merry Wives* 4.5.65–67); and the discussion of the Shakespearean scene in Patricia Parker, *Literary Fat Ladies: Rhetoric, Gender, Property* (London: Methuen, 1987), pp. 74–77. In a recent essay, Barbara Freedman has contested the dating that has enabled editorial identification of Shakespeare's stage character with the Duke of Württemberg. See her "Shakespearean Chronology, Ideological Complicity, and Floating Texts: Something Is Rotten in Windsor," *Shakespeare Quarterly* 45 (1994): 190–210. * * * whether or not the duke was satirized in Shakespeare, he was certainly a well-known figure in England during the 1590s.

5. *Historie of the Damnable Life and deserued death of Doctor John Faustus*, trans. P. F. (London, 1592); facsimile edition (New York: Da Capo, 1969), p. 9.

with a German duchy that was a hotbed of left-wing Protestantism rather than a place which had become, by the late sixteenth century at least, the center of a more conservative Lutheran orthodoxy.

The editorial suppression of "Wertenberg" elides a potentially significant historical difference between the two texts; it also obscures an interesting correlation between twentieth-century and Renaissance generational difference. W. W. Greg, who prefers the "Wittenberg" B text, chooses the version of the play that places it in a relatively conservative religious setting, at least by the standards of the 1590s. Kuriyama, Gill, and Warren, who prefer the A or "Wertenberg" version, do not concern themselves with the implications of the name, but nevertheless choose the version of the play which places Faustus in a locale associated with revolt against official Lutheran orthodoxy. Michael Keefer's recent edition of *Faustus* goes considerably further, appropriating Marlowe for the political left and decrying the B text's "deformation of the originally interrogative thrust of the play."[6] Modern editorial preference thus recasts elements of sixteenth-century religious and political controversy.

Considered in historical terms, "Wertenberg" is not the textual "accidental" Marlowe editors have taken it to be. It is, however, precious little to hang an argument on. We need to look at other elements of the A and B texts which seem to correlate, at least in terms of the implications they would have carried for late sixteenth and early seventeenth-century audiences, with the difference between "Wertenberg" and "Wittenberg." We will be dealing not with the places in themselves but with the ideological resonances they carried in England. We will be dealing in particular with the conflict between left-wing Protestant opinion and conservative Anglican orthodoxy as it was played out in the Marprelate controversy of the 1580s and 1590s, in later outbursts of a similar reforming "frenzy," and also in literary works like Spenser's "May Eclogue." Baldly summarized, it was a conflict that pitted the Anglican establishment — its advocacy of bishops, a set liturgy, ecclesiastical vestments, and ceremonial worship, its tendency (becoming more pronounced over time) to dilute or reject some of the most rigorous theological tenets of Calvinism—against more radical Protestant or "Puritan" opinion characterized by hostility to the established ecclesiastical hierarchy, rejection of all set liturgies and "supersti

---

6. Keefer, ed., p. lx. Keefer's edition appeared after this article was first published. There are, however, many points of agreement between us, and I have profited by his work in making revisions here. Curiously enough, however, despite his opposition to Greg, Keefer shares with the New Bibliography a confidence that he can reconstruct a single Marlovian "original" of the play.

tious" Anglican ceremonies, and insistence upon the full rigor of Calvinist doctrine.[7] That is not to say that either version of *Faustus* focusses directly on the conflict between religious ideologies, only that if we suspend the almost irresistible tendency to view one text as a defective image of the other, we will notice that the two present markedly different versions of what constitutes normative religious experience. In terms of the set of polarities I have suggested, the *Faustus* A text is clearly more "Protestant" and the B text more "Anglican" or Anglo-Catholic.

Both texts, and indeed all of the quartos before 1663, were issued, as the English Faustbook had been before them, in black letter—a type that was still quite common in the early seventeenth century for popular books of all kinds, but became less common for secular materials except for lawbooks as the century wore on. Particularly for readers of the 1620s and 1630s, we can speculate, the black-letter type may have given *Doctor Faustus* a faintly archaic and ecclesiastical air.[8] Both the Bishops' Bible (last edition 1602) and the King James Version (first edition 1611) were published in black letter. Whether fortuitously or by design, the title pages of the 1604 and 1616 versions of *Doctor Faustus* display some of the same differences we have already discussed in terms of the elaboration of visual effects. The 1604 *Faustus* is adorned only by a printer's device, albeit a fairly appropriate one for a play in which psychomachia figures prominently; the 1609 and 1611 quartos use a different device and add an ornamental border at the top but are otherwise equally plain. It is only with the publication of the 1616 version of the play that the famous picture of the Doctor, face to face with the devil he has just conjured up and surrounded by mysterious tools of the magician's trade, appears on the title page. After 1616, the picture of Faustus becomes a regular feature of seventeenth-century editions of the play, but the icon was associated only with the "ceremonial" B text, not with the more iconoclastic A.[9]

The doctrinal differences between the A and B versions of *Doctor Faustus* are encapsulated nicely in the two contrasting versions of

7. See, among many other discussions of the polarities, Christopher Hill, *Society and Puritanism in Pre-Revolutionary England*, 2nd edition (New York: Schocken, 1967); Patrick Collinson, *The Elizabethan Puritan Movement* (Berkeley: University of California Press, 1967); and J. Sears McGee, *The Godly Man in Stuart England: Anglicans, Puritans, and the Two Tables, 1620–1670* (New Haven: Yale University Press, 1976).
8. On the use of black-letter type, see Keith Thomas, "The Meaning of Literacy in Early Modern England," in Gerd Baumann, ed., *The Written Word: Literacy in Transition* (Oxford: Clarendon Press, 1986), pp. 97–131; and D. C. Greetham, *Textual Scholarship: An Introduction* (New York and London: Garland, 1992), pp. 228–36.
9. That is not to suggest that doctrinal difference was the only reason for the shift in title page.

the Old Man's appeal to Faustus.[1] He enters in both versions almost at the end of the play to try to win Faustus back from the devil. Here are both forms of the speech:

A: *Old.* Ah Doctor Faustus, that I might preuaile,
    To guide thy steps vnto the way of life,
    By which sweete path thou maist attaine the gole
    That shall conduct thee to celestial rest.
    Breake heart, drop bloud, and mingle it with teares,
    Teares falling from repentant heauinesse
    Of thy most vilde and loathsome filthinesse,
    The stench whereof corrupts the inward soule
    With such flagitious crimes of hainous sinnes,
    As no commiseration may expel,
    But mercie Faustus of thy Sauiour sweete,
    Whose bloud alone must wash away thy guilt.
                       (A 1302–13)

B: *Old man.* O gentle *Faustus* leaue this damned Art,
    This Magicke, that will charme thy soule to hell,
    And quite bereaue thee of saluation.
    Though thou hast now offended like a man,
    Doe not perseuer in it like a Diuell;
    Yet, yet, thou hast an amiable soule,
    If sin by custome grow not into nature:
    Then *Faustus*, will repentance come too late,
    Then thou art banisht from the sight of heauen;
    No mortall can expresse the paines of hell.
    It may be this exhoration
    Seemes harsh, and all vnpleasant; let it not,
    For gentle sonne, I speake it not in wrath,
    Or enuy of thee, but in tender loue,
    And pitty of thy future miserie.
    And so haue hope, that this my kinde rebuke,
    Checking thy body, may amend thy soule.
                       (B 1813–29)

Editorial opinion has focussed on the "inferior artistry" of the A version—which Greg called Senecan bombast (G p. 384)—but neither version is intrinsically preferable on aesthetic grounds alone. Rather, the two present strikingly different analyses of what Faustus must do to be saved. In A, the Old Man is a spiritual counsellor very much in the bracing Protestant or Puritan vein. He does not quite preach a doctrine of Calvinist predestination in that he

1. My argument here is dependent on Warren, pp. 129–39; and on Robert G. Hunter, *Shakespeare and the Mystery of God's Judgments* (Athens: University of Georgia Press, 1976), pp. 39–66.

describes heaven as a goal Faustus may "attaine" if he follows the "way of life," but his exhortation bears all the usual hallmarks of strenuous Protestant spirituality: the emphasis on sin as a state of "loathsome" inward corruption, the portrayal of spiritual experience as an arduous pilgrimage toward the goal of "celestial rest" and of repentance as a soul-searching individual struggle. The Old Man makes clear that his mere commiseration, though heartfelt, can accomplish nothing—everything depends on Faustus's inner condition and that is a matter between the sinner and God.

The B version is milder and gentler: it has been called semi-Pelagian, but perhaps a less inflammatory term like "Arminian" or "latitudinarian Anglican" would do.[2] In B, Faustus's sin is not an inborn condition, but a bad habit which is gradually becoming engrained. To be saved, he must give up his magic. Even at this perilously late stage in the game, the Old Man in B describes Faustus as having an "amiable soule" if "sin by custome grow not into nature." In contrast to A, the Old Man in B hopes that his words of admonition may have almost sacramental efficacy: "checking thy body," to "amend thy soule." His emphasis throughout is more on love than on punishment; he has the more priestly, confessional function of guiding the erring Christian into paths of right conduct.

There is no need to belabor the arresting contrasts between the speeches in A and B: a number of recent critics have begun to find them of interest.[3] What I would like to emphasize is their correlation with more scattered elements of each version of the play. The two texts of *Doctor Faustus* contain numerous editorial "accidentals" which can be read just as easily as configurations of ideological difference. Elsewhere in the A text, sin is portrayed in the "Genevan" mode as an ingrained condition of infected will. B emphasizes outward forms and "works": sin is incorrect action prompted by enemies outside the self. Early in the play, for example, the good angel in A says "Neuer too late, if Faustus can repent" (A 708). The B version has "if *Faustus* will repent" (B 649). In A, the Old Man leaves the stage "fearing the ruine of thy hopelesse soule"; in B, it is "Fearing the enemy of thy haplesse soule." Faustus's response in A is, "Accursed Faustus, where is mercie now?" In B, it is "Accursed *Faustus*, wretch what hast thou done?" (A 1328–29, B 1842–43). Damnation in A is a matter of inward conviction—a psychic event. Faustus utters his final speech alone on a bare stage and the devils enter only at the end to carry him off. In B, his damnation is sealed through outward ceremonies. The trinity of devils descends to claim him for themselves and Mephistopheles

2. See Hunter, p. 48.
3. In addition to Warren and Hunter, cited above, see Lawrence Danson, "Christopher Marlowe: The Questioner," *English Literary Renaissance* 12 (1982): 3–29.

reveals that he maliciously "Damb'd vp" the scriptural passage that
would have promised Faustus life (B 1990). The Good and Bad Angels orchestrate a pageant of heavenly throne and hell mouth that
shows Faustus his infernal destiny in hideously graphic form. In B
also, after the devils carry him off, the scholars return to find Faustus's fragmented body on stage—the outward signs of perdition. In
A, there are no visible remnants; the stage is empty.

Even though the spirituality of A appears more strenuous and
psychologically demanding throughout, the fate of Faustus is less
unequivocally established in that version than in B. The intimate,
introspective nature of Faustus's experience in A leaves open, as it
sometimes does in Puritan spiritual biography, the (admittedly
faint) possibility of salvation even at the very last instant and beyond the power of observers to perceive. Despite the chorus's pious
final speech about Faustus's "hellish fate," which closes the play in
both A and B, more than one reader has seen in the A text a potential for Faustus's escape even at the moment of his exit to the words
"ah *Mephastophilis*" (A 1508).[4] The ways of God remain inscrutable
to the end. The B text allows no such hope: damnation is enacted
as public ritual, imprinted upon Faustus's very body. Marjorie Garber and C. L. Barber have called attention to the play's insistence
on eucharistic imagery, which is particularly prominent in the B
version of the papal banquet (B 1085–94).[5] Also in B there is far
more emphasis than in A on Faustus's bodily fragmentation as a
symptom of spiritual decline: the removable head, the false leg. At
the end of B, his fragmented body on stage suggests the state of inner fragmentation associated in conservative eucharistic doctrine
with denial of the sacrament. The 1604 text presents a man in the
throes of psychic torment; the 1616 text enacts his literal dismemberment and encodes that bodily condition with ritual significance.[6]

I do not mean to suggest that the degree of Faustus's responsibility for his fate is altogether clear in either A or B, or that either text
delivers an unequivocal doctrinal message. Interpretation based on
comparison and contrast between two texts can easily make each
look more coherent in itself than it would if not measured against a

4. See Empson; graduate students of mine at the University of Wisconsin who were exposed to both versions of the play independently recognized the same possibility, though
not on the same grounds as his.
5. Marjorie Garber, " 'Here's Nothing Writ': Scribe, Script, and Circumscription in Marlowe's Plays," *Theatre Journal* 36 (1984): 301–20, Barber, ed. Wheeler, pp. 87–130.
6. For the suggestion about bodily fragmentation and the Eucharist, I am indebted to
Sonja Weiner, personal communication, May, 1988. See also Roslyn L. Knutson, "Influence of the Repertory System on the Revival and Revision of *The Spanish Tragedy* and
Doctor Faustus," *English Literary Renaissance* 18 (1988): 257–74, especially p. 273. For
comparison of other instances of Faustus's apparent loss of body parts, see B 1412–45
(which has no counterpart in A) and compare the A and B versions of the "false leg"
episode in Greg, ed., *Parallel Texts*, pp. 260–61 and 270–73.

massively different version. I would suggest, however, echoing Warren, that if lay readers or literary critics wish to discuss *Faustus's*
handling of doctrinal issues, we would do well to distinguish A from
B, inscribed as they are with very different configurations of religious experience. Much critical energy—including Greg's—has
been wasted over murky doctrinal issues that would unravel themselves readily if the interpreter were not burdened with a composite
text.

Conversely, however, the precise cause of Faustus's damnation
becomes much clearer if one conflates A and B. Edited versions of
the play have frequently identified Faustus's kiss of Helen of Troy
as the single experience that seals his hellish fate, using as evidence
the contrasting speeches by the Old Man before and after the kiss:
before the kiss, he implies that Faustus may yet be saved; after the
kiss, he characterizes him as irrevocably damned. That interpretation cannot be made with any certainty unless A and B are combined. In A the Old Man comes to admonish Faustus about the
"loathsome filthinesse" that has led him into sin and to entice him
toward repentance. Faustus vacillates and backslides, however, calling up Helen and praising her beauty in some of the most famous
lines of the play. During his encounter with Helen in A, the Old
Man returns and remarks:

> Accursed *Faustus*, miserable man,
> That from thy soule excludst the grace of heauen,
> And flies the throne of his tribunall seate
> (A 1377–79)

Devils enter to torment the Old Man, and after a few more lines he
exits, vowing "Hence hel, for hence I flie vnto my God" (A 1386).
The Old Man's speech appears to be a judgment upon Faustus's
eventual fate, but the Old Man's opinion cannot be definitive in the
A text because in his previous speech he has already defined repentance as an internal process of transformation. As we have seen,
other elements of the A version also support that definition. In A,
conversion is a psychic event, not a set of perceivable behaviors.

The B text offers even less evidence than A that the kiss is Faustus's undoing. In B the Old Man delivers his "semi-Pelagian"
speech to Faustus as we have already discussed it above: he emphasizes good works and outward behavior as a reliable gauge of spiritual health. Faustus vacillates, then calls upon Helen as in A. *But
in B the Old Man never returns.* Standard editions of the play have
adopted the B form of the Old Man's initial speech to Faustus, thus
establishing its standard of a "religion of works," in which outward
behavior reliably signifies inward condition. But in B, the fact that
the Old Man does not reenter to identify Faustus's behavior with

Helen as an exclusion of divine grace leaves Faustus's moral status uncertain even at this late stage of the play. Much too uncertain to be tolerable for traditional editors, who conclude that the necessary lines must somehow have become "lost" from the B text. But (to adopt the intentionalist language in which the discussion has usually been carried out) what if Marlowe never intended Helen's effect on Faustus to be absolutely clear? The play offers other signs that even thereafter, Faustus was not completely lost. After Faustus's encounter with Helen, editors have typically tidied up the uncertainty by inserting the Old Man's second speech as it appears in A. In the context of the B version's religion of works, the Old Man's judgment upon Faustus's spiritual condition becomes an unequivocal assertion of his damnation.

That is the pattern of meaning adopted in Greg's reconstruction, which is based on his 1946 article contending that Faustus is damned irrevocably by committing the mortal sin of demoniality with Helen.[7] Even more ingeniously, F. S. Boas's influential earlier edition had given several lines from the Old Man's initial speech in A to Faustus himself, as a response to the Old Man's speech in B. In Boas's version, the Old Man returns, as in A, and Boas comments in a note, "If A is correct, the Old Man in the background overhears the latter part of Faustus's apostrophe to Helen, and is thus convinced of his damnation."[8] This is more tentative than Greg but equally satisfying in its symmetry and clarity. Reading audiences of the 1604 and 1616 versions of the play received no such certainty that the scene with Helen was the precise moment in which Faustus's doom was sealed. Nor, I strongly suspect, did audiences in the late sixteenth and early seventeenth-century theater.

Is Greg necessarily correct in identifying Helen as a devil? In his and most other modern editions, the scene with Helen is editorially shaped to give us the seduction of Eve all over again, except that the temptress is not only inspired by a demon (as Eve was) but has become a demon herself. "Bad" texts, it would seem, can sometimes become acceptable if they confirm ancient wisdom about the danger of the feminine. Marlovian editors like Greg and Boas have willingly adopted elements of the "corrupt" and vilified A text if those elements help to tilt the play's meaning toward a desired clarity about the stages of Faustus's decline. But the clarity thus achieved is, in all likelihood, an artifact of twentieth-century rather than Renaissance sensibilities.

7. W. W. Greg, "The Damnation of Faustus," *Modern Language Review* 41 (1946): 97–107, reprinted in Clifford Leach, ed., *Marlowe: A Collection of Critical Essays* (Englewood Cliffs, New Jersey: Prentice Hall, 1964), pp. 92–107, and in Greg's *Collected Papers*, ed. J. C. Maxwell (Oxford: Clarendon Press, 1966), pp. 349–65.
8. Frederick S. Boas, ed., *The Tragical History of Doctor Faustus*, vol. 5 of R. H. Case, ed., *The Works and Life of Christopher Marlowe* (London: Methuen, 1932), pp. 163–64 n.

The "forme of *Faustus* fortunes good or bad" is, as I have tried to argue, differently shaped in the A and B texts in part because the two texts place such different valuations upon inward spiritual experience and ecclesiastical "forms." Perhaps because of *Doctor Faustus*'s highly loaded theological subject matter, the idea of original textual unity is particularly hard to resist for this play. In the early scene in which he gave up theology for magic, Faustus's mistake was to trust the literal words of a text as he read them on the page: "*Stipendium peccati, mors est*: ha . . . / The reward of sin is death; that's hard" (A 69–70; cited from B 66–67). He has, of course, cited the first part of Romans 6:23 but neglected the rest; further on in the speech, he similarly overlooks the second half of 1 John 1:8. In the A version of the play, we never know whether this blindness is the result of his own prejudice or of demonic tampering with the text. In the B version, however, he is manifestly the victim of Mephistopheles' textual contamination: the devil confesses that he "damb'd vp" the passages that promised Faustus life eternal (B 1990). Faustus has been betrayed by the material text before his eyes. The perceptible surface pattern of a book is posited as untrustworthy. Within the milieu of the B version of *Doctor Faustus*, the editorial task of filling in gaps to create a more reliable "original" becomes a praiseworthy undoing of demonic influence. God, his scripture, and his creation are unified and self-identical; it is the devil and demonic texts that are legion.

*   *   *

ERIC RASMUSSEN

The Nature of the B-Text†

Time's glory is . . .
To blot old books and alter their contents.
Shakespeare, *The Rape of Lucrece*

In 1600, Nottingham's Men (formerly the Admiral's Men) left the Rose, moved into the newly-built Fortune, and revived several old plays as showcases for Edward Alleyn who emerged from retirement to inaugurate the new playhouse. Revival was apparently accompanied by revision. In 1602, Henslowe records payments of £2 and part of £10 to 'bengemy Johnsone . . . for new adicyons for Jeronymo' and £4 to 'wm Bvrde & Samwell Rowle for ther adicy-

† From *A Textual Companion to Doctor Faustus* (Manchester and New York: Manchester University Press, 1993), pp. 40–46, 56–57. Reprinted with the permission of the author.

ones in docter fostes'.[1] Later that same year, Thomas Pavier published 'The Spanish Tragedy . . . Newly corrected, amended, and enlarged with new additions of the Painters part, and others, as it hath of late been diuers times acted'. This quarto introduced five additional passages, totalling 320 lines. In 1616, John Wright published a new edition of *Doctor Faustus*, the 'B-text' (advertised in 1619 as 'With new Additions'), that included seven new passages, expanding the text by some 676 lines.

It is certainly something of a rarity to have extant not only the records of payments for changes to two major texts, but (apparently) the changed texts as well. Although early editors assumed that the later texts of both plays preserved the additional passages mentioned by Henslowe, textual critics in the 1950s—who set out to 'seek simplicity and distrust it'[2]—found this situation was too good to be true. The Revels editor of *The Spanish Tragedy* seriously doubted that the 1602 additions were written by Jonson; and Greg concluded that 'none of the passages peculiar to [*Faustus*] B represent the additions paid for by Henslowe in 1602'.[3] More recent criticism has rediscovered simplicity. In 1984, Anne Barton argued persuasively that Pavier's additions were, in fact, those written by Jonson for Henslowe,[4] and, following the publication in 1973 of Bowers's 'Marlowe's *Doctor Faustus*: The 1602 Additions', most Marlowe scholars now believe that the B-text differs from the A-text mainly because it includes the Birde-Rowley 'adicyones'.[5]

The critical debate has tended to focus on questions of how much revision Henslowe would have expected for his money, and how valuable these new additions would then be both to the acting company and to the publishers. Greg confidently asserted that 'it is not at all likely that the Admiral's company, having paid a considerable sum for giving the play fresh attractions on the stage, would willingly have released the additions to the press' (*Parallel Texts*, p. 30). But Bowers countered with 'the inherent improbability that in 1616 John Wright would put out a new text . . . that would not include the substantial £4's worth of added 1602 matter' (*Complete Works*, ii.131–2). These rival claims, which effectively cancel each other out, demonstrate the

1. *Henslowe's Diary*, pp. 182, 203, 206. Roslyn L. Knutson provides a useful discussion of the relationship between commercial interests and the refurbishment of old scripts in 'Influence of the Repertory System on the Revival and Revision of *The Spanish Tragedy* and *Dr. Faustus*', *ELR*, XVIII (1988), 257–74. See also Carol Chillington Rutter, ed., *Documents of the Rose Playhouse*, The Revels Plays Companion Library (Manchester University Press, 1984), pp. 193–4.
2. Greg opens his *Parallel Texts* edition with this 'happy aphorism' of Whitehead's (p. vii).
3. Philip Edwards, ed. *The Spanish Tragedy* (London: Methuen, 1959), pp. lxi–lxvi; Greg, *Parallel Texts*, p. 26.
4. *Ben Jonson, Dramatist* (Cambridge University Press, 1984), pp. 1–15.
5. See Roma Gill, review of Bowers's *Christopher Marlowe: The Complete Works* in *RES*, n.s. XXV (1974), 459–64; Kuriyama, 'Dr. Greg and *Doctor Faustus*: The Supposed Originality of the 1616 Text'; Warren, '*Doctor Faustus*: The Old Man and the Text'.

limitations of attempting to resolve the issue with unprovable assertions of relative probabilities concerning external circumstances. A
more fruitful approach may be to concentrate on the internal evidence presented by the 676 lines that are unique to the B-text, and
see if it leads us to the Fortune playhouse in 1602.

The Additions

The seven passages that appear for the first time in the B-text of
Faustus are these:

(1) III.i.54–201 and III.ii.1–56 [verse]
   The rescue of Bruno, the rival Pope.
(2) IV.i.1–47 [verse and prose]
   The introduction of the new characters Frederick, Martino,
   and Benvolio.
(3) IV.ii and IV.iii [verse]
   Benvolio's revenge and Faustus's retaliation.
(4) IV.v and IV.vi.36–125 [prose]
   The Clowns in the tavern and their interruption at Vanholt.
(5) V.ii.1–23 [verse]
   Lucifer, Beelzebub, and Mephistopheles gloat over Faustus's
   imminent doom, after which Faustus and Wagner have a
   short interchange.
(6) V.ii.104–37 [verse]
   The Good and Bad Angel and their visions of heaven and
   hell.
(7) V.iii [verse]
   The scholars' discovery of Faustus's mangled body.

Interestingly, Samuel Rowley's authorship of part of the B-text has
never been in doubt. One of the striking features of the first B-text
passage, III.i–ii, is the extensive use of adjectives in -al to end verse
lines: *state pontifical* (III.i.91), *statues decretal* (l. 104), *authority
apostolical* (l. 144), *blessing apostolical* (l. 194). H. Dugdale Sykes
pointed out that this stylistic habit was characteristic of Rowley,
and noted four instances in Rowley's only extant play *When You See
Me, You Know Me* (1605): *pompe pontificall* (sig. A3r), *blessing Ap-
postolicall* (C4r), *pompe imperiall* (E4r), and *treason Cappitall*
(I4r);[6] Greg found another example, *Deitie supernall* (sig. G4r).[7]
(For the sake of completeness, we might add *nobilitie temporall*
(sig. H1r) as well, although this does not end a verse line.) A fur-

---

6. H. Dugdale Sykes, 'The Authorship of *The Taming of A Shrew, The Famous Victories of
   Henry V*, and the Additions to Marlowe's *Faustus*', in *Sidelights on Elizabethan Drama*
   (Oxford University Press, 1924), pp. 49–78, esp. 65–6.
7. *Parallel Texts*, pp. 133–4. See F. P. Wilson's Malone Society edition (Oxford, 1952).

ther link between Rowley and this B-text passage was then established by Leslie Oliver, who discovered that the Bruno scene derives from John Foxe's *Acts and Monuments*, the same source from which Rowley drew the Lutheran intrigue scenes in *When You See Me, You Know Me*.[8]

Greg concluded that Rowley could have been the original collaborator with Marlowe. Bowers, on the other hand, rightly points out that Rowley's special characteristics are found only in the scenes that are unique to the B-text and never in the work of Marlowe's original collaborator in scenes common to both texts.[9] Moreover, Bowers finds other stylistic evidence, such as the liberal use of rhymed couplets, that sets the unique B-scenes apart from the scenes where the A-text and B-text are textually close, adding to the overall impression that these passages are additions to the original play.[1] Bowers's conclusions have been further substantiated by David Lake, who observes that the additional passages contain three instances of the contraction *i'the*, a form that was extremely rare before 1599; thus, Lake concludes that the additions appear to date from the early seventeenth century.[2]

The converging evidence of Rowley's characteristics in the unique B-text Bruno scenes, the use of Foxe as a source, and the appearance of Rowley's name in Henslowe's record—combined with the evidence that the unique B-scenes are in fact later additions—make it appear likely that these particular scenes (III.i.54–201; III.ii.1–56) were commissioned by Henslowe and written by Rowley in 1602.[3] Still, it does not by any means follow that all of the additional passages were therefore written by Rowley. Bowers contends that 'the best test for the author of the new material is his penchant for rhyming couplets'. Although the unique B-text material is, indeed, heavily laden with couplets, the presence of rhymed couplets in both B III.i and B IV.ii–iii is not enough to justify Bowers's conclusion that 'little doubt can exist that these two

8. 'Rowley, Foxe, and the *Faustus* Additions', *MLN*, LX (1945), 391–4.
9. *Complete Works*, ii.133; 'Marlowe's *Doctor Faustus*: The 1602 Additions', 15n.
1. *Complete Works*, ii.133. However, Bowers misleadingly asserts that 'nowhere else in the play, whether in A or in B, is there a single couplet'. There are, in fact, a number of rhymed couplets in the original play: *please/these* and *scroll/soul* appear in Marlowe's portion of both texts (A II.i.86–7, 89–90; B II.i.86–9), as does *hell/hell* (A III.i.84–5; B III.ii.93–4); see also *bray/day* (A III.i.86–7) and the concluding *wits/permits* (Epilogue, 7–8).
2. 'Three Seventeenth-Century Revisions: *Thomas of Woodstock*, *The Jew of Malta*, and *Faustus B*', *N&Q*, n.s. XXX (1983), 133–43, esp. 143.
3. Kuriyama's evidence for Rowley's hand in the additions ('Dr. Greg and *Doctor Faustus*: The Supposed Originality of the 1616 Text', 191–6) reiterates Sykes's arguments that a number of phrases ('I warrant you', 'O brave', 'much ado') shared by the B-text additions and *When You See Me, You Know Me* serve to link *Faustus* and Rowley. But, as John Jump observes, these particular phrases 'were surely the commonest of common property' (*Doctor Faustus* (London: Methuen, 1962), p. xliv). Kuriyama seems unaware of the serious doubts cast upon Sykes's methodology by, among others, E. H. C. Oliphant in 'How Not to Play the Game of Parallels', *JEGP*, XXVIII (1929), 1–15.

scenes [IV.ii–iii] are the work of the author of the additions and revisions in III.i'.[4] Obviously, Rowley was not the only playwright in
the period who sometimes wrote in rhymed couplets. And, save for
the use of couplets, the other unique B-text passages are, stylisti-
cally, somewhat different from the Bruno scenes. For instance, only
one *-al* verse line ending is found elsewhere in the additions, *state
majestical* (IV.i.77);[5] a single occurrence can not be taken as a clear
sign of Rowley's authorship, especially when we remember that
Marlowe himself uses *demonstrations magical* in *Faustus* (A I.i.152;
B I.i.144) and *science metaphysical* in *2 Tamburlaine* (IV.ii.63).

One distinguishing feature of the additional scenes IV.i.1–47,
IV.ii–iii, and V.ii is the relative frequency with which a partial verse
line is completed by the opening part line of a new speech by a different character. This type of completion occurs ten times in these
235 added lines: IV.i.38, IV.ii.38, 44, 94, IV.iii.1, 11, V.ii.7, 21, 106,
109. In the 203 additional lines of the Bruno scenes attributed to
Rowley, there is only one shared verse line (III.i.89), and there is, at
most, one such divided line in Marlowe's original.[6] The evidence of
-al endings and divided verse lines is substantial and consistent
enough to make probable the conclusion that while Rowley may
have written the additions in III.i–ii, the additional verse scenes
IV.i–iii, and V.ii were probably written by someone else.

This other playwright (or playwrights) also seems to have been
responsible for the additional prose scenes. A recurring phrase links
the prose additions, IV.v and IV.vi.36–125, to IV.i. Nowhere in the
original text or in Rowley's additions is Faustus referred to as 'the
doctor'. The phrase does occur, however, twice in IV.i (lines 28 and
139), several times in the additional prose scenes under consideration (IV.v.54, 59, IV.vi.109), and in the short final verse scene
(V.iii.5). The playwright responsible for these added scenes may
have been the rather shadowy figure William Birde (alias 'Borne')
who apparently collaborated with Rowley on the lost play *Judas* for
Nottingham's Men late in 1601.[7] Although the new B-text passages
are now commonly referred to as the 'Birde-Rowley' additions, the
only evidence we have for linking them with Birde is Henslowe's
payment. Lacking any of Birde's identifiable writing, we have no
way of proving or disproving his authorship of any part of *Faustus*.

---

4. Bowers, 'Marlowe's *Doctor Faustus*: The 1602 Additions', 7.
5. This scene is technically not an addition but a revision of an existing scene in the original. The distinction will be discussed in the next section.
6. Boas, followed by several other editors, aligns A II.iii.43–4 (B II.iii.42–3) so that
   Mephistopheles and Faustus share a verse line 'Feigned, but are erring stars. / But have
   they all'. In the opinion of the present Revels editors, however, this was not Marlowe's
   intention.
7. *Henslowe's Diary*, p. 185.

The Revisions

Bowers speculates that, along with inserting new passages, Birde and Rowley may have substantially revised some of the original scenes. Although he approaches the 'question of less identifiable revision' more cautiously than the 'readily isolated new additions', Bowers points to these apparently revised scenes and episodes:[8]

(1) The Robin/Rafe scenes (A II.ii, III.ii) are heavily revised (B II.ii, III.iii), and Rafe is renamed Dick.
(2) III.Chorus is expanded.
(3) The scene with the German Emperor (A IV.i) is rewritten, Bruno is incorporated, and the 'injurious knight' is given the name Benvolio (B IV.i).
(4) Material from the original Horse-courser episode (A IV.i. 109–85) is transferred to the added scene of the Clowns at the tavern (B IV.v.35–54).
(5) Wagner's soliloquy (A V.i.1–8) is revised (B V.i.1–9).
(6) The Old Man's speech (A V.i.36–47) is heavily revised (B V.i.35–51), and his attack by devils is cut from the end of the scene (A V.i.111–19).

Bowers's admirably detailed analysis of these revisions stops short of claiming that Birde–Rowley went through and revised the entire play. Instead, Bowers continues to assume that in some of the scenes where there is only minor variation between the two texts, the differences are due to memorial corruption in the A-text. Yet, as I pointed out in the first chapter, in the brief passage concerning the Duchess of Vanholt and the grapes (A IV.ii.1–38; B IV.vi.1–35)—one of the scenes in which Bowers takes the variants to be due to corruption rather than revision—it is the A-text that is both closer to the source material and echoed in *The Taming of a Shrew*, leaving little doubt that the A-text preserves the original version of this scene and that its variant readings have independent authority. How then did equally intelligible variants find their way into the B-text?

Once again, the *Sir Thomas More* manuscript offers a useful glimpse into the mechanics of play revision in the Renaissance theatre. The analogue is particularly apt in that the dates of the original composition and later revision of *More* are, coincidentally, approximately the same as those of *Faustus*; More was originally written *c*. 1592 and the additions to the manuscript appear to date from *c*. 1603.[9] For the most part, the *More* revisers did not make

---

8. 'Marlowe's *Doctor Faustus*: The 1602 Additions', 11; *Complete Works*, ii.134–5.
9. The *More* dates are those adduced by Scott McMillin in *The Elizabethan Theatre and The Book of Sir Thomas More* (Ithaca: Cornell University Press, 1987), pp. 53–95.

their revisions and alterations on Munday's original manuscript, but re-transcribed entire scenes. Dekker copied out one of Munday's scenes from fol. 11v on to fol. 12r, and made a few minor changes. Another reviser, known only as 'Hand B', cancelled an entire scene of Munday's on fol. 5r and then transcribed it on to another page, fol. 7r, adding nine short speeches for a new character in the process.[1]

'Few authors can resist the opportunity to revise during the course of copying', writes Bowers.[2] E. A. J. Honigmann presents a book-length study aimed at demonstrating that 'little verbal changes, not necessarily always for the better' would come freely from the pen of a Renaissance playwright 'when the process of copying refired his mind'.[3] What is not always acknowledged, however, is that someone other than the original author might also introduce verbal changes while copying; the example of Dekker's revision of Munday's scene in *More* (discussed in Chapter 1) provides clear evidence of this. In making their additions and alterations, the reviser(s) who worked on *Faustus* may have copied out much of the text, and in so doing, intentionally or accidentally, introduced numerous verbal changes.

Lake points out that the revisers have left apparent traces even in passages that they were not necessarily rewriting. In the scene of Wagner and the Clown, the A-text reads 'I'll none of them' (I.iv.42), but the B-text has 'I'll none of 'em' (I.iv.31). The same change is made in the scene with the scholars: 'they hold them, they hold them' (A V.ii.33–4), becomes 'they hold 'em, they hold 'em' (B V.ii.62–3). According to Lake, 'this use of *'em* in a non-comic context is quite foreign to sixteenth-century usage, and reflects the Jonsonian revolution of 1599–1600'. It is difficult to reconcile Bowers's position, that these two scenes were not subjected to later revision, with Lake's conclusion, that these contractions 'point clearly to a post-1600 revision',[4] unless we posit some sort of transcriptional stage, which need not have amounted to a substantive revision, but in which minor changes might have been introduced. Such a fair copy transcript might have been necessary after the revisers had finished making their extensive cancellations, alterations, and insertions in the original play manuscript. And since we have some evidence that Henslowe would pay his playwrights only for fair copy scripts, it may

1. I suggest a possible motive for this revision in 'Setting Down What the Clown Spoke: Improvisation, Hand B, and *The Book of Sir Thomas More*', *The Library*, 6th. ser., XIII (1991), 126–36.
2. *On Editing Shakespeare* (Charlottesville: The University Press of Virginia, 1966), p. 19.
3. *The Stability of Shakespeare's Text* (London: Edward Arnold, 1965).
4. Lake, 'Three Seventeenth-Century Revisions: *Thomas of Woodstock, The Jew of Malta,* and *Faustus B*', 143.

be that a fair copy of *Faustus* was made by the revisers themselves.[5]

Sources of the B-Text Readings

Bowers and Kuriyama both assume that the alterations in the B-text
reflect a single revision undertaken in 1602. However, *Faustus* probably continued to be performed for more than a decade before the B-
text was printed in 1616. It is certainly possible that the text could
have been further revised at any time during this period.[6] If the B-
text additions were indeed composed sometime in 1602 or after, we
might expect them to show some indebtedness to sources that could
not have influenced the A-text because they had not yet been written.
To demonstrate that the unique B-text material could not have been
part of the original play, Bowers points to an apparent echo of Shakespeare in one of the additions. 'He took his rouse with stoups of
Rhenish wine' (B IV.i.19) may be compared with *Hamlet* I.iv.8–10:

> The King doth wake tonight and takes his rouse,
> Keeps wassail, and the swagg'ring upspring reels;
> And as he drains his draughts of Rhenish down . . .

Bowers seems not to have been aware that Greg had noticed the resemblance previously and declared that the *Faustus* passage 'must
be the earlier' (*Parallel Texts*, p. 362). In any case, Bowers, who
contends that the line is 'clearly a borrowing from *Hamlet*', concludes that this addition must have been written after the stage
production of *Hamlet* in 1600–1; Bowers opts for 1602, the date of
Henslowe's payment (*Complete Works*, ii.137).

Another previously unrecognized echo from Shakespeare, however, suggests that the date for one addition might be even later.
Benvolio's comment at B IV.ii.27, 'But yet my heart's more ponderous than my head', has the appearance of being an echo of Cor-
delia's aside in the Folio version of *King Lear*:

> And yet not so, since I am sure my love's
> More ponderous than my tongue.
>
> (I.i76–7; TLN 83–4)

The Quarto *Lear* version of these lines is significantly different:

> & yet not so, since I am sure
> My loues more richer then my tongue
>
> (sig. B2r)

---

5. See Bowers, *On Editing Shakespeare*, p. 15.
6. As Bentley notes, 'if a play had sufficient theatrical appeal to be kept in the repertory of
an Elizabethan, Jacobean, or Caroline acting company, it was normal for the text to be
revised for at least one of the revivals' (*The Profession of Dramatist in Shakespeare's Time*,
p. 263).

King Lear was first performed in 1606, but the revised version preserved in the Folio may not have been written until 1609–10.[7]
Shakespeare may, of course, be the debtor here. But if the phrase
was original with Shakespeare, then this addition to *Faustus* could
not have been written before 1606, and may be as late as 1609–10.
This late date of composition gains some small reinforcement from
the fact that the *Damnable Life*, from which the Benvolio scenes
draw heavily, was reprinted (perhaps for the first time since 1592)
in 1608. . . .

*   *   *

Conclusions

In 1602, Henslowe paid two playwrights to write additions for *Doctor Faustus*. Samuel Rowley, perhaps working in concert with
William Birde, extensively revised the original script. The text may
have been subjected to further revision at any point during the next
fourteen years; it was certainly expurgated of profanity, probably
some time after 1606. In 1616 (or shortly before), it seems that the
publisher John Wright had access to a composite manuscript that
contained all of the latest revisions and additions. Wright apparently had a transcript made with the aid of the printed version of
the play available in the A3 quarto, and it was from this transcript
that the B1 quarto was set into type.

---

7. The dates are those adduced by Taylor in '*King Lear*: The Date and Authorship of the
   Folio Version', in *The Division of the Kingdoms: Shakespeare's Two Versions of 'King Lear'*,
   pp. 351–468.

Early Performance

Philip Henslowe

Philip Henslowe's Diary[1] lists twenty-three performances of *Doctor Faustus* between September 30, 1594, and mid-October 1597. A characteristic entry reads:

¶9 of octob3 1594   Rd at docter ffostus . . . . . xxxxiiijs

The diary also has an inventory of props and clothing owned by the Lord Admiral's men. Two items refer specifically to productions of *Faustus*:

1. Inventory of props and apparel for the Lord Admiral's Men, 10 March 1598:

   Item, iij tymbrells, j dragon in fostes.

2. An undated inventory (probably 1602), in a section on the company's holdings of "Jerkings and Doublets" [i.e., vests and jackets]:

   17   faustus Jerkin his clok

Thomas Middleton

1604: T[homas]. M[iddleton]. *The Black Book* (London, 1604), sig. B4[r].

> Hee had a head of hayre like one of my Diuells in Doctor *Faustus* when the old Theater crackt and frighted the Audience.

---

1. *Henslowe's Diary*, ed. R. A. Foakes and R. T. Rickert (Cambridge: Cambridge University Press, 1961).

Anonymous

Early seventeenth century (?): A manuscript note in a book owned by J. G. R. and published by Thomas Vautollier (a French refugee publisher active in London and Edinburgh, 1562–87):

> Certain Players at Exeter, acting upon the stage the tragical storie of Dr. Faustus the Conjurer; as a certain nomber of Devels kept everie one his circle there, and as Faustus was busie in his magicall invocations, on a sudden they were all dasht, every one harkning other in the eare, for they were all perswaded, there was one devell too many amongst them; and so after a little pause desired the people to pardon them, they could go no further with this matter; the people also understanding the thing as it was, every man hastened to be first out of dores. The players (as I heard it) contrarye to their custome spending the night in reading and in prayer got them out of town the next morning.

John Melton

1620: John Melton, *Astrolagaster* (London, 1620), sig. E4^r.

> Another will fore-tell of Lightning and Thunder that shall happen such a day, when there are no such Inflamations seene, except men go to the *Fortune* [Theater] in *Golding-Lane* to see the Tragedie of Doctor *Faustus*: There indeede a man may behold shagge-hayr'd deuills runne roaring ouer the Stage with Squibs in their mouthes, while Drummers make thunder in the Tyring-house, and the twelue-penny Hirelings make artificial Lightning in the Heauens.

William Prynne

1633: William Prynne, *Histrio-mastix* (London, 1633), sig. ggg*4^r.

> the visible apparition of the Devill on the Stage at the Belsavage Play-house, in Queene Elizabeths dayes (to the great amazement both of the Actors and Spectators) whiles they were there prophanely playing the History of *Faustus* (*the truth of which I have herd from many now alive, who well remember it*) there being some distracted with that fearful sight.

The Faust Legend

ANONYMOUS

The source of Marlowe's play is an English translation of the anonymous *Historia von D. Johann Fausten, dem weitbeschreyten Zauberer
und Schwartkünstler*, published in 1587 in Frankfurt, and usually
known as the "Faustbuch." The earliest known English version was
published in London in 1592 by Thomas Orwin, the work of an anonymous translator identified only as "P. F., Gent." This seemingly places
the date of Marlowe's play sometime after that, composed sometime in
the year before his death in 1593. An earlier edition, however, must
have existed (the title page says that the 1592 edition was "Newly imprinted, and in conuenient places imperfect matter amended"), and indeed it seems that a translation was available at least by 1589, when
one appears in the inventory of possessions of Matthew Parkin, an Oxford scholar who died at twenty-one.[1] The following selections are
taken from Orwin's 1592 edition. The spelling and punctuation have
been modernized.

From The History of the Damnable Life and Deserved Death of Doctor John Faustus

Of his parentage and birth. Chap. 1

John Faustus, born in the town of Rhode, lying in the province of
Weimar in Germany, his father a poor husbandman and not able
well to bring him up, but having an uncle at Wittenberg, a rich man
and without issue, took this J. Faustus from his father and made
him his heir, in so much that his father was no more troubled with
him, for he remained with his uncle at Wittenberg where he was
kept at the university in the same city to study divinity. But Faustus,
being of a naughty mind and otherwise addicted, applied not his
studies but took himself to other exercises, the which his uncle oftentimes hearing, rebuked him for it as Eli oft times rebuked his
children for sinning against the Lord. Even so this good man la-

---

1. See R. J. Fehrenbach, "A Pre-1592 English Faust Book and the Date of Marlowe's *Doctor Faustus*," *The Library*, 7th ser., 2, (2001): 327–35.

bored to have Faustus apply his study of divinity that he might come to the knowledge of God and his laws. But it is manifest that many virtuous parents have wicked children, as Cain, Reuben, Absalom, and such like have been to their parents, so this Faustus having godly parents, and seeing him to be of a toward wit, were very desirous to bring him up in those virtuous studies, namely, of divinity. But he gave himself secretly to study necromancy and conjuration, in so much that few or none could perceive his profession.

But to the purpose. Faustus continued at study in the university and was by the rectors and sixteen masters afterwards examined how he had profited in his studies. And being found by them that none for his time were able to argue with him in divinity or for the excellency of his wisdom to compare with him, with one consent they made him Doctor of Divinity. But Doctor Faustus, within short time after he had obtained his degree, fell into such fantasies and deep cogitations that he was marked of many, and of the most part of the students was called the Speculator. And sometimes he would throw the Scriptures from him as though he had no care of his former profession, so that he began a very ungodly life, as hereafter more at large may appear. For the old proverb sayeth, Who can hold that will away? So, who can hold Faustus from the devil, that seeks after him with all his endeavor? For he accompanied himself with divers that were seen in those devilish arts and that had the Chaldean, Persian, Hebrew, Arabian, and Greek tongues, using figures, characters, conjurations, incantations, with many other ceremonies belonging to these infernal arts, as necromancy, charms, soothsaying, witchcraft, enchantment, being delighted with their books, words, and names so well that he studied day and night therein, in so much that he could not abide to be called Doctor of Divinity but waxed a worldly man and named himself an astrologian and a mathematician, and for a shadow sometimes a physician, and did great cures, namely with herbs, roots, waters, drinks, receipts, and clysters. And without doubt he was passing wise, and excellent perfect in the holy Scriptures, but he that knoweth his master's will and doth it not, is worthy to be beaten with many stripes. It is written, "No man can serve two masters," and "Thou shalt not tempt the Lord thy God." But Faustus threw all this in the wind and made his soul of no estimation, regarding more his worldly pleasure than the joys to come. Therefore at the day of judgment there is no hope of his redemption.

How Doctor Faustus began to practice in his devilish art, and
how he conjured the devil, making him to appear and meet him
on the morrow at his own house. Chap. 2.

You have heard before that all Faustus' mind was set to study the
arts of necromancy and conjuration, the which exercise he followed
day and night; and taking to him the wings of an eagle thought to fly
over the whole world and to know the secrets of heaven and earth.
For his speculation was so wonderful, being expert in using his vo-
cabula, figures, characters, conjurations, and other ceremonial actions, that in all the haste he put in practice to bring the devil before
him. And taking his way to a thick wood near to Wittenberg called in
the German tongue Spisser Wald, that is in English the Spissers
Wood (as Faustus would oftentimes boast of it among his crew being
in his jollity), he came into the same wood toward evening into a
crossway, where he made with a wand a circle in the dust, and
within that many more circles and characters. And thus he passed
away the time until it was nine or ten of the clock in the night. Then
began Doctor Faustus to call for Mephistopheles the spirit, and to
charge him in the name of Beelzebub to appear there personally
without any long stay. Then presently the devil began so great a ru-
mor in the wood as if heaven and earth would have come together
with wind, the trees bowing their tops to the ground. Then fell the
devil to blare as if the whole wood had been full of lions, and suddenly about the circle ran the devil as if a thousand wagons had
been running together on paved stones. After this, at the four corners of the wood it thundered horribly with such lightnings as if the
whole world, to his seeming, had been on fire. Faustus all this while
half amazed at the devil's so long tarrying, and doubting whether he
were best to abide any more such horrible conjurings, thought to
leave his circle and depart. Whereupon the devil made him such
music of all sorts as if the nymphs themselves had been in place,
whereat Faustus was revived and stood stoutly in his circle aspecting
his purpose and began again to conjure the spirit Mephistopheles in
the name of the prince of devils to appear in his likeness, whereat
suddenly over his head hung hovering in the air a mighty dragon.
Then calls Faustus again after his devilish manner, at which there
was a monstrous cry in the wood as if hell had been open and all the
tormented souls crying to God for mercy. Presently not three fath-
oms above his head fell a flame in manner of a lightning and
changed itself into a globe, yet Faustus feared it not but did persuade himself that the devil should give him his request before he
would leave. Oftentimes after to his companions he would boast
that he had the stoutest head (under the cope of heaven) at commandment, whereat they answered they knew none stouter than the

Pope or Emperor. But Doctor Faustus said "The head that is my servant is above all on earth," and repeated certain words out of Saint Paul to the Ephesians to make his argument good: The prince of this world is upon earth and under heaven. Well, let us come again to his conjuration where we left him at his fiery globe. Faustus, vexed at the spirit's so long tarrying, used his charms with full purpose not to depart before he had his intent, and crying on Mephistopheles the spirit. Suddenly the globe opened and sprang up in height of a man; so burning a time, in the end it converted to the shape of a fiery man. This pleasant beast ran about the circle a great while and lastly appeared in manner of a gray friar, asking Faustus what was his request. Faustus commanded that the next morning at twelve of the clock he should appear to him at his house, but the devil would in no wise grant. Faustus began again to conjure him, in the name of Beelzebub, that he should fulfill his request, whereupon the spirit agreed, and so they departed each one his way.

The conference of Doctor Faustus with the spirit Mephistopheles the morning following at his own house. Chap. 3.

Doctor Faustus having commanded the spirit to be with him, at his hour appointed he came and appeared in his chamber, demanding of Faustus what his desire was. Then began Doctor Faustus anew with him to conjure him that he should be obedient unto him, and to answer him certain articles, and to fulfill them in all points.

1 That the spirit should serve him and be obedient unto him in all things that he asked of him from that hour until the hour of his death.

2 Farther, anything that he desired of him he should bring it to him.

3 Also, that in all Faustus' demands or interrogations, the spirit should tell him nothing but that which is true.

Hereupon the spirit answered and laid his case forth, that he had no such power of himself until he had first given his prince (that was ruler over him) to understand thereof and to know if he could obtain so much of his Lord. "Therefore speak farther that I may do thy whole desire to my prince, for it is not in my power to fulfill without his leave." "Show me the cause why," said Faustus. The spirit answered, "Faustus, thou shalt understand that with us it is even as well a kingdom as with you on earth. Yea, we have our rulers and servants, as I myself am one, and we name our whole number the legion; for although that Lucifer is thrust and fallen out of heaven through his pride and high mind, yet he hath notwithstanding a legion of devils at his commandment that we call the oriental princes; for his power is great and infinite. Also there is an host in meridie, in septentrio, in occidente; and for that Lucifer hath his kingdom under heaven, we must change and give ourselves unto men to serve them at their pleasure. It is also certain, we have never as yet opened unto any man the truth of our dwelling, neither of our ruling, neither what our power is; neither have we given any man any gift or learned him anything except he promise to be ours."

Doctor Faustus, upon this, arose where he sat and said, "I will have my request, and yet I will not be damned." The spirit answered, "Then shalt thou want thy desire, and yet art thou mine notwithstanding. If any man would detain thee it is in vain, for thine infidelity hath confounded thee."

Hereupon spake Faustus, "Get thee hence from me, and take Saint Valentine's farewell and Crisam with thee, yet I conjure thee that thou be here at evening, and bethink thyself on that I have asked thee, and ask thy prince's counsel therein." Mephistopheles the spirit thus answered, vanished away, leaving Faustus in his study, where he sat pondering with himself how he might obtain his request of the devil without loss of his soul. Yet fully he was resolved in himself, rather than to want his pleasure, to do whatsoever the spirit and his lord should condition upon.

The second time of the spirit's appearing to Faustus in his house, and of their parley. Chap. 4.

Faustus continuing in his devilish cogitations, never moving out of the place where the spirit left him (such was his fervent love to the devil), the night approaching, this swift-flying spirit appeared to Faustus, offering himself with all submission to his service, with full authority from his prince to do whatsoever he would request if so be Faustus would promise to be his. "This answer I bring thee, and an answer must thou make by me again, yet will I hear what is thy desire because thou hast sworn me to be here at this time." Doctor Faustus gave him this answer, though faintly (for his soul's sake), that his request was none other but to become a devil, or at the least a limb of him, and that the spirit should agree unto these articles as followeth.

1 That he might be a spirit in shape and quality.

2 That Mephistopheles should be his servant and at his commandment.

3 That Mephistopheles should bring him anything, and do for him whatsoever.

4 That at all times he should be in his house, invisible to all men except only to himself, and at his commandment to show himself.

5 Lastly, that Mephistopheles should at all times appear at his command, in what form or shape soever he would.

Upon these points the spirit answered Doctor Faustus that all this should be granted him and fulfilled and more if he would agree unto him upon certain articles as followeth.

First, that Doctor Faustus should give himself to his Lord Lucifer, body and soul.

Secondly, for confirmation of the same he should make him a writing, written with his own blood.

Thirdly, that he would be an enemy to all Christian people.

Fourthly, that he would deny his Christian belief.

Fifthly, that he let not any man change his opinion, if so be any man should go about to dissuade or withdraw him from it.

Further, the spirit promised Faustus to give him certain years to live in health and pleasure, and when such years were expired that then Faustus should be fetched away; and if he should hold these articles and conditions that then he should have all whatsoever his heart would wish or desire; and that Faustus should quickly perceive himself to be a spirit in all manner of actions whatsoever. Hereupon Doctor Faustus' mind was so inflamed that he forgot his soul and promised Mephistopheles to hold all things as he had mentioned them. He thought the devil was not so black as they used to paint him, nor hell so hot as the people say, etc.

The third parley between Doctor Faustus and Mephistopheles about a conclusion. Chap. 5.

After Doctor Faustus had made his promise to the devil, in the morning betimes he called the spirit before him and commanded him that he should always come to him like a friar, after the order of Saint Francis, with a bell in his hand like Saint Anthony, and to ring it once or twice before he appeared, that he might know of his certain coming. Then Faustus demanded the spirit, what was his name? The spirit answered, "My name is as thou sayest, Mephistopheles, and I am a prince, but servant to Lucifer; and all the circuit from Septentrio to the Meridian I rule under him." Even at these words was this wicked wretch Faustus inflamed, to hear himself to have gotten so great a potentate to be his servant; forgot the Lord his maker and Christ his redeemer; became an enemy unto all mankind. Yea, worse than the giants whom the poets feign to climb the hills to make war with the gods, not unlike that enemy of God and his Christ that for his pride was cast into hell, so likewise Faustus forgot that the high climbers catch the greatest falls and that the sweetest meat requires the sourest sauce.

After a while, Faustus promised Mephistopheles to write and make his obligation, with full assurance of the articles in the chapter before rehearsed. A pitiful case, Christian reader, for certainly this letter or obligation was found in his house after his most lamentable end, with all the rest of his damnable practices used in his whole life. Therefore I wish all Christians to take an example by this wicked Faustus and to be comforted in Christ, contenting themselves with that vocation whereunto it hath pleased God to call them, and not to esteem the vain delights of this life, as did this unhappy Faustus in giving his soul to the devil. And to confirm it the more assuredly, he took a small penknife and pricked a vein in his left hand, and for certainty thereupon were seen on his hand these words written as if they had been written with blood, *O homo fuge:* whereat the spirit vanished, but Faustus continued in his damnable mind and made his writing as followeth.

*   *   *

The manner how Faustus proceeded with his damnable life, and of the diligent service that Mephistopheles used towards him. Chap. 8.

Doctor Faustus having given his soul to the devil, renouncing all the powers of heaven, confirming this lamentable action with his own blood, and having already delivered his writing not into the devil's hand, the which so puffed up his heart that he had forgot the mind of a man and thought rather himself to be a spirit. This Faustus dwelt in his uncle's house at Wittenberg, who died and bequeathed it in his testament to his cousin Faustus. Faustus kept a boy with him that was his scholar, an unhappy wag called Christopher Wagner, to whom this sport and life that he saw his master follow seemed pleasant. Faustus loved the boy well, hoping to make him as good or better seen in his devilish exercise than himself, and he was fellow with Mephistopheles. Otherwise Faustus had no more company in his house but himself, his boy, and his spirit, that ever was diligent at Faustus' command, going about the house clothed like a friar with a little bell in his hand, seen of none but Faustus. For his victual and other necessaries, Mephistopheles brought him at his pleasure from the Duke of Saxon, the Duke of Bavaria, and the Bishop of Salzburg; for they had many times their best wine stolen out of their cellars by Mephistopheles. Likewise their provision for their own table, such meat as Faustus wished for, his spirit brought him in. Besides that, Faustus himself was become so cunning that when he opened his window, what fowl soever he wished for came presently flying into his house, were it never so dainty. Moreover, Faustus and his boy went in sumptuous apparel, the which Mephistopheles stole from the mercers at Nuremberg, Augsburg, Frankfort, and Leipzig, for it was hard for them to find a lock to keep out such a thief. All their maintenance was but stolen and borrowed ware; and thus they lived an odious life in the sight of God, though as yet the world were unacquainted with their wickedness. It must be so, for their fruits be none other, as Christ saith through John where he calls the devil a thief and a murderer, and that found Faustus, for he stole him away both body and soul.

How Doctor Faustus would have married, and how the Devil had almost killed him for it. Chap. 9.

Doctor Faustus continued thus in his epicurish life day and night and believed not that there was a God, hell, or devil. He thought that body and soul died together and had quite forgotten divinity or the immortality of his soul, but stood in his damnable heresy day and night. And bethinking himself of a wife, called Mephistopheles to counsel, which would in no wise agree, demanding of him if he would break the covenant made with him or if he had forgot it. "Hast not thou," quoth Mephistopheles, "sworn thyself an enemy to God and all creatures? To this I answer thee, thou canst not marry; thou canst not serve two masters, God and my prince. For wedlock is a chief institution ordained of God, and that hast thou promised to defy, as we do all, and that hast thou also done; and moreover thou hast confirmed it with thy blood. Persuade thyself that what thou dost in contempt of wedlock, it is all to thine own delight. Therefore, Faustus, look well about thee and bethink thyself better, and I wish thee to change thy mind; for if thou keep not what thou hast promised in thy writing, we will tear thee in pieces like the dust under thy feet. Therefore, sweet Faustus, think with what unquiet life, anger, strife, and debate thou shalt live in when thou takest a wife; therefore change thy mind."

Doctor Faustus was with these speeches in despair; and as all that have forsaken the Lord can build upon no good foundation, so this wretched Faustus, having forsook the rock, fell in despair with himself, fearing if he should motion matrimony any more that the devil would tear him in pieces. "For this time," quoth he to Mephistopheles, "I am not minded to marry." "Then you do well," answered his spirit. But shortly, and that within two hours after, Faustus called his spirit, which came in his old manner like a friar. Then Faustus said unto him, "I am not able to resist nor bridle my fantasy. I must and will have a wife, and I pray thee give thy consent to it." Suddenly upon these words came such a whirlwind about the place that Faustus thought the whole house would come down. All the doors in the house flew off the hooks. After all this, his house was full of smoke and the floor covered over with ashes, which when Doctor Faustus perceived, he would have gone up the stairs. And flying up, he was taken and thrown into the hall, that he was not able to stir hand nor foot. Then round about him ran a monstrous circle of fire, never standing still, that Faustus fried as he lay and thought there to have been burned. Then cried he out to his spirit Mephistopheles for help, promising him he would live in all things as he had vowed in his handwriting. Hereupon appeared unto him an ugly devil, so fearful and monstrous to behold that Faustus durst not look on him. The devil said, "What wouldst thou have, Faustus? How likest thou thy wedding? What mind art thou in now?" Faustus answered, he had forgot his promise, desiring him of pardon, and he would talk no more of such things. The devil answered, "Thou were best so to do," and so vanished.

After appeared unto him his friar Mephistopheles with a bell in his hand, and spake to Faustus: "It is no jesting with us. Hold thou that which thou hast vowed and we will perform as we have promised; and more than that, thou shalt have thy heart's desire of what woman soever thou wilt, be she alive or dead, and so long as thou wilt thou shalt keep her by thee."

These words pleased Faustus wonderfully well, and repented himself that he was so foolish to wish himself married that might have any woman in the whole city brought to him at his command, the which he practiced and persevered in a long time.

Questions put forth by Doctor Faustus unto his spirit Mephistopheles. Chap. 10.

Doctor Faustus, living in all manner of pleasure that his heart could desire, continuing in his amorous drifts, his delicate fare, and costly apparel, called on a time his Mephistopheles to him; which being come, brought with him a book in his hand of all manner of devilish and enchanted arts, the which he gave Faustus, saying "Hold, my Faustus, work now thy heart's desire." The copy of this enchanting book was afterwards found by his servant, Christopher Wagner. "Well," quoth Faustus to his spirit, "I have called thee to know what thou canst do if I have need of thy help." Then answered Mephistopheles and said, "My Lord Faustus, I am a flying spirit, yea, so swift as thought can think, to do whatsoever." Here Faustus said, "But how came thy Lord and master Lucifer to have so great a fall from heaven?" Mephistopheles answered, "My Lord Lucifer was a fair angel, created of God as immortal, and being placed in the seraphins, which are above the cherubins, he would have presumed unto the throne of God, with intent to have thrust God out of his seat. Upon this presumption the Lord cast him down headlong, and where before he was an angel of light, now dwells he in darkness, not able to come near his first place without God send for him to appear before him as Raphael. But unto the lower degree of angels that have their conversation with men he was come, but not unto the second degree of heavens that is kept by the archangels, namely Michael and Gabriel, for these are called angels of God's wonders; yet are these far inferior places to that from whence my Lord and Master Lucifer fell. And thus far, Faustus, because thou art one of the beloved children of my Lord Lucifer, following and feeding thy mind in manner as he did his, I have shortly resolved thy request, and more I will do for thee at thy pleasure." "I thank thee, Mephistopheles," quoth Faustus. "Come let us now go rest, for it is night." Upon this, they left their communication.

How Doctor Faustus dreamed that he had seen hell
in his sleep, and how he questioned with his spirit of matters
as concerning hell, with the spirit's answer. Chap. 11.

The night following, after Faustus his communication had with Mephistopheles as concerning the fall of Lucifer, Doctor Faustus dreamed that he had seen a part of hell; but in what manner it was or in what place he knew not, whereupon he was greatly troubled in mind and called unto him Mephistopheles his spirit, saying to him, "My Mephistopheles; I pray thee resolve me in this doubt. What is hell, what substance is it of, in what place stands it, and when was it made?" Mephistopheles answered, "My Faustus, thou shalt know that before the fall of my Lord Lucifer there was no hell, but even then was hell ordained. It is of no substance, but a confused thing. For I tell thee that before all elements were made, and the earth seen, the Spirit of God moved on the waters and darkness was over all; but when God said, 'Let it be light,' it was so at his word, and the light was on God's right hand, and God praised the light. Judge thou further: God stood in the middle, the darkness was on his left hand, in the which my Lord was bound in chains until the day of judgment: in this confused hell is nought to find but a filthy, sulphurish, fiery, stinking mist or fog. Further, we devils know not what substance it is of, but a confused thing. For as a bubble of water flieth before the wind, so doth hell before the breath of God. Further, we devils know not how God hath laid the foundation of our hell, nor whereof it is: but to be short with thee, Faustus, we know that hell hath neither bottom nor end."

Another question put forth by Doctor Faustus to his spirit
concerning his Lord Lucifer, with the sorrow that
Faustus fell afterwards into. Chap. 13.

Doctor Faustus began again to reason with Mephistopheles, requiring him to tell him in what form and shape and in what estimation his Lord Lucifer was when he was in favor with God. Whereupon his spirit required him of three days' respite, which Faustus granted. The three days being expired, Mephistopheles gave him this answer: "Faustus, my Lord Lucifer (so called now, for that he was banished out of the clear light of heaven) was at the first an angel of God, he sat on the cherubins, and saw all the wonderful works of God, yea he was so of God ordained, for shape, pomp, authority, worthiness, and dwelling, that he far exceeded all other the creatures of God, yea our gold and precious stones, and so illuminated that he far surpassed the brightness of the sun and all other stars; wherefore God placed him on the cherubins, where he had a kingly office, and was always before God's seat, to the end he might be the more perfect in all his beings. But when he began to be high minded, proud, and so presumptuous that he would usurp the seat of his Majesty, then was he banished out from amongst the heavenly powers, separated from their abiding into the manner of a fiery stone that no water is able to quench but continually burneth until the end of the world."

Doctor Faustus, when he had heard the words of his spirit, began to consider with himself, having diverse and sundry opinions in his head, and very pensively (saying nothing) unto his spirit, he went into his chamber and laid him on his bed, recording the words of Mephistopheles, which so pierced his heart that he fell into sighing and great lamentation, crying out "Alas, ah, woe is me! What have I done? Even so shall it come to pass with me. Am not I also a creature of God's making, bearing his own image and similitude, into whom he hath breathed the spirit of life and immortality, unto whom he hath made all things living subject? But woe is me. Mine haughty mind, proud aspiring stomach, and filthy flesh hath brought my soul into perpetual damnation. Yea, pride hath abused my understanding, in so much that I have forgot my maker. The Spirit of God is departed from me. I have promised the devil my soul, and therefore it is but a folly for me to hope for grace, but it must be even with me as with Lucifer, thrown into perpetual burning fire. Ah, woe is me that ever I was born." In this perplexity lay this miserable Doctor Faustus, having quite forgot his faith in Christ, never falling to repentance truly, thereby to attain the grace and Holy Spirit of God again, the which would have been able to have resisted the strong assaults of Satan. For although he had made him a promise, yet he might have remembered through true repentance sinners come again into the favor of God, which faith the faithful firmly hold, knowing they that kill the body are not able to hurt the soul. But he was in all his opinions doubtful, without faith or hope, and so he continued.

*   *   *

*How Doctor Faustus made his journey through the
principal and most famous lands in the world. Chap. 22.*

Doctor Faustus having overrun fifteen years of his appointed
time, he took upon him a journey, with full pretence to see the
whole world; and calling his spirit Mephistopheles unto him, he
said, "Thou knowest that thou art bound unto me upon conditions,
to perform and fulfill my desire in all things, wherefore my pretence is to visit the whole face of the earth visible and invisible
when it pleaseth me: wherefore, I enjoin and command thee to the
same." Whereupon Mephistopheles answered, "I am ready, my lord,
at thy command," and forthwith the spirit changed himself into the
likeness of a flying horse, saying "Faustus, sit up, I am ready." Doctor Faustus loftily sat upon him, and forward they went. Faustus
came through many a land and province in which time he saw very
little that delighted his mind, whereupon he took a little rest at
home, and burning in desire to see more at large and to behold the
secrets of each kingdom, he set forward again on his journey upon
his swift horse Mephistopheles, and came to Treir, for that he
chiefly desired to see this town and the monuments thereof; but
there he saw not many wonders except one fair palace that belonged unto the bishop, and also a mighty large castle that was
built of brick, with three walls and three great trenches, so strong
that it was impossible for any prince's power to win it. Then he saw
a church wherein was buried Simeon and the Bishop Popo; their
tombs are of most sumptuous large marble stone closed and joined
together with great bars of iron. From whence he departed to Paris,
where he liked well the Academy, and what place or kingdom soever
fell in his mind, the same he visited. He came from Paris to Mentz,
where the river of Main falls into the Rhine; notwithstanding he
tarried not long there, but went to Campania in the kingdom of
Naples, in which he saw an innumerable sort of cloisters, nunner-
ies, and churches, great and high houses of stone, the streets fair
and large, and straight forth from one end of the town to the other
as a line; and all the pavement of the city was of brick, and the
more it rained in the town the fairer the streets were. There saw he
the tomb of Vergil and the highway that he cut through that mighty
hill of stone in one night, the whole length of an English mile.
Then he saw the number of galleys and argosies that lay there at
the city head, the windmill that stood in the water, the castle in the
water, and the houses above the water where under the galleys
might ride most safely from rain or wind. Then he saw the castle on
the hill over the town and many monuments within, also the hill
called Vesuvius, whereon groweth all the Greekish wine and most
pleasant sweet olives. From thence he came to Venice, whereas he

wondered not a little to see a city so famously built standing in the
sea, where through every street the water ran in such largeness that
great ships and barks might pass from one street to another, having
yet a way on both sides the water whereon men and horse might
pass. He marveled also how it was possible for so much victual to
be found in the town and so good cheap, considering that for a
whole league off nothing grew near the same. He wondered not a
little at the fairness of Saint Mark's place and the sumptuous
church standing therein called Saint Mark's: how all the pavement
was set with colored stones and all the rood or loft of the church
doubly gilded over. Leaving this, he came to Padua, beholding the
manner of their Academy, which is called the mother or nurse of
Christendom. There he heard the doctors and saw the most monuments in the town, entered his name into the university of the German nation, and wrote himself Doctor Faustus, the insatiable
speculator. Then saw he the worthiest monument in the world for a
church, named Saint Anthony's Cloister, which for the pinnacles
thereof and the contriving of the church hath not the like in Christendom. This town is fenced about with three mighty walls of stone
and earth, betwixt the which runneth goodly ditches of water.
Twice every twenty-four hours passeth boats betwixt Padua and
Venice with passengers as they do here betwixt London and
Gravesend, and even so far they differ in distance. Faustus beheld
likewise the counsel house and the castle with no small wonder.
Well, forward he went to Rome, which lay and doth yet lie on the
river Tiber, the which divideth the city in two parts: over the river
are four great stone bridges, and upon the one bridge called Ponte
S. Angelo is the Castle of S. Angelo, wherein are so many great cast
pieces as there are days in a year, and such pieces that will shoot
seven bullets off with one fire; to this castle cometh a privy vault
from the church and palace of Saint Peter, through the which the
Pope (if any danger be) passeth from his palace to the castle for
safegard. The city hath eleven gates, and a hill called Vaticinium
whereon Saint Peter's church is built. In that church the holy fathers will hear no confession without the penitent bring money in
his hand. Adjoining to this church is the Campo Santo, the which
Carolus Magnus built, where every day thirteen pilgrims have their
dinners served of the best: that is to say, Christ and his twelve
Apostles. Hard by this he visited the churchyard of Saint Peter's,
where he saw the pyramid that Julius Caesar brought out of Africa.
It stood in Faustus' time leaning against the church wall of Saint
Peter's, but now Papa Sixtus hath erected it in the middle of Saint
Peter's churchyard. It is twenty-four fathom long and at the lower
end six fathom foursquare, and so forth smaller upwards; on the
top is a crucifix of beaten gold; the stone standeth on four lions of

brass. Then he visited the seven churches of Rome, that were Saint Peter's, Saint Paul's, Saint Sebastian's, Saint John Lateran, St. Laurence, Saint Mary Magdalen, and Saint Marie Majora. Then went he without the town, where he saw the conduits of water that run level through hill and dale, bringing water into the town fifteen Italian miles off. Other monuments he saw, too many to recite, but amongst the rest he was desirous to see the pope's palace, and his manner of service at his table. Wherefore, he and his spirit made themselves invisible and came into the pope's court and privy chamber where he was. There saw he many servants attendant on his holiness, with many a flattering sycophant carrying of his meat, and there he marked the pope and the manner of his service, which he seeing to be so unmeasurable and sumptuous, "Fie," quoth Faustus, "why had not the devil made a pope of me?" Faustus saw notwithstanding in that place those that were like to himself, proud, stout, willful, gluttons, drunkards, whoremongers, breakers of wedlock, and followers of all manner of ungodly exercises. Wherefore he said to his spirit, "I thought that I had been alone a hog or pork of the devil's, but he must bear with me yet a little longer, for these hogs of Rome are already fattened and fitted to make his roast meat. The devil might do well now to spit them all and have them to the fire, and let him summon the nuns to turn the spits. For as none must confess the nun but the friar, so none should turn the roasting friar but the nun." Thus continued Faustus three days in the pope's palace, and yet had no lust to his meat, but stood still in the pope's chamber and saw everything whatsoever it was. On a time the pope would have a feast prepared for the Cardinal of Pavia, and for his first welcome the cardinal was bidden to dinner, and as he sat at meat the pope would ever be blessing and crossing over his mouth. Faustus could suffer it no longer, but up with his fist and smote the pope on the face, and withal he laughed that the whole house might hear him, yet none of them saw him nor knew where he was. The pope persuaded his company that it was a damned soul, commanding a mass presently to be said for his delivery out of purgatory, which was done. The pope sat still at meat, but when the latter mess came in to the pope's board, Doctor Faustus laid hands thereon, saying "This is mine." And so he took both dish and meat and fled unto the Capitol or Campadolia, calling his spirit unto him, and said, "Come, let us be merry, for thou must fetch me some wine and the cup that the pope drinks of, and here upon Monte Caval will we make good cheer in spite of the pope and all his fat abbey lubbers." His spirit, hearing this, departed towards the pope's chamber, where he found them yet sitting and quaffing; wherefore he took from before the pope the fairest piece of plate or drinking goblet and a flagon of wine, and brought it to Faustus. But when the pope and the rest of his crew perceived they were robbed, and knew not after what sort, they persuaded themselves that it was the damned soul that before had vexed the pope so and that smote him on the face; wherefore he sent commandment through all the whole city of Rome that they should say mass in every church and ring all the bells for to lay the walking spirit, and to curse him with bell, book, and candle, that so invisibly had misused the pope's holiness, with the Cardinal of Pavia and the rest of their company. But Faustus notwithstanding made good cheer with that which he had beguiled the pope of, and in the midst of the order of Saint Barnard's barefooted friars, as they were going on procession through the market place called Campa de Fiore, he let fall his plate dishes and cup, and withall for a farewell he made such a thunderclap and a storm of rain as though heaven and earth should have met together . . .

How the Emperor Carolus Quintus requested of Faustus to see some of his cunning, whereunto he agreed. Chap. 29.

The Emperor Carolus, the fifth of that name, was personally with the rest of his nobles and gentlemen at the town of Innsbruck where he kept his court, unto the which also Doctor Faustus resorted, and being there well known of divers nobles and gentlemen, he was invited into the court to meat, even in the presence of the emperor: whom when the emperor saw, he looked earnestly on him, thinking him by his looks to be some wonderful fellow, wherefore he asked one of his nobles whom he should be, who answered that he was called Doctor Faustus. Whereupon the emperor held his peace until he had taken his repast, after which he called unto him Faustus, into the privy chamber. Whither being come, he said unto him, "Faustus, I have heard much of thee, that thou art excellent in the black art, and none like thee in mine empire, for men say that thou hast a familiar spirit with thee and that thou canst do what thou list. It is therefore," saith the emperor, "my request of thee that thou let me see a proof of thine experience, and I vow unto thee by the honor of mine imperial crown, none evil shall happen unto thee for so doing." Hereupon Doctor Faustus answered his majesty that upon those conditions he was ready in anything that he could to do his highness's commandment in what service he would appoint him. "Well, then hear what I say," quoth the emperor. "Being once solitary in my house, I called to mind mine elders and ancestors, how it was possible for them to attain unto so great a degree of authority, yea so high that we the successors of that line are never able to come near. As for example, the great and mighty monarch of the world Alexander Magnus was such a lantern and spectacle to all his successors, as the chronicles make mention of so great riches, conquering, and subduing so many kingdoms, the which I and those that follow me (I fear) shall never be able to attain unto. Wherefore, Faustus, my hearty desire is that thou wouldst vouchsafe to let me see that Alexander, and his paramour, the which was praised to be so fair, and I pray thee show me them in such sort that I may see their personages, shape, gesture and apparel as they used in their lifetime, and that here before my face; to the end that I may say I have my long desire fulfilled and to praise thee to be a famous man in thine art and experience." Doctor Faustus answered, "My most excellent lord, I am ready to accomplish your request in all things, so far forth as I and my spirit are able to perform. Yet your majesty shall know that their dead bodies are not able substantially to be brought before you, but such spirits as have seen Alexander and his paramour alive shall appear unto you in manner and form as they both lived in their most flourishing time; and herewith I hope to please your imperial majesty." Then Faustus went a little aside to speak to his spirit, but he returned again presently, saying "Now if it please your majesty you shall see them, yet upon this condition that you demand no question of them nor speak unto them," which the emperor agreed unto. Wherewith Doctor Faustus opened the privy chamber door, where presently entered the great and mighty Emperor Alexander Magnus, in all things to look upon as if he had been alive, in proportion a strong thick-set man of a middle stature, black hair and that both thick and curled head and beard, red cheeks, and a broad face, with eyes like a basilisk; he had on a complete harness burnished and graven exceeding rich to look upon. And so passing towards the Emperor Carolus, he made low and reverent curtsy, whereat the Emperor Carolus would have stood up to receive and greet him with the like reverence, but Faustus took hold of him and would not permit him to do it. Shortly after, Alexander made humble reverence and went out again, and coming to the door his paramour met him, she coming in. She made the emperor likewise reverence. She was clothed in blue velvet wrought and embroidered with pearl and gold. She was also excellent fair like milk and blood mixed, tall and slender, with a face round as an apple. And thus she passed certain times up and down the house, which the emperor marking, said to himself, "Now have I seen two persons which my heart hath long wished for to behold, and sure it cannot otherwise be," said he to himself, "but that the spirits have changed themselves into these forms and have not deceived me," calling to his mind the woman that raised the prophet Samuel. And for that the emperor would be the more satisfied in the matter, he thought, "I have heard say that behind her neck she had a great wart or wen," wherefore he took Faustus by the hand without any words and went to see if it were also to be seen on her or not. But she, perceiving that he came to her, bowed down her neck, where he saw a great wart, and hereupon she vanished, leaving the emperor and the rest well contented.

How Doctor Faustus in the sight of the emperor conjured a pair of hart's horns upon a knight's head that slept out of a casement. Chap. 30.

When Doctor Faustus had accomplished the emperor's desire in all things as he was requested, he went forth into a gallery, and leaning over a rail to look into the privy garden he saw many of the emperor's courtiers walking and talking together. And casting his eyes now this way, now that way, he espied a knight leaning out at a window of the great hall, who was fast asleep (for in those days it was hot) but the person shall be nameless that slept, for that he was a knight, although it was done to a little disgrace of the gentleman. It pleased Doctor Faustus, through the help of his spirit Mephistopheles, to firm upon his head as he slept a huge pair of hart's horns; and as the knight awoke, thinking to pull in his head he hit his horns against the glass that the panes thereof flew about his ears. Think here how this good gentleman was vexed, for he could neither get backward nor forward: which when the emperor heard all the courtiers laugh, and came forth to see what was happened, the emperor also, when he beheld the knight with so fair a head, laughed heartily thereat and was therewithal well pleased. At last Faustus made him quit of his horns again, but the knight perceived how they came, etc.

How the above-mentioned knight went about to be revenged of Doctor Faustus. Chap. 31.

Doctor Faustus took his leave of the emperor and the rest of the courtiers, at whose departure they were sorry, giving him many rewards and gifts. But being a league and a half from the city he came into a wood, where he beheld the knight that he had jested with at the court with other in harness, mounted on fair palfreys, and running with full charge towards Faustus. But he, seeing their intent, ran toward the bushes, and before he came amongst the bushes he returned again, running as it were to meet them that chased him, whereupon suddenly all the bushes were turned into horsemen which also ran to encounter with the knight and his company, and coming to them, they closed the knight and the rest and told them that they must pay their ransom before they departed. Whereupon the knight, seeing himself in such distress, besought Faustus to be good to them, which he denied not, but let them loose. Yet he so charmed them that every one, knight and other, for the space of a whole month did wear a pair of goat's horns on their brows, and every palfrey a pair of ox horns on their head; and this was their penance appointed by Faustus, etc.

How Doctor Faustus deceived an Horse-courser. Chap. 34.

In like manner he served an horse-courser at a fair called Pheiffring, for Doctor Faustus through his cunning had gotten an excellent fair horse, whereupon he rode to the fair, where he had many chapmen that offered him money. Lastly, he sold him for forty dollars, willing him that bought him that in any wise he should not ride him over any water. But the horse-courser marveled with himself that Faustus bade him ride him over no water, but quoth he, "I will prove," and forthwith he rode him into the river. Presently the horse vanished from under him, and he sat on a bundle of straw, in so much that the man was almost drowned. The horse-courser knew well where he lay that had sold him his horse, wherefore he went angrily to his inn, where he found Doctor Faustus fast asleep and snorting on a bed. But the horse-courser could no longer forbear him, took him by the leg and began to pull him off the bed, but he pulled him so that he pulled his leg from his body, in so much that the horse-courser fell down backward in the place. Then began Doctor Faustus to cry with an open throat, "He hath murdered me!" Hereat the horse-courser was afraid and gave the flight, thinking none other with himself but that he had pulled his leg from his body. By this means Doctor Faustus kept his money.

How Doctor Faustus ate a load of hay. Chap. 35.

Doctor Faustus being in a town of Germany called Zwickau, where he was accompanied with many doctors and masters, and going forth to walk after supper, they met with a clown that drove a load of hay. "Good even, good fellow," said Faustus to the clown, "what shall I give thee to let me eat my belly full of hay?" The clown thought with himself, what a mad man is this to eat hay; thought he with himself, thou wilt not each much. They agreed for three farthings he should eat as much as he could: wherefore Doctor Faustus began to eat, and that so ravenously that all the rest of his company fell a-laughing, blinding so the poor clown that he was sorry at his heart, for he seemed to have eaten more than the half of his hay. Wherefore the clown began to speak him fair, for fear he should have eaten the other half also. Faustus made as though he had had pity on the clown, and went his way. When the clown came in place where he would be, he had his hay again as he had before, a full load.

How Faustus served the drunken clowns. Chap. 37.

Doctor Faustus went into an inn wherein were many tables full of clowns, the which were tippling can after can of excellent wine, and to be short, they were all drunken. And as they sat, they so sung and hallooed that one could not hear a man speak for them. This angered Doctor Faustus, wherefore he said to those that had called him in, "Mark, my masters, I will show you a merry jest." The clowns continuing still hallooing and singing, he so conjured them that their mouths stood as wide open as it was possible for them to hold them, and never a one of them was able to close his mouth again. By and by the noise was gone; the clowns notwithstanding looked earnestly one upon another and wist not what was happened; wherefore one by one they went out, and so soon as they came without, they were as well as ever they were. But none of them desired to go in any more.

How Doctor Faustus played a merry jest with the Duke of Anholt in his court. Chap. 39.

Doctor Faustus on a time came to the Duke of Anholt, the which welcomed him very courteously, this was in the month of January, where sitting at the table he perceived the duchess to be with child. And forbearing himself until the meat was taken from the table and that they brought in the banqueting dishes, said Doctor Faustus to the duchess, "Gracious lady, I have always heard that the great bellied women do always long for some dainties. I beseech therefore your grace hide not your mind from me, but tell me what you desire to eat." She answered him, "Doctor Faustus now truly I will not hide from you what my heart doth most desire, namely, that if it were now harvest, I would eat my belly full of ripe grapes, and other dainty fruit." Doctor Faustus answered hereupon, "Gracious lady, this is a small thing for me to do, for I can do more than this." Wherefore he took a plate and made open one of the casements of the window, holding it forth, where incontinent he had his dish full of all manner of fruits, as red and white grapes, pears, and apples, the which came from out of strange countries. All these he presented the duchess, saying "Madame, I pray you vouchsafe to taste of this dainty fruit, the which came from a far country, for there the summer is not yet ended." The duchess thanked Faustus highly, and she fell to her fruit with full appetite. The Duke of Anholt notwithstanding could not withhold to ask Faustus with what reason there were such young fruit to be had at that time of the year. Doctor Faustus told him, "May it please your grace to understand that the year is divided into two circles over the whole world, that when with us it is winter, in the contrary circle it is notwithstanding summer; for in India and Saba there falleth or setteth the sun so that it is so warm that they have twice a year fruit. And, gracious lord, I have a swift spirit, the which can in the twinkling of an eye fulfill my desire in anything, wherefore I sent him into those countries, who hath brought this fruit as you see." Whereat the duke was in great admiration.

* * *

How Doctor Faustus showed the fair Helena unto the students upon the Sunday following. Chap. 45.

The Sunday following came these students home to Doctor Faustus' own house and brought their meat and drink with them. These men were right welcome guests unto Faustus, wherefore they all fell to drinking of wine smoothly; and being merry, they began some of them to talk of the beauty of women, and everyone gave forth his verdict what he had seen and what he had heard. So one among the rest said, "I never was so desirous of anything in this world as to have a sight (if it were possible) of fair Helena of Greece for whom the worthy town of Troy was destroyed and razed down to the ground, therefore" sayth he, "that in all men's judgment she was more than commonly fair, because that when she was stolen away from her husband there was for her recovery so great bloodshed."

Doctor Faustus answered, "For that you are all my friends and are so desirous to see that famous pearl of Greece, fair Helena, the wife of King Menelaus and daughter of Tindalus and Laeda, sister to Castor and Pollux, who was the fairest lady in all Greece, I will therefore bring her into your presence personally and in the same form of attire as she used to go when she was in her chiefest flower and pleasantest prime of youth. The like have I done for the Emperor Carolus Quintus; at his desire I showed him Alexander the Great and his paramour. But," said Doctor Faustus, "I charge you all that upon your peril you speak not a word nor rise up from the table so long as she is in your presence." And so he went out of the hall, returning presently again, after whom immediately followed the fair and beautiful Helena, whose beauty was such that the students were all amazed to see her, esteeming her rather to be a heavenly than an earthly creature. This lady appeared before them in a most sumptuous gown of purple velvet, richly embroidered. Her hair hung down loose as fair as the beaten gold and of such length that it reached down to her hams, with amorous coal-black eyes, a sweet and pleasant round face, her lips red as a cherry, her cheeks of rose all color, her mouth small, her neck as white as the swan, tall and slender of personage, and in sum, there was not one imperfect part in her. She looked roundabout her with a rolling hawk's eye, a smiling and wanton countenance, which nearly had inflamed the hearts of the students but that they persuaded themselves she was a spirit, wherefore such fantasies passed away lightly with them. And thus fair Helena and Doctor Faustus went out again one with another. But the students at Doctor Faustus' entering again into the hall requested of him to let them see her again the next day, for that they would bring with them a painter and so take her counterfeit, which he denied, affirming that he could not always raise up her spirit, but only at certain times. "Yet," said he, "I will give you her counterfeit, which shall be always as good to you as if yourselves should see the drawing thereof," which they received according to his promise but soon lost it again. The students departed from Faustus' home everyone to his house, but they were not able to sleep the whole night for thinking on the beauty of fair Helena. Wherefore a man may see that the devil blindeth and inflameth the heart with lust oftentimes, that men fall in love with harlots, nay even with furies, which afterward cannot lightly be removed.

How an old man, the neighbor of Faustus,
sought to persuade him to amend his evil
life and to fall unto repentance. Chap. 48.

A good Christian, an honest and virtuous old man, a lover of the holy Scriptures, who was neighbor unto Doctor Faustus, when he perceived that many students had their recourse in and out unto Doctor Faustus, he suspected his evil life. Wherefore like a friend he invited Doctor Faustus to supper unto his house, unto the which he agreed. And having ended their banquet, the old man began with these words. "My loving friend and neighbor Doctor Faustus, I have to desire of you a friendly and Christian request, beseeching you that you will vouchsafe not to be angry with me but friendly resolve me in my doubt and take my poor inviting in good part." To whom Doctor Faustus answered, "My loving neighbor, I pray you say your mind." Then began the old patron to say: "My good neighbor, you know in the beginning how that you have defied God and all the host of heaven and given your soul to the devil, wherewith you have incurred God's high displeasure and are become from a Christian far worse than a heathen person. Oh, consider what you have done. It is not only the pleasure of the body but the safety of the soul that you must have respect unto, of which if you be careless then are you cast away and shall remain in the anger of almighty God. But yet is it time enough, Doctor Faustus, if you repent and call unto the Lord for mercy, as we have example in the Acts of the Apostles, the eighth chapter of Simon in Samaria, who was led out of the way, affirming that he was Simon Homo Sanctus. This man was notwithstanding in the end converted, after that he had heard the sermon of Philip, for he was baptized and saw his sins and repented. Likewise I beseech you, good brother Doctor Faustus, let my rude sermon be unto you a conversion, and forget the filthy life that you have led, repent, ask mercy, and live. For Christ saith, 'Come unto me all ye that are weary and heavy laden, and I will refresh you.' And in Ezekiel, 'I desire not the death of a sinner, but rather that he convert and live.' Let my words, good brother Faustus, pierce into your adamant heart, and desire God for his Son Christ's sake to forgive you. Wherefore have you so long lived in your devilish practices, knowing that in the Old and New Testament you are forbidden, and that men should not suffer any such to live, neither have any conversation with them, for it is an abomination unto the Lord, and that such persons have no part in the Kingdom of God." All this while Doctor Faustus heard him very attentively, and replied: "Father, your persuasions like me wondrous well, and I thank you with all my heart for your good will and counsel, promising you so far as I may to follow your discipline." Whereupon he took his leave. And being come home, he laid him very pensive on his bed, bethinking himself of the words of the good old man, and in a manner began to repent that he had given his soul to the devil, intending to deny all that he had promised unto Lucifer. Continuing in these cogitations, suddenly his spirit appeared unto him clapping him upon the head, and wrung it as though he would have pulled the head from the shoulders, saying unto him "Thou knowest, Faustus, that thou has given thyself body and soul unto my lord Lucifer, and has vowed thyself an enemy unto God and unto all men; and now thou beginnest to harken to an old doting fool which persuadeth thee as it were unto God, when indeed it is too late, for that thou art the devil's, and he hath good power presently to fetch thee: wherefore he hath sent me unto thee to tell thee, that seeing thou hast sorrowed for that thou hast done, begin again and write another writing with thine own blood; if not, then will I tear thee all to pieces." Hereat Doctor Faustus was sore afraid, and sayd, "My Mephistopheles, I will write again what thou wilt." Wherefore he sat him down and with his own blood he wrote as followeth, which writing was afterwards sent to a dear friend of the said Doctor Faustus being his kinsman.

* * *

*How Doctor Faustus made the spirit of fair Helena of
Greece his own paramour and bedfellow in his
twenty-third year. Chap. 55.*

To the end that this miserable Faustus might fill the lust of his
flesh and live in all manner of voluptuous pleasures, it came in his
mind after he had slept his first sleep and in the twenty-third year
past of his time, that he had a great desire to lie with fair Helena of
Greece, especially her whom he had seen and showed unto the students of Wittenberg, wherefore he called unto him his spirit
Mephistopheles, commanding him to bring him the fair Helena,
which he also did. Whereupon he fell in love with her and made
her his common concubine and bedfellow, for she was so beautiful
and delightful a piece that he could not be one hour from her if he
should therefore have suffered death, she had so stolen away his
heart. And to his seeming, in time she was with child and in the
end brought him a man child whom Faustus named Justus Faustus.
This child told Doctor Faustus many things that were to come and
what strange matters were done in foreign countries; but in the end
when Faustus lost his life, the mother and the child vanished away
both together.

*How Doctor Faustus made his will, in the which he
named his servant Wagner to be his heir. Chap. 56.*

Doctor Faustus was now in his twenty-fourth and last year, and
he had a pretty stripling to his servant, the which had studied also
at the University of Wittenberg. This youth was very well ac-
quainted with his knaveries and sorceries, so that he was hated as
well for his own knaveries as also for his master's, for no man
would give him entertainment into his service, because of his un-
happiness, but Faustus. This Wagner was so well beloved with
Faustus that he used him as his son, for do what he would his master was always therewith well content. And when the time drew
nigh that Faustus should end, he called unto him a notary and certain masters the which were his friends and often conversant with
him, in whose presence he gave this Wagner his house and garden.
Item, he gave him in ready money sixteen hundred guilders. Item, a
farm. Item, a gold chain, much plate, and other household stuff.
This gave he all to his servant, and the rest of his time he meant to
spend in inns and students' company, drinking and eating, with
other jollity. And thus he finished his will for that time.

*How Doctor Faustus having but one month of his
appointed time to come, fell to mourning and
sorrow with himself for his devilish exercise. Chap. 58.*

Time ran away with Faustus, as the hourglass, for he had but one month to come of his twenty-four years, at the end whereof he had given himself to the devil body and soul, as is before specified. Here was the first token, for he was like a taken murderer or a thief, the which findeth himself guilty in conscience before the judge have given sentence, fearing every hour to die; for he was grieved, and wailing spent the time, went talking to himself, wringing of his hands, sobbing and sighing; he fell away from flesh and was very lean, and kept himself close. Neither could he abide to see or hear of his Mephistopheles any more.

*   *   *

*How Doctor Faustus bewailed to think on hell, and
of the miserable pains therein provided for him. Chap. 61.*

Now thou Faustus, damned wretch, how happy wert thou if as an unreasonable beast thou mightest die without soul, so shouldst thou not feel any more doubts! But now the devil will take thee away both body and soul and set thee in an unspeakable place of darkness. For although other souls have rest and peace, yet I, poor damned wretch, must suffer all manner of filthy stench, pains, cold, hunger, thirst, heat, freezing, burning, hissing, gnashing, and all the wrath and curse of God, yea all the creatures that God hath created are enemies to me. And now too late I remember that my spirit Mephistopheles did once tell me there was a great difference amongst the damned, for the greater the sin, the greater the torment. For as the twigs of the tree make greater flame than the trunk thereof, and yet the trunk continueth longer in burning, even so the more that a man is rooted in sin the greater is his punishment. Ah thou perpetual damned wretch, now art thou thrown into the everlasting fiery lake that never shall be quenched; there must I dwell in all manner of wailing, sorrow, misery, pain, torment, grief, howling, sighing, sobbing, blubbering, running of eyes, stinking at nose, gnashing of teeth, fear to the ears, horror to the conscience, and shaking both of hand and foot. Ah that I could carry the heavens on my shoulders, so that there were time at last to quit me of this everlasting damnation! Oh who can deliver me out of these fearful tormenting flames, the which I see prepared for me? Oh there is no help, nor any man that can deliver me, nor any wailing of sins can help me, neither is there rest to be found for me day nor night. Oh woe is me, for there is no help for me, no shield, no defense, no comfort. Where is my hold? Knowledge dare I not trust, and for a soul to God wards that have I not, for I shame to speak unto him. If I do, no answer shall be made me, but he will hide his face from me, to the end that I should not behold the joys of the chosen. What mean I then to complain where no help is? No, I know no hope resteth in my groanings. I have desired that it should be so, and God hath said Amen to my misdoings: for now I must have shame to comfort me in my calamities.

An oration of Faustus to the students. Chap. 63.

My trusty and well beloved friends, the cause why I have invited you into this place is this: Forasmuch as you have known me this many years, in what manner of life I have lived, practicing all manner of conjurations and wicked exercises, the which I have obtained through the help of the devil, into whose devilish fellowship they have brought me, the which use the like art and practice, urged by the detestable provocation of my flesh, my stiff-necked and rebellious will, with my filthy infernal thoughts, the which were ever before me, pricking me forward so earnestly that I must perforce have the consent of the devil to aid me in my devices. And to the end I might the better bring my purpose to pass, to have the devil's aid and furtherance, which I never have wanted in mine actions, I have promised unto him at the end and accomplishing of twenty-four years, both body and soul, to do therewith at his pleasure. And this day, this dismal day, those twenty-four years are fully expired, for night beginning my hourglass is at an end, the direful finishing whereof I carefully expect. For out of all doubt this night he will fetch me, to whom I have given myself in recompense of his service, both body and soul, and twice confirmed writings with my proper blood. Now have I called you, my well beloved lords, friends, brethren, and fellows, before that fatal hour to take my friendly farewell, to the end that my departing may not hereafter be hidden from you; beseeching you herewith courteous and loving lords and brethren, not to take in evil part anything done by me, but with friendly commendations to salute all my friends and companions wheresoever, desiring both you and them, if ever I have trespassed against your minds in anything, that you would all heartily forgive me. And as for those lewd practices the which this full twenty-four years I have followed, you shall hereafter find them in writing. And I beseech you let this my lamentable end to the residue of your lives be a sufficient warning, that you have God always before your eyes, praying unto him that he would ever defend you from the temptation of the devil and all his false deceits, not falling altogether from God as I, wretched and ungodly damned creature, have done, having denied and defied baptism, the sacraments of Christ's body, God himself, all heavenly powers, and earthly men, yea, I have denied such a God that desireth not to have one lost. Neither let the evil fellowship of wicked companions mislead you as it hath done me. Visit earnestly and oft the church, war and strive continually against the devil with a good and steadfast belief on God and Jesus Christ, and use your vocation in holiness. Lastly, to knit up my troubled oration, this is my friendly request, that you would to rest, and let nothing trouble you. Also, if you chance to hear any noise or rumbling about the house, be not therewith afraid, for there shall no evil happen unto you. Also, I pray you, arise not out of your beds. But above all things I entreat you, if you hereafter find my dead carcass, convey it unto the earth, for I die both a good and bad Christian: a good Christian for that I am heartily sorry and in my heart always pray for mercy that my soul may be delivered— a bad Christian for that I know the devil will have my body, and that would I willingly give him so that he would leave my soul in quiet. Wherefore I pray you that you would depart to bed, and so I wish you a quiet night, which unto me notwithstanding will be horrible and fearful.

This oration or declaration was made by Doctor Faustus, and that with a hearty and resolute mind, to the end he might not discomfort them. But the students wondered greatly thereat, that he was so blinded, for knavery, conjuration, and such like foolish things, to give his body and soul unto the devil, for they loved him entirely and never suspected any such thing before he had opened his mind to them. Wherefore one of them said unto him, "Ah, friend Faustus, what have you done to conceal this matter so long from us? We would by the help of good divines and the grace of God have brought you out of this net and have torn you out of the bondage and chains of Satan, whereas now we fear it is too late, to the utter ruin of your body and soul." Doctor Faustus answered, "I durst never do it, although I often minded, to settle myself unto godly people, to desire counsel and help, as once mine old neighbor counselled me that I should follow his learning and leave all my conjurations. Yet when I was minded to amend and to follow that good man's counsel, then came the devil and would have had me away, as this night he is like to do, and said so soon as I turned again to God he would dispatch me altogether. Thus, even thus, good gentlemen and my dear friends, was I enthralled in that Satanical band, all good desires drowned, all piety banished, all purpose of amendment utterly exiled by the tyrannous threatenings of my deadly enemy." But when the students heard his words, they gave him counsel to do naught else but call upon God, desiring him for the love of his sweet Son Jesus Christ's sake, to have mercy upon him, teaching him this form of prayer: O God be merciful unto me, poor and miserable sinner, and enter not into judgment with me, for no flesh is able to stand before thee. Although, O Lord, I must leave my sinful body unto the devil, being by him deluded, yet thou in mercy mayest preserve my soul.

This they repeated unto him, yet it could take no hold, but even as Cain he also said his sins were greater than God was able to forgive; for all his thought was on his writing, he meant he had made it too filthy in writing it with his own blood. The students and the others that were there, when they had prayed for him they wept and so went forth, but Faustus tarried in the hall. And when the gentlemen were laid in bed, none of them could sleep for that they attended to hear if they might be privy of his end. It happened between twelve and one o'clock at midnight; there blew a mighty storm of wind against the house as though it would have blown the foundation thereof out of his place. Hereupon the students began to fear, and got out of their beds, comforting one another, but they would not stir out of the chamber; and the host of the house ran out of doors, thinking the house would fall. The students lay near unto that hall wherein Doctor Faustus lay, and they heard a mighty noise and hissing as if the hall had been full of snakes and adders. With that, the hall door flew open wherein Doctor Faustus was; then he began to cry for help, saying "Murder, murder," but it came forth with half a voice hollowly. Shortly after, they heard him no more. But when it was day, the students that had taken no rest that night arose and went into the hall in the which they left Doctor Faustus, where notwithstanding they found no Faustus, but all the hall lay besprinkled with blood, his brains cleaving to the wall. For the devil had beaten him from one wall against another: in one corner lay his eyes, in another his teeth, a pitiful and fearful sight to behold. Then began the students to bewail and weep for him and sought for his body in many places. Lastly they came into the yard, where they found his body lying on the horse dung, most monstrously torn and fearful to behold, for his head and all his joints were dashed in pieces.

The forenamed students and masters that were at his death, have obtained so much, that they buried him in the village where he was so grievously tormented. After the which, they returned to Wittenberg, and coming into the house of Faustus, they found the servant of Faustus very sad, unto whom they opened all the matter, who took it exceeding heavily. There found they also this history of Doctor Faustus noted, and of him written as is before declared, all save only his end, the which was after by the students thereto annexed; further, what his servant had noted thereof was made in another book. And you have heard that he held by him in his life the spirit of fair Helena, the which had by him one son, the which he named Justus Faustus. Even the same day of his death they vanished away, both mother and son. The house before was so dark that scarce anybody could abide therein. The same night Doctor Faustus appeared unto his servant lively, and showed unto him many secret things the which he had done and hidden in his lifetime. Likewise there were certain which saw Doctor Faustus look out of the window by night as they passed by the house.

And thus ended the whole history of Doctor Faustus his conjuration and other acts that he did in his life, out of the which example every Christian may learn. But chiefly the stiff-necked and high-minded may thereby learn to fear God, and to be careful of their vocation, and to be at defiance with all devilish works, as God hath most precisely forbidden, to the end we should not invite the devil as a guest nor give him place as that wicked Faustus hath done. For here we have a fearful example of his writing, promise, and end, that we may remember him: that we go not astray, but take God always before our eyes, to call alone upon him, and to honor him all the days of our life with heart and hearty prayer, and with all our strength and soul to glorify his holy name, defying the devil and all his works, to the end we remain with Christ in all endless joy. Amen, amen, that wish I unto every Christian heart, and God's name to be glorified. Amen.

SARA MUNSON DEATS

Doctor Faustus: From Chapbook to Tragedy†

Few works of English literature have evoked such violent critical controversy as Marlowe's *Doctor Faustus*. On one hand, Una Ellis-Fermor contends that *Doctor Faustus* is "the most nearly Satanic tragedy that can be found," while Leo Kirschbaum insists that "there is no more obvious Christian document in all Elizabethan drama than *Doctor Faustus*."[1] Although Ellis-Fermor's comment today seems somewhat hyperbolic, a modified version of the Satanic interpretation has attracted numerous adherents, including Harry Levin and Irving Ribner. In recent years, however, criticism has veered in the opposite direction, emphasizing the Christian ethos

---

† From *Essays in Literature* 3 (1976): 3–16. Reprinted by permission of *Essays in Literature*, a publication of Western Illinois University, Macomb, IL.
1. Ellis-Fermor, *The Frontiers of Drama* (New York: Oxford Univ. Press, 1946), p. 143; Kirschbaum, "Marlowe's *Faustus*: A Reconsideration," *Review of English Studies*, 19 (1943), 229.

of the play. This view has been given eloquent expression by Douglas Cole and has found persuasive exponents in Lily B. Campbell
and James Smith as well as Leo Kirschbaum. Paul H. Kocher has
chosen the *via media*, arguing that the play, while orthodox, presents the image of a mighty but wrathful Deity rather than the merciful, benevolent God of New Testament Christianity.[2]

In light of these contradictory readings, it is instructive to turn to
Marlowe's source for the play, *The English Faustbook*, translated
from the German by "P. F., Gent.," and published in 1592.[3] The
EFB has long been a rich mine for literary prospectors, but although this valuable lode has been generously tapped, its riches are
far from exhausted. Of the major editions of the play, only two,
those of John D. Jump and Frederick Boas, attempt a detailed treatment of the *EFB*.[4] The *EFB* has received more careful examination
in recent critical studies, but generally these source comparisons
are limited to one particular area of controversy or a critic's particular thesis.[5] Clearly, a careful, comprehensive analysis of Marlowe's
adaptation of his source (what he includes, what he omits, what he

2. See Levin, *The Overreacher* (Cambridge, Mass.: Harvard Univ. Press, 1952); Ribner, In-
troduction to *The Complete Plays of Christopher Marlowe* (New York: Odyssey, 1963);
Cole, *Suffering and Evil in the Plays of Christopher Marlowe* (Princeton, N. J.: Princeton
Univ. Press, 1962); Campbell, "Doctor Faustus: A Case of Conscience." *PMLA*, 67
(1952), 219–39; Smith, "Marlowe's Dr. Faustus," *Scrutiny*, 8 (1939–40), 36–55;
Kocher, *Christopher Marlowe: A Study of His Thought, Learning, and Character* (Chapel
Hill: Univ. of North Carolina Press, 1946).
3. Hereafter referred to as the *EFB*. References are to the edition modernized and edited
by William Rose (Notre Dame, Ind.: Univ. of Notre Dame Press, 1963). All page references to this source will be included within the text.
4. Jump, *Doctor Faustus* (London: Methuen, 1968), pp. xxxviii–xli, 123–40; Boas, *The
Tragical History of Doctor Faustus* (London: Methuen, 1932), pp. 6–11, 171–95. Roma
Gill in the New Mermaid edition of *Doctor Faustus* ([New York: Hill and Wang, 1966],
pp. xiii–xiv) relegates discussion of the *EFB* to a brief one-page summary in the introduction with occasional references in footnotes; Kirschbaum (*The Plays*, p. 101) and
Ribner (*Complete Plays*, p. xxiv) both award Marlowe's source for *Doctor Faustus* only a
half-page in their respective collections of Marlowe's dramas. Conversely, Boas and
Jump in their editions of *Doctor Faustus* have assembled in Appendixes those passages of
the *EFB* which they consider to be of chief importance in the composition of the play.
Neither has, however, made an effort to evaluate the relative correspondence between
play and source as this is clearly a task for a longer study. Jump's general critical evalua-
tion of the correspondence between play and source is condensed to three brief pages in
his introduction; Boas' discussion of this issue, although more detailed, is still far from
comprehensive.
5. Kocher (*Christopher Marlowe*, pp. 104–19) makes frequent references to the *EFB* in his
analysis of Marlowe's *Doctor Faustus*. His primary purpose, however, is to evaluate the
relative influence of the English witchcraft tradition and the *EFB* on Marlowe's portrait
of the archetypal witch, rather than to make a detailed comparison between play and
source. J. B. Brockbank (*Marlowe: Dr. Faustus* [Great Neck, N.Y.: Barron's, 1962]) presents an illuminating discussion of the origin and background of the Faust myth and
makes reference to the *EFB*, but his central emphasis is on the philosophical provenance of Marlowe's drama and its relationship to contemporaneous literary and theatrical tradition rather than on the relationship between the play and its source. The most
thorough and enlightening treatment of the correspondence between source and play
may be found in Cole's *Suffering and Evil* (pp. 191–243), but here again, Cole has limited his discussion of the source to those passages developing his own thesis.

accepts but modifies) would be a useful contribution to Marlowe scholarship.

The problems of a study of this kind are numerous, among them the disparity between the two texts (1604, 1616) and the disputed authorship of the comic sections of the play. Bearing in mind the space limitations of an essay as well as the manifold difficulties of the subject, this study will confine itself to the "tragic" portions of both play and source, thus focusing on those parts of the drama most undeniably from the pen of Marlowe, although even here there are a number of disputed passages.

I

A central crux of the tragedy concerns the motivation of its protagonist. What drive impels the eminent Doctor Faustus to devise his own destruction? Is it desire for worldly pleasure, forbidden knowledge, godlike power, or a combination of all three? Boas and Ribner adopt an heroic interpretation of the play, viewing Faustus as a type of Renaissance Prometheus, suffering eternal torment in the cause of humanistic enlightenment. Kocher, Levin, and Roma Gill all accept while modifying this heroic reading.[6] On the opposite end of the critical spectrum, Kirschbaum and Cole minimize the heroic aspects of the drama, insisting that Faustus' celebrated thirst for knowledge is a means rather than an end and that within the Christian framework of the play Faustus' transgression is unequivocally condemned.[7]

In the *EFB* there are two primary motivations for Faustus' fatal contract, a desire for worldly pleasure and a yearning for forbidden

---

6. Boas (Introduction to *The Tragical History*, p. 36) states:

> The Faust Book had been avowedly written as an awful warning but its author, in true Renaissance fashion, had created the Wittenberg Doctor with those qualities of intellectual curiosity, passion for beauty and ardour for classical antiquity which were dominant in Marlowe himself and had already found expression in *Tamburlaine*.

Ribner (*Complete Plays*, p. xxxvii) views Faustus' contract as an act of defiant humanism, and his tragedy that of a man "who will not surrender in return for the promise of salvation those heroic attributes—the craving for knowledge, wealth, power, and delight—for which Marlowe still sees it as in the nature of mankind to yearn." Kocher (*Christopher Marlowe*, p. 105) affirms curiosity as the primary drive, while not denying Faustus' pride and ambition. Levin (*Overreacher*, p. 110), like Kocher, identifies intellectual curiosity (*libido sciendi*) as the central activating force behind Faustus' contract, while also allowing, like Kocher, that "it cannot finally be detached from the secondary motives that entrammel it, the will to power and appetite for sensation." Gill (*Doctor Faustus*, pp. xxii, xix–xxvii), although recognizing Faustus' "obsession with luxury as a flaw in the nature of one dedicated to the search for knowledge," argues that its seriousness must not be magnified until it obscures the real issues, which she defines as superhuman knowledge and power, not wealth. Thus, although these critics vary in their respective emphases, they all focus on intellectual curiosity as Faustus' *hamartia*.

7. Kirschbaum, *Plays*, p. 103; Cole, *Suffering and Evil*, pp. 197–98.

knowledge, with the primacy of pleasure stressed throughout. The first chapter of the book explicitly defines the conflict of values: Faustus chooses Mammon over God, "regarding more his worldly pleasure than the joys to come." Later the magician prepares the diabolical covenant, revealing his drive for power over spirits, for pleasure, and for knowledge:

1. That the Spirit should serve him and be obedient unto him in all things that he asked of him from that hour until the hour of his death.
2. Farther, anything that he desired of him he should bring it to him.
3. Also, that in all Faustus his demands or Interrogations, the Spirit should tell him nothing but that which is true. (p. 68)

The didactic coda of Chapter V further cites Faustus' destructive esteem for the "vain delights of this life" (p. 73), and there is reiterated condemnation of his "swinish" and "Epicurish life" (pp. 79, 190), "his amorous drifts, his delicate fare, and costly apparel" (p. 82), and his voluptuous escapades (pp. 82, 96). Helen is certainly not Faustus' only amour; he enjoys, among others, the entire harem of the great Turk (pp. 139–40) and the seven fairest women in the world (p. 190). His feasting and wine-bibbing are recounted at length (Chaps. XLI, XLII, XLIII, XLIV) and infernal music twice sustains him in impenitence (pp. 76, 107). Ultimately, Faustus blames pleasure for luring him into the "weary labyrinth," blinding his eyes to true value, so that he could not find his way (pp. 196–97).

But the *EFB* sorcerer exhibits not only a voracious appetite for sybaritic delights but also a consuming thirst for forbidden knowledge. We first meet Faustus as the "insatiable Speculator" who, "taking to him the wings of an Eagle, thought to fly over the whole world, and to know the secrets of heaven and earth" (pp. 65–66). Furthermore, the third of his original requests demands true answers to his questions (p. 68). The magician, acknowledging curiosity as one of his egregious flaws, laments, "had not I desired to know so much, I had not been in this case" (p. 90), and is rebuked by Mephostophiles for having bartered his soul to the Devil "to have the pleasure of this world, and to know the secrets of hell" (p. 94). Moreover, Faustus' fatal curiosity, revealed through eight chapters of disputation (X–XVI, XVIII), is hardly satisfied after explorations of earth, the heavens, and hell, with a glimpse of paradise thrown in for good measure. Five later chapters (XXIV–XXVIII) display his learning under infernal tutelage and his expertise in astronomy and the occult.

But what of the Icarian aspiration traditionally associated with Faustus? "Give none the blame but thine own self-will, thy proud and aspiring mind, which hath brought thee into the wrath of God and utter damnation," reproaches Mephostophiles on one occasion (pp. 97–98). Faustus also berates himself, "woe is me, mine haughty mind, proud aspiring stomach, and filthy flesh, hath brought my soul into perpetual damnation" (p. 87). The author himself directly condemns the distorted aspiration whereby Faustus "forgot the mind of a man, and thought rather himself to be a spirit" (p. 77).

In the *EFB*, therefore, desire for pleasure, knowledge, and a certain type of power are all inducements to Faustus' damnation. Yet except for questions of astronomy (closely associated with astrology at this time), the lore he seeks is arcane and perverted (discussions of infernal subjects comprise six chapters, X–XV). The power he desires is similarly bizarre. It is certainly not political but consists rather in authority over spirits and the ability to peer and pry into the forbidden secrets of nature and the supernatural. In his farewell address to his students, Faustus summarizes his fatal flaws, urging the "detestable provocation of my flesh [pleasure], my stiff-necked and rebellious will [pride], with my filthy infernal thoughts [curiosity]," as the agents of his destruction (p. 201).

In his dramatic treatment of the Faust legend, Marlowe surpasses his source in deeply probing his hero's motivation. On four separate occasions during the first three scenes of the play, Marlowe allows his protagonist to rhapsodize on his dreams. The first of these occasions occurs in scene i, immediately following the rejection of divinity for "heavenly necromancy." In his ecstatic reverie, Marlowe's magician, like his fellow hedonist in the *EFB*, grants pleasure ("profit" and "delight") priority, but this pleasure is immediately expanded to include power, both human and divine:

> All things that move between the quiet poles
> Shall be at my command: emperors and kings
> Are but obey'd in their several provinces,
> Nor can they raise the wind or rend the clouds;
> But his dominion that exceeds in this
> Stretcheth as far as doth the mind of man:
> A sound magician is a demi-god;
> Here tire, my brains, to get a deity! (l.55–62)[8]

Conversely, the sorcerer of the *EFB* never presumes to control nature; although he desires to be a spirit (or devil), he never aspires to be a god.

8. Citations from *Doctor Faustus* in my text are to John D. Jump's edition. All references will henceforth be included within the text.

Following the departure of the Good and Bad Angels, Marlowe's Faustus again revels in visions of glory and wealth. Here again, he gives pleasure priority with emphasis on material "profit." The thrilling exuberance and eloquence of this passage should not obscure the basic materialism underlying his longing for "gold," "pearls," and "princely delicates." In his earlier soliloquy there had been no mention of knowledge; now, however, Faustus reveals not only the innate human desire for resolution of ambiguities, but also a penchant (like his predecessor in the *EFB*) for esoteric lore, in this case knowledge of "strange philosophy" and "the secrets of all foreign kings" (i.85–86). But this is only a passing reference. The concluding ten lines of the soliloquy (ll. 87–96) catalogue the "desperate enterprises" he hopes to undertake with his newly acquired power. They are a remarkable pastiche of adolescent fantasies and soaring ambitions, ranging from such enterprises of great pith and moment as ejecting the Prince of Parma from the land and altering the geography of Germany to such a whimsical undertaking as garbing the students in silk. Despite the ostensible patriotism of the speech, the entire soliloquy, like the previous one, concentrates on personal power and renown.

The succeeding dialogue with Valdes and Cornelius offers Faustus a third opportunity of sharing his fantasies with the audience. Indeed this scene, the only non-comic episode without correspondence in the source, was probably added specifically for this purpose. In this episode, treasure (i.129–31, 143–46) fame (ll. 118–19, 140–42) and control over spirits (ll. 120–25) are fervently anticipated, but the only learning mentioned is the occult skill necessary for acquiring wealth, power, and glory.

The conjurers of both play and source in their first meetings with their personal demons set forth the conditions of their contracts (cf. p. 68; iii. 89–103). Marlowe's hero, adhering to the previously established pattern, first requests material rewards, then knowledge, finally dominance. Although the first two articles closely resemble the original conditions in the *EFB* (p. 68), the third, demand for the power of reward and punishment (a prerogative normally reserved for God), has no counterpart in the source. Nor do the following ten lines of soaring rhetoric in which Faustus, like Tamburlaine, elevates the "sweet fruition of an earthly crown" above "knowledge infinite," envisioning himself not as a sage but as the "great emperor of the world" (iii. 104–13). There is absolutely no mention of political ambition in the *EFB*. By introducing this new element, Marlowe renders Faustus' later encounter with the Emperor (xii) trenchantly ironic. The Emperor episode is taken almost verbatim from the *EFB* (Chap. XXIX), but the original version lacks the ironic undertones Marlowe achieves by counterbalancing

Faustus' grandiose boast that "the Emperor shall not live but by my leave" with the magician's later subservience in the Emperor's presence.

In the latter portions of the play, the focus shifts from power to pleasure and fame. Faustus is tempted by the Bad Angel with visions of "honour and wealth" (v.22) and later yearns to be "cloy'd" with "all things that delight the heart of man," and to spend his "four-and-twenty years of liberty" in "pleasure" and in "dalliance" (viii.59–62). He also continues to pursue Fame, entreating Mephostophilis, "That Faustus' name, whilst this bright frame doth stand,/May be admired through the furthest land" (viii.63–64). Here, as so often, *hubris* and hedonism combine to doom Marlowe's hero.

But where is the "insatiable Speculator" of traditional criticism, the Renaissance martyr to man's search for knowledge? I suggest that this avid truth seeker is largely a projection from the original "speculator" of the *EFB*, although Marlowe's sorcerer does retain some shrunken vestiges of the keen curiosity of the *EFB* original. Like his predecessor in the source, Marlowe's Faustus disputes with Mephostophilis the metaphysics of hell, but, unlike the *EFB* magician, declines to accept the hard realities of his discovery. Furthermore, Marlowe's necromancer shows interest in astronomical lore, asking probing questions concerning the heavenly bodies and traveling the ornament in a dragon-drawn chariot "to find the secrets of astronomy" (Chorus 1.1–10), as does his *EFB* analogue. Yet, Faustus' astral journey, so vividly recounted in the source (pp. 113–17), is reduced in the play to fourteen lines of choral comment and a brief, mundane narration by the magician himself (viii.69–75). Marlowe's Faustus may wax eloquent on the beauty of Helen and the enchantments of infernal music, but his description of his cosmic flight is extremely pedestrian. Moreover, consonant with the drama's consistent minimizing of intellectual satisfaction, the five chapters in the source exhibiting Faustus' occult expertise (XXIV–XXVIII) have been condensed in Marlowe's tragedy to a mere six choral lines (Chorus 11.7–12).

Therefore, although it would be an oversimplification to say that Marlowe's hero reveals no desire for learning, the lure of forbidden knowledge emerges as a much more prominent feature of the *EFB* than of Marlowe's drama. Such intellectual curiosity as Marlowe's Faustus does exhibit is strongly vitiated by the yearning for power, fame, and wealth. Ultimately, in the tragedy, the desire for the kingdoms, the power, and the glory of the world is paramount, and Faustus seeks knowledge simply as an appurtenance to worldly pleasure and power or as a means of obtaining them. Thus, by shifting the emphasis from the sin of Prometheus to that of Lucifer, Marlowe ironically undercuts his hero's grandiose aspirations, largely invalidating the Satanic view of Faustus as a martyr to Renaissance humanism.

II

Another of Marlowe's provocative alterations in his source is the suggestion of willful self-deceit as a determinant in Faustus' damnation. There is a hint of this perversion of reason in the *EFB* (p. 72), but it occurs later than in the play and is not expanded. Initially, in the source Faustus is not deceived concerning the reality of damnation. Instead, he fears damnation and vainly seeks to obtain his request of the Devil without the loss of his soul (pp. 69–70). However, a change occurs after his second parley with the infernal Spirit, and his mind becomes so inflamed with greed that "he forgot his soul, and promised Mephostophiles to hold all things as he had mentioned them: he thought the Devil was not so black as they used to paint him, nor Hell so hot as the people say" (p. 72). After the compact and the enjoyment of some of its fruits, Faustus becomes passion's slave and his reason is completely overthrown:

> Doctor Faustus continued thus in his Epicurish life day and night, and believed not that there was a God, hell or Devil: he thought that body and soul died together, and had quite forgotten Divinity or the immortality of his soul. . . . (p. 79)

This brief reference, although not developed, was perhaps the embryo from which Marlowe evolved his complex treatment of the perversion of reason by appetite.

In the *EFB*, only after the infernal covenant does Faustus' reason become completely deluded; in Marlowe's tragedy, this perversion is manifest in Faustus' opening soliloquy, a masterly exemplum of reason pandering will. In his canvass of the traditional professions, Marlowe's divine rejects philosophy, physic, and law as unfulfilling, yet his specious rationale suggests that the limitation lies not in these studies but in himself. Thus one suspects that his rejection of these possible careers is simply a convenient rationalization for his future conduct. This tendency toward self-deception is most evident in the latter portion of the soliloquy. Here Faustus, turning to divinity, quotes Scripture out of context, ignoring the promise of grace expressed in the omitted complement of each of the cited verses in order to convince himself that he is already doomed to die eternally. Having persuaded himself of certain damnation, he is eager to exploit his inevitable situation. It is interesting to compare the Faustus of the source, pondering how he can secure both soul and pleasure (p. 70), to Marlowe's sorcerer declaiming, "Had I as many souls as there be stars, / I'd give them all to Mephostophilis" (iii.104–05). In the play, it is Faustus who proffers his soul to Lucifer (iii.92–93) and Mephostophilis who at one point seems reluctant to accept the offer (iii.83–84). Conversely, in the *EFB*, it is the fiend who demands the contract and Faustus who hesitates, attempting to obtain earthly pleasure without loss of spiritual salvation (pp. 69–70).

The self-delusion of Marlowe's Faustus is further reflected in his rationalizations about hell. Having convinced himself that damnation is ineluctable, he seeks to define it in palatable terms. Thus damnation initially terrifies him not at all; he judges hell a fable (v. 128) and confounds it with Elysium (iii.62). When confronted with undeniable evidence to the contrary, he employs casuistic reasoning to convince himself that Mephostophilis cannot be in hell, completely ignoring the definition of terms which would invalidate his logic (v.134–40), as he ignores anything which might impede his headlong career toward pleasure and power.

Similarly, Marlowe's protagonist dismisses all Mephostophilis' warnings. First, he ignores the account of Lucifer's fall by aspiring pride, presented as a kind of "mirror for magistrates" in which he may view his own image and possible fate (iii.65–71). The Lucifer analogy, although introduced at similar points in both play and source, is handled very differently in the two versions (cf. p. 69; iii.65–75). In the *EFB*, Lucifer's sin, although acknowledged, is understated while his glamour and puissance are exaggerated. It is only after the contract that Faustus is granted a fuller chronicle of Lucifer's physical and social descent. In the play, on the other hand, Lucifer's pride and insolence receive special stress and his power and eminence are largely ignored. Moreover, although the *EFB* demon gives an orthodox report of Lucifer's rebellion, before the compact he deletes any reference to the suffering of the fallen angels, whereas in the drama the suffering of the devils is graphically depicted. Secondly, and even more blindly, Marlowe's Faustus fails to heed Mephostophilis' passionate exhortation to "leave these frivolous demands" (iii.83) and remains unmoved by the demon's poignant description of the psychological pain of hell (iii.77–82). The unfortunate necromancer of the *EFB* receives no such cautionary advice and no portrait of damnation is offered before the signing of the bond, although much later hell is pictured with lurid particularly (pp. 84–85, 91–94).

Marlowe's reversal of traditional roles is obvious. The tempter of the *EFB*, like any good salesman, minimizes the liabilities and maximizes the advantages of his product until he has his victim's name on the dotted line, while the vacillating conjurer seeks the best bargain possible. Conversely, in the pre-contract scenes of the drama, Marlowe's Mephostophilis frequently speaks the truth and once even urges his "customer" to abstain from purchasing his product at such an exorbitant price, while it is Faustus himself who plays the Devil's advocate. Thus, Marlowe consistently alters his source to highlight Faustus' own responsibility for his damnation and to ironically undercut his hero's "aspiring mind."

III

Marlowe's Faustus is further undermined by his refusal, until the very end of the play, to acknowledge the vacuity of his bargain. The sorcerer's intransigence echoes that of his *EFB* counterpart, but again Marlowe has enhanced the irony by stressing the vast disparity between desire and achievement and thus Faustus' delusion in clinging to so empty a commitment.

From his initial encounter with his demon familiar, Marlowe's Faustus shows an inability to distinguish between mastery and servitude. In light of subsequent events, Faustus' "How pliant is this Mephostophilis, / Full of obedience and humility! / Such is the force of magic and my spells" (iii.31–33) is bitingly ironic. This confusion of slavery with power finds slight analogy in the *EFB*. In the source, moreover, Faustus' magic has some, although limited, efficacy, and the necromancer is able to constrain demons against their wills (p. 68). In the play, however, Mephostophilis denies Faustus even this satisfaction, immediately informing him that it is not magical coercion but moral corruption which calls the spirits from the vast deep (iii.46–56).

Not only does Faustus' magical power prove chimerical, but the eagerly anticipated rewards of the compact are also largely illusory. Ironically, Marlowe's magician actually achieves none of the conditions for which he barters his soul. In enumerating the first three articles of the bond, Marlowe adhers closely to his source (cf. p. 71; v.95–112). The first article states that Faustus may be a spirit in form and substance, the second that Mephostophilis shall be Faustus' servant and at his command, the third "that Mephostophilis shall do for him and bring him whatsoever." In both the *EFB* and the tragedy, the fulfillment of each condition is more apparent than real, although Marlowe consistently develops the incipient irony of his source.

In both play and source, the keeping of the first condition is equivocal. Although he receives the ultimate punishment of an infernal spirit, damnation, Faustus never really achieves the powers associated with spirits, and when he wishes to travel through space or become invisible, he must do so through the agency of his familiar.[9] Furthermore, the torn shreds of his body, displayed at the end of both tragedy and chapbook, testify to the humanity from which he could never escape.

The second proposition is more blatantly violated in both drama and source, although the ironic focus varies in the two versions. In both accounts, Faustus, instead of achieving dominion over spirits, is himself demonically manipulated. In Marlowe's tragedy, however, the power of the devils is largely psychological whereas the *EFB* is replete with lurid physical torments. Three comparisons are sufficient to illustrate this critical distinction. In scene v, Marlowe's conjurer is distracted from thoughts of connubial bliss by diversions and promises of sensual delights. The devil masquerade and the offering of the courtesans have their origin in the *EFB* (pp. 80–82), but in the source the devil is intended to terrify, not amuse, and the palliative of pleasure is preceded by the discipline of pain. Similarly, Faustus' interrogation concerning God and creation receives considerably milder punishment in the drama. The appearance of the infernal trinity is doubtless terrifying to Marlowe's magician, but his immediate recantation evokes instantaneous reward. Conversely, in the *EFB* (pp. 104–06), the hapless necromancer is first frozen and then cowed by a grotesque parade of fiends whose purpose is to horrify not, like Marlowe's masque of the Seven Deadly Sins, to delight. It is only after he is totally quelled with terror that he is offered the balm of music (p. 107). A similar strategy informs Faustus' abortive repentance with the Old Man. Again, the magician of the source is subjected to harrowing corporal punishment while the mere threat of physical violence causes Marlowe's Faustus to recant and propose a renewal of his bond (cf. xviii.74–81; pp. 183–84).

What is the significance of Marlowe's drastic modification of his source? One possibility is dramatic variety. In the first sequence, Marlowe's Faustus is cajoled; in the second, he is manipulated by both fear of pain and lure of pleasure; in the third, only threats are employed. There is no such carefully structured variety in the source where the necromancer is continually tortured into submission. Another possibility may be that consonant with the philosophical description of hell (v.122–27), which has no correspondence in the source, Marlowe's minimizing of physical punishment accentu-

9. For a discussion of the implications of the term "spirit" in the play, see W. W. Greg. "The Damnation of Faustus," *Modern Language Review*, 41 (1946), 103. Greg argues that in Marlowe's tragedy (as in the *EFB*) the term "spirit" always denotes "devil." For a provocative counterargument, see T. W. Craik, "Faustus' Damnation Reconsidered," *Renaissance Drama*, NS 2 (1969), 190–92. For a full and illuminating discussion of the powers traditionally associated with spirits in general and the limitations identified with devils in particular, see Robert West, *The Invisible World* (Athens: Univ. of Georgia Press, 1939), pp. 24–25.

ates the psychological nature of both Faustus' sin and his suffering, a psychological focus which Cole has so persuasively demonstrated.[1] Nevertheless, although perfectly valid, neither of these suggestions is completely satisfying in explaining Marlowe's radical deviation from his source-book. An additional explanation may be that in the given instances threats of pain are sufficient to control Marlowe's protagonist, rendering physical coercion unnecessary and causing Faustus' bondage in the drama to appear more degrading than in the *EFB*. Thus, the debasement inherent in any covenant with Satan and the ironic hiatus between Faustus' anticipated dominance and his actual servility are vividly dramatized.

Marlowe's ironic method is even more obvious in his treatment of the third article of the bond. This last condition is flagrantly violated in both play and source but the fatuity of Faustus' bargain is more glaringly spotlighted in Marlowe's tragedy. In the drama, Faustus' second request after signing the bond is denied (although the first, information about hell, is answered with disturbing candor). The necromancer is refused a wife and is offered instead surrogates innumerable as well as a book of magic. In the source, the denial of the wife occurs later, after the magician has enjoyed many fruits of his compact, including the entire harem of the Grand Turk (pp. 139–40). Thus the irony is considerably diminished. Faustus' questions concerning astronomy and creation are also evasively answered in both versions. The existence of the fiery and crystalline spheres was a subject of considerable controversy in the sixteenth century, and scholars have actively disagreed concerning the accuracy of Mephostophilis' dissertation on astronomy.[2] Nevertheless, however reliable or unreliable the fiend's data on second causes, his astronomical lecture ultimately proves unsatisfying because it withholds knowledge of the First Cause. On the analogous occasion in the *EFB* Faustus, although refused an account of the creation, is not denied knowledge of the Creator. Moreover, earlier (Chap. XI) the *EFB* sorcerer is offered the description of creation that he is later refused and is even allowed a glimpse of paradise (Chap. XXIII). All Marlowe's changes stress the emptiness of Faustus' bargain. Furthermore, in his dramatic rendering of this section, Marlowe compresses separate sequences from the source—one in which Faustus demands and receives astronomical information, and another in which he requests and is refused knowledge of cre-

1. *Suffering and Evil*, pp. 192–210, 229–30.
2. Some of the more authoritative discussions concerning this controversy include the following: F. R. Johnson, "Marlowe's 'Imperial Heaven,'" *ELH*, 12 (1945), 35–44, and "Marlowe's Astronomy and Renaissance Skepticism," *ELH*, 13 (1946), 241–54; Kocher, pp. 214–19; Greg, *Dr. Faustus: 1604–1616. Parallel Texts* (Oxford: Clarendon, 1950), p. 338, nn. 630–31; Brockbank, p. 47.

ation (Chaps. XVIII and XIX)—into one brief and moving scene. He also skillfully counterpoises two scenes of frustration, one in which Faustus is denied a wife, the other in which he is refused knowledge of creation. By compressing his material and skillfully juxtaposing two scenes of frustration (one sensual, one intellectual) and diversion (in both cases Faustus is distracted by nugatory substitutes), Marlowe again accentuates the reversal of expectation adumbrated but not clearly formulated in the *EFB*. Through this pervasive use of *peripety* Marlowe makes us acutely aware, as the *EFB* author does not, of the tragic falling off of Faustus and of the degree to which his overreach exceeds his grasp.

IV

And yet, critics have continually asked, is Faustus' obduracy in damnation the result of self-delusion, despair, or simple necessity? This leads us to the central crux of the play, the problem of repentance. What is the exact nature of Faustus' bondage? Is repentance really possible within the moral framework of the play? On this point there has historically been considerable dispute since Una Ellis-Fermor first asserted that "implicit in Marlowe's premise is the predestination of man to destruction by some determinate power capable of purpose and intention,"[3] a power she defined as sadistic. Levin endorses Ellis-Fermor, and Ribner although acknowledging the possibility of repentance finds it demeaning, as it would mean the rejection of all those human aspirations which led Faustus to make his bargain in the first place. Kirschbaum, Kocher, Smith, and Cole are of a different persuasion, insisting that repentance is always possible and laudable.[4] Again, a comparison of tragedy and chapbook is useful in resolving this controversy.

Because of the many differences in the fictional and dramatic forms, treatment of moral issues in these two genres must naturally differ considerably. The *EFB*, although containing elements of the jest-book, is essentially a didactic moral treatise. The author may intrude directly to guide the reader's response, and in several homiletic passages, most notably the comment concluding Chapter XIII, he does just that, denying the binding force of the compact while affirming the everpresent opportunity for repentance:

> In this perplexity lay this miserable Doctor Faustus, having quite forgot his faith in Christ, never falling to repentance truly, thereby to attain the grace and holy Spirit of God again, the which would have been able to have resisted the strong as-

3. Ellis-Fermor, p. 141.
4. Levin, p. 133; Ribner, p. xxxix; Smith, pp. 46–47; Kirschbaum, p. 103; Cole, pp. 202–03.

> saults of Satan: for although he had made him a promise, yet he might have remembered through true repentance sinners come again into the favour of God. (pp. 87–88)

Later, in one of the most sophisticated passages of the *EFB*, the author incorporates this concept into a dramatic context, expressing it, ironically, through the mouth of Satan's own emissary:

> (quoth Faustus) . . . tell me Mephostophiles, wouldst thou be in my case as I am now? Yes, saith the Spirit (and with that fetched a great sigh) for yet would I so humble myself, that I would win the favour of God. Then (said Doctor Faustus) it were time enough for me if I amended. True (said Mephostophiles), if it were not for thy great sins, which are so odious and detestable in the sight of God, that it is too late for thee. . . . (p. 98)

The implication is clear. Despite Mephostophiles' immediate denial, the speech confirms the demon's own conviction that grace is available, even to Faustus. In the wistful piety of this speech, do we perhaps find the inspiration for the passionate lamentation of Marlowe's demon over his damnation (iii.78–84)? Except for this one deviation, however, Mephostophiles, as the agent of the "father of lies," consistently rejects the possibility of penance while the author continually assures us that Faustus is always free to repent.

In adapting his source to the dramatic medium and in transforming a didactic moral treatise into a complex, psychological study of error and self-deception, Marlowe not only maintains the moral focus of his source but even makes salient additions and alterations to give this focus added impact. By manipulating character, plot, and structure with great variety and skill, he achieves a firm and unambiguous affirmation of man's freedom and responsibility while relying only minimally on direct choral statement.

One of Marlowe's most effective additions is to embody the alternatives facing his hero in two Morality play descendants, the Good and Bad Angels, who remind us constantly of the ubiquity of choice and of Faustus' personal onus. Furthermore, the very appearance of the Good Angel and Faustus' recurrent *psychomachiae* would seem to refute the magician's predestination to damnation by a malevolent Deity. There is absolutely no suggestion in the source for either the benign or malefic angel.

Another technique employed by Marlowe to clarify the options facing Faustus is to rearrange and modify various episodes from his source. Thus, the gift of Faustus' soul is contrasted with the gift of crowns (v), God's creation of the world with the Devil's creation of sin (vi), and the Old Man's counsel with Helen's temptation (xviii). Although the gift of crowns and the Masque of the Seven Deadly

Sins are totally original with Marlowe, both the Old Man and Helen derive from the source, but in the *EFB* the two sequences are separated by seven intervening chapters and several years. In the source, moreover, Helen does not appear at a time of spiritual crisis nor is she an agent of Faustus' damnation. She occupies a subordinate position as one of the long procession of Faustus' amours. In the play, however, the juxtaposition is patent. The Old Man, by word and by example, offers Faustus the hard road to salvation: only through present pain can Faustus achieve eternal bliss. Helen represents the alternative, the path of immediate pleasure leading to ultimate damnation. In turning from the Old Man to Helen, Faustus, consonant with his behavior throughout the play, rejects the Creator of the world for the god of his own appetite.

With brilliant dramatic economy, Marlowe also transforms the Old Man into a foil for Faustus as well as for Helen. In the *EFB*, the triumph of the Old Man is explicit. Not only is he triumphant but he is unharmed (p. 185). In the play, however, his final soliloquy is ambiguous. The lines, "I fly unto my God" (xviii.127), could foreshadow the Old Man's martyrdom or they could describe his flight to the sanctuary of God's protection. At any rate, in Marlowe's tragedy the Old Man's faith and courage in the face of imminent pain or even death provide a vivid contrast to Faustus' cowardice and lack of faith, thus magnifying both Faustus' responsibility and his frailty.

Marlowe further amplifies suggestions in the source and even introduces additional episodes to remind us of the "gift of God" so persistently ignored by Faustus. The first of God's miraculous interventions occurs during the critical contract scene (v). At this moment of spiritual crisis, the grace of God penetrates the web of delusion and error in which Faustus has enveloped himself, first congealing his blood, then inscribing on his arm the brief yet eloquent warning, *Homo fuge*. It is one of the most penetrating ironies of the play that this one evidence of reality in a mass of deception—the long desired "miracle"—should be rejected as hallucination. Here, as elsewhere, Faustus refuses to concede God's mercy or even to accept ocular proof of its existence, exclaiming, "My senses are deceiv'd, here's nothing writ" (v.79). Even when Faustus finally acknowledges the stigmatic script, he shows no awareness of the supernatural grace effecting this heavenly caveat, lamenting instead, "Whither whould I fly? / If unto God, he'll throw me down to hell" (v.77–78). The treatment of the analogous scene in the *EFB* is comparatively terse and undramatic (p. 73). The congealing of the blood was probably suggested by the sub-heading of Chapter VI, "How Doctor Faustus set his blood in a saucer on warm ashes, and writ as followeth" (p. 74), but there is no reference to the actual coagulation of the sorcerer's blood. The warning, *Homo fuge*, does appear in the source, but is not developed. From this exiguous treatment, Marlowe has evolved a dramatic and ironic scene, expanding the single miracle into two in order to affirm the validity of the very system his protagonist is rejecting. Similarly, in the final scene of the play when all seems lost and even the Good Angel admits defeat, Marlowe has introduced another miracle, a vision of Christ's blood streaming in the firmament, to remind Faustus, and the audience, of Christ's redeeming sacrifice.[5] There is no corresponding sign of grace in the *EFB*; Faustus appears doomed after his rejection of the Old Man and the author offers no ameliorating hope of eleventh-hour salvation. The scholars at Faustus' farewell dinner do insist that redemption is always available (pp. 203–04), but in the absence of any tokens of grace this assurance remains unconvincing. Marlowe, however, through the image of the ensanguined heavens, mitigates the *EFB* portrait of a stern, unyielding Deity and reminds the audience, as his source on this occasion does not, of God's infinite mercy. The latter miracle, like the earlier two, would be both dramatically and theologically gratuitous if Faustus were indeed predestined to damnation by the inscrutable Deity of the Satanic critics.

V

To summarize briefly, this analysis reveals several crucial changes which Marlowe has made in translating his source material into tragic dramatic meaning. Although worldliness remains Faustus' *harmartia*, the shift in emphasis from forbidden knowledge to power, from the sin of Prometheus to that of Lucifer, radically alters the nature of his transgression. Furthermore, by magnifying the hero's aspirations (making them vaster if not more lofty) and sharply curtailing his realization, Marlowe accentuates the vast disparity between the omnipotence of Faustus' dream and the impotence of his reward. By introducing elements of self-deception and rationalization, Marlowe adds psychological credibility to Faustus' irrational determination, while simultaneously reversing the roles of tempter and tempted to stress Faustus' personal onus for his

---

5. Some critics might argue that Faustus' reference to Christ's blood streaming in the firmament should be read metaphorically not literally. In this particular dramatic context, I find this interpretation untenable. The use of the word "streams" implicitly associates the vision of the ensanguined heavens with the earlier miracle of the coagulated blood. Earlier, divine grace impeded the stream of Faustus' blood that he might not endanger his salvation; now, divine grace sends another miracle, the vision of Christ's blood streaming in the heavens, to remind him that he is not irrevocably damned. Furthermore, the entire strategy of the scene suggests an actual vision. First, there is Faustus' prayer for the impossible miracle, that time would have a stop, answered by God's supernatural reminder that the miracle, the conquest of time by eternity, has already been effected through Christ's atoning blood.

damnation. By adapting Morality conventions and modifying dramatic structure, character, and action, Marlowe affirms the concepts of volition and responsibility which form the moral fulcrum of both play and source. Finally, by minimizing the physical power of the spirits and maximizing Faustus' increasing servility, Marlowe vividly illustrates the effect of error and compromise on the disintegration of the human ego. Every alteration Marlowe makes in his source intensifies the tragic emotion of the drama, exacerbating the pity and terror, stressing the enormity of Faustus' flaw and the immensity of his fall. Therefore, although the catastrophe of the play lacks the ghastly physical horror of the *EFB*, Marlowe's tragedy is the more terrible of the two accounts. It relates not the physical sunderance but the psychological dilaceration of the human personality by sin.

Renaissance Magic

HENRY CORNELIUS AGRIPPA

Henry Cornelius Agrippa (1486–1535), a German mystic and alchemist, was born near Cologne and studied both medicine and law there. In 1509, he set up an alchemical laboratory in Dole with the goal of synthesizing gold; for the next decade he traveled throughout Europe, displaying his alchemical skills. In 1520, he set up a medical practice in Geneva and in 1524 became physician to the queen mother at the court of King Francis I in Lyon. He wrote widely, his most important work being the three-volume *De Occulta Philosophiae* (written around 1510 and published in 1531), a defense of "hidden philosophy" (i.e., magic). Spelling and punctuation have been modernized.

From Three Books of Occult Philosophy

"The Life of Henry Cornelius Agrippa, Knight"

Henry Cornelius Agrippa, descended from a noble Family of Nettesheim in Belgia, Doctor of the Laws and Physic, Master of the Rolls, and Judge of the Spiritual Court, from his youth he applied his mind to learning, and by his happy wit obtained great knowledge in all arts and sciences; afterwards also he followed the Army of the Princes, and for his valor was created Knight in the Field. When he was by these means famous for learning and arms about 1530, he gave his mind to writing and composed *Three Books of Occult Philosophy*; afterward an *Invective or Cynical Declamation of the Uncertainty and Vanity of all Things*, in which he teacheth that there is no certainty in anything, but in the solid words of God, and that, to lie hid in the eminency of God's word. He also wrote a *History of the Double Coronation of the Emperor Charles*, and also of the excellency of the feminine sex, and of the apparitions of spirits; but seeing that he published commentaries on the *Ars Brevis* of Raymundus Lully [Ramon Lull], and was very much addicted to occult philosophy and astrology, there were those who thought that he enjoyed commerce with devils, whom notwithstanding he confuted in his published *Apology*, and showed, that he kept himself within the bounds of art. He wrote many learned orations, which manifest to all the excellency of his wit * * * and therefore by these monuments published, the name of Cornelius for his variety of learning was famous, not only amongst the Germans, but also other nations; for Momus himself carpeth at all amongst the gods; amongst the heroes, Hercules hunteth after monsters; amongst devils, Pluto the king of hell is angry with all the ghosts; amongst Philosophers Democritus laugheth at all things, on the contrary Heraclitus weepeth at all things; Pirrhias is ignorant of all things, and Aristotle thinketh he knoweth all things; Diogenes contemneth all things; this Agrippa spareth none, he contemneth, knows, is ignorant, weeps, laughs, is angry, pursueth, carps at all things, being himself a Philosopher, a Demon, a hero, a god, and all things.

To the Reader

I do not doubt but the title of our *Book of Occult Philosophy*, or *of Magic*, may by the rarity of it allure many to read it, amongst which some of a crazy judgment and some that are perverse will come to hear what I can say, who, by their rash ignorance may take the name of "magic" in the worse sense, and though scarce having seen the title, cry out that I teach forbidden arts, sow the seed of heresies, offend pious ears, and scandalize excellent wits; that I am a sorcerer, and superstitious and devilish, [and] indeed am a magician. To whom I answer, that a magician doth not amongst learned men signify a sorcerer, or one that is superstitious or devilish, but a wise man, a priest, a prophet; and that the Sybils were magicianesses, and therefore prophecied most clearly of Christ; and that Magicians, as wise men, by the wonderful secrets of the world, knew Christ, the author of the world, to be born, and came first of all to worship him; and that the name of "magic" was received by philosophers, commended by divines, and not unacceptable to the Gospel. I believe that the supercilious censors will object against the Sybils, holy magicians, and the Gospel itself sooner then receive the name of "magic" into favor; so conscientious are they, that neither Apollo, nor all the muses, nor an angel from heaven can redeem me from their curse. Whom therefore I advise, that they read not our writings, nor understand them, nor remember them. For they are pernicious and full of poison; the gate of Acheron is in this book. It speaks stones, let them take heed that it beat not out their brains. But you that come without prejudice to read it, if you have so much discretion of prudence, as bees have in gathering honey, read securely, and believe that you shall receive no little profit, and much pleasure; but if you shall find any things that may not please you, let them alone and make no use of them, for I do not approve of them, but declare them to you; but do not refuse other things, for they that look into the books of physicians do, together with antidotes and medicines, read also poisons. I confess that magic itself teacheth many superfluous things, and curious prodigies for ostentation. Leave them as empty things, yet be not ignorant of their causes. But those things which are for the profit of man, for the turning away of evil events, for the destroying of sorceries, for the curing of diseases, for the exterminating of phantasmes, for the preserving of life, honor, or fortune, may be done without offense to God or injury to religion, because they are, as profitable, so necessary . . .

*To R. P. D. Iohn Trithemius, an Abbot of Saint James in the
Suburbs of Herbipolis, Henry Cornelius Agrippa of
Nettesheym Sendeth Greeting.*

When I was of late (most reverend Father) for a while conversant with you in your monastery of Herbipolis, we conferred together of diverse things concerning chemistry, magic, and Kabbalah, and of other things, which as yet lie hid in secret sciences, and arts; and then there was one great question amongst the rest, why magic, whereas it was accounted by all ancient philosophers the chiefest Science, and by the ancient wise men and priests was always held in great veneration, came at last after the beginning of the Catholic Church to be always odious to and suspected by the holy Fathers, and then exploded by Divines, and condemned by sacred Canons, and moreover by all laws and ordinances forbidden. Now the cause, as I conceive is no other then this: *viz.* because by a certain fatal depravation of times and men, many false philosophers crept in, and these under the name of magicians, heaping together through various sorts of errors and factions of false religions, many cursed superstitions and dangerous rites, and many wicked sacrileges out of orthodox religion, even to the perfection of nature, and destruction of men, and injury of God, set forth very many wicked, and unlawfull books, such as we see carried about in these days, to which they have by stealth prefixed the most honest name, and title of "Magic." They therefore by this sacred title of "Magic," hoped to gain credit to their cursed and detestable fooleries. Hence it is that this name of "Magic," formerly honorable, is now in these days become most odious to good and honest men, and accounted a capital crime if any one dare profess himself to be a magician, either in doctrine or works—unless haply some certain old doting woman dwelling in the country would be believed to be skilful and have divine power, that (as saith Apuleius) she can throw down the

Heaven, lift up the earth, harden fountains, wash away mountains, raise up ghosts, cast down the gods, extinguish the stars, illuminate hell, or, as Virgil sings,

> She'll promise by her charms to cast great cares,
> Or ease the minds of men, and make the stars
> For to go back, and rivers to stand still,
> And raise the nightly ghosts even at her will,
> To make the earth to groan, and trees to fall
> From the mountains——

Hence those things, which Lucan relates of Thessala the magianess, and Homer of the omnipotency of Circe, whereof many I confess are as well of a fallacious opinion, as a superstitious diligence, and pernicious labor, as when they cannot come under a wicked art, yet they presume they may be able to cloak themselves under that venerable title of "magic." Since then these things are so, I wondered much, and was not less angry, that as yet there hath been no man, who did challenge this sublime and sacred discipline with the crime of impiety, or had delivered it purely and sincerely to us, since I have seen of our modern writers Roger Bacon, Robert [of York,] an English man, Peter [d'Abano], Albertus [Magnus] the Teutonich, Arnoldas de villa Nova, Anselm the Parmensian, Picatrix the Spaniard, Cicclus Asculus of Florence, and many others, but writers of an obscure name, when they promised to treat of magic, do nothing but irrational toys and superstitions unworthy of honest men. Hence my spirit was moved, and by reason partly of admiration and partly of indignation, I was willing to play the philosopher, supposing that I should do no discommendable work, who have been always from my youth a curious and undaunted searcher for wonderful effects and operations full of mysteries; if I should recover that ancient magic the discipline of all wise men from the errors of impiety, purify and adorn it with its proper luster, and vindicate it from the injuries of calumniators; which thing, though I long deliberated of it in my mind, yet never durst as yet undertake, but after some conference betwixt us of these things at Herbipolis, your transcending knowledge and learning, and your ardent adhortation put courage and boldness into me. There selecting the opinions of philosophers of known credit and purging the introduction of the wicked (who dissemblingly, with a counterfeited knowledge did teach, that traditions of magicians must be learned from very reprobate books of darkness, as from institutions of wonderful operations) and removing all darkness, have at last composed three compendious books of magic, and titled them *Of Occult Philosophy*, being a title less offensive, which books I submit (you excelling in the knowledge of these things) to your correction and censure, that if I have wrote any thing which may tend either to the contumely of nature, offending God, or injury of religion, you may condemn the error; but if the scandal of impiety be dissolved and purged, you may defend the tradition of truth; and that you would do so with these books, and magic itself, that nothing may be concealed which may be profitable, and nothing approved of which cannot but do hurt, by which means these three books having passed your examination with approbation, may at length be thought worthy to come forth with good success in public, and may not be afraid to come under the censure of posterity.

Farewell, and pardon these my bold undertakings.

Chap. 2 "What Magic Is, What Are the Parts Thereof, and How the Professors Thereof Must Be Qualified"

Magic is a faculty of wonderful virtue, full of most high mysteries, containing the most profound contemplation of most secret things, together with the nature, power, quality, substance, and virtues thereof, as also the knowledge of whole nature; and it doth instruct us concerning the differing and agreement of things amongst themselves, whence it produceth its wonderful effects, by uniting the virtues of things through the application of them one to the other and to their inferior sutable subjects, joining and knitting them together thoroughly by the powers and virtues of the superior bodies. This is the most perfect and chief science, that sacred and sublimer kind of philosophy, and lastly the most absolute perfection of all most excellent philosophy . . .

[A]ll regulative philosophy is divided into natural, mathematical, and theological. Natural philosophy teacheth the nature of those things which are in the world, searching and enquiring into their causes, effects, times, places, fashions, events, their whole and parts also.

> The number and the nature of those things,
> Called elements, what fire, earth, air forth brings:
> From whence the heavens their beginnings had;
> Whence tide, whence rainbow, in gay colors clad.
> What makes the clouds that gathered are, and black,
> To send forth lightnings, and a thundering crack;
> What doth the nightly flames, and comets make;
> What makes the earth to swell, and then to quake:
> What is the seed of metals, and of gold
> What virtues, wealth, doth nature's coffer hold.

All these things doth natural philosophy, the viewer of nature contain, teaching us according to Virgil's Muse.

> Whence all things flow,
> Whence mankind, beast; whence fire, whence rain and snow,
> Whence earthquakes are; why the whole ocean beats
> Over his banks and then again retreats;
> Whence strength of herbs, whence courage, rage of brutes,
> All kinds of stone, of creeping things, and fruits.

But mathematical philosophy teacheth us to know the quantity of natural bodies, as extended into three dimensions, as also to conceive of the motion and course of celestial bodies.

> As in great haste,
> What makes the golden stars to march so fast;
> What makes the moon sometimes to mask her face;
> The Sun also, as if in some disgrace.

And as Virgil sings:

> How the sun doth rule with twelve zodiac signs,
> The orb thats measured round about with lines,
> It doth the heaven's starry way make known,
> And strange eclipses of the sun and moon.
> Arcturus also, and the Stars of Rain,
> The Seven Stars likewise, and Charles his Wain,
> Why winter suns make towards the West so fast;
> What makes the nights so long ere they be past?

All which is understood by mathematical philosophy.

> Hence by the heavens we may foreknow
> The seasons all, times for to reap and sow,
> And when 'tis fit to launch into the deep
> And when to war, and when in peace to sleep,
> And when to dig up trees, and them again
> To set that so they may bring forth amain.

Now theological philosophy, or divinity, teacheth what God is, what the mind, what an Intelligence, what an angel, what a devil, what the soul, what religion, what sacred institutions, rites, temples, observations, and sacred mysteries are. It instructs us also concerning faith, miracles, the virtues of words and figures, the secret operations and mysteries of seals, and, as Apuleius saith, it teacheth us rightly to understand and to be skilled in the ceremonial laws, the equity of holy things, and rule of religions.

But to recollect myself, these three principal faculties magic comprehends, unites, and actuates, Deservedly therefore was it by the ancients esteemed as the highest and most sacred philosophy. It was, as we find, brought to light by most sage authors and most famous writers, amongst which principally Zamolxis and Zoroaster were so famous, that many believed they were the inventors of this science. Their track, Abbaris the Hyperborean, Charmondas, Damigeron, Eudoxus, Hermippus followed. There were also other eminent, choice men, as Mercurius Trismegistus, Porphyry, Iamblichus, Plotinus, Proclus, Dardanus, Orpheus the Thracian, Gog the Grecian, Germa the Babylonian, Apollonius of Tyana. Osthanes also wrote excellently in this art, whose books being, as it were, lost, Democritus of Abdera recovered and set forth with his own commentaries. Besides Pythagoras, Empedocles, Democritus, Plato, and many other renowned philosophers travelled far by sea to learn this art, and, being returned, published it with wonderful devoutness, esteeming of it as a great secret. Also, it is well known that Pythagoras and Plato went to the prophets of Memphis to learn it and travelled through almost all Syria, Egypt, Judea, and the schools of the Chaldaeans that they might not be ignorant of the most sacred memorials and records of magic, as also that they might be furnished with divine things. Whosoever, therefore, is desirous to study in this faculty, if he be not skilled in natural philosophy, wherein are discovered the qualities of things and in which are found the occult properties of every being; and if he be not skilful in the mathematics and in the aspects and figures of the stars, upon which depends the sublime virtue and property of every thing; and if he be not learned in theology, wherein are manifested those immaterial substances, which dispense and minister all things, he cannot be possibly able to understand the rationality of magic. For there is no work that is done by mere magic, nor any work that is merely magical, that doth not comprehend these three faculties.

KEITH THOMAS

Conjuring and the Magical Tradition†

Until the later seventeenth century the work of the practising wizard was sustained by the parallel activities of many contemporary intellectuals. Indeed the possibility of certain types of magic was a fundamental presupposition for most scientists and philosophers. Traditional cosmology portrayed an inanimate Earth or elemental world upon which played the influence of the heavenly bodies. This in itself was sufficient to encourage speculation about the astral reasons for earthly phenomena, and to give rise to much lore about the astrologically derived properties of plants and minerals. It also

† From *Religion and the Decline of Magic* (London: Orion Publishing Group, 1971), pp. 222–26. Reprinted by permission of The Orion Publishing Group Ltd.

suggested the possibility that the magician might find some means of tapping the influence of the stars and diverting it to other purposes. Throughout the Middle Ages there had been a continuous stream of magical speculation along these lines.

But the potentialities open to human ingenuity were greatly enhanced by the tide of Neoplatonism which swept through Renaissance Europe. The revival of this, the last school of ancient pagan philosophy, fostered a disposition to blur the difference between matter and spirit. Instead of being regarded as an inanimate mass, the Earth itself was deemed to be alive. The universe was peopled by a hierarchy of spirits, and thought to manifest all kinds of occult influences and sympathies. The cosmos was an organic unity in which every part bore a sympathetic relationship to the rest. Even colours, letters and numbers were endowed with magical properties. The investigation of such phenomena was the primary task of the natural philosopher, and their employment for his own purposes was the distinguishing mark of the magician. Three main types of magical activity thus lay open: natural magic, concerned to exploit the occult properties of the elemental world; celestial magic, involving the influence of the stars; and ceremonial magic, an appeal for aid to spiritual beings.

In this general intellectual climate it was easy for many magical activities to gain a plausibility which they no longer possess today. The doctrine of correspondences, or relationships between each part of the physical world, made possible the belief in systems of divination like palmistry and physiognomy; for, just as an individual man was believed to mirror the world in miniature, so the hand or the face mirrored the man. Such systems worked by what the German, Cornelius Agrippa, called 'the harmoniacal correspondency of all the parts of the body'.[1] From the disposition of the part one could infer that of the whole. In the same way one could accept the doctrine of signatures, according to which every herb bore a visible indication of its medical role. The work of the astrologers was similarly reinforced, for the influence of the celestial bodies upon the constitution of earthly ones could not be doubted. Even geomancy could be justified as the prophetic message of the soul communicated in a state of rapture.[2]

Further support for this kind of reasoning came from the doctrine of the magnet, set out by William Gilbert, himself a convinced believer in the theory that the world was alive. The magnet seemed

1. H. C. Agrippa, *Three Books of Occult Philosophy*, trans. J. F(reake?) (London, 1651), p. 107.
2. On signatures see, e.g., H. More, *An Antidote against Atheisme* (London, 1653), II. 6, and on geomancy, C. H. Josten, 'Robert Fludd's theory of geomancy and his experiences at Avignon in the winter of 1601 to 1602', *Journ. of the Warburg & Courtauld Institutes*, xxvii (1964): 327–35.

to open the possibility of telepathy, magical healing and action at a distance.[3] Sympathetic healing by the weapon-salve was easily acceptable, for it exploited the invisible effluvia and influences with which the world vibrated. It made sense to apply the ointment to the weapon rather than the wound because then the vital spirits in the blood congealed on the weapon would be drawn along in the air to rejoin the body. The technique, said Robert Fludd, was not 'cacomagical, but only naturally magical'. The Royal Society accordingly showed considerable interest in such 'magnetical cures' during its early years.[4] The use of the divining-rod was also stimulated by magnetical theory, for the instrument could be seen as a kind of lodestone, 'drawing iron to it by a secret virtue, inbred by nature, and not by any conjuration as some have fondly imagined'. It too was taken seriously by the Royal Society.[5] 'If we should consider the operations of this magnet,' wrote the virtuoso Elias Ashmole, 'there is no other mystery, celestial, elemental or earthly, which can be too hard for our belief.'[6]

Neoplatonic theory also emphasised the influence of the imagination upon the body, of the mind upon matter, and of words, incantations and written charms upon physical objects. By the exercise of his imagination, and the use of magic, symbols and incantations, the operator could transform either himself or his victim. Since the world was a pulsating mass of vital influences and invisible spirits, it was only necessary that the magician should devise the appropriate technique to capture them. He could then do wonders.

The intellectual study of magic was a European phenomenon emerging in the Florentine Italian Renaissance with the Platonism of such writers as Ficino and Pico della Mirandola, and spreading to Northern Europe through the works of Paracelsus and Cornelius Agrippa. A key role in the movement was played by Ficino's Latin translation of the *Corpus Hermeticum*, the supposed teachings of the ancient Egyptian god Thoth, or 'Hermes Trismegistus'. This compilation had been put together during the first few centuries after Christ, but was generally believed by Renaissance intellectuals to be pre-Christian, pre-Platonic and possibly even pre-Mosaic. It

3. W. Gilbert, *On the Magnet*, ed. D. J. Price (New York, 1958), V. xii; Kocher, *Science and Religion in Elizabethan England* (San Marino, Calif.: Huntington Library, 1953), pp. 181–2. There is a valuable discussion of the prospects raised by Gilbert's work in A. G. Debus, 'Robert Fludd and the use of Gilbert's *De Magnete* in the weapon-salve controversy', *Journ. of the Hist. of Medicine*, xix (1964).

4. R. Fludd, *Mosaicall Philosophy* (London, 1659), p. 289; T. Birch, *The History of the Royal Society of London* (London: A. Millar, 1756–7) i, pp. 25, 29, 31, 33; *Philosophical Trans.*, xix (1697), pp. 518–21.

5. (G. Plattes), *A Discovery of Subterraneall Treasure* (London, 1639), p. 13; Birch, op. cit., i, pp. 231–2, 234, 270.

6. E. Ashmole, *Theotrum Chemicum Britannicum* (London, 1652), p. 464.

taught that by mystical regeneration it was possible for man to re-gain the domination over nature which he had lost at the Fall. Its astrological and alchemical lore helped to create an intellectual en-vironment sympathetic to every kind of mystical and magical activ-ity.[7]

In England esoteric magical speculation was largely a derivative affair, stimulated by continental writings, but adding little of its own. It found no place in conventional Protestant education. Dee, Gilbert and Raleigh were deeply influenced, but Bacon was scepti-cal of the doctrines of sympathy and antipathy, which he thought but 'idle and most slothful conjectures', and he regarded talk of secret hidden virtues as an arrogant substitute for painstaking thought and investigation.[8] The most elaborate English hermeticist was Robert Fludd (1574–1637), whose misfortune it was to have been born at a time when the intellectual presuppositions of the system had already come under attack. Yet although Isaac Casau-bon's scholarship deprived the Hermetic books of their claim to be pre-Christian as early as 1614, the cult of Hermes Trismegistus had its English adherents throughout the seventeenth century, partly no doubt because Casaubon's discovery was tucked away in his polemic against the Counter Reformation historian, Baronius. Fludd wrote prolifically during the following decades, untroubled by Casaubon's findings, and John Everard's translation of the her-metic *Pymander* (1649) disseminated the tradition more widely. The preface unrepentantly asserted that the work had been written 'some hundreds of years before Moses'. In the latter half of the century astrologers and occult physicians continued to assert its antiquity and near-divinity: 'Hermes Trismegistus' even appears as a Christian name in a Hampshire parish register.[9]

But by the time this magical tradition had begun to make any

7. For modern editions see *Hermetica*, ed. Walter Scott (Oxford: Clarendon Press, 1924–36), and *Corpus Hermeticum*, ed. A. D. Nock and A.-J. Fustigière (Paris: Société d'édition "Les Belles Lettres," 1945–54). For a full account of the Hermetic tradition see Frances A. Yates, *Giordano Bruno and the Hermetic Tradition* (Chicago: University of Chicago Press, 1964), and Yates, *Occult Philosophy in the Elizabethan Age* (London: Routledge and Kegan Paul, 1979).

8. Francis Bacon, *The Works of Francis Bacon*, ed. James Spedding, Robert Leslie Ellis, and Douglas Denon Heath, 7 vols. (London: Longmans, 1887–1901), II, pp. 671–2; IV, pp. 84, 167, 255, 355, 366–68, 376 (views which were already held in 1601 by William Barlow, later Archdeacon of Salisbury, *H. M. C. Hatfield*, xi, 4). See also D. P. Walker, *Spiritual and Demonic Magic: From Ficino to Campanella* (London: Warburg Institute, 1958), pp. 199–202.

9. William Andrews Fearon and John Foster Williams, *The Parish Registers and Parochial Documents in the Archdeaconry of Winchester* (London: Warren and Sons, 1909), p. 24. For some seventeenth-century English Hermeticists see C. L. Marks, "Thomas Traherne and Hermes Trismegistus," *Renaissance News* 19 (1966); see also James Maxwell, *A New Eight-Fold Probation of the Church of England's Divine Constitution* (London, 1617); Henry Cornelius Agrippa, *His Fourth Book of Occult Philosophy*, trans. R. Turner (London, 1655); Henry More, *Tetractys Anti-Astrologia* (London, 1681); and John Case, *The Angelical Guide* (London, 1691).

substantial impact upon the population at large it was beginning to
lose its intellectual repute. Around the middle of the century most
serious scientists were moving over from an animistic universe to a
mechanistic one. Those virtuosi who continued to search for occult
virtues and correspondences were essentially outside the mainstream of scientific thinking which was to culminate with Isaac
Newton; though even Newton subscribed to the hermetic notion
that the true knowledge of the universe had been earlier revealed
by God to the ancients, the *prisci theologi*.[1] Natural science owed
much to the stimulus of hermetic thinking but its emancipation
from that tradition was accomplished in the later seventeenth century.[2]

* * *

1. J. E. Maguire and P. M. Rattansi, "Newton and the 'Pipes of Pan,' " *Notes and Records of the Royal Society* 21 (1966): 108–43.
2. Frances A. Yates, "The Hermetic Tradition in Renaissance Science," in *Art, Science, and History in the Renaissance*, ed. Charles S. Singleton (Baltimore: Johns Hopkins University Press, 1967), pp. 255–74; P. M. Rattansi, "The Intellectual Origins of the Royal Society," *Notes and Records of the Royal Society* 23 (1968): 129–43.

Religion

JOHN CALVIN

Calvin (1509–1564), born in France but working for most of his life in Geneva, was the most influential of the Continental reformers on the English church. *The Institution of the Christian Religion* (or *The Institutes*, as it later became known) was initially published in Latin in 1536. Thomas Norton's English translation appeared first in 1561 (the edition from which these selections are taken) and was published eight more times by 1632. Spelling and punctuation have been modernized. The biblical references inserted in brackets are transposed from Calvin's marginal notes.

From The Institution of the Christian Religion

From *Book 1, Chapter 1, Paragraph 1 (sig. A1ʳ)*

The whole sum, in a manner of all our wisdom, which only ought to be accounted true and perfect wisdom, consisteth in two parts: that is to say, the knowledge of God and of ourselves. But whereas these two knowledges be with many bonds linked together, yet whether [one] goeth before or engender the other is hard to discern. For first, no man can look upon himself but he must needs by and by turn all his senses to the beholding of God in whom he liveth and is moved, because it is plain that those gifts wherewith we be endowed are not of ourselves; yea, even that we have being is nothing else an essence in the one God. Finally, by these good things that are, as by dropmeal, poured unto us from heaven, we are led, as it were, by certain streams to the spraying head [i.e. fountain head] and so, by our own neediness, better appeareth that infinite plenty of good things that abideth in God. Specially, that miserable ruin, whereinto the first fall hath thrown us, compelleth us to lift our eyes, not only being foodless and hungry, to crave from thence that which we lack, but also being awakened with fear to learn humility.

From *Book 1, Chapter 17, Paragraph 11 (sig. H8ᵛ–I1ʳ)*

But when that light of God's providence hath once shined upon a godly man, he is now relieved and delivered not only from the extreme anguish and fear wherewith he was before oppressed, but also from all care. For, as justly as he feareth fortune, so he dare boldly commit himself to God. This is (I say) his comfort: to understand that the heavenly father doth so hold in all things with his power, so ruleth them with his authority and countenance, so ordereth them with his wisdom, that nothing befalleth but by his appointment, and that he is received into God's tuition and committed to the charge of angels and cannot be touched with any hurt of water nor fire nor weapon, but so far as it shall please God the governor to give them place . . . Now if their safety be assailed either by the devil or by wicked men, in that case if they were not strengthened with remembrance and meditation of providence they must needs be discouraged. But when they call to mind that the devil and all the rout of the wicked are so every way holden in by the hand of God as with a bridle, that they can neither conceive any mischief against us, nor go about it when they have conceived it, nor if they go never so much about it, can stir one finger to bring it to pass but so far as he shall suffer, yea, so far as he shall command, and that they are not only holden fast bound with fetters, but also compelled with bridle to do service; here have they abundantly wherewith to comfort themselves. For as it is the Lord's work to arm their fury and to turn and direct it whither it pleaseth him, so is it his work also to appoint a measure and end, that they do not alter their own will licentiously triumph.

From *Book 2, Chapter 4, Paragraph 3 (sig. M4ᵛ–5ʳ)*

It is oftentimes said that God blindeth and hardeneth the reprobate, that he turneth, boweth, and moveth their hearts, as I have elsewhere taught more at large. But of what manner that is, it is never expressed, if we flee to free foreknowledge or sufferance. Therefore we answer that it is done after two manners. For first, whereas when his light is taken away, there remaineth nothing but darkness and blindness, whereas when his spirit is taken away, our hearts wax hard and become stones, whereas when his direction ceaseth, they are wrested into crookedness. It is well said that he doth blind, harden and bow them from whom he taketh away the power to see, obey and do rightly. The second manner, which cometh near to the property [i.e. proper sense] of the words, is that for the executing of his judgments by Satan, the minister of his wrath, he both appointeth their purposes to what end it pleaseth him, and stirreth up their wills, and strengtheneth their endeavors.

So when Moses rehearseth that King Sehon [Simon] did not give passage to the people because God had hardened his spirit and made his heart obstinate, he by and by adjoineth the end of his purpose: that he might (sayeth he) give him unto our hands. Therefore because it was God's will to have him destroyed, the making of his heart obstinate was God's preparation for his destruction.

From *Book 3, Chapter 3, Paragraph 21* (*sig. BB6^{r-v}*)

[I]n Isaiah [42:17], when the faithful complain and lament that they are forsaken of God, they reckon this as a token of being reprobates, that their hearts were hardened by God. The Apostle also meaning to exclude apostates from hope of salvation, appointeth this reason, that it is impossible for them to be renewed unto repentance [Heb. 6:6] because God, in renewing them whom he will not have perish, showeth a token of his fatherly favor, and in a manner draweth them unto him with the beams of his cheerful and merry countenance. On the other side, with hardening them, he thundereth against the reprobate, whose wickedness is unpardonable. Which kind of vengeance the Apostle threateneth to wilful apostates, which when they depart from the faith of the gospel do make a scorn of God, reproachfully despise his grace, and defile and tread under feet the blood of Christ, yea as much as in them as they crucify him again. For he doth not (as some fondly rigorous men would have it) cut off hope of pardon from all wilful sins, but teacheth that apostasy is unworthy of all excuse; so that it is no marvel that God doth punish a contempt of himself so full of sacrilege, with unappeasable rigor. For he sayeth that it is impossible that they which have once been enlightened, have tasted of the heavenly gift, having been made partakers of the Holy Ghost, having tasted the good word of God and the powers of the world to come, if they fall, should be renewed to repentance, crucifying again of new and making a scorn of the son of God.

From *Book 3, Chapter 3, Paragraph 24* (*sig. BB7^{v}*)

But whereas some do think it too hard, and too far from the tender mercifulness of God, that any are put away that flee to beseeching the Lord's mercy, that is easily answered. For he doth not say that pardon is denied them if they turn to the Lord: but he utterly denieth that they can rise unto repentance, because they are by the just judgment of God stricken with eternal blindness for their unthankfulness. And it maketh nothing to the contrary that afterward he applieth to this purpose the example of Esau, which in vain attempted with howling and weeping to recover his right of the first begotten. And no more doth that threatening of the Prophet. When they cry, I will not hear [Zech. 7:13]. For in such phrases of speech is meant neither the true conversion nor calling upon God, but that carefulness of the wicked, wherewith being bound, they are compelled in extremity to look unto that which before they carelessly neglected, that there is no good thing for them but in the Lord's help. But this they do not so much call upon, as they mourn that it is taken from them. Therefore the Prophet meaneth nothing else by crying, and the Apostle nothing else by weeping, but that horrible torment which by desperation fretteth and vexeth the wicked. This it is good to mark diligently, for else God should disagree with himself, which crieth by the Prophet that he will be merciful so soon as the sinner turneth [Ezek. 18:21]. And as I have already said, it is certain that the mind of man is not turned to better, but by God's grace preventing it. Also his promise concerning calling upon him will never deceive. But that blind torment wherewith the reprobate are diversely drawn when they see that they must needs seek God, that they may find remedy for their evils, and yet do flee from his presence, is unproperly called conversion and prayer.

The Thirty-Nine Articles

Agreement to these statements of basic belief was required from all members of the clergy in the Church of England. They were intended less as a systematic theology than as an effort to establish uniformity in the treatment of certain controversial matters. The statements were approved by Convocation in 1563 and confirmed by statute in 1571. In 1628, King Charles I proposed these for all his "loving subjects to continue in the uniform profession thereof." Spelling and punctuation have been modernized.

1 Of faith in the Holy Trinity

There is but one living and true God, everlasting, without body, parts, or passions; of infinite power, wisdom, and goodness; the maker and preserver of all things both visible and invisible. And in unity of this Godhead there be three persons, of one substance, power, and eternity: the Father, the Son, and the Holy Ghost.

2 Of the word or Son of God, which was made very man

The Son, which is the word of the Father, begotten from everlasting of the Father, the very and eternal God, of one substance with the Father, took man's nature in the womb of the Blessed Virgin, of her substance, so that two whole and perfect natures, that is to say, the godhead and manhood, were joined together in one person, never to be divided; whereof is one Christ, very God and very man; who truly suffered, was crucified, dead, and buried, to reconcile his Father to us, and to be a sacrifice, not only for original guilt, but also for all actual sins of men.

3 *Of the going down of Christ into hell*

As Christ died for us, and was buried, so also it is to be believed that he went down into hell.

4 *Of the resurrection of Christ*

Christ did truly arise again from death, and took again his body, with flesh, bones, and all things appertaining to the perfection of man's nature; wherewith he ascended into heaven, and there sitteth, until he return to judge all men at the last day.

5 *Of the Holy Ghost*

The Holy Ghost, proceeding from the Father and the Son, is of one substance, majesty, and glory, with the Father and the Son, very and eternal God.

6 *Of the sufficiency of the Holy Scriptures for salvation*

Holy Scripture containeth all things necessary to salvation, so that whatsoever is not read therein, nor may be proved thereby, is not to be required of any man, that it should be believed as an article of the faith, or be thought requisite or necessary to salvation. In the name of the Holy Scripture we do understand those canonical books of the Old and New Testament, of whose authority was never any doubt in the church.

Of the names and number of the canonical books: *Genesis, Exodus, Leviticus, Numbers, Deuteronomy, Joshua, Judges, Ruth, the First Book of Samuel, the Second Book of Samuel, the First Book of Kings, the Second Book of Kings, the First Book of Chronicles, the Second Book of Chronicles, the First Book of Esdras, the Second Book of Esdras, the Book of Esther, the Book of Job, the Psalms, the Proverbs, Ecclesiastes or Preacher, Cantica or Songs of Solomon, Four Prophets the greater, Twelve Prophets the less.*

And the other books (as Jerome saith) the church doth read for example of life and instruction of manners, but yet doth it not apply them to establish any doctrine. Such are these following: *the Third Book of Esdras, the Fourth Book of Esdras, the Book of Tobias, the Book of Judith, the rest of the Book of Esther, the Book of Wisdom, Jesus the Son of Sirach, Baruch the Prophet, the Song of the*

Three Children, the Story of Susanna, Of Bel and the Dragon, the Prayer of Manasses, the First Book of Maccabees, the Second Book of Maccabees.

All the books of the New Testament, as they are commonly received, we do receive and account them canonical.

7 Of the Old Testament

The Old Testament is not contrary to the New: for both in the Old and New Testament everlasting life is offered to mankind by Christ, who is the only mediator between God and man, being both God and man. Wherefore they are not to be heard which feign that the old fathers did look only for transitory promises. Although the law given from God by Moses, as touching ceremonies and rites, do not bind Christian men, nor the civil precepts thereof ought of necessity to be received in any commonwealth; yet notwithstanding, no Christian man whatsoever is free from the obedience of the commandments which are called moral.

8 Of the three Creeds

The three creeds, Nicene Creed, Athanasius's Creed, and that which is commonly called the Apostles' Creed, ought thoroughly to be received and believed: for they may be proved by most certain warrants of Holy Scripture.

9 Of original or birth-sin

Original sin standeth not in the following of Adam (as the Pelagians do vainly talk), but it is the fault and corruption of the nature of every man, that naturally is engendered of the offspring of Adam; whereby man is very far gone from original righteousness, and is of his own nature inclined to evil, so that the flesh lusteth always contrary to the spirit; and therefore in every person born into this world, it deserveth God's wrath and damnation. And this infection of nature doth remain, yea in them that are regenerated; whereby the lust of the flesh . . . is not subject to the law of God. And although there is no condemnation for them that believe and are baptized, yet the apostle doth confess that concupiscence and lust hath of itself the nature of sin.

10 Of Free-Will

The condition of man after the fall of Adam is such that he cannot turn and prepare himself by his own natural strength and good works to faith and calling upon God. Wherefore we have no power to do good works pleasant and acceptable to God, without the grace of God by Christ preventing us, that we may have a good will, and working with us, when we have that good will.

11 Of the justification of man

We are accounted righteous before God, only for the merit of Our Lord and Saviour Jesus Christ, by faith, and not for our own works or deservings; Wherefore, that we are justified by faith only is a most wholesome doctrine, and very full of comfort, as more largely is expressed in the Homily of Justification.

12 Of good works

Albeit that good works, which are the fruits of faith, and follow after justification, cannot put away our sins and endure the severity of God's judgment; yet are they pleasing and acceptable to God in Christ and do spring out necessarily of a true and lively faith, insomuch that by them a lively faith may be as evidently known as a tree discerned by the fruit.

13 Of works before justification

Works done before the grace of Christ, and the inspiration of his Spirit, are not pleasant to God, forasmuch as they spring not of faith in Jesus Christ, neither do they make men meet to receive grace, or (as the school-authors say) deserve grace of congruity. Yea rather, for that they are not done as God hath willed and commanded them to be done, we doubt not but they have the nature of sin.

14 Of works of supererogation

Voluntary works besides, over and above God's commandments, which they call works of supererogation, cannot be taught without arrogancy and impiety: for by them men do declare, that they do not only render unto God as much as they are bound to do, but that they do more for his sake than of bounden duty is required: whereas Christ saith plainly, when ye have done all that are commanded to you, say, we are unprofitable servants.

15 Of Christ alone without sin

Christ in the truth of our nature was made like unto us in all things, sin only except, from which he was clearly void, both in his flesh and in his spirit. He came to be the Lamb without spot, who, by sacrifice of himself once made, should take away the sins of the world, and sin (as St. John saith) was not in him. But all we the rest (although baptized, and born again in Christ) yet offend in many things; and if we say we have no sin, we deceive ourselves and the truth is not in us.

16 Of sin after baptism

Not every deadly sin willingly committed after baptism is sin against the Holy Ghost and unpardonable. Wherefore the grant of repentance is not to be denied to such as fall into sin after baptism. After we have received the Holy Ghost, we may depart from grace given and fall into sin, and by the grace of God we may arise again and amend our lives. And therefore they are to be condemned, which say, they can no more sin as long as they live here, or deny the place of forgiveness to such as truly repent.

Between Calvinism & Catholicism

17 Of predestination and election

Predestination to life is the everlasting purpose of God, whereby (before the foundations of the world were laid) he hath constantly decreed by his counsel secret to us, to deliver from curse and damnation those whom he hath chosen in Christ out of mankind, and to bring them by Christ to everlasting salvation, as vessels made to honor. Wherefore, they which be endued with so excellent a benefit of God be called according to God's purpose by his Spirit working in due season: they through grace obey the calling: they be justified freely: they be made sons of God by adoption: they be made like the image of his only-begotten Son Jesus Christ: they walk religiously in good works, and at length, by God's mercy, they attain to everlasting felicity.

As the godly consideration of predestination, and our election in Christ, is full of sweet, pleasant, and unspeakable comfort to godly persons, and such as feel in themselves the working of the spirit of Christ, mortifying the works of the flesh, and their earthly members, and drawing up their mind to high and heavenly things, as well because it doth greatly establish and confirm their faith of eternal salvation to be enjoyed through Christ, as because it doth fervently kindle their love towards God: So, for curious and carnal persons, lacking the spirit of Christ, to have continually before their eyes the sentence of God's predestination, is a most dangerous downfall, whereby the Devil doth thrust them either into desperation, or into wretchlessness of most unclean living, no less perilous than desperation.

Furthermore, we must receive God's promises in such wise, as they be generally set forth to us in Holy Scripture; and, in our doings, that will of God is to be followed, which we have expressly declared unto us in the word of God.

follow the Bible, not the Pope

18 Of obtaining eternal salvation only by the name of Christ

They also are to be had accursed that presume to say, That every man shall be saved by the law or sect which he professeth, so that he be diligent to frame his life according to that law, and the light of nature. For Holy Scripture doth set out unto us only the name of Jesus Christ, whereby men must be saved.

19 Of the church

The visible church of Christ is a congregation of faithful men, in the which the pure word of God is preached and the sacraments be duly ministered according to Christ's ordinance in all those things that of necessity are requisite to the same. As the churches of Jerusalem, Alexandria, and Antioch have erred; so also the church of Rome hath erred, not only in their living and manner of ceremonies, but also in matters of faith.

20 Of the authority of the church

The church hath power to decree rites or ceremonies, and authority in controversies of faith. And yet it is not lawful for the church to ordain any thing that is contrary to God's word written; neither may it so expound one place of scripture that it be repugnant to another. Wherefore, although the church be a witness and a keeper of holy writ, yet, as it ought not to decree any thing against the same, so besides the same ought it not to enforce any thing to be believed for necessity of salvation.

21 Of the authority of general councils

General councils may not be gathered together without the commandment and will of princes. And when they be gathered together (forasmuch as they be an assembly of men, whereof all be not governed with the spirit and word of God), they may err, and sometimes have erred, even in things pertaining unto God. Wherefore things ordained by them as necessary to salvation have neither strength nor authority, unless it may be declared that they be taken out of Holy Scripture.

22 *Of purgatory*

The Romish doctrine concerning purgatory, pardons, worshipping, and adoration as well of images as of relics, and also invocation of saints, is a fond thing, vainly invented, and grounded upon no warranty of scripture, but rather repugnant to the word of God.

23 *Of ministering in the congregation*

It is not lawful for any man to take upon him the office of public preaching, or ministering the sacraments in the congregation, before he be lawfully called and sent to execute the same. And those we ought to judge lawfully called and sent, which be chosen and called to this work by men who have public authority given unto them in the congregation, to call and send ministers into the Lord's vineyard.

24 *Of speaking in the congregation in such a tongue as the people understandeth*

It is a thing plainly repugnant to the word of God, and the custom of the primitive church, to have public prayer in the church, or to minister the sacraments in a tongue not understood of the people.

25 *Of the sacraments*

Sacraments ordained of Christ be not only badges or tokens of Christian men's profession, but rather they be certain sure witnesses and effectual signs of grace and God's good will towards us, by the which he doth work invisibly in us, and doth not only quicken, but also strengthen and confirm our faith in him.

There are two sacraments ordained of Christ Our Lord in the gospel: that is to say, baptism and the supper of the Lord. Those five commonly called sacraments, that is to say, confirmation, penance, orders, matrimony, and extreme unction, are not to be counted for sacraments of the gospel, being such as have grown partly of the corrupt following of the apostles, partly are states of life allowed in the scriptures; but yet have not like nature of sacraments with baptism and the Lord's Supper, for that they have not any visible sign or ceremony ordained of God.

The sacraments were not ordained of Christ to be gazed upon or to be carried about, but that we should duly use them. And in such only as worthily receive the same they have a wholesome effect or operation, but they that receive them unworthily, purchase to themselves damnation, as St. Paul saith.

26 Of the unworthiness of the ministers, which hinders not the effect of the sacrament

Although in the visible church the evil be ever mingled with the good, and sometime the evil have chief authority in the ministration of the word and sacraments, yet forasmuch as they do not the same in their own name, but in Christ's, and do minister by his commission and authority, we may use their ministry, both in hearing the word of God, and in the receiving of the sacraments. Neither is the effect of Christ's ordinance taken away by their wickedness nor the grace of God's gifts diminished from such as by faith and rightly do receive the sacraments ministered unto them, which be effectual, because of Christ's institution and promise, although they be ministered by evil men.

Nevertheless, it appertaineth to the discipline of the church, that enquiry be made of evil ministers, and that they be accused by those that have knowledge of their offences; and finally being found guilty, by just judgement be deposed.

27 Of baptism

Baptism is not only a sign of profession and mark of difference, whereby Christian men are discerned from others that be not christened, but it is also a sign of regeneration or new birth, whereby, as by an instrument, they that receive baptism rightly are grafted into the church; the promises of forgiveness of sin, and of our adoption to be the sons of God by the Holy Ghost, are visibly signed and sealed; faith is confirmed, and grace increased by virtue of prayer unto God. The baptism of young children is in any wise to be retained in the church, as most agreeable with the institution of Christ.

28 Of the Lord's Supper

The supper of the Lord is not only a sign of the love that Christians ought to have among themselves one to another; but rather it is a sacrament of our redemption by Christ's death: insomuch that to such as rightly, worthily, and with faith receive the same, the bread which we break is a partaking of the body of Christ; and likewise the cup of blessing is a partaking of the blood of Christ.

Transubstantiation (or the change of the substance of bread and wine) in the supper of the Lord, cannot be proved by holy writ, but is repugnant to the plain words of scripture, overthroweth the nature of a sacrament, and hath given occasion to many superstitions. The body of Christ is given, taken, and eaten, in the supper, only after an heavenly and spiritual manner. And the means whereby the body of Christ is received and eaten in the supper is faith.

The sacrament of the Lord's supper was not by Christ's ordinance reserved, carried about, lifted up, or worshipped.

29 Of the wicked which do not eat the body of Christ in the use of the Lord's Supper

The wicked, and such as be void of a lively faith, although they do carnally and visibly press with their teeth (as St Augustine saith) the sacrament of the body and blood of Christ, yet in no wise are they partakers of Christ: but rather, to their condemnation, do eat and drink the sign or sacrament of so great a thing.

30 Of both kinds

The cup of the Lord is not to be denied to the lay-people: for both the parts of the Lord's sacrament, by Christ's ordinance and commandment, ought to be ministered to all Christian men alike.

31 Of the one oblation of Christ finished upon the cross

The offering of Christ once made is the perfect redemption, propitiation, and satisfaction, for all the sins of the whole world, both original and actual; and there is none other satisfaction for sin, but that alone. Wherefore the sacrifices of masses, in the which it was commonly said, that the priest did offer Christ for the quick and the dead, to have remission of pain or guilt, were blasphemous fables and dangerous deceits.

32 Of the marriage of priests

Bishops, priests, and deacons are not commanded by God's law, either to vow the estate of single life or to abstain from marriage; therefore it is lawful also for them, as for all other Christian men, to marry at their own discretion, as they shall judge the same to serve better to godliness.

33 Of excommunicate persons, how they are to be avoided

That person which by open denunciation of the church is rightly cut off from the unity of the church and excommunicated ought to be taken of the whole multitude of the faithful as an heathen and publican, until he be openly reconciled by penance and received into the church by a judge that hath authority thereunto.

34 Of the traditions of the church

It is not necessary that traditions and ceremonies be in all places one or utterly like; for at all times they have been divers, and may be changed according to the diversity of countries, times, and men's manners, so that nothing be ordained against God's word. Whosoever through his private judgement, willingly and purposely, doth openly break the traditions and ceremonies of the church, which be not repugnant to the word of God, and be ordained and approved by common authority, ought to be rebuked openly (that other may fear to do the like) as he that offendeth against the common order of the church, and hurteth the authority of the magistrate, and woundeth the consciences of the weak brethren.

Every particular or national church hath authority to ordain, change, and abolish ceremonies or rites of the church ordained only by man's authority, so that all things be done to edifying.

35 *Of homilies*

The second Book of Homilies . . . doth contain a godly and wholesome doctrine, and necessary for these times, as doth the former Book of Homilies, which were set forth in the time of Edward the Sixth; and therefore we judge them to be read in churches by the ministers, diligently and distinctly, that they may be understood of the people. [Names of the Homilies follow.]

36 *Of Consecration of bishops and ministers*

The Book of Consecration of Archbishops and Bishops, and Ordering of Priests and Deacons, lately set forth in the time of Edward the Sixth, and confirmed at the same time by authority of parliament, doth contain all things necessary to such consecration and ordering, neither hath it any thing, that of itself is superstitious or ungodly. And therefore, whosoever are consecrate or ordered according to the rites of that book, since the second year of the aforenamed King Edward unto this time, or hereafter, shall be consecrated or ordered according to the same rites. We decree all such to be rightly, orderly, and lawfully consecrated and ordered.

37 *Of the civil magistrates*

The queen's majesty hath the chief power in this realm of England and other her dominions, unto whom the chief government of all estates of this realm, whether they be ecclesiastical or civil, in all causes doth appertain, and is not, nor ought to be, subject to any foreign jurisdiction.

Where we attribute to the queen's majesty the chief government, by which titles we understand the minds of some slanderous folks to be offended, we give not to our princes the ministering either of God's word, or of the sacraments, the which thing the Injunctions

also lately set forth by Elizabeth our queen do most plainly testify;
but that only prerogative, which we see to have been given always
to all godly princes in Holy Scriptures by God himself; that is, that
they should rule all estates and degrees committed to their charge
by God, whether they be ecclesiastical or temporal, and restrain
with the civil sword the stubborn and evil-doers.

The Bishop of Rome hath no jurisdiction in this realm of England. The laws of the realm may punish Christian men with death,
for heinous and grievous offences. It is lawful for Christian men, at
the commandment of the magistrate, to wear weapons, and serve in
the wars.

38 Of Christian men's goods which are not common

The riches and goods of Christians are not common, as touching the
right, title, and possession of the same, as certain Anabaptists do
falsely boast. Notwithstanding, every man ought, of such things as he
possesseth, liberally to give alms to the poor, according to his ability.

39 Of a Christian man's oath

As we confess that vain and rash swearing is forbidden Christian
men by Our Lord Jesus Christ, and James his apostle, so we judge,
that Christian religion doth not prohibit, but that a man may swear
when the magistrate requireth, in a cause of faith and charity, so it
be done according to the prophet's teaching, in justice, judgment,
and truth.

WILLIAM PERKINS

Perkins (1558–1602) was a Cambridge-based, nonconformist theologian whose his ideas were not wildly divergent from the Calvinist consensus that defined the character of the English church in the 1590s.
Marlowe would have overlapped with Perkins at Cambridge and no
doubt heard him preach. *A Golden Chain*, initially published in Latin
in 1590, was published in English the following year and quickly became a best-seller, not only in England but, unusual for a book by an
Englishman, also on the Continent. Spelling and punctuation have
been modernized.

From A Golden Chain, or The Description of Theology

From *Of Predestination and Creation*, sig. B4[r]

God's decree, in as much as it concerneth man, is called predestination, which is the decree of God by which he hath ordained all

men to a certain and everlasting estate: that is, either to salvation or condemnation for his own glory.

From *Of Election, and of Jesus Christ the Foundation Thereof,* sig. D2^r

Predestination hath two parts: election and reprobation (I Thessalonians 5:9). Election is God's decree, whereby on his own free will he hath ordained certain men to salvation, to the praise of the glory of his grace (Ephesians 1:4–6): *He hath chosen us in him, before the foundation of the world, according to the good pleasure of his will . . .*

From *Concerning the First Degree of the Declaration of God's Love,* sig. P4r–8^r

The declaration of God's love in those of years of discretion hath especially four degrees (Romans 8:30; I Corinthians 1:30). The first degree is an effectual calling, whereby a sinner being severed from the world, is entertained into God's family (Ephesians 2:17, 19). Of this there be two parts. The first is election, which is a separation of a sinner from the cursed estate of all mankind (John 15:19). The second is the reciprocal donation or free gift of God the father, whereby he bestoweth the sinful man to be saved upon Christ, and Christ again actually and most effectually upon that sinful man, so that he may boldly say this thing, namely Christ, both God and man, is mine, and I for my benefit and use enjoy the same. The like we see in wedlock: the husband saith, this woman is my wife, whom her parents have given unto [me], so that, she being fully mine, I may both have her and govern her. Again, the woman may say, this man is mine husband, who hath bestowed himself upon me, and doth cherish me as his wife (Romans 8:32; Isaiah 9:6; John 17:2, 6–7; John 10:29).

Hence cometh that admirable union, or conjunction, which is the engrafting of such as are to be saved into Christ, and their growing up together with him; so that after a peculiar manner, Christ is made the head, and every repentant sinner, a member of his mystical body (John 17:20–1; Ephesians 2:20; John 25:1–2; Ephesians 2:20–2) . . .

A member of Christ is diversely distinguished, and is so either before men or God. Before men they are the members of Christ, who outwardly professing the faith are charitably reputed by the church as true members. But such deceiving at length both themselves and the church, may be reprobates: and therefore in God's presence they are no more true members, than are the noxious humours in a man's body, or a wooden leg or other joint cunningly fastened to another part of the body. * * *

Again, members before God, they are such as either are decreed to be so, or actually are so already. Such as are decreed to be so, are they, who, being elect from all eternity, are either as yet not born, or not called (John 10:16). Actual members of Christ are either living or dying members. An actual living member of Christ is every one elected, which being engrafted by faith and the spirit into Christ, doth feel and shew forth the power of Christ in him.

An actual dying or decaying member is every one truly engrafted into Christ, and yet hath no feeling of the power and efficacy of the quickening spirit in him. He is like unto a benumbed leg without sense, which indeed is part of a man's body, and yet receiveth no nourishment. Such are those faithful ones, who for a time do faint and are overcome under the heavy burden of temptations and their sins; such are also those excommunicate persons, who in regard of their engrafting are true members, howsoever in regard of the external communion with the church and efficacy of the spirit they are not members, till such time as, they being touched with repentance, do begin, as it were, to live again.

God executeth this effectual calling by certain means. The first is the saving hearing of the word God . . . The second is the mollifying of the heart, the which must be bruised in pieces, that it may be fit to receive God's saving grace offered unto it. * * * The third is faith, which is a miraculous and supernatural faculty of the heart, apprehending Christ Jesus, being applied by the operation of the Holy Ghost, and receiving him to itself (John 1:12; 6:35; Romans 9:30) . . .

In the work of faith there are four degrees, or motions of the heart, linked and united together, and are worthy the consideration of every Christian.

The first is knowledge of the gospel, by the illumination of God's spirit (Isaiah 53:11; John 7:3) . . . The second is hope of pardon, whereby a sinner, albeit he yet feeleth not that his sins are certainly pardoned, yet he believeth that they are pardonable (Luke 15:18). The third is an hungering and thirsting after that grace which is offered to him in Christ Jesus, as a man hungereth and thirsteth after meat and drink (John 6:35; 7:37; Revelation 21:6; Matthew 5:6). The fourth is the approaching to the throne of grace, that there flying from the terror of the law, he may take hold of Christ and find favour with God (Hebrews 4:16) . . . The fifth, arising of the former, is an especial persuasion imprinted in the heart by the Holy Ghost, whereby every faithful man doth particularly apply unto himself those promises which are made in the gospel (Matthew 9:2; 15:28; Galatians 2:20). This persuasion is, and ought to be, in every one, even before he have any experience of God's mercies (Matthew 15:22–7; John 20:29; Hebrews 11:1).

In philosophy, we first see a thing true by experience, and afterward give our assent unto it. As in natural philosophy: I am persuaded that such a water is hot, because when I put mine hand into it, I perceive by experience an hot quality. But in the practice of faith it is quite contrary. For first, we must consent to the word of God, resisting all doubt and diffidence, and afterward will an experience and feeling of comfort follow (II Chronicle 20:20) . . .

From *Of the Decree of Reprobation*, sig. T6r–7ᵛ

[N]ow followeth the decree of Reprobation whereby God in his just judgment hath determined eternally to reject some to the praise of his justice (1 Peter 2:8; Jude 5:4; 1 Thessalonians 5:9; Romans 9:21) . . . First, it is untrue that God would have all men saved in Christ, for no man can be said to be elected if God will that all men should be elected in Christ. For election is a singling out of some from others, and he that electeth or chooseth cannot be said to receive all . . . If any man reason out of 1 Timothy 2, "That God would that all men would be saved," he must know that this sentence is not meant generally of all men, but indefinitely of some, and therefore must not be understood of every singular and particular man but of every singular and particular estate and condition of man.

From *Concerning the Execution of the Decree of Reprobation*, sig. V2r–V4ᵛ

Reprobates are either infants or men of riper age. In reprobate infants, the execution of God's decree is this: as soon as they are born, for the guilt of original and natural sin being left in God's secret judgement unto themselves, they dying are rejected of God for ever (Romans 5:14; 9:11). Reprobates of riper age are of two sorts: they that are called (namely by an uneffectual calling) and they that are not called. In the reprobates which are called the execution of the decree of reprobation hath three decrees, to wit, an acknowledgement of God's calling, a falling away again, and condemnation.

The acknowledgement of God's calling is whereby the reprobates for a time do subject themselves to the calling of God, which calling is wrought by the preaching of the word (Matthew 22:14). And of this calling there are five other degrees.

The first is an enlightening of their minds, whereby they are instructed of the Holy Ghost to the understanding and knowledge of the word (Hebrews 6:4; 2 Peter 2:20).

The second is a certain penitency, whereby the reprobate: (1) doth acknowledge his sin; (2) is pricked with the feeling of God's wrath for sin; (3) is grieved for the punishment of sin; (4) doth confess his sin; (5) acknowledgeth God to be just in punishing sin; (6) desireth to be saved; (7) promiseth repentence in his misery or affliction, in these words, 'I will sin no more' (Matthew 27:3; Hebrews 12:17; I Kings 21:27; Numbers 23:10; Psalms 78:32–5).

The third degree is a temporary faith, whereby the reprobate doth confusedly believe the promises of God made in Christ. I say *confusedly*, because he believeth that some shall be saved, but he believeth not that he himself particularly shall be saved, because he being content with a general faith, doth never apply the promises of God to himself, neither doth he so much as conceive any purpose, desire, or endeavor to apply the same, or any wrestling or striving against security or carelessness and distrust (James 2:19; Matthew 13:20–1; John 2:23–4).

The fourth is a tasting of heavenly gifts: as of justification and of sanctification, and of the virtues of the world to come. This tasting is merely a sense in the hearts of the reprobates, whereby they do perceive and feel the excellency of God's benefits, notwithstanding they do not enjoy the same. For it is one thing to taste of dainties at a banquet, and another thing to feed and to be nourished thereby (Hebrews 6:4).

The fifth degree is the outward holiness of life for a time, under which is comprehended a zeal in the profession of religion, a reverence and fear towards God's ministers, and amendment of life in many things (Mark 6:20; Acts 18:13; Hosea 6:4).

The second degree of the execution of God's counsel of reprobation in men of ripe age which are called, is a falling away again, which for the most part is effected and wrought after this manner. First, the reprobate is deceived by some sin. Secondly, his heart is hardened by the same sin. Thirdly, his heart being hardened, it becommeth wicked and perverse. Fourthly, then followeth his incredulity and unbelief, whereby he consenteth not to God's word, when he hath heard and known it. Fifthly, an apostacy, or falling away from faith in Christ, doth immediately follow this unbelief (Hebrews 3:12–13; I Timothy 1:9). . . . After apostacy followeth pollution, which is the very fullness of all inquiry, altogether contrary to sanctification (Genesis 15:16).

The third degree is damnation, whereby the reprobates are delivered up to eternal punishment. The execution of damnation beginneth in death, and is finished in the last judgement (Luke 16:22) . . .

From *Of the Application of Predestination*, sig. V7ᵛ–X1ᵛ

The judgement and discerning of a man's own predestination is to be performed by means of these rules which follow.

I. The elect alone, and all they that are elect, not only may be, but also in God's good time are, sure of election in Christ to eternal life (I Corinthians 2:12; II Corinthians 13:5).

II. They have not this knowledge from the first causes of election, but rather from the last effects thereof; and they are especially two: the testimony of God's spirit, and the works of sanctification (II Peter 1:10; Romans 8:16).

III. If any doubt of this testimony it will appear unto them, whether it come from the spirit of God, or of their own carnal presumption.

IV. If the testimony of God's spirit be not so powerful in the elect, then may they judge of their election by that other effect of the Holy Ghost, namely, sanctification. Like as we use to judge by heat that there is fire when we cannot see the flame itself.

V. And of all the effects of sanctification, these are most notable: (1) To feel our wants, and in the bitterness of heart to bewail the offense of God in every sin. (2) To strive against the flesh; that is, to resist and to hate the ungodly motions thereof, and with grief to think them burdenous and troublesome. (3) To desire earnestly and vehemently the grace of God and merit of Christ to obtain eternal life. (4) When it is obtained, to account it a most precious jewel (Philippians 3:8). (5) To love the minister of God's word in that he is a minister, and a Christian in that he is a Christian; and for that cause, if need require, to be ready to spend our blood with them (Matthew 10:41; I John 3:16). (6) To call upon God earnestly, and with tears. (7) To desire and love Christ's coming and the day of judgement, that an end may be made of the days of sin. (8) To fly all occasions of sin, and seriously to endeavour to come to newness of life. (9) To persevere in these things to the last gasp of life. Luther hath a good sentence for this purpose: 'He that will serve God, must', saith he, 'believe that which cannot be seen, hope for that which is deferred, and love God, when he showeth himself an enemy, and thus remain to the end'.

VI. Now, if so be all the effects of the spirit are very feeble in the godly, they must know this, that God trieth them, yet so, as they must not therewith be dismayed, because it is most sure, that if they have faith but as much as a grain of mustard seed, and be as weak as a young infant is, it is sufficient to engraft them into Christ; and therefore they must not doubt of their election because they see their faith feeble and the effects of the Holy Ghost faint within them.

VII. Neither must he, that as yet hath not felt in his heart any of these effects, presently conclude that he is a reprobate, but let him rather use the word of God and the sacraments, that he may have an inward sense of the power of Christ drawing him unto him, and an assurance of his redemption by Christ's death and passion.

VIII. No man may peremptorily set down that himself or any other is a reprobate. For God doth oftentime prefer those which did seem to be most of all estranged from his favour, to be in his kingdom above those who in man's judgement were the children of the kingdom. Hence is it that Christ saith: 'The publicans and harlots go before you', and 'many a one is called at the eleventh hour', as appeareth by that notable example of the thief upon the cross.

The uses which may be made of this doctrine of predestination are very many. First, for our instruction, we are taught these things:

I. That there is neither any justification by works, nor any works of ours that are meritorious. For election is by the free grace of God and therefore in like sort is justification. For, as I said before, the cause of the cause is the cause of the thing caused. And for this reason, in the work of salvation grace doth wholly challenge all to itself (Romans 11:5; 2 Timothy 1:9; Philippians 1:29; Romans 3:24; Titus 3:5; Ezekiel 36:27; Romans 6:23).

II. That astrology, teaching by the casting of nativities what men will be, is ridiculous and impious, because it determineth that such shall be very like in life and conversation, whom God in his predestination hath made unlike . . .

III. That God is most wise, omnipotent, just and merciful (Ephesians 1:5).

Secondly, being the servants of God we are admonished:

I. To fight against all doubting and diffidence of our salvation, because it neither dependeth upon works, nor faith, but upon God's decree which is immutable (Matthew 24:24; Luke 10:20; Romans 8:33; 2 Timothy 2:19). This teacheth that the anchor of hope must be fixed in the truth and stability of the immutable good pleasure of God, so that, albeit our faith be so tossed as that it is in danger of shipwreck, nevertheless it must never sink to the bottom, but even in the midst of danger take hold upon repentance, as on a board, and so recover itself.

II. To humble our souls under the mighty hand of God, for we are as clay in the hand of the potter (Romans 9:21).

III. To give all glory to God (Thessalonians 2:13).

IV. To bear crosses patiently (Romans 8:29; Philippians 3:10).

V. To do good works (Ephesians 2:10).

JOHN D. COX

From The Devil and the Sacred in English Drama, 1350–1642†

* * *

All [Marlowe's] major characters are willfully and aggressively competitive—"overreachers," to use Harry Levin's irreplaceable term—even though their aggression is never rewarded with unambiguous success.[1] Whether or not the portrait of a young man at Marlowe's Cambridge college, Corpus Christi, is really of Marlowe, its motto captures the ambiguity of Marlowe's life and that of his heroes as well: "Quod me nutruit me destruit" ("What nourishes me destroys me").[2] Where Faustus is concerned, one might even say that what nourishes and destroys him is his competitive ambition itself, and this ambiguity about Faustus so affects the world of his play that it is what distinguishes Marlowe's devils most strikingly from any preceding devils on the English stage.

To be sure, Marlowe was well aware of the tradition he was borrowing, and he acknowledges it in several ways. His acknowledgments, however, indicate change as well as continuity. Traditionally, for example, Lucifer was believed to have fallen because of overweening ambition, and Marlowe acknowledges this tradition when Faustus questions Mephistopheles about Lucifer:

> *Faustus.* Was not that Lucifer an angel once?
> *Mephistopheles.* Yes, Faustus, and most dearly loved of God.
> *Faustus.* How comes it then that he is prince of devils?
> *Mephistopheles.* O, by aspiring pride and insolence,
> For which God threw him from the face of heaven.
>
> (1.1.66–70)

Marlowe may well have encountered the idea of Lucifer's *libido dominandi* in his own reading of Augustine at Cambridge,[3] but he

† From *The Devil and the Sacred in English Drama, 1350–1642* (Cambridge: Cambridge University Press, 2000), pp. 110–18. Copyright © 2000 Cambridge University Press. Reprinted with the permission of Cambridge University Press.
1. Harry Levin, *The Overreacher* (Cambridge, Mass.: Harvard University Press, 1952).
2. Charles Nicholl, *The Reckoning* (New York: Harcourt Brace, 1992), pp. 5–9.
3. On the Cambridge curriculum when Marlowe was in residence there as a student, see John Bakeless, *The Tragical History of Christopher Marlowe*, 2 vols. (Cambridge, Mass.: Harvard University Press, 1942) 1:56–61. On Augustine in particular, see Douglas Cole, *Suffering and Evil in the Plays of Christopher Marlowe* (Princeton University Press, 1962), pp. 194–95. In Appendix D, "Libido," of *The Overreacher*, Levin outlines the history of *libido dominandi*. Despite allusions to Augustine's *Confessions*, however, Levin omits Augustine's contribution and attributes the phrase to Pascal (p. 202), who almost certainly learned it from *The City of God*. Augustine first uses the phrase in the preface to Book 1; his influential account of Lucifer's fall is in Book 11 and 12.

could have found it in innumerable other places as well (there is a hint of it in his source, the English Faustbook), and it is pervasive in early religious drama. Milton's memorable and influential interpretation of Lucifer's lust to dominate in *Paradise Lost* indicates that the idea was still vital almost a century after Marlowe. Whether or not Marlowe saw any of the mystery plays, they were still being staged in some places when he entered Cambridge in 1580, so his earliest audiences might well have imagined easily what Mephistopheles describes, because they had literally seen Lucifer's fall in a pageant performed within ten years of the time *Dr. Faustus* first alluded to it on the public stage.

The archetypal *libido dominandi* that Mephistopheles describes is a central but troubled idea in *Dr. Faustus*. From a traditional point of view, Faustus perpetuates the stage convention by repeating Lucifer's sin in his own turn, as innumerable personified abstractions had done before him. According to Mephistopheles, "pride and insolence" (a strangely orthodox phrase for a devil to use) led to Lucifer's overthrow, and pride is the key concept in Faustus' story: initially he wishes to go beyond the bounds of received knowledge because it is "too servile and illiberal for me" (1.1.36), and he believes the conjuring of devils will afford him "a world of profit and delight, / Of power, of honour, of omnipotence" in which "All things that move between the quiet poles / Shall be at my command" (1.1.55–57). Pride is the first in the pageant of the seven deadly sins, complementing the Evil Angel's temptation to Faustus: "Be thou on earth as Jove is in the sky, / Lord and commander of these elements" (1.1.78–79), a temptation that in turn answers Faustus' own ambition to "gain a deity" (1.1.65). No less than Tamburlaine before him, Faustus is a hero who rises from an inauspicious background ("Now is he born, his parents base of stock" [Pro. 11]), and eventually comes to believe that he can have the means to "reign sole king" over everyone he encounters (1.1.96), including the Duke of Parma, Catholic oppressor of Protestants in the Netherlands.

But aspiring pride and insolence are not as straightforward as they appear to be in *Dr. Faustus*. For one thing, Mephistopheles' account of Lucifer's being thrown from the face of heaven is closely anticipated by the opening Chorus' description of Faustus as "swoll'n with cunning of a self-conceit" and mounting on waxen wings, till "heavens conspired his overthrow" (Pro. 20–22). The Chorus' description is not neutral; it is as strongly slanted as Mephistopheles' language to connote mere power in the "heavens": "God threw him" and "heavens conspired his overthrow." In similar terms, the power-hungry Tamburlaine sees God as a competitor, imagining that the "frame of Heaven" might "conspire my overthrow."[4] Moreover, the emphasis on mere power reappears in the closing Chorus of *Dr. Faustus*, which refers again to "the hellish" fall of Faustus:

> Whose fiendful fortune may exhort the wise
> Only to wonder at unlawful things
> Whose deepness doth entice such forward wits,
> To practise more than heavenly power permits. (Epi. 5–8)

Traditionally, damnation had been understood as a logical necessity of divine love, yet the defining characteristic of God in *Dr. Faustus* is not love but overwhelming power.[5] And this characteristic cannot be explained as a perception of a guilty conscience, because the Chorus uses the same terms. In Marlowe's rendering of the story, Lucifer and Faustus are not willful rejecters of creative and loving goodness; they are merely losers in a struggle for power.

Marlowe alludes once more to Lucifer's fall in *Dr. Faustus*, introducing still another characteristic ambiguity: homoerotic wit. When Mephistopheles describes the women he can supply to Faustus, he promises that

> She whom thine eye shall like, thine heart shall have,
> Be she as chaste as was Penelope,
> As wise as Saba, or as beautiful
> As was bright Lucifer before his fall.   (2.1.158–61)

The switch from female chastity and wisdom to male beauty is understated in the exotic catalog, which has the same witty quality as a similar catalog in *Hero and Leander*:

> There might you see the gods in sundrie shapes,
> Committing headdie ryots, incest, rapes:
> For know, that vnderneath this radiant floure
> Was *Danaes* statue in a brazen tower,
> *Ioue* slyly stealing from his sisters bed,
> To dallie with *Idalian Ganimed*.[6]

Another gender switch occurs in the intense eroticism of the scene with Helen, whom Faustus apostrophizes:

> O, thou art fairer than the evening air,
> Clad in the beauty of a thousand stars.
> Brighter art thou than flaming Jupiter,

4. *Doctor Faustus A- and B-Texts*, ed. David Bevington and Eric Rasmussen (Manchester: Manchester University Press, 1993), Pro. 22 n.
5. Paul Kocher makes the same point about *Tamburlaine* in *Christopher Marlowe* (Chapel Hill: University of North Carolina Press, 1946), p. 71, and later compares "Jove" of the earlier play to the God of *Faustus* (p. 118).
6. *Hero and Leander*, ed. C. F. Tucker Brooke, *The Works of Christopher Marlowe* (Oxford: Clarendon Press, 1910), I, 143–48. I have used this edition in quoting works by Marlowe other than *Dr. Faustus*.

When he appeared to hapless Semele,
More lovely than the monarch of the sky
In wanton Arethusa's azured arms,
And none but thou shalt be my paramour. (5.1.104–10)

Orthodox readings of *Dr. Faustus* are severely strained by the rhetorical power of such passages and by their similarity to the undisguised homoeroticism of *Hero and Leander*.[7] To suggest that the beauty of the unfallen Lucifer was powerfully erotic is to read his fall very differently from the way it had been understood by Augustine or by the tradition indebted to Augustine.[8]

The devils of *Dr. Faustus* are also subversively ambiguous as they interact with Faustus in his struggle for power. For if Faustus is "overthrown" on one hand by an absent, punitive, malignant, and merely powerful God, he is destroyed on the other by the lying promises and empty threats of demons. The result is less an opposition of good and evil than of one overwhelming cosmic power and another. Faustus' bid for power is thus hopeless from the outset, and his condition has been aptly described in Constance Kuriyama's clever neologism, "omnimpotence" (*Hammer or Anvil*, pp. 95–135). The devils are the only effective influence on Faustus, and they appear in large numbers in this play: eight out of thirty-five characters in the character list of the A-text are devils, and nine others are personified vices. The most powerful agents who oppose them are the Good Angel and the Old Man, who make brief, intermittent, and ineffectual appearances, in contrast to Mephistopheles' ubiquitous presence.[9]

Marlowe thus recreates a simulacrum of familiar oppositional thinking in order to deconstruct it. He does this, in part, by identifying even the ineffectual Old Man rhetorically with the struggle

7. Edward Snow, "Marlowe's *Dr. Faustus* and the Ends of Desire," in *Two Renaissance Mythmakers* (Baltimore: Johns Hopkins University Press, 1977), pp. 70–110, also sees Faustus' repeated midnight invocation, "Come, Mephistopheles" (2.1.26–29) as erotic (p. 72). Constance Kuriyama first noticed the gender switch in Faustus' hyperbolic descriptions (*Hammer or Anvil* [New Brunswick, N.J.: Rutgers University Press, 1984], pp. 119, 123), and her explanation is neither that the wit is mimetic nor intentionally heterodox, but that it is a subconscious expression of Marlowe's own sexually ambivalent imagination. See also Nicholas Davidson, "Christopher Marlowe and Atheism" in *Christopher Marlowe and the English Renaissance*, ed. Darryll Grantley and Peter Roberts (Aldershot: Scolar Press, 1996), pp. 141–42.

8. C. L. Barber argues that *Dr. Faustus* depends for its effect on a lively sense of blasphemy, as an angry way of acknowledging the power of the sacred, " 'The form of Faustus' fortunes, good or bad,' " *TDR* 8 (1964): 92–119. Barber cites Mephistopheles' lines about the beauty of Lucifer as an example of language which condemns its users "by the logic of a situation larger than they are" (p. 99). He is referring to Lucifer's pre-fallen happiness, not to the gender switch, but in context it also depends on blasphemy for its effect.

9. Huston Diehl sees God's absence as a reflection of Calvinistic iconoclasm and resistance to ritual in the 1580s, in *Staging Reform, Reforming the Stage* (Ithaca: Cornell University Press, 1997), pp. 73–81. Still, as part of a traditional opposition in *Dr. Faustus*, stage devils are themselves visible remnants of sacred culture, and the ritual of invoking the devil is as potent as any staged miracle.

for power. The Old Man's final speech is a cry of victory with more than a hint of gloating in it, as well as an echo of the Chorus' allusions to the powerful heavens:

> My faith, vile hell, shall triumph over thee.
> Ambitious fiends, see how the heavens smiles
> At your repulse, and laughs your state to scorn! (5.2.116–18)

This is Marlowe's version of the idealized defiance of tortured and dying martyrs in Foxe's *Acts and Monuments*, including their ready memory for biblical quotations. (The Old Man alludes to Psalm 2:1.) But it is far removed from precedents in Protestant drama.[1] In context, the Old Man's declaration of victory culminates a sequence of similar triumphs, all made by Faustus himself, which begin with a mockery of traditional ritual in the scurrilous terms that Bale had introduced into virulently anti-Catholic drama:

> How? Bell, book, and candle, candle, book, and bell,
> Forward and backward, to curse Faustus to hell.
> Anon you shall hear a hog grunt, a calf bleat, and an ass bray,
> Because it is Saint Peter's holy day. (3.2.84–87)

Protestants were accustomed to believing that traditional religion was an instrument of Satan, but *Dr. Faustus* is a rare (if not unique) Elizabethan instance of the devil intervening explicitly on the Protestant side. Faustus appropriates a power superior to the Pope's to make the Pope look like a gull and an asshead, just as the Old Man will appropriate a power apparently superior to the devil's to smile at hell's repulse and laugh its state to scorn. Marlowe's implicit reduction of the reformation to a struggle for power is an acute response to the secularization introduced by the Tudors, not because struggles for power were invented by Protestants but because Protestants made religion a matter of crown policy and thus, comparatively, a matter of mere power.

Staged between Faustus' victory over the Pope and the Old Man's over the devil are four more, all won by Faustus in league with Mephistopheles. The first vindicates learning against courtly arrogance (4.1.1–99); the second similarly vindicates learning against clownish aspiration (4.1.100–89); the third demonstrates intellectual prowess before a duke (4.2); the fourth demonstrates similar prowess before fellow academics (5.1.100–10). Like the sequence

1. Several critics have noticed differences between the Old Man in the A and B versions of *Dr. Faustus*, and Leah Marcus argues that the A version is closer to militant Protestantism than the B version, in *Unediting the Renaissance* (London and New York: Routledge, 1996), pp. 47–51 (citing other references). My point is that either version compromises the oppositional clarity of militant Protestantism by identifying the Old Man as just another contestant in a pervasive cosmic struggle for mastery. Marcus anticipated this point, observing that the devil's championing of Protestant policy "massively undercuts the 'official' ideology of the play" (p. 61).

of victories in *1 Tamburlaine*, all of Faustus' victories are sympathetic but ambiguous, beginning with his victory over the Pope: he
is courted by the most powerful ruler in Europe and demonstrates
his invulnerability to courtly detraction; he vanquishes lower-class
demands for justice with an ease that might have made Martin
Luther envious;[2] he handily wins the unfeigned admiration of the
powerful and the learned. In short, his career embodies a fantasy of
upwardly mobile Protestant power in the sixteenth century, and the
demonic motivation of this career is one of the play's most subversive ironies.

Viewed in the context of the sequential victories that make up
the second half of the play, the Old Man's ultimate victory has less
to do with a triumph of faith over despair (or of cosmic goodness
over evil) than it does with making sure one joins the winning side
from the outset—provided, that is, that one can know what the
winning side is going to be. When Faustus torments and humiliates
an anonymous knight, for example (4.1), it is because the knight
refuses to believe in the power of Faustus' magic. But the refusal to
believe in a certain kind of superhuman power is precisely what the
Old Man, the Good Angel, and the Chorus say is Faustus' problem,
and his torment of the anonymous knight is therefore a direct parallel to his own torment at the hands of heavenly power as the play
ends. If devils are the means of torment in Faustus' case (as he
seems to believe), then his case parallels the anonymous knight's
even more closely, since Mephistopheles is also the means of the
knight's torment at Faustus' hands.

The deconstructive ambiguity of traditional oppositions in *Dr.
Faustus* is enhanced by Marlowe's secularization of the fiend's traditional equivocation. Faustus' determination to enhance his power
leads him naturally to reject traditional affirmations of human limitation, because to acknowledge them would be to give up before
he begins. Having recognized the cosmic determinism of traditional
theology, as he sees it, Faustus scorns the theological truisms he
hears from Mephistopheles:

> What, is great Mephistopheles so passionate
> For being deprivèd of the joys of heaven?
> Learn thou of Faustus manly fortitude,
> And scorn those joys thou never shalt possess. (1.3.85–88)

If one's dominion that exceeds in magic is to stretch as far as does
the mind of man, it will have to stretch farther than traditional
hopes and fears about the human condition, even when those are

---

2. On the Protestant response to peasant demands for social justice, see Stephen Greenblatt, "Murdering Peasants: Status, Genre, and the Representation of Rebellion," in
   Learning to Curse (New York: Routledge, 1999), pp. 99–130.

voiced in apparent sincerity by the devil himself. In retrospect and from an orthodox perspective, Faustus' refusal to listen to what Mephistopheles tells him is fatal and ironic.[3] In context, however, it is an affirmation of the manly fortitude that set him on his course in the first place. Given the triumph he enjoys as a consequence of his choice, he appears to have chosen rightly, despite occasional doubts, because he is clearly on the winning side: successful, admired, powerful, Protestant, and fully aware of his deserving superiority.

Yet the devils who seem to offer Faustus a means to escape traditional limitations are apparently the means of his undoing in the end, the duplicitous source of his "omnimpotence." The demons play a role in *Dr. Faustus* that is analogous to the Vice of the morality play and that therefore parallels the role of Vice-derived characters in other plays by Marlowe, such as Barabas in *The Jew of Malta* or Mortimer in *Edward II*.[4] The point of contact for all these characters is their essential hypocrisy and their *libido dominandi*, which is the origin of both devils and vices in English stage tradition. But as in other points where Marlowe deconstructs the tradition, the effect of his equating devils in *Dr. Faustus* with the Vice is strikingly different from anything in earlier drama. The defeat of Faustus in the cosmic power struggle offers no evidence of a good and loving God who opposes evil with redemptive power, any more than Barabas' defeat in the human power struggle is proof of justice in human affairs. For all Marlowe lets us know in *Dr. Faustus*, God is no better than Ferneze: what both indubitably have in common is that they win in the end, and in a struggle for power, winning is all that counts. The difference in *Dr. Faustus* is that Barabas' dramaturgical analogues (i.e., the devils) are not defeated either, or at least not in the short term. Despite allusions to their one-time defeat by God, they triumph maliciously over the only character who is defeated in this play—a mortal loser in the stakes for cosmic dominance.

To be sure, Mephistopheles as a tempter does not seem like an equivocating Vice, because he is so solemn and seldom takes us into his confidence.[5] His method of temptation is actually more like that of the devil in the mystery plays, who tends to be less comical than the Vice and infrequently reveals his purpose. Lucifer's temp-

---

3. T. McAlindon, *Dr. Faustus Divine in Show* (New York: Twayne Publishers, 1994), pp. 45–61.
4. On Marlowe's adaptation of morality-play conventions, see David M. Bevington, *From "Mankind" to Marlowe* (Cambridge, Mass.: Harvard University Press, 1962), pp. 199–262.
5. McAlindon, in *Dr. Faustus Divine in Show* (1994), sees Mephistopheles as "an entirely original kind of devil" whose early behavior "is totally at variance with both his intentions and his conduct as shown later" (p. 38), but this underestimates the sophistication of Marlowe's devil and ignores Mephistopheles' important aside, quoted in the text below.

tation of Eve in the cycle plays is closer to Mephistopheles' temptation of Faustus than, say, to Titivillus' temptation of Mankind. Mephistopheles seldom uses dramatic asides, but he does so once with telling effect: "O, what will I not do to obtain his soul?" (2.1.73). Otherwise, Marlowe's devil presents the same face to us that he presents to Faustus, thus creating uncertainty about when he is lying and when he is not.

The focus of demonic dissimulation in *Dr. Faustus* is the bargain itself. That the pact is really a means to make Faustus *submit* (rather than giving him the means to dominate, as he hopes to do) seems apparent from the moment Mephistopheles explains blasphemy as a sign of potential interest in submission to demons (1.3.47–55). Yet even this claim may merely be a demonic feint in Mephistopheles' incessant battle to control Faustus, because Mephistopheles always seeks to dominate Faustus rhetorically and always succeeds. Like Tamburlaine, he is a master of "working words" by which he overpowers his victim, and he serves a power-seeker, as Theridamas does, whose sole aim is to "enlarge his kingdom" (2.1.40).

Take Mephistopheles' phrase to describe the motive for Lucifer's rebellion, for example: "aspiring pride and insolence" (1.3.69), which captures God's view of the matter, as it had been traditionally understood. Since Mephistopheles presumably does not hope to convert Faustus to God's view, his use of traditional diction is presumably to tempt Faustus to persevere in "manly fortitude," because that kind of perseverance is really a submission to the devil. The rhetorical effect of this reverse psychology on the audience is the same as it is on Faustus: to make us feel the limiting restrictions of orthodoxy.

The bargain thus appears to be another demonic feint, as the Good Angel and the Old Man suggest in their assurance of divine mercy long after Faustus has signed. For their assurance clarifies one point: we can assume that the devil is telling the truth about the bargain only if we assume that the Good Angel and the Old Man are lying. If the bargain were indeed what Mephistopheles claims it is, he would not pursue his victim after the signing but would expend his energy elsewhere, confident that he could abandon Faustus to his already accomplished damnation.[6] Mephistopheles "serves" Faustus not in good faith according to a bargain but because he is vigilant to "obtain his soul," that is, to dominate him by pretending to serve him.

This is why Mephistopheles' threats are empty but effective.

6. This point is well made by T. McAlindon, *"Doctor Faustus*: the Predestination Theory," *English Studies* 76 (1995), 215–16.

Threats (including the bond) are the stick in his approach; temptations to power, the carrot. If the devils literally harmed Faustus, they would be less likely to obtain his soul, that is, to secure his unswerving allegiance, because physical pain could break the victim but not "turn" him, and the threat of torture is useful in persuading him when he wavers, because it convinces him of the threateners' power. This is why the Old Man does not fear the "sifting" of Satan: secure in his allegiance to the other side, the Old Man knows the devils can torture and destroy him, but they cannot "obtain his soul," as Mephistopheles admits:

> His faith is great. I cannot touch his soul.
> But what I may afflict his body with
> I will attempt, which is but little worth. (5.1.79–81)

The Old Man even sees the "furnace" of demonic torture as God's hand trying his faith (5.1.115)—a telling comment on divine and demonic instrumentality in the destruction of Faustus as well, and a deconstructive view of martyrdom.

At the same time, as long as Faustus still thinks he has something to gain from Mephistopheles, he does not want to abandon the opportunity to gain it. Lies and truth thus become intermingled and difficult to distinguish:

Faustus. Come, I think hell's a fable.
Mephistopheles. Ay, think so still, till experience change thy mind.
Faustus. Why, think'st thou then that Faustus shall be damned?
Mephistopheles. Ay, of necessity, for here's the scroll
  Wherein thou hast given thy soul to Lucifer. (2.1.130–34)

Mephistopheles seems to take one step backward, as he affirms the real existence of hell, in order to take two steps forward in lying about the efficacy of the bargain in Faustus' domination. But if the reality, as Marlowe presents it, is that God and Lucifer are locked in a power struggle, then the truth of what opposes the devil is not guaranteed either, any more than Ferneze's truth is guaranteed simply because he is a Christian. If the aim of both sides is to catch Faustus' soul, what will they not do to obtain it? In *Dr. Faustus* Marlowe reproduces the effect of ubiquitous dissimulation in the quest for power that he also creates in *The Jew of Malta*, but the effect appears on a cosmic scale, and the stakes are correspondingly higher.[7]

* * *

7. Coburn Freer, "Lies and Lying in *The Jew of Malta*," in *"A Poet and a Filthy Play-maker"*: *New Essays on Christopher Marlowe*, ed. Kenneth Friedenreich, Roma Gill, and Constance Kuriyama (New York: AMS Press, 1988), pp. 143–65, especially the following: "When a majority of characters in a play lie to each other and themselves, their verbal behavior will not only shape the action but will also give that action a multitude of meanings, some of them inevitably contradictory" (p. 145).

CRITICISM

Early Critics

THOMAS WARTON

From The History of English Poetry: From the Close of the Eleventh to the Commencement of the Eighteenth Century†

* * *

Marlowe's wit and spriteliness of conversation had often the un-happy effect of tempting him to sport with sacred subjects; more perhaps from the preposterous ambition of courting the casual ap-plause of profligate and unprincipled companions, than from any systematic disbelief of religion. His scepticism, whatever it might be, was construed by the prejudiced and peevish puritans into ab-solute atheism: and they took pains to represent the unfortunate catastrophe of his untimely death, as an immediate judgment from heaven upon his execrable impiety. He was in love, and had for his rival, to use the significant words of Wood, 'a bawdy servingman, one rather fitted to be a pimp, than an ingenious *amoretto*, as Mar-lowe conceived himself to be.' The consequence was, that an affray ensued; in which the antagonist having by superior agility gained an opportunity of strongly grasping Marlow's wrist, plunged his dagger with his own hand into his own head. Of this wound he died rather before the year 1593. One of Marlowe's tragedies is 'The tragical history of the life and death of doctor John Faustus'. A proof of the credulous ignorance which still prevailed, and a speci-men of the subjects which then were thought not improper for tragedy. A tale which at the close of the sixteenth century had the possession of the public theatres of our metropolis, now only fright-ens children at a puppet-show in a country-town. But that the learned John Faust continued to maintain the character of a con-juror in the sixteenth century even by authority, appears from a 'Ballad of the life and death of doctor Faustus the *great congerer*,'

† (London: J. Dodsley et al., 1775), vol. 4, p. 261.

which in 1588 was licenced to be printed by the learned Aylmer bishop of London.

SIR WALTER SCOTT

On *Doctor Faustus*†

Christopher Marlowe's *Tragicall History of Dr Faustus*—a very remarkable thing. Grand subject—end grand.

CHARLES LAMB

From Specimens of English Dramatic Poets Who Lived about the Time of Shakespeare‡

* * *

The growing horrors of Faustus are awfully marked by the hours and half hours as they expire and bring him nearer and nearer to the exactment of his dire compact. It is indeed an agony and bloody sweat.

Marlowe is said to have been tainted with atheistical positions, to have denied God and the Trinity. To such a genius the history of Faustus must have been delectable food: to wander in fields where curiosity is forbidden to go, to approach the dark gulf near enough to look in, to be busied in speculations which are the rottenest part of the core of the fruit that fell from the tree of knowledge. Barabas the Jew, and Faustus the conjurer, are offsprings of a mind which at least delighted to dally with interdicted subjects. They both talk a language which a believer would have been tender of putting into the mouth of a character though but in fiction. But the holiest minds have sometimes not thought it blameable to counterfeit impiety in the person of another, to bring Vice in upon the stage speaking her own dialect, and, themselves being armed with an Unction of self-confident impunity, have not scrupled to handle and touch that familiarly, which would be death to others. Milton, in the person of Satan has started speculations hardier than any which the feeble armoury of the atheist ever furnished: and the precise strait-laced Richardson has strengthened Vice, from the mouth of Lovelace, with entangling sophistries and abstruse pleas

† Notebook entry dated May 26, 1797, in J. G. Lockhart, ed., *Memoirs of the Life of Sir Walter Scott* (Philadelphia: Carey, Lea, and Blanchard, 1837), vol. 1, p. 264.
‡ (London: Longman, Hurst, Rees, and Orme, 1808), p. 40.

against her adversary Virtue which Sedley, Villiers, and Rochester, wanted depth of Libertinism sufficient to have invented.

WILLIAM HAZLITT

From Lectures Chiefly on the Dramatic Literature of the Age of Elizabeth†

Marlowe is a name that stands high, and almost first in this list of dramatic worthies. He was a little before Shakespear's time, and has a marked character both from him and the rest. There is a lust of power in his writings, a hunger and thirst after unrighteousness, a glow of the imagination, unhallowed by any thing but its own energies. His thoughts burn within him like a furnace with bickering flames; or throwing out black smoke and mists, that hide the dawn of genius, or like a poisonous mineral, corrode the heart. His 'Life and Death of Doctor Faustus,' though an imperfect and unequal performance, is his greatest work. Faustus himself is a rude sketch, but it is a gigantic one. This character may be considered as a personification of the pride of will and eagerness of curiosity, sublimed beyond the reach of fear and remorse. He is hurried away, and, as it were, devoured by a tormenting desire to enlarge his knowledge to the utmost bounds of nature and art, and to extend his power with his knowledge. He would realise all the fictions of a lawless imagination, would solve the most subtle speculations of abstract reason; and for this purpose, sets at defiance all mortal consequences, and leagues himself with demoniacal power, with 'fate and metaphysical aid.' The idea of witchcraft and necromancy, once the dread of the vulgar and the darling of the visionary recluse, seems to have had its origin in the restless tendency of the human mind, to conceive of and aspire to more than it can achieve by natural means, and in the obscure apprehension that the gratification of this extravagant and unauthorised desire, can only be attained by the sacrifice of all our ordinary hopes, and better prospects to the infernal agents that lend themselves to its accomplishment. Such is the foundation of the present story. Faustus, in his impatience to fulfil at once and for a moment, for a few short years, all the desires and conceptions of his soul, is willing to give in exchange his soul and body to the great enemy of mankind. Whatever he fancies, becomes by this means present to his sense: whatever he commands, is done. He calls back time past, and anticipates the future: the visions of antiquity pass before him, Babylon in all its glory, Paris and Oenone: all the projects of

† (London: Stodart and Stewart, 1820), pp. 56–59, 64.

philosophers, or creations of the poet pay tribute at his feet: all the delights of fortune, of ambition, of pleasure, and of learning are centered in his person; and from a short-lived dream of supreme felicity and drunken power, he sinks into an abyss of darkness and perdition. This is the alternative to which he submits; the bond which he signs with his blood! As the outline of the character is grand and daring, the execution is abrupt and fearful. The thoughts are vast and irregular; and the style halts and staggers under them, 'with uneasy steps';—'such footing found the sole of unblest feet.' There is a little fustian and incongruity of metaphor now and then, which is not very injurious to the subject. . . . The intermediate comic parts, in which Faustus is not directly concerned, are mean and grovelling to the last degree. One of the Clowns says to another: 'Snails! what hast got there? A book? Why thou can'st not tell ne'er a word on 't.' Indeed, the ignorance and barbarism of the time, as here described, might almost justify Faustus's overstrained admiration of learning, and turn the heads of those who possessed it, from novelty and unaccustomed excitement, as the Indians are made drunk with wine! Goethe, the German poet, has written a drama on this tradition of his country, which is considered a master-piece. I cannot find, in Marlowe's play, any proofs of the atheism or impiety attributed to him, unless the beliefs in witchcraft and the Devil can be regarded as such; and at the time he wrote, not to have believed in both, would have been construed into the rankest atheism and irreligion. There is a delight, as Mr. Lamb says, 'in dallying with interdicted subjects'; but that does not, by any means, imply either a practical or speculative disbelief of them . . .

GEORGE HENRY LEWES

From The Life and Works of Goethe†

The reader who opens 'Faustus' under the impression that he is about to see a philosophical subject treated philosophically, will have mistaken both the character of Marlowe's genius and of Marlowe's epoch. 'Faustus' is no more philosophical in intention than the 'Jew of Malta', or 'Tamburlaine the Great'. It is simply the theatrical treatment of a popular legend,—a legend admirably characteristic of the spirit of those ages in which men, believing in the agency of the devil, would willingly have bartered their future existence for the satisfaction of present desires. Here undoubtedly is a philosophical problem, which even in the present day is constantly

† (London: David Nutt, 1855), pp. 319–20.

presenting itself to the speculative mind. Yes, even in the present day, since human nature does not change,—forms only change, the spirit remains; nothing perishes,—it only manifests itself differently. Men, it is true, no longer believe in the devil's agency; at least, they no longer believe in the power of calling up the devil and transacting business with him; otherwise there would be hundreds of such stories as that of 'Faust'. But the spirit which created that story and rendered it credible to all Europe remains unchanged. The sacrifice of the future to the present is the spirit of that legend. The blindness to consequences caused by the imperiousness of desire; the recklessness with which inevitable and terrible results are braved in perfect consciousness of their being inevitable, provided that a temporary pleasure can be obtained, is the spirit which dictated Faust's barter of his soul, which daily dictates the barter of men's souls. We do not make compacts, but we throw away our lives; we have no Tempter face to face with us offering illimitable power in exchange for our futurity: but we have our own Desires, imperious, insidious, and for them we barter our existence,—for one moment's pleasure risking years of anguish.

ANONYMOUS

Faust on the Stage†

'The Tragical History of Doctor Faustus' is then the earliest literary work extant purporting to treat of the Wittenberg savant and conjuror—terms almost synonymous in the age in which he lived. To the average mind of the fifteenth century, astronomy and astrology, chemistry and alchemy, signified exactly the same thing; in fact, our prosaic and matter-of-fact ancestors cared very much more for the arts of divination, the transmutation of metals, and the secret of perpetual youth, than for any abstract idea of science. What may be called the poetry of science, the love of knowledge for its own sake, is a recent invention, like the love of picturesque scenery, and the arts of spelling accurately, and speaking decently and modestly. Some of these last are not very widely distributed even now, any more than a knowledge of the difference between science and quackery. In queer lower strata lurk 'survivals' of the thoughts and customs of centuries long gone by, changed a little as to outward form and expression, but in essentials just as of old. There are thousands of people now in England who know no more difference between astronomy and astrology than their ancestors of four hun-

† *All the Year Round* (June 28, 1879): 40–41.

dred years ago. White witches are yet to be found in Devonshire, and gipsies everywhere that a silver spoon is to be picked up. More than this, the present Astronomer Royal, like Flamsteed, who lived a century and a half before him, is besieged with requests to find lost linen and spoons, to 'take the stars off' a favourite son who has a strange knack of losing his watch when he goes to market, to 'fix the planets' for a pet daughter, or to find the whereabouts of stolen property. A yearly average arrives at the Observatory at Greenwich of letters containing droll requests of this kind, proving that vulgar human nature is profoundly penetrated with the wisdom of Buckle's apothegm that 'the chief use of knowledge of the past is to predict the future.' In a rough kind of way these good people agree with the philosopher, albeit they import the revelations of the planets into their calculations. In Marlowe's time nobody doubted his own star for an instance. During the lifetime of the English poet, the greatest living woman saving Elizabeth herself, Catherine de Medicis, spent a part of every day with Ruggieri, her necromancer, in the tower since built into the wall of the Paris corn-market, or in his loftier observatory at Blois. It was in the latter that the Italian juggler cast the horoscope of Henry of Navarre, and found that he would reign in France; a prediction which absolutely drew away the queen from the Huguenots, the natural allies of the monarchy against the overweening Guises, backed by Spain and the Pope. It was, therefore, not astonishing that the world should have a lively sense of the personal presence of Lucifer, at the time Kit Marlowe tippled sack at Deptford. Honest Kit himself never doubted the personality of angel or devil. He presents us with the personality of Tamburlaine the Great, after the fashion caricatured by Shakespeare, and gives us Doctor Faustus in all good faith, without sceptical reservation, cold realism, or metaphysical abstraction. To Marlowe Faustus is an entity—a genuine living man, as unlike Goethe's Faust as may be; a real personage, making a real compact with a real devil, and paying the penalty with body and soul. In reading Marlowe's remarkable work it is impossible to imagine that the author doubted the possibility of the events he puts before the spectator. This simple faith gives a genuineness to the 'Tragical History of Doctor Faustus', that one is far from finding in the great work of Goethe. Marlowe's work is the outcome of an undoubting mind—not the statement of a great problem yet unsolved. After the old simple fashion, Marlowe points his moral before he begins to adorn his tale, and tells us, through the medium of the chorus, how Faustus is

> graced with Doctor's name,
> Excelling all, and sweetly can dispute
> In the heavenly matters of theology:

Till swoln with cunning, and a self-conceit,
His waxen wings did mount above his reach,

and so 'surfeits on the cursed necromancy.' Marlowe wrote, as
Goethe could not write, in the firm belief of the possibility of what
he wrote. Goethe's earth and air spirits are abstractions; Marlowe's
are concrete actualities, and throughout the Englishman's wonderful play there is no hint, any more than there is in a mediaeval mystery, that the events in it are either impossible or even improbable.
There is another curious point of difference; not with the last
thought of Goethe in the second part of Faust, but in the first or
dramatic part—a difference clearly ascribable to the fervent religious faith of the sixteenth century. Throughout Marlowe's play
there is the constant interposition of good counsel and warning to
repentance. Faustus signs the contract, but it is throughout suggested that it might have been annulled had he turned back in
time; the Christian doctrine of repentance is never forgotten, and
Faustus is constantly opened a loophole of escape.

Weary of success as a learned doctor, he asks:

Are not thy bills hung up as monuments,
Whereby whole cities have escaped the plague,
And thousand desperate maladies been cured?

Human knowledge being compassed, he aspires to the supernatural, and accordingly calls in two doctors learned in the art magical,
'the German Valdes,' whose name hath a most un-Teutonic sound,
and Cornelius. These worthies instruct him how to use the works
of Bacon and Albertus Magnus, in conjunction with the Hebrew
Psalter and New Testament, so as to raise spirits more potent than
those whom Owen Glendower (teste Hotspur) called in vain. His
interview with Mephistopheles is marked by several peculiarities,
notably one not overlooked by Milton:

FAUST. Where are you damned?
MEPH. In hell.
FAUST. How comes it then that thou art come out of hell?
MEPH. Why, this is hell, nor am I out of it;
Think'st thou that I, that saw the face of God
And tasted the eternal joys of Heaven,
Am not tormented with ten thousand hells
In being deprived of everlasting bliss?

This Mephistopheles is not the mocking fiend of Goethe, but
rather the awful Lucifer of Milton. He is determined to secure the
soul of Faustus, and during his twenty-four years of service realises
every kind of impossibility for his temporary master. Some persis-
tence on the part of the fiend is required, for Marlowe's Faustus is

a shabby client, ever trying to escape performance of his bond. This
is not astonishing when the spirit of the age is taken into consideration. The mystic and comprehensive answer to Where is hell?

> Hell hath no limits, nor is circumscribed
> In one self place: but where we are is hell,
> And where hell is there must we ever be,

must not be understood too literally. Nothing would have been farther from Marlowe's purpose than to shake popular belief in an actual fixed place of eternal punishment. Firstly, such doctrine would
have been utterly opposed to the theology of his day; secondly, it
would have made an end of his tragedy. The reality of the infernal re-
gions is as necessary to Marlowe as to Dante. Neither doubted their
existence, while, on the other hand, Goethe held what are called 'advanced views' on such subjects, and, whether he chose openly to
avow his disbelief in eternal punishment or not, treats his angels and
spirits in Faust as mere poetical machinery, just as Julius Caesar, according to Sallust, treated the old Pagan gods in that memorable
speech in the senate house, touching the conspiracy of Catiline.
There is no real good or evil spirit in Goethe's wonderful work, and
the malicious Mephistopheles is rather recollected as a saver of good
things than as a malignant fiend. Now Marlowe, on the contrary, is
very real. Not only is Faustus duly handed over to the foul fiend at
the conclusion of the tragedy, but a perpetual conflict is maintained
between his good and bad angels. He is warned over and over again,
and it is implied that even such contract as he has signed with Lucifer may be voided by prompt renunciation and repentance. He is
shown, within the compass of eight days, the face of heaven, of
earth, and of hell. The seven deadly sins appear before him, and describe their attributes; he is given every chance of repentance in vain.
Yet he is not shown to be oppressed by the Greek destiny. On the
contrary, his power to decide is assumed by the frequency of the appeals made to him. He is vanquished by one weakness—sensuality.

A. C. BRADLEY

From English Poets: Selections with Critical Introductions by Various Writers†

* * *

[T]here is that incommunicable gift which means almost everything,
style; a manner perfectly individual, and yet, at its best, free from ec-

† (New York: Macmillan, 1880), vol. 1, pp. 413–14.

centricity. The 'mighty line' of which Jonson spoke, and a pleasure, equal to Milton's, in resounding proper names, meet us in the
very first scene; and in not a few passages passion, instead of vocif-
erating, finds its natural expression, and we hear the fully-formed
style, which in Marlowe's best writing is, to use his own words,

> Like his desire, lift upward and divine.

'Lift upward' Marlowe's style was at first, and so it remained. It
degenerates into violence, but never into softness. If it falters, the
cause is not doubt or languor, but haste and want of care. It has the
energy of youth; and a living poet has described this among its
other qualities when he speaks of Marlowe as singing

> With mouth of gold, and morning in his eyes.

As a dramatic instrument it developed with his growth and acquired variety. The stately monotone of 'Tamburlaine,' in which the
pause falls almost regularly at the end of the lines, gives place in
'Edward II' to rhythms less suited to pure poetry, but far more rapid
and flexible. In 'Dr. Faustus' the great address to Helen is as different in metrical effect as it is in spirit from the last scene, where the
words seem, like Faustus' heart, to 'pant and quiver'. . . .
The expression 'lift upward' applies also, in a sense, to most of
the chief characters in the plays. Whatever else they may lack, they
know nothing of half-heartedness or irresolution. A volcanic self-
assertion, a complete absorption in some one desire, is their characteristic. That in creating such characters Marlowe was working
in dark places, and that he developes them with all his energy, is
certain. But that in so doing he shows (to refer to a current notion
of him) a 'hunger and thirst after unrighteousness,' a desire, that is,
which never has produced or could produce true poetry, is an idea
which Hazlitt could not have really intended to convey. Marlowe's
works are tragedies. Their greatness lies not merely in the conception of an unhallowed lust, however gigantic, but in an insight into
its tragic significance and tragic results; and there is as little food
for a hunger after unrighteousness (if there be such a thing) in the
appalling final scene of 'Dr. Faustus,' or, indeed, in the melancholy
of Mephistopheles, so grandly touched by Marlowe, as in the catastrophe of 'Richard III' or of Goethe's 'Faust.'

A. C. SWINBURNE

"Prologue" to *Doctor Faustus*†

Light, as when dawn takes wind and smites the sea,
Smote England when his day bade Marlowe be.
No fire so keen had thrilled the clouds of time
Since Dante's breath made Italy sublime.
Earth, bright with flowers whose dew shone soft as tears,
Through Chaucer cast her charm on eyes and ears:
The lustrous laughter of the love-lit earth
Rang, leapt, and lightened in his might of mirth.
Deep moonlight, hallowing all the breathless air,
Made earth and heaven for Spenser faint and fair.
But song might bid not heaven and earth be one
Till Marlowe's voice gave warning of the sun.
Thought quailed and fluttered as a wounded bird
Till passion fledged the wing of Marlowe's word.
Faith born of fear bade hope and doubt be dumb
Till Marlowe's pride bade light or darkness come.
Then first our speech was thunder: then our song
Shot lightning through the clouds that wrought us wrong.
Blind fear, whose faith feeds hell with fire, became
A moth self-shrivelled in its own blind flame.
We heard in tune with even our seas that roll,
The speech of storm, the thunders of the soul,
Men's passions clothed with all the woes they wrought,
Shone through the fire of man's transfiguring thought.
The thirst of knowledge, quenchless at her springs,
Ambition, fire that clasps the thrones of kings.
Love, light that makes of life one lustrous hour,
And song, the soul's chief crown and throne of power,
The hungering heart of greed and ravenous hate,
Made music high as heaven and deep as fate.
Strange pity, scarce half scornful of her tear,
In Berkeley's vaults bowed down on Edward's bier.
But higher in forceful flight of song than all
The soul of man, its own imperious thrall,
Rose, when his royal spirit of fierce desire
Made life and death for man one flame of fire.
Incarnate man, fast bound as earth and sea
Spake, when his pride would fain set Faustus free.
Eternal beauty, strong as day and night,

† Written for William Poel's production of 1896, from *"The Tragical History of Doctor Faustus" by C. Marlowe, as Revised by The Elizabethan Stage Society under the Direction of William Poel* (London: H. Bullen, 1904), p. 4.

Shone, when his word bade Helen back to sight.
Fear when he bowed his soul before her spell,
Thundered and lightened through the vaults of hell.
The music known of all men's tongues that sing,
When Marlowe sang, bade love make heaven of spring;
The music none but English tongues may make,
Our own sole song, spake first when Marlowe spake;
And on his grave, though there no stone may stand,
The flower it shows was laid by Shakespeare's hand.

GEORGE SANTAYANA

From Three Philosophical Poets†

Marlowe's public would see in Doctor Faustus a man and a Christian like themselves, carried a bit too far by ambition and the love of pleasure. He is no radical unbeliever, no natural mate for the devil, conscienceless and heathen, like the typical villain of the Renaissance. On the contrary, he has become a good Protestant, and holds manfully to all those parts of the creed which express his spontaneous affections. A good angel is often overheard whispering in his ear; and if the bad angel finally prevails, it is in spite of continual remorse and hesitation on the Doctor's part. This excellent Faustus is damned by accident or by predestination; he is browbeaten by the devil and forbidden to repent when he has really repented. The terror of the conclusion is thereby heightened; we see an essentially good man, because in a moment of infatuation he had signed away his soul, driven against his will to despair and damnation. The alternative of a happy solution lies almost at hand; and it is only a lingering taste for the lurid and the horrible, ingrained in this sort of melodrama, that sends him shrieking to hell.

What makes Marlowe's conclusion the more violent and the more unphilosophical is the fact that, to any one not dominated by convention, the good angel, in the dialogue, seems to have so much the worse of the argument. All he has to offer is sour admonition and external warnings:

> O Faustus, lay that damnèd book aside,
> And gaze not on it lest it tempt thy soul,
> And heap God's heavy wrath upon thy head.
> Read, read, the Scriptures; that is blasphemy. . . .
> Sweet Faustus, think of heaven, and heavenly things.

† (Cambridge: Harvard University Press, 1910), pp. 147–49.

To which the evil angel replies:

> No, Faustus, think of honour and of wealth.

And in another place:

> Go forward, Faustus, in that famous art,
> Wherein all nature's treasure is contained.
> Be thou on earth as Jove is in the sky,
> Lord and commander of these elements.

There can be no doubt that the devil here represents the natural ideal of Faustus, or of any child of the Renaissance; he appeals to the vague but healthy ambitions of a young soul, that would make trial of the world. In other words, this devil represents the true good, and it is no wonder if the honest Faustus cannot resist his suggestions. We like him for his love of life, for his trust in nature, for his enthusiasm for beauty. He speaks for us all when he cries:

> Was this the face that launched a thousand ships
> And burnt the topless towers of Ilium?

Even his irreverent pranks, being directed against the pope, endear him the more to an anti-clerical public; and he appeals to courtiers and cavaliers by his lofty poetical scorn for such crabbed professions as the law, medicine, or theology. In a word, Marlowe's Faustus is a martyr to everything that the Renaissance prized,—power, curious knowledge, enterprise, wealth, and beauty.

Modern Critics

CLEANTH BROOKS

The Unity of Marlowe's *Doctor Faustus*†

In his *Poetics*, Aristotle observed that a tragedy should have a beginning, a middle, and an end. The statement makes a point that
seems obvious, and many a reader of our time must have dismissed
it as one of the more tedious remarks of the Stagirite, or indeed put
it down to one of the duller notes taken by the student whom some
suppose to have heard Aristotle's lectures and preserved the substance of them for us. Yet the play without a middle does occur, and
in at least three signal instances that I can think of in English literature, we have a play that lacks a proper middle or at least a play
that *seems* to lack a middle. Milton's *Samson Agonistes* is one of
them; Eliot's *Murder in the Cathedral*, another; and Marlowe's *Doctor Faustus*, the third. Milton presents us with Samson, in the
hands of his enemies, blind, grinding at the mill with other slaves,
yet in only a little while he has Samson pull down the temple roof
upon his enemies. There is a beginning and there is an end, but in
the interval between them has anything of real consequence happened? *Murder in the Cathedral* may seem an even more flagrant
instance of an end jammed on to a beginning quite directly and
without any intervening dramatic substance. Thomas has come
back out of exile to assume his proper place in his cathedral and act
as shepherd to his people. He is already aware of the consequences
of his return, and that in all probability the decisive act has been
taken that will quickly lead to his martyrdom and death.

Marlowe's *Doctor Faustus* may seem to show the same defect, for
very early in the play the learned doctor makes his decision to sell
his soul to the devil, and after that there seems little to do except to

---

† From *To Neville Coghill from Friends*, ed. J. Lawlor and W. H. Auden (London: Faber
and Faber, 1966), pp. 110–24. Reprinted by permission of the publisher.

fill in the time before the mortgage falls due and the devil comes to collect the forfeited soul. If the consequence of Faustus's bargain is inevitable, and if nothing can be done to alter it, then it doesn't much matter what one puts in as filler. Hence one can stuff in comedy and farce more or less *ad libitum*, the taste of the audience and its patience in sitting through the play being the only limiting factors.

*   *   *

For their effectiveness, *Doctor Faustus, Samson Agonistes* and *Murder in the Cathedral*, all three, depend heavily upon their poetry. One could go further: the poetry tends to be intensely lyrical and in the play with which we are concerned arises from the depths of the character of Faustus himself; it expresses his aspirations, his dreams, his fears, his agonies, and his intense awareness of the conflicting feelings within himself. The poetry, it ought to be observed, is not a kind of superficial gilding, but an expression—and perhaps the inevitable expression—of the emotions of the central character. If there is indeed a 'middle' in this play—that is, a part of the play concerned with complication and development in which the character of Faustus becomes something quite different from the man whom we first meet—then the 'middle' of the play has to be sought in this area of personal self-examination and inner conflict, and the poetry will prove its most dramatic expression. . . .

But before attempting to get deeper into the problem of whether *Doctor Faustus* has a proper middle, it will be useful to make one or two general observations about the play. *Doctor Faustus* is a play about knowledge, about the relation of one's knowledge of the world to his knowledge of himself—about knowledge of means and its relation to knowledge of ends. It is a play, thus, that reflects the interests of the Renaissance and indeed that looks forward to the issues of the modern day. There is even an anticipation in the play, I should suppose, of the problem of the 'two cultures'. Faustus is dissatisfied and even bored with the study of ethics and divinity and metaphysics. What has captured his imagination is magic, but we must not be misled by the associations that that term now carries for most of us. The knowledge that Faustus wants to attain is knowledge that can be put to use—what Bertrand Russell long ago called power knowledge—the knowledge that allows one to effect changes in the world around him. When Faustus rejects philosophy and divinity for magic, he chooses magic because, as he says, the pursuit of magic promises 'a world of profit and delight, / Of power, of honour, of omnipotence'. He sums it up in saying: 'A sound Magician is a mighty god.' But if one does manage to acquire the technical knowledge that will allow one to 'Wall all Germany with brass' or to beat a modern jet plane's time in flying in fresh grapes from the tropics, for what purpose is that technical knowledge to be used? How does this knowledge of means relate to one's knowledge of ends? Marlowe is too honest a dramatist to allow Faustus to escape such questions.

This last comment must not, however, be taken to imply that Marlowe has written a moral tract rather than a drama, or that he has been less than skilful in making Faustus's experiments with power knowledge bring him, again and again, up against knowledge of a more ultimate kind. Marlowe makes the process seem natural and inevitable. For example, as soon as Faustus has signed the contract with the devil and has, by giving himself to hell, gained his new knowledge, his first question to Mephistopheles, rather naturally, has to do with the nature of the place to which he has consigned himself. He says: 'First will I question with thee about hell, / Tell me, where is the place that men call hell?' In his reply, Mephistopheles explodes any notion of a local hell, and defines hell as a state of mind; but Faustus cannot believe his ears, and though getting his information from an impeccable source, indeed from the very horse's mouth, he refuses to accept the first fruits of his new knowledge. He had already come to the decision that stories of hell were merely 'old wives' tales'—one supposes that this decision was a factor in his resolution to sell his soul. Yet when Mephistopheles says that he is an instance to prove the contrary since he is damned, and is even now in hell, Faustus cannot take in the notion. 'How? Now in hell? / Nay and this be hell, I'll willingly be damned here. . . .'

The new knowledge that Faustus has acquired proves curiously unsatisfactory in other ways. For instance, Faustus demands a book in which the motions and characters of the planets are so truly set forth that, knowing these motions, he can raise up spirits directly and without the intervention of Mephistopheles. Mephistopheles at once produces the book, only to have Faustus say: 'When I behold the heavens, then I repent / . . . Because thou has deprived me of those joys.' Mephistopheles manages to distract Faustus from notions of repentance, but soon Faustus is once more making inquiries that touch upon the heavens, this time about astrology; and again, almost before he knows it, Faustus has been moved by his contemplation of the revolution of the spheres to a more ultimate question. 'Tell me who made the world,' he suddenly asks Mephistopheles, and this thought of the Creator once more wracks Faustus with a reminder of his damnation. Marlowe has throughout the play used the words *heaven* and *heavenly* in a tantalizingly double sense. *Heavenly* refers to the structure of the cosmos as seen from the earth, but it also has associations with the divine—the sphere from which Faustus has cut himself off.

Thus, technical questions about how nature works have a tendency to raise the larger questions of the Creator and the purposes of the creation. Faustus cannot be content—such is the education of a lifetime—or such was Marlowe's education, if you prefer—cannot be content with the mere workings of the machinery of the universe: he must push on to ask about ultimate purposes. Knowledge of means cannot be sealed off from knowledge of ends, and here Faustus's newly acquired knowledge cannot give him answers different from those he already knew before he forfeited his soul. The new knowledge can only forbid Faustus to dwell upon the answers to troubling questions that persist, the answers to which he knows all too well.

To come at matters in a different way, Faustus is the man who is all dressed up with no place to go. His plight is that he cannot find anything to do really worthy of the supernatural powers that he has come to possess. Faustus never carries out in practice his dreams of great accomplishments. He evidently doesn't want to wall all Germany with brass, or make the swift Rhine circle fair Wittenberg. Nor does he chase the Prince of Parma from Germany. Instead, he plays tricks on the Pope, or courts favour with the Emperor by staging magical shows for him. When he summons up at the Emperor's request Alexander the Great and his paramour, Faustus is careful to explain—Faustus in some sense remains to the end an honest man—that the Emperor will not be seeing 'the true substantial bodies of those two deceased princes which long since are consumed to dust'. The illusion is certainly life-like . . . ; but even so, Alexander and his paramour are no more than apparitions. This magical world lacks substance.

With reference to the quality of Faustus's exploitations of his magical power, one may point out that Marlowe is scarcely answerable for some of the stuff that was worked into the middle of the play. Yet to judge only from the scenes acknowledged to be Marlowe's and from the ending that Marlowe devised for the play, it is inconceivable that Faustus should ever have carried out the grandiose plans which he mentions in scene iii—such matters as making a bridge through the moving air so that bands of men can pass over the ocean, or joining the hills that bind the African shore to those of Spain. Faustus's basic motivation—his yearning for self-aggrandisement—ensures that the power he has gained will be used for what are finally frivolous purposes.

I have been stressing the author's distinction between the different kinds of knowledge that Faustus craves, and his careful pointing up of the inner contradictions that exist among these kinds of knowledge. I think that these matters are important for the meaning of the play, but some of you may feel that in themselves they scarcely serve to establish the requisite middle for the play. To note the confusions and contradictions in Faustus's quest for knowledge may make Faustus appear a more human figure and even a more modern figure. (I am entirely aware that my own perspective may be such as to make the play more 'modern' than it is.) Yet, if Faustus is indeed doomed, the moment he signs with his own blood his contract with the devil, then there is no further significant action that he can take, and the rest of the play will be not so much dramatic as elegiac, as Faustus comes to lament the course that he has taken, or simply clinical, as we watch the writhings and inner torment of a character whose case is hopeless. Whether the case of Faustus becomes hopeless early in the play is, then, a matter of real consequence.

On a purely legalistic basis, of course, Faustus's case *is* hopeless. He has made a contract and he has to abide by it. This is the point that the devils insist on relentlessly. Yet there are plenty of indications that Faustus was not the prisoner of one fatal act. Before Faustus signs the bond, the good angel twice appears to him, first to beg him to lay his 'Damned book aside' and later to implore him to beware of the 'execrable art' of magic. But even after Faustus has signed the bond, the good angel appears. In scene vi he adjures Faustus to repent, saying: 'Repent yet, God will pity thee.' The bad angel, it is true, appears along with him to insist that 'God cannot pity thee.' But then the bad angel had appeared along with the good in all the early appearances too.

There are other indications that Faustus is not yet beyond the possibility of redemption. The devils, in spite of the contract, are evidently not at all sure of the soul of Faustus. They find it again and again necessary to argue with him, to bully him, and to threaten him. Mephistopheles evidently believes that it is very important to try to distract Faustus from his doleful thoughts. The assumption of the play is surely that the devils are anxious, and Mephistopheles in particular goes to a great deal of trouble to keep Faustus under control. There is never any assumption that the bond itself, signed with Faustus's blood, is quite sufficient to preserve him safe for hell. At least once, Lucifer himself has to be called in to ensure that Faustus will not escape. Lucifer appeals to Faustus's sense of logic by telling him that 'Christ cannot save thy soul, for he is just, / There's none but I have interest in the same.' But Lucifer employs an even more potent weapon: he terrifies Faustus, and as we shall see in scene xviii, a crucial scene that occurs late in the play, Faustus has little defence against terror.

In scene xviii, a new character appears, one simply called 'an Old Man'. He comes just in the nick of time, for Faustus, in his despair, is on the point of committing suicide, and Mephistopheles, apparently happy to make sure of Faustus's damnation, hands him a dagger. But the Old Man persuades Faustus to desist, telling him: 'I see an angel hovers o'er thy head, / And with a vial full of precious grace, / Offers to pour the same into thy soul: / Then call for mercy, and avoid despair.'

The Old Man has faith that Faustus can still be saved, and testifies to the presence of his good angel, waiting to pour out the necessary grace. But Faustus has indeed despaired. It may be significant that Faustus apparently does not see the angel now. At this crisis when, as Faustus says, 'hell strives with grace for conquest in my breast', Mephistopheles accuses him of disobedience, and threatens to tear his flesh piecemeal. The threat is sufficient. A moment before, Faustus had addressed the Old Man as 'my sweet friend'. Now, in a sudden reversal, he calls Mephistopheles sweet — 'Sweet Mephistopheles, intreat thy lord / To pardon my unjust presumption, / And with my blood again I will confirm / My former vow I made to Lucifer.' The answer of Mephistopheles is interesting and even shocking. He tells Faustus: 'Do it then quickly, with unfeigned heart, / Lest greater danger do attend thy drift.' There is honour among thieves, among devils the appeal to loyalty and sincerity. 'Unfeigned heart' carries ironically the very accent of Christian piety.

Faustus, for his part, shows himself now, perhaps for the first time, to be truly a lost soul. For he suddenly rounds upon the Old Man and beseeches Mephistopheles to inflict on him the 'greatest torments that our hell affords'. The pronoun is significant. Faustus now thinks of hell as 'our hell', and the acceptance of it as part of himself and his desire to see the Old Man suffer mark surely a new stage in his development or deterioration. The shift-over may seem abrupt, but I find it credible in the total context, and I am reminded of what William Butler Yeats said about *his* Faustian play, *The Countess Cathleen*. The Countess, as you will remember, redeemed the souls of her people from the demons to whom they had sold their souls by selling her own. Many years after he had written the play, Yeats remarked that he had made a mistake, he felt, in his treatment of the Countess. As he put it in his *Autobiography*: 'The Countess sells her soul, but [in the play] she is not transformed. If I were to think out that scene to-day, she would, the moment her hand had signed, burst into loud laughter, mock at all she has held holy, horrify the peasants in the midst of their temptations.' Thus Yeats would have dramatized the commitment she had made. The comment is a valid one, and I think is relevant here. Yeats, in making the signing of the bond the decisive and effective act, is of course being more legalistic than is Marlowe, but he vindicates the psychology of the *volte face*. When Faustus does indeed become ir-recoverably damned, he shows it in his conduct, and the change in conduct is startling. Faustus has now become a member of the devil's party in a sense in which he has not been before.

I think too that it is a sound psychology that makes Faustus demand at this point greater distractions and more powerful narcotics than he had earlier required. Shortly before, it was enough for Faustus to call up the vision of Helen. Now he needs to possess her. And if this final abandonment to sensual delight calls forth the most celebrated poetry in the play, the poetry is ominously fitting. Indeed, the poetry here, for all of its passion, is instinct with the desperation of Faustus's plight. Helen's was the face 'that launched a thousand ships and burnt the topless towers of Ilium'. If the wonderful lines insist upon the transcendent power of a beauty that could command the allegiance of thousands, they also refer to the destructive fire that she set alight, and perhaps hint at the hell-fire that now burns for Faustus. After this magnificent invocation, Faustus implores Helen to make his soul immortal with a kiss, but his soul is already immortal, with an immortality that he would gladly—as he says in the last scene—lose if he could.

It may be worth pointing out that the sharpest inner contradictions in Faustus's thinking are manifest in the passage that we have just discussed. Faustus is so much terrified by Mephistopheles's threat to tear his flesh piecemeal that he hysterically courts the favour of Mephistopheles by begging him to tear the flesh of the Old Man. Yet Mephistopheles in his reply actually deflates the terror by remarking of the Old Man that 'His faith is great, I cannot touch his soul'. He promises to try to afflict the Old Man's body, but he observes with business-like candour that this kind of affliction amounts to little—'it is but little worth'.

Perhaps the most powerful testimony in the play against any shallow legalistic interpretation of Faustus's damnation occurs in one of the earlier speeches of Mephistopheles. If Mephistopheles later in the play sees to it, by using distractions, by appealing to Faustus's sense of justice, by invoking terror, that Faustus shall not escape, it is notable that early in the play he testifies to the folly of what Faustus is proposing to do with his life.

When Faustus asks Mephistopheles why it was that Lucifer fell, Mephistopheles replies with complete orthodoxy and with even Christian eloquence: 'Oh, by aspiring pride and insolence'. When Faustus asks him 'What are you that live with Lucifer?' Mephistopheles answers that he is one of the 'unhappy spirits that fell with Lucifer', and that with Lucifer he is damned forever. It is at this point that Faustus, obsessed with the notion that hell is a place, expresses his astonishment that Mephistopheles can be said at this very moment to be in hell. Mephistopheles's answer deserves to be quoted in full:

> Why this is hell, nor am I out of it:
> Think'st thou that I who saw the face of God,
> And tasted the eternal joys of Heaven,
> Am not tormented with ten thousand hells,
> In being deprived of everlasting bliss?
> Oh Faustus, leave these frivolous demands,
> Which strike a terror to my fainting soul.

Faustus is surprised that great Mephistopheles should be, as he puts it, 'so passionate' on this subject, and the reader of the play may himself wonder that Mephistopheles can be so eloquent on the side of the angels—of the good angels, that is. But Marlowe has not been careless nor is he absent-minded. The psychology is ultimately sound. In this connection, two points ought to be observed. Though there is good reason to believe that Marlowe expected his audience to accept his devils as actual beings with an objective reality of their own and not merely as projections of Faustus's state of mind, in this play—as in any other sound and believable use of ghosts, spirits, and other such supernatural beings—the devils do have a very real relation to the minds of the persons to whom they appear. Though not necessarily merely projections of the character's emotions, they are always in some sense mirrors of the inner states of the persons to whom they appear.

The second point to be observed is this: Faustus does learn something in the course of the play, and in learning it suffers change and becomes a different man. At the beginning of the play, he does seem somewhat naïve and jejune. He is fascinated by the new possibilities that his traffic with magic may open to him. Mephistopheles's use of the phrase 'these frivolous demands' is quite justified. But in a sense, the very jauntiness with which he talks to Mephistopheles is proof that he is not yet fully damned, has not involved himself completely with the agents of evil. As the play goes on, he will lose his frivolousness: he will learn to take more and more seriously the loss of heaven. Yet at the same time, this very experience of deeper involvement in evil will make more and more difficult any return to the joys of heaven.

At any rate, there is a tremendous honesty as the play is worked out. Faustus may appear at times frivolous, but he is honest with himself. With all of his yearning for the state of grace that he has lost, he always acknowledges the strength of his desire for illicit pleasures and powers. At one point in the play, before he signed the fatal bond, Faustus says to himself that he will turn to God again.

But immediately he dismisses the notion: 'To God?' he asks incredulously, and then replies to himself: 'He loves thee not, / The God thou servest is thine own appetite.'

Most of all, however, Faustus is the prisoner of his own conceptions and indeed preconceptions. It is not so much that God has damned him as that he has damned himself. Faustus is trapped in his own legalism. The emphasis on such legalism seems to be a constant element in all treatments of the Faustian compact. It occurs in Yeats's *The Countess Cathleen*, when the devils, trusting in the letter of the law, are defeated and at the end find they have no power over the soul of the Countess. Legalism is also a feature of one of the most brilliant recent treatments of the story, that given by William Faulkner in *The Hamlet*.

Faustus's entrapment in legalism is easily illustrated. If the devils insist that a promise is a promise and a bond is a bond that has to be honoured—though it is plain that they are far from sure that the mere signing of the bond has effectively put Faustus's soul in their possession—Faustus himself is all too easily convinced that this is true. Apparently, he can believe in and understand a God of justice, but not a God of mercy. If Faustus's self-knowledge makes him say in scene vi, 'My heart's so hardened, I cannot repent', his sense of legal obligation makes him say in scene xviii: 'Hell calls for right, and with a roaring voice / Says, Faustus come, thine hour is come / And Faustus will come to do thee right.' Even at this point the Old Man thinks that Faustus can still be saved. The good angel has reiterated that he might be saved. The devils themselves would seem to fear that Faustus even at the last might escape them: but Faustus himself is convinced that he cannot be saved and his despair effectually prevents any action which would allow him a way out.

In one sense, then, this play is a study in despair. But the despair does not paralyze the imagination of Faustus. He knows constantly what is happening to him. He reports on his state of mind with relentless honesty. And at the end of the play, in tremendous poetry, he dramatizes for us what it is to feel the inexorable movement toward the abyss, not numbed, not dulled with apathy, but with every sense quickened and alert. (Kurtz, in Conrad's *Heart of Darkness*, shows these qualities. He is damned, knows that he's damned, indeed flees from redemption, but never deceives himself about what is happening, and mutters, 'The horror, the horror'.)

One may still ask, however, whether these changes that occur in Faustus's soul are sufficient to constitute a middle. Does Faustus act? Is there a sufficient conflict? Is Faustus so incapacitated for choice that he is a helpless victim and not a conscious re-agent with circumstance?

Yet, one must not be doctrinaire and pedantic in considering this concept of decisive action. As T. S. Eliot put it in *Murder in the Cathedral*, suffering is action and action is suffering. Faustus's suffering is not merely passive: he is constantly reaffirming at deeper and deeper levels his original rash tender of his soul to Lucifer. Moreover, if Faustus's action amounts in the end to suffering, the suffering is not meaningless. It leads to knowledge—knowledge of very much the same sort as that which Milton's Adam acquired in *Paradise Lost*—'Knowledge of good bought dear by knowing ill'— and through something of the same process. Early in the play, Mephistopheles told him: 'Think so still till experience change thy mind.' Perhaps this is the best way in which to describe the 'middle' of the play: the middle consists of the experiences that do change Faustus's mind so that in the end he knows what hell is and has become accommodated to it, now truly damned.

My own view is that the play does have a sufficient middle, but this is not to say that it is not a play of a rather special sort—and that its dependence upon its poetry—though a legitimate dependence, I would insist—is very great.

There is no need to praise the poetry of the wonderful last scene, but I should like to make one or two brief observations about it. The drama depends, of course, upon Faustus's obsession with the clock and his sense of time's moving on inexorably, pushing him so swiftly to the final event. But this final scene really grows integrally out of the play. The agonized and eloquent clock-watching matches perfectly the legalism which has dominated Faustus from the beginning of the play. What Faustus in effect tries to do is to hold back the hand of the clock, not to change his relation to God. Incidentally, what Faustus does not notice is that like Mephistopheles earlier, he himself is now already in hell. The coming of the hour of twelve can hardly bring him into greater torment than that which now possesses him and which the poetry he utters so powerfully bodies forth.

Everybody has commented on Marlowe's brilliant use of the quotation from Ovid: 'O lente, lente currite noctis equi', in the *Amores* words murmured by the lover to his mistress in his wish that the night of passion might be prolonged, in this context so jarringly ironic. But the irony is not at all factitious. The scholar who now quotes the lines from Ovid in so different a context is the same man who a little earlier had begged the phantasm of Helen to make his soul immortal with a kiss. Now, in his agony, he demands of himself: 'Why wert thou not a creature wanting soul? / Or, why is this immortal that thou hast?'

Again, the great line, 'See, see where Christ's blood streams in the firmament', echoes a significant passage much earlier in the play. (I do not insist that the reader has to notice it, or that Marlowe's audience would have necessarily been aware of the echo, but

I see no reason why we should not admire it if we happen upon it ourselves or if someone calls it to our attention.) When Faustus prepares to sign the document that will consign his soul to the devil, he finds that he must sign in blood, and he pierces his arm to procure the sanguine ink. But his blood will hardly trickle from his arm, and he interprets his blood's unwillingness to flow as follows: 'What might the staying of my blood portend? / Is it unwilling I should write this bill? / Why streams it not, that I might write afresh?' His own blood, in an instinctive horror, refuses to stream for his damnation. Now, as he waits for the clock to strike twelve, he has a vision of Christ's blood *streaming* in the firmament for man's salvation. But in his despair he is certain that Christ's blood does not stream for his salvation.

In short, the magnificent passage in the final scene bodies forth the experience of Faustus in a kind of personal *dies irae*, but it is not a purple patch tacked on to the end of a rather amorphous play. Rather, the great outburst of poetry finds in the play a supporting context. It sums up the knowledge that Faustus has bought at so dear a price, and if it is the expression of a creature fascinated with, and made eloquent by, horror, it is still the speech of a man who, for all of his terror, somehow preserves his dignity. Faustus at the end is still a man, not a cringing wretch. The poetry saves him from adjectness. If he wishes to escape from himself, to be changed into little water drops, to be swallowed up in the great ocean of being, he maintains to the end—in spite of himself, in spite of his desire to blot out his personal being—his individuality of mind, the special quality of the restless spirit that aspired. This retention of his individuality is at once his glory and his damnation.

G. K. HUNTER

Five-Act Structure in *Doctor Faustus*†

The original and substantive texts of Marlowe's *Doctor Faustus* (the Quartos of 1604 and 1616) present the play completely without the punctuation of act division or scene enumeration. This is common enough in the play-texts of the period. Indeed it is much the commonest form in plays written for the public theatres.[1] Shakespeare's

---

† From *Tulane Drama Review* 8.4 (1964). Reprinted by permission of George Hunter.

1. W. T. Jewkes notes that 'of the 134 plays written for the public stage [*and printed before 1616*], 30 are divided, as against 104 undivided'. (*Act Division in Elizabethan and Jacobean Plays, 1583–1616* [Hamden, Conn., 1958], p. 96.) See, however, my 'Were there act-pauses on Shakespeare's stage?' in *English Renaissance Drama*, ed. Henning, Kimbrough, Knowles (1976).

Henry V and *Pericles* are without divisions in their quarto texts, but we know that they were written with a five-act structure in mind— the choruses tell us that.

What is exceptional in the textual history of *Doctor Faustus* is not the lack of division in the original texts; it is rather the reluctance of modern editors to impose an act-structure on the modern texts. This is curious, but it seems possible to discern why the reluctance exists and a survey of the modern editions of *Faustus* throws some interesting light on critical attitudes to the subject matter of the play.

Marlowe (like other Elizabethan dramatists) was 'rediscovered' by the educated English public in an atmosphere which played down his specifically dramatic and theatrical powers. Charles Lamb's *Specimens of the English dramatic poets who lived about the time of Shakespeare* (1808) established him primarily as a poet. This, as I say, did not distinguish him from other dramatists of the period. But the attitudes implied by Lamb's volume were more difficult to shake off in the case of *Doctor Faustus* than in other Elizabethan plays; for here they were reinforced, later in the century, by a second wave of anti-theatrical (or at least a-theatrical) influence. In 1887 the young Havelock Ellis (then a medical student) suggested to Henry Vizetelly, well known in 'advanced' circles as a courageous though rather *risqué* publisher, that he should put out a series of unexpurgated (key word!) texts of the Elizabethan dramatists—the famous 'Mermaid' series. The *Marlowe*, the first volume in the series, was edited by Ellis himself, and may be taken as a manifesto of the whole new movement. It bore proudly on the title-page the legend *Unexpurgated*, not simply because the usual casual indecencies of clown conversations were preserved, but rather because an appendix carried the full testimony of the informer Richard Baines 'concernynge [Marlowe's] damnable opinions and judgment of Religion and scorne of Gods worde', to which Ellis added the even more offensive comment that such 'damnable opinions . . . have, without exception, been substantially held, more or less widely, by students of science and the Bible in our own days'. To say this of remarks like 'Moses was but a juggler', 'that Christ better deserved to die than Barabas', etc., was to push Marlowe into the front line of the late Victorian battle against bourgeois values. Marlowe appears as a social rebel and religious freethinker (like Ellis himself) and this comes to reinforce the earlier view that he was primarily a poet. The two attitudes join together, in fact, to suggest that he was a poet *because* he was a freethinker, rejecting social conventions in order to achieve his individual and personal vision. He becomes the morning-star of the 1890s, a harder and more gem-like Oscar Wilde.

In order to preserve the image of Marlowe as a cult-figure of this kind it is necessary to discount the theatrical, and so popular, provenance of his work. If he was the laureate of the atheistical imagination, he must have stood at a considerable distance from his rudely Christian audience; and this assumption presses especially heavily upon *Doctor Faustus*, whose hero is himself a free-thinker and (by implication at least) a poet. It is not surprising therefore to find Ellis saying in his headnote to *Faustus*: 'I have retained the excellent plan introduced by Professor Ward and adopted by Mr. Bullen, of dividing the play into scenes only; it is a dramatic poem rather than a regular drama.' In the face of this critical assurance, and with the *Zeitgeist* exerting the kind of pressure that I have described, the earlier editorial practice of presenting the play in five acts, derived from the 1663 Quarto by Robinson (1826) and continued in Cunningham (1870), Wagner (1877), and Morley (1883), withered away. It was not until the bibliographical breakthrough[2] of Boas, Kirschbaum, and Greg (1932, 1946, 1950) that the play reappeared in the five-act form. Even after their labours the old attitudes persist. The edition by Kocher (1950) is divided into scenes only, and the recent replacement of Boas by the 'Revels' edition of J. D. Jump (1962) avoids the act divisions: 'Neither A1 [1604] nor B1 [1616] makes any attempt to divide the play into acts and scenes, so no such distribution is given prominence in the present edition' (xxxv). It may be sufficient reply to this to quote the recent comment of W. T. Jewkes, who has analysed the act structure of all the plays in the period:

> The plays of the 'University wits', however, appear both undivided and divided. On a closer inspection it was evident that the clearly divided texts from this group were those which showed least sign of playhouse annotation, while those which retained fragmentary division, or none at all, showed signs of adaptation for performance. It is evident then that these dramatists divided their plays originally, but that adaptation for the stage resulted in either the total or partial loss of act headings.[3]

2. I mean the perception that the 1616 text must be the basis of any modern recension. In this text the nature of the structure is much clearer; and it was, in fact, the reading of Greg's *editio minor* that first made clear to me the precision with which the play moved. Greg himself, however, hedges his bets. He finds the act division 'convenient in discussing the construction of the play' (parallel text edition, p. 153) and so presents it to the reader; but he confides to us in a footnote that 'I see no reason to suppose that any act division was originally contemplated' (p. 153, n. 5). His argument is that there is too great a disproportion between the numbers of lines to be found in the different acts for these to make just divisions. A rereading of *The Winter's Tale*, in which Act IV is two and a half times as long as Act III, ought to convince us of the peculiarity of this mode of assessment. It may be, of course, that Shakespeare also ought to be presented without act-division. But no editor has yet had the courage to present his text in this way.
3. Op. cit., p. 97. Cf. my article cited above.

This argument might well be augmented, in the particular case of *Doctor Faustus*, by reference to the choruses which mark the beginnings of some of the acts, or by repeating Boas's observations about the material taken from the Faustbook. But it is not my purpose here to argue in detail the textual or theatrical probability that *Faustus* is in five-act form. I rather wish to look at the developing movement of the play to see if the act divisions accepted by Boas and others correspond to anything in the inner economy of the work, marking progressive stages in an organized advance through the material. Since Goethe remarked, 'How greatly is it all planned' in 1829,[4] many have been found to repeat his encomium, but few to justify it. I would suggest that the play *is* planned greatly, even precisely, in five clear stages (or acts), moving forward continuously in a single direction. I am assuming, when I say this, that the text as we have it in the 1616 Quarto is the product of a unified organizing intelligence. Marlowe *may* have had a collaborator, but I do not believe that we can detect his work—and a stroke of Occam's razor makes him disappear.

The first point I should like to make is that the action (I deal only with the main plot at the moment) moves through clearly separable stages. Act I is concerned (as is usual) with setting up the situation and introducing the principal characters. Here we learn the nature of Faustus's desires, set against the limiting factor of his nature; we meet Mephistophilis and the contrast between the two is made evident. Act II begins with a preliminary reminder (found before each act of the play) of the stage at which the action has arrived:[5]

> Now Faustus must thou needs be damned,
> And canst thou not be saved.
> What boots it then to think on God or heaven?
> (II. i. 1–3)

In Act I, the temptation to think of heaven is hardly present; but the subject here announced is the warp on which much of the main-plot action of Act II is woven. The conflict is now entered upon in real earnest. The introductory note to Act III is more obvious, being handled by the 'Chorus'. He tells us that 'Learned Faustus', having searched into the secrets of Astronomy, now is gone to prove Cosmography. He is in fact completing his Grand Tour when we meet him, having taken in Paris, Mainz, Naples, Venice, and Padua, and is newly arrived in Rome, 'Queen of the Earth' as Milton's Satan calls it,[6] and the summation of worldly grandeur.

---

4. Recorded in the *Diary* of H. Crabb Robinson, for 2 August 1829.
5. Text and line numbers of quotations from Marlowe are taken from Irving Ribner's text (1963).
6. *Paradise Regained*, IV. 45. Cf. William Thomas, who calls Rome 'the onelie jewell, myrrour, maistres, and beautie of the worlde' (*Historie of Italie* [1549]).

Mephistophilis describes the sights, and then conducts his master into the highest social circles in the city, and so in the world.

Act III is spent in Rome; Act IV in the courts of Germany. The introductory Chorus makes clear the distinction between 'the view / Of rarest things' which is the substance of Act III and the 'trial of his art' which is what we are to see in Act IV. The introductory speech to Act V is spoken by Wagner, Faustus's servant, who is confused in one text with the Chorus, and who is exercising here what is clearly a choric function. His first line marks the change of key: 'I think my master means to die shortly.' Act V is concerned with preparations and prevarications in the face of death.

It is obvious enough, I suggest, that each act handles a separate stage in Faustus's career. But it is not obvious from what I have said that the stages move forward in any single and significant line of development. To see that they do requires a fairly laborious retracing of the action, seen now in the light of what was more obvious to Marlowe and his audience than to us—the supposed hierarchy of studies.

The opening lines of the play show us Faustus trying to *settle his studies*; the opening speech, with this aim in mind, moves in an orthodox direction through the academic disciplines, beginning with logic, here representative of the whole undergraduate course of Liberal Arts, through the *Noble Sciences* of Medicine and Law and so to the *Queen of Sciences*, Divinity. So far, the movement has been, as I say, completely orthodox, and a frame of reference has been neatly established. But, having reached Divinity, Faustus still hopes to advance, and can only do so in reverse:

> . . . Divinity, adieu!
> These metaphysics of magicians
> And negromantic books are heavenly[7]
> (I. i. 49–51)

At this point he passes, as it were, through the looking glass; he goes on trying to evaluate experience, but his words of value (like 'heavenly') now mean the opposite of what they should. The 'profit and delight . . . power . . . honour . . . omnipotence' that he promises himself through the practice of magic are all devalued in advance. By embracing negromancy he ensures that worthwhile ends cannot be reached; and the rest of the play is a demonstration of this, moving as it does in a steadily downward direction.

The route taken by Faustus in his descent through human activi-

---

7. I preserve the original form *negromantic*, though most modernizing editors change it to *necromantic*. This seems to me to be a greater change than is warranted by a licence to modernize. It is the 'black art' in general that Faustus is welcoming, not the power to raise the dead.

ties was, I think, intended to be easily understood by the original
audience, and again I suggest that it is the structure of knowledge
as at that time understood that provides the key. Divinity was, as I
have noted, the 'Queen of the Sciences'. Not only so, but it was the
discipline which gave meaning to all other knowledge and experience. Hugh of St Victor expresses the idea succinctly: 'all the natural arts serve divine science, and the lower order leads to the
higher'.[8] In Marlowe's own day the same point is made, more elaborately, in the popular *French Academy* of La Primaudaye:

> What would it availe or profit us to have and attaine unto the
> knowledge and understanding of all humane and morall Phi-
> losophy, Logicke, Phisicke, Metaphisicke, and Mathematick . . .
> not to bee ignorant of any thing, which the liberall arts and
> sciences teach us, therewith to content the curious minds of
> men and by that means to give them a tast, and to make them
> enjoy some kind of transitory good in this life: and in the
> meane time to be altogether and wholy ignorant, or badly in-
> structed, in the true and onely science of divine Philosophy,
> whereat all the rest ought to aime.   (Preface to Book IV)

But if one rejects the final cause here supposed, what happens to
the rest of knowledge? This is the question that the play asks and
pursues. In what direction does the Icarus of learning fall when he
abandons the orthodox methods of flight? The order of topics in the
medieval encyclopaedias gives one some clue here. These regularly
begin with God and divine matters. Vincent of Beauvais' *Speculum*
starts from the Creator, then moves to 'the empyrean heaven and
the nature of angels', then to 'the formless material and the making
of the world; the nature and the properties of things created', then
to the human state and its ramifications. The *De Rerum Natura* attributed to Bede and William of Conches's *Philosophia Mundi*[9]
have the same four-book order. Book I deals with God; Book II with
the heavens; Book III with the lower atmosphere; Book IV with the
earth, so down to man and his human activities. The *Proem* to
Book IV (identical in both works) gives a fair indication of the nature of the movement assumed:

> The series of books which began with the First Cause has now
> descended to The Earth, not catering for itching ears nor loi-
> tering in the minds of fools, but dealing with what is useful to
> the reader. For now is that verse fulfilled: 'For the time will
> come when they will not endure sound doctrine; but after their

8. *De Sacramentis* (Prologue), in Migne's *Patrologia Latina*, vol. clxxvi, col. 185.
9. The first is to be found in *P.L.* xc, cols 1127 ff., and the second (attributed to Honorius
   Augustodunensis) in vol. clxxii, cols 39 ff. I am indebted to Dr Hans Liebeschütz for
   pointing these out to me.

own lusts shall they heap to themselves teachers, having itch-ing ears.' (2 Timothy, iv, 3). But since the mind of the honest man does not turn after wickedness, but conforms itself to the better way, let us turn to the remaining subjects, in the interest of a mind of this kind, estranged from wickedness and con-formable to virtue.

In Marlowe's own day this order of topics appeared in works as popular as the Baldwin-Palfreyman *Treatise of Moral Philosophy* (in-numerable editions from 1557 to 1640), in Palfreyman's compan-ion *Treatise of Heavenly Philosophy*, and in William Vaughan's *The Golden Grove* (1600, 1608). *The French Academy*, which Marlowe has been supposed to have known, uses the same organization of topics but treats them in reverse order, upwards from (1) 'the insti-tution of manners and callings of all estates', through (2) 'concern-ing the soule and body of man', and (3) 'a notable description of the whole world . . . Angels . . . the foure elements . . . fowles, fishes, beasts . . . ' etc. to (4) 'Christian philosophy, instructing the true and onely meanes to eternall life'. It seems reasonable to suppose that Marlowe knew this system of knowledge; and it is my assertion that he used it to plan the relationship of the parts of *Doctor Fau-stus*.

When Faustus has signed away his soul, the first fruits of his new 'power . . . honour . . . omnipotence' appear in the knowledge of as-tronomy that he seeks. Astronomy is a heavenly art, no doubt—it appears early in the encyclopaedias—but it is one that is not obvi-ously dependent on divinity. Yet here it leads by the natural process that the encyclopaedists describe to the question of first cause. If the heavens involve more than the tedium of mechanics ('these slender questions Wagner can decide') then astronomy leads straight back to the fundamental question: Who made the world? But, under the conditions of knowledge that Faustus has embraced, this basic question cannot be answered, for it is 'against our king-dom'. The trap closes on the pseudo-scholar and forces him back-wards and downwards.

This is the movement—backwards into ever more superficial shallows of knowledge and experience—which continues inexorably throughout the whole play, as it must, given the initial choice. Baulked in Act II from the full pursuit of astronomy, in Act III Fau-stus turns to cosmography, from the heavens to the earth. But the charms of sightseeing pall, and a magical entrée even to the 'best' society in the world involves only a tediously superficial contact. Marlowe's age had serious doubts about the importance of cosmog-raphy (or geography) as an object of human endeavor. *The French Academy* treats it under the heading of 'curiosity and novelty', as a destructively unserious pursuit. The drop in the status of Faustus's activities is nicely caught by the change of tone between the Chorus at the beginning of Act III and that introducing Act IV. The first tells us that

> Learnèd Faustus
> To find the secrets of astronomy
> Graven in the book of Jove's high firmament
> Did mount him up to scale Olympus' top.
>   (III, Prol. 1–4)

We seem here still to be dealing with a genuine search for knowledge. But in the later chorus we hear only that:

> When Faustus had *with pleasure*[1] ta'en the view
> Of rarest things and royal courts of kings,
> He stay'd his course and so returned home.
>   (IV, Prol. 1–3)

The emphasis is no longer on the search after knowledge, with discovery, presumably, as the aimed-for end, but with what is more appropriate to the diabolical premise ('that is not against our kingdom'), with pleasure taken and then given up, without reaching forward to the final causes. Faustus's merry japes among the cardinals are enjoyed by the protagonist, and are clearly meant to be enjoyed by the audience; but nothing more than pleasure is involved, and given the giant pretensions of the first act, the omission is bound to be a factor in our view of the Roman scenes.

Faustus not only views Rome. He also dabbles in state-craft, rescuing the Antipope Bruno and transporting him back to his supporters in Germany. The step from cosmography to statecraft is similar to that from astronomy to cosmography. In each case we have a reduction in the area covered, and an increasing remoteness from first causes. The panoply of state is not here (as it usually is in Shakespeare) an awesome and a righteous thing. It is not approached through the lives of those who must live and suffer inside the system, but via the structure of knowledge, so that it is the relationship to divinity rather than the power over individual lives that is the determining factor in our attitude. The ludicrous antics at the Papal court have usually been seen as a simple piece of Protestant propaganda, pleasing to the groundlings and inserted for no better reason. Yet one can see that this episode (placed where it is) has its own unique part to play in the total economy of the work. It is proper to start Faustus's descent through the world from the highest point, in Rome; it is equally proper to begin his social and political descent with the Vicar of Christ (and so down to Emperor, to Duke, and back to private life). By turning the conduct of the pa-

---

1. Italics added.

pal court into farce Marlowe devalues *all* sovereignty and political activity in advance. Bruno (and his tiara) are saved; but there is no suggestion that *he* has any more virtue to recommend him; he has no real function in the play except to reduce the title and state of the Pope to a mere name.

There is no suggestion in this act that Faustus himself is aware of the startling discrepancy between the actual happenings and the promises he made to himself (and to us) at the beginning of the play. The audience, however, can hardly forget so soon; and our memory is reinforced in the papal palace by the ritual threats of damnation uttered by the Pope and friars. It is no doubt comic that the Pope should be boxed on the ear and exclaim, 'Damn'd be this soul for ever for this deed', but we should not fail to notice the sinister echo reverberating behind the horseplay; the curse is comic at this point, but sinister in the context of the whole action.

Act IV carries the descent of Faustus one more clear step, by still further reducing the importance of the area in which he operates. I have mentioned the social descent to the secular courts of Emperor and Duke of Vanholt. At the same time there is a descent in terms of the kind of activity that the magic procures. Faustus's anti-Papal activities can be seen as political action of a kind, and this aspect would be more obvious to the Elizabethans than it is to us (involved, as they were, in the kind of struggle depicted). But in Act IV he is presented quite frankly as a court entertainer or hired conjurer. In the court of Charles V, of course, there is still some intellectual dignity in his activities. Charles's longing, to see 'that famous conqueror, Great Alexander, and his paramour', is a kingly interest in a paragon of kingship. But when Faustus goes on to the court of the Duke of Vanholt he is reduced to satisfying nothing more dignified than the pregnant 'longings' of the duchess for out-of-season grapes. At the same time his side activities are brought down by a parallel route. At the court of the Emperor he was matched against the disbelieving knights, Frederick, Benvolio, etc.; at Vanholt his opponents are clowns, the Horse-courser, the Hostess.[2]

The last act of *Faustus* is often thought of as involving restoration of dignity and brilliance to the sadly tarnished magician. In terms of poetic power there is something to be said on this side; but the poetry that Faustus is given in this act serves to do more than simply glorify the speaker. The fiery brilliance of the Helen speech is lit

---

2. I find that this general point has been made by Kirschbaum in his paperback *The Plays of Christopher Marlowe* (New York: Meridian, 1962): 'Surely Marlowe means to stress the magician's continuing degradation by showing him first playing his tricks with the spiritual head of all Roman Christendom and then ultimately declining, to play them with the clowns' (p. 119).

by the Fire of Hell (as has been pointed out by Kirschbaum[3] and others). The imminence of eternal damnation gives strength and urgency to the action, but the actions that Faustus himself can initiate are as trivial and as restricted as one would expect, given the moral development that I have described as operating throughout the rest of the play. There is no change of direction. In Acts III and IV we saw Faustus sink steadily from political intrigue at the Curia to fruit-fetching for a longing duchess. The last act shows a consistent extension of this movement. It picks up the role of Faustus as entertainer, but reduces the area of its exercise still further; it is now confined to the enjoyment of some 'two or three' private friends, and as an epilogue to what Wagner characterizes by 'banquet . . . carouse . . . swill . . . belly-cheer'. Helen appears, in short, at the point where one might have expected dancing-girls.

The nature of the object conjured in Act V, no less than the occasion of the conjuring, shows the same logical development of the movement in the preceding acts. Charles V had longed to satisfy an intellectual interest; the Duchess of Vanholt longed for the satisfaction of a carnal but perfectly natural appetite; but the desire to view Helen of Troy is both carnal and (as the ironic word *blessed* should warn us) reprehensible, and leads logically to the further and final depravity of:

> One thing, good servant, let me crave of thee
> To glut the longing of my heart's desire—
> That I may have unto my paramour
> That heavenly Helen which I saw of late,
> Whose sweet embracings may extinguish clear
> Those thoughts that do dissuade me from my vow
> And keep mine oath I made to Lucifer.
>
> (v. i. 90–96)

The circle in which Faustus conjures has now shrunk from the *urbs et orbis* of Rome to the smallest circle of all. When the dream of power was lost, the gift of entertainment remained; but even this has now faded. The conjuring here exists for an exclusively self-interested and clearly damnable purpose. The loneliness of the damned, summed up in Mephistophilis's cryptic '*Solamen miseris socios habuisse doloris*'—this now is clearly Faustus's lot. Left alone with himself and the mirror of his own damnation[4] in Helen ('Her lips suck forth my soul: see where it flies!'), he is in a situation that cannot be reached by either the Old Man or the students. His descent has taken him below the reach of human aid; and there is a certain terrible splendour in this, as the poetry conveys, but the

3. 'Marlowe's Faustus: a reconsideration', *R.E.S.* xix (1943).
4. See W. W. Greg, 'The damnation of Faustus', *M.L.R.* xli (1946).

moral level of this splendour is never in doubt; it is something that the whole weight of the play's momentum presses on our attention, moving steadily as it does, through the clearly defined stages of its act-structure, away from the deluded dream of power and knowledge and downward, inevitably, coherently, and logically, into the sordid reality of damnation.

I have sought to show that the movement of the main plot of *Faustus* is controlled and splendidly meaningful. It moves in a single direction (downwards) through a series of definite stages which it would be wilfully obscurantist not to call acts. Indeed it conforms, by and large, to the strict form of five-act structure which was taught in Tudor grammar schools, out of the example of Terence. The structural paradigm was, of course, concerned with comedy, and especially the comedy of intrigue, and could not be applied very exactly to a moralistic tragedy like *Faustus*. But it is easy to see that Act I of *Faustus* gives us the introductory materials, Act II the first moves in the central conflict (Faustus versus the Devil), Acts III and IV the swaying back and forward of this conflict, and Act V the catastrophe.

What is more, these stages of the main plot are reinforced or underlined by a parallel movement going on simultaneously in the subplot. The general relation between the two levels of the plot, the level of spiritual struggle and that of carnal opportunism, is one of parody—a mode of connection that was common in the period. And I should state that by 'parody' I do not mean the feeble modern reduction of characteristics to caricature, but rather that multiple presentation of serious themes[5] which relates them both to the man of affairs and to the light-minded clown.

It is not only in the detail of individual scenes that the subplot parodies the main plot: the whole movement of the subplot mirrors that social and intellectual descent that I have traced in the career of Faustus. The first subplot scene concerns Wagner, a man close to Faustus himself. The second comic scene involves Wagner and *his* servants, Robin and Dick. The third and subsequent scenes show Robin and Dick by themselves, Wagner having disappeared (he reappears—though not as part of the subplot—in v. i). It has been argued that this very descent, and the disappearance of Wagner, 'suggests a different hand' [*not Marlowe's*] for the Robin and Dick scenes.[6] This provides an interesting parallel to the assumption that Marlowe cannot be responsible for the main-plot scenes in the middle of the play. At both levels the action descends to triv-

5. See G. K. Hunter, *John Lyly* (London: Routledge and Kegan Paul, 1962), pp. 135–40. The significance of the parody in *Faustus* is denied by Jump (op cit. lix–lx).
6. *Doctor Faustus*, ed. F. S. Boas (London: Methuen, 1932), p. 27.

ialities, and the critics close their eyes in dissent. But if the movement is deliberate at one level it seems likely that it is so at the
other level also.

Even more impressive than this general movement in the subplot
is the accumulation of details in which the action of the subplot
scene mirrors that of the contiguous main plot. Thus Act I, scene i,
shows us Faustus using his virtuosity in logic to deceive himself.
Scene ii shows us Wagner as no less able to chop logic and so to
avoid the plain meaning of words. As a development from this we
see Faustus raising Mephistophilis and arranging that he should be
his servant. The following scene shows us Wagner trying to control
Robin, who would not 'give his soul to the devil for a shoulder of
mutton', unless it were 'well roasted, and good sauce to it, if I pay
so dear'. Wagner too has learned how to raise spirits and makes
Robin his servant by a parody compact, promising to teach him 'to
turn thyself to a dog, or a cat, or a mouse, or a rat, or any thing'. It
may be noted that the general effect of this and the preceding
comic scene is to reduce in status and to 'place' for us Faustus's
pretensions to have conquered a new art by the force of his learning, and to have gained important new powers. When such as Wagner can raise Banio and Belcher, and all for the sake of terrifying
Robin, then neither the means nor the ends of magic can be considered sufficient, by themselves, to make the magician a hero.

In Act II, scenes i and ii, Faustus signs his pact with the Devil
and has the first fruits of his 'new' knowledge. In scene iii we meet
Robin again. The power of raising spirits has declined from Faustus's servant Wagner to Wagner's servant, Robin. He and his fellow, Dick, plan to use one of the conjuring books to get free drink.
In Act III the first two scenes show Doctor Faustus surveying the
great cities of Europe and conjuring at Rome. The third scene
shows Robin and Dick enjoying *themselves* in their own clownish
way; but it is not now a way that is so remote from that of Faustus.
He 'took away his holiness' wine', 'stole his holiness' meat from the
table', 'struck Friar Sandelo a blow on the pate'; they steal the Vintner's cup, and when pursued for it they rely (as Faustus does) on
magic as a rescue from their scape.

The play began with Faustus and Robin at opposite ends of the
spectrum. One was 'glutted . . . with learning's golden gifts', powerful and renowned; the other was ignorant, 'out of service', and
'hungry'. But the process of logical development in the main plot,
as I have described it, has by the end of Act III brought Faustus
down through the diminishing circles of his capacity to the point
where his powers and Robin's are no longer incommensurate. Up
to this point, of course, Faustus and the clowns have never appeared together in any one scene. Such a conjunction would be un-

thinkable at the beginning of the play. But by Act IV Faustus has himself sunk to the level of a comic entertainer. His relationship to Frederick, Martino, and Benvolio is entirely without dignity or intellectual pretension, and the intrusion of the clowns, Robin, Dick, Carter, Horse-courser, Hostess, into the court of the Duke of Vanholt marks a natural and inevitable climax in the downward movement of the main plot. The comic 'Doctor Fustian' is now all the figure that Faustus can cut in the world; the 'success' that he has bought so dearly is to be the leader of a troupe of clowns.

There is no doubt a *frisson* intended between the last line of Act IV and the first line of Act V—between the duchess's appreciation of Faustus's powers: 'His artful sport drives all sad thoughts away', and (set against that) Wagner's 'I think my master means to die shortly'. The contrast between the two lines catches much of the movement from Act IV to Act V. Act IV is the climax of the subplot interest. Almost the whole act is taken up with triviality of one kind or another, and it ends with the confrontation of main plot and subplot characters, reducing them to one level. Act V, on the other hand, is without comic relief; and one can see why, in the terms I have outlined, this should be so. Through Act IV we see Faustus's life enmeshed in the triviality that was inherent in the original stipulation of 'any thing . . . that is not against our kingdom'. Act V, as it begins with the mention of death, so continues to move in the shadow of a tragic conclusion. Faustus has now fallen *beneath* the level of the clowns and horse-courser:

> Why wert thou not a creature wanting soul?
> . . .
> Ah, Pythagoras' *metempsychosis*, were that true,
> This soul should fly from me and I be changed
> Into some brutish beast. All beasts are happy,
> For when they die
> Their souls are soon dissolved in elements.
>
> (v. ii. 169. 171–5)

The movement of the subplot helps to confirm this veiw of the general direction of Faustus's development. The constant looming presence of the clownish common man, with his attention set on immediate comforts, serves as a norm against which we may observe and judge the splendours and the miseries of the overweening intellectual.

*   *   *

DOUGLAS COLE

Doctor Faustus and the Morality Tradition†

The supernatural context of Faustus' tragedy, and the central importance of theological concepts of evil and suffering within that context, distinguish it from all other tragedies of the time, and suggest a relationship to the English morality play. Even though Marlowe's play seems by and large to grow directly from the English Faust-Book rather than from the stage tradition of the moralities, there is no doubt that the morality tradition provided Marlowe with both a thematic precedent and devices of dramaturgy on which to draw. Hardin Craig's definition of the morality play as the presentation of man in the postlapsarian situation, where he is destined to die in sin unless he be saved by the intervention of divine grace and by repentance,[1] is certainly applicable to *Doctor Faustus*, though it by no means exhausts the meaning and effect of Marlowe's play. This general thematic import of the morality play was characteristically embodied in a dramatic structure defined by the conflict of abstract forces of good and evil over the soul of the hero, who represented all mankind. Undoubtedly the conflict between the forces of good and evil provides the major dramatic tension in *Doctor Faustus*, and Faustus himself stands (and falls) as the central figure in the conflict, the *only* human figure of real dramatic importance. But we have already reached the point where distinctions must be drawn. Is Faustus truly representative of mankind, or even of a general class of men, as the strict morality hero always was? And is the conflict of good and evil, which Marlowe has certainly heightened in his departures from the Faust-Book, the characteristic conflict of the morality?

There are many things about Faustus which would appear at first to put him outside the realm of a representative man: his uncommon intellectual attainments, his extraordinary reach of imagination and ambition, his arcane pursuits of forbidden magic, his bold and conscious arrogance in the face of the divinely established order. The dreams and desires that spur him to his fatal exercise of freedom are more superhuman than they are human; their very singularity helps to establish Faustus as one of the most individualized of Elizabethan stage characters. Nevertheless, the qualities and motivations which make Faustus an individual, especially in the way Marlowe has chosen to present them, make him at the same

† From *Suffering and Evil in the Plays of Christopher Marlowe* (New Jersey: Princeton University Press, 1962), pp. 231–43. Reprinted by permission of the author.
1. "Morality Plays and the Elizabethan Drama," *SQ*, 1 (1950), 67.

time a figure of more than particular or personal significance. Some critics have sought to identify Faustus' desires with the personal desires of Marlowe, but the whole dramatic structure with its burden of inescapable irony denies that argument. There are two aspects of Faustus' desires which give them a more universal application: the degree to which they fit the spirit of the Elizabethan age, and the degree to which they are exhibited by the most common of men. The first involves the goals of wealth, honor, and omnipotence, goals which Faustus and his fellow-magicians foresee as attainable through geographical and military exploits: India, the Orient, Spain and America, the conquest of the seas and dominion over foreign powers—all these were part of what was fast becoming a national dream for the Elizabethans. There is also the second aspect, the aspect of rock-bottom sensuality involved in Faustus' goal of a personal life of "all voluptuousnesse" (317). The universal appeal of this most common human inclination is made concrete in the comic scenes of low life which parody the learned but sensual Doctor's career. It must be emphasized that neither of these aspects appear in the Faust-Book; they are therefore indications of a conscious artistic effort toward dramatic universalization of the Faustian theme.

There is also a deeper and more general sense in which the Faustian figure stands for more than himself, and this is responsible for the enduring fascination which the figure, under one name or another, has exercised on the human imagination for centuries before and after Marlowe. It is bound up with the mythic pattern of the forbidden quest for superhuman knowledge and power, the quest which more often than not carries with it the seeds of its own destruction.[2] The application to Marlowe's Faustus has been made best perhaps by Professor Heilman: "[Faustus] is Everyman as Intellectual, with the axiological choice centered in the problem of knowledge. As Everyman Faustus embodies a perennial human aspiration—to escape inhibitions, to control the universe, to reconstruct the cosmos in naturalistic, non-theistic terms. As intellectual he is also aware of the exploit in its philosophical dimensions. In Everyman the tragic flaw—pride, wilfulness—causes blindness to the nature and destiny of man; in the intellectual, *hubris* destroys the understanding of the nature and limitations of knowledge."[3]

Marlowe has further shaped this fundamental pattern of human

2. For examples of this pattern before and after Marlowe's *Faustus*, see Philip Mason Palmer and Robert Pattison More, *The Sources of the Faust Tradition: From Simon Magus to Lessing* (New York: Oxford University Press, 1936). Arpad Steiner examines the Christian awareness and interpretation of the pattern in "The Faust Legend and the Christian Tradition," *PMLA*, LIV (1939), 391–404.

3. Robert Heilman, "The Tragedy of Knowledge: Marlowe's Treatment of Faustus," *Quarterly Review of Literature* 2 (1946): 331.

experience by making it grow out of a freely repeated moral choice, linking Faustus' sin with the primal or original sin of Christian theology. It is this burden and responsibility of moral choice in a Christian context which adds the final degree of universality to his figure and his career.

Faustus, then, for all his individuality, still represents humanity caught up in a conflict which, though extraordinary in its detail, is nevertheless fundamental in the experience of men. We have already seen how Marlowe has emphasized the conflict of good and evil through the two Angels who crystallize the alternatives Faustus continually faces. Their presence in the play has often been attributed to the influence of the morality tradition, and certainly to the extent that they are concrete embodiments of the conflict in Faustus' mind they appear to be a characteristic device of the morality play. But that by no means exhausts their significance and function. In the first place, angels and devils in Marlowe's time were not considered abstractions or even metaphors for the operations of the human mind; they were conceived as real spiritual beings created by God and granted certain powers and functions. Among these was the power to influence by suggestion, though not constrain, the mind of man. Now it will be noticed that Faustus never directs his attention to the Good and Evil Angels as dramatic entities; he neither speaks directly to them nor shows any sensible awareness of their physical presence. Their words are suggestive, however, of the drift of his own thought; hence their activity remains on a spiritual rather than physical level insofar as Faustus is concerned.[4]

This lack of physical interaction or even direct dialogue with the central human figure distinguishes the Angels' behavior from the characteristic dramatic activity of morality vices and virtues, and also from the dramaturgical conduct of the personified mental forces in such plays as *Horestes* and *Appius and Virginia*. A further distinction lies in the absence of any interaction between the Angels themselves. In direct contrast to the conventional behavior of morality vices and virtues, they never engage in physical contact with each other, and never appear except in the presence of the human protagonist, upon whom their attention is always centered. In this they also differ strikingly from the contending personifications of human faculties in Nathaniel Woodes' *The Conflict of Conscience* (1581), where the protagonist Philologus is torn between

4. See the analysis of this problem by Robert H. West, *The Invisible World: A Study of Pneumatology in Elizabethan Drama* (Athens: University of Georgia Press, 1939), pp. 102–104. The one appearance of the Angels peculiar to the 1616 text, in the spectacular scene preceding Faustus' final monologue (1995–2034), is exceptional: here the spirits call Faustus' attention to a visible heavenly throne and a picture of hell; they no longer represent two possible alternatives, but demonstrate the now inevitable consequences of Faustus' past decisions.

Conscience and Sensual Suggestion. Philologus' personified conscience not only tries to persuade him to deny Sensual Suggestion, but also presents an explanation of the situation directly to the audience, and even engages in direct debate with Sensual Suggestion, during which Philologus is merely a bewildered bystander.[5]

Marlowe's use of the Angels, then, differs radically from the conventional employment of abstract or metaphorical figures in the morality plays. Even more important, however, is the fact that their very appearance in sixteenth-century English drama is unique. Nowhere in the extant morality plays dated after 1500 do good and evil angels contend for the soul of man. And even among the very early moralities such angels are found in only one play, *The Castle of Perseverance* (1400–1425). If Marlowe drew his angels from a dramatic tradition rather than from theological thought regarding the nature and functions of spirits, he either made use of plays no longer extant or reverted to a much older tradition of religious drama extending through the mystery-cycles and back to the Latin drama of the medieval Church.

The first dramatic appearances of good and evil spirits in relationship with human figures are found in two Latin plays recorded in a thirteenth-century manuscript.[6] In a Christmas play the shepherds at the time of Christ's birth are urged by angels to visit the Saviour, and by evil spirits to stay away. In the second example, a Passion Play brings an angel and a demon into the story of Mary Magdalene, but only the angel speaks to Mary, moving her finally to conversion. The durability of this convention in the Magdalene story is witnessed by the English play of *Mary Magdalene* (1480–1490) in the Digby manuscript; the good angel admonishes, but the bad angel remains silent, tempting Mary only indirectly through Lechery, the personification of one of the Seven Deadly Sins. Here the spirits themselves are not paired for the dramatization of conflict and choice. This condition is more closely approximated in the Towneley Lucifer play and the Newcastle play of Noah's Ark. In the former, both good and evil angels present their arguments to Lucifer after he has aspired to usurp the majesty of God, but these are arguments after the choice has been made. In the Noah play, the strife between Noah and his wife is brought about at the devil's suggestion, but resolved by the admonition of an angel; in this case, however, the evil spirit acts upon one figure, the wife, while the good spirit acts upon the other.

The "purest" use of angels as representatives of opposing moral

5. Nathaniel Woodes, *The Conflict of Conscience*, ed. Herbert Davis and F. P. Wilson (Oxford: Malone Society, 1952), ll. 1728 ff.
6. Karl Young, *The Drama of the Medieval Church*, corrected reprint ed. (Oxford: Oxford University Press, 1951), i, 535.

alternatives facing a single human figure is found in *The Castle of Perseverance*, where the good angel assigned to Humanum Genus heads the threefold forces of Conscience, Confession, and Penance, as well as the subsidiary forces of the Seven Virtues, against the evil angel, who commands the World, the Flesh, the Devil, and the Seven Sins. Aside from this elaborate symmetrical antagonism, the angels argue with each other at the start of the play for the allegiance of Humanum Genus, and at the end of the play contend for the possession of his soul. It is clear that the more abstract conventions of the morality conflict predominate in *The Castle of Perseverance*; the more impressive dramatic strife is waged outside and around the human protagonist; even the opposing spirits direct themselves more to the argument with each other than to the decisions of Humanum Genus. Thus, the dramaturgical conduct of the good and evil angels in the one English morality play that employs them is at a farther remove from Marlowe's treatment of these spirits than is the non-dramatic theological formulation concerning the activities of angels and demons.

Both the external nature of the conflict in *Perseverance* and its pattern of alternating victory and defeat were to become the staple features of the battle between good and evil in the later morality plays, but both are foreign to Marlowe's handling of the conflict. In *Faustus*, the activities of the Angels are confined to the attempt to sway the Doctor's will to the side of good or evil. Unlike Humanum Genus and many of his later counterparts, Faustus himself is never separated from the conflict, and he himself is the only one to resolve it. In his case there is no alternating pattern—without exception he finally chooses the way of evil. Thus, the end result of Marlowe's staging of the Angels is to stress the Doctor's own will and responsibility in acting against his own best interests.

The introduction of the Seven Deadly Sins is another device in *Doctor Faustus* often linked with the morality tradition. Here again Marlowe is indebted not to the contemporary morality play, but to the early moralities before 1500. The Seven Deadly Sins, cast in the role of militant aggressors, are found in *The Castle of Perseverance*, the Digby *Mary Magdalene*, and Medwall's *Nature* (1490–1501), and there is evidence of dramatic pageants no longer extant illustrating the Seven Sins, in documents of the fourteenth and fifteenth centuries.[7] After the turn of the century, however, the morality play characteristically exhibits a more select number of sins or vices, adapted often to the more specialized homiletic stresses of the Reformation period. But throughout the development of the

7. See Bernard Spivack, *Shakespeare and the Allegory of Evil* (New York: Columbia University Press, 1958), p. 60.

tradition the vices retain both their aggressive character as destructive agents intent on seducing the human hero, and their essential strategy of deceit, disguising their vicious qualities under more attractive names. In Marlowe's play, not only are the Seven Deadly Sins presented *en masse*, which by that time had become an unusual thing in the drama, but they are also limited to one ironic episode of pageantry, and do not act as destructive agents plotting the downfall of Faustus.[8] They are presented rather as a delight and gratification to him, not in any ameliorating disguise, but in the raw, vulgar expression of their true natures (669–730). Faustus does not even get the dubious credit of being attracted to evil under the guise of an apparent good; he delights in it for what it really is, and under circumstances which present it as a "reward" for his obedience to the devil. Faustus, therefore, needs no deception to lead him to sin; he is his own worst deceiver, his own worst enemy, his own worst tempter.

Thus there is hardly any need in Marlowe's play for the most vital of morality conventions, the character of the Vice. This arch-deceiver and chief agent of destruction is entirely absent. Faustus' chief aggressor is the devil, a devil whose language and behavior bear little resemblance either to the habitual behavior of the Vice or to that of any devil who had ever trod the English stage. The devil, as Spivack has pointed out, holds but a negligible place in morality drama;[9] he appears in only nine of the almost sixty surviving plays of the morality convention, and has a significant role as tempter in only two early plays, *Wisdom* and *Mankind* (both c. 1461–1485). For the most part he is a grotesque, ludicrous figure, descended from the roaring fiends of the mystery-cycles, and having no direct contact with the human protagonist; often he is the object of the Vice's scurrilous humor and contempt. Spivack suggests that he does not fit in with the abstract morality pattern because he is "historical" and represents too undifferentiated an evil for the homiletic purposes of the morality play.[1] In *The Conflict of Conscience* (1581), Sathan himself opens the play, and gives his reason for not partaking of the main dramatic action: his ugly shape will attract no one, he says, and so he must send out the more alluring vices to destroy man.[2] We are reminded of how Fau-

---

8. A contemporary two-part play, in which the Seven Sins apparently functioned as symbolic figures in a series of scenes presenting historical and legendary characters who illustrated the Sins' effects, is known through a surviving stage "platt" or plot called "The Platt of the Second Part of the Seven Deadly Sins." There is little indication of how the Sins acted, but the play clearly had no central protagonist. See C. Walter Hodges, *The Globe Restored: A Study of the Elizabethan Theatre* (London: E. Benn, 1953), pp. 99–100, 182–184.
9. P. 130.
1. P. 132.
2. *Ed.cit.*, ll. 1–114. The same argument is given by Sathan in Thomas Garter's *The Com-*

stus recoiled, seeing the ugliness of Mephostophilis, but nevertheless persisted in his "devilish exercise" after demanding the devil to
assume a more pleasing and pious shape. Marlowe's irony of a disguise that is no disguise uses an old convention in a new way and
dramatically underlines the *self-imposed* moral blindness of his protagonist.

Marlowe's Mephostophilis has a seriousness and intensity which
is unparalleled in any previous theatrical representation of the diabolic, and unmatched in the Faust-Book as well. He is memorable
not so much for the threats and the delights with which he "serves"
Faustus, but for the brief yet telling witness that he gives to the
pains of hell. Nowhere in the English dramatic tradition had the
devil ever been used to express the suffering of damnation in this
way; nowhere had the pain of loss been given such intense and lu-
cid expression as in the words of Mephostophilis. Like the demons
of which Chrysostom wrote, he cries out in testimony of his torment—and this in the face of the very man he is supposed to lead
to hell. Mephostophilis' behavior in these instances is curiously at
odds with the more conventional fireworks, pranks, spectacular appearances, and threats in which he and the other devils indulge in
other sections of the play. Here the more typical qualities of the
stage devil are thrust into the background, and he emerges as a real
and suffering individual being. The dramaturgical conduct of Marlowe's devil on these occasions is closer to the theology of the diabolic and of damnation than to the behavior of any devil in the
mystery and morality plays. Marlowe's theology in this case is indeed orthodox; it is based on teaching that was even older than the
liturgical drama. But the originality with which he sets his theological knowledge into dramatic form is the mark of his genuine het-
erodoxy.[3]

Marlowe makes the father of lies tell the truth to Faustus, an
unheard-of tactic for any representative of evil in the morality tradition. That Faustus should proceed to his own damnation in the
face of such testimony sets him at an infinite distance from any of

---

mody of the moste vertuous and Godlye Susanna (printed 1578), ed. J. Johnson (Oxford:
Malone Society, 1937), ll. 26–50. In the fifteenth-century play Wisdom Lucifer changes
his form to that of a "goodly galont" when he undertakes his temptation of Mind, Will,
and Understanding: The Macro Plays, ed. F. J. Furnivall and Alfred W. Pollard, EETS, ex.
ser. XCI (London: Early English Text Society, 1904), p. 48.

3. Spivack (p. 240) asserts that the "deepest suffering of the sinner in the early moralities
is very little different [from that in Marlowe's Faustus and in Dante's Commedia] though
it is scarcely so well expressed. He too is cut off by his sins from the divine source of his
being and the vision that gives meaning to life." This may be so according to what can be
assumed doctrinally, but when it comes to actual dramatic expression within the plays,
there is nothing in the early moralities that approaches the explicit and precise formulation of the pain of loss (poena damni) that one finds in the speeches of Mephostophilis
and Faustus—even though the directly homiletic character of the morality play invited
open and precise statements of doctrine.

the beguiled human victims of the Vice in the moralities. There need be no Vice in Marlowe's play, nor even a deceitful devil, for Faustus is his own destroyer. What Marlowe has done to stress this point, by his handling of Mephostophilis as well as of the Deadly Sins, is to *reverse* the normal devices of the morality play. That he knew how to employ those devices in the regular way is manifest in the dramatic behavior of Barabas and Lightborn. Here, however, he is after a different form of ironic effect, a form which emphasizes at every opportunity Faustus' *willful* blindness to the overt evil before him.

There is yet another constitutional feature of the morality play which does not appear in Marlowe's *Faustus*: explicit didacticism which takes the form of direct homiletic address to the audience. It is true that the epilogue draws a moral from the action, indeed that the action itself carries a powerful exemplary force, but *within* the play there is none of the bald didacticism directed at the audience that always characterized the morality play. The closest approach to this homiletic quality is found in the Old Man's sermon to Faustus, in the admonitions of the Good Angel, and perhaps in the self-revelations of the Seven Deadly Sins. But nowhere is the audience itself addressed openly either in general admonition or in doctrinal commentary on Faustus' actions. In the case of the speeches of the Deadly Sins, the effect is primarily satirical and comically imaginative. Marlowe has replaced homily with dramatic irony. The solidly intellectual concepts of sin and damnation, of evil and suffering, which form the basis of his play are never preached; they are dramatized. The ironic dimensions of that dramatization carry to the audience the inescapable message implicit in Faustus' career; the dramatic *exemplum* stands without need of any homiletic elaboration.

While both the character and career of Faustus exhibit a fundamental quality which is both representative and universal in human experience, and while the nature of his conflict is the familiar tension holding his salvation or damnation in precarious balance, it is clear that this conflict is not set forth in the characteristic dramaturgical mode of the morality play. The moral forces and principles that were once abstracted from man's nature and presented separately as external agents are now within his own being. The battle between good and evil is fought in Faustus' own mind, and the only true abstractions that are given life in the play—the Seven Deadly Sins—are merely symbolic ornaments rather than major movers of the dramatic action. The springs of action in *Doctor Faustus* are coiled within the moral center of Faustus' soul: his imagination, his intellect, his exercise of choice begin the movement of the play and carry it to its tragic conclusion.

Here is the tragedy of moral choice wrought to its highest pitch, simple, stark, uncomplicated by the myriad relationships of human intercourse. *The Tragical History of Doctor Faustus* stands unique among the plays of its time in that all significant conflicts, struggles, delights, decisions, and pains are packed within one man, one character who is both victim and executioner. Doctor Faustus, for all his solitary stature, is no less human than any other tragic protagonist who plays his part in a world thronged with other men. He is no less human, because he bears the paradoxical twofold burden that all men must bear: unavoidable responsibility for his freely-made choices, and final helplessness in the face of a universal order that encompasses more than can the mind of man.

Ultimately, it is precisely this burden of his humanity that is the root of his suffering. In this he is unlike all other creations of Marlowe's imagination. Dido suffers as a lover who has lost her beloved; Tamburlaine, because he loses what is dear to both conqueror and lover; the Jew and the Guise suffer when their own treachery has backfired; Edward, when his friends and his kingship are no more. But only Faustus suffers because of his humanity, because he cannot escape the consequences of his human acts of mind and will, because by those acts he has eternally separated himself from the only power that can fulfill and perfect his humanity. It is perhaps just this essentially human quality of his suffering that has made it endure as Marlowe's most powerful dramatic statement.

The quality of evil and of suffering inherent in Marlowe's Faustus establishes him as neither hero nor villain, but as man.

SUSAN SNYDER

Marlowe's *Doctor Faustus* as an Inverted Saint's Life†

Critics have long recognized that *Doctor Faustus* is both a tragedy and a morality play. Because Faustus despairs, tragedy wins out in the end; but along the way semi-allegorical characters periodically wrestle over the soul of Faustus, reminding us of the contrasting medieval pattern of fall and redemption. Mr. Clifford Davidson[1] sees significance in Faustus' Wittenberg background and relates his hardened heart to the Lutheran emphasis on the bondage of the will. Such an emphasis, with its concomitant insistence that fallen

† From *Studies in Philology* 63: 514–23. Copyright © 1966 by the University of North Carolina Press. Used by permission of the publisher.
1. "Doctor Faustus of Wittenberg," *SP*, LIX (1962), 514–23.

man has no power to initiate his own repentance, is surely present in the play, underlying the sense of tragic inevitability. On the other hand, the speeches of the Good and Evil Angels, the Old Man, and Faustus himself convince us dramatically, if not theologically, that repentance is a constant possibility. This plays against the overly deterministic first element and helps to restore the balance of initiative between hero and opposing force important to the tragic effect. Contributing to and sustaining this tragic balance is a third structural pattern: the inverted saint's life.

Marlowe was accused in his own time of holding unorthodox religious views. One target of his attacks, according to both the Kyd deposition and the Baines memorandum, was Scriptural miracles. Kyd and Baines report statements by Marlowe that such miracles were not the work of God but of clever conjurors who could trick simple people with their arts: "Moyses was but a Jugler and . . . one Heriots being Sir W Raleighs man Can do more than he"; "it was an easy matter for Moyses being brought up in all the artes of the Egiptians to abuse the Jewes being a rude and grosse people."[2] We cannot know how seriously these assertions were made; but even if they were only jesting tavern talk it may have been this idea of the saint as magician that led Marlowe to see in his magician, Faustus, a kind of inverted saint. In any case, the events and language of the play present a parody of the conventional saint's life so consistent that it can hardly be an accident.

The saint's life is a didactic biography. As biography it follows the course of the subject's life. As a didactic work, however, it tends to stress certain features of every holy life, so that a kind of predictable pattern usually emerges, containing some or all of the following elements: early life (sometimes worldly and sinful), conversion to God, sacramental reception into the church, struggle against various temptations of the devil (sometimes overcome with the direct aid of God or his agents), miracles and mystic experiences (sometimes climaxed by a form of the beatific vision), holy death. *Doctor Faustus* turns the whole pattern upside down to tell the story of a man who after an orthodox early life is "converted" to the devil and seals his pact with a diabolic sacrament; who undergoes a series of "temptations" by the Good Angel and his own conscience, from which his mentor Mephostophilis "rescues" him; who performs "miracles" that are quite literally conjuring tricks; whose heavenly vision is a Greek strumpet; who is received at his death by his eternal master, Lucifer.[3]

2. Quoted by Paul Kocher, *Christopher Marlowe* (Chapel Hill, 1946), pp. 34–35. The admired "Heriots" is Thomas Harriot, mathematician, sceptic, one of the Raleigh circle which also included Marlowe.
3. The parody gives new, if ironic, life to the ancient identification of magician and holy

Thus one can see three dramatic movements operating simultaneously in *Doctor Faustus*. As a Christian soul, Faustus is caught
between his two angels, swinging between remorse and desperate
pleasure-seeking, not lost until the final moment. In theological
terms he is not damned until he dies; deliverance is always possible
if he will repent and call for mercy, and in the dramatic tradition of
the morality such deliverance was often postponed until the last
minute. At several points Faustus seems capable of breaking
through to God before the devils return him to spiritual insensibil-
ity.

But against the hope for an eleventh-hour rescue raised by the
morality elements is the increasing sense of inevitability in Faustus'
downward career. The morality upswing demands only a change of
heart; but Faustus loses his freedom to change as he hardens into
the constricting mold of proud despair. It is his pride (like Lucifer's
before him) that initiates the despair—and it is, of course, this
same pride that gives him heroic stature in the tragic context: that
is, in human terms rather than divine. Faustus respects reason and
justice, the great human distinction and the great human achievement. It follows that when he turns to *"Jeromes* Bible" in the opening scene he finds not the message of grace to the humble but the
cold logic of damnation: *"Stipendium peccati, mors est . . . Si peccasse, negamus, fallimur, et nulla est in nobis veritas."* And if the
wages of sin is death and all are sinners, the proud human intellect
can come to only one conclusion:

> Why then belike we must sinne,
> And so consequently die,
> I, we must die, an everlasting death.[4]

The interaction of pride and despair directs Faustus' course
throughout the play. Having made the diabolic pact he often longs
to repent, but pride in reason and justice still blinds him to the
mercy that lies beyond them. Christian theologians have always

man. E. M. Butler has traced the "myth of the magus" back to the sacrificial king-god of
the seasonal fertility rites and to the tribal witch-doctor [*The Myth of the Magus* (Cambridge, 1948), pp. 1–11]. The main features of the magus myth can be discerned in the
Biblical accounts of Moses and Christ as well as in the legends of Pythagoras and
Zoroaster. The line between magic and miracle is largely a Christian invention (p. 78).
Once drawn, however, it placed a wide gulf between saint and Magician, and the latter
suffered inevitable degradation. There is little in the *Faustbuch* to suggest a saint or even
an anti-saint. The stature of Faustus is Marlowe's gift.

4. I, i, 65–73. All *Doctor Faustus* references, unless otherwise noted, are to the B text of
1616 in W. W. Greg's edition of the parallel texts (Oxford, 1950). The B text is generally
accepted by modern editors as more reliable than the A quarto of 1604. Probably neither
version is entirely Marlowe's work, but the main plot displays a unity and progression
which indicate that his collaborator or collaborators, however inferior as poets, did not
misunderstand the play's design. The authorship problem is thus not crucial to this discussion.

In all quotations I have expanded abbreviations and regularized *i* and *j*, and *u* and *v*.

recognized the arrogance at the core of despair, the stiff-necked refusal to beg as a gift the salvation one cannot earn.[5] Faustus is by
turns anguished, hysterical, remorseful—but never humble.

It is the peculiar nature of Faustus' sin that allows tragedy to op-
erate in a Christian morality context. The grace is offered but the
protagonist personally blocks his own escape to it. Despair renders
his vision intensely subjective, thus allowing dramatically for a dual
view of God—tyrannic antagonist as well as loving father—without
outrage to orthodoxy. It is possible, depending on one's predilec-
tions, to see one or the other God as existing only in Faustus' diseased mind. God does not appear in his own person, unequivocally.
The Good Angel and the Old Man may be taken as his agents, but
they may also be merely a delusive inner voice and a fallible human
being. The *certitude* of God, a hindrance to the questioning spirit
of tragedy, is blurred in a haze of subjectivity.

Faustus' career as an anti-saint performing an exact parody of the
traditional words and deeds of the third pattern, shares with the
tragic pattern an inevitable progression to a preordained end; and
with the morality pattern the down-and-up movement of temptation and triumph. A more detailed analysis of the play will serve to
clarify the parody strain and its interaction with the other two kinds
of structure.

The prologue begins the parody of sainthood by describing Faustus' early devotion to divinity (ll. 14–19). As the man destined for
heroic virtue eventually becomes dissatisfied with lesser endeavors,
so Faustus starts by turning away from the limitations of divinity.
These limitations are, from the orthodox point of view, mainly in
himself; his use of logic in reasoning from the wages-of-sin and
all-men-are-sinners texts shows him reducing God to a level with
earthly concerns. That his whole study of divinity has been poisoned with pride is evident from his boast to Valdes and Cornelius:

> And I, that have with subtle Sillogismes
> Gravel'd the Pastors of the *Germane* Church
> And made the flowring pride of *Wittenberg*
> Sworne to my Problemes . . . (I, i, 134–137).

For Faustus, theology was merely a field in which to display his gifts
of reasoning. It is fitting that his "subtle Sillogismes" should lead
him away from the divinity he never really understood in its
essence. The inversion is complete when he turns to magic, finding

---

5. For example, Augustine, *De sermone Domini in monte I*, XXII, 74, in Migne (ed.), *Pa-
trologiae cursus completus . . . series latina*, XXXIV, 1266–1267. It was pride, says Augustine, that turned Judas' repentance (Matt. 27:3–5) into despair; he could not humble his
heart. The pride at the center of despair emerges clearly in one *locus classicus*, Cain's defiant declaration to God after killing Abel: "Maior est iniquitas mea, quam ut veniam
merear" (Gen. 4:13).

a new heaven in "Lines, Circles, Letters, Characters" (I, i, 75–78).
The saint aspires through faith to be God's child; Faustus parodies
the idea in his determination to father a god.

> A sound Magitian is a Demi-god,
> Here tire my braines to get a Deity.[6]

There is deep irony in his delighted imaginings:

> Shall I make spirits fetch me what I please?
> Resolve me of all ambiguities?
> Performe what desperate enterprise I will?   (I, i. 106–108)

He will. All ambiguities will be resolved in the end, only too clearly;
all enterprises will be desperate because Faustus will live in despair; spirits will fetch him what he has pleased to choose—damnation.

Valdes and Cornelius are the first of Faustus' "spiritual advi-
sors."[7] They encourage the new ambitions of their convert with rewards significantly phrased:

> Val.: *Faustus*, these bookes, thy wit, and our experience,
> shall make all Nations to *Canonize* us
> . . . .
> Cor.: The *miracles* that magick will performe,
> Will make thee vow to study nothing else.[8]

These preceptors indoctrinate Faustus in his anti-religion. They
promise to supply him with books: Roger Bacon and "Albanus"
(probably Albertus Magnus), the Hebrew Psalter and the New Testament—for incantations. They will teach him the rites and ceremonies, instruct him in the rudiments of his new discipline. They
are, in fact, preparing their catechumen for his formal reception
into the "church," in the manner of a saint's life. There is even a reminder, as one would expect in the case of a saint, that this candi-
date will in time go beyond his instructors:

> Val.: First I'le instruct thee in the rudiments,
> And then wilt thou be perfecter than I   (I, i, 103–184).

6. I, i, 88–89. The reading of A and B², "to gaine a deitie," loses half the point. Both Greg
and Boas favor B's "get," in the sense of "beget."

7. Unless we count Mephostophilis, who in the B text later confesses (V, ii, 1989–1992)
that before his visible entry he had guided Faustus' eyes to the fatal Scripture passages.

8. I, i, 141–142 and 158–159. Italics mine, excluding proper names. C. L. Barber [" 'The
form of Faustus fortunes good or bad,' " *Tulane Drama Review*, VIII (Summer, 1964),
99] gives another, not necessarily conflicting, interpretation of the constant use of religious language for Faustus' necromantic pursuits: the repeated, involuntary invocation
of heaven and things divine by Faustus, Valdes and Cornelius, and Mephostophilis
shows the inadequacy of blasphemous magic as a substitute for the lost joys of heaven.
"In repeatedly using such expressions, which often 'come naturally' in the colloquial language of a Christian society, the rebels seem to stumble uncannily upon words which
condemn them by the logic of a situation larger than they are."

In scene iii Faustus' first rite is a parody of baptism. Instead of renouncing the devil and all his works, Faustus renounces the Trinity ("valeat numen triplex Jehovae").[9] When he performs the two central symbolic acts of baptism, sprinkling holy water and making the sign of the cross, the object is to invoke not God but Mephostophilis. The parody continues with the entrance of Mephostophilis garbed, by Faustus' order, in a Franciscan habit, to match his role as spiritual guide. The guidance itself carries on the mockery, for Faustus is told how to win hell:

> Therefore the shortest cut for conjuring
> Is stoutly to abjure all godlinesse,
> And pray devoutely to the Prince of hell   (I, iii, 278–280).

Periodically Marlowe suspends the parody and turns the values right side up again. Thus, in between Faustus' conversion to magic and his mock baptism is a short scene in which two scholars fear for the soul of their colleague. Their brief conversation gives the sense of danger necessary to balance and intensify the blasphemous comedy of the conjuring scene. In the conjuring scene itself, the danger is again asserted, this time even more tellingly, by Mephostophilis. He abandons his role as hell's advocate long enough to describe movingly the fall of the angels and their endless despair:

> Why this is hell: nor am I out of it.
> Think'st thou that I that saw the face of God,
> And tasted the eternall Joyes of heaven,
> Am not tormented with ten thousand hels,
> In being depriv'd of everlasting blisse?   (I, iii, 301–305)

The words have a double impact because they are so incompatible with the role of the speaker. He concludes with an almost involuntary plea that Faustus abandon the desires that terrify even a devil (II. 306–307). Faustus is too exhilarated to heed the warning, but it registers with the audience.

The second act[1] shows Faustus' ceremonial reception into the devil's church and his temptations by hope. Following are the third and fourth acts describing his conjuring miracles. The order of events is significant, for in the saint's life a period of trial and temptation often precedes activity as an instrument of grace, just as in Christ's life, the model for these others, the temptation in the wilderness comes before the ministry.

---

9. I, iii, 242–243. On "numen triplex Jehovae" as the Trinity, see Boas' note on this passage in the Arden edition.
1. I follow Boas' act divisions, believing with him that "the prevalent practice of a merely scenic division . . . has . . . done injustice to the structural quality of the play" (p. vi).

The first soliloquy of Act II presents Faustus in despair, wavering between stoic resolution and the desire to escape into hope. He starts wistfully, trying to think of a way out, then stiffens, wavers again at the thought of repentance, falls back once more with a recollection of the diabolic syllogism (God does not love sinners), and finally resolves to be loyal to Belzebub.

> Now *Faustus*, must thou needs be damn'd?
> Canst thou not be sav'd?
> What bootes it then to thinke on God or Heaven?
> Away with such vaine fancies, and despaire,
> Despaire in GOD, and trust in *Belzebub*,
> Now go not backward *Faustus*, be resolute.
> Why waverst thou? O something soundeth in mine eare.
> Abjure this Magicke, turne to God againe.
> Why he loves thee not:
> The God thou serv'st is thine owne appetite
> Wherein is fixt the love of *Belzebub*,
> To him, I'le build an Altar and a Church.
> And offer luke-warme bloud, of new borne babes (II, i,
>   390–401).

The language of the passage suggests the spiritual trials of the saint: "vaine fancies"; "be resolute"; "I'le build an Altar and a Church." When the Angels enter, Faustus is again tempted by "Contrition, Prayer, Repentance" (II, i, 405). The Bad Angel assures him they are merely lunatic illusions; he must turn his thoughts from heaven to earth. So Faustus relapses into his former state, rejoicing at his deliverance: "*Faustus* thou art safe. / Cast no more doubts" (II, i, 413–414).

Once tested, Faustus is ready for his sacramental entry into Lucifer's church. He invokes Mephostophilis as one would the Holy Ghost ("*Veni veni Mephostophile*"),[2] and hears from him that Lucifer is ready to receive his votary.

In the course of this sacramental shedding of blood, Faustus becomes a demonic Christ. He repeats the words "*Consummatum est*," to signify that his blood like Christ's has done its work (II, i, 417).[3] But that work is to sell what Christ bought, to give back to hell the soul that Christ won from it with his blood. W. W. Greg points out that by the terms of the contract Faustus' nature is altered. He keeps his human soul but becomes "a spirit [*i.e.* a devil] in forme and substance."[4] This amalgam of human and diabolical

2. II, i, 417.
3. See John 19:30.
4. "The Damnation of Faustus," *MLR*, XLI (1946), 103; II, i, 488.

suggests a parody of the dual nature of Christ, at once human and divine.

The congealing of Faustus' blood and the mysterious *"Homo fuge"* represent his second temptation by grace. He wavers again, but stays in despair, and Mephostophilis is quick to produce "somewhat to delight his minde," a dance of devils. The latter phenomenon is to offset the effect of the congealed blood and the strange inscription, which come from God. In the play's total inversion, it is the inscription that seems an evil hallucination. Faustus thinks his senses deceived when he sees it (l. 467); for this anti-saint, the true visions are the "shews" of Mephostophilis. The latter, still the preceptor, concludes the scene by presenting his pupil with a book, to be perused well and guarded carefully. Faustus has his false Gospel and the sacrament is complete.

The next two "temptations" continue the inversion principle, but they are not simply repetitions of the first ones. They show the progressive hardening of Faustus' despair, preparing for the last scene when its weight will pull him down from a frantic leap to heaven. His conversation with Mephostophilis about heaven (II, ii, 570–580) shows him once more the anti-saint, tempted by heaven as true saints are tempted by the world and the flesh. "When I behold the heavens then I repent" (l. 570); that is, I am tempted to hope. His guardian devil assures him that heaven is not half so fair as earthly man. Still Faustus desires it; he makes an intellectual rejection of his magic. But the core of pride is still there. Faustus thinks his own will can turn him from evil. Because he lacks humility to ask for grace, the short essay into repentance is abortive. His heart refuses to follow his mind.

> My heart is hardned, I cannot repent:
> Scarce can I name salvation, faith, or heaven[5]
>
> (II, ii, 580–590).

In this dilemma his thoughts turn to suicide. The next four lines recreate verbally the traditional allegorical figure of Despair, carrying the instruments of self-destruction:[6]

> Swords, poyson halters, and invenomb'd steele,
> Are laid before me to dispatch my selfe:

---

5. Other passages suggest a Christ-parody: Faustus' desire to raise the dead and grant eternal life (I, i, 51–53), and his "graveling" of the German pastors (I, i, 134–135), perhaps meant to recall the youthful Christ confounding the doctors of the law.

6. Despair is represented in medieval and Renaissance iconography as a figure in the act of self-destruction. In allegorical narrative and drama, Despair or a similar figure usually presents the hero with a choice of weapons for suicide (see Skelton's *Magnyfycence*, Book I of *The Faerie Queene*, and Arnoul Greban's *Mystère de la passion*; in the latter case the victim is Judas). Cf. also Arieh Sachs, "The Religious Despair of Dr. Faustus," *JEGP*, LXIII (1964), 625–47.

> And long e're this, I should have done the deed,
> Had not sweete pleasure conquer'd deepe despaire.

This is perhaps spelling out his condition almost too obviously, but it does create the desired impression of despair settling about him like a permanent aura, always with its implication of death. The suicide motif will reappear later. Faustus does not take his own life in the physical sense, but he is committing spiritual suicide. Now, however, he is recalled again by "sweete pleasure" to unconsciousness.

The fourth temptation takes Faustus a step further. Calling on Christ is his first open rebellion against the diabolic trinity: "O Christ my Saviour, my Saviour, / Helpe to save distressed *Faustus* soule" (II, ii, 652–653). Realizing his need for help, he is close to breaking out of despair. The devils must abandon persuasion and distraction for threats. The Bad Angel warns that they will tear him to pieces (l. 650); Lucifer, Belzebub, and Mephostophilis appear, to frighten him into submission.

The parodic element in this rebellion is less apparent than elsewhere, until we recall the Protestant insistence on man's utter helplessness, of which God periodically reminds him. Lucifer's open show of power is equivalent in a sense to the God-directed sufferings that chastise and humble the souls of the elect. More openly parodic are Faustus' abject plea for pardon and his vow "never to looke to heaven" (II, ii, 665–666). Lucifer rewards his obedient servant with an appropriate vision. As Faustus prepares to watch the Seven Deadly Sins, he himself reminds us with unintentional irony of the contrast between this vision and that of the saints: "That sight will be as pleasant to me, as Paradise / was to Adam the first day of his creation" (II, ii, 673–674).

Acts III and IV, as we have them, have always been viewed as the weak part of the play, in terms of structure and dramatic interest. In the structure of the parodied saint's life, the pranks and tricks do have their place as the "miracles" that demonstrate the saint's peculiar gifts of grace. As God's favorites can sometimes prophesy the future, the devil's saint can recreate the past—Alexander and his paramour, for example. As Jesus and his saints used miracles to convince scoffers, Faustus uses his conjuring to discomfit the scornful Benvolio with a pair of horns. Faustus performs his cheap illusions to show the powers he has gained from the devil. That they amount to so little underlines for the audience the tragedy of Faustus' degeneration. Nevertheless, these scenes do not hold the interest dramatically (as spectacle they can be more successful, as a recent New York production showed). The ideas are not worked out and we lose sight of Faustus the man in all the buffoonery. It is significant that he has become a buffoon, but more inner characterization is needed if we are to feel the pity of it.

Faustus does not approach consciousness of his state in these two acts, except for a curious brief soliloquy which interrupts his practical joke on the horse-courser:

> What art thou *Faustus* but a man condemn'd to die?
> Thy fatall time drawes to a finall end;
> Despaire doth drive distrust into my thoughts.
> Confound these passions with a quiet sleepe:
> Tush Christ did call the Theefe upon the Crosse,
> Then rest thee *Faustus quiet in conceit*   (IV, v, 1546–1551).

This is startling enough in the middle of a prank, and critics have made various attempts to justify it or to blame it on an unskillful collaborator. It is certainly introduced without preamble, but Greg's condemnation of its "combined piety and bad taste"[7] misses the point. The good thief was traditionally invoked against despair, as Lily B. Campbell notes.[8] The passage thus reminds us of Faustus' despair and impending fate (tragic inevitability) and suggests at the same time that he may still be saved (morality promise of last-minute rescue). Unfortunately for Faustus, the story of the good thief is itself double-edged. It can be an antidote to despair, but it can also be a devilish encouragement to postpone repentance until the last breath, relying on God's great love. It is the latter application that prevails with Faustus, who makes no move to repent but "rests quiet." Unable to find the middle way of hope, he falls into the opposite extreme of presumption.

In Act V we are again involved in the human tragedy. As the play moves toward its agonizing close, the parodic element is less important than the hero's intense inner experience; but it is still there. The rapturous lines to Helen of Troy, with their allusions to heaven, immortality, and ecstatic self-abandonment, are a blasphemous parody of the supreme mystical union with God:[9]

> Sweet *Hellen* make me immortall with a kisse:
> Her lips sucke forth my soule, see where it flies.
> Come *Hellen*, come, give me my soule againe,
> Here will I dwell, for heaven is in these lippes,
> And all is drosse that is not *Helena*   (V, i, 1876–1880).

The great beauty of the poetry only increases its shock value. The tension between orthodoxy and blasphemy which runs through the whole play is at its strongest here.

7. Greg, *Doctor Faustus* (parallel texts), p. 118.
8. "*Doctor Faustus*: A Case of Conscience," *PMLA*, LXVII (1952), 236. One example is woodcut 4 of the *Ars moriendi*, a popular late medieval tract, in which the good thief appears with Peter, Paul, and Mary Magdalene to preserve Moriens from despair [facs. of *editio princeps*, *c.* 1450, ed. W. Harry Rylands (1881)].
9. The spelling "Hellen" in B (A has "Helen") may be just a typesetter's whim, but it affords a neat epitome of the heaven-hell inversion.

Afterwards, the inevitability of the anti-saint's career works mainly to reinforce the tragic end of Faustus the man. Even before Helen the Old Man has come, bringing Faustus to an anguished awareness of sin in an abrupt switch from the drunken pleasures of the banquet. So dangerous is this emissary that Mephostophilis quickly hands Faustus a dagger in the hope that suicide will damn forever the soul the devil is in danger of losing. "Hell claimes his right" (l. 1832), and Faustus, always responsive to the dictates of justice, is about to execute himself when the Old Man stops him:

> O stay good *Faustus*, stay thy desperate steps.
> I see an Angell hover ore thy head,
> And with a vyoll full of pretious grace,
> Offers to poure the same into thy soule,
> Then call for mercy, and avoyd despaire   (V, i, 1834–1838).

Faustus is moved to ponder his sins, but now the only result can be the hopeless, sterile remorse of Judas: "I do repent, and yet I doe despaire" (l. 1844). When Mephostophilis intervenes, his language ("traytor," "disobedience")[1] suffices to remind Faustus of his contract and to turn him from mercy through the invocation of justice. Faustus succumbs fearfully and is rewarded with Helen.

Tension builds on the last night, as the devils await their prize and the scholars urge Faustus to repent, to "looke up to heaven" (V, ii, 1935). He cannot. His answer is that of Cain: my offence is too great to be pardoned (ll. 1937–1939).[2] As for reaching to heaven, "I would lift up my hands, but see they hold 'em, they hold 'em" (ll. 1953–1954).

In the final soliloquy, morality play, tragedy, and demonic saint's legend fuse in a terrible conclusion. We watch Faustus search frantically for a way out, knowing that he himself blocks that way. He cannot leap up to heaven ("who puls me downe?").[3] He can look, at last, and for a moment he sees redemption:

> See see where Christs blood streames in the firmament,
> One drop would save my soule, halfe a drop, ah my Christ
>   (A, ll. 1463–1464).[4]

But the verb is conditional. One drop "would" save him, if he had hope. He has none, and the vision is replaced by the angry face of God the Judge. Only justice is left.

The travestied saint's life in *Doctor Faustus* intensifies its tragic effect, increasing the stature of the hero while ensuring his down-

---

1. V, i, 1847–1848.
2. See note 5, p. 315, above.
3. V, ii, 2048.
4. Line 1463 does not appear in B, but even the staunchest foes of the A quarto refuse to omit it from their editions.

fall. By hinting at a possible "divine comedy" pattern of last-minute
redemption, Marlowe calls attention to his ultimate overthrow of
that pattern. Together with the great poetry and the portrayal of
Faustus' grandly inquiring mind, the travesty establishes within
Doctor Faustus the center of rebellion necessary in tragedy. It asserts definitely the freedom of the mind, to balance or at least
protest the inevitable working of evil in Faustus and his world.

JONATHAN DOLLIMORE

Dr. Faustus (c. 1589–92): Subversion through Transgression†

One problem in particular has exercised critics of *Dr. Faustus*: its
structure, inherited from the morality form, apparently negates
what the play experientially affirms—the heroic aspiration of 'Renaissance man.' Behind this discrepancy some have discerned a
tension between, on the one hand, the moral and theological im-
peratives of a severe Christian orthodoxy and, on the other, an affirmation of Faustus as 'the epitome of Renaissance aspiration . . .
all the divine discontent, the unwearied and unsatisfied striving after knowledge that marked the age in which Marlowe wrote' (Roma
Gill, ed. *Dr. Faustus*, p. xix).

Critical opinion has tended to see the tension resolved one way
or another—that is, to read the play as ultimately vindicating either
Faustus or the morality structure. But such resolution is what *Dr.
Faustus* as interrogative text[1] resists. It seems always to represent
paradox—religious and tragic—as insecurely and provocatively ambiguous or, worse, as openly contradictory. Not surprisingly Max
Bluestone, after surveying some eighty recent studies of *Dr. Faustus*, as well as the play itself, remains unconvinced of their more or
less equally divided attempts to find in it an orthodox or heterodox
principle of resolution. On the contrary: 'conflict and contradiction
inhere everywhere in the world of this play' ('*Libido Speculandi*:
Doctrine and Dramaturgy in Contemporary Interpretations of Marlowe's *Dr. Faustus*', p. 55). If this is correct then we might see it as
an integral aspect of what *Dr Faustus* is best understood as: not an
affirmation of Divine Law, or conversely of Renaissance Man, but
an exploration of subversion through transgression.

† From *Radical Tragedy: Religion, Ideology, and Power in the Drama of Shakespeare*
(Durham, NC: Duke University Press, 1984) 109–19. Reprinted by permission of the
publisher.
1. This concept, originating in a classification of Benveniste's, is developed by Catherine
Belsey in *Critical Practice* (London: Methuen, 1980), chapter 4.

Limit and Transgression

Raymond Williams has observed how, in Victorian literature, individuals encounter limits of crucially different kinds. In *Felix Holt* there is the discovery of limits which, in the terms of the novel, are enabling: they vindicate a conservative identification of what it is to be human. In complete contrast *Jude the Obscure* shows its protagonist destroyed in the process—and ultimately because—of encountering limits. This is offered not as punishment for hubris but as 'profoundly subversive of the limiting structure' ('Forms of English Fiction in 1848', p. 287). *Dr. Faustus*, I want to argue, falls into this second category: a discovery of limits which ostensibly forecloses subversive questioning in fact provokes it.[2]

What Erasmus had said many years before against Luther indicates the parameters of *Dr. Faustus'* limiting structure:

> Suppose for a moment that it were true in a certain sense, as Augustine says somewhere, that 'God works in us good and evil, and rewards his own good works in us, and punishes his evil works in us' . . . Who will be able to bring himself to love God with all his heart when He created hell seething with eternal torments in order to punish His own misdeeds in His victims as though He took delight in human torments?
> (*Renaissance Views of Man*, ed. S. Davies, p. 92)

But Faustus is not *identified* independently of this limiting structure and any attempt to interpret the play as Renaissance man breaking out of medieval chains always founders on this point: Faustus is constituted by the very limiting structure which he transgresses and his transgression is both despite and because of that fact.

Faustus is situated at the centre of a violently divided universe. To the extent that conflict and contradiction are represented as actually of its essence, it appears to be Manichean; thus Faustus asks 'where is the place that men call hell?', and Mephostophilis replies 'Within the bowels of these elements', adding:

> when all the world dissolves
> And every creature shall be purify'd,
> All places shall be hell that is not heaven.
> (v. 117, 120, 125–7)

If Greg is correct, and 'purified' means 'no longer mixed, but of one essence, either wholly good or wholly evil' (*Marlowe's Dr. Faustus*, Parallel Texts, p. 330), then the division suggested is indeed

2. Still important for this perspective is Nicholas Brooke's "The Moral Tragedy of Doctor Faustus," *Cambridge Journal* 5 (1952): 662–87.

Manichean.[3] But more important than the question of precise origins is the fact that not only heaven and hell but God and Lucifer, the Good Angel and the Bad Angel, are polar opposites whose axes pass through and constitute human consciousness. Somewhat similarly, for Mephostophilis hell is not a place but a state of consciousness:

> Hell hath no limits, nor is circumscrib'd
> In one self place, but where we are is hell,
> And where hell is, there must we ever be.
>
> (v. 122–4)

From Faustus' point of view—one never free-ranging but always coterminous with his position—God and Lucifer seem equally responsible in his final destruction, two supreme agents of power deeply antagonistic to each other[4] yet temporarily co-operating in his demise. Faustus is indeed their subject, the site of their power struggle. For his part God is possessed of tyrannical power—'heavy wrath' (i. 71 and xix. 153), while at the beginning of scene xix Lucifer, Beelzebub and Mephostophilis enter syndicate-like 'To view the *subjects* of our monarchy'. Earlier Faustus had asked why Lucifer wanted his soul; it will, replies Mephostophilis, 'Enlarge his kingdom' (v. 40). In Faustus' final soliloquy both God and Lucifer are spatially located as the opposites which, *between them*, destroy him:

> O, I'll leap up to my God! Who pulls me down?
>
> see where God
> Stretcheth out his arm and bends his ireful brows
>
> My God, my God! Look not so fierce on me!
>
> Ugly hell, gape not! Come not, Lucifer.
>
> (ll. 145, 150–1, 187, 189)

Before this the representatives of God and Lucifer have bombarded Faustus with conflicting accounts of his identity, position and destiny. Again, the question of whether in principle Faustus can re-

---

3. The Manichean implications of protestantism are apparent from this assertion of Luther's: "Christians know there are two kingdoms in the world, which are bitterly opposed to each other. In one of them Satan reigns. . . . He holds captive to his will all who are not snatched away from him by the Spirit of Christ. . . . In the other Kingdom, Christ reigns, and his kingdom ceaselessly resists and makes war on the kingdom of Satan" (*Luther and Erasmus: Free Will and Salvation*, ed. E. Gordon Rupp [London: SCM, 1969], pp. 327–28; see also Peter Lake, *Moderate Puritans and the Elizabethan Church* [Cambridge: Cambridge University Press, 1982], pp. 144–45).

4. Cf. Michael Walzer, *The Revolution of the Saints: A Study in the Origin of Radical Politics* (London: Weidenfeld and Nicolson, 1966): "The imagery of warfare was constant in Calvin's writing" (p. 65); specifically, of course, warfare between God and Satan.

pent, what is the point of no return, is less important than the fact
that he is located on the axes of contradictions which cripple and
finally destroy him.

By contrast, when, in Marlowe's earlier play, Tamburlaine speaks
of the 'four elements/Warring within our breasts for regiment' he is
speaking of a dynamic conflict conducive to the will to power—one
which 'Doth teach us all to have aspiring minds' (l. II. vii. 18–20)—
not the stultifying contradiction which constitutes Faustus and his
universe. On this point alone *Tamburlaine* presents a fascinating
contrast with *Dr Faustus*. With his indomitable will to power and
warrior prowess, Tamburlaine really does approximate to the self-
determining hero bent on transcendent autonomy—a kind of fantasy on Pico's theme of aspiring man. But like all fantasies this one
excites as much by what it excludes as what it exaggerates. Indeed
exclusion may be the basis not just of Tamburlaine as fantasy projection but *Tamburlaine* as transgressive text: it liberates from its
Christian and ethical framework the humanist conception of man
as essentially free, dynamic and aspiring; more contentiously, this
conception of man is not only liberated from a Christian framework
but reestablished in open defiance of it. But however interpreted,
the objective of Tamburlaine's aspiration is very different from
Pico's; the secular power in which Tamburlaine revels is part of
what Pico wants to transcend in the name of a more ultimate and
legitimate power. Tamburlaine defies origin, Pico aspires to it:

> A certain sacred striving should seize the soul so that, not con-
> tent with the indifferent and middling, we may pant after the
> highest and so (for we can if we want to) force our way up to
> with all our might. Let us despise the terrestrial, be unafraid of
> the heavenly, and then, neglecting the things of the world, fly
> towards that court beyond the world nearest to God the Most
> High.   (*On the Dignity of Man*, pp. 69–70)

With *Dr. Faustus* almost the reverse is true: transgression is born
not of a liberating sense of freedom to deny or retrieve origin, nor
from an excess of life breaking repressive bounds. It is rather a
transgression rooted in an *impasse* of despair.

Even before he abjures God, Faustus expresses a sense of being
isolated and trapped; an insecurity verging on despair pre-exists a
damnation which, by a perverse act of free will, he 'chooses'. Arrogant he certainly is, but it is wrong to see Faustus at the outset as
secure in the knowledge that existing forms of knowledge are inadequate. Rather, his search for a more complete knowledge is
itself a search for security. For Faustus, 'born, of parents base
of stock', and now both socially and geographically displaced
(Prologue, ll. 11, 13–19), no teleological integration of identity,

self-consciousness and purpose obtains. In the opening scene he
attempts to convince himself of the worth of several professions—
divinity, medicine, law, and then divinity again—only to reject each
in turn; in this he is almost schizoid:

> Having commenc'd, be a divine in show,
> Yet level at the end of every art,
> And live and die in Aristotle's works.
> Sweet Analytics, 'tis thou hast ravish'd me!
>
> When all is done, divinity is best.
>
> Philosophy is odious and obscure,
> Both law and physic are for petty wits,
> Divinity is basest of the three,
> Unpleasant, harsh, contemptible, and vile.
>
> (i. 3–6, 37, 105–8)

As he shakes free of spurious orthodoxy and the role of the conventional scholar, Faustus' insecurity intensifies. A determination to
be 'resolved' of all ambiguities, to be 'resolute' and show fortitude
(i. 32; iii. 14; v. 6; vi. 32, 64) is only a recurring struggle to escape
agonised irresolution.

This initial desperation and insecurity, just as much as a subsequent fear of impending damnation, suggests why his search for
knowledge so easily lapses into hedonistic recklessness and fatu-
ous, self-forgetful 'delight' (i. 52; v. 82; vi. 170; viii. 59–60). Wagner cannot comprehend this psychology of despair:

> I think my master means to die shortly:
> He has made his will and given me his wealth
>
> I wonder what he means. If death were nigh,
> He would not banquet and carouse and swill
> Amongst the students.   (xviii. 1–2, 5–7)

Faustus knew from the outset what he would eventually incur. He
willingly 'surrenders up . . . his soul' for twenty-four years of 'voluptuousness' in the knowledge that 'eternal death' will be the result (iii.
90–4). At the end of the first scene he exits declaring 'This night I'll
conjure though I die therefor'. Later he reflects: 'long ere this I should
have done the deed [i.e., suicide] / Had not sweet pleasure conquer'd
deep despair' (vi. 24–5). This is a despairing hedonism rooted in the
fatalism of his opening soliloquy: 'If we say that we have no sin, we
deceive ourselves, and there's no truth in us. Why, then, belike we
must sin, and so consequently die' (i. 41–4). Half-serious, half-
facetious, Faustus registers a sense of human-kind as miscreated.

Tamburlaine's will to power leads to liberation through transgression. Faustus' pact with the devil, because an act of transgression without hope of liberation, is at once rebellious, masochistic and despairing. The protestant God—'an arbitrary and wilful, omnipotent and universal tyrant' (Walzer, p. 151)—demanded of each subject that s/he submit personally and without mediation. The modes of power formerly incorporated in mediating institutions and practices now devolve on Him and, to some extent and unintentionally, on His subject: abject before God, the subject takes on a new importance in virtue of just this direct relation.[5] Further, although God is remote and inscrutable he is also intimately conceived: 'The principal worship of God hath two parts. One is to yield subjection to him, the other to draw near to him and to cleave unto him' (Perkins, *An Instruction Touching Religious or Divine Worship*, p. 313). Such perhaps are the conditions for masochistic transgression: intimacy becomes the means of a defiance of power, the new-found importance of the subject the impetus of that defiance, the abjectness of the subject its self-sacrificial nature. (We may even see here the origins of sub-cultural transgression: the identity conferred upon the deviant by the dominant culture enables resistance as well as oppression.)

Foucault has written: 'limit and transgression depend on each other for whatever density of being they possess: a limit could not exist if it were absolutely uncrossable and, reciprocally, transgression would be pointless if it merely crossed a limit composed of illusions and shadows' (*Language, Counter-Memory, Practice*, p. 34). It is a phenomenon of which the anti-essentialist writers of the Renaissance were aware: 'Superiority and inferiority, maistry and subjection, are joyntly tied unto a naturall kinde of envy and contestation; they must perpetually enter-spoile one another' (Montaigne, *Essays*, III. 153).

In the morality plays sin tended to involve blindness to the rightness of God's law, while repentance and redemption involved a renewed apprehension of it. In *Dr. Faustus* however sin is not the error of fallen judgement but a conscious and deliberate transgression of limit. It is a limit which, among other things, renders God remote and inscrutable yet subjects the individual to constant surveillance and correction; which holds the individual subject terrifyingly responsible for the fallen human condition while disallowing

5. Cf. C. Burges, *The First Sermon* (London, 1641): "A man once married to the Lord by covenant may without arrogancy say: this righteousness is my righteousness . . . this loving kindness, these mercies, this faithfulness, which I see in thee . . . is mine, for my comfort . . . direction, salvation, and what not" (p. 61; quoted from Conrad Russell, *The Crisis of Parliaments* [London: Oxford University Press, 1971], p. 204).

him or her any subjective power of redemption. Out of such conditions is born a mode of transgression identifiably protestant in origin: despairing yet defiant, masochistic yet wilful. Faustus is abject yet his is an abjectness which is strangely inseparable from arrogance, which reproaches the authority which demands it, which is not so much subdued as incited by that same authority:

> *Faustus*: I gave . . . my soul for my cunning.
> *All*:   God forbid!
> *Faustus*: God forbade it indeed; but Faustus hath done it.
>
> (xix. 61–4)

Mephostophilis well understands transgressive desire; it is why he does not deceive Faustus about the reality of hell. It suggests too why he conceives of hell in the way he does; although his sense of it as a state of being and consciousness can be seen as a powerful recuperation of hell at a time when its material existence as a *place* of future punishment was being questioned, it is also an arrogant appropriation of hell, an incorporating of it into the consciousness of the subject.

A ritual pact advances a desire which cancels fear long enough to pass the point of no return:

> Lo, Mephostophilis, for love of thee
> Faustus hath cut his arm, and with his proper blood
> Assures his soul to be great Lucifer's,
> Chief lord and regent of perpetual night.
> View here this blood that trickles from mine arm,
> And let it be propitious for my wish.
>
> (v. 54–8)

But his blood congeals, preventing him from signing the pact. Mephostophilis exits to fetch 'fire to dissolve it'. It is a simple yet brilliant moment of dramatic suspense, one which invites us to dwell on the full extent of the violation about to be enacted. Faustus finally signs but only after the most daring blasphemy of all: 'Now will I make an end immediately / . . . *Consummatum est*: this bill is ended' (v. 72–4). In transgressing utterly and desperately God's law, he appropriates Christianity's supreme image of masochistic sacrifice:[6] Christ dying on the cross—and his dying words (cf. John xix. 30). Faustus is not liberating himself, he is ending himself: 'it is finished'. Stephen Greenblatt is surely right

---

6. Margaret Walters reminds us how Christian iconography came to glorify masochism, especially in its treatment of crucifixion. Adoration is transferred from aggressor to victim, the latter suffering in order to propitiate a vengeful, patriarchal God. See her *The Nude Male: A New Perspective* (London: Paddington Press, 1978), pp. 10, 72–75. Faustus' transgression becomes subversive in being submissive yet the reverse of propitiatory.

to find in Marlowe's work 'a subversive identification with the alien', one which 'flaunts society's cherished orthodoxies, embraces what the culture finds loathsome or frightening' (*Renaissance Self-Fashioning*, pp. 203, 220). But what is also worth remarking about this particular moment is the way that a subversive identification with the alien is achieved and heightened through travesty of one such cherished orthodoxy.

Power and the Unitary Soul

For Augustine the conflict which man experiences is not (as the Manichean heresy insisted) between two contrary souls or two contrary substances—rather, one soul fluctuates between contrary wills. On some occasions *Dr. Faustus* clearly assumes the Augustinian conception of the soul; on others—those expressive of or consonant with the Manichean implications of universal conflict—it presents Faustus as divided and, indeed, constituted by that division. The distinction which Augustine makes between the will as opposed to the soul as the site of conflict and division may now seem to be semantic merely; in fact it was and remains of the utmost importance. For one thing, as *Dr. Faustus* makes clear, the unitary soul—unitary in the sense of being essentially indivisible and eternal—is the absolute precondition for the exercise of divine power:

> O, no end is limited to damned souls.
> Why wert thou not a creature wanting soul?
> Or why is this immortal that thou hast?
> Ah, Pythagoras' *metempsychosis*, were that true,
> This soul should fly from me and I be chang'd
> Unto some brutish beast: all beasts are happy,
> For when they die
> Their souls are soon dissolv'd in elements;
> But mine must live still to be plagu'd in hell.
>
> (xix. 171–9)

Further, the unitary soul—unitary now in the sense of being essentially incorruptible—figures even in those manifestations of Christianity which depict the human condition in the most pessimistic of terms and human freedom as thereby intensely problematic. In a passage quoted below, the English Calvinist William Perkins indicates why, even for a theology as severe as his, this had to be so: if sin were a corruption of man's 'substance' then not only could he not be immortal (and thereby subjected to the eternal torment which Faustus incurs), but Christ could not have taken on his nature (see p. 168).

Once sin or evil is allowed to penetrate to the core of God's sub-ject (as opposed to being, say, an inextricable part of that subject's fallen *condition*) the most fundamental contradiction in Christian theology is reactivated: evil is of the essence of God's creation. This is of course only a more extreme instance of another familiar prob-lem: how is evil possible in a world created by an omnipotent God? To put the blame on Adam only begs the further question: Why did God make Adam potentially evil? (Compare Nashe's impudent gloss: 'Adam never fell till God made fools' [*The Unfortunate Trav-eller*, p. 269]).

Calvin, however, comes close to allowing what Perkins and Au-gustine felt it necessary to deny: evil and conflict do penetrate to the core of God's subject. For Calvin the soul is an essence, im-mortal and created by God. But to suggest that it partakes of *God's* essence is a 'monstrous' blasphemy: 'if the soul of man is a portion transmitted from the essence of God, the divine nature must not only be liable to passion and change, but also to ignorance, evil de-sires, infirmity, and all kinds of vice' (*Institutes*, I. xv. 5). Given the implication that these imperfections actually constitute the soul, it is not surprising that 'everyone feels that the soul itself is a recep-tacle for all kinds of pollution'. Elsewhere we are told that the soul, 'teeming with . . . seeds of vice . . . is altogether devoid of good' (I. xv; ii, iii). Here is yet another stress point in protestantism and one which plays like *Dr. Faustus* (and *Mustapha*) exploit: if human beings perpetuate disorder it is because they have been created dis-ordered.

The final chorus of the play tells us that Dr. Faustus involved himself with 'unlawful things' and thereby practised 'more than heavenly power permits' (ll. 6, 8). It is a transgression which has re-vealed the limiting structure of Faustus' universe for what it is, namely, 'heavenly *power*'. Faustus has to be destroyed since in a very real sense the credibility of that heavenly power depends upon it. And yet the punitive intervention which validates divine power also compromises it: far from justice, law and authority being what legitimates power, it appears, by the end of the play, to be the other way around: power establishes the limits of all those things.

It might be objected that the distinction between justice and power is a modern one and, in Elizabethan England, even if enter-tained, would be easily absorbed in one or another of the paradoxes which constituted the Christian faith. And yet: if there is one thing that can be said with certainty about this period it is that God in the form of 'mere arbitrary will omnipotent' could not 'keep men in awe'. We can infer as much from many texts, one of which was Lawne's *Abridgement* of Calvin's *Institutes*, translated in 1587—

around the time of the writing of *Dr. Faustus*. The book presents and tries to answer, in dialogue form, objections to Calvin's theology. On the question of predestination the 'Objector' contends that 'to adjudge to destruction whom he will, is more agreeable to the lust of a tyrant, than to the lawful sentence of a judge'. The 'Reply' to this is as arbitrary and tyrannical as the God which the Objector envisages as unsatisfactory: 'it is a point of bold wickedness even so much as to inquire the causes of God's will' (p. 222; quoted from Sinfield, p. 171). It is an exchange which addresses directly the question of whether a tyrannical God is or is not grounds for discontent. Even more important perhaps is its unintentional foregrounding of the fact that, as embodiment of naked power alone, God could so easily be collapsed into those tyrants who, we are repeatedly told by writers in this period, exploited Him as ideological mystification of their own power. Not surprisingly, the concept of 'heavenly power' interrogated in *Dr. Faustus* was soon to lose credibility, and it did so in part precisely because of such interrogation.

Dr. Faustus is important for subsequent tragedy for these reasons and at least one other: in transgressing and demystifying the limiting structure of his world without there ever existing the possibility of his escaping it, Faustus can be seen as an important precursor of the malcontented protagonist of Jacobean tragedy. Only for the latter, the limiting structure comes to be primarily a socio-political one.

Lastly, if it is correct that censorship resulted in *Dr. Faustus* being one of the last plays of its kind—it being forbidden thereafter to interrogate religious issues so directly—we might expect the transgressive impulse in the later plays to take on different forms. This is in fact exactly what we do find; and one such form involves a strategy already referred to—the inscribing of a subversive discourse within an orthodox one, a vindication of the letter of an orthodoxy while subverting its spirit.

MICHAEL NEILL

From Anxieties of Ending†

* * *

In *Doctor Faustus*, where mortal limitation is an even more persistent theme, the anxiety of ending becomes proportionately more intense; but here it is compounded by a gathering horror of no-

† From *Issues of Death: Morality and Identity in English Renaissance Tragedy* (Oxford: Oxford University Press, 1997), pp. 206–11. Reprinted by permission of Oxford University Press.

end.[1] What results is a frenzied climax in which longing for closure and dread of the end are almost evenly poised. In the big soliloquy that opens the play, the hero announces a beginning fraught with the consciousness of ending, where every aim appears simply to define a limit, and every *telos* is realized as a *finis*:

> Settle thy studies, Faustus, and *begin*
> To sound the depth of that thou wilt profess:
> Having commenced, be a divine in show,
> Yet level at the *end* of every art . . .
> Is, to dispute well, logic's chiefest *end*?
> Affords this art no greater miracle?
> Then read no more; thou hast attained that *end*. . . .
> The *end* of physic is our body's health.
> Why, Faustus, hast thou not attained that *end*? . . .
> Yet art thou still but Faustus, and a man.
> Couldst thou make men to live eternally,
> Or, being dead, raise them to life again,
> Then this profession were to be esteemed.
> Physic, farewell!   (I. i. 1–27; emphasis added)

At the furthest point of all his studies (an 'end' which is also the starting-point of the play) Faustus discovers not revelation but the ironic confinement of divinity, whose doctrine appears to promise him only the fearful oxymoron of ending without end:

> Why, then, belike we must sin,
> And so consequently die:
> Ay, we must die *an everlasting death*.
>   (lines 45–7; emphasis added)

Not the least significant of the powers that Faustus attributes to magic is an ability to confound divinity by reversing this threat. For magic seems to hold out the promise of achieving ends without end—a teleological 'omnipotence' (line 55) capable of surpassing all limit. But the supposedly unconditional 'whatsoever' of Faustus' pact with Lucifer absurdly conflicts with the 'wheresoever' of the Devil's counter-claim, and is effectually nullified by the strict 'four and twenty years' of its 'conditions' (II. i. 95–111). The signing of the pact itself is accomplished in language that notoriously confuses two kinds of ending:

> Now will I make an end immediately.

---

1. In my reading of *Faustus* I am considerably indebted to the seminal essays by Marjorie Garber (' "Infinite Riches in a Little Room": Closure and Enclosure in Marlowe') and Edward A. Snow ('Marlowe's *Dr Faustus* and the Ends of Desire'), both in Alvin Kernan (ed.), *Two Renaissance Mythmakers* (Baltimore: Johns Hopkins University Press, 1977), 3–21, 70–109.

. . . . .
Consummatum est, this bill is ended.
(ii. i. 71–3)

For *consummatum* read *finitum*. The writing of the bill in blood is meant to signal a new beginning, invoking a blasphemous analogy with the spiritual rebirth made possible by Christ's blood-sacrifice. Indeed in the following scene the born-again Faustus will compare himself to 'Adam [on] the first day | Of his creation' (ii. ii. 116–17); but the parodic misapplication of Christ's last words on the cross ('Consummatum est') serves as a reminder that the magician is dooming himself to an end that excludes consummation.

Christ's words will be punningly echoed once more at the beginning of Faustus' passion in Act V, when Wagner announces the conclusion of his master's diabolic Last Supper: 'Belike *the feast is done*' (v. i. 9; emphasis added)—not *consummatum* here, but *consumptum*. The magic circle that is at once the symbol and the agent of Faustus' infinite desire now becomes the sign of his fatal limitation, marking his painfully human position 'in the middest' between the rival infinities of Heaven and Hell. 'Hell', Mephostophilis warns him, with a sardonic quibble, 'hath no limits, nor is *circumscribed*' (ii. i. 121); and, as the protagonist's career 'draws towards a final end' (iv. iii. 24), the horror of an endlessness which he so easily dismissed ('I think hell's a fable'; ii. i. 127) will come to embrace the dispensation of God himself—as in Faustus' tormented vision of the heavens, red with sacrificial blood at once infinitely abundant, infinitely potent, and infinitely unattainable ('See, see where Christ's blood streams in the firmament! | One drop would save my soul, half a drop'; v. i. 287–8). By this time, the various reminders of God's 'infinite' mercies, the 'eternal joy and felicity' of heaven, its 'Innumerable joys', 'Pleasures unspeakable, bliss *without end*' (lines 174, 203, 241, 248; emphasis added) serve only as reminders of eternal death, everlasting pain, and perpetual damnation (lines 165–6, 243, 258, 276). The language of Faustus' last speech is dense with apocalyptic suggestion, and in his panic the magus is made to quote the demented kings of the earth in Revelation as they face the terrors of the End: 'mountains and rocks, Fall on us, and hide us . . . from the wrath of the Lamb' (Rev. 6: 16). But in Faustus' case it is less the prospect of punishment and suffering than the vertigo of endlessness that is felt as so unbearable. He beats his head, like Lear, against those stony words that mark the unimaginable boundary between the mortal and the infinite, time and eternity:

. . . and must remain in hell *for ever*—hell, oh, hell *for ever*! Sweet friends, what shall become of Faustus, being in hell *for ever*?

> Now has thou but *one bare hour* to live,
> And then thou must be damned *perpetually*!
> Stand still, you *ever* moving spheres of heaven,
> That time may cease, and midnight *never* come;
> Fair nature's eye, rise, rise, again, and make
> *Perpetual* day . . .
>
> Impose some *end* to my *incessant* pain;
> Let Faustus live in hell a thousand years,
> A hundred thousand, and *at last* be saved!
> No *end* is *limited* to damned souls!
>   (v. i. 187–9, 275–80, 309–12; emphasis added)

In the *mise-en-abîme* of Faustus' last soliloquy the terror of ending is locked in struggle with the even greater terror of 'no end', just
as in its final lines the fearful closure of midnight is poised against
the ghastly opening of Hell.[2] The A text of the play seeks to resolve
this tension by an act of violent scission—the sudden silencing
of Faustus' cry as the devils drag him into the hell-mouth ('Ah,
Mephostophilis!')—and by the intervention of an Epilogue that
puts striking prosodic emphasis on the sudden abruption of his career ('*Cut* is the branch. . . . Faustus is *gone*'). But these gestures
seem to have been insufficiently powerful to contain the anxieties
let loose by Faustus' torment; for the author of the B text additions
sought to allay them further in a coda that is full of the rhetoric of
ceremonial closure. 'Faustus' end', for all its fearful signs of reprobation, is to be clad in the decencies of mourning:

> We'll give his mangled limbs due burial;
> And all the students, clothed in mourning black,
> Shall wait upon his heavy funeral.
>   (lines 348–50)

The funeral pageant announced by the Second Scholar is designed
to transform the arbitrary violence of ending into a ritual of con-
summation. But even these reduplicated signs of closure need to be
reinforced in the printed text by the conclusive tolling of the motto
that adorns both versions of the play: 'Terminat hora diem; terminat Author opus.' It is as if the vertigo of Faustus' dying moments,
his dizzy gaze into the shapelessness of the infinite, had threatened
the very form of drama itself; and only by an inscription which ex-

---

2. Faustus' paradoxical terror of and longing for the end is echoed in Tourneur's D'Amville,
whose gathering terror of death comes to express itself in a similar longing for annihila-
tion or unconsciousness: 'O were my body circumvolv'd | Within that cloud, that when
the thunder tears | His passage open, it might scatter me | To nothing in the air!'; IV. iii.
248–51); 'I shall steal into my grave without | The understanding or the fear of death, |
And that's the end I aim at' (v. ii. 174). Robert Watson's 'Duelling Death', in *The Rest is
Silence*, 156–252, exposes similar contradictions in Donne's attitudes to ending.

pressly returns us to the scene of writing, insisting on the dramatist's power to write an end to his own creation, can stability be restored.

* * *

ROMA GILL

"Such Conceits as Clownage Keeps in Pay": Comedy and *Dr. Faustus*†

The buskined scorn of the Prologue to *1 Tamburlaine* would be more appropriately addressed to a reader of the play than to any contemporary audience, who appear to have demanded the customary

> jigging veins of rhyming mother-wits,
> And such conceits as clownage keeps in pay. (1–2)[1]

Offering the public a printed text in 1590, Richard Jones confessed to having personally expurgated 'some fond and frivolous gestures, digressing and, in my poor opinion, far unmeet for the matter . . . though haply they have been of some vain-conceited fondlings greatly gaped at, what times they were showed upon the stage'. No further evidence comes from the play itself, or from the comments of spectators, to identify *Tamburlaine's* 'frivolous gestures'; their digression must have been so complete that excision left no scars. Yet *Tamburlaine* is not without its moments of comedy—as in Part 1 when the conqueror mounts to his throne on the subdued back of Bajazeth (IV,ii); or where, at the height of his career in Part 2, he drives the bridled kings who draw his chariot (IV,iii). There is even a comic parallel to the main action in the scene (III,iii) in Part 1 where Zenocrate berates Zabina whilst Tamburlaine, offstage, trounces Bajazeth. But the comedy of such jokes underlines the cruelty of the play, releasing tension into near-hysteria rather than relaxation. It is immediately recognisable as Marlowe's own humour, differing only in a degree of subtlety from the refined, sardonic comedy which forms an integral part of *The Jew of Malta* and *The Massacre at Paris*.

The same style and intention characterise moments in *Dr. Fau-*

† From *The Fool and the Trickster: Studies in Honour of Enid Welsford*, ed. Paul V. A. Williams (Boydell & Brewer, 1979), pp. 55–63. Reprinted by permission of Boydell & Brewer.

1. Quotations from all Marlowe's plays except *Dr. Faustus* are taken from my own edition, *The Plays of Christopher Marlowe* (Oxford, 1971). *Dr. Faustus* is quoted from the *Parallel Texts* edition of W. W. Greg (Oxford, 1950). Quotations from Shakespeare's plays are taken from the New Arden editions.

stus. They may be comparatively light-hearted, as when the Doctor, too eager in his conjuring to specify that the devil should assume a personable appearance, orders the *'Dragon'* that responds to his invocation to

> Goe and returne an old Franciscan Frier,
> That holy shape becomes a diuell best.   (A269–70; B253–4)[2]

More sinister is the dramatic irony with which Mephostophilis deflates Faustus's pride in his new-found skill; far from being compelled to appear, the spirit explains that he 'came now hither of [his] owne accord' (A289; B270), thereby anticipating Faustus's next question, which was designed to be merely rhetorical: 'Did not my conjuring speeches raise thee?' (A290; B271). Such moments, however, are rare; and it is idle to speculate whether Marlowe was unable to sustain this manner through five acts, or whether the encounter at Deptford brought his writing of *Dr. Faustus* to an untimely end. In the event, the actors appear to have been presented with the beginning and ending of a great tragedy, and the problem of how to bridge the twenty-four years 'of profite and delight, Of power, of honour, and omnipotence' (B80–1; A83–7) for which Faustus has sold his soul.

Marlowe left enough pointers to indicate that the middle of his tragedy should be anticlimactic, faithful to its source in *The English Faustbook*[3] and showing Faustus's increasing disillusion with the vanity of his human wishes, and frustration at the limitations of supernatural (diabolic) knowledge. Comedy was inevitable; but it need not have led to the unhappy chaos that once prompted an undergraduate to adapt Aristotle's definition and describe *Dr. Faustus* as a play with 'a beginning, a muddle, and an end'. The trouble is caused largely by a lack of homogeneity in the different comic episodes, which appear to have been added by different authors at different times, and not always with the same purpose. But whilst this is greatly to be lamented on particular aesthetic grounds relating to *Dr. Faustus*, the situation has considerable general interest for the information it affords about Elizabethan modes of stage comedy.

I shall restrict my discussion here to a single scene—Act I, scene iv in modern editions—because as the site for an archaeological 'dig' it is unequalled for its variety of sherds and levels! It is the first comic scene in the play, apart from the brief interlude in scene ii where Wagner entertains the audience and bemuses the Scholars—

---

2. Normally line references for both A and B texts are given, and the accidentals are those of A; where B's reading is preferred, the B line number precedes that of A.
3. *The Historie of the damnable life, and deserued death of Doctor John Faustus*, translated into English by 'P. F. *Gent.*' in 1592.

and allows time for Valdes and Cornelius to instruct Faustus in the rudiments of their art. Scene iv is common to both A and B texts of *Dr. Faustus*, so there is no need to debate the possible authorship of Birde and Rowley, whose 'adicyones' to the play cost Henslowe £4 in 1602;[4] these are incorporated in the B text, but totally absent from A.[5] However, A and B do give slightly differing versions of this scene; in all probability, the printing of B was supervised by an 'editor' who took it upon himself to curb some of A's verbosity and repetitiveness (the stigmata of a 'reported' text), and to delete such out-dated jokes as the Horse-courser's observation that 'Doctor *Lopus* was neuer such a Doctor' (A1176), which would be topical only for a short time after the execution of Dr. Lopez in 1594.

Dr. Faustus is an ambitious and frustrated man. Despite his mastery of all human learning, he is forced to recognise that he is 'still but *Faustus*, and a man' (A53; B50). Turning his back on orthodox scholarship, he resorts to black magic, and after elaborate rituals of conjuring Mephostophilis appears. The unhappy, tormented spirit tries unsuccessfully to prevent Faustus from selling his soul to the devil, but at the end of Act I, scene iii Faustus leaves the stage rapt with a vision of supernatural power for which no price (he believes) could be too high:

> Had I as many soules as there be starres,
> Ide giue them al for *Mephastophilis*:
> By him Ile be great Emprour of the world,
> And make a bridge through the moouing ayre,
> To passe the *Ocean* with a band of men,
> Ile ioyne the hils that binde the *Affricke* shore,
> And make that land continent to *Spaine*,
> And both contributory to my crowne.
>
> (A347–54; B327–34)

Nothing but comedy could follow these mighty lines, for reasons that are not only aesthetic. Marlowe expects a *critical* sympathy for his protagonist, a balanced ambivalence of attitude arising from a rare inwardness with the character's frustrations and aspirations, together with a moral sense that is both practical and common. The parodic elements in the scene that follows re-assert the moral norm, which was first stated in the Prologue's uncompromising censure.

The scene features an interchange between Wagner and an unnamed 'Clown', and as such has many parallels among the *zanni* scenes of the Italian *Commedia dell'arte* as they are described by

4. *Henslowe's Diary*, ed. R. A. Foakes and R. S. Rickert (Cambridge, 1961), p. 206.
5. I outlined my theory of the relationship between the A and B texts in my edition of *Dr. Faustus* (London, 1965), and I have not retracted these views; a similar position was described by Fredson Bowers in his edition of the *Works* of Marlowe (Cambridge, 1973).

K. M. Lea in her study of *Italian Popular Comedy* (Oxford, 1934). One of the two traditional *zanni* is 'an awkward booby' who pretends to misunderstand what is said to him (I,63) and who 'would perjure himself for a plate of macaroni' (II,441). The other *zanni* is astute and witty, often a servant who parodies the actions of his master. When the word was introduced into English, it became synonymous with 'ape' or 'mimic'; Drayton intends pleonasm when he writes 'To Mr. Henry Reynolds'

> th' *English*, Apes and very Zanies be
> Of everything, that they doe heare and see.

The character of Wagner is developed from *The English Faustbook*, and is most probably the work of Thomas Nashe, whose pet phrases are common in his mouth.[6] The introduction of Wagner in Act I, scene ii established him in the mould of Miles, Friar Bacon's 'subsizar' in Greene's *Friar Bacon and Friar Bungay* (?1589). The relationships between Miles and Bacon, Wagner and Faustus, are academic rather than feudal—pupil:teacher and not servant: master. Impoverished undergraduates, both Miles and Wagner are repaid for their domestic services with a smattering of education; they show a cheerful pride in their positions of confidence, and in their scholastic attainment—quite unlike the grievance of Flamineo in Webster's *The White Devil* (1612) that for lack of parental means he was 'fain to heel [his] tutor's stockings At least seven years' whilst he was at the university (I,ii,322–3).[7] Wagner's first appearance was almost a solo act, as he paraded his Latin and his logic (in mimicry of Faustus) before the bewildered Scholars. But now, although he intends to imitate his master by becoming himself a master, he in fact plays 'straight man' to the Clown.

Especially in the A text, this scene reads as though it has been extemporised: Hamlet might have used it as an object-lesson in his advice to the players to 'let those that play your clowns speak no more than is set down for them' (III,ii,45–7). But the extemporising might have been permitted—perhaps even intended—by the dramatist. Letoy in Brome's *Antipodes* (1638) glances superciliously back to

> the days of Tarlton & Kempe,
> Before the stage was purg'd from barbarisme,
> And brought to the perfection it now shines with.
> Then fooles & jesters spent their wits, because
> The Poets were wise enough to save ther owne
> For profitabler uses.   (D3ᵛ)

6. Cf. Paul Kocher, 'Nashe's Authorship of the Prose-Scenes in *Faustus*', *MLQ* 3 (1942): 17–40.
7. Ed. John Russell Brown (London, 1960).

Certainly, in the scene with the Vintner and his goblet (III,iii) one of the servants, Rafe, is instructed to provide his own terms of abuse: 'I scorn you: and you are but a &c' (A995; the licence has been revoked in the B text).

The control of Act I, scene iv belongs to the Clown; he is self-indulgent in his wisecracks, but when Wagner feeds him the key line that justifies the entire scene, his professionalism is valuable. Wagner, his attention drawn to the Clown's ragged clothing, observes

> the vilaine is bare, and out of seruice, and so hungry, that I know he would giue his soule to the Diuel for a shoulder of mutton, though it were blood rawe.   (A367–9; B346–8)

The Clown repeats Wagner's remark, thereby underlining the parody of Faustus's deed and emphasising the moral norm implied in his own capping line:

> How, my soule to the Diuel for a shoulder of mutton though twere blood rawe? not so good friend, burladie I had neede haue it wel roasted, and good sawce to it, if I pay so deere.
>   (A370–3; B351–2)

The B text, here based on an 'edited' copy of A, omits the repetition, replacing it with 'Not so neither' (B350) which sadly weakens the joke and its import.

B's 'editor' also deleted most of the sequence (A391–405) immediately following Wagner's attempt to give the Clown money as an earnest of his apprenticeship. The Italians called such sequences '*lazzi*'—a term which English scholarship might find useful. Miss Lea cites a definition of *lazzi* as 'ces inutilités, qui ne consistent que dans le jeu que l'acteur invente suivant son génie'.[8] Here in *Dr. Faustus* the *lazzo* takes first the familiar form of mistaking words: Wagner offers 'gilders', and the Clown pretends to hear 'Gridyrons'. It is a form of comedy that this Clown has already used, when he pretended to understand 'knaues acre' for Wagner's 'staues acre' (A377–8). The humour is scarcely original: in *Two Gentlemen of Verona* (*c*. 1594–5) Shakespeare's Speed seems weary when Launce will not distinguish between 'Mastership' and 'Master's ship': 'Well, your old vice still: mistake the word' (III,i,285). The Clown queries Wagner's 'gilders', and the *lazzo* continues with another familiar topic. In response to his 'Gridyrons, what be they?' he is told that the coins are 'french crownes', and is able to riposte

---

8. Kathleen M. Lea, *Italian Popular Comedy: A Study in the Commedia dell' Arte, 1560–1620*, 2 vols. (Oxford: Clarendon Press, 1939), I, 68.

Mas but for the name of french crownes a man were as good
haue as many english counters.   (A394–5)

The Elizabethan chronicler, William Harrison, vouches for the re-
spectability (and antiquity) of the joke in his *Description of England*
(1587), where he writes that French and Flemish crowns are 'onlie
currant among vs, so long as they hold weight' (Book II, ch. xxv). It
is significant that there are no overtones here of the kind that
Shakespeare plays with in *Measure for Measure* (1604), when Lu-
cio's reference to 'A French crown' brings from the First Gentleman
the immediate response 'Thou art always figuring diseases in me'
(I,ii,49).

Some juggling brings this *lazzo* to an end, with both Wagner and
the Clown calling upon the audience to 'Beare witnesse' that neither is holding the gilders.

Wagner now introduces what the Italians would have called a
burla, which in the *commedia dell'arte* would have brought the
scene to an uproarious conclusion.[9] He invokes two devils, '*Baliol*
and *Belcher*' (A405; B371), and orders them to carry the Clown off
to hell. The B text is more or less true to the Italian convention: the
devils arrive, and the terrified Clown agrees to serve his conjuror
master. A's Clown, however, has more *lazzi*—an insignificant, mildly
obscene comment on the sex of the devils, after they have been
called to heel and he is safe; and, which is much more interesting,
a refusal to be scared by them:

> Let your *Balio* and your *Belcher* come here, and Ile knocke
> them, they were neuer so knockt since they were diuels, say I
> should kill one of them, what would folkes say? do ye see yon-
> der tall fellow in the round slop, hee has kild the diuell, so I
> should be cald kill diuell all the parish ouer.   (A406–11)

Predictably, when the devils enter this braggadocio is exposed: according to the stage-direction '*the clowne runs up and downe crying*'. There is nothing uncommon in the humour; but these lines
provide the key to the Clown's identity. What textual editors call
a 'reported text' is a version of the play achieved by memorial reconstruction on the part of one or more of the actors who had
performed it. In this *lazzo*, however, the Clown is recalling not
the words of *Dr. Faustus* but those of the moralistic comedy *A
Looking-Glass for London*, written by Thomas Lodge and Robert Greene, which was entered in the Stationers' Register in
March 1593/4.[1]

Lodge and Greene owed a considerable debt to Marlowe, having

9. Lea, I, 66.
1. Ed. W. W. Greg, Malone Society Reprints (Oxford, 1932).

taken much of Faustus's final soliloquy to give to their repentant
Usurer in scene xvii of *Looking-Glass*. Now their comedian, vari-
ously called 'Clown' and 'Adam', makes some little repayment.
Scene xiv in *Looking-Glass* shows Adam escorting his master's wife
home from the inn. The devil appears, and offers to carry Adam—
who has in him some traces of the Morality Vice—away to hell. His
confidence strengthened by alcohol and incantation, the Clown
stands his ground: '*Nominus patrus*, I blesse me from thee, and I
coniure thee to tell me who thou art' (G3ʳ). Reaching for his 'cud-
gell', he attacks until the devil pleads that he is mortally wounded,
and then triumphs with the boast

> Then may I count my selfe I thinke a tall man, that am able to
> kill a diuell. Now who dare deale with me in the parish, or
> what wench in *Ninivie* will not loue me, when they say, there
> goes he that beate the diuell.   (G3ᵛ)

Although in *Dr. Faustus* the action of calling up the devil parodies
that of the main plot, the Clown's lines do not arise naturally from
the situation, as they do in *Looking-Glass*; there is consequently no
doubt where the lines originated.

A further connexion between the two Clowns might be made
through their costumes. By drawing attention to his 'round slop'—
baggy trousers—the Clown permits identification with the slops he
wears in *Looking-Glass for London*, which are capacious enough to
hold a side of beef and a bottle of beer, in protest against the
Lenten fasting laws: the stage-direction instructs '*Enters Adam solus, with a bottle of beere in one slop, and a great peece of beefe in an
other*', and the Clown demonstrates to the audience '*Ecce signum*,
this right stop is my pantry' (12ᵛ). Did the baggy trousers become,
thus early, a traditional costume for the stage clown? If so, we can
recognise, some years later, a type-figure behind Jonson's Bobadill
in *Every Man In His Humour* [2] who is mocked by Downright for his
'huge tumbrell stop' and 'GARAGANTVA breech' (II,ii,24–5), until
Jonson makes the term generic when Downright calls to the poetic
Master Mathew, who is accompanied by Bobadill, 'Sirrha, you,
ballad-singer, and slops, your fellow there' (IV,ii,119–21).

In passing, certain resemblances may also be noted between the
Clown's lines in *Dr. Faustus* and those of 'Sander' (or 'Saunders')
in the anonymous *Taming of A Shrew* (Q1594).[3] Sander is the equivalent of Grumio in Shakespeare's *Taming of The Shrew*. When he is
called by another servant, 'Come hither sirha boy', he replies with
indignation

---

2. *The Works of Ben Jonson*, ed. C. H. Herford and Percy Simpson (Oxford, 1927).
3. *Narrative and Dramatic Sources of Shakespeare*, ed. Geoffrey Bullough (London, 1957).

> Boy; oh disgrace to my person, souns boy
> Of your face, you have many boies with such
> Pickadevantes I am sure.   (scene viii)

Wagner supplies the same feed-line, and receives an almost identical retort:

> How, boy? swowns boy, I hope you haue seene many boyes with such pickadevaunts as I haue. (A362)

The B text has acquired the exclamation 'O disgrace to my person' (B342), although the 'editor' has changed the (?obsolescent), 'pickadevaunts' for 'beards'. Like *A Looking-Glass for London*, *The Taming of A Shrew* is indebted to *Dr. Faustus* for many of its serious passages, but there is no need to postulate two-way traffic in the borrowing here. Quite possibly the 'pickadevaunts' opening lines come from an earlier 'level' of *Dr. Faustus* Act I, scene iv than that of the 'kill deuil' *lazzo*; they could have been transposed to *A Shrew* by quite a different clown—who was perhaps himself called Sander or Saunders. It must be admitted, however, that the actor-lists in Chambers' *Elizabethan Stage* (Oxford, 1923) record no suitable person.

Still, Chambers does identify an actor called John Adams, who played with Sussex's Men in 1576, and with The Queen's Men in 1583 and 1588 (II,296). These are the only available facts, but the actor's reputation was good enough to link him with Richard Tarlton in the memory of the Stage-keeper in Jonson's *Bartholomew Fair* (1614).[4] The Stage-keeper's recollection proves beyond a shadow of doubt that this was the Clown in *Dr. Faustus*:

> And Adams, the rogue, ha' leaped and capered upon him [Tarlton], and ha' dealth his vermin about as though they had cost him nothing.   (Induction, 38–40)

After the Clown has dropped his play with 'knaues acre' (A371), he returns to Wagner's promise that, if he enters upon his apprenticeship, he will be dressed 'in beaten silk and staues acre' (A377; B355). In the B text the Clown explains: 'Staues-aker? that's good to kill Vermine: they be-like if I serue you, I shall be lousy' (B356–7). He has understood correctly; a common insect-repellent, staves-acre [the seeds of a plant of the species *Delphinium Staphisagria*] was recommended to travellers by Thomas Nashe in the Epistle Dedicatory to his *Lenten Stuffe* (1599):[5] 'Looke how much Tobacco wee carry with vs to expell cold, the like quantitie of Staues-aker wee must prouide vs of to kill lice'.

4. Ed. G. R. Hibbard (London, 1977).
5. *The Works of Thomas Nashe*, ed. R. B. McKerrow (Oxford, 1904–10).

Wagner, his implications having been grasped, proceeds to a new threat:

> sirra, leaue your iesting, and binde your selfe presently vnto me for seauen yeeres, or Ile turne al the lice about thee into familiars, and they shal teare thee in peeces.
> (A385–8; B359–61)

The origin of the Stage-keeper's remark that Adams used to handle his 'vermin' 'as though they had cost him nothing' is to be found in the Clown's answer to Wagner, typically mistaking his meaning:

> they are too familiar with me already, swowns they are as bolde with my flesh, as if they had payd for my [B 'their'] meate and drinke.   (A390–1; B363–4)

Adams, one can deduce, was the kind of clown scathingly described by Hamlet in the Q1 advice to the players, who 'keepes one sute of jeasts, as a man is known by one sute of Apparell' (III,ii).

In *Dr. Faustus*, however, the idea of the 'familiars', and the fear of being torn to pieces by them, is alarmingly apt, since they parody— in retrospect and prospect—the substance of the play. Dr. Faustus has acquired his 'familiar', Mephostophilis, and with him the constant threat that 'diuels shall teare thee in peeces' (A709; B650). In his confession to the Scholars at the end of the play, Faustus tells them how he had often, during the twenty-four years, intended to speak of his bargain with Lucifer and ask for their prayers, 'but the diuell threatned to teare mee in peeces, if I namde God, to fetch both body and soule, if I once gaue eare to diuinitie' (A1431–3; B1966–9). With this statement, the ironic reversal of *Dr. Faustus* is completed: the scholar who boasted that he could 'commaund great *Mephastophilis*' (A276) is reduced to the level of a clown tormented by fleas, and the servant has become the master.

Ideas and Ideologies

CHARLES G. MASINTON

[Faustus and the Failure of Renaissance Man]†

* * *

Out of the ancient myth of the magician who sells his soul to the Devil for occult powers, Marlowe has fashioned a veritable fable of

---

† From *Christopher Marlowe's Tragic Vision* (Athens: Ohio University Press, 1972) 113–22. Reprinted by permission of the author.

Renaissance man—of his dreams and aspirations and, more particularly, his failures and illusions. For in Faustus we find the elements most suggestive of the Renaissance innovations in European thought. He is partly an artist, who wishes not to glorify God, as his medieval predecessors did, but to applaud and please man; he is partly a scientist and philosopher, whose hope is to make man more godlike and not to justify his miserable state on earth; and, most significantly, he is a Protestant, a Lutheran by training, who has attempted through the Reformation to escape the evils he associates with the Roman Catholic Church, only to become obsessed with the pervasive evil he sees in man's nature: an inability to avoid sin, an inborn depravity that makes damnation inescapable. Given this theological position, Faustus loses faith that his soul will be saved through God's grace, despairs, and indulges in magic in a desperate attempt to transcend his mortal state. His adventure with the powers of darkness is thus characterized by the desire to escape the conditions imposed by his religious heritage—which pictures man as a finite, suffering, damned creature—and to improvise a new, omnipotent self which will not be subject to mortality. Faustus' concerns with pagan culture, his flying, and his tricks are all designed to leave the past further and further behind, to forget what it represents. He plans to nullify his old identity as an imperfect being by originating a new context in which he can devise an ideal self. He yearns for a life of power and pleasure and is convinced that he can reach this goal merely because he commits himself to the arts of black magic. Faustus embodies the Renaissance notion that man can infinitely improve and develop himself.[1] He is an ironic figure, of course, since his attempts to be more than man by throwing over the teachings of his religious training damn him: his humanistic concern with man alone does not make room for God's mercy, and he perishes in his isolation.

Marlowe uses the form of a morality play in *Doctor Faustus*, but it is not enough to say that he follows orthodox Christian doctrine with regard to his protagonist's fate. The play does more than simply dramatize the damnation of the Christian sinner who becomes an apostate: it is also a mythic representation of the post-medieval condition of Western man as he tries to destroy or disregard the cultural influences that have shaped him in order to realize his most radical dreams. Marlowe demonstrates that the individual who disengages himself from his intellectual, social, and spiritual patrimony not only experiences a painful personal isolation from the communion of his race, but also encounters the problems of anxiety, dread, and meaninglessness. Since he chooses to usurp the

---

1. See C. S. Lewis' discussion of magic in *English Literature in the Sixteenth Century Excluding Drama* (Oxford: Clarendon Press, 1954), pp. 1–14.

power of God, Faustus has no one to blame but himself for his suffering; responsibility for his tragic failure to overreach human limitations rests with him alone. Without faith in God to give life
meaning, his vision of heroic freedom from man's estate quickly
dissolves—and in its place is left the metaphysical void. What purposes, then, can Faustus find in existence? He turns to the pleasures of magic and art and the power of scientific knowledge as
substitutes for the Christian faith he has lost. He has accepted the
temporal and secular world as all, and now he faces the hopeless
task of satisfying his yearning spirit by earthly means.

Faustus believes easily enough in the reality of the Devil, for his
Lutheran education at Wittenberg has taught him that the world,
the achievements of men, and even such traditionally dependable
inner resources as conscience and reason are under the Evil One's
control. He also believes that he lacks the means to earn God's
grace (which can save man from the Devil), for he has been taught
that man has no free will by which to achieve salvation: the will too
is in bondage to the Devil.[2] Man alone can do nothing to make
himself worthy of being saved. Faustus' only hope, according to
Lutheranism, lies in the doctrine of justification by faith. Not by
means of good works but only through faith in the mercy of a sovereign God can he be forgiven his sins and look forward to an everlasting life.[3] But Faustus, the skeptic who is completely committed
to the possibilities of this world, does not possess the requisite
faith. Since, then, he believes that men are by nature guilty, have
no free will by which to resist evil, and are therefore damned, Faustus loses hope and despairs. His soul starves because the divine
source of its sustenance is missing. And all his magic and power
over nature cannot feed his perishing spirit. His damnation is the
existential plight of the radical humanist: he is isolated from God
and must create meaning in life by imposing his individuality on
the world. The Good Angel and the Bad Angel dramatize Faustus'
conflict of soul and show that his belief in unavoidable sin out-
weighs his faith in God's grace and the efficacy of prayer.

He is a man typical of the Renaissance and modern periods because his tragedy occurs as a consequence of possessing too much
knowledge: his development as an empirical and skeptical thinker
leaves no room for faith.[4] Like his mythical predecessors in the

2. For Luther's denial of free will and his belief in man's complete inability to save himself
   without the grace of God, see *The Bondage of Will* [*De Servo Arbitro*, 1525], trans. J. I.
   Packer and O. R. Johnson (London: James Clarke, 1957), esp. pp. 144–49 and 154–56.
3. See Clifford Davidson, "Doctor Faustus of Wittenberg," *Studies in Philology* 59 (1962):
   514–23; see also Lily B. Campbell, "*Doctor Faustus*: A Case of Conscience," *PMLA* 67
   (1952): 219–39.
4. See Robert B. Heilman, "The Tragedy of Knowledge: Marlowe's Treatment of Faustus,"
   Quarterly Review of Literature 2 (1946): 316–32.

dim, Edenic past, he is fated to eat the fruit of the tree of the knowledge of good and evil, and in doing so he reluctantly becomes the Devil's disciple and loses sight of the image of God in his soul. Sad Mephistophilis is, in one sense, that nostalgic but proudly resistant side of his nature which persists in its lonely course toward damnation, the memory of lost blessedness its constant reminder of the futility of all attempts to achieve true happiness. But in another sense, the magician's evil companion is that instinct for total pleasure which man's puritanical conscience tortures and represses until hell is created within.

In the Prologue the Chorus explains, in terms of the Icarus myth, that it is pride—the rebellious spirit of self-glorification—that leads Faustus to throw over his theology and proceed to black magic. A short summary of his life shows that his background and training have formed in him a Reformation Protestant conscience, which, however, does not prevent him from turning to witchcraft:

> Now is he born, of parents base of stock,
> In Germany, within a town called Rhode;
> At riper years to Wittenberg he went,
> Whereas his kinsmen chiefly brought him up.
> So much he profits in divinity,
> The fruitful plot of scholarism graced,
> That shortly he was graced with doctor's name,
> Excelling all whose sweet delight disputes
> In th' heavenly matters of theology;
> Till, swollen with cunning of a self-conceit,
> His waxen wings did mount above his reach,
> And melting, heavens conspired his overthrow.
> For, falling to a devilish exercise,
> And glutted now with learning's golden gifts,
> He surfeits upon cursèd necromancy;
> Nothing so sweet as magic is to him,
> Which he prefers before his chiefest bliss.
> (11–27)[5]

It is precisely this strict religious conscience which, though he unconsciously plays the role of the fallen Lucifer in an attempt to do so, Faustus can never obliterate. His theological training has convinced him of his bondage to the Devil, and he cannot escape from its teachings because they are the very forms of consciousness through which he views the human condition.

His knowledge and studies have not brought him contentment because they have only reminded him of human limitation. He

---

5. All references to the play are taken from W. W. Greg's *Conjectural Reconstruction of "The Tragical History of the Life and Death of Doctor Faustus"* (Oxford: Clarendon Press, 1950).

therefore desires something more than the knowledge of philosophy or medicine: though he might "heap up gold, / And be eternized for some wondrous cure" (I.i.14–15), even that does not appeal to him. His discontent cannot be relieved, for what really disturbs him is being human, possessing only finite attributes. Being a god is the only thing that will satisfy him:

> Yet art thou still but Faustus, and a man.
> Couldst thou make men to live eternally
> Or being dead raise them to life again,
> Then this profession [i.e., medicine] were to be esteemed.
>   (I.i.23–26)

Faustus' mistake, from the theological point of view which both his religious training and the morality-play elements of the drama require us to take, is the error—a humanistic assumption—that in man's limited sciences, arts, and philosophies lie the means to satisfy his profoundest spiritual needs, though according to Christian tradition they are fulfilled only in God. Ironically, the Wittenberg Protestantism that Faustus knows is itself preoccupied with man—his guilt, his sinful nature, his great unworthiness to be saved by God, and his powerlessness before the Devil.[6] Faustus knows that he will be saved only if he has faith that through Christ he can expect mercy, but here too Faustus is blocked: faith is possible only as a gift from God,[7] and Faustus cannot imagine that God will show mercy to a creature as sinful as he. The famous scholar is convinced so strongly of his sin that hope for salvation is impossible. Faustus is put in the paradoxical predicament of damning himself by his theology:

> *Stipendium peccati mors est.* Ha! *Stipendium . . .* The reward of sin is death: that's hard. *Si peccasse negamus, fallimur, et nulla est in nobis ueritas.* If we say that we have no sin, we deceive ourselves, and there's no truth in us. Why, then belike, we must sin, and so consequently die.
>
> > Ay, we must die an everlasting death.
> > What doctrine call you this? *Che serà, serà:*
> > What will be, shall be! Divinity, adieu!
> >   (I.i.39–46)

Through a false syllogism he arrives at a deterministic conclusion about man's fate. He is so intent on the first part of the New Testament passage he reads from Romans 6:23 that he fails to notice what follows: "but the gifte of God *is* eternal life through Iesus

---

6. See *Luther's Works*, 55 vols., gen. eds. Jaroslav Pelikan and Helmut T. Lehmann (Philadelphia: Muhlenberg Press, 1958–67), XXXIV, 164–65, and 178–87.
7. *Luther's Works*, XXXI, 362–63 and XXXIV, 173–74.

Christ our Lord." Faustus here seems—as Luther often does—to be more Manichean than Christian, since he assumes that the power of evil has complete sway over the forces of good in the world.[8] In the second passage he reads (I John 1:8), he again deceives himself, because its message is tempered with these reassuring words from the following verse: "If we acknowledge our sinnes, he is faithful and iust, to forgive vs our sinnes, & to clense vs from all vnrighteousness" (I John 1:9).[9] Faustus sees only that half of revealed truth that, as a Lutheran who accepts the doctrine that it is impossible for man to overcome sin, his argument permits him to see. Like Tamburlaine, he is fooled by his rhetoric into imagining a false fate for himself. This illusion about inevitable damnation so terrifies him that he turns to magic as an escape. But magic, too, is illusory, and Faustus damns himself by confining his consciousness to a world of fantasy. He chooses twenty-four years of entertainment and the distractions of flimsy tricks to keep his mind from brooding over his "everlasting death." But he soon finds that he cannot surpass his status as a creature and that finally he must accept the end to which all men are subject.

Since he can do nothing to relieve his fate as a man, he will commune with spirits and attempt to become a god. But it is a mad course that he chooses—futile and ridiculous from the beginning. Just as he is about to receive the magicians Cornelius and Valdes, who teach him their lore, his *psychomachia* is dramatized by the Good Angel and the Bad Angel. The former counsels him to read the Bible; his evil counterpart, however, urges Faustus, in terms that hint at the myth-making powers of the artist, to usurp divine power through magic:

> Go forward Faustus, in that famous art
> Wherein all nature's treasury is contained:
> Be thou on earth as Jove is in the sky,
> Lord and commander of these elements.
> (I.i.72–75)

And Faustus answers,

> How am I glutted with conceit of this!
> Shall I make spirits fetch me what I please,
> Resolve me of all ambiguities,
> Perform what desperate enterprise I will?
> I'll have them fly to India for gold,
> Ransack the ocean for orient pearl,

8. J. P. Brockbank, *Marlowe: "Dr. Faustus"* (London: Edward Arnold, 1962, pp. 13–15, 39, and 54.
9. For these two passages I have used the Geneva Bible (1560), which was the most widely used translation during Marlowe's life.

> And search all corners of the new-found world
> For pleasant fruits and princely delicates.
>
> (I.i.76–83)

If this speech suggests the imaginative soaring of the artistic spirit,
Faustus' speech of welcome to the two magicians Cornelius and
Valdes makes it doubly clear that he thinks of himself as a sort of
artist. In it he compares himself to Musaeus, the legendary Greek
poet who was said to be either the pupil or the son of Orpheus.
(Musaeus was also the name given the author of a late fifth-century
or early sixth-century Greek poem on the love of Hero and Leander—the work which gave Marlowe the outline for his poem.) The
reference to the poet's descent into hell—though Marlowe probably
confuses it with the famed visit to the underworld by the mythical
poet-musician Orpheus—ironically prepares us for the fate that
awaits Faustus:

> Valdes, sweet Valdes, and Cornelius,
> Know that your words have won me at the last
> To practise magic and concealèd arts;
> Yet not your words only, but mine own fantasy,
> That will receive no object, for my head
> But ruminates on necromantic skill.
> Philosophy is odious and obscure,
> Both law and physic are for petty wits,
> Divinity is basest of the three,
> Unpleasant, harsh, contemptible, and vild;
> 'Tis magic, magic, that hath ravished me.
> Then, gentle friends, aid me in this attempt,
> And I, that have with concise syllogisms
> Gravelled the pastors of the German church,
> And made the flowering pride of Wittenberg
> Swarm to my problems as the infernal spirits
> On sweet Musaeus when he came to hell,
> Will be as cunning as Agrippa was,
> Whose shadows made all Europe honour him.
>
> (I.i.98–116)

Art is a kind of magic which transforms the world, and the close
relationship between art and the occult is here intimated in the reference to Cornelius Agrippa, the sixteenth-century German physician and student of magic, whose namesake teaches the forbidden
knowledge to Faustus in the play. Agrippa's name follows that of
Musaeus so closely that a comparison of the two men is suggested:
they both control elements of the spiritual world and are therefore
apparently able to transcend the boundaries of ordinary mortals.
The artist and the magician can live as God in fantasies of their

own creation, forgetting for a time the limitations of mortality. Marlowe's picture of Faustus is, at least here, probably autobiographical. A former student of theology who openly questioned Christian beliefs, the creator of sixteenth-century England's best known erotic poem, *Hero and Leander*, Marlowe must have felt deeply the pain that attends the loss of religious conviction and welcomed the temptation to indulge in an imaginative reconstruction of the world. And so it is with Faustus, who has decided to abandon a deterministic theology in favor of the freedom he thinks magic offers. He will become a god, as he tells us in his opening soliloquy:

> A sound magician is a demi-god;
> Here tire my braines to get a deity!
> (I.i.60–61)

This usurpation of the powers of God is, of course, a mortal sin— and a fearsome irony; for in trying to ignore the possibility of damnation altogether, Faustus condemns himself by reenacting Lucifer's archetypal sin.[1] And though he at first seems willing to give his soul as the price for accepting the black art, he later sees his mistake and falls into the worse sin of despair.

The short second scene comically reflects the specious logic by which Faustus justifies his turning to magic. His servant Wagner discourses lengthily and almost meaninglessly when the two scholars ask him where Faustus is, yet finally informs them that Faustus is in the company of Cornelius and Valdes. This scene does not advance the action, but it serves to put the first scene into perspective. Faustus is not a very much better logician than Wagner; both substitute a high-sounding rhetoric for exact discourse.

The powerful scene in which Faustus blasphemes the Holy Trinity and conjures comes next. His Latin incantations are no less than a Black Mass, a perverted form of ritualistic worship in which evil spirits are called upon. Mephistophilis appears as an ugly dragon, but the surprised magician charges him to "Go, and return an old Franciscan friar" (I.iii.25)—a command whose anti-clerical satire reminds us of Ithamore's blunt statement to Barabas, "Look, look, Mr. here come two religious Caterpillers" (IV.1529), at the approach of Friar Bernardine and Friar Jacomo. Faustus feels that his power as a conjurer has raised the diabolical spirit, but Mephistophilis tells him that the devils come to tempt a soul whenever they hear the Trinity blasphemed. Yet Faustus is not convinced of his powerlessness to command supernatural beings, nor does he fear the results of his evil commitment:

---

1. See Helen Gardner, "Milton's 'Satan' and the Theme of Damnation in Elizabethan Tragedy," *English Studies*, NS, 1 (1948) 49–51; see also Brockbank, pp. 37–38.

> There is no chief but only Beelzebub,
> To whom Faustus doth dedicate himself.
> This word 'damnation' terrifies not me,
> For I confound hell in Elysium:
> My ghost be with the old philosophers!
> (I.iii.56–60)

He imagines a pleasant fate for himself after death because he rejects the Christian view of what awaits the unrepentant sinner and, in its place, turns for comfort to the myth of the dwelling place of the blessed shades offered by classical mythology. Faustus again partakes of the spirit of the artist—and resembles particularly the Renaissance artist, who joined the humanist scholars in joyously rediscovering the world of Greece and Rome. It is only speculation, but surely here all of Marlowe's sympathies are engaged, as he looks back longingly, through the eyes of Faustus, to the once-fresh world of pagan antiquity, before the Christian awareness of sin came between man and the pure, sensuous enjoyment of his life.

The nostalgic tone that is evident at times during the play, and is again present in the famous Helen speech (V.i.98–117), corresponds to Faustus' (and Marlowe's) sense of the loss of some earlier, original experience of psychological wholeness or of unity between man and nature. The ideally beautiful past, which can never be recaptured but seems to hold the secret of happiness, is a minor motif running throughout Marlowe's dramas; it reveals a playwright aware of the end of an epoch. As the medieval synthesis of philosophy, science, and religion crumbles and Marlowe intuits the threat of personal chaos in the brave new world of the Renaissance, he gazes wistfully back into the distant, classically serene past for the innocence and newness which are missing from his age of intellectual upheaval. Caught between one world dying and another yet unborn, he feels the emptiness and lack of faith that pervade a culture as it loses the traditional values that give it a sense of order. The typical action of his plays thus describes the tragic fate of a protagonist who fails to cope with the radically new circumstances that—though he has arrogantly created them in the hope of possessing enormous powers and endless delights—deprive him of his sustaining dreams. Tamburlaine once enjoyed Zenocrate and the illusions of never-ending conquest. Barabas had his wealth and his commercial empire; Edward was King of England; Dido was happy with her lover Aeneas; and Faustus was the great Doctor of Divinity who astounded the scholars at Wittenberg. But now these joys are gone, and Marlowe's protagonists suffer the severe sense of deprivation and melancholy this loss inflicts upon them. Ironically, their misled attempts to break through the limitations of their original conditions of being bring only an increased awareness of limitation—and a tragic end besides. In a sense, they set out on radically independent journeys away from the center of an older, more serene world in an attempt to find personal meaning or fulfillment; they are all protestors—Protestants, if you will—discontented questers who throw over the Old Order to discover a new one. And Faustus is the arch-Protestant, in whose eccentric course is the summing-up of the experience of the others. What he and they discover is not a newer, braver kind of salvation in their own designs but the lack of coherence to which Donne's *First Anniversary* testifies. They are lonely figures who find that both psychologically and philosophically the center cannot hold when they serve their anarchic impulses through the furious drive to replace what they sense to be man's lost perfection.

* * *

ALAN SINFIELD

Reading Faustus's God†

The Tragical History of Doctor Faustus has afforded a marvelous interpretive challenge to Christian humanists who feel they should discover Marlowe to be endorsing a nice, decent kind of god.[1] However, my argument thus far should suggest another plausible Christian reading. Elizabethan orthodoxy would make Faustus's damnation more challenging than most modern readers might expect, by denying that Faustus had a choice anyway: it would regard Faustus, not as damned because he makes a pact with the devil, but as making a pact with the devil because he is already damned. "Before the foundations of the world were laid," it says in the seventeenth of the Thirty-nine Articles, "he hath constantly decreed by his counsel secret to us, to deliver from curse and damnation those whom he hath chosen." And Faustus, an Elizabethan might infer from his blasphemous, dissolute,

† From *Faultlines: Cultural Materialism and the Politics of Dissident Reading* (Berkeley: University of California Press, 1992) 230–37. Reprinted by permission of the University of California Press.

1. For a good selection of critics on the play, including James Smith, W. W. Greg, J. C. Maxwell, Helen Gardner, Cleanth Brooks, J. B. Steane, and L. C. Knights, see John Jump, ed., *Marlowe: "Dr Faustus": A Casebook* (London: Macmillan, 1969). However, Una Ellis-Fermor found the God of *Faustus* to be "sadistic" and revolt against him only proper (Jump, ed., *Marlowe*, p. 43). For more recent attitudes, see Stephen Greenblatt, *Renaissance Self-Fashioning: From More to Shakespeare* (Chicago: University of Chicago Press, 1980), ch. 5; Jonathan Dollimore, *Radical Tragedy: Religion, Ideology, and Power in the Drama of Shakespeare and His Contemporaries* (Brighton: Harvester, 1984), ch. 6; Simon Shepherd, *Marlowe and the Politics of Elizabethan Theatre* (New York: St Martin's Press, 1986), pp. 100–108, 136–41.

and finally desperate behavior, exemplifies the fate of the reprobate.
The article continues: "So, for curious and carnal persons, lacking
the Spirit of Christ, to have continually before their eyes the sentence of God's predestination is a most dangerous downfall, whereby
the devil doth thrust them either into desperation, or into wretchlessness of most unclean living, no less perilous than desperation." In
Kyd's *The First Part of Hieronimo* (c. 1585), the villainous Lazarotto
declares himself just such a person:

> Dare I? Ha! ha!
> I have no hope of everlasting height;
> My soul's a Moor, you know, salvation's white.
> What dare I not enact, then? Tush, he dies.[2]

That Faustus might be in such a condition is supported by Mephostophilis's claim:

> 'Twas I that, when thou were't i' the way to heaven,
> Damm'd up thy passage; when thou took'st the book
> To view the scriptures, then I turn'd the leaves
> And led thine eye.
>
> (5.2.86–89)

If Faustus was guided by Mephostophilis, the decision was God's.
For protestant thought could not tolerate devils wandering round
the world at whim: God does not just allow their activities, he contracts out tasks to them. They are "God's hang-men," King James
wrote, "to execute such turns as he employs them in."[3] However,
Calvin says, it is only the reprobate who are ultimately subject to
them—God "does not allow Satan to have dominion over the souls
of believers, but only gives over to his sway the impious and un-
believing, whom he deigns not to number among his flock" (*Institutes* 1.14.18). So Mephostophilis's intervention would be part of
Faustus's punishment within the divine predetermination.

The issue is focused in Faustus's first speech when he juxtaposes
two texts: "The reward of sin is death," and "If we say that we have
no sin we deceive ourselves, and there is no truth in us." It appears
that it has been arranged who shall sin and die; Faustus concludes:

> Why then, belike we must sin, and so consequently die.
> Ay, we must die an everlasting death.
> What doctrine call you this? *Che sera, sera.*
> What will be, shall be.
>
> (1.1.40–46)

2. Kyd, *First Part of Hieronimo and The Spanish Tragedy*, ed. Andrew Cairncross (Lincoln: University of Nebraska Press, 1967), *First Part of Hieronimo*, 3.59–62.
3. King James I, *Daemonologie (1597), Newes from Scotland (1591)* (London: Bodley Head, 1924), p. 20.

Christians who wish usually manage to evade this discouraging thought. Douglas Cole says Faustus's texts are "glaring half-truths, for each of the propositions he cites from the Bible is drawn from contexts and passages which unite the helplessness of the sinner with the redeeming grace of God"; Cole's implication is that Faustus is so eager to damn himself that he disregards God's generous offers.[4] To be sure, "the wages of sin is death" continues: "but the gift of God is eternal life"; and the second quotation, about everyone sinning and dying, continues: "If we confess our sins, he is faithful and just to forgive us our sins, and to cleanse us from all unrighteousness." But Calvin uses the first text—all of it—to emphasize that salvation is entirely God's decision: the desert of all is death but some receive eternal life through "the gift of God" (*Institutes* 3.14.21). And Tyndale in his *Exposition of the First Epistle of St John* (1531) uses the second text to demonstrate that we have no say in the success of our confession: "our nature cannot but sin, if occasions be given, except that God of his especial grace keep us back: which pronity to sin is damnable sin in the law of God."[5] So God may indeed forgive us our sins if we repent, but some at least will be damned for sins to which they have, in their nature, a "pronity." Faustus's summary, "What will be, shall be," may be irreverent, but it is in the mainstream of Reformation thought. If he draws not comfort but blasphemy from his reading, that will perhaps be for the reason given by Tyndale in a rubric in the Prologue to the first edition of his *Exposition of . . . John*: "If God lighten not our hearts, we read the scripture in vain."[6]

If Faustus is damned from before the start (to pursue the hypothesis), what then of his efforts to repent? For modern readers and audiences who do not already know the story, there is a question: will he change or not? For Elizabethan orthodoxy the answer was the same again: repentance is not something for the individual to achieve, but a divine gift. "It is not in our powers to repent when we will. It is the Lord that giveth the gift, when, where, and to whom it pleaseth him," Phillip Stubbes declares.[7] So if Faustus does not have it, there is nothing he can do. Yet there are the injunctions of the Good Angel, which appear to represent, like the personifications in a morality play, a choice open to Faustus:

4. Douglas Cole, *Suffering and Evil in the Plays of Christopher Marlowe* (Princeton: Princeton Univ. Press, 1962), p. 198. Cole recognizes that Faustus's behavior is typical of the reprobate, but still believes he makes "his original choice by himself" (pp. 199–201). See also Helen Gardner and J. B. Steane, in Jump, ed., *Marlowe*, pp. 95, 181–82. Malcolm Kelsall says Faustus's tone and failure to complete his quotations show a superficial attitude and "would be picked on by any school child" (*Christopher Marlowe* [Leiden: Brill, 1981], p. 163). The texts are 1 John 1:8–9 and Rom. 6:23.

5. T. H. L. Parker, *English Reformers* (London: SCM Press, 1966), p. 111.

6. G. E. Duffield, ed., *The Work of William Tyndale* (Appleford, Berks: Sutton Courtenay Press, 1964), p. 175.

7. Stubbes, *Anatomie of Abuses*, 1:190. However, Calvin seems uneasy at *Institutes* 3.3.24.

GOOD ANGEL:	Faustus, repent; yet God will pity thee.
BAD ANGEL:	Thou art a spirit [sc. devil]; God cannot pity thee.
FAUSTUS:	Who buzzeth in mine ears I am a spirit?
	Be I a devil, yet God may pity me;
	Yea, God will pity me if I repent.
BAD ANGEL:	Ay, but Faustus never shall repent.

Exeunt Angels.

FAUSTUS: My heart's so harden'd I cannot repent.

(2.2.12–18)

If Faustus's heart is hardened and he cannot repent, who has hardened it? This was a key question in the theology of election and reprobation. In Exodus (chapters 7–14) it is stated repeatedly that God hardens Pharoah's heart against the Israelites, so that he refuses to let them go despite divine smiting of the Egyptians with diverse plagues. This was taken as a paradigm of the way God treats the reprobate. Paul alludes to it when he confronts the question in the Epistle to the Romans: "Therefore hath he mercy on whom he will have mercy, and whom he will he hardeneth" (Rom. 9:18). Luther stressed this text, and Erasmus was obliged to admit that it appears to leave nothing to human choice.[8] For Calvin it was plain: "When God is said to visit in mercy or harden whom he will, men are reminded that they are not to seek for any cause beyond his will" (*Institutes* 3.22.11). Hence Donne's lines: "grace, if thou repent, thou canst not lack; / But who shall give thee that grace to begin?" (Holy Sonnet 4). And that is why Faustus can speak repentant words and it makes no difference. He actually calls upon Jesus: "Ah, Christ my saviour, my saviour, / Help to save distressed Faustus' soul." But the response is the entrance of Lucifer, Belzebub, and Mephostophilis: "Christ cannot save thy soul, for he is just," says Lucifer (2.2.83–85). Is this a devilish manipulation or a theological commonplace? It may be both—as Banquo says, instruments of darkness may tell us truths; it is the argument offered by Lawne's apologist for the *Institutes*.

Why then the appeals of the Good Angel? "What purpose, then, is served by exhortations?" Calvin asks himself. It is this: "As the wicked, with obstinate heart, despise them, they will be a testimony against them when they stand at the judgment-seat of God; nay,

---

8. E. Gordon Rupp and Philip S. Watson, eds., *Luther and Erasmus: Free Will and Salvation* (Philadelphia: Westminster Press, 1969), pp. 230–31, 64. Sidney's theory of poetry centers upon the claim that people are moved by it, but he accepts nevertheless that in Alexander Pheraeus, it "wrought no further good in him" beyond that he "withdrew himself from hearkening to that which might mollify his hardened heart" (Philip Sidney, *Miscellaneous Prose of Sir Philip Sidney*, ed. Katherine Duncan-Jones and Jan van Dorsten [Oxford: Clarendon Press, 1973], pp. 96–97).

they even now strike and lash their consciences" (*Institutes* 2.5.5). On this argument, the role of the Good Angel is to tell Faustus what he ought to do but cannot, so that he will be unable to claim ignorance when God taxes him with his wickedness. This may well seem perverse to the modern reader, but is quite characteristic of the strategies by which the orthodox deity was said to maneuver himself into the right and humankind into the wrong. Perkins declares:

> Now the commandment of believing and applying the Gospel, is by God given to all within the Church; but not in the same manner to all. It is given to the Elect, that by believing they might indeed be saved; God inabling them to do that which he commands. To the rest, whom God in justice will refuse, the same commandment is given not for the same cause, but to another end, that they might see how they could not believe, and by this means be bereft of all excuse in the day of judgment.[9]

Such doctrine was preached from almost every pulpit.

Faustus is amenable at every point, I think, to a determined orthodox reading. Yet the play might do more to promote anxiety about such doctrine than to reinforce it. For although I have felt it necessary to argue for the Reformation reading, *Faustus* is in my view *entirely ambiguous*—altogether open to the more usual, modern, free-will reading. The theological implications of *Faustus* are radically and provocatively indeterminate.

A good deal might depend on which version is being used, for many of the exchanges added in the B text seem to sharpen the theological polarity. They include the lines where Lucifer, Belzebub, and Mephostophilis gloat over Faustus (5.2.1–19), and the speeches where Mephostophilis says he led Faustus's eye when he read the Bible and where the Good and Bad Angels vaunt over Faustus (5.2.80–125). These additions enhance the impression that the Reformation god is at work; William Empson argues that they were demanded by the censor, who wanted it clear that Faustus must suffer and be damned for his conjuring. Empson calls them "the sadistic additions," finding their "petty, spiteful, cosy and

9. William Perkins, "A Discourse of Conscience," in Thomas F. Merrill, ed. *William Perkins, 1558–1602, English Puritanist: His Pioneer Works on Casuistry* (Nieuwkoop: B. De Graaf, 1966), pp. 20–21; see William Lawne, *An Abridgement of the Institution of Christian Religion*, trans. Christopher Fetherstone (London, 1585), pp. 53, 72–73, 221. Apropos of the second commandment, where God promises to visit "the iniquity of the fathers upon the children unto the third and fourth generation" (Deut. 5:9), Lawne's objector is told that children are justly punished for the iniquity they themselves commit "when God taketh away grace and other helps of salvation from a family" (Lawne, *Abridgement*, pp. 86–87).

intensely self-righteous hatred" untypical of Marlowe.[1] Given the intermittent nature of the evidence, Empson's theory must be regarded as a stimulating indication of the awkward status of orthodoxy in the play, rather than as right or wrong. In any event, what Empson does not quite take on board is that the B text adds also two major passages that are *more* sympathetic to Faustus: the kind and gentle exhortation of the Old Man (5.1.36–52), and the scene after Faustus's removal to hell in which the Scholars resolve to mourn and give him due burial (5.3). These passages plant in the play a moral perspective alternative to God's. The Old Man and the Scholars pray for Faustus right up to the end, though theologians like Tyndale say we should not pray for apostates—except for their destruction, "as Paul prayed for Alexander the coppersmith (the ii Timothy, the last), 'that God would reward him according to his works.' "[2] The Old Man speaks

> not in wrath,
> Or envy of thee, but in tender love,
> And pity of thy future misery.
> (5.1.48–50)

Unlike in the A text at this point, the Old Man is far gentler than the Good Angel, who anyway has not visited Faustus for nine hundred lines and has only reproaches left to contribute (5.2.92–108; B text only). The Scholars, in the face of the horrific evidence of Faustus's destruction ("See, here are Faustus' limbs, / All torn asunder by the hand of death" [5.3.6–7]), agree to hold a noble funeral. It is rather like the endings of Euripides' *Hippolytus* and *Bacchae*, where the gods stand aside after their disastrous intrusions upon human affairs and the people draw together in sorrow and compassion.

This is why I say the B text sharpens the theological polarity, whereas Empson says it is only more sadistic: both the Reformation god and a more genial alternative are presented more vividly. This produces the possibility, which would also fit the sense most readers have of Marlowe as an author, that at some stage at least the play was written to embarrass protestant doctrine. Richard Baines alleged that in order to persuade men to atheism, Marlowe "quoted a number of contrarieties out of the scripture,"[3] and the strenuous efforts of Christian humanist critics to tame the play to their kind

---

1. William Empson, *Faustus and the Censor* (Oxford: Basil Blackwell, 1987), p. 168 and ch. 6. Empson dismisses as insignificant Faustus's uncompleted biblical quotations (discussed above), on the ground that "to accept the promises of God requires a miracle" anyway, "and it had been vouchsafed to Luther but not to Faust" (p. 169).
2. In Parker, ed., *English Reformers*, p. 142.
3. Richard Baines's allegation, quoted from Paul Kocher, *Christopher Marlowe: A Study of His Thought, Learning, and Character* (New York: Russell & Russell, 1962), p. 36.

of order suffice to make it worth considering whether *Faustus*
dwells provocatively upon such contrarieties. However, as I have argued in earlier chapters, there need not have been a precise intention in either direction, and no version of the play may represent,
or ever have represented, a single coherent point of view. Substantial texts are in principle likely to be written across ideological
faultlines because that is the most interesting kind of writing; they
may well not be susceptible to any decisive reading. Their cultural
power was partly in their indeterminacy—they spoke to and facili-
tated debate. But whoever rewrote parts of *Faustus*, and from whatever motive, the revisions indicate an unease with Reformation
theology and help to make plain the extent to which any extended
treatment cannot but allow contradictions to be heard—by those
situated to hear them.

A similar confusion appears in the text of Nathaniel Woodes's
The Conflict of Conscience (1581), a play usually adduced to set off
Marlowe's superior verse and humanity. It is based on the story of
one Francesco Spiera, which was translated in 1550 and reissued
in 1569–70 with a preface by Calvin. In Woodes's play, Philologus,
despite good protestant beginnings, is tempted and indulges in
worldly delights, and concludes that he is "reprobate" and cannot
be saved: "I am secluded clean from grace, my heart is hardened
quite."[4] But the play appeared in print in 1581 in two issues of the
same quarto edition, and with two contrasting endings. In the first
Philologus kills himself and is indeed damned; in the second, a joyful messenger reports that he renounced his blasphemies at the last
moment. (Both versions are headed on the title page "An excellent
new Commedie.") Evidently someone involved in the publication
was worried. The two endings of *The Conflict of Conscience* correspond to the main alternatives in the Christian dilemma: either
God must know who is to be damned and therefore, since he created everyone, must be responsible for people going to hell; or God
has set the world going but has left it to myriad individual people to
decide how it will all turn out. In the former version it is hard to
discern his goodness; in the latter, he may be good but is disconcertingly impotent (perhaps rather than paring his fingernails, as
James Joyce has it, he is gnawing them in suspense). Historically,
each of these two theologies has fed on the inadequacy of the
other. And so with the predestinarian and free-will readings of *Faustus*. In Marlowe's play they are, in effect, simultaneously present,
but they cannot be read simultaneously; instead they obstruct, en-

4. Nathaniel Woodes, *The Conflict of Conscience* (Oxford: Malone Society, 1952), lines
2116, 2151. See Celesta Wine, "Nathaniel Wood's *Conflict of Conscience*," *PMLA* 50
(1935): 661–78; Lily B. Campbell, "*Dr Faustus*: A Case of Conscience," *PMLA* 67
(1952): 219–39.

tangle, and choke each other. In performance, one or the other may be closed down, but the texts as we have them offer to nudge audiences first this way then that, not allowing interpretation to settle. *Faustus* exacerbates contrarieties in the protestant god so that divine purposes appear not just mysterious but incoherent.

Even critics who believe Faustus is able to choose freely do not thereby prevent the play from provoking embarrassment about God. They cannot settle the point at which Faustus is irrevocably committed, and this is related to God's goodness—the later the decision, the more chance Faustus seems to have. Many theologians have held apostasy to be irrevocable—the "sin against the Holy Ghost," the one that cannot be forgiven. The homily "Of Repentance" declares, "they that do utterly forsake the known truth do hate Christ and his word, they do crucify and mock him (but to their utter destruction), and therefore fall into desperation, and cannot repent." Richard Hooker said the same.[5] If this is so, Faustus's fate is settled very early, and most of the play shows God denying him further chance to repent; the effect is quite close to a predestinarian reading. No doubt this is why others have maintained that Faustus's situation becomes irretrievable when he conjures; or when he signs; or when he rejects the Good Angel; or when he visits hell; or when he despairs; or when he consorts with Helen; or not until the last hour. Such interpretive scope hardly makes for a persuasive theology. It may lead to the thought that there is no coherent or consistent answer because we are on an ideological faultline where the churches have had to struggle to render their notions adequate. It may suggest not only that Faustus is caught in a cat-and-mouse game played by God at the expense of people, but also that God makes up the rules as he goes along.

Finally, *Faustus* disrupts any complacent view of orthodox theology through its very nature as a dramatic performance. Even for an audience that finds Faustus's blasphemy horrifying, an actor might very well establish a sufficient empathic human presence to make eternal damnation seem unfair. Faustus himself manifests at one point a morality provocatively superior to God's. Anticipating the terror of his last hour, he refuses the support of the Scholars: "Gentlemen, away, lest you perish with me" (there is no knowing what God might do)—"Talk not of me, but save yourselves and depart" (5.2.67–70). At this moment, when human companionship might be most desired, Faustus puts first his friends' safety. As with the Old Man and the Scholars, a generous concern for others is shown

---

5. *Certain Sermons or Homilies* (London: Society for Promoting Christian Knowledge, 1899), p. 568; Hooker, *Of the Laws of Ecclesiastical Polity*, intro. C. Morris (London: Dent, 1969), 1:295. See also Calvin, *Institutes* 3.3.22; Ian Breward, ed., *The Work of William Perkins* (Abingdon: Sutton Courtenay Press, 1970), p. 254.

persisting in people beyond the point (whenever that is) where the Reformation god has decided that eternal punishment is the only proper outcome. It is one thing to argue in principle that the reprobate are destined for everlasting torment, but when Faustus is shown wriggling on the pin and panic-stricken in his last hour, members of an audience may think again. If this is what happened, for some at least, then there are two traps in the play. One is set by God for Dr. Faustus; the other is set by Marlowe, for God.

MARJORIE GARBER

[Writing and Unwriting in *Doctor Faustus*]†

* * *

"What means this show? Speak, Mephistophilis," demands Faustus in his peremptory—and slightly querulous—fashion. "Nothing," replies the equable and witty Mephistophilis, a born deconstructer. "Nothing, Faustus, but to delight thy mind, / And let thee see what magic can perform" (*Doctor Faustus* II. i, 82–84). Yet Mephistophilis, of course, does not mean "nothing"—or means it only in a deliberately ironic and doubling sense. For the magic show he produces to delight and distract Faustus's mind comes at a crucial point in the dramatic action—the point when Faustus has just attempted to sign away his soul. When Faustus stabs his arm and begins to write in blood his "deed of gift of body and of soul" to Lucifer, he exclaims, "My blood congeals, and I can write no more" (II. i. 61), and Mephistophilis, drily acknowledging the legendary thermal properties of hell, announces he will "fetch thee fire to dissolve it straight." Faustus's problematic effort at inscribing and subscribing is one of the key signatures of the play. Faustus must write in order that he be damned.

But even in his failure to write, Faustus is caught up in a ceremony of signing that puts him into conflict and competition with, as well as mimetic parody and imitation of, not one but two other authors, or authorities—the author of the play, and the Author of the Universe, who is also the Author of the Scriptures. For it is the unwilled appearance of an inscription on Faustus's arm, advising-him to flee, that sets Mephistophilis on to his diversionary tactics, and produces the magic demonstration—a representation which is, in turn, described as "nothing." At this pivotal moment, the play be-

† From "'Here's Nothing Writ': Scribe, Script, and Circumscription in Marlowe's Plays," *Theatre Journal* 36 (1984): 308–14. Reprinted by permission of Johns Hopkins University Press.

comes a plot of simultaneous writing and unwriting—the more
Faustus would write, the more "here's nothing writ."

Marlowe's *Doctor Faustus* begins, not with an act of writing, but
with a scene of *reading*. "Settle thy studies, Faustus, and begin,"
says the protagonist to himself (I. i. 1), invoking, as he does so often, his own magic name—throughout the play he will address
himself in this curious and characteristic vocative third person. He
reviews the possible primary texts of study—Aristotle's *Analytics*,
written in Greek, Galen's medical treatises, in Latin, Justinian's *Institutes* on Roman law, and "Jerome's Bible"—the Vulgate—all the
classic works of the humanistic heritage—and he rejects them all in
favor of magic. What does he mean by magic?

> Lines, circles, letters, and characters;
> Ay, these are those that Faustus most desires.
> Oh, what a world of profit and delight,
> Of power, of honor, and omnipotence,
> Is promised to the studious artisan!
>
> [I. i. 52–56]

Lines, circles, letters and characters—these are indeed the signs
and signifiers of magical arts. But more specifically and locally in
Marlowe's play they are the elements of *language*, of writing. "Oh,
what a world of profit and delight." We do not need the reminder of
Horace here to see Faustus as a man enraptured by the idea of
making, of poesis, of poetry—of becoming author of himself.

"O Faustus, lay that damned book aside, / And gaze not on it"
(71–72) urges the Good Angel. "Read, read the Scriptures" (74).
But Lucifer and Mephistophilis are always at hand to offer him
other texts. Throughout the play, Faustus's reading is bound up
with questions of textual authority. Even when, at the close of the
play, he pledges in a famous gesture to "burn my books!" (V. i. 331),
he is corrected, overruled, and overwritten by the Chorus in the
Epilogue: "Burned is Apollo's laurel bough / That sometime grew
within this learned man." (Ep. 2–3). Although Faustus himself
vows to become "conjuror-laureate," in his own dangerous phrase,
in the opening moments of the play he is counseled by his fellow
conjurors, Valdes and Cornelius, to first learn "the words of art"
by means of which he will soon become "perfecter" than they at
conjuring (I. iv. 34; i. 159). Advised by Valdes to carry with him
not only "Bacon's and Albanus' works," traditional medieval texts
of magic, but also "the Hebrew Psalter and New Testament"
(155–56), he withdraws with his colleagues to dinner, where "after
meat / They'll canvass every quiddity" (164–165).

When we next see Faustus he is a practicing conjuror, and also
explicitly a writer, an inscriber as well as a circumscriber, accompa-

nied by Lucifer and four attendant devils. "Faustus, begin thine incantations," he counsels himself, echoing and transmuting his first
line in the play, "and try if devils will obey thy hest":

> Within this circle is Jehovah's name,
> Forward and backward anagrammatized;
> Th'abbreviated names of holy saints,
> Figures of every adjunct to the heavens,
> And characters of signs and erring stars,
> By which the spirits are enforced to rise:
>
> [I. iii. 8–13]

Writing the name of Jehovah is a manifestly taboo or forbidden
act. Faustus's blasphemous enterprise is, however, doomed to self-
subversion. For to anagrammatize the name of Jehovah—to rearrange its letters so as to form a new word—is merely to replicate
the original pious replacement of the tetragrammaton, YWVH—a
term the Jews considered too holy for utterance, and therefore
pointed with vowels from the Hebrew word "Adonai," or "Lord," as
a direction to the reader to substitute a permissible euphemism for
the ineffable name. Jerome actually incorporates this substitution
when he speaks of "Jehovah" in his vulgate translation of Exodus 6:3, and he is followed in this practice by Wyclif and other English translators.

Moreover, the sacred tetragrammaton itself signified God's power
by virtue of its ambiguities. The most widely accepted etymological
explanation of YWVH associates the word with the Hebrew *hayah*,
"to be," construing the term as it might be written or pronounced
in full as either *Yahveh*, "He who causes to be," or *Yahuah*, "He who
indeed will (show himself to) be," employing the third person singular masculine of the imperfect tense of the verb "to be" in its oldest form. As the complexity of tense and syntax in the English
rendering indicates, the name of God was itself a multivalent sign,
declaring by its linguistic and grammatical form that God tran-
scended the ordinary limits of time and individual history.[1] Faustus
attempts to undo the existence and power of the Author of the
Scriptures by placing His name in time, by writing the Name forward and backward inside a circle, and thereby asserting his own
role as a new author and a new authority. In doing so, however, he
performs an inadvertently pious transcription of a name which had
always been ineffably multiple and indeterminate.

At the same time, Faustus's attempt to invert the name of God is
doomed by the very nature of the written language itself. For to a
reader and speaker of English (or, indeed, of German, the language

---

1. W. Gunther Plaut and Bernard J. Bamberger, *The Torah: A Modern Commentary* (New
York: Union of Hebrew Congregations, 1981), pp. 425–26.

of Faustus's Wittenberg) Hebrew writing *is* backward, its characters inscribed from right to left upon the page. Correctly understood, correctly read, backward is forward and forward is backward—as it will be, indeed, throughout *Doctor Faustus*. The Bad Angel repeatedly urges Faustus to "Go forward in that famous art" of magic (I, i. 75; II. i. 15), while the Good Angel and the Old Man implore him to repent and go back to God. Likewise the Chorus points darkly in the Epilogue to Faustus as an unhappy example of those "forward wits" who suffer a "hellish fall" because they are enticed "To practice more than heavenly power permits" (Ep. 7–8).

The idea that language can be made to go forward and backward at will, continually writing and unwriting itself, is one that we will hear Faustus frequently express in one form or another. When, for example, Mephistophilis suggests that because of his sacrilegious pranks the Pope will have him excommunicated with bell, book, and candle, Faustus answers merrily, "Bell, book and candle—candle, book, and bell,—/Forward and backward, to curse Faustus to hell!" (III. ii. 97–98), and at the beginning of Act II as he waits in his study to see if Lucifer will accept the terms of his bargain, we hear him caution himself, "Now go not backward; Faustus, be resolute" (II. i. 6).

If Faustus is able to "be resolute" to "go not backward," it is by vowing to invert, or "unwrite," the ritual and the sign at the heart of Christ's contract. He continues his self-address:

> The God thou serv'st is thine own appetite,
> Wherein is fixed the love of Belzebub:
> To him I'll build an altar and a church,
> And offer lukewarm blood of new-born babes.
> [II, i. 11–14]

This mockery of the Mass is only one of several hinted at in the play. Another will come when Faustus, made invisible, snatches the "meat" and "wine" from the Pope, who should himself be dispensing the Eucharist. The friars with bell, book, and candle intone "Cursed be he that stole his Holiness' meat from the table!" and "Cursed be he that took away his Holiness' wine!" (III. ii. 103, 113), and this rather comic malediction is immediately followed by a scene in which Robin and Dick enter with a cup they have stolen from the vintner. The pregnant Duchess of Anholt requests that Faustus procure her "no better meat than a dish of ripe grapes" (IV. v. 18).[2] Indeed, when Faustus first takes up conjuring, he does

2. The sacramental interchangeability of the two species, bread and wine (or in *Faustus'* terms "meat" and "grapes"), had been firmly asserted by the Council of Trent: "It is most true that there is as much contained under either species as under both, for Christ exists whole and entire under the species of bread, and under every part of the species, whole too and entire under the species of wine and under its parts." (*Council of Trent*,

so over "meat" shared with his disciples, Valdes and Cornelius, an event to which his servant Wagner's "wine, if it could speak," could testify (I. ii. 7). That off-stage meal is not self-evidently a Last Supper, or a parody of one. But when we look at all these Eucharistic gestures in the light of the central writing scene with which we began, each apparently trivial incident suggests and contributes to a prevailing pattern. For the writing of Faustus's "deed of gift of body and of soul" is the making of a testament—a last testament and a new testament. Written in blood, substituting blood for ink, it superscribes—or rather, attempts to superscribe—Christ's own testament of body and blood.

In law a testament is a will, a formal declaration, usually in writing, of a person's wishes as to the disposal of his property after his death. Faustus writes not one but two such testaments in the course of the play. One, explicitly described as "Faustus' latest will" (V. i. 154) and "my will" (156), bequeaths his real property, his "wealth, / His house, his goods, and store of golden plate, / Besides two thousand ducats ready coined" to his servant Wagner (V. i. 2–4). The other, the "deed of gift" (II. i. 59, 89), is likewise in law "an instrument of writing," and has, as we have seen, been written and signed previously; it pledges "body and soul, flesh, blood, or goods" (110–111) to Lucifer and his agent Mephistophilis. Prefaced by study and reading, then, the dramatic life of Faustus is demarcated within the play by these two acts of writing, which are in several senses equally acts of playwriting.

A third sense of "testament," of course, is that described in the Scriptures: a covenant between God and man. This is the primary meaning of the word in the passage from St. Mark—the source for the rite of the Holy Eucharist—where Jesus says to his disciples, giving them bread, "Take, eat, this is my body," and giving them wine, "This is the blood of the new testament, which is shed for many." The new testament of Christ renews and fulfills the old testament of Moses and the prophets, and the Epistle to the Hebrews combines the two latent meanings of testament as "covenant" and "will," explaining that Christ "is the mediator of the new testament, that by means of death, for the redemption of the transgressions that were under the first testament, they which are called might receive the promise of eternal inheritance. For where a testament is, there must also of necessity be the death of the testator. For a testament is of force after men are dead; other wise it is of no strength at all while the testator liveth. Whereupon neither the first testament was dedicated without blood" (Hebrews 9:15–18).

By Marlowe's time a "testament" was clearly a book or text as

Sess. 13, cap. 3. Cited in Matthew Britt, ed., *The Hymns of the Breviary and Missal* [New York: Benzinger Brothers, 1948], pp. 167–68.)

well as a "deed," a speech-act committed to writing. As we have seen, Valdes refers to the "New Testament" as a "work" that can be carried into a secret place as an instrument of magic, together with the works of Bacon and Albanus, and in the *Faerie Queene* Red Crosse gives Prince Arthur "a booke, wherein his Saveours testament / Was writ" (I. ix. 19). But in the play, the insistent, or at least repeated, act of making a will reifies the implicit analogy (and disjunction) between Christ's written testament and Faustus's will-ful deed, a conjunction of word and practice which is itself repli-cated by the act of writing—and performing—the play. Both words, "*will*" and "*deed*," incarnate the speech-acts they embody, trans-forming by the very act of executing them a spoken pledge into an inscribed written artifact. "What might the staying of my blood por-tent?" asks Faustus when his blood congeals. "Is it unwilling I should write this bill? / Why streams it not, that I may write afresh? / Faustus gives to thee his soul" (II. i. 63–66).

"See, see, where Christ's blood streams in the firmament" he will later cry, when hell is discovered and the clock strikes eleven. "One drop would save my soul, half a drop" (V. i. 286–287). "Why streams it not?" "See . . . where Christ's blood streams." Faustus's timely writer's block is yet another sign he will not heed, or read, and so he *signs*. As the Old Man will point out, now only the sacra-ment of Christ can correct or erase this error in writing: "thy Savior sweet / Whose blood alone must wash away thy guilt" (V. i. 63).

It is frequently observed that in *Doctor Faustus* Marlowe demon-strates his indebtedness to the morality tradition, in the retention and subversion of such figures as the Good and Bad Angels, the Seven Deadly Sins, and the repentant Old Man.[3] Yet his play also owes—and pays—a debt to the other native dramatic heritage of the English Renaissance stage, the miracle or cycle play, performed on the Feast of Corpus Christi, that celebrates the Eucharistic mir-acle of transubstantiation. And the doctrine of transubstantiation is itself, manifestly, the quintessential metaphor. According to that doctrine, the bread and wine of the Eucharist *are* the body and blood of Christ, though their exterior semblance remains the same as before, just as Christ on earth *is* the Word made Flesh. As we shall see all these metaphors of transformation participate in the writing and unwriting—the re-signing—of Marlowe's text.[4]

3. E.g., David M. Bevington, *From Mankind to Marlowe: Growth of Structure in the Popu-lar Drama of Tudor England* (Cambridge, Mass.: Harvard University Press, 1962); Nicholas Brooke, "The Moral Tragedy of *Doctor Faustus*," *Cambridge Journal*, 5 (1952) 662–87; David Kaula, "Time and the Timeless in *Everyman* and *Doctor Faustus*," *College English* 22 (1960), 9–14.
4. See C. L. Barber. " 'The form of Faustus' fortunes good or bad," *Tulane Drama Review* 8 (1964), 92–119. Barber suggests that "We can . . . connect the restriction of the impulse for physical embodiment in the Protestant worship with a compensatory fascination in

When Marlowe went up to Cambridge in 1580–81, it was as a member of "the Ancient and Religious Foundation of Corpus Christi and the Blessed Virgin Mary," so named after the medieval Guilds which had united for the founding. Marlowe entered Corpus Christi College as a Canterbury scholar under a provision made by the celebrated Archbishop Matthew Parker, Master of Corpus from 1544 to 1553. In the library of Corpus, endowed with Parker's magnificent bequest of books and manuscripts, Marlowe read plots and exotic place names which he would incorporate into *Tamburlaine* and *Edward II*; there, too, he might have found and transposed the haunting, disembodied final line of *Doctor Faustus*, "*Terminat hora diem; terminat Author opus*"—a phrase that occurs in precisely that form in a manuscript from the Archibishop's collection.[5]

But Corpus Christi College itself, its eponymous sacrament, and its Name-Day Festival in celebration of that sacrament, offered a potential source and text of a somewhat different kind, and one equally relevant to Marlowe's work. In the 1550s, the College found itself besieged by the complex and troublesome question of the nature of the Eucharistic sacrament, the doctrine of transubstantiation and the Real Presence of Christ's body and blood. For a College founded and named in honor of the Guild of the Precious Body of Jesus Christ such an issue was inevitably a sensitive one. In his official revision of Cranmer's Forty-Two Articles, Archbishop Parker struck a precarious balance between claims for a real, corporeal presence and the reformer's reduction of the sacrament to a purely figurative sign: "The Body of Christ is given, taken, and eaten in the Supper, only after an heavenly and spiritual manner. And the mean whereby the Body of Christ is received and eaten in the Supper is Faith." H. C. Porter wryly observes, "that was a hit—a palpable hit—at the Real Absence."[6]

When we consider such theoretical and doctrinal issues as the Real Presence (or Absence) and the dogma of transubstantiation in terms of the semiotics of theatre,[7] we can see the remarkable, though risky, opportunity offered to the dramatist—especially a

the drama with magical possibilities and the incarnation of meaning in physical gesture and ceremony" (p. 97), and argues persuasively that the imagery of orality and devouring, eating and being eaten in *Faustus* is linked to the protagonist's own "blasphemous need, in psychoanalytic terms" (p. 107).

5. Parker MS, 281, fol.78*v*. Cited in John Bakeless, *The Tragicall History of Christopher Marlowe* (Cambridge, Mass.: Harvard University Press, 1942), 1, 293.
6. H. C. Porter, *Reformation and Reaction in Tudor Cambridge* (Cambridge: Cambridge University Press, 1958), p. 67.
7. Barber suggests the connection between sacramental doctrine and a major shift in semiotic perspective when he speaks of the "semantic tensions" involved in viewing the Eucharist as a "bare sign": "the whole great controversy centered on fundamental issues about the nature of signs and acts, through which the age pursued its new sense of reality," "Faustus' Fortunes," 97.

young and daring dramatist like Marlowe, who had almost surely, by the terms of his scholarship, studied for holy orders, and who could not in any case have avoided the ferment or the controversy, whatever his own ultimate religious choice. If the Corpus Christi Day procession was the most picturesque event in medieval Cambridge's civic drama, the Mass was English Christendom's purest moment of theatre. In fact, the Protestant liturgical reformers' attempt to turn the Mass into a communion was directly analogous to the Tudor and Elizabethan dramatists' efforts to transform the nature of the theatrical experience. The Protestant reformers set out to alter the central ceremony of Christian worship in England from a sacrifice offered to God by a priest on behalf of the people to one which suggested, in both words and actions, a feast in which the worshippers entered into communion with Christ by receiving the elements of the Eucharist.[8] The worshippers became, in effect, a participating audience, whose belief insured the efficacy of the performance.

In a manifest way, the theatrical medium offered a special opportunity for articulating—or disarticulating—semiotic problems of presence and absence, since by the convention of dramatic transactions a character may be at once "absent" and "present" from the stage, like the ghost of Old Hamlet in Gertrude's closet, or Banquo at the banquet in *Macbeth*.[9] For Marlowe, the "invisible" presence of Faustus at the Pope's feast in Act III, scene ii provides a telling, and, at the same time, safely comic, commentary on presence and absence in the Mass. The feast as staged in *Faustus* is doubly an anti-Mass, both because the Pope approaches the meat and wine in an epicurean rather than a sacramental manner, and because he is physically prevented from partaking of the "troublesome banquet" (80) by Faustus's prankish intervention. Neither locally nor spiritually, then, is a "real presence" distributed or consumed. Faustus himself becomes a visible absent presence who effects a series of locally present absences.

The visual element of tour-de-force and practical joke in this scene would very likely have been intensified by the onstage appearance of the cowled friars, for the canonical office for Corpus Christi was written, at the request of Pope Urban IV, by the most illustrious of Dominican Friars, Saint Thomas Aquinas. The text of *Faustus* is not explicit about the order to which the Pope's attendant friars belong, but the Dominicans, or Black Friars, were the traditional Preaching Friars. Moreover, Marlowe's company would al-

8. T. M. Parker, *The English Reformation to 1558*, 2nd ed. (London: Oxford University Press, 1966), pp. 99–100.
9. See Thomas Cartelli, "Banquo's Ghost: The Shared Vision," *Theatre Journal* 35:3 (1983): 389–405.

ready have possessed a set of black friars' robes, since the friars in *The Jew of Malta* are described as "friars of Saint Jaques" (III. iii. 33), so-called after the Dominican church of St. Jacques in Paris. That the Pope's bumbling friars would belong to the same order as the learned and eminent Friar who set the office for Corpus Christi Day and defined the Eucharistic sacrament is an incidental, but perhaps not accidental, irony whose effect would be more directly felt by a sixteenth century audience than by a modern one.

For any audience interested in semiotics and the magical properties of signs, however, it is instructive to consider Saint Thomas's compositions for Corpus Christi Day as a kind of subtext for *Doctor Faustus*. The festival's magnificent hymns explicitly acknowledge an analogy between the transforming power of language (the word and the Word) and the transubstantiation of bread and wine into flesh and blood. The hymn *Pange, lingua, gloriosi* declares, "*Verbum caro, panem verum / Verbo carnem efficit / Fitque sanguis Christi merum*" ("By his word, the Word-made-Flesh changes true bread into flesh / And makes wine into the blood of Christ"). The conspicuous word-play on word (*Verbum, verum, Verbo*) and flesh (*caro, carnem*) offers a poetic equivalent to the transubstantiation of the two species, bread and wine, into their divine counterparts. Here, then, is yet another version of sacred writing, Eucharistic magic words at work, the opposite of Faustus's "anagrammatized" and inverted Black Mass on Jehovah's name.

Perhaps even more suggestive are lines from another of Saint Thomas's Corpus Christi hymns, "*Panis angelicus fit panis hominum*; / *Dat panis caelicus figuris terminum*" ("Thus Angels' bread is made the bread of man; / the heavenly bread puts an end to types and figures").[1] In this case the concept of ending (*terminum*) familiar throughout *Faustus* is expressed as a paradoxical form of beginning—the end of the Old Testament in the realization of the New, the end to types and figures itself figured forth in the Incarnation of Christ. "This Sacrament, the embodied fulfillment of all the ancient types and figures," Saint Thomas calls it.[2] And this is just what Faustus, for all his vainglory, is not; he *is* a figure, a representation, a terminable fiction, a dramatic creation who perversely tries to turn blood into ink as an act of willful self-inscription—the antithesis of a creating Word who selflessly transforms wine into blood as an act of grace.[3]

1. "*Sacris solemniis juncta sint gaudia.*" Texts and commentaries on the Corpus Christi hymns can be found in Britt, *Hymns*, pp. 166–93. I am indebted to Michael J. O'Loughlin for this suggestion.
2. Thomas Aquinas, "Sixth Lesson for Corpus Christi Day," in *Selected Writings*, ed. M. C. D'Arcy (London: Dent, 1939, rev. ed., 1964), p. 40.
3. A passage in the *Summa Theologica* comments with provocative pertinence on the whole question of metaphor and metonymy as it relates to the Eucharistic sacrament. "*Hic est calix sanguinis mei* is a figurative expression, which can be understood either by

The play's instrumental triad of blood/wine/ink is thus divisible into two binarisms, blood/wine and blood/ink, where one is associated with Christ and seems clearly holy, the other associated with Faustus's devilish bargain, and therefore unholy. Yet this division will not stay divided. *Someone* intervenes, inscribing Faustus's arm with a warning, yet another sign:

> But what is this inscription on mine arm?
> *Homo, fuge!* whither should I fly?
> If unto God, he'll throw me down to hell.
> My senses are deceived; here's nothing writ:
> Oh yes, I see it plain; even here is writ,
> *Homo, fuge!* Yet shall not Faustus fly.
>
> [II. i. 73–78]

Moreover, the determinedly blasphemous "*Consummatum est,* this bill is ended," (II. i. 73), pronounced as he signs his name to the deed of gift, once again indicates the incommensurability of the devilish and the divine, now through Faustus's radical misunderstanding of time and sequence. Christ on the cross could put a period, a point, an end, to the sentence that was God on earth, the Word made Flesh, just as His sacrifice, emblematized in the sacrament of the Eucharist, "put an end to types." But, as Faustus will later discover, "no end is limited to damned souls" (V. 1: 312). The continually iterated word "limit," which for Faustus means both scope and bound, is both his temptation and his downfall. He strives to limit others and in himself to exceed all limits, to write his life backward and forward as he chooses. And, like the hapless victims of fairy tale wish-fulfillment trials, he gets, ironically, just what he bargains for, the letter of the law, and has to suffer the excessive consequences. His is a *life sentence*, both compound and complex, as well as a sentence of death.

Stanislavski suggested to the actors in his theatre that they think of their characters in terms of verbs rather than nouns, since "every objective must carry in itself the germ of action." Thus the actor should express himself in some form of the sentence "I wish to do [X]."[4] Michael Goldman has justly observed that "what ravishes the Marlovian actor can never be contained within what a method ac-

---

metonymy or by metaphor. Metonymy signifies the container for the contained, and the sense, which is then, *This is my blood contained in the chalice,* is justifiable, for Christ's blood is sacramentally consecrated as drink for the faithful, an idea better conveyed by the term *cup* than *blood.* By metaphor Christ's Passion is signified, as when he himself said, *Father, if it be possible, let this chalice pass from me.* This sense of the consecration formula is then, *This is the chalice of my Passion*" (*Summa Theologica,* 3a, lxxviii, 3.1). Quoted in Thomas Aquinas, *Theological Texts,* ed. and trans., Thomas Gilby (London: Oxford University Press, 1955), pp. 370–71.

4. Constantin Stanislavski, *An Actor Prepares,* trans. Elizabeth Reynolds Hapgood (New York: Theatre Arts Books, 1936), p. 116.

tor would call an 'objective,'" since "the ravished man's desire
swells beyond any specific goal."[5] For Faustus, however, this act of
striving is both more boundary breaking and more doomed, because the verb after which he strives, that which he wishes to *do*, is
God's verb; the verb intrinsic and implicit in Jehovah's name, the
verb "to be," "to pre-exist," which has neither beginning nor end.
"Stand still, you ever moving spheres of heaven, / That time may
cease, and midnight never come, / . . . / The stars move still, time
runs, the clock will strike, / The devil will come, and Faustus must
be damned" (V. i. 277–285).

Faustus's "will" becomes, at the last, both a noun and a verb. His
deed of gift is not a divine metaphor like Christ's Eucharist, but instead a fallen, time-bound, and limited dramatic metonymy, based
upon an accidental or contingent connection with magic and magical power, rather than an essential similarity. His power is tran-
sumptive rather than authoritative; his will and deed are not the
plot of the play, but a counterplot countenanced by another author.
Thus, though he claims that "a sound magician is a demi-god,"
(I. i. 63) his own powers are derived from his perverse testament,
and rather than integration and transubstantiation he incurs dispersal and displacement at the play's end.

The comic scenes in Act IV have shown the audience a Faustus
with a false head and leg, both of which are removed without personal injury, and with apparently magical effect. But this dismemberment is repeated in a different spirit in the final scene, when an
appalled and awestruck scholar discovers the necromancer's scattered remains. "Oh, help us heaven!" he cries, "See, here are Faustus' limbs / All torn asunder by the hand of death," and a few
moments later, "We'll give his mangled limbs due burial" (V. i.
337–338, 348). Here once again we find a curious intertextual relation between *Doctor Faustus* and the liturgical office for Corpus
Christi Day. In the Fifth Breviary Lesson Saint Thomas writes of
the miracle of the Eucharist, "Nothing more marvellous, for there
it comes to pass that the substance of bread and wine is changed
into the body and blood of Christ. He is there, perfect God and perfect man, under the show of a morsel of bread and a sup of wine.
He is eaten by his faithful, *but not mangled*. Nay, when this Sacrament is broken, in each piece he remains entire."[6] The Latin phrase
is *sed minime laceratur*, and *laceratur* is usually rendered as "mangled" in English translation. The ceremony of Faustus's dispersal—
which is the play—offers, then, one more disjunction, rather than

---

5. "Marlowe and the Histrionics of Ravishment," in Alvin Kernan, ed., *Two Renaissance
   Mythmakers: Christopher Marlowe and Ben Jonson* (Baltimore: Johns Hopkins University
   Press, 1977), p. 22.
6. Thomas Aquinas, *Theological Texts*, p. 366.

conjunction, with the Eucharistic rite. "The appearance of bread and wine remain, but the Thing is not bread or wine," continues the lesson. Yet it is precisely Faustus's tragedy that he is reduced to the "accidents" of his appearance, the ironic stage buffoonery of the clown, less than the sum of his parts.

Early in the play, Wagner anticipates this radical dismemberment when he threatens a Clown with punishment unless the Clown agrees to bind himself as his servant: "I'll turn all the lice about thee into familiars, and make them tear thee in pieces" (I. iv. 22–23). Even at this point the trope of fragmentation is firmly tied to the blasphemous de-centering of the Eucharist; the Clown equably replies, "you may save yourself a labor, for they are as familiar with me as if they had paid for their meat and drink." An audience inclined to dismiss this exchange as merely low and not very forceful banter might find itself disconcerted to hear Mephistophilis echo it, much later, in a characteristic inversion of forward-backward language: "Revolt [i.e., turn back to Satan from God] or I'll in piecemeal tear thy flesh" (V. i. 85). Rather than being integrated into the metaphor of the body and blood of Christ, Faustus is excluded and decentered, displaced. To the triad of blood/wine/ink we can here perhaps add a second, equally concerned with the metatheatrical materials of Marlowe's art: flesh/bread/ and props or stage properties: a wooden leg, a false head. Faustus is incarnated as a dramatic character, not an autonomous author, and, as Marlowe's written supplement to his play, *terminat Author opus*, declares, the author, not the self-inscribed character, ends the work. Marlowe signs his own writ, which must be executed. "The clock will strike, / The devil will come, and Faustus must be damned."[7]

*   *   *

KATHARINE EISAMAN MAUS

[Marlowe and the Heretical Conscience]†

*   *   *

[T]he nature of theater in Marlowe's plays is refracted through what I would call a "heretical conscience." This "heretical conscience" does not, however, merely refer to Marlowe's own actual, now irrecover-

7. For another perspective on the dismemberment of Faustus, see Edward A. Snow. "*Doctor Faustus* and the Ends of Desire," in *Mythmakers*, p. 94ff.
† From *Inwardness and Theater in the English Renaissance* (Chicago: U of Chicago P, 1995), pp. 87–93. Reprinted with the permission of the University of Chicago Press and the author.

able, opinions or behaviors. Nor is it simply a matter of his use of precedents—the influence upon him, for instance, of Foxe's *Acts and Monuments*, one of the sources for *Tamburlaine* and *Dr. Faustus*. Rather it is a matter of Marlowe's recognizing that the primary political and religious crises of his time are closely related to the issues that make the Renaissance theater seem so promising and so dangerous.

In *Dr. Faustus*, Marlowe adapts an indigenous morality drama that in its original or pure form seems to fulfill all the criteria of pedagogical theater as the protheatricalists Sidney and Heywood imagine it. Dramas like *Everyman* attempt to convey lessons to the audience about problems of general concern. Everybody is going to die. Everybody worries about it, or ought to. The effect of universality in the morality play is intensified by its allegorical technique. Groups of people may be represented by a single character, like John Commonweal in Lindsay's *Satire of the Three Estates*. On the other hand, the traits, moods, or psychic components of an individual may be dispersed into various allegorical personifications, like Fancy, Despair, and Good Hope in Skelton's *Magnificence*, so that the message of the play seems to be reinforced by an entire community of characters. This dramaturgy is the product of a culture in which the difference between an individual and a group has not become highly charged, in which the boundaries between one individual and another are neither rigid nor ethically decisive. In the theatrical universe of the morality play, it is reasonable to imagine the audience as an essentially unanimous group that sees exemplary versions of itself mirrored in the abstract, generalized situations acted before it.

Well before Marlowe's time, however, morality drama had begun to change. Sixteenth-century morality plays are increasingly likely to treat relatively specialized topics, like the dilemma of the youthful prodigal or of the unwise ruler. As Bernard Spivack writes, "The human situation . . . is treated from some partial point of view, and restricted to the vices characteristic of some mode or station of life."[1] This particularizing tendency begins to confound the rather simple kinds of identification between character and spectator that Renaissance defenders of the theater take for granted. For instance, Heywood recommends chronicle history plays for stirring the patriotism of English kings:

> What English prince should he behold the true portraiture of that famous King Edward the third, foraging France . . . and would not suddenly be inflamed with so royal a spectacle, being made apt and fit for the like achievement.[2]

1. Bernard Spivack, *Shakespeare and the Allegory of Evil* (New York: Columbia University Press, 1958), p. 207.
2. Thomas Heywood, *An Apology for Actors* (London, 1612), B4ʳ.

In the same vein, Sidney reminds us that Alexander took his copy of
Homer with him on his campaigns, in order to be inspired by the
example of Achilles. It might be obvious why Alexander would learn
from Homer, or why an English king would be thrilled by a play
about Edward III, or why every man would want to see *Everyman*.
It is less obvious what a butcher, or a merchant's wife, or an apprentice would find compelling about the *Iliad*, or about a history
play that deals entirely with the lives of the nobility. Sidney and
Heywood presume that the social usefulness of theater flows from
audiences' perception of a close resemblance between their own
lives and the lives depicted onstage. As I mentioned in the last
chapter, however, the unprecedented successes of the English Renaissance theater are grounded upon the surprising willingness of
mass audiences to interest themselves in situations and in kinds of
characters remote from anything they encountered outside the
Globe or the Swan. Although, as we have seen, Kyd muses upon
the curious workings of fellow feeling in *The Spanish Tragedy*,
nothing in late sixteenth-century writing about the theater explicitly acknowledges the challenge contemporary dramaturgy poses to
conventional accounts of audience response.

Marlowe, however, seems to recognize that his innovative theater
must work its sweet violence from an oblique angle. At the conclusion of *Dr. Faustus*, the fate of the protagonist is described as
straightforwardly edifying:

> Regard his hellish fall,
> Whose fiendful fortune may exhort the wise
> Only to wonder at unlawful things,
> Whose deepness doth entice such forward wits,
> To practice more than heavenly power permits.
>
> (5.3.23–27)

But what, exactly, are spectators supposed to learn from Faustus? It
is not clear that his "fortune" fits the pattern of exemplary instruction upon which the epilogue depends. In the play's opening lines,
the Chorus announces his uniqueness in ways that suggest limitation:

> Not marching in the fields of Thrasimene,
> Where Mars did mate the warlike Carthagens,
> Nor sporting in the dalliance of love
> In courts of kings where state is overturned,
> Nor in the pomp of proud audacious deeds,
> Intends our muse to vaunt his heavenly verse.
>
> (Prologue 1–6)

Faustus's story is only one among many possible stories, marked off
grammatically ("not . . . nor . . . nor") and generically from epic,

erotic, or chivalric plots. The Chorus emphasizes disparities, not similarities, among possible theatrical protagonists; so that Faustus's own tendency to cast himself as Everyman seems characteristically egoistical and myopic. If, however, each individual's story is different from every other's, then the exhortatory value of other people's experiences becomes questionable.

Throughout *Faustus*, Marlowe makes the individualist and naturalistic conventions of tragedy collide abruptly with the collectivist, allegorical procedures of the morality play, deliberately emphasizing the irreconcilability of the two genres.[3] The generic dislocation creates a series of dilemmas or equivocations where none seemed to exist before. W. W. Greg does not know what to make of Faustus's body: on the one hand Faustus seems to become a "spirit" upon signing the contract with the devil; on the other hand, much later in the play, Faustus "commits the sin of demoniality [with Helen], that is, bodily intercourse with demons."[4] Likewise Wilbur Sanders disapproves of Marlowe's inconsistent representation of Hell.[5] As the play proceeds toward its terrifying climax the physical location of hell and its corporeal horrors are increasingly emphasized, particularly in the B version, even though Mephistophilis earlier maintains that hell is not a place, but a state of mind: "Why, this is hell, nor am I out of it" (1.3.78). Such complaints may seem merely obtuse, since hell may be for the orthodox believer simultaneously a physical place and a state of mind, and damnation both a material and spiritual condition. Inadvertently Greg and Sanders identify, however, a consistent strain of inconsistency in *Faustus*: equivocations structured by theologico-political disputes over the relationship between bodies and minds, matter and spirit. These are the very controversies that, as we have already seen, dominate the heresy trial and its conceptualization by dissident and orthodox alike.

The imagery of Communion in *Faustus*, for instance, works in the same ambiguous way.[6] It is entirely consistent with Marlowe's tactics elsewhere in *Faustus* that the two quasisacramental moments in which the facts of the body seem most vividly present are also possibly but not necessarily moments of delusion: when Faustus's blood clots on his arm, and he momentarily sees *"homo fuge"* written there, and then again when Christ's blood streams in the firmament, apparently forever out of reach. For here again, con-

3. For a contrary view, which sees *Faustus* as essentially continuous with the morality tradition and its "movement . . . therefore inevitably towards orthodoxy rather than iconoclasm," see Michael Hattaway, "The Theology of Marlowe's *Dr. Faustus*," *Renaissance Drama* new series 3 (1970): 51–78.
4. W. W. Greg, "The Damnation of Faustus," *Modern Language Review* 41 (1946): 97–107.
5. Wilbur Sanders, *The Dramatist and the Received Idea: Studies in the Plays of Marlowe and Shakespeare* (Cambridge: Cambridge University Press, 1968), pp. 194–242.
6. C. L. Barber notes the importance of Communion imagery in "The Form of Faustus' Fortunes Good or Bad." *Tulane Drama Review* 8 (1964): 92–119.

temporary debates focus upon whether the elements undergo a material change (the Catholic position) or a change in spiritual character (the Lutheran position) or merely a transformation in the minds of the believers (the Zwinglian position). Renaissance disputes over the nature and power of devils run along similar lines. Some argue that devils can bring about material changes; others that they are at best masters of illusion; others that devils are pure hallucinations, projections of a guilty imagination.[7] These debates involve not merely disagreements about the source and efficacy of supernatural phenomena, but disagreements over the nature of, and the possibility of interaction between, matter and spirit. Thus when Faustus is dismembered and then reconstitutes himself in the comic scenes with the Horse-Courser, or when "Helen passes over the stage"—perhaps a resurrected historical Helen, perhaps a devil inhabiting Helen's corpse, perhaps a devil metamorphosed as Helen's duplicate—the uncanny fluidity of supernaturally controlled bodies obscure what exactly is happening and also, at the same time, whether the categories for specifying what might be happening are even appropriate. As in the heresy trial, it is not just a matter of labeling particular phenomena, of dividing or refusing to divide the realm of the body from the realm of the spirit, but of deciding what the terms of such classification are to signify.

The two texts we have of *Faustus*, the relative authority of which is endlessly debated among textual editors, inflects the action in opposite directions: the largely inner and spiritual struggles of the A text become extroverted, theatrical, and corporeal in the B text. The different versions exploit, that is, alternative interpretive options for the allegorical, psychomachic conventions of the morality play: one which tends to imagine the action as essentially internal to a single mind, the other of which tends to reify the allegorical abstractions and treat them as agents in their own right. The Good and Evil Angels, the Old Man, the mysterious force that holds Faustus down as he attempts to leap up to his God, even Mephistophilis himself: are these to be considered "natural persons," characters in their own right, or are they allegories, or are they guilty illusions? Perhaps these seem silly or hairsplitting questions: asked of an ordinary morality play, they would certainly be beside the point. And Renaissance drama, like its morality predecessors, often deliberately obscures the difference between natural and symbolic characters, so much so that the attempt to make the distinction itself can seem naive. But Marlowe makes it hard to discard such categories,

---

7. For the first of these three positions see, for instance, Jean Bodin, *De la Demonomanie des sorciers* (Paris, 1580); for the second, see Lewis Lavater, *Of ghostes and spirites walking by nyght* (London, 1572), and Lambertius Danaeus, *A dialogue of witches* (1575); for the third, see Reginald Scot, *The Discovery of Witchcraft* (1584).

unsatisfactory as they may be. Central to the critical debate about *Faustus* have long been the play's entirely ambiguous, but nonetheless unavoidable, claims about the freedom of Faustus's will.[8] Is he coerced, or is he persuaded? Is he responsible, or is he not? Is his fate in his own power, or is it imposed upon him? It is impossible to answer these questions, or even to ask them, without some rough rules for differentiating between what is proper to Faustus and what is not. But even as the distinctions are made they destabilize themselves, just as they do in the sixteenth-century heresy trial.

Both texts of *Faustus* employ allegorical conventions in deeply unsettling ways, dissolving any intuitions about "natural" or universally accepted boundaries between inside and outside, between soul and body, between self and other, even while insisting upon the importance of those boundaries. Marlowe wants it both ways, dramatizing a story of individual autonomy and radical alienation, but at the same time subjecting the assumptions upon which that story seems premised to a rigorous, suspicious critique.

The two *Tamburlaine* plays pose even more clearly than *Faustus* the problem of what exemplary theater might mean in a world of radically diverse individuals. Zenocrate, spokesperson of pious orthodoxy, constantly underscores the connections among human beings:

> I fare, my lord, as other empresses
> That, when this frail and transitory flesh
> Hath sucked the measure of that vital air
> That feeds the body with his dated health,
> Wanes with enforced and necessary change.
>
> (*Tamburlaine II* 2.4.42–46)

Zenocrate sees herself as hemmed in by ordinary human weakness. Her days are numbered, her changes enforced and necessary. Her sense of fellow feeling proceeds, moreover, from a conception of her own body and the bodies of others as "frail and transitory": subject to capture, rape, torment, death. This frame of mind encourages her to derive lessons from the spectacles of those around her, especially when those spectacles emphasize physical vulnerability. In part I, for instance, she comes upon the corpses of Bazajeth and Zabina, and moralizes upon their fate:

8. For a variety of views on this issue, attempting to align Marlowe's view with a range of possible doctrines, see, for example, Lily Campbell, "Dr. Faustus: A Case of Conscience," *PMLA* 67 (1952): 219–39; Douglas Cole, *Suffering and Evil in the Plays of Christopher Marlowe* (Princeton: Princeton University Press, 1962); Richard Waswo, "Damnation, Protestant Style: Macbeth, Faustus, and Christian Tragedy," *Journal of Medieval and Renaissance Studies* 4 (1974): 63–99; Roy T. Eriksen, *The Form of Faustus Fortunes': A Study of the Tragedy of Dr. Faustus (1616)* (New Jersey: Humanities Press International, 1987), pp. 26–58.

> Those that are proud of fickle empery
> And place their chiefest good in earthly pomp,
> Behold the Turk and his great empress!
> Ah, Tamburlaine my love, sweet Tamburlaine,
> That fights for sceptres and for slippery crowns,
> Behold the Turk and his great empress!
>
> (*Tamburlaine I* 5.2.291–96)

Zenocrate behaves as Sidney or Heywood would expect a theater spectator to behave, generalizing from specific vivid cases in order to apply them to her own situation.

Zenocrate is not, however, at the hub of *Tamburlaine*. Her lover and husband dominates the plays, a man entirely insensitive to the sufferings of others, because he considers himself to be of a different kind. The stars that reigned at his birth, he declares, will never conjoin again until the end of the world. Whereas the body signifies common human weakness for Zenocrate, it expresses in Tamburlaine's case a transcendence of ordinary human frailty. Other bodies are wounded, but Tamburlaine's remains miraculously unscathed. Menaphon describes him as taller, larger, stronger, than anyone else: "in every part proportioned like the man/ Should make the world subdued to Tamburlaine" (1.1.27–28). Even at the moment of his death Tamburlaine imagines not a failure, but a reconfiguration of the body to allow a more perfect expression of and reward for the "fiery spirit" that no longer consents to terrestrial confinement.

ALISON FINDLAY

Heavenly Matters of Theology: A Feminist Perspective†

* * *

The Tragicall History of Doctor Faustus by Christopher Marlowe does not offer much to the feminist reader at first glance.[1] Female characters play only small roles in contrast to that of the male protagonist, whose spiritual struggle is at the centre of the morality pattern. Faustus's quest for infinite knowledge and bargain with the devil is modelled on the Fall. In Marlowe's rewriting of the story and in his source, *The English Faust Book*, female characters are

† From *A Feminist Perspective on Renaissance Drama* (Oxford: Blackwell, 1999), pp. 14–25. Reprinted by permission of the publisher.
1. Christopher Marlowe, *Doctor Faustus: A and B Texts (1604, 1616)*, ed. David Bevington and Eric Ramussen, Revels Plays (Manchester: Manchester University Press, 1993). All quotations are taken from the B text.

depicted after the legacy of Eve, personifying the combination of sin, desire and death. *The English Faust Book* tells that whenever Faustus thinks of turning to God, 'straightways the devil would thrust him a fair lady into his chamber, which fell to kissing and dalliance with him through which means he threw his godly motions in the wind, going forward still in his wicked practices to the utter ruin both of his body and soul'.[2] Marlowe's play follows the same pattern. Indeed, Kay Stockholder sees Faustus driven by a simultaneous desire for and fear of women.[3] Both Lucifer and Mephistopheles use women to tempt Faustus into hell. Mephistopheles promises Faustus 'the fairest courtesans' to satisfy his 'wanton and lascivious' desires (2.1.144–57) and Lucifer's pageant of the seven deadly sins comes to a climax with Lechery, a 'Mistress Minx' (2.3.157). The most important female character, Helen of Troy, appears at a key moment in Faustus's damnation: first, before the Old Man tries to persuade Faustus to 'leave this damned art' and return to God (5.1.35–51), and again when Faustus rejects his advice. Marlowe seems to confirm misogynist gender oppositions, presenting Helen as a demonic counterpart to the godly patriarch who is Faustus's only chance of salvation. It is her embraces which will 'extinguish clear' any thoughts of repentance (5.6.89). Helen seals Faustus's damnation with a kiss:

> Sweet Helen, make me immortal with a kiss.
> [They kiss]
> Her lips suck forth my soul. See where it flies!
> Come, Helen, come, give me my soul again.
> [They kiss again]
>
> (5.2.96)

By tasting the fruit of Helen's lips, Faustus repeats Adam's sin, trying to become immortal and all-knowing. W. W. Greg argues that Helen is a spirit from the demonic world, and that by choosing to commit intercourse with her, Faustus cuts himself off from any possible redemption.[4] Helen of Troy was often included alongside Eve in lists of 'wicked' women in the formal controversy, so her use as a figure of final temptation and damnation is not surprising.

Even the Duchess of Vanholt, an apparently innocent female character, is depicted after the legacy of Eve. In Act 4, Scene 6, the Duchess is significantly pregnant, embodying the punishment in-

2. *The English Faust Book: A Critical Edition Based on the Text of 1592*, ed. John Henry Jones (Cambridge: Cambridge University Press, 1994), p. 112.
3. Kay Stockholder, ' "Within the massy entrailes of the earth": Faustus's Relation to Women', in Kenneth Friedenreich, Roma Gill and Constance B. Kuriyama (eds.), *A Poet and a Filthy Playmaker* (New York: AMS Press, 1988), pp. 203–20.
4. W. W. Greg, 'The Damnation of Faustus', in John Jump (ed.), *Marlowe, Doctor Faustus: A Casebook* (Basingstoke: Macmillan, 1969), pp. 71–88; pp. 86–87.

flicted on women to bring forth children in sorrow. When Faustus promises her what she most desires, the grapes he offers hold the same mysterious danger as the apple. The Duchess's greedy consumption of the fruit is part of a wider pattern of eating and drinking in the play. Filling the body with food is an attempt to compensate for lack: the lost paradise of Eden and, especially for female spectators, the unsatisfied appetite for knowledge. She perhaps speaks for that audience when she says 'we are much beholding to this learned man' (4.6.122).

In encouraging spectators to identify with Faustus as an everyman figure, the play appears to gender its audience (or readers) as male. Indeed, the prologue to the 1604 text addresses them as 'Gentlemen'. It seems that to empathize with Faustus's experience, women spectators must become transvestite readers who condemn their own sex as the cause of his downfall. The misogynist bias of the text inclines them to regard themselves as responsible, according to Calvin, for 'the ruin and confusion of mankind'. More interestingly, though, the play also allows female spectators to see their own situations represented in the protagonist. Read alongside the Eden story, *Doctor Faustus* can be seen as a tragedy of knowledge which debates women's relationship to learning as much as men's. The prologue to the second quarto (1616) modifies its mode of address from 'Gentlemen' to 'gentles', as if in recognition of the fact that its daring ideas were addressed as much to female spectators as to male. In terms of the quest for knowledge, it is Eve rather than Adam who is the progenitor for Marlowe's central character, so although he is male, female experience is encoded into the play's structure. Faustus repeats Eve's sin in seeking knowledge which God deems is beyond his scope. He says 'A sound magician is a demigod. Here, tire my brains to get a deity' (1.1.61). The play shows that such an enterprise is damned. The epilogue moralizes

> Faustus is gone. Regard his hellish fall.
> Whose fiendful fortune may exhort the wise
> Only to wonder at unlawful things,
> Whose deepness doth entice such forward wits
> To practise more than heavenly power permits.
> (Epilogue.4)

True wisdom consists in keeping strictly within the limits of the law, defining oneself according to its strictures, and not seeking to know more than one's allotted place.

The 'evil' of knowledge is highlighted by the use of books as demonic props in *Doctor Faustus*. Mephistopheles offers Faustus a book to contemplate (2.1.158), as does Lucifer after the pageant of the seven deadly sins (2.3.168). Learning and sexual pleasure are equated in the verb 'ravished', used to describe the exciting effect of knowledge. For women, reading forbidden texts and 'ravishment' were connected in an even more literal way, since it was believed that from secular literature, especially romances, they would learn promiscuity. The growth in published fiction and plays from the 1580s suggests that such recreational reading by women was on the increase.[5] Through repeated reference to books as 'damned', the play cautions female spectators that contact with such literature is dangerous. Even the most liberal books on women's education recognized this. Vives's *Instruction of a Christian Woman* warned that secular fiction was sure to corrupt, and that 'a woman should beware of all these books, likewise as of serpents or snakes'.[6] Reading supposedly destroyed innocence, taught wives and daughters how to cuckold their husbands, arrange assignations with their lovers, and subvert paternal authority. When Lady Arbella Stuart secretly married William Seymour, for example, King James purportedly said that she had 'etne of the forbidden trie'.[7]

Doctor Faustus picks up on male insecurity about women's 'knowledge' in the cuckoldry jokes Faustus plays on Frederick, Martino and Benvolio (4.1), and in the scene where Robin boasts that his master's wife has become his mistress in both senses of the word (2.1.19–25).[8] In a speech unique to the first quarto text (1604), her infidelity is linked explicitly to learning. Robin boasts 'my master and mistress shall find that I can read—he for his forehead, she for her private study' (A Text, 2.3.17–18). Robin's ability to read and conjure allows him to cuckold his master, but it is the mistress's addiction to learning which makes her vulnerable to Robin's advances. Her private study is both a physical place in which they can meet secretly to have sex, and the reading which teaches her how to transgress.

Writing was even more condemnable than reading for women. Vives was opposed to all forms of original composition, recommending that when a girl learned handwriting she should restrict herself to copying 'some sad sentence, prudent and chaste, taken out of the holy scripture' which would remind her of her subordinate position.[9] Any writing which moved beyond the passive repe-

5. Anne Laurence, *Women in England 1500–1760: A Social History* (London: Weidenfeld and Nicolson, 1994), p. 174.
6. Kate Aughterson (ed.), *Renaissance Woman: Constructions of Femininity in England, A Sourcebook* (New York: Routledge, 1995), pp. 170–71.
7. *The Letters of Lady Arbella Stuart*, ed. Sara Jayne Steen (New York: Oxford University Press, 1994), p. 292.
8. On the cuckoldry jokes, see Stockholder, ' "Within the massy entrailes of the earth" ', pp. 210–11.
9. Aughterson (ed.), *Renaissance Woman*, p. 169. See also Valerie Wayne, 'Some Sad Sentence: Vives' *Instruction of a Christian Woman*', in Margaret P. Hannay (ed.), *Silent But for the Word: Tudor Women as Patrons, Translators and Writers of Religious Works* (Kent, Ohio: Kent State University Press, 1985), pp. 15–29.

tition of conventional spiritual wisdom invited an autonomous expression of self. The play implicitly reminds women that this is
damnable through the use of writing at pivotal moments of Faustus's history. To confirm his pact with the devil, Faustus has to 'bequeath' his soul by writing a deed of gift. It is a legal document
whose importance would strike all spectators, but the act of writing, as that which seals his fate, would have had special significance for women. Marlowe increases the dramatic tension in Act 2,
Scene 1 by showing how Faustus experiences difficulty in writing as
his blood congeals:

> What might the staying of my blood portend?
> Is it unwilling I should write this bill?
> Why streams it not, that I may write afresh?
> 'Faustus gives to thee his soul'—O, there it stayed!
> Why should'st thou not? Is not thy soul thine own?
> Then write again: 'Faustus gives to thee his soul'
>
> (2.1.65)

The anxiety of authorship which Faustus experiences is akin to that
felt by any woman in the Renaissance who ever considered putting
pen to paper. The opportunities which this deed opens up, the self-
possession it represents, would have excited spectators who enter-
tained ideas of moving beyond their allotted positions as wives or
daughters, and thinking as authors of themselves. 'Why should'st
thou not? Is not thy soul thine own?' voices their own emergent desire for autonomy, their claim, by rights, to determine their own fu-
tures rather than simply be guided by the men in their families.
The congealing of the ink-blood graphically dramatizes the agonizing process of self-expression, difficult enough for any author, but
for women whom convention relegated to silence and chastity, even
more traumatic.

Faustus's writing of his death warrant would find an echo in the
minds of female spectators with regard to their own reputations.
Women could not even speak or write publicly in their own defence, since to do so would be rather to confirm a slander than to
discredit it. Constantia Munda neatly summarizes the impossible
position they were placed in:

> Nay, you'll put gags in our mouths and conjure us all to si-
> lence; you will first abuse us, and then bind us to the peace.
> We must be tongue-tied, lest in starting up to find fault, we
> prove guilty of those horrible accusations.[1]

Through the fate of its author-scholar protagonist, *Doctor Faustus*
seems to warn women again of the dangers of writing, learning,

---

1. Simon Shepherd (ed.), *The Women's Sharp Revenge: Five Women's Pamphlets from the
   Renaissance* (New York: St. Martin's, 1985), p. 137.

self-possession. Faustus's damnation gives a vivid picture of the fate that awaits them if they dare to follow their desires and trespass into the forbidden world of knowledge. Seen as a moralistic play, *Doctor Faustus* conjures women to silence for fear of losing their souls, or at least their reputations. It persuades them to accept their inheritance from Eve and their subsequent role as the weaker vessel. Only by complete subjugation to male authority and instruction (which would, of course, confirm these ideas of guilt and inferiority) could they mitigate their position as daughters of the woman who had plucked the forbidden fruit.

The possibility of sympathy for Faustus and for Mephistopheles opens up another, less conservative way of reading the play with more appeal for feminist sympathizers. The upward trajectory of Faustus's progress and the simultaneous sense of loss represented by Mephistopheles lead back to a radical reinterpretation of the Eden narrative and Eve's role. In this sense, as much as in the charges of atheism raised against Marlowe, the text constitutes a rebellion against conventional church wisdom. Female spectators in the Renaissance, and even now, could see their own situations represented in Mephistopheles and Faustus.

Mephistopheles is a feminized figure in that he represents lack. In Freudian and Lacanian theory, and in culture more generally, woman has been read in negative terms: lacking a penis rather than having a womb. Female identification with nothingness (the symbol 0) serves to guarantee male superiority in the Symbolic Order, the language system governing social exchanges which privileges the phallus as a primary signifier. Lack is accompanied by desire, in Freudian terms 'penis envy', on the woman's part. The story of the Fall defines Eve in similar terms. God tells her 'thy desire shall be to thy husband, and he shall rule over thee' (Genesis 3.16). Eve's inferior role, her lack, brings with it a desire for (to be like) her husband. Although Mephistopheles is a male character, all that we learn about him places him in the 'female' position of lack and its concomitant presence of desire. Since Faustus cannot understand that Mephistopheles can be in hell and still be talking to him, Mephistopheles explains:

> Why, this is hell nor am I out of it.
> Think'st thou that I, that saw the face of God
> And tasted the eternal joys of heaven,
> Am not tormented with ten thousand hells
> In being deprived of everlasting bliss?
>
> (1.3.78)

Mephistopheles speaks like one who has had a taste of the Tree of Knowledge, become like a god and seen the bliss, but who is

then deprived of access to such blessings, having to watch in silence while men like Faustus enjoy the pursuit of learning. As
Mephistopheles explains, hell is not a physical space; it is a state of
lack:

> Hell hath no limits, nor is circumscribed
> In one self place, for where we are is hell,
> And where hell is must we ever be.
>
> (2.1.124)

The experience of hell that Mephistopheles describes was shared,
consciously or subconsciously, by women spectators. Hell is the
loss or lack of autonomy experienced in the family, under the control of one's father or husband. At least one character in Renaissance drama, Jessica in *The Merchant of Venice*, feels 'our house is
hell' (2.3.2), and although she is escaping from a Jewish father, her
words may well have struck a chord with Christian daughters or
wives in the playhouse. Mephistopheles, like women spectators, is
subject to the commands of men. The contract he makes with
Faustus mirrors the unequal relationship between the sexes after
the Fall. Faustus tastes the 'fruit' offered by Mephistopheles, the
temptations of power, and sells his soul in return for twenty-four
years of all-encompassing mastery: the ability to command at home
and abroad and a virtual monopoly on learning. Mephistopheles,
like Eve, is relegated to a subordinate position by the terms of the
contract:

> First, that Faustus may be a spirit in form and substance.
> Secondly, that Mephistopheles shall be his servant, and be by
> him commanded.
> Thirdly, that Mephistopheles shall do for him and bring him
> whatsoever.
> Fourthly, that he shall be in his chamber or house invisible.
> Lastly, that he shall appear to the said John Faustus at all times
> in what shape and form soever he please.
>
> (2.1.95)

The roles assigned to Mephistopheles would have been immediately recognizable to women as the duties prescribed for them in
household conduct books. William Gouge's popular guide, *Of Domesticall Duties* (1622), pointed out that a wife should always be
willing to yield to her husband's command and *'performe what busi-
nesse he requireth of her'*. To show reverence for him, she should
follow the pattern set by Rebecca in the Bible, who covered her
face with a veil (Genesis 24.65). The wife's gesture and speech,
such as it was, was a metaphorical veil to obscure her and glorify
her husband; like Mephistopheles, she was to be practically invisi-

ble in her lord's chamber or house.[2] An earlier conduct book, Dod and Cleaver's *A godly form of household government* (1598), pointed out that 'a certain discretion and desire [was] required of women to please the nature, inclinations and manners of their husbands, so long as the same importeth no wickedness.'[3] By echoing this in the last term of the demonic contract, *Doctor Faustus* implies that such domination does import wickedness, that it is necessarily evil. Identifying with Mephistopheles as a victim is undoubtedly difficult for an audience whose spiritual framework is Christian, but the lines which Marlowe gives the character are moving, and do allow women readers or spectators to read against the grain of the play's morality structure.

While Mephistopheles is a devil, and therefore immediately suspect, Faustus is an 'everyman' with whom the audience are encouraged to identify. Those women who felt trapped by the conventions laid down in conduct books must have had some sympathy with his frustration at the beginning of the play, when he complains that the sphere in which he is confined makes his work 'too servile and illiberal' (1.1.34). Because his study of books is a space normally forbidden to them, they recognize his quest for forbidden knowledge. Faustus's ability to transcend boundaries enacts a basic human fantasy, but one which must have seemed all the more wonderful to those whose gender necessarily put them in thrall. His pact with the devil opens up a wealth of wisdom which appears dangerously attractive in the play. Faustus's magnificent verse embodies the pleasures of secular learning and literature even as it describes them, threatening to 'ravish' the audience just as much as the protagonist (2.3.24–30). As Faustus's fellow scholar realizes, 'wondrous knowledge' (5.5.16) exerts its own magnetic pull on the hearts of those who witness the tragical history, making simple moral judgements inadequate. Even in the epilogue passing sentence on Faustus, the value of learning shines stubbornly through:

> Cut is the branch that might have grown full straight
> And burned is Apollo's laurel bough
> That sometime grew within this learned man.
>
> (Epilogue.1)

We are tempted to celebrate the 'learned man', to lament an overwhelming sense of loss, a waste of potential and intellectual riches. In spite of the play's condemnation of Faustus, we sense the possibility of reading his thirst for knowledge as laudable rather than damnable.

2. William Gouge, *Of Domesticall Duties* (London, 1622), The English Experience (Amsterdam: Walter Johnson Inc., Theatrum Orbis Terrarum, 1976), pp. 319 and 277.
3. Aughterson (ed.), *Renaissance Woman*, p. 81.

Hermetic philosophy offered Renaissance audiences a way of interpreting Faustus's quest in positive terms. Taken up by occult thinkers such as Bruno, Agrippa and Ficino, it claimed that a scholar could expand the mind to become like God and, through learning, actually unite with him:

> unless you make yourself equal to God, you cannot understand God; for the like is not intelligible save to the like. Make yourself grow to a greatness beyond measure, by a bound free yourself from the body; raise yourself above all time, become Eternity; then you will understand God. Believe that nothing is impossible for you, think yourself immortal and capable of understanding all, all arts, all sciences, the nature of every living being.[4]

Marlowe would have been familiar with these ideas from the occult tradition through his links with Walter Ralegh's circle, as John Mebane points out, so it is not surprising that he should draw on them in *Doctor Faustus*.[5] Much of the protagonist's thinking is based on the hermetic idea of transcendence through mental self-improvement. For women it has special significance.

Reading the acquisition of knowledge as a step towards God reverses patriarchal interpretations of the Eden story. Femininity, as represented by Eve, symbolizes openness to experience and growth, whereas paternal law is prohibition and confinement. A feminist re-reading produces a fable about maturation instead of fall, with Eve as a leading figure in human progress. Lyn M. Bechtel argues that Genesis 2.4–3.24 can be better understood as a story of growth from childhood to adulthood, where knowledge of sex, desire and death is a natural progression through adolescence rather than the result of sin.[6] Given the fact that girls usually mature more quickly than boys, Eve is naturally the first to taste the apple. According to this view, she is not the weaker vessel or the second sex but the primary one: she opens the gateway to maturation and, through her knowledge of desire and death, begins the process of renewing life. Feminist readings of Genesis which regard Eve and women's relationship to knowledge positively were to be found in the Renaissance. Rachel Speght's *Moralities Memorandum, with a Dreame Prefixed* (1621) confidently asked 'wherefore shall / A woman have her intellect in vaine, / Or not endeavor *Knowledge* to attaine'.[7] By

4. Quoted in John S. Mebane's lively discussion of the play in *Renaissance Magic and the Return of the Golden Age* (Lincoln: University of Nebraska Press, 1992), p. 123.
5. Ibid., pp. 113–14.
6. Lyn M. Bechtel, 'Rethinking the Interpretation of Genesis 2.4b—3.24', in Athalya Brenner (ed.), *A Feminist Companion to Genesis* (Sheffield: Sheffield Academic Press, 1993), pp. 77–118; p. 103.
7. Rachel Speght, *Moralities Memorandum, with a Dreame Prefixed* (1621), in Germaine Greer, Jeslyn Medoff, Melinda Sansone and Susan Hastings (eds.), *Kissing the Rod: An Anthology of Seventeenth-century Women's Verse* (London: Virago, 1988), pp. 68–78; p. 71.

focusing on the most radical example, Aemelia Lanyer's poem *Salve Deus Rex Judaeorum*, we can see how women watching *Doctor Faustus* might have identified with the protagonist's quest in opposition to the play's morality pattern.

Lanyer's defence of Eve is the centrepiece of her poem's project to promote the interests of learned women, herself included. She tells Queen Anne of Denmark that it is a serious piece of exegesis 'which I have writ in honour of your sex'.[8] Lanyer, like Bechtel and like Faustus, sees knowledge as a means of development. In a cheeky reversal of the usual gendered associations, she says that Adam fell for the sensual beauty of the fruit, whereas 'If Eve did err, it was for knowledge sake' (l. 797). Eve is the more mature character. Rather than offering an apple to her teacher, she gives it like a teacher to her pupil, anxious to educate him and raise him to her level of understanding. Generosity is the only fault she can be charged with:

> . . . Eve, whose only fault was too much love
> Which made her give this present to her dear,
> That what she tasted he likewise might prove,
> Whereby his knowledge might become more clear.
> He never sought her weakness to reprove,
> With those sharp words which he of God did hear;
> Yet men will boast of knowledge, which he rook
> From Eve's fair hand, as from a learned book.
>
> (l. 801)

The conventional labels of 'fault' and 'weakness' are brought into question by Lanyer's account. There is nothing intellectually weak about an Eve whose hand offers lessons like a 'learned book'. Her only 'fault', or mistake, is in trusting Adam. Her unselfish act is rewarded by Adam's selfish one: snatching knowledge and power for himself while condemning her to a life without learning or autonomy. Since Eve was obviously the intellectual pioneer, her subsequent deprivation is both unjust and tragic. In a passionate outburst which reminds us of the pain of loss expressed by both Mephistopheles and Faustus, Lanyer proclaims 'Then let us have our liberty again / And challenge to yourselves no sov'reignty' (l. 825). In *Doctor Faustus* Marlowe re-presents Eve's tragedy; from a male perspective, it is true, but one in which female spectators could see themselves. Faustus's growth and self-determination, cut off so brutally, offers an image of the way in which their potential for development is repressed and their power is demonized by a

---

8. 'To The Queen's Most Excellent Majesty', in Diane Purkiss (ed.), *Renaissance Women: The Plays of Elizabeth Cary; the Poems of Aemilia Lanyer* (London: Pickering & Chatto, 1994), p. 243.

society which took its ultimate authority from patriarchal interpretations of the Bible.

Aemelia Lanyer extends her feminist reading of the Eden narrative in the final section of her poem, 'The Description of Cookeham', where she describes an all-female 'paradise' (l. 21) of scholarly activity. Cookeham was the family home of Margaret Clifford, Countess of Cumberland, for whom *Salve Deus Rex Judaeorum* was written. Its garden is a place where women's reading and writing are blessed with grace. At the centre of the garden, as in Eden, is a 'stately tree' (l. 53), which is associated with the beneficial powers of knowledge. It allows Margaret 'goodly prospects' (l. 54), not unlike the vast horizons that are opened up to Faustus; it welcomes and elevates her so that all the surrounding countryside seems to kneel in salute. As well as giving her command over the material world, the tree enables the Countess to understand the Creator's majesty, and here, Lanyer's view of knowledge is very close to the hermetic idea. Lanyer recounts how she, Margaret and her daughter Anne are forced to leave Cookeham and take up their positions in the wilderness of patriarchal society. In another line that recalls Mephistopheles's sense of loss, Aemelia Lanyer laments being robbed of Anne Clifford's company: 'Whereof deprived, I evermore must grieve' (l. 125). Anne, who leaves to get married, chooses to say goodbye at the tree. The poem's feminist ideas on female learning, sisterhood and loss all come together here:

> Where many a learned book was read and scanned;
> To this fair tree, taking me by the hand,
> You did repeat the pleasures which had passed,
> Seeming to grieve they could no longer last.
>
> (l. 161)

The feminist interpretation of Genesis put forward by Lanyer suggests that alternative views about knowledge were in circulation when *Doctor Faustus* was being performed, and may have had a special appeal to women. Like Marlowe, Lanyer uses a conventional Christian tale, the form of writing most acceptable for women, as a vehicle for the promotion of radical ideas. Her passionate celebration of female learning and literacy points to the possibility of an unorthodox response to *Doctor Faustus* on the part of some women.

Approaching the play via these ideas about Eve and knowledge produces very different readings of Faustus's journey and Helen's role. The audience can understand that the access to wisdom, beauty and pleasure which Faustus has been given is too valuable to lose, so he cannot repent. Faustus asks 'Why should I die, then, or basely despair?' (2.3.29). While the audience recognize that he is deceiving himself, they are tempted to share his belief that immersion in the classics will allow him to transcend the Christian heaven and hell. Helen represents the climax of this alternative existence:

> Here will I dwell for heaven is in these lips,
> And all is dross that is not Helena.
> I will be Paris, and for love of thee
> Instead of Troy shall Wittenburg be sacked . . .
> O, thou art fairer than the evening's air,
> Clad in the beauty of a thousand stars.
> Brighter art thou than flaming Jupiter
> When he appeared to hapless Semele,
> More lovely than the monarch of the sky
> In wanton Arethusa's azured arms;
> And none but thou shalt be my paramour.
>
> (5.2.99)

Helen embodies knowledge, sexuality and pleasure. Read using the feminist interpretation of Eve, she is not the demon who causes Faustus's downfall but the summit of his intellectual and sensual experience; his coming of age or maturity. (Interestingly, the B text omits the Old Man's damning commentary on the couple, leaving this speech more open to positive responses from the audience.) Faustus's knowledge stretches across time and space, from the ancient world of Trojan history to the Wittenberg of the present, from classical myth to nature and astronomy. That Faustus is moving closer to heaven through this vast panorama of experience, as in the hermetic tradition, does not seem ridiculous. It is possible to share, or at least understand his view that he does not need anything beyond the wealth that is Helen, since the 'heaven' of knowledge 'dwells in these lips'. Heaven is no longer a patriarchal space since Helen outshines Jupiter, and Arethusa cradles the 'monarch of the sky' in her arms like a mother. 'Feminine' knowledge is an overwhelming force which envelops the human subject in pleasure rather than fear.

The hermetic idea of human development collapses the moral framework of *Doctor Faustus*, as Nicholas Brooke demonstrates in one of the most powerful anti-orthodox readings. He argues that Christian doctrine's insistence on subjection to the will of a superior god is anathema to the individual wishing to grow and explore independently, and that in Marlowe's play the human desire to create an autonomous self is inimical to divine will because the order of God is 'an order of servitude'. From this perspective 'Heaven is the subjection of self, Hell in this sense is the assertion of the self.'[9]

9. Nicholas Brooke, 'The Moral Tragedy of Doctor Faustus' (1952), in Jump (ed.), *Marlowe, Doctor Faustus: A Casebook*, pp. 101–33; pp. 118–19.

The play's preoccupation with a quest for selfhood is an intrinsic part of its appeal to audiences of women struggling to establish identities in the face of paternal laws which demanded servitude. Women like Aemelia Lanyer, seeking to move beyond the roles assigned to them, can sympathize with Faustus's goal to 'be admired through the furthest land' (3.1.63). His tragic loss and downfall mirrors their own story as daughters of Eve, but his very daring in transgressing the heavenly Father's law so confidently, so absolutely, offers a beacon of possibility to those women anxious to strike out and pursue their own 'bright fame' (3.1.62), against all the rules.

* * *

STEPHEN ORGEL

[Magic and Power in *Doctor Faustus*]†

* * *

Thomas Kyd's charges against Marlowe explicitly associate him with the Ralegh circle, which included not only [Thomas] Hariot, but John Dee and Henry Percy, the 'Wizard Earl' of Northumberland (of whom the *DNB* says he was 'passionately addicted to tobacco smoking'). With Ralegh we are back to atheism and sex, but with Hariot, Dee, and Northumberland we have arrived at conjuring and science.

It is easy to see the ambitions of this group summed up in and refracted through the figure of Doctor Faustus, not least because his drama is one of overreaching ambition combined with relentless failure. What is more difficult to see is how the author of this famous and perennially successful morality could be accused of atheism. The play itself became a powerful argument for belief. But magic and theater have a complex and contradictory interrelationship in the age. The transition from *Doctor Faustus* to *The Tempest* in only two decades records something like a paradigm shift: Faustus's magic, after all, is not the empiricism of Hariot, or the mathematics of Dee, it is theology, whereas Prospero's magic is art and science. Shakespeare seems to say that if magic has any validity, any reality, it is because it deals not with metaphysics and the occult but with the facts of nature—storms, astronomy, human disease; the body, the mind, and the passions, not the soul. There is

† From *The Authentic Shakespeare and Other Problems of the Early Modern Stage* (New York: Routledge, 2002), pp. 222–29. Reproduced by permission of Routledge/Taylor & Francis Books, Inc.

nothing whatever in *The Tempest* about magic leading to damnation; even Sycorax's putative liaison with the devil eventuates only in Caliban. The worst that can be said about magic in the play is that it is in the end a retreat from reality and responsibility: that is why it must be renounced—not because it is damnable, but because it is finally just as unsatisfactory as it had been for Faustus twenty years earlier. Ben Jonson offered the audiences of 1610 an alternative way of looking at Renaissance magic in *The Alchemist*, written within a year of *The Tempest*, in which the charlatan magicians—a butler, a con-man, and a whore—and the gullible public that believes in them are all equally culpable. The only person who is not represented as culpable in this proto-capitalist system is also the only person who ultimately profits from it, the master, who is out of town while his servant delivers the goods. Lovewit's acquisition of the rich widow is the real magic in the play.

What urges are these plays satisfying in a culture in which magic still seems a real possibility? The question, of course, is moot since the magic in all three cases is theater, and in that respect, at least, it proved superlatively effective. *Faustus* in particular became one of the most famous plays of Renaissance England, a kind of cultural artifact. As a literary text it survives in two quite different published versions, both involving collaborators, but these are surely only indices to a continuous process. The text must have been revised and augmented constantly, in production after production, thereby becoming more and more detached from any particular author. Scenes apparently kept being added to it (the play's structure seems designed to allow for this: a beginning and an end, and an infinitely expandable and variable middle). It was produced pretty much continuously, from the early 1590s until the closing of the theaters in 1642, and was played again after the Restoration. In both published versions, Marlowe's name is as truncated as the play, and grows increasingly nebulous: it appears first, in 1604, as 'Ch. Marl.' and then, in 1616, as 'Ch. Mar.'—and in the only surviving copy of the latter, the name has been expanded with pen and ink to read 'Macklin' or 'Marklin.' The author, the sense of an author, disappears. In its own time it is less a text than a continuous event.

Something of the nature of that event can be seen in a characteristic group of stories about the play. In one version, during a performance in Exeter, as Faustus was conjuring surrounded by a group of devils, the actors became aware that there was one devil too many, and stopped the play and fled from the town in fear for their lives and souls. In other less stylish versions of the story, Satan himself actually appeared during a performance. These stories are part of the mythology of anti-theatricalism, intended to demon-

strate how inherently profane and dangerous an amusement theater is; but they also indicate the extent to which theater was in
touch with an aspect of reality that was beyond rational control—
they are stories about the power of theater, even of a theater of
charlatans, about theater as magic, with *Doctor Faustus* as the par-
adigmatic instance.

The play as it survives is a strange combination of great poetry
and clowning, everything Sidney was describing when he attacked
the 'mongrel tragicomedy, mixing clowns and kings.' Faustus himself is both hero and clown. If the play is about unbounded ambition, it is also about insufficient imagination—every reader, every
audience has felt that Faustus doesn't make enough of his bargain,
doesn't even really know what to ask for. For all its talk of the perils
of boundless ambition, there is a continuous sense of disappoint-
ment in the play, a sense that Faustus isn't ambitious enough—that
he isn't, in fact, as ambitious as any of us would be in the same situation.

The play is in this respect much more a temptation than a warning. In his opening soliloquy, Faustus rejects philosophy, medicine,
and law, and comes at last to divinity, and he quotes St. Jerome's
Bible: '*Stipendium peccati mors est*. Ha! / . . . The reward of sin is
death. That's hard' (A 1.1.40–41).[1] It has often been observed that
the unspoken second half of the biblical sentence promises eternal
life through Christ; what Faustus omits—or ignores—is the promise of grace through repentance, a promise that will be in the mind
of every Elizabethan spectator. Faustus is throughout the play convinced that he won't be *allowed* to repent, but this is because he
simply hasn't read far enough; he hasn't read as far as we have.
Theological arguments citing strict Calvinist doctrine about the impossibility of repentance for the confirmed sinner are doubtless
technically correct, but dramatically irrelevant: the point is surely
not that God's mercy isn't infinite, but that, even at the end, Faustus still doesn't believe in it. For an audience, this has a curious
double edge: it means that we're always on top of the action, that
we understand from the beginning why Faustus is doomed to failure and we fully approve of his damnation; but it also means that
we see that we could do it better, make the bargain and get away
with it, have the world and have repentance too. This is the sense
in which the play is as much a temptation as a warning.

Marlowe starts with a fantasy of unlimited desire and unlimited
power to satisfy it. When Faustus summons Mephistophilis, he ar-
ticulates a megalomaniac dream—to live in all voluptuousness, to

1. Quotations from *Doctor Faustus* are from the edition edited by David Bevington and Eric
Rasmussen (Manchester University Press, 1992); the 1604 text is A, the 1616 text B.

be the emperor of the world, to control nature and the supernatural: this is what the diabolical deal promises him. But four scenes
later, when his bad angel urges him to think on the wealth he can
have, his eager reply is 'The seignory of Emden shall be mine!'
(A 2.1.23)—Emden is a rich commercial port; the dream is already
a good deal less ambitious than ruling the world, and he hasn't
even signed the bond yet. By the end of the same scene his voluptuousness has diminished significantly too: 'Let me have a wife, the
fairest maid in Germany, for I am wanton and lascivious, and cannot live without a wife' (143–5). But Mephistophilis will not supply
a wife, presumably because marriage is a sacrament. He produces
instead a devil dressed as a woman furnished with fireworks, at
once an allegory of lust and of theater (the only beautiful women
this stage provides are sparkling female impersonators); and a bit of
clowning ensues that calls the whole assumption of omnipotence
into question. Faustus's indignation in the 1604 text—'A plague on
her for a hot whore' (153)—by 1616 includes a revelation of the
limits of his bargain: 'Here's a hot whore indeed; no, I'll no wife'
(B 2.1.149)—if this is a woman, I don't want any. Mephistophilis
then produces an alternative proposal, to bring Faustus the fairest
courtesans in the world to sleep with. These will be entirely poly-
morphous, chaste as Penelope and wise as Sheba, but beautiful as
Lucifer: the moral and intellectual ideals are female, but the ideal
of beauty is male. This sounds like a much more attractive proposition than marriage for a truly wanton and lascivious voluptuary, especially one with sexual tastes like Marlowe's; but Faustus doesn't
even comment on it, and Mephistophilis effortlessly moves him on
to what it turns out he really wants, books. The books are books of
incantations, astronomy, and natural history: universal power is
construed as power over the supernatural, the celestial, the natural,
but epitomised in the written word—the power is literacy, the pact
with the devil is an allegory of Marlowe's own education, the search
for the right books.

What do you do with power in Marlowe's world? Faustus's initial instincts are altruistic. A good deal of the play's appeal is to
English anti-Catholic sentiments—deeply felt, obviously; the feelings Burghley must have appealed to when he recruited Marlowe
into government service. All the horseplay with the pope is the
other side of the ambition to build a wall of brass around Protestant Germany. The real English fear of the danger of Catholic
power is disarmed by magic's ability to make fools of its audience.
From this aspect, the play can be seen as part of the long history of
English Protestant militancy: Faustus's magic is the fantasy of Sidney's aborted political and military career, Leicester's momentary
triumph in the Netherlands, Essex's and Nottingham's minuscule

Spanish campaigns, Prince Henry's fantasmic Protestant army of European liberation. Faustus is, for a little while, a version of the Protestant hero—the damnable magic is on our side, working for us; the megalomaniac Faustus, the megalomaniac Marlowe, is playing it both defensive and safe.

But where do the real ambitions lie? At the play's center, after all, is a confrontation with Catholic power itself in the person of the Holy Roman Emperor. The visit to Charles V ought to be a triumphant entry: Faustus has humiliated the pope; in the B text he has even freed Bruno the antipope and flown him to the imperial court; he is more powerful than any earthly monarch. Why isn't this a scene of two emperors, either paying homage to each other or threatening each other? But Faustus appears instead as an entertainer, 'The wonder of the world for magic art' (B 4.1.11), and from the sorcery materializes not a promise of infinite power but simply a magic show—he produces, at the emperor's request, 'the royal shapes / Of Alexander and his paramour' (93–4). Only shapes, however, impersonated by spirits; so the emperor's wish to embrace, or even to question, Alexander, is disappointed—there's simply nothing there. All he can do, all he finally wants to do, is look for a mole on the phantom lady's neck. The really satisfying show is what follows: the spectacle of the taunting unbeliever knight Benvolio getting his comeuppance, furnished by Faustus's magic with horns—the greatest triumph isn't ruling the world, it's revenge; the best joke is sexual subversion, cuckolding your enemy. But then it turns out that Faustus *hasn't* cuckolded Benvolio—the horns are a pointless joke: as the emperor immediately points out, Benvolio isn't even married. So Faustus has his joke, but the transgressiveness is harmless: nobody's wife has been debauched, Faustus hasn't committed lechery; there is nothing here that the most moral of Elizabethan audiences can't laugh at with a clear conscience.

What Faustus presents is nothing but what Marlowe's stage presents, the mongrel tragicomedy that Sidney abhorred, the wondrous adulterated with the clownish. Faustus comes to Charles V as Dr. Dee came to the emperor of Hungary, not in triumph but as a petitioner, a supplicant. What he seeks is a job in the emperor's service—the dream of glory and power is finally only an upwardly mobile lower-middle-class Elizabethan dream: Spenser's dream of a good civil service job, Jonson's dream of the Mastership of the Revels; not even Sidney's dream of political influence and independence. Most of all, it is the dream of Marlowe the working-class boy with a high-class university education which somehow didn't get him the kind of life he thought it would, Marlowe trying to find a niche in the bureaucracy, a place in the service of some powerful courtier impressed by his learning and poetry, but also able to see beyond it to his shrewdness, unscrupulousness, willingness. The fantasies of unlimited power are consistently scaled down in the play, until they finally seem to represent something that really ought to be obtainable—do you have to make a pact with the devil just to get a decent job or someone to go to bed with? But the only job Faustus gets turns out to be Marlowe's job, inventing theatrical spectacles for rich audiences.

Here then is the progression of fantasies: imperial power is almost immediately abandoned for money, and not even for what we would call 'real money,' all the gold in the New World or the riches of Asia, but something much more modest and localized, the revenues of the profitable commercial city of Emden. Women get short-circuited as soon as it turns out marriage is impossible—if marriage is impossible, so is sex: Faustus turns out to have the most conventional middle-class morals. There's no megalomaniac fantasy here, nothing irregular or transgressive, not even Marlowe's interest in boys. The desire for books certainly shouldn't be a problem, but even there Faustus doubts that he's got what he's asked for—when Mephistophilis produces the books containing all earthly knowledge, Faustus's reaction is 'Oh thou art deceived,' you don't know what you're talking about; and the devil has to reassure him, 'Tut, I warrant thee,' I guarantee it (A 2.2.181–2). But this too doesn't satisfy him; obviously there's got to be more to life than books. So we start again, with less material, more free-floating ambitions: he wants to fly, to go to Rome, to be invisible, to humiliate the pope, to be mischievous without consequences. And then he wants, not to be emperor, but to *impress* the emperor, to get secure employment, to be noticed, successful, admired—by the middle of the play this is what magic can do for you.

It also, however, puts you in mortal danger, not for your soul but for your life. The greatest danger isn't damnation, it's human envy, the other courtiers who resent your success—the attempt on Faustus's life appears only in the B text, but it's implicit in the whole premise of the play. Running parallel with the dream of success, therefore, is necessarily a dream of invulnerability: the magic that damns you is also, quite simply, the only thing that can save your life. The invulnerability is limited in time to the twenty-four years of the contract; but given the dangers of a fantasy life such as Faustus's (and, it follows, such as Marlowe's) a pretty good bargain nevertheless, especially considering Marlowe's other career as a government spy—the career that got him murdered, at the age of twenty-nine, presumably on orders from someone with real power. If Marlowe had made Faustus's deal he would have lived another twenty-four years, and died in 1617, the year after and a year older than Shakespeare. Consider the life expectancy in this period: if

you were male and made it past adolescence without succumbing
to childhood diseases, smallpox, plague, miscellaneous fevers, wild
animals, duels, highwaymen, fires, food poisoning, whatnot, you
had a chance of reaching a reasonable age, which in the early seventeenth century was not the threescore and ten stipulated by the
Word of God but anything over forty-five—Shakespeare died at
fifty-two, and nobody deploring his death claimed that this was especially premature. Obviously it helped a lot if you could make a
deal with the devil; it was clear you couldn't make one with God.

For all the play's talk of power, its principal theme is survival.
The eventual love scene, conjuring up Helen of Troy to be Faustus's
paramour, is unquestionably a triumph; but it isn't really Faustus's
triumph. The project is not even Faustus's idea: it's suggested to
him by his two scholars—even now, he doesn't know what to ask
for. If the initial failure was artistic, lack of imagination, perhaps
the ultimate failure is scholarly, lack of originality. But Marlowe
rescues him with some of the greatest verse in the language:

> Was this the face that launched a thousand ships . . .
>   (A 5.1.91)

All the disastrous consequences of epic lust provide the language of
love poetry; and there's no indication here that the woman who appears this time, whatever she is, is an inadequate reward for Faustus's pains. He really does, finally, get what he wants. But notice
what he wants. Mephistophilis has offered him the most beautiful
women in the world, all he can handle, every morning. What he
wants instead is a literary allusion, a paragon from his classical education, Homer's ideal. Helen *is* a spirit, the quintessential emana-
tion of humanist passion—for the best book, the best poem, the
best text. What's desirable about her is that she *isn't* a woman.

The damnation scene is of course a foregone conclusion, but in
its evasions and ambivalences it replicates the movement of the
play as a whole. If it is true that, doctrinally, Faustus cannot repent,
it is a doctrine that Faustus is either unaware of or denies. What he
says, several times, is that he is *afraid* to repent, afraid that the devils will tear him to pieces if he does—as if this were worse than, or
different from, being carried off to hell. Is the failure to repent one
more failure of imagination, and by the same token one more temptation for the audience? The scene is another love scene, too: 'O
lente lente curite noctis equi' (A 5.2.74), Faustus, trying to survive a
little longer, quotes (actually, misquotes) the *Amores*. Ovid, making
love to Corinna, implores night's horses to run slowly; but the allusion is more elaborate than this. Ovid is not addressing Night but
Aurora, Dawn, and urges her to imagine herself in bed not with her
aged husband Tithonus but with her young and handsome lover

Cephalus; the line, 'Stay night, and run not thus' in Marlowe's translation (1.13.40), is spoken by Aurora in a love scene within a love scene, and it implores more time with the beautiful youth, not with the mistress—Marlowe's textual arabesque provides Faustus with a boy after all. In the final moment of frustration, seeing Christ's blood stream in the firmament and convinced that 'One drop would save my soul,' Faustus calls out 'I'll leap up to my God: who pulls me down?' (77). The answer might be obduracy, pride, despair, or even Calvinist doctrine; but as Edward Snow once mischievously remarked to me, it could also be simply gravity.[2] The play still tempts us to smart-aleck comebacks.

* * *

PERFORMANCE

DAVID BEVINGTON

Staging the A- and B-Texts of *Doctor Faustus*†

To what extent, and in what ways, do the staging requirements for the A- and B-texts of *Doctor Faustus* differ? Those texts differ substantially as to the nature of their respective authorities. Eric Rasmussen and I argue, in our Revels edition of 1993, that the A-text is closer than the B-text to Marlowe's original, having been based on the authorial papers of Marlowe and his collaborator, rather than being a "reported" or memorially reconstructed text as argued earlier by Leo Kirschbaum and W. W. Greg, among others.[1] Marlowe's collaborator, possibly Henry Porter, wrote most of the comic scenes on separate manuscript pages that were then inserted into the composite playscript, thereby making possible the misplacement of some scenes by the printer (Valentine Simmes). Philip Henslowe probably sold these papers to the stationer Thomas Bushell in 1600, at a time

2. Snow's brilliant essay on the play is "Marlowe's *Doctor Faustus* and the Ends of Desire," in Alvin Kernan, ed., *Two Renaissance Mythmakers* (Baltimore, 1977), pp. 70–110.
† From *Marlowe's Empery: Expanding His Critical Contexts*, ed. Sarah Munson Deats and Robert A. Logan (Newark: University of Delaware Press, 2002), pp. 43–60. Reprinted by permission of Associated University Presses.
1. Leo Kirschbaum, "The Good and Bad Quartos of *Doctor Faustus*," *The Library*, 4th series, 26 (1946), 272–94, and W. W. Greg, ed., *Marlowe's "Doctor Faustus," 1604–1616: Parallel Texts* (Oxford: Clarendon Press, 1950), 63–97. All citations in this present essay are to *Christopher Marlowe: "Doctor Faustus." A- and B-Texts (1604–1616)*, ed. David Bevington and Eric Rasmussen, The Revels Plays (Manchester: University of Manchester Press, 1993).

when the Admiral's Men sold four plays from their repertory to London publishers. *Faustus* was still popular, but Henslowe may have felt that he no longer needed the A-text papers since a fair copy had (presumably) been made into a playbook; moreover, he seems to have been on the point of commissioning a new version of the play with additions by William Birde (or Borne) and Samuel Rowley. "A booke called the plaie of Doctor Faustus" was entered in the Stationers' Register on 7 January 1601, and the A-text was published in 1604. It was republished in 1609 and again in 1611 by George Eld for John Wright; rights in the play were transferred by Bushell to Wright on 13 September 1610.[2]

Birde and Rowley were paid £4 for their "adicyones in doctor fostes" on 22 November 1602.[3] The resulting version is almost surely the B-text, published in 1616 and then reprinted at least six times between 1616 and 1631. Both the A- and B-text versions enjoyed a long popularity, onstage and in print. The B-text became the "received" version of the play. It omits some 36 lines of the A-text, while at the same time introducing thousands of verbal changes, including the alterations of some characters' names. Most notably, it expands the text by some 676 lines, mainly in detailing Faustus's rescue of the rival Pope Bruno and in the expansion of the comic antics having to do with Benvolio, Martino, Frederick, the Carter, and the Hostess.

The contention of Kirschbaum, Greg, and others[4] that the B-text best represents Marlowe's authorial intentions was based in good part on a rejection of the A-text as a "bad quarto." Once we see that the evidence for such a claim is unsubstantial, we have every reason to conclude that the B-text is the theatrically revised version of 1602 or thereabouts, doubtlessly including alterations from a variety of sources besides the additions provided by Birde and Rowley. The B-text is often attentive to practical matters of staging like thunder, music, processions, *exeunts* "*several ways,*" action "*above,*" descents from the "*heavens,*" and the like, whereas the A-text is silent or vague. The printer of the 1616 text may have been provided with a new copy prepared especially for the printing process, based on the playhouse manuscript containing the Birde-Rowley additions, along with a copy of the A-text published in 1611 to aid the scribe of the printer's copy in interpreting the playbook when it proved difficult to decipher.[5] Some of the revisions may have oc-

2. Greg, ed., *Doctor Faustus*, 11–12.
3. *Henslowe's Diary*, ed. R. A. Foakes and R. T. Rickert (Cambridge: Cambridge University Press, 1961), p. 206. Cited in E. K. Chambers, *The Elizabethan Stage*, 4 vols. (Oxford: Clarendon Press, 1923), 3.423.
4. In addition to the works cited in note 1 above, see also *The Tragical History of Doctor Faustus*, ed. Frederick S. Boas (London: Methuen, 1932), xiii.
5. See *Faustus*, ed. Bevington and Rasmussen, 77, and Eric Rasmussen, *A Textual Companion to "Doctor Faustus,"* The Revels Companion Series (Manchester: University of Manchester Press, 1993), 40–61.

curred after 1608. Birde and Rowley found materials for their additions in *The History of the Damnable Life and Deserved Death of
Doctor John Faustus* (London, 1592), a free translation of the German *Historia von d. Johann Fausten, dem weitbeschreiten Zauberer
und Schwartzkünstler* (Frankfurt am Main, 1587, known widely as
the *Faustbuch*) that had served as the source for the A-text original
but which also provided many of the episodes still to be exploited in
an expanded dramatic version.[6] The revisers also turned to John
Foxe's *Acts and Monuments*, popularly known as *The Book of Martyrs*, especially for the scenes involving Bruno and the German emperor.[7]

Such an account of the origin and nature of the A- and B-texts
invites us to look at the staging differences of the two versions.
Henslowe's impetus for an expanded revision of his money-making
property was presumably that audiences clamored for more of
the comic business that Marlowe and his collaborator had begun to provide in the A-text version and that could easily be elaborated. The loose-knit nature of the play's middle, long deplored by
classically-minded critics, made possible the insertion of more
comic high jinks and patriotic Protestant bravado. Conceivably, the
theater space in which the A-text play originally appeared was lacking in certain architectural and mechanical features that Henslowe
later realized he could remedy and exploit in the years following
1602. A look at the staging requirements of the A- and B-texts
ought to be able to afford us, then, materials for a kind of brief
sketch of certain changes in theater design, staging methods, and
audience taste or expectations during the years from 1588–89
down into the 1600s.

The staging of the opening scenes, wherein the two texts are for
the most part alike, is generally similar in the two versions. Faustus
is first seen *"in his study"* in both texts (1.1.0.1). Yet the absence of
the word *"Enter"* in the B-text, normally sensitive to staging issues,
may possibly indicate an option in the method of Faustus's first appearance. In both texts he is presented to the audience by the Prologue, saying, "And this the man that in his study sits." As he
departs, the Prologue gestures in the direction of the protagonist,
now visible in the theater. Does the B-text, by omitting the word
"Enter," perhaps suggest that the Prologue draws back a curtain
concealing a discovery space? Faustus could, of course, simply enter onstage through a door as his presence is invoked, in either text.
Conversely, he could have been "discovered" by being suddenly revealed in a discovery space; the A-text's word *"Enter"* is not neces-

6. *Faustus*, ed. Bevington and Rasmussen, 3–4, 77.
7. John Foxe, *Acts and Monuments*, 2d ed., 3 vols. (London: John Daye, 1570); new ed. by
George Townsend, 3 vols. (London: Seely and Burnside, 1841).

sarily inconsistent with that option. Still, the lack of *"Enter"* in the B-text is intriguing.

In either event, Faustus presumably comes forward in the theater, not limiting his physical location to a "discovery" space if one was in fact used, making the whole stage his "study" in the imaginative, flexible concept of Elizabethan staging. He is visited there by the Good and Evil Angels—called "Angel" and "Spirit" in the B-text—and by Valdes and Cornelius. A comic scene intervenes at this point, involving Wagner and the two scholars (1.2) for which staging requirements are identical in the two versions, during which action we are invited to suppose the speakers to be in Faustus's house (since Wagner is carrying wine, presumably for his master).

The scene of Faustus's conjuring of Mephistopheles (1.3) is verbally alike in the two texts for the most part. Yet the opening stage direction reflects a marked change in staging, and it is a change that affects our sense of theology. To replace the A-text's brief *"Enter* FAUSTUS *to conjure,"* with its rather literary way of describing Faustus's intent rather than instructing the acting company what is to happen at this point or how Faustus is to be accoutered (he needs to be holding a book), the B-text is graphic about sound effects, company roster, and order of entering. *"Thunder. Enter* LUCIFER *and four Devils,* FAUSTUS *to them with this speech,"* reads the stage direction, calling for added devils and specifying that Faustus enters after them. Since they have no speeches in the present scene, and since Faustus gives no indication of being aware of them, the likelihood is that they enter *"above."* Lucifer is explicitly named, suggesting that his appearance is such as to indicate that he is identifiably the chief devil; the name, not mentioned in the dialogue here, would otherwise be superfluous. Presumably, the others might include Beelzebub, who appears later in the company of Lucifer and Mephistopheles (2.3.84.1, 5.2.0.1), and Demogorgon, mentioned in this scene at line 19. The fourth devil mentioned in Faustus's incantation at 16–23 is Mephistopheles, raising the possibility that Mephistopheles enters *"above"* as one of the four devils at the scene's beginning and that he then withdraws in order to be able to reenter at line 23.2.

The staging effect of the B-text revisers is at all events reasonably plain, and theologically significant. The devils are waiting for Faustus, all four of them. Mephistopheles's explanation to Faustus that "I am a servant to great Lucifer / And may not follow thee without his leave" (B-text, 39–40, identical in A-text) is given an objective correlative onstage. Indeed, we can imagine the dramatic irony resulting from the audience's ability to see Lucifer and his cohorts while Mephistopheles goes on to make clear to Faustus that this di-

abolical visitation is a tribute not to Faustus's magical power but to
the readiness of all the devils to come whenever a person abjures
the Scriptures and Christ. As Mephistopheles puts it, using a theatrically meaningful plural, "We fly in hope to get his glorious soul,
/ Nor will we come unless he use such means / Whereby he is in
danger to be damned" (47–49). Perhaps Lucifer and his cohorts
nod in gleeful acquiescence at this point. The text is unchanged
from the A-text here; what has happened is that the B-text revisers
have found a way to exploit the theatrical potential of the language
by bringing on all the devils at the earliest possible point.

A similar dramatic irony continues, in the B-text, to hover over
Mephistopheles's following lines, giving them added pain:

> Unhappy spirits that fell with Lucifer,
> Conspired against our God with Lucifer,
> And are for ever damned with Lucifer.
>
> (1.3.69–71)

How is Lucifer, still presumably visible to the audience, to respond
to this warped tribute? How do his fellows express their feelings
about this unhappy reminder of their damnation? Almost certainly
they remain visible to the audience for the entire scene of conjuration and of explanation about the all-encompassing nature of being in hell, serving as a kind of obscene chorus, silently whetting
Mephistopheles on in his work and gloating at Faustus's aptness to
be instructed. Perhaps they exit when Mephistopheles leaves at line
100, or else stay on until Faustus finishes the scene.

When Mephistopheles makes his entrance to the conjuring Faustus at 1.3.23.2, he may appear in the B-text as a "*dragon*." This
word occurs in the B-text alone. It does so, to be sure, as part of
Faustus's conjuration: "*surgat Mephostophilis Drago.*" Editors have
long regarded the word as a misplaced stage direction; however, as
Eric Rasmussen and I argue in our Revels edition (p. 212), the misplacement may point to a more suitable location at 23.2: "*Enter a
Devil Dragon*," i.e., in the shape of a dragon. Faustus's objection
that "Thou art too ugly to attend on me" supports such a conjecture; so too, interestingly, does the title-page woodcut of the 1616
B-text quarto, not printed in any of the earlier A-text editions,
showing a splendid black, winged dragon in front of the conjuring
Faustus and safely outside Faustus's conjuring circle. This is not
to argue that the A-text performances did not also conceive of
Mephistopheles as a dragon, since the 1598 inventory of the Admiral's Men included "j dragon in fostes,"[8] but it does suggest that the
B-text is specifically attentive to stage business here. The title-

---

8. *Henslowe's Diary*, 320.

page's illustration thus may well feature an aspect of production so compelling that audiences clamored for more.

Despite the silence of all but Mephistopheles in 1.3, the devils have been introduced as vitally operative figures in a drama of damnation and as a part of the stage "picture" depicting that conflict. This circumstance casts its shadow over the subsequent action and alters the way the two texts are to be read. When in scene 4, for example, both texts specify "*Enter two Devils*" to Wagner and Robin, the B-text encourages the visual identification in the theater of these figures with those already seen onstage in 1.3. Perhaps the excision of the A-text's reference to these figures in scene 4 as "a he devil and a she devil," with subsequent obscene joking on the idea that she devils have "clefts and cloven feet" (A-text, 1.4.55–57), is to be understood as allowing for a reentry of devils already visually familiar to the audience. Clearly, in the B-text the devils are already in costume, ready for a quick entrance. Because they are more continually at hand and more visually recognizable than in the A-text, the implications of a malign conspiracy of evil lying in wait for Faustus are more marked.

The scene of Faustus's selling of his soul to the devil (2.1) offers few variants between the A- and B-texts, in dialogue or in staging. The A-text's vivid stage directions are preserved in the later text, albeit with an added theatrical particularity that is characteristic of the B-text elsewhere. Whereas the A-text specifies, "*Enter with* Devils, *giving crowns and rich apparel to Faustus, and dance and then depart*" (2.1.82.1–2), not directly naming Mephistopheles, who has just exited to fetch amusing distractions for his victim and who must indeed reenter, the B-text removes the ambiguity: "*Enter* MEPHISTOPHELES." Similarly, when in the A-text Mephistopheles exits and then quickly reenters "*with a chafer of coals*" (A-text, 69.1) to unthicken Faustus's congealed blood, the B-text changes the language to "*with the chafer of fire.*" The alteration seems insignificant at first, and points indeed to identical stage business, and yet the substitution of "*the*" for "*a*" sounds consciously theatrical; the B-text instructs Mephistopheles to return to the stage with *the* chafer, the one in the company's possession, the one that the actor will know is waiting for him backstage. *Fire* instead of *coals* may suggest, similarly, that the thing has to be lighted before it is brought onstage like a *flambeau* dish in a fancy restaurant, providing the desired spectacular effect. Again, this is not to argue that the coals of the A-text were unlit—obviously they were lit—but that the language of the B-text stage direction is attentive to theatrical contingencies.

Even when the B-text changes appear to move in a less theatrically conscious direction, they are in fact aware of theatrical contingency. Toward the end of 2.1, for example, when Faustus complains that he is "wanton and lascivious and cannot live without a wife" (A-text, 144–45), Mephistopheles assures him, in the A-text, "Well, thou shalt have one. Sit there till I come. I'll fetch thee a wife, in the devil's name." A stage direction follows: "*Enter with a* Devil *dressed like a woman, with fireworks.*" The B-text omits mention of the fireworks, a seeming impoverishment in theatrical terms. Yet the B-text's simpler, "Well, Faustus, thou shalt have a wife," and simpler stage direction, "*He fetches in a* woman Devil," are clearer for the acting company. The A-text fails to note an exit, and then specifies "*Enter*" without indicating who is to enter. The purport is clear enough, but the B-text language is unambiguous and to the point. The B-text phrase "*a* woman Devil" is utilitarian, as distinguished from the A-text's literary and metaphorical "*a* Devil *dressed like a woman.*" From the audience's point of view, the entering figure is "*a* woman Devil"; the surmise that it is in fact a Devil dressed like a woman is safe enough, but it is an interpretive statement. What the company must provide here is an actor dressed like a woman Devil, not a Devil dressed like a woman.

Similarly, the ending of 2.1, in which the B-text truncates a discourse about magical books, leaving out a series of vivid stage directions specifying that Mephistopheles is to turn the pages in those books that Faustus desires to see—"*There turn to them,*" "*Turn to them,*" "*Turn to them*"—seems to take away a sequence of compelling stage images. Yet the revisers have done so, it would seem, because the ending of the A-text proceeds so abruptly into what follows. "Tut, I warrant thee," says Mephistopheles to Faustus's voicing of doubts about the efficacy of the books shown him, at which point the dialogue ceases without any indication of an "*Exeunt.*" Instead, the A-text introduces a lengthy dialogue, chiefly between Faustus and Mephistopheles, that has every appearance of being an entirely separate scene mistakenly placed at this spot. Perhaps the comic scene of Robin and Rafe (or Robin and Dick in the B-text) with Faustus's conjuring book had gotten misplaced in the shuffle of manuscript pages and should have been placed here to separate the two long scenes of Faustus and Mephistopheles. In any event, the passage as it stands in the A-text is theatrically abrupt and incomplete. Even its piquant stage directions are characteristically ambiguous: "*Turn to them.*" Is Mephistopheles or Faustus to turn the pages, or both? What does "*them*" signify? The intent is more or less clear, but as theatrical language the stage directions are more characteristic of the A-text than of the B-text.

The omnipresence of the devils in the B-text, and the distressing theological implications of that phenomenon, take the form of giving Beelzebub more lines of dialogue. In 2.3, when Faustus's

attempt to call on Christ prompts the sending of diabolical rein-
forcements, Beelzebub is made partner with Lucifer in a rapid-fire
exchange of threats and warnings to their victim (2.3.91–95),
whereas in the A-text these lines are Lucifer's alone.[9] Shortly thereafter, as well, when Lucifer calls for the seven Deadly Sins to enter,
it is Beelzebub who says to Faustus, "Now, Faustus, question them
of their names and dispositions" (108–9), rather than Lucifer.
Mephistopheles is also more of a partner in this sequence: he is
bidden to escort in the Deadly Sins, and does so, whereas in the
A-text Lucifer simply calls offstage for them to come.

The major additions to the B-text are found, of course, in the
second half of the play, especially in the phase of the play repre-
senting Faustus's travels and stunts as a magician. Here the
Damnable Life was at hand for further exploitation; it seems clear
that Henslowe's instructions to Birde and Rowley were to add
marvels of the sort that audiences demanded. They did so, with
resulting theological emphases that may have been doctrinally
conscious but that may just as well have been the unintended result of showbiz stratagems. The bent in this direction is plainly sig-
naled by the chorus to act 3, considerably expanded to tell us of
Faustus's viewing the cosmos and all quarters of the earth, and of
his further travels "mounted then upon a dragon's back, / that with
his wings did part the subtle air" (18–19). Wholesale revision begins only moments later, as Faustus arrives at the Pope's chambers
in Rome.

In staging terms, the visit to the Pope's chamber in the B-text is
markedly longer than that of the A-text, and requires a considerably
expanded cast. Whereas the A-text is content to show us the Pope
and the Cardinal of Lorraine at a banquet, attended by Friars, the
B-text introduces the Cardinals of France and Padua, the Bishops
of Lorraine and Rheims, Monks, Pope Adrian (i.e., Hadrian IV),
Raymond King of Hungary, and Bruno the rival pope. The procession is visually more elaborate, not only in the number of church-
men and aristocrats present but in the appurtenances of rank
brought to accompany them. The procession enters, "*some bearing
crosiers, some the pillars*" (3.1.88.2–3). The order of entry in the
stage direction bespeaks the dignity of the occasion, with cardinals
first, then the bishops, then the monks and friars "*singing their procession,*" then the Pope and King Raymond, with "Saxon Bruno" led
on in chains. The alterations bespeak an enlarged capacity of the
acting company around 1602, and point at once to the enhanced
symbolic importance of Faustus's Rome journey. He is to be made a

9. Bernard Beckerman, "Scene Patterns in *Doctor Faustus* and *Richard III*," in *Shakespeare
and His Contemporaries: Essays in Comparison*, ed. E. A. J. Honigmann (Manchester:
University of Manchester Press, 1986), 31–41.

Protestant hero, doing battle with the papacy on behalf of German (and hence, by implication, English) nationalism.

Whereas the A-text does of course have its fun at the Pope's expense, making a kind of cheap appeal to English audiences, the B-text turns this moment into a major enterprise. Mephistopheles, in this version, openly encourages Faustus to use his magic "to cross the Pope" and "dash the pride of this solemnity" (80–81). Considerable stage business is devoted to the humiliation of the captive Bruno at the hands of Pope Adrian: he is made to kneel in front of the papal throne so that Adrian can use Bruno as a footstool to reach his throne, to the accompaniment of trumpets: "*A flourish while he ascends*" (97.1). Bruno's addressing Adrian as "Proud Lucifer" (92) plays upon the frequent presence onstage of the actual Lucifer and his fellow devils. The reference to Bruno as "Saxon Bruno" (89) elides the difference between a German hero confronting the papacy and an implied hero of Anglo-Saxon Britain. Indeed, the whole story is loosely taken out of Foxe's *Acts and Monuments* (2.195–96) by a similar sleight of hand: Foxe's account of the Emperor Frederick Barbarossa's unsuccessful attempt to set up a rival pope (Victor IV) in defiance of Pope Alexander III (successor to Hadrian IV in 1159–81) is converted into material for the present occasion. All of these changes enhance Faustus's role as champion of Protestant nationalism at the expense of the ultramontane church.

Faustus's antics in defense of Protestantism are designed to be theatrically varied and entertaining for English audiences even while putting down the papacy. Faustus repeatedly takes the initiative. It is his idea to have Mephistopheles accompany the cardinals to their consistory and overwhelm them with drowsiness so that Faustus and Mephistopheles can then enter to the Pope dressed "*like the cardinals*" (160.1) and misrepresent what the consistory has decided. The comic effect is to undercut ridiculously the defiant speech of the Pope threatening to depose the German Emperor and threaten his loyal subjects with excommunication. The Pope is made to seem gullible as well, believing the misrepresentations of Faustus as false cardinal and delivering Bruno into the hands of Faustus and Mephistopheles, thereby making possible the escape of Bruno on a "proud-paced steed" that flies over the Alps "as swift as thought" to the Emperor (3.2.4–6). Even Bruno's "triple crown" is delivered into the hands of the supposed cardinals. A magic girdle then enables Faustus, no longer dressed as a cardinal, to watch invisibly as the cardinals are humiliated and hauled off to prison for their seeming malfeasance in letting Bruno go. Only at the conclusion of this long episode do the B-text revisers go back to the original play and the business of Faustus's snatching dishes and wine from the Pope's table, while the Friars sing their "dirge" of male-diction and exorcism.

The comic business of discomfiting the obstreperous Knight with a pair of horns is also greatly expanded in the B-text, but presumably for reasons that are those of vaudeville rather than of polemical controversy. In the A-text, the unnamed Knight is little more than a skeptical observer of Faustus's entertaining the emperor with the show of Alexander and his paramour (4.1). From the start of the scene, the Knight is given ironic asides ("I'faith, he looks like a conjurer," [12]) that lead to his discomfiture with the horns but that also usefully introduce a note of ambiguity as to the ethical nature of Faustus's inventive magic. When he challenges Faustus directly, and suggests wryly that Faustus's claim of being able to produce Alexander and his paramour is just about as true "as Diana turned me to a stag" (62), he presumably gives Faustus the idea for a comic revenge that will demonstrate once more the power of magical art. The Knight departs rather than abuse his patience with the conjuring (65.1), and then has to be summoned at Faustus's request in order for the Emperor to see the effects of magic: "*Enter the* KNIGHT *with a pair of horns on his head*" (76.2). Thus the business ends in the A-text. It is simply another demonstration of the tricks that Faustus can do with the devil's assistance, and a warning that academics can be vindictive if they are crossed.

The B-text enhancement takes several forms. It is much longer, requires an expanded cast, and puts new demands on the acting space. The Knight, now christened Benvolio, takes on the dimensions of a major, even legendary, character, suggesting that the Knight had by this time become a central part of the play for many viewers. Indeed, one can imagine that some of the added material had made its way into performances through ad-libs even before Birde and Rowley were set to work. Benvolio is talked about before he enters by his friends Martino and Frederick, who are accompanied by other officers and gentlemen. They enter "*at several doors*" in act 4 to set the scene, and it is to be a scene as much about Benvolio as about Faustus and the Emperor. Indeed, Faustus and Benvolio are discussed as polar types: Faustus has rescued Bruno, "our elected pope," from Rome's clutches, while Benvolio is reported to be "Fast asleep," having taken "his rouse with stoups of Rhenish wine." The line is patently a steal from *Hamlet* 1.4.8–10; Birde and Rowley, with theatrical timeliness, are quoting from a recent and successful London play.

When Benvolio makes his heralded appearance, it is "*above at a window, in his nightcap, buttoning*" (4.1.23.1). All signs point to a theatrical notoriety. Benvolio is elaborately characterized as a drunkard, a user of profanity, and a boaster who will "stand" in his "window" to see the conjuring, though he professes to be bored at the prospect. His asides are enriched with pungent metaphors of a Falstaffian sort ("He looks as like a conjurer as the Pope to a coster-monger," [73]). During Faustus's magic show, Benvolio does not exit from the window; instead, he goes to sleep in full view of the audience. The show itself is described in a lavish stage direction, recounting how "*Darius is thrown down. Alexander kills him, takes off his crown,*" whereupon Alexander embraces his paramour, "*sets Darius's crown upon her head,*" and embraces the German Emperor, all to the accompaniment of trumpets and other "*music*" (102.2–9), none of which is required in the A-text. When Faustus then calls attention to the "strange beast" that "thrusts his head out at win-dow" (119–20), the comic situation invites the hung-over Benvolio to wake with a start and bang his head on the window frame. And whereas the A-text had allowed the Knight to exit in order to facili-tate a reentrance "*with a pair of horns on his head*" (A-text, 4.1.76.2), the B-text requires a *trompe-l'oeil* effect of horns that seem to have sprouted on Benvolio's head as he lay asleep in the window.

Not content with these enlargements, Birde and Rowley pursue the vendetta of Faustus and Benvolio past the episode of the horns. Benvolio is attacked, at Faustus's behest, by "a kennel of devils" with names like Belimoth, Argiron, and Ashtaroth (146–52). Al-though the horns are eventually removed (another *trompe-l'oeil* ef-fect, this one preserved from the A-text), Benvolio is anything but appeased, and vows revenge. The ensuing scenes riot in the stage ramifications of this intent. A large cast of Benvolio, Frederick, Martino, "*and* Soldiers" (4.2.0.2) lie in ambush for Faustus in a "grove," "behind the trees" (16–18). When Faustus enters the scene where they conspire to kill him, he does so "*with the false head*" (37.1), the word "*the*" again signaling (as in the case of "*the chafer of fire,*" B-text [2.1.69.1]) a specific playhouse property, an item in the inventory of props. The false head makes possible the *trompe-l'oeil* effect of striking off Faustus's head, an elaboration of stage business modeled perhaps on the Horsecourser's pulling off Faustus's leg in the A-text (4.1.174.1).

Evidently one cannot have too much of a good thing in the the-ater. At the same time, the thematic ramifications are not inappro-priate to a story of a blaspheming conjurer. Faustus's rising from apparent death prompts Benvolio to exclaim, "Zounds, the devil's alive again!" (4.2.67); Faustus has indeed performed parodic mira-cles not unlike those of Christ's raising of Lazarus. The equating of him with the devil is reinforced by his conjuring of various devils to mount "these traitors" on their "fiery backs," taking them "as high as heaven" and then pitching them "headlong to the lowest hell"

(79–80). Faustus plays the role, anticipating that of the very devils who will eventually throw him down into damnation. The reiterated devils' names of Ashtaroth and Belimoth (78, 84), not present in the A-text but named earlier in the B-text at 4.1.149, expand the dimensions of a diabolical conspiracy and give immediacy in the theater to those otherwise disembodied spirits that hover over the action.

When the *"ambushed* SOLDIERS*"* (i.e., soldiers placed in ambush) come forward on command to attempt to end the life of Faustus, the B-text seemingly obliges with one of its most spectacular stage effects: the trees of the grove are seen to move. "For lo, these trees remove at my command / And stand as bulwarks 'twixt yourselves and me," Faustus defiantly proclaims (101–2). However this *trompe-l'oeil* effect was carried off, it must have required some stage ingenuity; Henslowe was not paying his revisers to indulge in verbal gymnastics only. Graphic stage directions immediately following this moment insist on stage action. "FAUSTUS *strikes the door, and enter a* Devil *playing on a drum, after him another bearing an ensign, and divers with weapons;* MEPHISTOPHELES *with fireworks. They set upon the* SOLDIERS *and drive them out"* (4.2.105.1–4). And immediately in the next scene, *"Enter at several doors* BENVO-LIO, FREDERICK, *and* MARTINO, *their heads and faces bloody and besmeared with mud and dirt, all having horns on their heads"* (4.3.0.1–3). One can never have too many horns—especially when, as in this instance, they set up the tried and true joke about persons who are suddenly disfigured thus and laugh scornfully at each other until they realize, from the others' laughter, that they too have been made to look like fools.

The episode of Faustus and the Horse-courser in the B-text generally follows the outlines of the account in the A-text, except that once again it is elaborated and repeated. Whether or not Mephistopheles is present for the first scene together with Faustus and the Horse-courser is a puzzle; the B-text rearranges the only dialogue involving Mephistopheles in the A-text so that the Horse-courser directly beseeches Faustus to sell his horse for forty dollars, rather than asking Mephistopheles to intervene in his behalf (A-text, 4.4.117–21), and yet the B-text's indication that Mephistopheles is to enter at 4.4.1 seems reason enough to leave him onstage. The business of pulling off Faustus's leg is actually shortened in the B-text somewhat, but is more than compensated for by a long added scene (4.5) that brings back the Horse-courser in the company of Robin, Dick, a Carter, and the Hostess of a tavern—the latter two being added characters to the play. The Horse-courser's reappearance makes possible the repeating of his entire story (35–56), as though the staging of the event were not enough to satisfy audiences; they are regaled with a narrative description after the fact. Nothing could testify more eloquently to the fame that this business seems to have acquired. The Horse-courser and the horse had become legend by the time Birde and Rowley were paid to write it all up in loving repetition.

The Horse-courser's recital of his story provides the occasion, moreover, for another such account, this one being of the Carter and his load of hay, which the good doctor has managed to consume down to the last straw on a bet that he could eat as much as he wished for three farthings (24–31). We see how one addition leads to another, and then to the improbable appearance of "*The* CLOWN[S]" at the Duke of Vanholt's palace (4.6.35.1). The nature of their ensuing conversation as a comic extension of the A-text's scene of Faustus's fetching of grapes from India seems apparent when we notice how ambiguously a sense of place is suggested in the theater. The clowns call loudly for beer, as though still in the hostess's tavern; when she arrives, she does so "*with drink*" as though from her own establishment (67–76, 99.1). The apparent inconsistency about location can be explained if we assume that Faustus has charmed the clowns and dulled their senses so that they do not know where they are, prompting them to behave with comic indecorum in the presence of the Duke of Vanholt, but the effect is dislocating in a way that also suggests textual improvisation.

There is still one joke too good not to revisit: that of Faustus's leg being pulled off by the Horse-courser. Whereas the A-text chastely settles for a direct presentation of that comic action onstage (4.1.174.1), the B-text, by bringing the Horse-courser and Faustus together one more time at the Duke of Vanholt's palace, provides occasion for the Horse-courser to make sly insinuations about Faustus's presumed wooden leg (accompanied, of course, by punning on the idea of "standing upon" such a leg in the sense of attaching importance to it, or standing on ceremony, or literally standing on one's legs) and for Faustus to refute the clowns' laughter in the most direct way possible. He curtsies, draws out their curiosity to the full, and then shows them his apparently restored limb. "But I have it again now I am awake. Look you here, sir" (107–8). The effect is pure theater. Faustus manages it as though it were another of his magic tricks, like allowing a false head to be severed or a false leg to be pulled off. What a trickster! And yet all that is required of the actor is that he pull up his gown and show the two legs he has enjoyed all along. So much for the magic of theater.

Faustus's last hours in this world are oppressively weighed down in the B-text by an overseeing presence of devils that are not a

consistent part of the A-text version. Act 5 begins in the B-text with
"Thunder and lightning. Enter Devils *with covered dishes.*
MEPHISTOPHELES *leads them into Faustus's study. Then enter* WAG-
NER." This replaces the A-text eloquently simple *"Enter* WAGNER *so-
lus."* Even Faustus's food is supplied by devils. We know that
Faustus relies on spirits to supply all his needs, of course, but the
B-text staging makes the diabolical presence explicit. When Helen
is brought in to Faustus a second time by Mephistopheles, the
B-text is at pains to specify that they are *"passing over between two
Cupids"* (93.1). These Cupids must be devilish spirits. To be sure,
the B-text does excise a passage at the end of 5.1 in which, in the
A-version, devils menace the Old Man to no avail, but the B-text
more than compensates for this cut by a new beginning of 5.2.

   "Thunder. Enter LUCIFER, BEELZEBUB, *and* MEPHISTOPHELES," the
B-text specifies, evidently intending that these devils appear *"above"*
as they seemingly did at the beginning of Faustus's conjuring scene
in 1.3. Their conversation in 5.2 strongly determines Faustus's
outcome and casts him in the unsympathetic light of a "Fond
worldling" whose "store of pleasures must be sauced with pain"
(5.2.12, 16). This is the theology of the A-text as well, to be sure,
but the insistent and homiletic tone here provides a kind of choric
commentary that the A-text eschews for the most part in the action
of the play, leaving commentary of this kind to the actual chorus
figure of the epilogue.

   The B-text's most extensive addition to act 5 is certainly no less
didactic. Mephistopheles gladly takes credit for tempting Faustus
into damnation: " 'Twas I that, when thou were i' the way to
heaven, / Dammed up thy passage." All hope is past: Faustus must
now "Think only on hell, / For that must be thy mansion, there to
dwell" (93–99). To underscore the hopelessness of Faustus's situation, spectacular stage contrivances are brought into use as means
of visual demonstration. The Good and Bad Angels enter *"at several
doors"* to join forces for the first time in denouncing Faustus and
his foolish choice. (In the A-text, they always speak in symmetrical opposition to each other: "Too late" versus "Never too late,"
2.3.78–79, etc.) Music plays *"while the throne descends"* displaying
the bright heavenly joys that Faustus has forfeited, while the Good
Angel points out its salient features: "yonder throne" and "those
bright shining saints," all set in "resplendent glory" (110–20). The
"throne" is presumably let down from the "heavens"; those "heavens" display above, in the theater, a vision of heavenly harmony re-
capitulated in the descending throne. The "saints" may be mute
actors, or puppets, or some pictorial representation; whatever the
means, the representation is clearly intended to remind viewers of
the ascent of the blessed souls at the time of the Last Judgment, in

a portrayal such as any parishioners might have seen on the west walls of their churches. Evidently the throne reascends once its saintly vision has been presented for all to witness.

As the Good Angel concludes his homily by saying, "The jaws of hell are open to receive thee," hell is *"discovered"* (B-text, 5.2.120.2). The Good Angel's utterance affords visual clues: hell is backstage, provided with a vivid representation of damnation and then suddenly revealed by means of a backcloth. The Admiral's Men included a "Hell mought" in their inventory for 1598 (*Henslowe's Diary*, p. 319). Such a hellmouth presumably resembled those seen in medieval illustrations, with a leviathan-shaped aperture leading back into the bowels of the underworld, filled with black smoke, din, and misery. Again, we cannot be certain whether this was achieved in Henslowe's theater by means of a painting or other more lifelike representations; but there can be little doubt as to the purport of it all, since the Bad Angel instructs Faustus in what his eyes are to see, including "Furies tossing damnèd souls / On burning forks," bodies boiled in lead, live quarters of carcasses "burning on the coals," and an "ever-burning chair" or throne meant to serve as the visual counterpart for the heavenly throne that Faustus will never enjoy (121–32).

One odd, even jarring, effect of this theatrical display in the B-text is to put a highly pictorial construction on the nature of hell. What hell is actually like is a question that consumes Faustus throughout the play; it is in fact his first question once he has signed the contract with the devil (A- and B-texts, 2.1.119–20). Can hell be all that bad, if it means conversing about first causes and astronomy, as he and Mephistopheles are doing? (A-text, 11.141–42). Faustus has every reason to wonder if hell is "a fable" (130), since, if accounts of hell are nothing but old wives' tales, his selling of his soul cannot come to any serious account. Yet Mephistopheles is at pains to explain to Faustus that hell is a state of being absent eternally from God ("Why, this is hell, nor am I out of it," [A-text, 1.3.78; see also 2.1.140]). Calvin was insistent on the idea that humans, because they see through a glass darkly in this mortal life, cannot comprehend the true nature of heaven or hell and thus are driven to childish pictorial depictions of that which goes utterly beyond the human imagination. This is a wonderfully sophisticated idea of hell that informs the A-text pretty much from start to finish (even if hell is also described by Mephistopheles as "within the bowels of these elements" where "we are tortured and remain for ever," [2.1.122–23]). The B-text, especially in 5.2, ends the play by bringing its audience back to the very kinds of garish visualization that both Calvin and Mephistopheles seem to resist.

That same graphic pictorializing informs the ending of the play in the B-text. Although the terrifying striking of the clock, and the entering of the devils to carry Faustus off to hell, is essentially the same in the two texts, the B-version then adds a scene of three scholars entering Faustus's chambers to view the unnerving evidence of his damnation. Having experienced a night of "fearful shrieks and cries," they now inform us what they behold: "See, here are Faustus's limbs, / All torn asunder by the hands of death" (5.3.4–7). The text does not inform us precisely how this effect was conveyed in the theater, but we can guess that Henslowe and his revisers did not rely solely on the Second Scholar's verbal report. At hand for the revisers' work was the gruesome account of the *Damnable Life*: "The hall lay besprinkled with blood, his brains cleaving to the wall, for the devil had beaten him from one wall against another. In one corner lay his eyes, in another his teeth . . . They found his body lying on the horse dung, most monstrously torn and fearful to behold, for his head and all his joints were dashed to pieces."[1] Some of this could have been made visible in the theater by means of a backdrop suddenly revealed by the drawing back of a curtain, thereby visually replacing the scene of hell-mouth displayed in 5.2.

The B-text thus reaches for a climax in physically compelling evidence of the horrors of hell. The move is of a piece with the revisers' plan throughout: give 'em blood and guts and theatrical novelties. The impulse strikes us as at once commercial and doctrinal; by giving audiences more of what they found titillating and entertaining, the B-text also appeals to a kind of popular theology insistent on reprisals for sinners and on a Calvinistic assumption that the reprobate are irrevocably damned. The B-text thus sacrifices some of the A-text's stunning ambiguity throughout as to whether it is indeed too late, or not too late, for Faustus to repent. The B-text does this in return for what are evidently seen as solid theatrical gains in spectacle and laughter.

The A- and B-texts thus show us, with unusual clarity, the early stage history of a play in transition as theater space developed new methods and as popular demands helped determine the shapes of plays mounted for its benefit. The exploitation of new stage machinery takes the form of a descent from the "heavens" of the heavenly throne in act 5. Appearances of devils "above" exploit theatrical space while simultaneously enhancing the ominous presence of a kind of diabolical chorus, resulting in a B-text that is manifestly more deterministic and less ambiguous as to whether

1. *The History of the Damnable Life and Deserved Death of Doctor John Faustus* (London, 1592). See *Faustus*, ed. Bevington and Rasmussen, 285.

Faustus can be saved than is the A-text version. Expanded casting requirements and elaborated comic action involving especially the German Pope, Benvolio, and the Horse-courser seem motivated by commercial factors and audience demand, to which Henslowe was clearly attuned. *Trompe-l'oeil* effects are more common and spectacular in the B-text; vaudeville routines have a field day. Stage directions reflect the practicalities of playhouse action in their references to specific props presumably owned by the company. At the same time, all this showbiz serves the purposes of an enhanced patriotic Protestantism of the sort that Henslowe's audiences were evidently demanding. The homiletic heavyhandedness of the B-text's act 5 aligns itself with the kind of popular Puritan-leaning religious sentiment that was becoming increasingly strident in the last years of Elizabeth's reign. In every way, the story of the theatrical shift from the A-text to the B-text of *Doctor Faustus* is a saga of its time.

GEORGE BERNARD SHAW

Review of *Doctor Faustus*, July 2, 1896, Acted by Members of the Shakespeare Reading Society†

Mr. William Poel, in drawing up an announcement of the last exploit of the Elizabethan Stage Society, had no difficulty in citing a number of eminent authorities as to the superlative merits of Christopher Marlowe. The dotage of Charles Lamb on the subject of the Elizabethan dramatists has found many imitators, notably Mr. Swinburne, who expresses in verse what he finds in books as passionately as a poet expressed what he finds in life. Among them, it appears, is a Mr. G. B. Shaw, in quoting whom Mr. Poel was supposed by many persons to be quoting me. But though I share the gentleman's initials, I do not share his views. He can admire a fool: I cannot, even when his folly not only expresses itself in blank verse, but actually invents that art form for the purpose. I admit that Marlowe's blank verse has charm of color and movement; and I know only too well how its romantic march caught the literary imagination and founded that barren and horrible worship of blank verse for its own sake which has since desolated and laid waste the dramatic poetry of England. But the fellow was a fool for all that. He often reminds me, in his abysmally inferior way, of Rossini. Rossini had just the same trick of beginning with a magnificently

† *Saturday Review* (July 11, 1896); rpt. in *Dramatic Opinions and Essays* (New York: Brentano's, 1909), pp. 36–43.

impressive exordium, apparently pregnant with the most tragic de-
velopments, and presently lapsing into arrant triviality. But Rossini
lapses amusingly; writes 'Excusez du peu' at the double bar which
separates the sublime from the ridiculous; and is gay, tuneful and
clever in his frivolity. Marlowe, the moment the exhaustion of the
imaginative fit deprives him of the power of raving, becomes childish in thought, vulgar and wooden in humor, and stupid in his attempts at invention. He is the true Elizabethan blank-verse beast,
itching to frighten other people with the superstitious terrors and
cruelties in which he does not himself believe, and wallowing in
blood, violence, muscularity of expression and strenuous animal
passion as only literary men do when they become thoroughly de-
praved by solitary work, sedentary cowardice, and starvation of the
sympathetic centres. It is not surprising to learn that Marlowe was
stabbed in a tavern brawl: what would be utterly unbelievable
would be his having succeeded in stabbing any one else. On paper
the whole obscene crew of these blank-verse rhetoricians could
outdare Lucifer himself: Nature can produce no murderer cruel
enough for Webster, nor any hero bully enough for Chapman, de-
vout disciples, both of them, of Kit Marlowe. But you do not believe in their martial ardor as you believe in the valor of Sidney or
Cervantes. One calls the Elizabethan dramatists imaginative, as
one might say the same of a man in delirium tremens; but even that
flatters them; for whereas the drinker can imagine rats and snakes
and beetles which have some sort of resemblance to real ones, your
typical Elizabethan heroes of the mighty line, having neither the
eyes to see anything real nor the brains to observe it, could no more
conceive a natural or convincing stage figure than a blind man can
conceive a rainbow or a deaf one the sound of an orchestra. Such
success as they have had is the success which any fluent braggart
and liar may secure in a pothouse. Their swagger and fustian, and
their scraps of Cicero and Aristotle, passed for poetry and learning
in their own day because their public was Philistine and ignorant.
To-day, without having by any means lost this advantage, they enjoy
in addition the quaintness of their obsolescence, and, above all, the
splendor of the light reflected on them from the reputation of
Shakespeare. Without that light they would now be as invisible as
they are insufferable. In condemning them indiscriminately, I am
only doing what Time would have done if Shakespeare had not rescued them. I am quite aware that they did not get their reputations
for nothing; that there were degrees of badness among them; that
Greene was really amusing, Marston spirited and silly-clever, Cyril
Tourneur able to string together lines of which any couple picked
out and quoted separately might pass as a fragment of a real organic poem, and so on. Even the brutish pedant Jonson was not

heartless, and could turn out prettily affectionate verses and fool-
ishly affectionate criticisms; whilst the plausible firm of Beaumont
and Fletcher, humbugs as they were, could produce plays which
were, all things considered, not worse than 'The Lady of Lyons.'
But these distinctions are not worth making now. There is much
variety in a dust-heap, even when the rag-picker is done with it; but
we throw it indiscriminately into the 'destructor' for all that. There
is only one use left for the Elizabethan dramatists, and that is the
purification of Shakespeare's reputation from its spurious elements.
Just as you can cure people of talking patronizingly about 'Mozart-
ian melody' by showing them that the tunes they imagine to be his
distinctive characteristics were the commonplaces of his time, so it
is possible, perhaps, to cure people of admiring, as distinctively
characteristic of Shakespeare, the false, forced rhetoric, the callous
sensation-mongering in murder and lust, the ghosts and combats,
and the venal expenditure of all the treasures of his genius on the
bedizenment of plays which are, as wholes, stupid toys. When Sir
Henry Irving presently revives 'Cymbeline' at the Lyceum, the numerous descendants of the learned Shakespearean enthusiast who
went down on his knees and kissed the Ireland forgeries will see no
difference between the great dramatist who changed Imogen from
a mere name in a story to a living woman, and the manager-
showman who exhibited her with the gory trunk of a newly be-
headed man in her arms. But why should we, the heirs of so many
greater ages, with the dramatic poems of Goethe and Ibsen in our
hands, and the music of a great dynasty of musicians, from Bach to
Wagner, in our ears—why should we waste our time on the rank
and file of the Elizabethans, or encourage foolish modern persons
to imitate them, or talk about Shakespeare as if his moral plati-
tudes, his jingo claptraps, his tavern pleasantries, his bombast and
drivel, and his incapacity for following up the scraps of philosophy
he stole so aptly, were as admirable as the mastery of poetic speech,
the feeling for nature, and the knack of character-drawing, fun, and
heart wisdom which he was ready, like a true son of the theatre, to
prostitute to any subject, any occasion, and any theatrical employment? The fact is, we are growing out of Shakespeare. Byron declined to put up with his reputation at the beginning of the
nineteenth century; and now, at the beginning of the twentieth, he
is nothing but a household pet. His characters still live; his word
pictures of woodland and wayside still give us a Bank-holiday
breath of country air; his verse still charms us; his sublimities still
stir us; the commonplaces and trumperies of the wisdom which age
and experience bring to all of us are still expressed by him better
than by anybody else; but we have nothing to hope from him and
nothing to learn from him—not even how to write plays, though he

does that so much better than most modern dramatists. And if this is true of Shakespeare, what is to be said of Kit Marlowe?

Kit Marlowe, however, did not bore me at St. George's Hall as he has always bored me when I have tried to read him without skipping. The more I see of these performances by the Elizabethan Stage Society, the more I am convinced that their method of presenting an Elizabethan play is not only the right method for that particular sort of play, but that any play performed on a platform amidst the audience gets closer home to its hearers than when it is presented as a picture framed by a proscenium. Also, that we are less conscious of the artificiality of the stage when a few well-understood conventions, adroitly handled, are substituted for attempts at an impossible scenic verisimilitude. All the old-fashioned tale-of-adventure plays, with their frequent changes of scene, and all the new problem plays, with their intense intimacies, should be done in this way.

The E.S.S. made very free with 'Doctor Faustus.' Their devils, Baliol and Belcher to wit, were not theatrical devils with huge pasteboard heads, but pictorial Temptation-of-St.-Anthony devils such as Martin Schongauer drew. The angels were Florentine fifteenth-century angels, with their draperies sewn into Botticellian folds and tucks. The Emperor's bodyguard had Maximilianesque uniforms copied from Holbein. Mephistophilis made his first appearance as Mr. Joseph Pennell's favorite devil from the roof of Notre Dame, and, when commanded to appear as a Franciscan friar, still proclaimed his modernity by wearing an electric bulb in his cowl. The Seven Deadly Sins were *tout ce qu'il y a de plus fin de siècle*,[1] the five worst of them being so attractive that they got rounds of applause on the strength of their appearance alone. In short, Mr. William Poel gave us an artistic rather than a literal presentation of Elizabethan conditions, the result being, as always happens in such cases, that the picture of the past was really a picture of the future. For which result he is, in my judgment, to be highly praised. The performance was a wonder of artistic discipline in this lawless age. It is true, since the performers were only three or four instead of fifty times as skilful as ordinary professional actors, that Mr. Poel has had to give up all impetuosity and spontaneity of execution, and to have the work done very slowly and carefully. But it is to be noted that even Marlowe, treated in this thorough way, is not tedious; whereas Shakespeare, rattled and rushed and spouted and clattered through in the ordinary professional manner, all but kills the audience with tedium. For instance, Mephistophilis was as joyless and leaden as a devil need be—it was clear that no stage-

---

1. All those most in the style of our time (French).

manager had ever exhorted him, like a lagging horse, to get the long speeches over as fast as possible, old chap—and yet he never for a moment bored us as Prince Hal and Poins bore us at the Haymarket. The actor who hurries reminds the spectators of the flight of time, which it is his business to make them forget. Twenty years ago the symphonies of Beethoven used to be rushed through in London with the sole object of shortening the agony of the audience. They were then highly unpopular. When Richter arrived he took the opposite point of view, playing them so as to prolong the delight of the audience; and Mottl dwells more lovingly on Wagner than Richter does on Beethoven. The result is that Beethoven and Wagner are now popular. Mr. Poel has proved that the same result will be attained as soon as blank-verse plays are produced under the control of managers who like them, instead of openly and shamelessly treating them as inflictions to be curtailed to the utmost. The representation at St. George's Hall went without a hitch from beginning to end, a miracle of diligent preparedness. Mr. Mannering, as Faustus, had the longest and the hardest task; and he performed it conscientiously, punctually, and well. The others did no less with what they had to do. The relief of seeing actors come on the stage with the simplicity and abnegation of children, instead of bounding on to an enthusiastic reception with the 'Here I am again' expression of the popular favorites of the ordinary stage, is hardly to be described. Our professional actors are now looked at by the public from behind the scenes; and they accept that situation and glory in it for the sake of the 'personal popularity' it involves. What a gigantic reform Mr. Poel will make if his Elizabethan Stage should lead to such a novelty as a theatre to which people go to see the play instead of to see the cast!

WILLIAM TYDEMAN

[*Doctor Faustus* on the Stage]†

When in 1959, in his autobiography *A Life in the Theatre*, Sir Tyrone Guthrie wrote that one of the minor tragedies of the historical development of European culture had been 'the divorce between the theatrical performance and the literary study of drama', he could scarcely have foreseen the present upsurge of interest in the staging of plays among academics. Few scholars or critics would now come to the discussion of dramatic literature without an acute

† From *Doctor Faustus: Text and Performance* (London: Macmillan, 1984), pp. 78–83.

interest in its stage realisation, or in many cases without some practical knowledge of plays in production, albeit at the amateur level.
Yet one drawback to this desirable situation is that, whereas scholarly commentators are frequently prone to perceive and bring out
ambiguities and paradoxes within a playtext, and to emphasise the
multiplicity of available responses to them, the director of a play in
the theatre usually feels obliged to take concrete decisions on what
to stress and what to play down. With a work such as *Faustus*, over-
emphasis on ambivalence, however admirable in academic terms,
can leave spectators baffled; on the other hand, over-insistence on
a particular reading can lay a producer open to the charge of limiting our response to a full range of meanings.

There can be little doubt, as Verna Ann Foster points out in her
stimulating survey 'Dr *Faustus* on the Stage', that early presenta-
tions divide into those which treat the story as that of an idealised
Renaissance hero whose faults, if any, are those of the justified sinner, and those which view the work as an Elizabethan morality play
in which the old lesson of the wages of sin being death is incul-
cated. William Poel, as we have seen, ignored much that was base
or trivial in Faustus's character, and cast him as a serious seeker after truth, reinforcing the point by permitting him to be viewed as
both astronomer and cosmographer, and thus anticipating Nicholas
Brooke's argument that the middle scenes may not depict Faustus
in such a harsh light as some orthodox commentators claim. But in
order to achieve this impression directors have had to cut heavily
into the text to suppress such slapstick incidents as the fooling with
the Horse-Courser, or have played up the solemn majesty of such
sights as the vision of the Emperor Alexander. Failure to do the former creates too great a dichotomy between romantic scholar and
cocksure magician, as in Wade's production in 1925 and Walter
Hudd's in 1946; failure to do the latter reinforces what has been
the much more general attitude to the play, that Faustus achieves
nothing of real lasting worth from his bargain, just as Lucifer intends.

This of course has been an important feature in the argument of
those who interpret *Faustus* as a morality piece: by making his im-
moral pact with the Devil, the Doctor turns his back on legitimate
satisfactions, trading them in for a bag of tricks. Nugent Monck's
1929 presentation, by coupling the play with *Everyman*, fore-
shadowed the critical approach developed by James Smith, Leo
Kirschbaum, Sir Walter Greg and others, but to do so a ruthless
line had to be taken with the more commendable, less selfish, motives behind Faustus's decision to hand himself over to diabolic
agents. To treat the work as an updated morality does less than justice to the challenge *Doctor Faustus* presents to orthodoxy, and to

the picture it offers of a living personality rather than a doctrinal statistic.

In this respect Nevill Coghill's attempt to do justice both to the morality framework and to the integrity of the character-portrait it contains was important: seeing the play as a study of the wages of excessive intellectual curiosity, Coghill was able to unify the aspiring scholar with the conjuring showman by suggesting that any abuse of his magic powers sprang from Faustus's vocational frustrations expressing themselves in pranks and showing-off rather than solid achievements. What did not come across in 1957 or 1966 was that Faustus is partly an heroic figure, even if not the dignified titanic rebel of Poel's version. Neither Dobtcheff's sorcerer nor Burton's bookworm quite measured up to the Renaissance dimension.

Michael Benthall came closest in recent times to a reading of the play which suggested in some measure that Faustus received value for his disastrous bargain. The ceremonial pomp and processions of the Edinburgh version not only ensured that the middle of the play was held together by spectacle, but meant that Faustus himself increased his stature as one who had risen from scholarly obscurity to mingle with the highest in the land, albeit in the case of the Pope to mock them. Certainly, amid the impressive trappings of the imperial court, Faustus came across as a conjuror still, but one expert and awe-inspiring enough to be invited to give a command performance. Paul Daneman here created something of the favourable impact some commentators feel Faustus would have achieved on the Elizabethan stage: the splendid surroundings certainly diminished the sense of his having sacrificed his soul for a few parlour tricks, at least at Edinburgh. At the Old Vic the inevitable reduction in pageantry renewed one's sense that Faustus was a small-time entertainer after all.

Furthermore, Daneman's performance was too genial and openhearted to convince one as to the scale of his revolt or the poetic justice of his punishment: Benthall seemed to treat the story as that of the misfortune of a nice chap who had experienced a thoughtless moment of rashness, and could not get himself out of the resultant mess. Presentation and performance minimised the egocentric, spiteful, irresponsible, vulgar traits in the hero: the result was to lessen the tragedy of a man in whom good and bad tendencies are inextricably mixed.

No such reservations could honestly be expressed about Clifford Williams's interpretation in 1968, or about Eric Porter's valiant attempt to suggest the medley of motives and emotions at war within the protagonist's brain. Here one had the intelligent, arrogant genius the text seems to demand, the sense of bored discontentment with the legitimate road to the glittering prizes, the enjoyment of the grotesque and the contemptuously sardonic delight in the humiliation of others. What was missing was the passionate desire for power and knowledge which lay behind the negotiations with Lucifer; like Mannering, Hardwicke and Burton before him, and Kingsley later, Porter failed to suggest the capacity of magic to 'ravish' its devotees. Nor did Williams altogether succeed in reconciling his designer's brilliantly idiosyncratic images of Hell—most notably the memorably evil Deadly Sins—with the obvious perceptive intelligence of his Faustus. The infernal machinery was perhaps a self-indulgence in the context, being too repellent to enable us to comprehend this ascetic Faustus's fascination with it. More seductive were some of the magical effects: Alexander and his Paramour were silvered statues moving in mimed dance; at the Pope's banquet a slimy grey hand appeared from His Holiness's dish; when Mephostophilis spat out a grape-seed it exploded. Like Coghill in 1957, Williams devised these ingenious routines in order to emphasise his vision of Faustus as exuberant as well as scholarly; the joy in scoring off the supreme Pontiff must be given as much weight as the pleasure of hearing Homer sing, and Williams almost made it work.

John Barton was in some respects more successful in creating a unified theme for the play, but often at some expense to its texture. The concept of the action as the diseased fantasy of a weak neurotic helped to stress the hollowness of Faustus's recompense for his sacrifice, while the use of puppets and masks cleverly reinforced the manipulation of man by devils. But, for those who reject the image of Faustus as deluded victim merely, and see him as possessing at least some of the lofty hopes and the eager spirit of enterprise of the age in which he was conceived, Barton's treatment ceased to create a sense of tragedy and declined into bathos. McKellen's Faustus was not even allowed to befool the Pope or fling the fireworks: he shrank to a twitching neurotic in a tinsel cloak, and as a result the play became a powerful study of a psychotic temperament with no counterbalancing features. The richness of the clash of conflicting values, the fascination of a personality combining disparate and warring impulses, was lost. Barton united the various elements of the original only by rejecting ambiguity.

Christopher Fettes too was able to achieve an impression of unity with his scaled-down text of 1980 and his view of the play as embodying the frustrations of a contemporary adolescent. Indeed, the work's relevance for today was perhaps exaggerated by some of the ruthless updating he permitted himself. Faustus, a 'typical' student with portable cassette recorder, smoking a cigarillo, his tutor a blind man in a wheelchair, was accompanied by a blend of classical and popular music, and a variety of sound-effects, including voices of American spacemen backing the concluding lines. Some of this seemed merely distracting. There were also worthier novelties, the most striking being the casting of David Rappaport, an actor 3 feet 6 inches tall, as the Pope. Here the notions of man's tenuous hold on temporal achievement, of the corrupt abuse of authority as a means of compensation, were more tellingly conveyed than in more conventional productions: one saw a parallel between Faustus and his adversary. Yet the play too shrank under this treatment; its full resonance was lost despite the erudite programme note's emphasis on the Greek concept of *pothos*, 'the longing for that which cannot be obtained'. *Pothos* was seen as essentially a juvenile passion: part of Faustus's triumph is surely that he never loses this longing even in his maturity.

Productions of the play have come far since *The Times* said of Poel's 1896 version, '*Dr Faustus* seems scarcely fitted for representation on the modern stage'. Few would take so gloomy a view today. Even if they have rarely been content to take the text on trust, directors can scarcely be blamed for their vigorous wielding of the scissors or the felt pen. Nor must the problems of creating a coherent Faustus, of making the notions of Hell and damnation meaningful to a modern audience, of spanning the presumed 'gulf between the peaks', be minimised. A conflation of the best features of all the productions reviewed here—Benthall's spectacle, Williams's consistent concept of a complex Faustus, Barton's puppetry, Fettes's economy (and his Mephostophilis)—might prove rewarding, but they illustrate the obvious truth that no single production of *Doctor Faustus* in recent times can be deemed truly satisfactory. Yet the play has inspired some exciting theatrical moments, and much of its power is still untapped, particularly its contemporary relevance. All who have participated in its realisation, as spectators, actors or directors, Christian or agnostic, might well unite in agreeing that this play's continuing power to move and stir us lies in Wilde's penetrating aphorism, 'When the Gods wish to punish us, they answer our prayers.'

Christopher Marlowe: A Chronology

Life and Career of Marlowe	Literary, Theatrical, and Historical Events
1558	Accession of Queen Elizabeth
1560	Publication of the Geneva Bible
1563	Church of England adopts *The Thirty-Nine Articles*; first edition of John Foxe's *Acts and Monuments* published
1564 Born, February 6, to John and Catharine Marlowe (baptized February 26)	Shakespeare born April 23
1568	Publication of Bishops' Bible
1570	Queen Elizabeth excommunicated by Pope Pius V
1572	St. Bartholomew's Day Massacre in Paris
1576	Opening of the Theatre in Shoreditch; Lord Admiral's acting company formed
1577	Drake sets off on round-the-world voyage
1579 Admitted to the Kings School, Canterbury	Publication of Spenser's *Shepheardes Calendar*
1580	Drake returns
1581 Enters Corpus Christi College, Cambridge	
1583	Queens' Men formed
1584 Receives BA at Cambridge	Failure of Sir Walter Raleigh's Virginia Colony
1586	Death of Philip Sidney from wounds received at battle of Zutphen (October 17)

1587	Receives MA at Cambridge (March 31); *Tamburlaine* first performed (?)	Execution of Mary, Queen of Scots; Rose Theatre built
1588		Defeat of the Spanish Armada
1589	Imprisoned for street brawl resulting in death of William Bradley (September 18; released October 1); *Doctor Faustus* first performed (?)	Richard Hakluyt's *Principal Navigations, Voyages, and Discoveries of the English Nation* first published
1590	*Tamburlaine* published	Spenser's *The Faerie Queene* published (Books 1–3); Sidney's *Arcadia* published
1591		Edward Allyn leaves Lord Admiral's Men for Lord Strange's Company
1592	In Netherlands, arrested for counterfeiting in February; *The Jew of Malta* first performed at the Rose Theater; *Edward II* first performed (?)	
1593	In May, "Dutch Libel" discovered; Marlowe interrogated by Privy Council on May 20; Marlowe killed in barroom fight in Deptford (May 30); Marlowe buried June 1; Baines Letter attacking Marlowe for blasphemy delivered June 2.	Theatres closed for plague from February to December
1594	*The Massacre at Paris* published; *Edward II* published; *Tragedy of Dido, Queen of Carthage* published	Henry of Navarre crowned Henry IV of France; Lord Chamberlain's Men formed
1595		Swan Theatre built
1596		Spenser's *Faerie Queene* published (with Books 4–6)
1598	*Hero and Leander* published	

1599		Bishops order burning of various books, including Marlowe's translation of Ovid's *Elegies*; Globe Theatre built
1600	Marlowe's translation of Lucan published	
1603		Death of Queen Elizabeth and Accession of King James; Lord Chamberlain's Men re-formed as the King's Men
1604	*Doctor Faustus* (A-Text) published	
1613		First Globe playhouse burns down
1616	*Doctor Faustus* (B-Text) published	Death of Shakespeare (April 23)
1623		Publication of Shakespeare's First Folio
1633	*The Jew of Malta* published	Herbert's *The Temple* published; Donne's *Poems* published

Selected Bibliography

EDITIONS OF *DOCTOR FAUSTUS*

The Early Texts

The Tragicall History of D. Faustus as it hath bene Acted by the Right Honorable the earle of Nottingham his Seruants (London: Thomas Bushnell, 1604) [The A-Text; rpt. for John Wright, 1609, 1611].

The Tragicall History of the Life and Death of Doctor Faustus (London: John Wright, 1616) [The B-Text; rpt. 1619, 1620, 1624].

In Collected Works

Bevington, David, and Eric Rasmussen, eds. Christopher Marlowe, *Doctor Faustus and Other Plays*. Oxford: Clarendon Press, 1995.

Brooke, C. F. Tucker, ed. *The Works of Christopher Marlowe*. Oxford: Clarendon Press, 1919.

Burnett, Mark Thornton, ed. Christopher Marlowe, *The Complete Plays*. London: Dent, 1999.

Bowers, Fredson, ed. *The Complete Works of Christopher Marlowe*, 2 vols. New York and London: Cambridge University Press, 1973.

Gill, Roma, ed. *The Complete Works of Christopher Marlowe*. Oxford: Clarendon Press, 1987.

Kirschbaum, Leo, ed. *The Plays of Christopher Marlowe*. Cleveland and New York: World Publishing, 1962.

Pendry, E. D., and J. C. Maxwell, eds. *Christopher Marlowe: Complete Plays and Poems*. London: Dent; Totowa, NJ: Roman & Littlefield, 1976.

Ribner, Irving, ed. *The Complete Plays of Christopher Marlowe*. New York: Odyssey, 1963.

Steane, J. B., ed. *Christopher Marlowe, The Complete Plays*. Harmondsworth, UK: Penguin, 1969.

Single-Play Editions

Bevington, David, and Eric Rasmussen, eds. *Doctor Faustus: A- and B-Texts (1604, 1616)*. Manchester and New York: Manchester University Press, 1993.

Boas, F. S., ed. *The Tragicall History of Doctor Faustus*. London: Methuen, 1932. *Doctor Faustus 1604 and 1616: A Scolar Press Facsimile*. Menstton: Scolar Press, 1970.

Gill, Roma, ed. *Dr Faustus*. London: Earnest Benn, 1965.

Greg, W. W. ed. *Marlowe's "Doctor Faustus" 1604–1616: Parallel Texts*. Oxford: Clarendon Press, 1950.

Jump, John D., ed. *The Tragical History of the Life and Death of Doctor Faustus*. London: Methuen, 1962.

Keefer, Michael, ed. *Doctor Faustus: A 1604-Version Edition*. Peterborough, Ont.: Broadview Press, 1991.

Ormerod, David, and Christopher Wortham, eds. *Christopher Marlowe: "Dr Faustus": The A-Text*. Nedlands: University of Western Australia Press, 1985.

Ribner, Irving, ed. *'Doctor Faustus': Text and Major Criticism*. New York: Odyssey Press, 1966.

Walker, Keith, ed. *Doctor Faustus*. Edinburgh: Oliver & Boyd, 1973.

CRITICAL AND TEXTUAL STUDIES

• indicates works included or excerpted in this Norton Critical Edition.

Alexander, Nigel. "The Performance of Christopher Marlowe's *Dr Faustus.*" *Proceedings of the British Academy* 57 (1971): 331–49.

Arber, Edward, ed. *Transcript of the Registers of the Company of Stationers of London 1554–1640*, 5 vols. Birmingham: Privately printed, 1875–94.

Barber, C. L. "The Form of Faustus' Fortunes Good or Bad." *Tulane Drama Review* 8 (1964): 92–119.

Bartels, Emily C., ed. *Critical Essays on Christopher Marlowe*. New York: G. K. Hall, 1997.

• Bevington, David. "Staging the A- and B-Texts of *Doctor Faustus*." In Sarah Munson Deats and Robert A. Logan, eds., *Marlowe's Empery: Expanding His Critical Contexts*. Newark: University of Delaware Press, 2002.

———. *From "Mankind" to Marlowe: Growth and Structure in the Popular Drama of Tudor England*. Cambridge: Harvard University Press, 1962.

Bluestone, Max. "*Libido Speculandi*: Doctrine and Dramaturgy in Contemporary Interpretations of Marlowe's Doctor Faustus." In *Reinterpretations of Elizabethan Drama: Selected Papers from the English Institute*. Ed. Norman Rabkin. New York: Columbia University Press, 1969, pp. 33–88.

Bowers, Fredson. "The Text of Marlowe's *Faustus*." *Modern Philology* 49 (1952): 195–204.

Brockbank, J. P. *Marlowe: "Dr. Faustus."* London: Edward Arnold, 1962.

Brooke, Nicholas. "The Moral Tragedy of Doctor Faustus." *Cambridge Journal* 7 (1952): 662–87.

• Brooks, Cleanth. "The Unity of Marlowe's *Doctor Faustus*." In J. Lawlor and W. H. Auden, eds., *To Neville Coghill from Friends*. London: Faber, 1966.

Brown, Constance Kuriyama. *Christopher Marlowe: A Renaissance Life*. Ithaca, NY: Cornell University Press, 2002.

Campbell, Lily B. "*Doctor Faustus*: A Case of Conscience." *PMLA* 67 (1952): 219–39.

Cheney, Patrick. *Marlowe's Counterfeit Profession: Ovid, Spenser, Counter-Nationhood*. Toronto: University of Toronto Press, 1997.

• Cole, Douglas. *Suffering and Evil in the Plays of Christopher Marlowe*. Princeton, NJ: Princeton University Press, 1962.

• Cox, John D. *The Devil and the Sacred in English Drama, 1350–1642*. Cambridge: Cambridge University Press, 2000.

Craik, T. W. "Faustus's Damnation Reconsidered." *Renaissance Drama* ns 2 (1969): 189–96.

• Deats, Sara Munson. "*Doctor Faustus*: From Chapbook to Tragedy." *Essays in Literature* 3 (1976): 3–16.

• Deats, Sara Munson, and Robert A. Logan, eds. *Marlowe's Empery: Exploring His Critical Contexts*. Newark: University of Delaware Press, 2002.

• Dollimore, Jonathan. "*Dr. Faustus* (c. 1589–92): Subversion through Transgression." In *Radical Tragedy: Religion, Ideology, and Power in the Drama of Shakespeare*. Durham, NC: Duke University Press, 1984.

Downie, J. A., and J. T. Parnell, eds. *Constructing Christopher Marlowe*. Cambridge: Cambridge University Press, 2000.

Empson, William, ed. *Faustus and the Censors: The English Faust-Book and Marlowe's "Doctor Faustus,"* Oxford: Blackwell, 1987.

Farnham, Willard, ed. *Twentieth Century Interpretations of "Doctor Faustus."* Englewood Cliffs, NJ: Prentice-Hall, 1969.

• Findlay, Alison. *A Feminist Perspective on Renaissance Drama*. Oxford: Blackwell, 1999.

Foster, Verna Ann. "*Dr Faustus* on the Stage." *Theatre Research* 14 (1974): 18–44.

Friedenreich, Kenneth, Roma Gill, and Constance Brown Kuriyama, eds. "*A Poet and a Filthy Play-Maker*": *Essays on Christopher Marlowe*. New York: AMS Press, 1988.

• Garber, Marjorie. " 'Here's Nothing Writ': Scribe, Script, and Circumscription in Marlowe's Plays." *Theatre Journal* 36 (1984): 301–20.

Gardner, Helen Louise. "Milton's Satan and the Theme of Despair in Renaissance Literature." *Essays and Studies* n.s. 1 (948): 46–66.

Greg, W. W. "The Damnation of Faustus." *Modern Language Review* 41 (1946): 97–107 [Reprinted in John Jump, ed. *"Dr Faustus"*: A Casebook. London: Macmillan, 1969, pp. 71–88.]

• Gill, Roma. " 'Such Conceits as Clownage Keeps in Pay': Comedy and *Dr. Faustus*." In Paul V. A. Williams, ed., *The Fool and the Trickster: Studies in Honour of Enid Welsford*. Suffolk, UK: Boydell, 1979.

Hamlin, William M. "Casting Doubt in Marlowe's Faustus." *Studies in English Literature* 41 (2001): 257–75.

Hammill, Graham. "Faustus' Fortunes: Commodification, Exchange, and the Form of Literary Subjectivity." *ELH* 63 (1996): 309–36.

Hattaway, Michael. "The Theology of Marlowe's *Doctor Faustus*." *Renaissance Drama*, n.s. 3 (1970): 51–78.

Healy, Thomas E. *Christopher Marlowe*. Plymouth: Northcote House/British Council, 1994.

Henslowe's Diary. Ed. R. A. Foakes and R. T. Rickert. Cambridge: Cambridge University Press, 1961.

Honigmann, Ernst. "Ten Problems in *Dr Faustus*." In *The Arts of Performance in Eliza-bethan and Early Stuart Drama*. Ed. Murray Biggs, Philip Edwards, Inga-Stina Ewbank, and Eugene M. Waith. Edinburgh: Edinburgh University Press, 1991, pp. 173–91.

Hunter, G. K. *Dramatic Identities and Cultural Tradition*. Liverpool: Liverpool University Press, 1978.

• ———. "Five-Act Structure in *Doctor Faustus*." *Tulane Drama Review* 8.4 (1964).

Jump, John, ed. *"Marlowe: Doctor Faustus": A Casebook*. London: Macmillan, 1969.

Kirschbaum, Leo. "The Good and Bad Quartos of *Doctor Faustus*." *The Library* 26 (1946): 272–94.

Knutson, Rosalyn I. " 'Influence of the Repertory System on the Revival and Revision of *The Spanish Tragedy* and *Dr. Faustus*." *English Literary Renaissance* 18 (1988): 257–74.

Kott, Jan. "The Two Hells of Dr. Faustus: A Plytheatrical Vision." In *The Bottom Transla-tion: Marlowe and Shakespeare and the Carnival Tradition*. Trans. Daniela Miedzgrzecka and Lillian Vallee. Evanston: Northwestern University Press, 1987, pp. 1–27.

Kuriyama, Constance Brown. "Dr. Greg and Doctor Faustus: The Supposed Originality of the 1616 Text." *English Literary Renaissance*, 5 (1975): 171–97.

Levin, Harry. *The Overreacher: A Study of Christopher Marlowe*. Cambridge: Harvard Uni-versity Press, 1952.

MacLure, Millar, ed. *Christopher Marlowe: The Critical Heritage*. London: Routledge & Kegan Paul, 1979.

Marcus, Leah. *Unediting the Renaissance: Shakespeare, Marlowe, Milton*. New York: Rout-ledge, 1996.

• Marcus, Leah. "Textual Instability and Ideological Difference: *The Case of Doctor Fau-stus*." *Renaissance Drama* 20: 38–54.

Matalene, H. W. "Marlowe's Faustus and the Comforts of Academicism." *ELH* 39 (1972): 495–519.

• Masinton, Charles G. *Christopher Marlowe's Tragic Vision*. Athens: Ohio University Press, 1972.

• Maus, Katharine Eisaman. *Inwardness and Theater in the English Renaissance*. Chicago: Chicago University Prerss, 1995.

McAlindon, T. *Doctor Faustus: Divine in Show*. New York: Twayne, 1994.

Mebane, John. *Renaissance Magic and the Return of the Golden Age*. Lincoln: University of Nebraska Press, 1989.

• Neill, Michael. "Anxieties of Ending." In *Issues of Death: Morality and Identity in English Renaissance Tragedy*. Oxford: Oxford University Press, 1997.

Nuttall, A. D. "Raising the Devil: Marlowe's *Doctor Faustus*." In *The Alternative Trinity: Gnostic Heresy in Marlowe, Milton, and Blake*. Oxford: Clarendon Press, 1998, pp. 78–85.

Oliver, Leslie. "Rowley, Foxe, and the Faustus Additions." *Modern Language Notes* 60 (1945): 391–45.

• Orgel, Stephen. *The Authentic Shakespeare and Other Problems of the Early Modern Stage*. New York: Routledge, 2002.

Ornstein, Robert. "Marlowe and God: The Tragic Theory of *Doctor Faustus*." *PMLA* 83 (1968): 13.

Palmer, D. J. "Magic and Poetry in *Doctor Faustus*." *Critical Quarterly* 6 (1964): 56–67.

• Rasmussen, Eric. *A Textual Companion to Doctor Faustus*. Manchester and New York: Man-chester University Press, 1993.

Ricks, Christopher. "Doctor Faustus and Hell on Earth," *Essays in Criticism* 35 (1985): 101–20.

Rozett, Martha Tuck. *The Doctrine of Election and the Emergence of Elizabethan Tragedy*. Princeton, NJ: Princeton University Press, 1984.

Sales, Roger. *Christopher Marlowe*. Basingstoke, UK: Macmillan, 1991.

Sanders, Wilbur. "Marlowe's Doctor Faustus." *Melbourne Critical Review* 7 (1964): 78–91.

• Sinfield, Alan. *Faultlines: Cultural Materialism and the Politics of Dissident Reading*. Berke-ley: University of California Press, 1992.

Snow, Edward. "Marlowe's *Doctor Faustus* and the Ends of Desire." In *Two Renaissance Mythmakers: Christopher Marlowe and Ben Jonson*. Ed. Alvin Kernan. Baltimore: The Johns Hopkins University Press, 1977, pp. 70–110.

• Snyder, Susan. "Marlowe's Doctor Faustus as an Inverted Saint's Life." *Studies in Philology* 63 (1966): 565–77.

Steane, J. B. *Christopher Marlowe: A Critical Study*. Cambridge: Cambridge University Press, 1964.

Streete, Adrian. " '*Consummatum Est*': Calvinist Exegesis, Mimesis, and *Doctor Faustus*." *Literature and Religion* 15 (2001): 140–58.

• Thomas, Keith. "Conjuring and the Magical Tradition." In *Religion and the Decline of Magic*. London: Orion, 1971.

• Tydeman, William. *"Doctor Faustus": Text and Performance*. London, Macmillan, 1984.

- Warren, Michael J. *"Doctor Faustus*: The Old Man and the Text." *English Literary Renaissance* 11 (1981): 111–47.

  Waswo, Richard. "Damnation, Protestant Style: Macbeth, Faustus, and Christian Tragedy." *Journal of Medieval and Renaissance Studies* 4 (1974): 63–99.

  Webb, David C. "Damnation in *Doctor Faustus*: Theological Striptease and the Histrionic Hero." *Critical Survey* 11 (1999): 31–47.

  West, Paul. "The Impatient Magic of Dr. Faustus." *English Literary Renaissance* 4 (1974): 218–40.
- White, Paul Whitfield, ed. *Marlowe, History, and Sexuality: New Critical Essays on Christopher Marlowe.* New York: AMS Press, 1998.